MW00440534

By the same author

Fiction

Pieces of Silver

The Unfair Advantage

Non-fiction

Road Trip

The Track Day Manual

FASTER *than the* BULLET

MIKE BRESLIN

Pie Shop Publishing

Pie Shop Publishing, London

Cover design: Bespoke Book Covers
(www.bespokebookcovers.com)

Main cover image: LAT Photographic/Motorsport Images

Contact Mike Breslin: www.bresmedia.co.uk

This is for Jassy, my wife, best friend and travelling companion

South of Kamieńsk, Poland. September 1939

At that very moment no one was quite as alive as Ingo Six. The throttle was wide open, there was not a millimetre of space left in its travel, it was jammed to its stop, his wrist bent back on the twist grip, the engine note a high, steely rasp. The motorcycle and sidecar combination could go no faster. This was perfect.

Ingo was escaping from nothing. He was merely living life the only way he knew how. Fast. The field-grey painted BMW R12 kicked out at a rut, and he made an instant steering correction, as natural to Ingo Six as blinking out sudden light. The bike's passage over the gravel and sand track shook his bones, as if they were a part of the machine's steel frame, and jangled the equipment tied to the motorcycle itself and to the sidecar, while the hits of tiny flies pricked his cheeks, one larger insect becoming a custard smudge on the left lens of his goggles. Because of the space the 750cc boxer twin engine took beneath him he sat with his legs wide astride the bike, pressing his thighs against the fuel tank to help him keep his seat as the BMW rattled and skipped across the surface of the uneven track. He leant forward, his arms well spread and bent a little to hold the bullhorn-shaped handlebars. His stahlhelm was loosely fixed to the back seat behind him, clonking like a cow bell, a helmet was not for him; goggles alone were enough for Ingo. His Kar 98 rifle was slung over his back like a heavy sash. He had still not used it, and he hoped he never would.

Small stones rattled against the bottom of the bike and its sidecar like shotgun pellets and the speeding air pummelled his face, smelling of dry grass, the summer breathing its last warm breath. He could also smell the baking steel of the three-wheeled machine beneath him, the hot oil, and the burning petrol the engine greedily slurped. He could feel the dust and sand caking on the skin of his face, thick in the creases carved by his smile, gritty in his teeth. Ahead, the unsealed road ran straight to a slight rise; a level crossing he realised. According to the speedometer affixed to the bowl of the headlamp in front of him the bike was going close to 95km/h, a very good speed on this sort of surface.

Ingo glanced at his passenger, sitting in the sidecar on the right side of the machine, below and slightly behind him. Pop looked up, as cool as a beer at the Augustiner Keller back in Ingo's home city of Munich. He raised an eyebrow beneath the jutting brim of his helmet – only an idiot would not wear one, he had said earlier, as they had set out to find a stray Panzer II that had lost touch with the regiment, its radio broken, it had turned out.

On the first day of the invasion, three days ago, the corporal's bike had been destroyed, his passenger wounded, when they had run into the Polish army at Mokra. Ingo had been pleased when Pop had asked to ride in his sidecar this morning, pleased that he had not insisted on taking the controls, too. Because Ingo wanted to show Pop what he could do.

They had completed their mission, found the tank and pointed it in the right direction, and Ingo had simply continued to ride. To ride fast. The older man had said nothing about that, and the older man was not complaining about the speed; but then he knew all about speed. The bike kicked out again, the revs singing, as the rear tyre spun across the surface of the sandy track.

The level crossing was now racing towards them like a poke in the eye. The railway was built up on a bed of stones, so the crossing was also raised, like a shallow humpback bridge, the sort of thing one might slow for. But Ingo kept the throttle fully open; the engine snarling metallically; the springs in the seat creaking. There was an acrid pong from the clutch – but not the brakes, for he had hardly touched them. And he was not about to do so now.

Ingo raised his behind from the saddle, to take the shock of the landing through bended legs, and as the BMW hit the forward slope it settled on its haunches like a leopard about to leap. Then it was launched from the ramp of the hump. It was a heavy machine – he did not need an excuse to keep it flat out, but if he had it would be momentum – yet it was a beautiful experience to fly it. The engine note changed, sharper, higher, as the parallel lines of tracks fell away beneath the combination while it cleared the railway and flew for maybe fifteen metres, the handlebars no longer juddering and strangely light in Ingo's hands. It landed with a thump that compressed the springs, the equipment tied to the bike rattling and clanking, before it bounced back into the air for a moment, slightly askew now so that when it again hit the road he had to fight it, the machine out of shape, a hastily steered correction, the sidecar slightly wide of the track, scything a confetti of yellow wild flowers from the roadside.

Ingo settled back into the seat and then once again stole a glance at Pop. The older man – twenty-nine, old enough to be given his nickname, ten years older than Ingo – looked unflustered, examined a grimy crescent at the end of a fingernail, and whistled; though it was a silent whistle, against the blast of the airstream, the rattle of the bike and the rasp of the engine. Ingo laughed.

They sped towards a cluster of stained-wood farm buildings with dirty thatched roofs, and the track was soon funnelled through a narrow section with a deep ditch to the right, a ragged stone wall to the left. But Ingo did not slow. Just then Pop started to slap Ingo's right leg. He glanced down and back to see his upturned face. Pop did not look so calm now, there was concern in his eyes. It felt faster, with the jagged wall close by, and Ingo wondered if he had scared the older man with his speed, thought it funny that he might have. Him of all people.

But Pop pointed at the map that was folded on his lap, weighted down with his Bergmann MP 28 sub machine gun. His finger stabbed at a point that was a little above and to the right of a line of pencilled hatching. Ingo realised they had strayed too far, too fast. He looked ahead again and thought, at last, that maybe he should slow. But then, directly in front of them, out of the cover of a wooden farm building at the end of the wall, a strange machine crawled in to the road. Ingo recognised it instantly. A Polish tankette.

The TKS, a flat-topped tiny tank with no turret and just two men inside, about the size of a small car but shorter in both length and height, was halfway through its jerking turn on to the narrow track, its observation slits, periscope aperture and the barb of its forward facing machine gun not yet pointing down the road. Ingo immediately understood what he needed to do, it came to him with that rush of life, that shock of exquisite electricity within, he was now getting used to as soon as he saw the green and brown painted machine. He knew there was no time to stop and turn, and that the Hotchkiss machine gun would come to bear in a second or so. All he could do was keep the throttle wide open and aim for the tiny gap to the left of the small tank, the gap between the tankette and the plank wall of the building that was just a little wider than the gap to the right between the tankette and the deep ditch. That gap on the left, Ingo judged instinctively, which was *just* wide enough.

The TKS was almost straight when Ingo was fifty metres and two seconds from it, and he could hear the rattle of its tracks and the crunching bite of its weight, on what was now a broken stone road. Twenty-five metres; one second. The gap he aimed for still looked extremely narrow, but he did not, could not, hesitate. The air was suddenly filled with the rattle of machine gun fire and the snatching stench of bullet propellant as Pop hosed the front of the tankette with his MP 28, the sidecar shivering to the recoil, bright sparks dancing on the armour of the squat little tank.

Ten metres. The machine gun at the front of the tankette opened up, a blossom of bright light, the rush of displaced air close to Ingo's cheek, the clang of a bullet ricocheting off a part of the bike's frame behind him. But in that same packed moment the combination was alongside the tankette, the gap between the two so tight that the butt of its handlebars just scraped the wooden building, rattling a plank. Then they were through.

Once past Ingo almost immediately found himself hurtling through the cluster of wooden farm buildings, with a curve ahead that took the track around a large barn. He braked with right hand and right foot, clutched with his left hand, the machine snaking on the loose surface, then he had to let go of the throttle to snick the BMW down a gear with the H-pattern lever to the right of the fuel tank, before pitching it into the right hand turn and taking it in a long slide, steering the motorcycle on the throttle with Pop – who knew his stuff alright – leaning out of the sidecar to stop the machine toppling. When they were through the turn, the barn now covering their escape, Ingo shifted up a gear with a solid clunk and twisted the throttle to its stop again.

A few kilometres further on and Pop pointed to a small wood. Ingo drove off the track and across the grass, which was cropped and brittle here and buzzed against the tyres, before coming to a halt amidst the trees.

Life at speed still coursed through Ingo's veins, and he laughed, laughed loud, as he killed the ignition and the engine hiccupped once, then died. Pop got out of the sidecar, holding his Bergmann by its wooden rifle-like grip and the steel magazine that came out of its side, his finger tickling the trigger. He had a quick look round, the perforated muzzle of the sub machine gun indicating his line of sight. It did not take long, they could see for miles across the flat, yellow land here. If the tankette followed, they would spot it in plenty of time.

"That was interesting," Pop said, as Ingo's laughter spluttered out in a series of little half coughs.

Pop took his helmet off, and immediately combed his hair with his fingers; it was thinning and precious, once red, now like copper filaments. There was a shiny bald patch on the crown of his head, which is why, as always, he soon put the helmet back on. He was not a tall man, but he was muscular, which made him seem like an elongated and inverted triangle from a distance. He always looked as though a joke had been played on him, and he was taking it well, the hint of a smile, a lazy nod, or an equally lazy shake of the head. He did not look flustered now, but then Pop was a cool one in action, Ingo had seen that already, seen it when they'd come up against the Polish armoured train at Mokra. In fact, the only time he did not seem calm was when there were women around. His eyes were green-grey, the same colour as the BMW, and the German army uniforms they both wore.

Ingo knew that Pop had raced motorcycles and cars before the war, when he was a member of the NSKK, the Nazi's motoring organisation; had even finished the famous 2000 Kilometres of Germany Rally in '33, on a DKW bike, and come fourth in the sports car class at the Grossglockner hillclimb in a BMW 328 in '38. That had intrigued Ingo, as he knew a little about racing, but wanted to know much more.

"Yes, interesting," Pop repeated, taking a slosh from his water bottle.

"Were you worried?" Ingo said. "I thought I might scare you, but the others said that was impossible."

"I was more scared of the tank than you, Pup."

"That was not a real tank, it was a baby tank," Ingo said.

"The machine gun looked grown up."

"We were too quick."

"No one is faster than a bullet, Pup," Pop said, again using the nickname Feldwebel Kroh had given Ingo, then he looked thoughtful, shook his head and smiled.

"What?"

"Nothing." Pop plucked a cigarette out of a pack of Reemtsma R6 and lit it. "We'll wait here, it's too dangerous to head back with that sardine can out there; and there will be cavalry with it, somewhere, that's for sure. Our panzers will be here soon enough. Best we sit tight."

"No, let's go cross country," Ingo said, sitting tight did not suit Ingo Six. "This thing can outrun a tin can and some horses, any day." Ingo reached out and laid his hand flat against the warm steel of the petrol tank, held it there for a few seconds, a habit of his; not superstition, but something else.

"Idiot," Pop said.

Ingo laughed again. Laughed until he could not stop laughing. And Pop laughed too, because when Ingo laughed like this it was impossible for others not to laugh with him.

***

4

Chillar, Argentina. October 1949

The clock ticked slowly. That could not be so, he knew. A second is a second is a second. But the clocked ticked slowly. There had once been a dripping tap that had not quite kept time with it, but not for long; it was a job that filled an hour or so, and that was always welcome. He ran his fingers through his thick beard. He was used to it now, used to his new name, too: Enrique Hohberg. It was the name that was on his Red Cross passport, the document that had got him on to the ship in Genoa; the ship that had got him out of Europe. There had always been many German-Argentinians, now there were also many 'old comrades' in this country.

The sun had risen above the low hills and the grass was golden-green. The day ached to be filled, but there was not much to fill it with. Breakfast had been taken, lunch was long hours away. Dinner; a distant future where men went to The Moon. He sat in the kitchen, which was simple: a stove, a table, and some cupboards. It smelt of coffee and cigarettes, and the earthy tang of the grass outside the open window that the rising sun had brought to life. There was nothing of him in this kitchen, nor in any other part of the small farmhouse – which was just a living room, bathroom and a single bedroom.

He had bought the farm, the house and a barn. Bought it with cash. But there was little land with it, that had been sold to a larger estancia, which now worked it; but here at least that meant cows rather than people. The closest people were ten kilometres away, in Chillar. He rarely went in to the tiny town, four-hundred kilometres south of Buenos Aires and in the province that bore the capital's name. It was a nothing place, Chillar, far from anywhere, really – and that was exactly why he had chosen to live here.

The snub-nosed Colt .38 sat on the kitchen table, alongside the chipped coffee mug and the pot that had been drained. The butts of three cigarettes were squashed into an ashtray that had once been a hub cap. He could afford a proper ashtray, could afford for it to be of the finest crystal; he could afford a gold-stemmed cigarette holder, too, but he had no need for such things. He had bought the thirty-eight in Mar del Plata, from a man at a bar in the port who had guessed what he was. Because of this it had been expensive.

Enrique picked up the short revolver, almost enjoying the weight of it in his hand. He spun the cylinder, its slickly, clickety movement sounding like a rattlesnake in the quiet kitchen. The Colt was well cared for, and smelt of gun oil and a tiny trace of cordite, though he sometimes thought he imagined that, or that perhaps his nasal passages would never be free of that particular smell – he had breathed deeply of air soaked in propellant for such a long time, perhaps it had become a part of him? War never lets you go, and it uses every trick to remind you it's still with you. You can travel twelve-thousand kilometres to try to escape it. But it's always there.

He pulled back the hammer, the steel cold against his thumb, then pressed the short and ugly barrel against his temple, allowing it to dig into his skin. He pulled the trigger.

Click.

The same as before. No surprise. No relief. No disappointment. It had been a joke the first time he had done it, but he had not laughed. He did not laugh now. It was a morning ritual, like emptying his bowels. And there was no danger, no thrill to it. The rounds were placed on the table, in a neat row like copper-capped tombstones. He would reload the revolver now, another part of his daily routine. He always kept it loaded and ready.

When the day grew a little warmer, which it would in an hour or so, he thought he might ride his horse, Zündapp. But he knew he would not take his yellow-painted Jeep out today. It was low on fuel, and he was putting off a trip in to Chillar until he needed a few things, not just gas for the only car that made sense when you've a driveway like the one that led up to the farmhouse – another reason he had chosen the place, no one arrived here quickly or quietly, there was always plenty of warning when a car rattled up that rocky track.

He started to insert the bullets into the chambers of the revolver. He would never use the thirty-eight on himself, of that he was certain. Ingo Six was not done with life yet. He still had hope. And that in itself was a miracle.

***

Warsaw, Poland. November 1939

As Lidka and Kassia left the tottering building in which they shared an apartment on Piwna a squad of German soldiers marched by, their boots crunching the cobbles in almost complete unison, crisp footfalls echoing in the narrow confines of the tight, stony-cold canyon of the old street, ringing like volleys of rifle fire. It was strange how quickly the people had become used to it. German soldiers were everywhere, it seemed to Lidka Wadalowska, and now their field grey uniforms had started to blend in with the stone and the cobbles of the city – that stone which the Stukas had not turned to dust, at least. She still hated them, every Pole in Warsaw hated them. But she also chose to ignore them, for there was nothing else she could do.

Kassia did not ignore them: "Look at them; most of them are just boys, how could they have beaten us?" she said, though not too loud. The young German soldiers did not ignore Kassia, either, because Kassia was beautiful. That was a simple fact. Lidka was not beautiful, but she was told that she was pretty, and that was enough for her. She did not worry too much about it, she liked makowiec cake, and she liked pierogi, and she would eat both often – though that was rarely possible now – without concerning herself about a little extra weight on her behind. Kassia seldom ate things like cake, that could be the price of being close to perfection, Lidka supposed, but sometimes she thought that not eating sweet things had made Kassia a little bitter, too. They had few things in common, except for the flat they shared and having grown up in the same town, Wagrowiec. That was how they had become friends, discovering they had common ground, when they had both moved to Warsaw; Lidka to teach, Kassia because she was bored. It had seemed only natural that they should share the apartment. They were also both around the same age, Lidka twenty-three and Kassia a year older.

The two friends continued to walk down the cool canal of Piwna Street, Kassia in that way of hers; a beautiful girl walking, knowing she's a beautiful girl walking, as the German soldiers watched her, her heels ringing out like whip cracks on the cobbles, demanding attention. Lidka did not think the war would change Kassia. It was not yet winter, but it was already getting cold. The pastel-painted houses had a dirty laundry look to them, stained by the greasy drizzle; as if they had been left out to dry, and forgotten. There was a slight rotting vegetable smell to the street, which seemed strange as few could afford to let food spoil these days. The Germans marched away from them.

"Any word on Jósef?" Kassia said, quite suddenly.

"No."

"He'll show up."

Lidka nodded. Jósef was in the air force; he had been her boyfriend, though *he* had thought there was more to it than that, had hinted at marriage. She had been about to call it off when the Germans invaded. But it was hard to call it off when a boy was at the front. Now she had no idea where he was. There were Polish soldiers who had escaped to France to continue to fight, she had heard. Or perhaps he was in neighbouring Romania, where many had fled to, or in a German POW camp. Or a Russian one. Or perhaps he was dead. That thought made her a little ashamed of the relief she felt that he was out of her life.

"Yes, he'll show up," Lidka said, as they took a tight turn to the right, her heels slithering a little against the slippery cobblestones, then walked up a narrow side-street and in to the Rynek Starego Miasta, which since the Germans had come had reverted to its old role of a market square on some days, though this only amounted to a few covered tables, the canvas stretched above them stained miserable by the drizzle.

The produce was predictable, mostly spuds. The square had not been damaged too much during the fighting and the bombing, though there was still a mask of wooden scaffolding obscuring the façades of some of the four- and five-storey old buildings that edged it. The painted walls that were still visible, and undamaged, cheered Lidka a little; they seemed to mock the grey Germans, she thought. A stiff wind blew across the Vistula, from the direction of Russia – Lidka hated the Russians, too, and their pact with the Nazis. But *they* were not in Warsaw. A German soldier stared at her, winked. She was blonde, 'homely', the Nazis liked that, she knew. She looked the other way, to where a mongrel pissed against the wall: it was very good ignoring, she thought.

"At least this war will help you lose weight," Kassia said, as she picked up a misshapen potato from a stall and studied it as if it was a rock from Mars. "There is no makowiec to be seen now."

"I'm not on a diet," Lidka said.

"No?" Kassia said. "I thought we all were."

"If you're not buying, put it back," the woman tending the potato stall snapped, and Kassia turned away from Lidka before she could reply, dropping the spud. Then she spotted someone she knew halfway across the square, a man in an expensive looking woollen coat.

"Jacek!" she shouted. "A moment, Lidka," she added, hurrying over to the smiling man.

Lidka watched Kassia greet him. He kissed her cheek, a lingering kiss she thought, then she turned away from them and looked again at the market stalls. It was a shame there was no makowiec. The poppy seed pastry was just one of the things Lidka loved that the war had taken away, or at least made hard to find. Chopin, too. Chopin had been banned by the Nazis, as they tried to strip away all that was Polish from the Poles. She loved Chopin above all else, even makowiec and pierogi. Lidka lived for Chopin. She had never been able to master the piano, and a part of her did not really want to now, she had recently realised, for that would take some of the magic away. Besides, people who could play Chopin well were like gods, or goddesses. Not even Kassia, who of course could play the piano – and look serene and beautiful as she did so – could play Chopin well.

Because she had been thinking about Chopin it was in her head; *The Raindrop Prelude*, one of her favourites. She often wondered how music could be in her head, for there was not a piano in her head. It seemed proof that it was of the soul – she still believed in God, she thought, but since September she had not been to mass. There was a stronger breath of wind from across the Vistula, from the treacherous east, stinging her skin a little, and the music was lost in the cold gust for a moment. And she realised then, with quite a start, the music had not been in her head after all.

The gust died and the music returned. It was perfect. She had not heard such perfection for a long time, and she was drawn towards the source of the music, all thoughts of shopping for potatoes forgotten. The perfect pitter-patter notes were like little fishhooks, and she gladly let them snag at her, as the hypnotic music led her down Krzywe Koło.

Lidka followed the street, and then turned hard left when it did, too. The music was quite clear now, and it was, she thought, perhaps the most beautiful piano playing she had ever heard. And yet it was not coming from a concert hall, or even a church, but rather a tiny café with steamed up windows, and a small sign that read 'Café Kasper' over the door. The café was in a salmon-coloured three-storey building with typical six-panel windows, the frames painted a dark green. The heavy wooden door was set into an oval-headed doorway with a keystone-capped stone arch. She walked in, the feeling of stepping into a cloud accentuated by the fug of cigarette smoke. No one looked her way as she entered, even though the base of the door squealed a little against the stone step, for all those within faced in one direction only; the corner of the room where someone played an upright piano that did not look capable of the sublime music that was coming from it.

The young man at the keyboard was smiling, a joy she knew and recognised. She very suddenly welled up, and had to wipe a tear from her eye. He was handsome, dark hair a little long and untidy. His eyes were the green of a sunlit forest, she thought, full of life and tricks, sparkling like emeralds. His smile was white, with one cheeky tooth out of place, an endearing defect. His skin was tanned, and she thought he might be a labourer, for he wore a simple vest, with the three buttons at its throat undone, but – and she was no snob – could a labourer play like this? Could anyone other than an angel play piano like this? He was the only man in the café not smoking.

The way his fingers caressed the keyboard was almost sexual, and she felt a flutter within her, another tear swelled and burst, and this time she let it slide down her cheek, like a comforting caress. She had never felt like this before. Never. Right then he seemed to notice her, and he smiled wider. Then winked. And in a smooth movement which should have been impossible he merged the sacred *Raindrop Prelude* into a jazz piece that shocked and amazed everyone, so much so that one old man shouted "Bravo!" as old men sometimes did.

But for Lidka the spell was broken. The child, for he seemed a child now, had spoilt it; ruined her Chopin. It was now that she saw that on the back of the chair on which he sat was a field grey German army tunic, there was also a soldier's cap on the top of the piano.

She turned and left the café, and a moment later the jazz piece stopped abruptly and she heard a chair topple. She walked away quickly, but sensed he came after her, and so she stepped in to the doorway of a hat shop, a bell dinging her entrance. She heard the scraping clash of steel heel guards on army boots against the wet cobbles as someone ran by outside, ran very quickly, shouting in the German she understood: "Wait! Where have you gone?"

*

Lyon, France. November 1939

The wind that blew across the Bron airfield, around ten kilometres from the centre of the city, was steely cold, and it thrummed through the radio wires of the single Morane-Saulnier parked up close to the new Polish headquarters. The wind was strong enough to make the modern-looking French monoplane fighter shudder, and chilly enough to make Jósef Sczcepanski shiver.

Jósef was in a long queue of Polish Air Force personnel; all of them had somehow made their way from their homeland to fight on with the French. He estimated there were at least three hundred of his comrades gathered here, none of them in uniform – Jósef wore a beige jacket over a thin shirt, cream flannels and deck shoes. The line of men slowly shuffled into the shelter of a space between two brick-built buildings, which was covered with corrugated iron that fluted and vibrated as the wind raced through it. The narrow space smelt of stale sweat and pungent French tobacco smoke, issuing from the De Troupe cigarettes that had been handed out on their arrival. A single lightbulb swung from the tinny ceiling, stirring the shadows beneath it. There were large sheets of thick paper affixed to boards on the walls, each with lists of positions to be taken. There was room to write a name, experience and qualifications. One was headed *Aircrew Training.*

It had been a long journey, and Jósef felt as if he had been swept along, without once making a decision of his own. But now here was one right in front of him, a big one; and it was one he was not ready to take. If he had taken decisions, he would have been back in Warsaw by now, with Lidka. But then he had heard bad things about Warsaw, about the beating it had taken. If he had taken decisions, then perhaps he would not have followed Kapitan Wysocki. But Wysocki was decisive, as a pilot should be, and Jósef had followed him because he was ordered; because he did not know what else to do; but mostly because he had been afraid.

Wysocki had flown a PZL 23, a Karaś, while Jósef, as a fitter, had looked after the same light bombers on the ground. Wysocki had been shot down, had baled out of his burning plane; he was lucky to be alive, though you would not think it. He had lost his young wife in the bombing of Warsaw, wanted nothing more now than to kill Germans. He had dark eyes, dark hair, and a humour that matched. He never lost his temper, but was more cold than cool. Jósef supposed he was a hero, but he wore no medal, as there was no one left to give them out. There were burns on his hands, from the blazing Karaś that he had jumped from. Wysocki never mentioned them, never seemed to notice them. But Jósef always did, all the more when he tried not to.

A group of them, led by Wysocki, had crossed into Romania, where they had been interned in a town called Babadag. From there Wysocki had persuaded them to escape, then led them to Bucharest, where they had obtained civilian papers from the Polish embassy. Then they had all managed to find a berth on a small coaster called the *Transylvania*, bound for Beirut. In Beirut, after weeks of trying, they had found some space on a larger French ship, the *Champollion*, which had taken them to France. It had then been a slow and uncomfortable train journey up from Marseilles. Jósef had not been sleeping well and was tired to his core, an iron tired that seemed to be a part of him now. He wondered if he would ever feel rested again, ever feel warm. Or safe.

He shuffled on, in the same group, Wysocki leading the way again, not seeming to notice the cold. There were pencils in pots with which to fill in the spaces on the large sheets. Jósef looked at the list for aircrew training. He thought of how proud Lidka would be of him, if he were aircrew. She did not know if he was still alive, of course. He did not know for sure that she was, either, and there was no way of finding out: Poland was now a part of Germany and Germany was at war with France. But he hoped there might be a way to send a letter soon, somehow. He stared at the blank space on the list for aircrew training.

"We have plenty of aircrew, Sczcepanski," Wysocki said. "Not so many aeroplanes."

"There will be planes, soon, sir," Jósef said.

"That's true. But *you* would be of better use on the ground, the more planes we get, the more mechanics we'll need."

Jósef nodded.

"Besides ..." Wysocki started, but left the word float there, like a lonely artillery spotter plane in a big sky, warning of danger to come.

"Besides?"

"Nothing; do as you will."

Jósef nodded, as Kapitan Wysocki scrawled his rank and experience in the box marked *pilot*. The burn on his right hand flashed red raw in the harsh electric light, and Jósef looked away.

Jósef thought again of how he would look with a wing sewn to the breast of a smartly cut uniform, then thought of Lidka. Then he picked up the pencil.

*

Warsaw. November 1939

General von Rundstedt grunted.

"Left you say?" Ingo took the left turn, the BMW's tyres slithering on the greasy cobbles. General von Rundstedt seemed to be enjoying his ride in the sidecar now, but it was difficult to know for sure if a pig was enjoying anything, really. He would be bacon soon – that was Kroh's plan for the good general – so Ingo hoped he was making the most of his final hours in the lemony autumn sunlight. The General smelt of the farmyard, and pig-shit, but he guessed he would not be pleased to know that soon he would smell so much better. Ingo's mouth flooded with saliva at the thought of sizzling pork.

Ingo had offered to pick up the pig in Solec, where Kroh did most of his dodgy deals. The pig was payment for something, the feldwebel had not said what and Ingo knew better than to ask. Ingo had assumed it would already have been slaughtered, but it had not. He was not keen on killing animals, but after two hours he had managed, with the help of some Polish lads and a rope, to tie the general into the sidecar. He had offered to pick up the pig because he was bored, and Feldwebel Kroh had said that he could take one of the BMWs. But he had also offered because he was in love, and he wanted to take a detour to the Old Town to look for her.

He had never been in love before, but he thought this might be the real thing, because it had happened fast; at over one hundred and fifty kilometres per hour. For Ingo that was the way with everything, he never understood why anyone could take more than an eighth of a second to make a decision. He could understand even less how someone could then change their mind. Life wasn't that difficult, for Ingo Six.

Ingo opened the throttle and the big bike and sidecar sped up a narrow side street, the cold airstream washing away the smell of the pig, a little. He assumed she must be somewhere here; he had seen her in the Old Town, so he had returned to the Old Town. Five times now. When he found her he would apologise for *Tiger Rag*, then all would be well. He was sure. Pop had said, 'what if she has a husband, a boyfriend?' Ingo had decided not to think about that. Besides, garrison life in Warsaw was tedious, but searching for the girl, with a pig in the sidecar, was fun.

There were military policemen, 'chained dogs', at the end of the street, their hated profession betrayed by the steel gorgets, like small crescent-shaped breastplates, that hung from chains around their necks. With a black market pig in the sidecar they were best avoided, and so he stamped on the rear brake, spun the BMW, and headed away from them, slotting the combination through a tight turn, and then another, the tyres thrumming against the cobbles.

"You led me into an ambush, Herr General," he told the pig.

Then he saw her.

She was walking in to another side street. She did not look in his direction, although most others did – he supposed it was difficult to ignore a pig in a sidecar. He slowed the BMW and took it in to the narrow lane, where doors met the street and the sunlight was blocked out by the buildings. It was chilly in the tight street, and smelt of last night; damp and arthritic, as if the stone was in pain, aching for the sun it seldom saw. She walked quickly, a mac hid her clothes; it was tightly belted, which emphasised her curves. He pulled up alongside her, allowed the machine to idle, the valves *ticker-ticking* loudly, and then kept level with the walking girl; her shoes were flat and soft and made little squidgy noises on the cobbles. He could see that she wore no ring.

"Hey!" he said, sharply.

She looked straight ahead, obviously ignoring him.

General von Rundstedt snorted, and the unusual sound startled her, forcing her to turn her head towards him. She saw the pig, then him. He thought she recognised him, something in her blue eyes – the eyes of a summer sky, with whisky flecks of extra warmth. The eyes he had easily read the other day, in the café; the eyes that loved Chopin, but not *Tiger Rag*. Eyes surprised now, to see him, to see General von Rundstedt.

He grinned at her.

"So, two Germans on a motorcycle," she said.

"You speak German?"

"Only when I have to," she said, sniffing and wrinkling her nose at the smell of the pig, but making a point at looking at him when she did so.

"You're Volksdeutsche?"

With that she came to a sharp halt. "I am Polish," she said.

She was annoyed, he could see that. Volksdeutsche were those Poles seen as German, ethnic Germans. Poles the Nazis liked, in other words. But he filed that sort of thing under politics, so somewhere below having a haircut and waiting for a train on his list of dislikes. And from the look on her face, the spark in her eyes, being referred to as Volksdeutsche was close to the bottom of her list. But at least she was talking to him. He had brought the machine to a halt as she had stopped, and now he switched off the engine. General von Rundstedt settled down in the seat of the sidecar like a tired gundog, the ropes that held him in slightly slackening around his thick pink body.

"Yes, of course," Ingo said. "Polish."

"I was brought up in the west, many speak German in the west."

"It must be useful; now."

"Only if I want to speak to murderers," she said.

"Murderers?"

"Murderers, soldiers, with you Germans it's all the same."

"I'm no murderer, not sure I'm even much of a soldier," he said.

"So what's that for, then?" she said, nodding her head at the rifle barrel that was poking above his shoulder.

He shrugged, and with that the Kar 98 that was slung over his back shifted a little. "That? I've never even used it."

"I don't believe you," she said, but he saw that she had cocked her head, ever so slightly, as if she was reconsidering. Ever so slightly.

"It's true. I'm only along for the ride, you see."

"You make it sound like a holiday."

He shrugged: "I always try to make the best of things, why wouldn't you?"

"Well, that explains the pig."

"You mean the general?" he said. "I couldn't even kill him."

She finally smiled. It was a beautiful smile, glowing against a skin made peachy in the cold air. Her teeth were white and neat. Her long blonde hair was tied back beneath a beret. Her nose was strong rather than pretty; not big – yet there was enough of it to stop her eyes staring at each other, turning her crossed-eyed by falling in love with themselves.

"I saw you in the café, playing Chopin. Playing it so ..." she trailed off, obviously regretting that she had spoken of the café, and then started to walk again. The street was on a slope so he eased off the brake and let gravity do the work, the heavy tyres creaking against the cobbles, the suspension squeaking.

"You like Chopin?"

She nodded, crisply.

"He wasn't so bad, I suppose," Ingo said, and her shoulders stiffened through the tight stretch of the mac.

"Why did you do what you did, why did you change the music?"

"I'm not sure; I get bored," he said. "It just happened."

"Bored of Chopin?"

"I'll play it for you again, if you want?" he said, ignoring the question, for that road was taking him nowhere, wasn't fast, and had few interesting turns. "Chopin, I mean."

"You play well; where did you learn?" she said.

"Home, Munich. My father sells pianos, my mother wanted me to be a pianist," he said.

"And you *didn't*?"

He paused before replying, he did not want to go into all *that* now, and so he said: "I'm *restless*, need to be moving, me." They were coming to the end of the street now, and he could see the walls of the old Barbican. "Say, what if you come to that same café, next Saturday evening, I'll play Chopin again?"

"I'm busy."

"Busy with what?" Ingo said.

"This and that."

"You work?"

"Not now."

"No?"

"I was a teacher," she said.

"Was?"

"You haven't been paying much attention to current affairs, have you?"

He grinned: "What do you teach?"

"What *did* I teach," she said. "Languages, Polish history; nothing that would interest you, though; you don't strike me as the studious type."

"Depends on the teacher; I find most subjects are easy enough, if I have a good teacher."

"Most subjects; how about humility?"

"I'm a champion at that."

"And leaving people be?"

"Not so good," he said.

"Well, let me teach you a lesson," she said, then stopped again. He tugged at the brake lever and the BMW came to a standstill with a lurch, fuel sloshing in the tank. "I have a boyfriend," she said. "Jósef, he is ... Well, I'm not sure; but he *is*."

For some reason Ingo was not concerned. She did not care for this Jósef, he could see that in her eyes – in the same way he had seen the love for Chopin in her eyes. Well, Mother had always said that one day he would be thankful for his musical gift.

"But you will still come, to hear me play; play Chopin?" he said.

She did not answer, just shook her head.

"In Bulgaria that means yes," he said, and General von Rundstedt grunted in agreement.

*

Feldwebel Christian Kroh was looking for something in particular. He walked some metres in front of Ingo and Pop, down the pavement of Świętojerska in the Jewish quarter, in the direction of the Krasinski Gardens. The street was lined with five- and six-storey brick-built apartment buildings and its steeply cambered road was surfaced in smooth old cobbles. Sud-flecked water trickled along a bone-white stone gutter and into a drain. The day was cloudy and it was cold in the street. The air smelt of the soapy water someone had recently poured into the gutter; and raw onion.

Kroh was carrying his fancy camera in one hand while he munched on a raw onion that was in the other; a thing of his. He had given up cigarettes because Hitler didn't smoke, onions filled the gap, he always said. Pop walked beside Ingo, and smoked. Ingo doubted he would ever give up his Reemtsmas, even if the Führer actually ordered him to. The only thing he liked more than fags was motor racing. And women.

"Pretty, eh," Pop said.

The girl was hurrying along on the other side of the street. Ingo could not see much of her face, for she had turned her head away from them, so he could not say if she was pretty or not. She wore a red coat, from which dark-stockinged legs scissored, and her gleaming shoes clicked along the pavement. Ingo started to think about the girl from the café again. He wondered if she would turn up at Kasper's tomorrow. Hoped, again, she would.

"Probably a Yid, 'round here," Kroh said, about the girl in the red coat, having stopped now, to look at a burnt-out building, a reminder of September.

Pop shrugged, puffed at his cigarette.

"Can't fuck Jews, Pop. Right?"

"Right," Pop said. But Ingo knew Pop had nothing against Jews. Neither did he. They had had many Jewish customers at his father's piano shop in Schwabing in Munich, before it had moved to Wagmüllerstrasse and what Father had believed was a much better location, in the well to do district of Lehel. They were mostly decent people. But that had been before his father had joined the Party. It was only then that there was, somehow, something different about them; though Ingo could never work out what that was.

Kroh dropped his half-eaten onion on the floor and it rolled off the sloping shoulder of the kerb and into the gutter water. He placed the viewfinder of the camera close to his eye and stepped back into the street, to get the burnt-out apartment building in the frame. Ingo did not doubt that the fancy little camera he used was stolen, but the enthusiasm for his art was all his own.

Kroh's hobby was photography. His camera was a Leica III, and he was a specialist. Other soldiers called such pictures 'tourist photographs'. They were usually of dead bodies and destruction – soldiers' humour is often camouflaged. But Kroh took it all a little more seriously than most. It was just a skeleton of a building now. The ribs of three of its storeys were sticky-looking with shining burnt wood that seemed to almost sag under thick carpets of ash and piles of rubble. Kroh took his picture, but Ingo knew that this was not what he was looking for; he had many photographs of gutted buildings and charred tanks, bloated dead horses and corpses in each and every state of decay. No, Kroh was after something else.

Ingo was not afraid of much, he knew that now. While the newspapers made out Poland had been a walkover, and the myth of cavalry charging panzers had taken hold quickly, for the 4th Panzer Division it had been anything but an easy ride. Their tanks had been chewed up on the outskirts of Warsaw, and while Ingo had still not used his rifle – and now that Pop said the war was as good as over probably never would, thank God – he had fed the ammunition belts into Pop's MG 34 when they had dismounted to fight, and had heard, and even felt, the pass of enemy rounds. That, he had admitted to Pop, had been exciting. He had not been afraid at any time, then. So, no, Ingo Six was not afraid of much at all. But he was afraid of Feldwebel Christian Kroh.

The 4th had left plenty of wrecks in and around Warsaw. Kroh, who had dirt on everyone, had managed to see to it that he and some others from the Aufklärungsgruppe, the reconnaissance group of the 35th Panzer Regiment, were kept in the city when the others had gone back to Bamberg, kept back to help with the salvage. Kroh wanted to stay because he had found lots of juicy trade in Solec, where in the heavy shadow of the western reaches of the Poniatwoski Bridge there was always shady business to do. They had taken their time with their official task and had mostly worked for Kroh on his black market deals in Solec, and elsewhere. He was not the type you could refuse; but then he always made sure they had a share, and if one day soon Ingo was to race then, as Pop always said, they would need money for that. At least to begin with.

Someone had done bad things to Kroh, once. Ingo had to believe that, otherwise he would lose faith in humanity. There had to be a reason for such malice in a man. Despite this, Kroh smiled a lot, just never more so than when he was inflicting punishment; official or unofficial. It could seem a friendly smile, too, at first; which meant that often people would not take him seriously. A serious mistake. Once you got to know him you soon realised there was a slight but barbed hook at the edge of his smile; it was a warning. He was a little short, but not as short as Pop, and quite stocky. He had blond hair and blue eyes, the Nazi ideal, but the blond was more like damp straw, and the blue was without life, like daubs of matt paint dried on to a discarded palette. Someone had told Ingo that Kroh had been a thief before he had joined the army. He still was. He was also a fully paid up member of the Party, had been from early on. This was one of his proudest boasts.

The camera clicked, then Kroh let it drop on its leather strap as a man stepped out of one of the doorways. Kroh's eyes would never light up, but his smile hooked viciously at the sight of the old Jew.

"Just the thing," Kroh said, to no one in particular.

The old Jew looked like he'd slid off a Nazi propaganda poster; a long thick beard and a hooked nose. He was dressed entirely in black with a tall cap with a very short peak. The old man turned quickly in the other direction but Kroh shouted "Halt!", the shout as sharp and loud as a gunshot in the street, stopping the man dead. It was echoed by a slamming shutter, some way down

Świętojerska, high in a building. The Jew turned, and fear mixed with resignation in his eyes.

"This old lad needs a shave, eh Pop?" Kroh said. He held his gleaming black and chrome camera out in front of him, worked the winding knob on the top of its body.

"Sure there's a barbershop around here somewhere," Pop said.

Kroh nodded at the bayonet on Pop's belt, and Pop sighed, unsheathed it from its leather frog. "Hope you've kept it sharp; make it smooth Pop, like a baby's behind, right?"

"Come on, leave him be, he's just —" Ingo started.

"Just what, Pup?"

"He's an old man, that's all."

"He's a Jew."

"But —"

"Yes, just a Jew," Pop cut in, facing the old man and shrugging a little as he said it. The Jew seemed to understand – Yiddish was quite close to German – and he nodded, very slightly; in a 'get it over with' sort of way. Pop and Ingo saw this, but Kroh did not, as he was still glaring at Ingo. But that was forgotten when Pop grabbed a handful of beard and then began to slice off chunks of it, letting them drop in the gutter while Kroh took his photographs. Ingo knew it was time for him to keep quiet.

It was an old joke, Germans had been cutting the beards off Jews since they'd arrived in Poland, but bored soldiers would laugh at anything. Ingo thought of the girl from the café again. He hoped now she was not around, as he felt the acid of shame burn within him.

Those other Jews on the street hurried along, looking in the other direction. The old Jew said nothing, he just stood very still, with no sign of any emotion on his face, as Pop hacked away handfuls of wiry hair. Because the Jew did not weep, and did not even move, Kroh was soon bored, and it was far from a smooth shave when he told Pop to stop.

"I've got my pictures," Kroh said.

Then he punched the old man in the nose.

The old man fell to the ground, blooms of rose-red blood vibrant against the iron-grey cobbles. He still did not make a sound, but his right arm was outstretched, his hand palm up on the pavement. Kroh stamped on it, small bones crunched, and he let out a high cry. Anger rose within Ingo like bile and his hands tightened into fists. But Kroh was already walking on, content with the old man's scream, whistling his strange whistle, which was not really a whistle at all, but more like leaking air.

"Come on, Pup, nothing we can do here," Pop said. "The old lad's been lucky, I'd say."

"Lucky?"

"Yes, lucky. But Kroh's in a good mood now, let's see if we can persuade him to let us have a car for the afternoon – I can teach you how to do racing down-shifts," Pop said, then walked after Kroh.

Ingo looked once more at the Jew in the gutter, hesitated for a while. "I'm sorry," he said, softly, then jogged after Pop and Kroh.

**

Seville, Spain. November 1949

Sundermann stared at Sarah Malka through the smoke of his cigarette. His eyes were green, a little bloodshot, and watery from the booze. She knew he was in his late forties, yet his hair was not thinning, and was brushed over from a side parting, slicked with brilliantine. His face was deeply lined, though, around the eyes in particular. He did not look like a man who slept well – but she didn't mind that. He wore a suit that looked expensive, but was worn, and old, and a tie with navy blue stripes on a paler blue, which was now a little crooked.

They sat in Morales, a bar close to the bullring, over the road from the canalised diversion of the Guadalquivir River. It was decorated with pictures of matadors and picadors, and also hung with mirrors in which the candlelight swam. The floor was tiled and clicked to hard leather shoe soles which punctuated impassioned conversations; while the smell was cigars and cigarettes, the wood of the sherry casks, and the aroma of the huge hams that were hung above the bar. It was a place of smoke.

A woman was unusual in a bar like this, a woman like her more so; Latin tan and luscious hair, loose blouse (all tools of her trade), and Sundermann was clearly enjoying the hot and envious stares from the Spaniards. He was also enjoying the pale fino sherry, and the plate of Jambon Iberico. She did not share the plate of cured ham. She was working, and she only ate to stay alive these days, anyway. Her fino, she sipped. Tiny sips.

"You drink like a lady," Sundermann said, in very good, if slurred, Spanish. It was meant to be a joke, she thought.

She smiled, and then covered her mouth as she yawned. On the other side of the room a young man looked at his watch, then drained his glass of Cruzcampo beer and left the bar.

"Tired?" Sundermann said.

"Not *too* tired," she replied, also in Spanish. Languages were another tool of her trade.

His eyes were glassy with booze, but her hint lit them up like green lights. "We could go to my place?" he said.

"Yes, your place," she answered, then stood.

He stood too, and brought the table with him, toppling the glass of fino in his haste. He was drunker than she had realised; but it did not matter, if it all worked the way she thought it would, he would still pay.

A little later they had walked through the slightly chilly narrow streets to Sundermann's apartment in the Arenal district, which was in a three-storey house at the end of a row. She paused a little outside, making a show of taking a look at the building. The two upper floors had single iron-railed balconies. The stone was painted white and the windows, like the house itself, were narrow. The building was old, with sores on its skin where patches of paint had fallen away like scabs.

"It's not much, but it's home," he said.

"Home?"

"For now," he said, and even in the silver moonlight she thought she saw the tug of a regretful, wry smile at the corner of his mouth.

"Are you on the top floor?" she asked, raising her voice a little.

"Yes, why?"

"Let's go up," she said. "I'm cold."

He let her in then led her up the stairs and in to his apartment. There was nothing much to it, just an easy chair, a wood-encased Telefunken radio set the shape of a church window and a drinks cabinet with a glass front; the levels in the bottles of spirits lined up in a diminishing bar graph of preference. There were pictures on the wall, of flamenco dancers, their swirling red skirts smears in the paint, but she did not believe they were his, thought that they probably came with the flat. As she took in the details of the room she took off her coat and dropped it on the chair and then kicked off her shoes. It took her an instant more to find the bedroom. It was at the front. The iron bed was unmade, and the shutters and the windows shut.

Sarah switched on the light. He was behind her. She took off her blouse, then her skirt, allowing both to fall to her feet. Then her bra and panties, quickly. He stared at her naked reflection, which was thrown on to the window by the lightbulb. She knew she had him. She was in complete control. In the reflection she could see what he saw; the cream pale skin, a ghost of her bathing suit, and the tanned limbs. Her breasts were taut and tight, the nipples hard, because it was cold in the room.

"Undress," she said, turning to face him.

He did so, quickly. From the sound his jacket made when it hit the floor she knew there was something hard in his pocket, as there was under his shorts. But she did not look at that for long, instead she looked at his left arm. He moved to kiss her, hold her, and she took his arm, twisted it a little, which was easy, as he was drunk, and pliant. Then she saw it, on the underside of the arm near the armpit, the mark of the devil: *AB*.

She stepped away from him, pushing him back. Because he was intoxicated and off balance he fell on to the bed, the tired springs wheezing like an asthmatic donkey. Surprise painted his face, but not yet anger, and she knew she had to move fast, while he was still confused. She quickly stepped into her panties and put on her bra and was out of the bedroom door and into her skirt by the time he had recovered.

"What's wrong?" he said, loudly, and she heard the bed creak as he stood up from it. "Is it something I said?" She pulled on her blouse, then reached for her coat.

But he was with her now, still naked. He had a knife, clutched tight across his chest so he knew she could see it. Sarah recognised it instantly. An SS dagger, the motto '*My Honour is Loyalty*' in German, clear on the blade.

"I'm not finished with you," Sundermann said.

"I've changed my mind."

"No, you haven't," he said, moving towards her, the lamplight splashing on the gleaming blade.

"What's that?" she said. "A souvenir?"

"Take off your clothes."

"A souvenir of Treblinka?"

That stopped him, dead. He stared at her for some stretched seconds, and Sarah stared back.

"Who are you?" he said, almost whispering it.

Sarah did not reply, but reached for the cold iron door handle. It was as she turned it that he attacked. She did not doubt he would kill her, for she now knew for sure that this man had killed many. And that this man must now have figured out just why she was there.

He was drunk, and angry, and she heard and sensed his movement, was able to duck away from the passage of the knife, which swished past her, an inch from her cheek, then thudded in to the now open door, carving a yellow notch in the dark wood. Sarah dodged behind him as he stumbled, then regained his balance. Now he was in-between her and the door.

Sundermann looked at her, held the knife out in front of him, aiming it like a pistol. "I said take off your clothes."

Yitzhak crept in through the open door. He carried a short club, the lead-weighted truncheon he kept in the lining of his jacket, and he moved like the night. He would have waited outside the bar, and then followed them.

Sarah shrugged off her blouse and Sundermann smiled again. "That's better, and the bra."

Yitzhak was right behind Sundermann now. But he simply grinned, and then nodded.

"Take it off!" Sundermann ordered, and Yitzhak again nodded, briskly. She did so, quickly, trying not to look at Yitzhak, and Sundermann stared at her breasts. Yitzhak did not stare, just took a quick look, then there was another nod that she caught through the corner of her eye, slow and appreciative this time.

Then the game was done. Yitzhak clouted Sundermann with the club, aiming for the axis, the delicate bones at the base of the skull, the noise of the hit a muted crack. Sundermann folded, as if his legs had turned to cooked spaghetti, and fell face first. Such a hit could kill instantly, she knew, but in matters like this Yitzhak did not leave things to chance. He hit Sundermann again, and again, and again, as he lay on his back on the tiled floor. He swung the club with the cool passion of a man who was content with his work.

Sarah put her bra back on, and her blouse, while Yitzhak closed the door and then felt for a pulse in Sundermann's neck.

"He's still with us ... Just ..."

"Yes?"

"Now gone," Yitzhak said, taking his finger from the dead man's neck, grinning at Sarah.

"Arsehole," she said, "why the wait?"

Yitzhak just grinned: "Not often you get an eyeful of a married woman's titties. Let's say perks of the job, eh? Very perky, actually."

Sarah shook her head, as she finished dressing. "This is messy, is there anyone else around?" she said, looking at the corpse. They had planned to finish him later, once she was sure they had their man, to come back on another day when no-one would have seen him with her. Then hang him. Slowly. Make it look like suicide. But a dead Nazi is a dead Nazi, and Sarah could not regret that.

"Doesn't seem so," Yitzhak said. "The apartment below is empty, and I've heard nothing."

"Then it's a drunken fall, from the balcony?"

"That should do it, yes. Nasty accident," Yitzhak said, picking up the SS dagger and looking down at Sundermann's now flaccid penis. "Hmm, I could make him kosher first, wouldn't take much cutting?"

"Just get on with it," Sarah ordered.

*

Chillar, Argentina. November 1949

Horses aren't like motorbikes, Ingo thought, as he tugged at the rein, flicked a heel into Zündapp's flank. They are unpredictable, could be bad tempered – well, Zündapp could. Like most Criollos he was also tough, squat and could run forever, but unlike most Criollos he could be a bit of a jerk. That, Ingo had soon realised, was why he had come with the farmhouse, and why no one had ever returned to collect him.

But the horse had one redeeming feature. He was seldom boring.

Zündapp was a glossy deep chestnut, blending in to an almost-black at his mane and at the legs – though one of his socks was odd, an off-white colour. The hair between his now-stiff ears was also black, and swept to one side, like Hitler. That might have been a better name for him, *Hitler*, but even though he did not behave like a motorcycle, Ingo had named him after one.

What made riding this horse all the more tricky, and, yes, all the more exciting, was that at times Zündapp could be friendly, docile even. Sometimes he would even jump for Ingo. But this was the first time he had tried to jump him over the cross-braced five-bar gate that now raced towards them, growing bigger, like a wooden wave cresting on a pale green sea.

The horse snorted, and Ingo smelt its sweat, the leather of its tack, which jangled and creaked as Zündapp flicked his head to one side, tugging the rein through Ingo's hand, burning it slightly. They had been going hard for almost half an hour and wisps of silver steam curled off the horse's body. He was cantering well now, the thump of his hooves ringing hollow on the ground. Ingo checked the horse, judging its pace, then loosened his grip on the reins a bit, giving it its head.

As Zündapp cantered towards the gate Ingo tried to feel for a hint of hesitation, of malice, though his calves, which brushed against the flanks of the stocky Criollo, but the canter never checked, the horse seemed sure, and Ingo raised himself out of the saddle, taking his weight on his feet in the iron stirrups. Readying himself for the jump.

They were just a few metres from the five-bar gate when Zündapp decided to stop, ploughing deep furrows in the ground and sliding into the gate which crunched and shuddered to the impact. Ingo was thrown over the horse's head, and the gate, and his world was just a marbled-blue sky for a moment as he tipped head over heels, before he landed hard on his behind, the hit jarring his body. The horse whinnied from the other side of the gate, then turned and galloped away, sods of grassy earth thrown from its pounding hooves, the beat of its gallop fading fast. Zündapp would be back at the farmhouse in an hour. It would take Ingo a little longer.

"Bastard horse," he said aloud.

Ingo eased himself up on to his feet, checked himself for damage; there would be bruises, he thought, nothing worse. Then he started to walk back in the late spring warmth. He wore shorts and boots, a thin shirt and no hat, and he had a canvas bag slung over his shoulder which contained water and food. He thought it might rain later, perhaps a storm. There was a thin dark line on the distant horizon; a lead filament lining the edge of the vast sky.

There was a cluster of trees, but otherwise the land was flat here in three directions, with a rise to the west. There was nothing but fields and a network of rough farm tracks used by the farmers and the farm workers who sometimes saw him, and stared; wondering who the bearded man with no hat was, he supposed. It was noon, a Sunday, he thought – he had to count back, still wasn't sure, but the silence seemed to confirm it. Even the birds had taken a rest. Not a sound, except the omnipresent, steely, shrill noise in his head that had been a part of him since Kursk. He could smell his own sweat, and the hot grass, and the hunk of cold beef in the bag slung around his neck – from the joint he had cooked up two nights before and lived on since. He often just ate beef, and apples. He was glad he had not yet bought a saddle bag for Zündapp, for if he had then today there would be no lunch.

Ingo decided to eat under the scant shade of one of the trees, pulling the beef from his canvas bag and unwrapping it as he walked. He ate it slowly.

He was bored of beef, but he savoured every morsel. That was something he had learnt long ago … No, not so long ago.

He crunched on the apple, drank some of the water, glad that the bottle had not smashed when he'd fallen from the horse, and then sat with his back against the slender trunk of the tree. When you can sleep in a trench or a panzer you can sleep anywhere, even if your behind is sore because you've been thrown by an arsehole of a horse. He dozed off. And dreamt of Russia. Again. He hated that dream; and he awoke to a shell strike. Had he screamed? He wasn't sure. Maria, the whore who helped him with his Spanish and with other things – because he was still alive – said he yelled out in his sleep sometimes. He was not surprised at that. But he hoped that if he *talked* in his sleep it would be in German, and not Spanish, he would not want poor Maria to know what he had seen.

The cloud had closed in while he had been asleep, it was a little colder, and he could smell static in the air. Hear the rumble of thunder, too …

"No, that's not it," he said, to himself, aloud again, a habit of the bored and lonely. "That's …" Yet Ingo was not sure what *that* was. It sounded like an engine, he thought, but not in one of the docile sedans that were seldom driven quickly here. But it might easily have been a tuned straight-six, driven hard; he had a good ear for such things. The sound fluctuated, and it came from the other side of the rise. For a moment he hesitated. Something told him not to go and look. But he could not stop himself. He started to walk to the rise in the ground; he heard a sharp rise in revs from beyond it, and his heart rate leapt with that. He sped up, then broke into a run. He thought the noise was diminishing and he ran faster, until he was sprinting by the time he came to the top of the rise.

The cloud of dust stretched across the pampas like a huge dirty quill; and at its nib there was a bright point of colour. His eyesight was still good and he could see it was a pale green car; an old Chevrolet Master Coupe. Its suspension was impossibly extended so it could deal with the rough track and it was going at an astonishing speed for the road surface, sometimes flying for many metres as it was launched over a hump. There was signwriting along its side and there was a large number 23 on it, too. It was a racing car.

He followed its swift passage until it slowed for a corner, the roughly-crisp engine blips of racing down-changes carrying across the empty space. The car kicked left, then right, then took the turn with a rooster tail of dirt spraying from its rear wheels. And then it was lost from Ingo's sight, hidden by the dust which it trailed behind it. The air held its smell, a hint of acrid, hot clutch, and burnt fuel. He relished it, sniffed it inside him, like a starving man savouring the aroma of sizzling bratwurst.

Right then it started to rain, a heavy cold drop landing on Ingo's hand, a wet tattoo beating against his head and shoulders soon after. It was ten kilometres back to the old farmhouse, he would be cold and wet by the time he had walked home, but he hardly cared. His face felt strange, the skin of his cheeks stretched. He realised he was smiling.

***

Warsaw. November 1939

Why did she go? Chopin, of course. Why did she stay?

Ingo, it was his name. He was laughing. Lidka was laughing, too, it was difficult not to laugh when he laughed. He had stopped playing Chopin some time ago, but she had not left. She had not believed she would go to the café on Krzywe Koło, but she had gone to the market in the square, because they were almost out of potatoes – that's what she had told Kassia, that's what she had told herself. Once in the square the music – one of the Nocturnes, Opus 9, Number 2 – hooked her, reeled her in. Again. She did not fight it. Performing Chopin publicly was banned by the Nazis, but she supposed the soldiers who heard the music would not care, or perhaps would not know it for what it was. And then some would surely love it too much to betray it anyway.

He had not played the frivolous music this evening, just Chopin. Café Kasper was packed. The windows were steamed up, but someone had wiped a porthole in one with a sleeve, so she could see it was now raining hard outside, and hear the slap of it against the cobbles. The place smelt of strong tea, sour rye soup, and cigarette smoke. It was small, not much bigger than a regular drawing room, and was dotted with tiny brass-topped circular tables, around which four people could just about gather, with their cups of tea, or little glasses of vodka.

Some had not found seats at the small tables and had stood to listen to the music instead. No one seemed to care that he was a German soldier, if indeed they had even realised, they only cared to hear Chopin played well, played well on a poor piano – he had performed two magic tricks in one there. People were hungry for Chopin, and Kasper, the café owner – a man with a bushy grey-black moustache, like a little raincloud over the rolling pale fields of his fat face, and the nous and means to find and provide Łańcut vodka – had been happy to allow Ingo to play his piano. It pulled in a crowd, and he sold plenty of vodka, żur and pierogi. Once she had seen Ingo wink at him, and the always slouching Kasper had given him the famous two-fingered Polish army salute, before bending a thumb and turning his fingers into a gun, then puffing out his cheeks and making a popping sound with his mouth; a thing of his, she now realised, for whatever the situation may be.

"It's good vodka, where does he get it?" Lidka asked, taking a sip – the peppery burn of it warming, further corroding the lead weight of doubt within her. He did not wear his tunic, this was slung atop the upright piano, with its marks of interlocking teacup rings and cigarette burns – which made it hard to believe the music she had heard could have possibly come from it. They sat at one of the tiny tables. His hair seemed long, for a German soldier; unruly, thick and dark, curling at the ends like surf; an inverted question mark of it floated above his smooth forehead.

"I've no idea," he replied. "But it's what brought me here in the first place."

"The vodka?"

Ingo nodded. "Feldwebel Kroh, I guess he's my boss, some fella down in Solec told him Kasper was the man for good vodka, I come up here, to load up the sidecar with a few bottles, and then after that the wheels of commerce turn, I suppose. I think a lot of it gets sent back to Germany."

"Black market?"

"Kroh doesn't care much what colour the market is; though I suppose the blacker the better, with that one."

"You don't like him?"

"He's a difficult man to like, is Kroh," Ingo said, after a slight hesitation. "But then you get all sorts in the army, that's what my pal Pop always says."

"But it's illegal?"

"Maybe, but Kroh's more dangerous than the military police. Pop says that, too."

She was about to tell him to be careful, but then she thought it was not her place, and that he would only laugh anyway, and so she said what had been on her mind for a little while. "You're not like a soldier, do you know that?"

"Kroh says it all the time, doesn't seem to understand I'm only along for the ride."

"So, you were called up?"

"No, I enlisted."

"But, why?"

"I was bored. I saw a poster for the Wehrmacht. There was a motorcycle on it; and so I went straight to the recruiting office near the Feldherrnhalle; and signed up there and then."

"You didn't even think it over?"

"No, I always trust to instinct. It never fails me," he said, his grin widening.

"Really, a big decision like that – so simple?"

"Well, not quite that simple, I admit. One day, maybe I'll tell you about it," he said, and for a fraction of a moment his smile slipped slightly, she thought.

"Why not tell me now?"

"Have some more vodka," he said, and poured some into the small glass. "The army's not so bad, you know, it has its moments."

"But it's all such a waste, you play the piano so ..." She let the words die, shook her head.

"I can play piano when I'm an old man, or when there's time, perhaps. But, for now, I intend to live."

She thought to tell him that she had never felt more alive than she had just half an hour ago, when he had somehow turned dull wire into heaven, but she did not.

"Besides," he added. "If I'd not volunteered, I'd have been called up anyway, sooner or later, and then I might have ended up on a horse and cart rather than a motorbike; which, despite what the newsreels show, is the way most of the German army gets around. So it made sense."

"None of it makes sense," she said, quietly. Some of the Poles began to leave now. A middle-aged man in a postman's uniform thanked Ingo for playing Chopin, in Polish; Ingo did not understand but he smiled back. His companion, a man with iron-filing bristles on a scarlet face, smoking a pipe of evil-smelling local tobacco and wearing a peaked leather cap, also spoke Polish. "You play well, German," he said. Then he turned to Lidka. "He has finished with Chopin, girl. And it's curfew soon." He smiled as he said it, but there was a warning in his steely eyes. Or a threat.

"What did he say?" Ingo asked.

"He said you play well."

The man had left now. Others followed, and the discarded field grey tunic thrown on top of the piano suddenly seemed to stand out.

"I want to ask you something, Ingo."

"Go ahead."

"I have heard things, seen things. The way the Germans have been, the way they have treated Poles, and Jews; you must have seen this?"

"Yes, I've seen it, too much of it; there are some real thugs in the army. In any army, I would have thought. But there are far more decent people, like my pal Pop – you'd like Pop, he'd like you ..." He paused for a moment, shook his head slightly, and then continued. "But men like Kroh seem to enjoy inflicting pain, and the Nazis have given them an excuse, I guess. So, yes, I've seen it. But I don't understand it. Doubt I ever will."

Just then a gang of young boys ran by, they could hear their shoes slapping against the wet cobbles, laughter and shrieks echoing along the narrow street.

"Hear that?" he said.

"Kids, always noisy."

"Kids, *always* kids. German, Pole, Jew or Eskimo; but always kids. The only thing that changes is that as we grow we get fed full of ... Well, in the end, or rather, in the beginning, we're all pretty much the same, that's what I believe."

"Most Germans don't think like that," she said.

"There, see? You're the same! 'Most Germans'. I'm a German, I think that, and many others will too. I have faith in humanity, there are more good people than bad. And Germans, Poles, Jews; well, like I said, we're all the same, in the end. Or the beginning."

"You forgot the Eskimos."

He grinned at that. "Oh yes, and the Eskimos. Let's drink to the Eskimos!" He raised his glass, and they clinked a toast to people far away. Then drank a little more vodka.

She wished all Germans *were* like Ingo, but did not say so. Instead, she said: "You didn't mean what you said, did you? About waiting until you're an old man before you play the piano; I mean, play it seriously?"

"*Seriously*? I'm not sure you can ever play it *seriously*," he said. "But I know what you mean, and yes, there are other things to do first. I have plans, you know?"

She thought he was going to go on, but instead he just threw a vodka down his throat – he didn't seem the type for sipping – and then poured another into the tiny glass from the bottle at the centre of the table.

"What plans?" she asked, after a small lull in the conversation measured by the ding of a bicycle bell outside, the hiss of its tyres over wet stone, and the scrape of a chair leg along the floor.

"My pal Pop use to race motorbikes, and cars, before the war," Ingo said, just a little more seriously now, though his eyes still smiled – with passion rather than mirth. "He took part in the 2000 Kilometres of Germany Rally, racing all around the country. Can you imagine that?"

"No," she said, though she could imagine that he had imagined that. Often.

"Well, Pop says there's money in racing, once you've made a name; if you're good."

"And you're good?"

"Pop says so."

"And you say?"

"I would like to find out." He laughed again, and she noticed an old man in the far corner smiling at his laughter. It was so easy to forget that Ingo was a German soldier.

"But surely there's money in playing the piano, too?"

"Well, it's not the money I'm interested in, that's Pop's thing. I just want to race."

"But will there will be racing now, there's a war on?"

"No, not for us soldiers, anyway. But this can't last long, they say it's already fizzled out in France, it hardly got started there; and it's done and dusted here, it seems. Pop has promised to teach me all he knows about riding motorcycles and driving cars in the meantime, and Pop knows plenty."

Just then Kasper brought two steaming plates of pierogi, the ravioli-like delicacy of pasta filled with whatever's to hand. He placed it on the table, then did that two-fingered salute thing of his, again turning it into a popping pistol, and Ingo laughed. The food smelt wonderful, and saliva flooded her mouth. Lidka was starving, and took a fork and began to dig in without a word. It was filled with spiced minced meat and cabbage, and she wondered if Ingo had brought the ingredients, for she had seen little meat lately. They did not talk so much as they ate.

"So, you like your food, but then who doesn't?" Ingo said after they had both finished. "But that's all I know about you. Oh, and that you're a teacher."

She dabbed at the corner of her mouth with a napkin to give her time to think about her reply. She did not think she had to fear him, but the teaching she now did was illegal, and as absurd as it seemed, he was still a German soldier. But she saw no reason to lie to someone who had bought her such excellent pierogi.

"The school was destroyed in the bombing in September," she said, and that was the truth.

"So, you don't work, now?"

She shook her head: "You Germans have closed most of the schools."

"We have?"

"You really don't know?"

"They don't tell us much," he said.

"No, I can believe that." There was a pause in the conversation that somehow seemed longer than it was. She realised that others had left now, and she glanced at the clock on the wall. It would be curfew soon.

"So, how do you manage, with no work?" he finally said.

She shrugged. "I manage."

"Do you miss it?" he asked.

She nodded. "Yes. You know, I have always wanted to be a teacher; I used to teach my dolls," she said, laughing.

"You did?"

"Yes, back in Wagrowiec, when I was a child."

"Your home?"

"I left just last year. Bad timing, to come to Warsaw then."

"Good timing, I'd say."

She smiled.

"Your family, they still there?"

"Just Father, my mother died some years ago, giving birth to a baby brother who died that same night." It was a long time ago, but it still hurt, and she paused for a moment. "He married again, but I never could get along with her, was glad to get away."

"Wicked stepmother?"

"Not really, no. Now I'm far away I realise it was only because she was not my mother, and we both knew it. I was glad to move to Warsaw to work, I think they were glad, too. Father writes, but less often now, what with everything that's happened here, and there. Maybe I will go and see him, soon."

"So, you're an independent woman, a modern woman: I like that," he said. "Where do you live now?"

"I share an apartment with a friend," she said. "She's from Wagrowiec, too."

"Another teacher?" Ingo asked.

"No, she's not a teacher."

"Tell me about her," he said.

"There's not much to tell. She likes clothes, fine things …"

"And what do you like?" he said, perhaps sensing that she did not want to talk about her flat mate.

"Isn't it obvious? Chopin. Why else would I be here?"

"And pierogi?"

"And pierogi," she said. "And that's me, there's nothing more to tell."

"You have left one thing out," Ingo said.

"I have?"

"Last time, when I was with the general; you said there was someone?"

"I did?"

He nodded.

She was about to say he was far away, which is what she supposed. But she did not want to talk about Józef, because she was not sure there was anything to say now. And also because she wanted to hear Ingo play Chopin again; she wanted to eat pierogi with him again; and to drink more of Kasper's pepper vodka with him. She realised then she had spent a happy couple of hours.

"I must be going," she said, "it's almost curfew."

"I'll walk with you," he said, reaching for the army tunic from the top of the piano.

"No. Please, it's best for me if we're not seen together," she said, pushing her chair back and pulling on her mac.

"Tuesday, then. Here? I'll play *Heroic*, it's my favourite."

She smiled, she was not surprised that that was his favourite. Then she left the café.

***

Chillar. November 1949

He waited. He had waited here every day for two weeks. On none of those occasions had he set out to come to this place, but he could not kid himself that Zündapp had led him here. The horse stood some metres away, munching noisily on the coarse grass in the warm sunshine. The day was beginning to die, slowly. Ingo knew all about that …

Tonight, Maria the whore would be visiting, so he would not wait for too long. It was a long ride back to the old farmhouse filled with emptiness.

He could hear an engine in the distance, but it was a pump, asthmatic and labouring, not the tuned six-cylinder he listened out for. It had rained heavily since that last time and the ground smelt richer, the now deep-brown rough track on which he had seen the Chevy was streaked with long caramel-coloured puddles where the water had filled the furrows carved by the wheels of what little traffic there was. He chose a spot low in the sky and vowed to wait until the sun had crossed it before he rode back to the farmhouse. He had no watch. No time for the torture of time; the clock in the kitchen he could just about put up with, because sometimes it was useful to know how many hours were left in a day.

The ground at the top of the slope was broken and he sat on a stone and ate an apple. The distant pump chugged softly, a beat to the high pitched, twanging-wire whistle between his ears that had been a part of him since the war.

After about half an hour he saw something moving on the horizon, on the eastward leg of the track before it turned north, coming towards him. For a moment, no more, his heart sped up. But his eyes were still good and his ears were okay, too, despite the tinnitus. It was a tractor. Its driver stared at Ingo as he drove towards him, and Ingo stared back, but after the tractor took the long turn to the left its driver did not turn back to look at the bearded man in shorts with no hat. The corner was interesting, there was a rise before it that would pitch a speeding car into the air, Ingo thought, leaving plenty for the driver to do to get the car turned in. At the outer edge of the corner there was a rocky stream, the reason for the turn in the first place.

The sun touched the invisible point in the sky. Ingo let it caress the patch of blue, then tenderly hold its hand until fingers slipped and sun and piece of sky could only hold each other's gaze ... The sun had bowed politely, dipped a little more, before Ingo finally stood up to leave.

And then he heard it. Steely, as if the noise of it sliced through the very fabric of the air, rasping then burbling, the driver on and off the throttle. The green car, the harsh sun behind it so that Ingo had to form a peak with his hand to see it, was side on as it slid into view; sliding a little too much, Ingo thought. The driver held the skid, straightened the car, and accelerated. Huge toffee-coloured splashes exploded from the car's wheels as it surged through the long puddles, the driver bringing it up through the 'box with crisp gear-changes. Even with the sun in his eyes Ingo could see the driver was smiling; a crescent of polar white beneath a Zorro moustache. The car was heading to what Ingo already thought of as the jump ...

The Chevrolet took flight over the hump in the road, a metre of sky below it, its wheels drooping far beneath it on its long suspension travel, so that it seemed to stretch itself like a man just out of bed. But it was in the air for just a second, and then it landed, its leaf springs compressing and the car seemingly shrugging. Ingo looked at the driver, saw that he in turn was looking at him, and he knew in that split second of the other man's distraction that he would not make the corner.

The driver's head snapped left, looking through the turn and beyond, which showed he knew what he was about, and at the same time the nose of the car dipped on its springs as if to kiss the rough, wet track, one wheel locking solid and skidding.

By the time the no-longer-smiling driver, his forehead now furrowed with concern, had come off the brake the Chevy had slid too wide, first at the front, before its tail overtook its nose as it skidded towards the rocky stream. It was side on to him now and Ingo could read some of the yellow signwriting on the green car; *Di Rossi Auto Repairs*. Then the car's outer wheels dug in to the stony ground. It tipped over on to its side, then on to its roof, and then finished its single rollover on its wheels, right in the centre of the shallow stream.

Ingo did not hesitate. Even the slowest rollover could kill or maim a man, and he sprinted down the slope, slipping in the mud his side of the stream before splashing through the ankle deep water.

The driver was already pulling himself out of the window, though, the car's door either damaged or welded shut; Ingo suspected the latter. He was a tall man, neither young, nor old. His skin was tanned, and his eyes were chestnut.

His hair was losing a battle with his forehead, was making a tactical withdrawal, but it had opened a second front at the rear, where it advanced to the man's broad shoulders. His moustache was neat, straight, and sharply clipped, underlining a strong nose. He wore a pale blue shirt, and tan whipcord trousers. He pulled a small silver case out of his pocket, took a cheroot from it then lit it with a match he struck against a rock.

"You distracted me," he said, as Ingo slowed to a walk and splashed towards him, the water was icy cold.

"You locked up; then came off the brake too late," Ingo said.

"The German; you're the German?"

"The car is damaged," Ingo said. His Spanish was still improving, but it was good enough for conversation now. He was concerned that people in Chillar might be aware of him, though, as the man seemed to suggest.

"Just a few more dings, to join the others," the man said. Close up, Ingo now saw the green paint was faded and the car was indeed very battered; it was clear this was not its first accident. "You don't race from Buenos Aries to Lima – and back – without picking up a few dents."

"Uh, uh," Ingo mumbled, suddenly realising, with a shock, he had fallen into a conversation.

"Ten-thousand kilometres, a long way that, you know? Do they have such races in Germany?"

"We had something tougher, in Russia," Ingo said, and immediately regretted it. He bent down low, so that his knees were in the cold water, too, but he hardly noticed that. Instead he noticed something else, a silver gleam where steel was broken clean in half.

"Your steering arm's sheared."

"They have a habit of breaking, I carry a spare."

"And some tools?"

The driver nodded, then said: "Racing in Russia?"

"If you want me to help you'd best shut up and roll up your sleeves," Ingo said. He heard the clop of Zündapp's hooves on the stones at the edge of the far side of stream.

"Nice horse," the man said.

"No, he's an arsehole. Spanner?"

It took them an hour or so to make the repairs, a job made difficult by the car being stranded in the stream, then for a moment they stood in the setting sun inspecting their handiwork.

"You know, you've saved my life," the driver said. "That was not a job for one man."

"A walk from here would not have killed you." He had guessed from some of the signage on the car that it came from Chillar.

"No, but my wife would, if she knew I'd been with Sophia again," with that his suntanned face split into a white grin. "The car."

Ingo saw the painted *Sophia* above the door on the driver's side. On the door itself, above the number 23, were the names *Carlo Rossi* and *Carlos Rojo*.

"Rossi, that's me; Italian – well, we moved here when I was a child – and Carlos, Argentinian forever, or so he said. He was my co-driver, but he is dead now. An accident …"

Ingo thought Rossi wanted him to say something. Perhaps here people dying still meant something. All he said was: "I have to go."

"Why not stay a while … sorry, your name?"

But Ingo was already splashing through the stream towards Zündapp.

"I'll let you drive Sophia, as payment for your help – she's quite a ride my friend!" Rossi shouted after him.

Ingo heard him, but said nothing as he mounted the horse.

*

Lampeter, Wales. November 1949

They called him Joe the Pole, as *Joe* was about all they could pull out of the tangle of *C*s and *S*s, and *Z*s of his name. It did not worry him. He even thought of himself as simply Joe now, as if the other half of his name, of who he was, had been burnt away with his skin. No one from back then, when it had happened – wherever they might be, if they might be – would recognise him for who he really was now, anyway. So Joe would do.

He had found a regular job, at last. He liked the idea of working on engines. It's hard to see a man's face when it's under the beige bonnet of a Standard Ten. But he could see their faces. He could hear them, too, understand them. They would not know that.

"Complicated name, he has," David Davies, known here in Lampeter as Dai Twice, said.

"Polish, see," his son and apprentice, Huw, put in. "They all have complicated names; but why on Earth would you put a Z, *there?*" They were standing by a work bench that was clamped with a big blue vice as they looked again at the letter of recommendation from Ifor Pugh's cousin, the letter that had got Joe the job. The work top was scattered with car parts, some wrapped and new, others old and oily. The place smelt of petrol and grease, but this only just cut through an almost spicy smell of wood-smoke, which came through the red-painted steel garage door, slid open on its rusty rollers. Outside, on the apron of gravel-strewn asphalt where the single Esso petrol pump stood, three vehicles awaited their turn inside the small workshop: a green Ford Eight, a scarlet Morris van with white signwriting that said *DC Williams A'i Fab*, and an ugly but new-looking Singer SM1500 in a gleaming blue that was dark as black.

Davies & Son (Dai Twice was actually the son on the sign, the garage was almost as old as the motor car), sat at the edge of the small market town, which was known – in west Wales and vicarages across the principality at least – for its old college with its stark quadrangle. The River Teifi carved its way through green fields nearby and the road from Carmarthen joined the road from Llandovery just across the stern stone bridge that spanned the river. The town was overlooked by a cluster of green hills, one of which was capped with a tonsure of trees.

Dai Twice and Huw wore overalls camouflaged in grease and oil stains, Joe had been given a new set. They were tight, and chafed the burns on his body, but he would not mention that. Dai Twice had been a bit too old to fight, his son a bit too young. They were lucky, and had lucky faces, and dark curly hair, the elder with a little grey in it, the younger with a little length in it. They both had almost exactly the same shape of grease stain on their left cheek, as if it was a family badge, but that was of course a coincidence. It was like the outline of a harp, and Joe wondered how that would look on Mrs Davies, who he had met briefly, and who had also called him Joe; before turning away, just a little too quickly. But then they all turned away soon enough, the women. They did not like to see that side of the war. Joe's war.

It still amused Joe that people who spoke a language stuffed with double Ls and double Fs in the strangest of places could have trouble getting their tongues around his surname. They did not know he could understand Welsh, and they spoke as if he was English, or another foreigner, which he was. He had only ever spoken to them, and everyone else in the town, in English. Knowing Welsh was just another little secret of his.

He had learnt his Welsh at the farm near Llandysul, where he had lived for two or three years. There had been no home to go back to, he knew, and so he had worked with Ifor Pugh, worked hard, and then when old Pugh had died he had moved to Lampeter, doing odd jobs for cash at first, then helping with the hay making in the farms around the town. Just last week he had answered an advertisement for a mechanic in the *Carmarthen Journal*.

He knew the job he was doing on the Zenith carburettor of the old Standard Ten was good, even though it was painful to grip its parts in his burnt fingers. He thought he could make something of working here, with David Davies and his son, enough cash to get through each day as it came. And hope that the pain did not get too bad. He could ask for no more from life.

"Wonder what happened to his face; and hands?" Dai Twice said, as Joe fitted the float mechanism back in the chamber. With the mention of his highly visible wounds he felt the burns flare; the pain of it was always there, but sometimes others' reaction to it hurt him almost as much.

"Fighter pilot, I expect," Huw said. "A lot of Poles were pilots; lot of pilots were burnt. Read that, I did."

Joe did not mind if they thought that.

"Pilot is it? Then why here?" Dai Twice said.

"Hiding, isn't it? Wouldn't you? I mean ..."

"Well, he's come to the right place," Dai Twice said. "And he certainly knows his way round a carburettor."

*

Tel Aviv, Israel. November 1949

There was a café on Allenby Street, close to the busy junction with King George Street, Sheinkin Street and the Carmel Market; a junction the German immigrants had nicknamed Potsdamer Platz. Bendel's served the bagels and babka that came closest to those that Saul Gabriel had eaten on Rochstrasse in Berlin, long before the war. Sarah Malka would often meet him at the café, it was a twenty-minute walk from the Bauhaus apartment on Dizengoff Street in which she lived with her husband and child. Gabriel lived and worked from an apartment and office on Montefiore Street. He had helped her, spotted her talent when she was with a splinter group of the Nakam back in Europe, her gift for languages – and other things. Gabriel had found her work, with The Group, and a life that seemed normal. From the outside.

There was nothing angelic about Gabriel's appearance. He seemed to reflect all the evil he'd seen, to remind the world of what it was capable of. But reminding wasn't enough for men like Gabriel, women like Sarah. He stooped over his black coffee, which he took with a pinch of cardamom, and Sarah found that she was half-listening out for a snap, so brittle he seemed. He sat in the shade, she sat in the warming late-autumn morning sunlight. His skin looked as dry as old scrolls, almost combustible. His hair was pale and thick, a little like raw wool, and his eyes were a dark mahogany colour that seemed black in some lights, with a shine to them that made them look like little pools of oil. Yes, they gleamed, the one part of him that was so obviously alive, a light that spoke of the fire within him that had seen him through Terezin and Belzec; he was one of the very few to have survived the latter. Vengeance was now the fuel for that fire. Saul Gabriel, like all of them in The Group, lived for vengeance.

The Group did not, officially, exist.

Gabriel sipped his coffee, gave a tight but content grimace at the bitter taste of it, then sat back against the steel frame of the chair. The buildings across the street were headache-white in the slanting sunlight; Bauhaus, with curved balconies and gleaming rails, like the superstructure of a bright ship. A soldier, carrying a rifle, his girl's arm through his, a beret stuffed into an epaulette, walked by. The girl was also in army uniform, which clashed with her curls, makeup and emergency red lipstick. A Sten gun was slung over her shoulder, as if it was a handbag. A taxi honked a horn and a donkey hauling a trailer, hooves like maracas on the bitumen, stoically ignored it. The road was dusty, the air was gritty. Sarah could smell the sea, not so far away, but mainly she could smell freshly baked bread. It was a smell that reminded her of a time before the other war.

"How is David?"

"He's fine," Sarah said.

"The boy?"

"He is well."

That would be it, as far as pleasantries were concerned. She would not tell him that her husband wanted her to stop. He wanted her to stop what he believed she was doing; working as a translator for the government, which she occasionally did as it was a cover which allowed her to travel to wherever The Group might need her to be. The boy? Benjamin was two, and had known only happiness, and for that reason, as wrong as she knew this was, she could not love him. The boy had been a mistake, for her, but David had wanted a son. Now he wanted another. That was just another thing to argue about.

"What happened?" Gabriel said.

"I had to be sure it was him."

Gabriel nodded, he knew what that meant. They did not all carry the SS mark, the blood group tattoo on the left arm; some just the scar where it had been removed, some had never had it. But some still bore the sign of the devil, and it could often be the final jagged piece in a jigsaw of broken glass.

"And he would not let you leave?"

This time she nodded, it had happened before.

"It's good you have Yitzhak to watch your back."

"Yitzhak's a clown," she said.

"Yitzhak's a soldier."

"A fool."

"But a gifted assassin."

"Yes, that's true," she said. "He used a club. Then we dressed the corpse, poured whiskey over it, dropped it from the balcony, into the street."

"Our friends in Spain say it made the local papers, a drunk falling to his death."

"It's a pity we were forced to kill him too soon, that we were unable to make him suffer, to let him know he was going to die; it was too clean an end, for him."

"He's dead, so it was for the best. You did well."

"But the world does not know – it does not know we've had our vengeance."

"Once the world knows, we will be stopped. They are building a modern state here, and revenge is not seen as a modern trait," he said. He had said it before, many times.

A freshly squeezed orange juice and a bagel was placed in front of her. The waiter then placed a bagel in front of Gabriel, too. A beige-painted Fargo army truck rumbled past, the fumes from its exhaust fugging the air. Gabriel took another sip of his coffee, a small but slow sip, and she waited until he placed the cup back on its saucer before she asked what she always asked.

"Is there anything?"

Gabriel sighed. She knew by now that he would not prolong this with questions of who; and he just said what he always now said when she asked this question: "No."

Sarah nodded sharply. Thought about taking a bite from the bagel, but sipped some orange juice instead.

35

"You, know, maybe he's dead," Gabriel said, as he had also said many times before. "It is quite likely."

"*He* is still alive," she said. "I know it."

"*He* is just one of them."

"They are all *just* one."

"And thanks to you and Yitzhak, one is one dead one," he said, with a laugh as dry as sawdust. It was as close to humour as Gabriel was likely to get, he sipped a little more coffee, then continued. "You know something; to some – even here – we're just killers."

"It's a word that means nothing in this context."

"Perhaps, but we must tread carefully."

"Just promise me, if you hear anything. Anything at all." she said. "Promise you will tell me."

Gabriel nodded. "I will tell you," he said.

*

Chillar. November 1949

Rossi was waiting for him. The green Chevrolet was parked up by the stream. Ingo stood at the crest of the rise and hesitated for a moment. It was hot and still, and the only sound was Zündapp munching on the dry grass some metres before the top of the small hill. Rossi had opened a bottle of wine, and there was a hamper sat on a flat rock. But it was the sight of the car that compelled Ingo to walk down the slope, leaving Zündapp to his lunch.

Soon Ingo was at the foot of the slope and Rossi was grinning, as he poured the rich red wine into tin mugs, the sun shining through it as it was decanted, making it ruby bright. Ingo splashed through the ankle deep stream. The car's body was ticking as it cooled and he could smell the hot brake linings and the good oil – he felt like a starving man, walking into a restaurant, but he knew he should turn back. Now.

"You'll take some wine?"

"Why?"

"Because it's wine," Rossi said, raising his eyes to the sky and shaking his head.

Ingo said nothing, just stared at the car.

"Okay, you helped me fix Sophia," Rossi added. "So, I thought I'd show my appreciation, and what better way? But I don't know your name?"

"Wine, you said?"

Rossi handed him the mug. Ingo took a deep gulp of it, it was robust and fruity, wine to make you feel alive, and so he drank some more. He would not be staying long, so he might as well make the most of it, he thought, as he continued to study the car.

"Your name?" Rossi repeated.

"Enrique."

Rossi nodded. "That's all I need to know, my friend. I'm more interested in your loving touch with this old girl," he tapped the tinny roof, "than European history – that's all been rather tedious these last few years."

"Depends where you were standing, I'd say."

"Sure, of course. It's Carlo by the way."

"Yes, I know, you said. But not Carlos, he's dead."

Carlo nodded, took his first gulp of wine, a deep gulp.

"In this?" Ingo said.

"Yes, in Sophia. We were driving through dust, it was always mud or dust on those trans-continental races. It was somewhere in Bolivia. I'd pulled out to overtake a slower car, still in the dust cloud. Of course, you can never slow down, you need to get past —"

"Never lift," Ingo interrupted, surprising Carlo as much as he surprised himself.

"Exactly, I thought you would understand," Carlo said, before he continued: "The road was wide enough, wide enough for three cars, I'd say. It was so dusty I never even realised it was a Ford we were passing, we could hear it, somewhere inside its own yellow cloud, rather than see anything of it – there was a hint of blue as we went by, that's all. Perhaps I was momentarily distracted by this ..." He trailed off, drank some more wine.

Ingo knew that this was where he should say, 'and what then?', for the man was a showman, and knew how to tell a tale, but instead he took a little more wine himself. Carlo continued anyway: "There was a dried up river bed in front of us, a bridge across it. It narrowed the road; I had a second to make a decision: the car to my left, head on into the stone buttress, or the river bed to the right."

"And you went to the right?"

"Right," Carlo said. "It was a longer drop than I anticipated, to the riverbed, and we were going," he shrugged to show an estimation, "perhaps 100 kilometres per hour, maybe more, even though I stood on the brakes. The old girl flew like a condor, gliding like she was born to it, but she's a fat assed bird, and she did not land so well. She rolled over, then on to her wheels. I held on tight to the wheel, but there was nothing for poor Carlos to hold on to. I swear I heard his neck snap."

Ingo said nothing. Drank a little more wine.

"I should have been more careful."

"Sometimes you simply can't slow, you have to keep the momentum," Ingo said. The words weren't his, he just agreed with them. Even now.

Carlo placed the tin mug on the roof of the car. "Some food?" He did not wait for an answer, just walked over to the basket and pulled out some cold sausage – a local chorizo – a loaf of bread, a wedge of parmesan-like reggianito cheese and some baked empanadas. Ingo's time on the Eastern Front had made it a reflex, taking offered food, so he accepted a piece of the sausage, a slice of bread and some cheese. The sausage smelt fatty and good, bringing both saliva and homesickness. It was excellent, as was the cheese; granular and tangy, tingling with that sort of intensity of flavour that can almost hurt.

"Tell me, Carlo, how often do you race her?" It was the first time he had referred to the car as 'her', and Carlo as 'Carlo'.

"I never race her, my friend."

"Why not?"

"My wife. After Carlos was killed she made me swear that I would never race again. I promised, at the time it seemed a small thing. We had our first child by then, Aldo, and now there is little Anna, so …" he shrugged. "But …"

"But now you're not so sure?"

"No, I'm sure. I never break my word, so I'm sure."

"Yet I've seen you drive it; drive it fast, too?"

Carlo seemed pleased with the compliment wrapped in the question. "I never promised not to *drive* Sophia again, though I make sure my wife does not know, of course. And I never promised to sell her, either. Besides, the old girl is past it now, she would hardly be competitive, even with Fangio or Gálvez at the wheel, and it's been ten years since I last raced."

"That's a long time."

"How long for you? I feel you have, haven't you?"

Ingo did not answer, instead taking an empanada, biting into it, then slowly chewing on the piece of pastry filled with ground beef and onion.

Carlo shrugged and poured himself another tin mug of wine, and then did the same for Ingo. Neither of them said a thing, but they both raised their mugs in a silent toast, then dinged them together.

"I drive the car now only when my wife's away. She's at her sister's in Tres Arroyos this weekend – and it's so difficult to resist Sophia, once you're tried her."

Ingo nodded, and took another deep gulp of wine.

"Why don't you drive her, Enrique?" Carlo said.

***

Warsaw. December 24, 1939

"Why do you stare at the piano, Miss Wadalowska? Sarah asked.

"Oh, but it's a wonderful piano," Lidka said, startled to realise that she had been staring at it. Sarah Vogler looked at her if she was a little crazy. She was a good student, very good with languages, especially French, which was what Lidka had taught before the world had been turned upside down. She was 14 and pretty in a way that was nudging in to beautiful. Dark eyes, luscious long, black hair with hints of deep bronze, like threaded filaments within it.

Sarah was also Jewish, and when she had arrived for the lesson she had worn a white armband showing a blue Star of David on the sleeve of her coat, as did all Jews in the city now, on the orders of the Germans. The Voglers had been forced to move from their house in the pleasant northern district of Żoliborz, as the Germans had banned Jews from owning any property there. They had had to sell the smart house for a fraction of its worth and had moved to a rented apartment on Sienna, which was in a Jewish district favoured by professionals and businessmen, such as Sarah's father, Sol, a jeweller. But it was not Żoliborz.

Lidka had always believed she was not supposed to have favourites – although in truth there were no rules for this clandestine teaching – but Sarah certainly was her favourite, of the six she taught in these secret lessons.

The Nazis had imposed their own version of schooling, and only Volksdeutsche would get this education now – which would not include Polish history. The others would have to make do with technical or practical subjects, because the Germans saw Slavs – as they mislabelled the Poles – as workers for the Reich; Slavs, slaves, much the same. But for the Jews, not even this; there was to be no education for Jews. They could only now find schooling in little underground classes like this one, which were springing up across the city, across the country, where Polish children and Polish Jewish children could learn in secret. Teaching, teaching of any value at any rate, was now illegal.

"I suppose it is a nice piano," Sarah said.

"It's a Pleyel; the same make that Chopin used," Lidka said.

The smart upright did not look out of place in the parlour of Mr Paczkowski's home on Mochnackiego, in the well-to-do district of Ochota. Mr Paczkowski's son, Andrzej, was one of her pupils, and had been before all this, at the school she had worked in, also in Ochota, which is how Lidka knew the Paczkowskis. Andrzej was not a keen student, but because he was part of the class they were able to use the Paczkowski parlour as a classroom. It was a fine classroom, in a fine house, a townhouse, which had been in the Paczkowski family for decades. The house was the colour of the stone it was made of and the front door was actually to the side of the building. It had once been split into apartments, Lidka had been told, and because of this there was a second staircase at the rear. It looked a little Georgian, with three tall windows on each floor, shorter windows on the top floor and a single neo-classical arched full-length window in the centre of this room, which was on the first floor, where a thick duvet of snow now lay on the shallow, shelf-wide, Juliet balcony.

Through another window, on the side of the house, she could see the naked oak that reached for the glass, branches arthritic and trembling from the cold. The tree was growing in one of the few gaps in the line of buildings, mostly upmarket apartment blocks and townhouses, along the graceful crescent of Mochnackiego. The street was unusual, in that it was a crescent, and lucky, in that it had been spared in the fighting and bombing in September.

The ground floor was given over to Mr Paczkowski's trade as an art dealer – office, library, storeroom and what was once a gallery – plus a kitchen and a bathroom. There was a room for the maid in the attic, bedrooms and bathrooms on the top floor, while this floor was all about the room they were now in and the dining room.

This room, the parlour as Mrs Paczkowska insisted on calling it, made a fine classroom, though Lidka would admit that the paintings hanging from its yellow walls – including a blue landscape by Zak and a nude by Kramsztyk – were a distraction. There were also many other paintings, by less well-known painters. In fact, the room was full of paintings, of every different kind, its bright yellow walls studded with rectangles of colour, the highly polished parquetry showing reflected versions of the same, which looked drowned and smeared. Even on a winter's day like today, when hesitant snow floated in the wind like ash above a fire, it could seem like summer in the Paczkowskis' parlour. Now there was also a Christmas tree, which Mr Paczkowski and Andrzej had put up earlier, decorated with gingerbread shapes and baubles, and a slight scent of pine perfumed the parlour.

She glanced at Andrzej, assumed he would be staring at the nude – a thin woman with a cigarette in a holder, wearing a necklace and nothing else, the colours vibrant and breathing – he was of that age when such things crammed a boy's mind. But he was not staring at the Kramsztyk. He looked down at the book in front of him, too quickly. Lidka thought he might have been staring at Sarah, rather than the nude. It would make more sense; but then fifteen-year-old boys seldom make much sense.

"Andrzej, would you read, please?" Lidka said, and the boy stood up and started to read.

She looked at the art in the room as Andrzej stumbled through his poor translation of the passage she had given them, written in her own hand, as there were few textbooks. The parlour was full of art because, she had heard from the maid, Magda, Mr Paczkowski was a soft touch, for an art dealer, and would rather buy a piece himself than see an artist starve. But looking at the pictures now, Lidka wondered at that, and thought that it was rather that sometimes he could hardly bear to part with them. None of that mattered now anyway, because since the Germans had taken Warsaw no one was interested in buying paintings.

Mr Paczkowski also loved music, and he played piano well himself. She had told him about Ingo, when she had said she had arranged this recital as a Christmas gift. But she had not told him he was German. She hoped his playing would do the talking for her. In truth, she just desperately wanted to hear Ingo play Chopin on a fine piano. They had met six times in Café Kasper now, and each time it had been wonderful to hear him play. But she was greedy for Chopin, even more than she had once been for makowiec; she simply *needed* to hear Ingo play the Pleyel. She was normally so sensible, but this one desire had made her take this risk. She was anxious. But not scared, for she knew the acid taste of fear from when the bombs had fallen in September, and there was none of that. Just a nervous excitement.

Andrzej mumbled the last line of his translation just as a soft chime from a clock on the mantel marked the end of the lesson.

"That's it, for today," Lidka said.

"Homework, Miss Wadalowska?" The other five pupils thrust sabre stares at Sarah for that – she was the only one who perhaps truly understood the risk their parents took to educate them, and that they should make the most of it. Lidka had a mathematics task she had copied from a single book, six times, and she handed the sheets out. Andrzej then led the secret students out of the parlour, while Sarah helped place the chairs they had used for the lesson in a crescent around the piano. She always stayed a little late after the lesson, always had a question to ask.

"Will someone be playing the piano?" was the question today.

"Yes."

"Oh, that will be nice ... I should be getting back, then," Sarah said, just enough of the little girl left in her that it should come out slightly sulkily.

"Uh-uh," Lidka murmured, and Sarah nodded, then picked up her satchel, packed her books and then put on her coat, and Lidka once again caught sight of the Star of David armband sewn on to the right sleeve. Sarah walked slowly towards the double doors to the parlour.

"Wait, Sarah," Lidka said. "I'm sure Mr Paczkowski wouldn't mind if you stay, as long as you're quiet and keep out of the way."

"Really, Miss?" Sarah's eyes lit up with excitement. "Who will be playing?"

"Oh, a young man, from out of town I believe," Lidka said. "But you mustn't bother him with too many questions, Sarah, he's very shy."

Very shy.

How could she have believed Ingo might have pulled *very shy* off? He had come in, grinning, some 20 minutes after the lesson had finished and the small audience had arrived. He wore civilian clothes, a rather sharp suit with lapels like Stuka wings, razor creased trousers, and gleaming brogues. She thought he might have borrowed the suit, it was a little short in the sleeves, while he didn't seem the type to waste time on ironing.

"Don't speak, just play," she now said to him, quiet but sharp.

"*Tiger Rag?*"

"You know what to play," she said. The others were watching them, Mr Paczkowski, his wife, Jadwiga, two of her friends and a doctor whose name Lidka had not caught, in her nervousness. Mr Paczkowski was a serious but kindly man, who often held his head at a light tilt, which made it seem he was always balancing something within it, an effect of intelligence that his slightly unruly hair and beard and round thick lens spectacles accentuated. He often wore cardigans, some with suede patches at the elbows, and had a penchant for bright ties – the only clue to his work with colour.

In the sepulchral silence of the parlour it was no surprise that Mr Paczkowski picked out the sharp edges of the German they whispered, and he slid his chair back on the parquet flooring, a shriek of wood on wood that went with the sudden and untypical panic in his eyes.

"He's German?" he said.

Lidka shook her head, was about to say he was Volksdeutsche, to ease the shock a little. But it suddenly didn't matter. Ingo just beamed his widest grin, the sort of grin that cannot go unanswered, and they all smiled back. He sat at the piano, cracked his fingers, stretched them in front of him as if examining his nails, and then paused for a long moment; acting the part, she thought, for he did not need to compose himself to have the composer within. He could breathe this stuff, she knew, even on the tin can piano in the café. She felt a spasm of anticipation, then a slight panic that he might indeed play *Tiger Rag*. And then he began.

Mr Paczkowski's wife cried first. Then Mr Paczkowski. Ingo played *Raindrop* and then *Fantaise-impromptu*, and then *Heroic*, and then much more, managing to slide each piece in to the next with hardly a pause. Every now and then he would look at her, for approval, and she knew he was playing his very best, for her. It was wonderful, even better than she had imagined. But she did not cry, she was too full of joy for that; bursting with joy.

Lidka had never met anyone as alive as Ingo, she knew that. Everybody else in Warsaw, everybody in the world, was half dead compared to Ingo. She glanced at Sarah, who was ensnared in the music, tears in her eyes, too, her attention wholly on the young man at the piano. *She looks in love*, Lidka suddenly thought, *silly girl*. And then there was a twist in Lidka's belly, hot and raw. She realised then that it was she that was the silly girl, here, not Sarah. And she was suddenly scared. She turned to see a slight crease of concern on Ingo's brow, one note not quite perfect. But only she noticed that, she thought.

When it was over they clapped, and Ingo stood by the piano for some long moments, the palm of his hand pressed against the upper panel of the Pleyel. It seemed so intimate, as if he was feeling the piano's soul, thanking it, and she suddenly wished he was pressing his hand against her skin; it shocked her, but excited her, too. Lidka looked at Sarah, who stared dreamily at Ingo, caught her attention and tilted her head sharply, letting her know it was time to go. Sarah beamed and mouthed a thank you, then quietly slipped away.

"You took a risk, bringing a German to my house," Mr Paczkowski said, but his words were matter of fact, rather than a rebuke.

"Was it worth it?" she asked.

Mr Paczkowski nodded.

None of them, other than Lidka and Mr Paczkowski, spoke German well enough for a conversation and she made an excuse that Ingo needed to be somewhere, that he had played for them too long, that she had not noticed the time pass, and then they left. They would not know he was a soldier, at least. And she thought they could not think badly of anyone who had played the Chopin the Nazis had banned, and played it so well.

There was a tram stop close by and he said he would walk her to it. But she needed to go to the City Centre, and so she turned left on leaving the house, said she would catch the tram from Grójecka. Ingo was billeted in one of the forts, near Mokotów, so could take the Filtrowa tram back, and so she was pleased when he still insisted on walking with her; along the elegant crescent of three- and four-storey houses and apartment blocks that was Mochnackiego and then on to Grójecka. They then strolled down the wide cobbled avenue towards the tram stop that was a concrete island in the centre of the street. There was snow on the ground, but the road and the broad pavement had been cleared. The sky was steely grey, and the air was cold and crisp. An iron wind whispered through the battle-scarred modern apartment blocks of more snow to come, soon, and little wispy particles of frozen drizzle stung her face like icy wasps.

"Wait, stand there," he said, holding her by the arm suddenly and stopping her. "With that undamaged building in the background."

"The background to what?" she said.

"Smile," he said, whipping a small camera out of his coat's inside pocket, and quickly taking a picture of her. "You didn't smile!" he said, winding the film on with the knob on the top of the camera body.

"I wasn't ready!" she said, with a laugh now, and he clicked again. "That's a fine camera," she said.

"Not mine; it's Kroh's. It's a Leica, proper expensive he says. He'd kill me if he knew I'd borrowed it – now take off your head scarf, so I can get a proper picture."

He took his photograph and then she tied her scarf around her head again. They walked on. Ingo did not wear a hat and he did not seem to care about the cold. There were many Germans on the street, all in uniform. She guessed he was taking a risk, wearing civilian clothes; it was sure to be against some regulation or other, as the Nazis seemed to have a rule for everything, but he did not seem at all concerned, and he certainly made no effort to hide the fact that he was German, as he carried on chatting. She was happy that he wanted a picture of her, felt warm inside, and was pleased to be walking with him, and in other times she would have been proud, she supposed. He looked good in the suit and coat; and it was much more Ingo than his field grey uniform. She simply could not think of him as a soldier and she saw now that what he said – *I just came along for the ride* – was entirely true.

"Are you sure you're a soldier?" she said, smiling.

"So they tell me."

She was silent for a moment, then said: "I can't imagine you killing someone."

"Neither can I."

"But you might have to, one day."

He smiled. "I've told you before, I've not even fired my rifle since the war started."

"Is that true; never?"

"It's true, and Pop says there's not much of this war left now, anyway, so I doubt I ever will, which suits me just fine. But let's not talk about the war and killing; tell me, who was the pretty girl?"

She feigned bewilderment, for a moment or two. Ingo knew about the work she did now, she had seen no reason in not telling him, he was not a threat; he was not really even a soldier. "Oh, that's Sarah; one of my pupils."

"She will break hearts when she's older, that's for sure."

"Perhaps, but she is very young now; just a child really."

She didn't want to talk about Sarah, not now, remembering the stab of jealousy she had felt. They walked past one of the large dome-capped concrete billboard cylinders that had once displayed adverts and pages from newspapers, but was now just pasted with overdone posters of evil-looking Semites, which told Poles how everything that had happened to Warsaw in September was really the fault of the Jews. She looked away from the posters and sniffed at the air, which smelt of frying mince and onion. "I think someone's cooking pierogi," she said, glad of the opportunity to change the subject.

"You love pierogi, don't you?"

"Almost as much as Chopin," she said, as they reached the tram stop.

"We don't get pierogi at the barracks," he said.

"No, what do you get?"

"Mostly pork, cabbage, potatoes. German food." A bell clanged and she could hear the clank and shriek of the wheels of the tram and the swish of its connecting frame against the cables.

"Fresh meat?" she asked, as she turned to see the red and yellow tram approach.

"Mostly tinned; blood sausage, liver sausage, schinkenwurst. But yes, fresh meat, when we can get it," Ingo said, and she remembered the pig in the sidecar.

"And cake?"

"Yes, but the cook uses too many almonds."

"Too many almonds? Where does he get almonds?"

Ingo shrugged: "I don't know, but he uses too many. I swear the smell of almonds is now a part of me; my nose is so full of the smell of almonds it actually *smells* of almonds!"

She laughed, loud: "That's absurd."

"It's true, here, smell my nose."

She did as he said, having to tilt her face to move her nose close to his, as if she was … kissing him. As she thought it his lips touched hers, she fell into his trap, and she could feel his laughter quiver through the kiss. She made no move to back away, just kissed him as he kissed her, right in the middle of Grójecka, without a care for those on the tram now pulling up who must be watching. She could not smell almonds.

***

Near Chillar. December 24, 1949

The pedal was pressed to the limit of its play. The Chevrolet could go no faster. Ingo glanced at Carlo sat in the passenger seat. *Is he scared?* He didn't look scared. He looked the way Ingo felt. Happy. He had once been told it was rude to turn down a Christmas present, and so he had finally accepted Carlo's offer to drive Sophia. He wondered now if this was the best gift he had ever been given …

The car floated on the loose gravel surface, so that Ingo was always making tiny corrections, his fingers loose on the huge steering wheel, caressing its wooden rim as they once caressed the keys of a piano. Inside the cabin of the Chevy it smelt of hot steel, hot oil and his own sweat, for driving very fast in a tin can in the heat of an Argentine high-summer December is hard work indeed. The gravel hit the floor-pan like hail on a corrugated iron roof; the modified 3.2-litre Stovebolt straight six rasped away, harsh yet crisp-edged; the tyres thrummed loudly against the surface of the un-metalled road. It was music.

And as with all good music there was variety, and complexity; a rise and a curve like the sensual base of a gleaming cello, followed by a dip to a slithery double S of bends, the road bordered by stout trees and a jagged boulder the size of a van. Ingo braked, softly at first, and then more firmly, the car dipping at the front, biting in to the broken road surface, rising a little at the rear as the weight shifted forwards, Ingo balancing it perfectly, allowing the back end to bob and shift, movement he felt through his behind. He double-declutched down through two gears while still braking, pivoting the heel of his right foot to blip the throttle as the car was between gears, to match the revs and stop the rear axle locking, timing the change perfectly, a skill he had honed when driving 25-tonne tanks, where perfect gear changes are vital. It was all done in a blur of hands and feet, so that it took under a second to move the long-throw gearshift through two slots, and then he was easing off the brake a little, the rear of the car already turning so that he took the first part of the curves with opposite lock on, steering the car on the throttle as much as with the wheel, then purposely over correcting the steering at the end of the initial section of the sequence to pitch the car in the opposite direction, the chassis at forty-five degrees to the roadway beneath him. He did the same through the next two parts of this serpentine section of road. It was perfect, he knew.

He exited the final turn and had the car out of its slide as soon as the road was straight, not wasting a moment in sideways driving where it was not necessary. It had taken him time to learn that discipline, he remembered.

Soon the road joined the highway, which was straight and metalled, and Ingo reluctantly slowed, having noticed that the needle on the temperature gauge was beginning to almost nudge the red band, smelling the acrid heat from the engine. The tyres hummed against the tarmac and the engine burbled rather than roared now, so Carlo did not have to shout to be heard.

"I've never seen driving like that. You're a natural!"

Ingo just smiled, he had heard that before. It had meant much then. Now it could take him nowhere.

"I have promised my wife not to go all the way with Sophia, but you my friend, you must have her. You must race this car, Enrique."

"I cannot," Ingo said, feeling the smile slide from his face.

"You have to, it's a crime to waste such talent."

Ingo had heard that before, too, but that had been a different talent. The car smelt heavily of a hard drive, scorched brake linings and hot steel, it was intoxicating. Dangerously so. He shook his head.

"The past is the past, no one cares about all that here," Carlo said.

Ingo just stared ahead, and slowed the car a bit more, easing off the throttle, allowing the brakes to cool.

"Where did you learn to drive so well, Enrique?" Carlo said, changing tack. "The Nürburgring? Spa? Maybe the Mille Miglia?" There was true reverence in his voice when he said the last.

"You would not believe where I learnt to drive fast, Carlo."

"You must race, Enrique. You must!"

Ingo faced him now, saw the fire in his eyes, the sort of fire he'd seen in other eyes. Little good came of that passion, in his experience, but he would admit to himself – and take it as a warning – that he felt a little, maybe more than that, of the same. "Call me Ingo," he said. "It's one secret I can let go. Because today you allowed me to be Ingo again."

"I'll call you Ingo, and you'll race Sophia. I know it, you know it; even the goddamned car knows it – listen to how she purrs!"

***

Fort Piłsudski, Warsaw. Christmas Day 1939

"You tried the lemon trick?"

"Almonds."

"Why not lemon?"

"There's a shortage," Ingo said, and Pop smiled and shook his head.

They had eaten their Christmas dinner of roast goose and bread dumplings, with red cabbage on the side. Ingo had wrapped up some extra goose with its apple, date, chestnut and onion stuffing in a piece of paper, and was now taking a generous slice of stollen. The air was saturated with the thick aroma of the roasted meat. There were wooden tables in the canteen, connected into thick stripes on a cold concrete floor, the walls were painted in an off-white, and the windows were frosted; it was like eating inside a refrigerator. It was cold enough to believe that, too. But the food was hot and, this evening at least, it was good, although there were few in the canteen to enjoy it, as many had gone back to

Germany for Christmas and most of the others had eaten their meal at lunchtime, when Pop was taking his turn on guard at the main gate and Ingo had been on punishment duty, cleaning the latrines, after he was spotted sneaking back into the fort in improper uniform, the borrowed suit, the day before. Luckily, it had not been Kroh dishing out the punishment.

"Better not let her see you take so much extra cake, she's a ball-breaker that one," Pop said. Ingo looked up to see one of the canteen staff, a plump Polish-German girl with big breasts and a red face. "I wouldn't mind warming my hands there, mind," Pop added, staring at the girl, while running his fingers lightly over his bald patch.

"Why don't you talk to her?" Ingo said.

"I will, I will … Then I'll thaw the witch out, sure of it …" he trailed off as the girl realised he was staring at her, then he turned away, fast, took a swig from his bottle of local Haberbusch beer, then lit a Reemtsma R6.

"Well, tell me all about it then," Pop said, quickly. "After the almonds?"

"I kissed her. That was the point, wasn't it?"

"Just a kiss, that's never the point – come on, you must have felt her tits, at least?" he said, his voice a little higher now.

"Of course I didn't, on a tram stop!"

"I've had a girl on a tram stop, twice."

"Well I haven't," Ingo said, a little loud now, so that the two radio operators sat at the table opposite looked up from their plates of roast goose.

"No, you *haven't*, have you, Pup?"

He shook his head.

"Tomorrow's close enough to Christmas, you take her goose and stollen; she gives you plum and dumplings. Only fair, I'd say."

"Dumplings? Any good?" Kroh had a habit of creeping up on people.

"Great dumplings," Ingo said, and Pop laughed. Kroh coloured, thinking the joke was on him. Ingo could see the anger rise in his face, like port poured in a glass.

"We're talking about girls," Pop said.

"Her?" Kroh said, tossing his head in the direction of the canteen worker.

"No, not her," Ingo said.

"Then who?"

"Pup has his randy eyes on some tart," Pop said.

"Local?"

"Volksdeutsche," Pop put in, before Ingo could answer.

"But of course. Germans can't fuck untermensch Slavs, it's a crime against purity, right?" Kroh said. "Only good for raping, them," he added, then laughed. They both laughed with him, synthetic laughs they had found they could concoct on demand, because that's the sort of thing you learnt in this outfit damned quickly.

"Anyway, I have a job for you two, tomorrow night," Kroh said, suddenly serious.

"Tomorrow?"

"What, other plans?"

Ingo did, but said nothing, just shook his head and doused a sigh with a swig of Haberbusch.

"You know where Wawer is, right?"

Pop nodded.

"There's an inn there. I need you to get there for ten-thirty. There will be some Polish lads. They will load up the back of the Polski with vodka, right? Count the bottles in the crates very carefully, then pay them. I'll give you the cash to take along."

"Sounds simple enough," Pop said. "Official?"

"Don't be cute, Grandad," Kroh said.

"And our cut?"

"The usual," Kroh said, and Pop nodded. The usual was usually fair; there was always a strange honour in Kroh's dishonesty.

"Oh, and just make sure you drive carefully, Pup, vodka bottles are fragile; as fragile as an idiot's nose – got it?

"Got it, Feldwebel."

"Take some irons, get yourself a couple of Lugers – here." He gave them a chit, which he had signed. "Keep them in your coat, easier than taking a rifle in a boozer, right?"

"Why, it's just business, isn't it?" Pop said, because they hadn't had to carry guns at all times for a little while now – there had been little resistance in Warsaw since the city had fallen, other than the odd slogan daubed on a wall.

"Some people just don't know when they're beat, that's all; and lads can do silly things after a few beers, right?"

Pop nodded, but Ingo could see he was concerned. He hated doing this sort of work for Kroh, but he was not the sort of man you could refuse, and the extra money was always welcome. They were both putting it aside, as the war was about over, Pop reckoned, and soon there would be racing to be done, and to start off with that might cost, until Ingo had proved himself. Ingo usually didn't mind Kroh's errands quite so much anyway, for as well as bringing in extra cash they also beat boredom. But he had had big plans for tomorrow night, and Kroh did not listen to reason, especially if the reason wasn't even Volksdeutsche.

"I'd do it myself, but I'm needed here tomorrow night, right?"

"Yes, of course," Pop said.

"There are some papers you will need, to see you past the chained dogs if they stop you. Come and collect them from my office tomorrow, I'll give you directions to the inn then. Oh, and Pup, get a haircut."

With that he left them, whistling as he went. Only it wasn't really whistling, there was no real whistle to it, just air escaping, almost like a hiss. He whistled, like this, all the time. And it might have been endearing. If it was not Kroh.

"Hasn't anyone ever told him he can't whistle?" Ingo said.

"Someone did, once," Pop said.

"Yes?"

"Kroh said to him: 'I like to whistle, do you like to breathe?' Then he punched him in the throat."

"In the throat?"

Pop nodded. "Ended up in hospital – that's an accident, you know?"

"Yes, I suppose it would be," Ingo said.

"I saw another *accident* once, in Nuremberg, when I was with the NSKK a few years back. I learnt a lot about Nazis at that time; I was one, on paper at least. But it was worth it, as without them I would never have raced." Ingo knew that Pop had started racing with the Nazi motoring corps, which had led to his transfer to the Heer to help train army motorcyclists, then ultimately the 4th, a move which Pop hinted had had something to do with an Oberstleutnant's daughter. "Any road," Pop continued, "one night I saw a bunch of Brownshirts beating up a little fella, a Jew or a red, most likely, I never asked. There were about six of them, outside Zum Gulden Stern, you know it?"

Ingo shook his head.

"Well, they mashed up this Jew, or red, good and proper. There was nothing I could do, but I was drunk enough to watch them, maybe I was even trying to find the courage to help the poor bastard out. Not sure; can't remember. But I recognised one of the Brownshirts, a lad I'd known for years. Back in the bar I asked him why it took so many of them to kick the shit out of one little guy like that. Know what he said?"

"They were all drunk?"

"Well, there's always that with Brownshirts," Pop said. "But no, what he said was that they all joined in so that if the police got involved – though to be honest even *then* that was unlikely – then they would all have to take the punishment. It was almost like a covenant. That's the way real Nazis work, and it's the way Kroh works; everyone needs to get their hands good and dirty. The thing is, if you're not a part of it, if you don't play ball, then you're as good as the enemy. You know, when you think about it, it's like being in a gang."

"I'm not sure I want to be in Kroh's gang," Ingo said.

"I'm not sure you have a choice, so long as you're in Hitler's gang, and if I remember rightly you joined that one on your own accord."

Ingo took a swig of beer, ignored that. "Seems to me Kroh's in the wrong gang anyway," he said. "You'd think he'd be SS, what with all that Nazi guff."

"He was," Pop said. "But did a little too much business on the side, got himself kicked out. Yet he has a great respect for those two little slithery letters, does our Kroh, would do anything to get back in, I hear."

"I'd gladly pen a letter of recommendation for him," Ingo said.

Pop smiled. "You know that raw onion thing of his?"

Ingo nodded.

"An SS doctor told him it was good for him, would help him give up smoking; a very Nazi thing that. If it had been anyone else, he would have used the onion on them the very same way our cook used one on the goose. But as I said, those two little letters only spell out good things to Feldwebel Christian Kroh."

At the mention of goose Ingo sighed, then said: "I don't suppose we could leave a little early, tomorrow?"

"I've been waiting for that suggestion, Pup."

"You have?"

"How else will she get her goose, eh?"

Ingo nodded, smiled. They had arranged to meet in Kasper's, as usual. Lidka had told him her friend was away for Christmas. He had wondered why she had said so, as she boarded the tram, but later he had figured it out.

"Shouldn't take too long, I should think," Pop said, with a grin.

"Thanks, Pop, I owe you."

There was a clatter of pans falling to the floor in the kitchen, the smash of a plate, and the girl with the big breasts pushed her way through the swing doors, shouting before she had even gone through. Pop's gaze was fixed to her arse, as he said: "Don't thank me, Pup. Just tell me all about it after, yes? *All* about it. Every. Single. Little. Detail."

*

Warsaw. December 26, 1939

Pop talked about it all the time. Yet Ingo had picked up nothing about how to actually do it listening to him. But Lidka had known what to do, and had taken charge. Now she lay on the bed alongside him, on her back, staring at the ceiling, her breasts quivering to her laboured breath, a fine dew of sweat coating her skin. It was cold in the room, but their loving had been hot. The light was off, but in the snow-reflected moonlight her naked body was a dim, pure white. Lidka had not been quite so pure, but that had not been a disappointment. Her appetites stretched far beyond pierogi and makowiec, and the roast goose and the stollen remained wrapped in paper in the little kitchen of her apartment in the Old Town. But he did not mind that his girl – yes, that had to be so, now – had lived a life, and supposed it was this Jósef she now never mentioned. She turned her head, smiled.

"That was wonderful," she said. He reached for a breast, the red-brown nipple as hard as a nut in his fingers.

"Are we together, now?" he asked.

She paused before answering. "I suppose we are."

"And when I'm gone?" he said, taking his finger from her nipple.

"You're going?"

"Some time, I should think."

"Soon?"

"Not too soon, I hope. But when I go, will you wait?"

"I will wait," she said, without hesitation.

"You promise?"

"I promise," she said. "And you?"

"Yes, me too," he said. "Pop says this war is nearly done, things will be different here, then. I think."

She said nothing. Turned her head slightly away, shivered.

"What is it, are you too cold?" he said.

"No, not too cold."

A clock chimed, somewhere out in the night.

"Shit!"

He rolled off the bed and was already reaching for his underwear as he fell to the floor with a bone-jarring thump.

"What is it?"

"I have to go, I'm late; I need to be at Wawer at ten-thirty – Kroh will kill us if we mess this up," he said as he tugged on his uniform, then kissed her, on the mouth, on each breast, then on the mouth again.

"Thank you," he said, as he left the room and rushed through the living room, bumping against a chair as he pulled on his greatcoat.

"When will I see you again?" she shouted after him.

"I will leave a message at Kasper's, as always," he shouted back, pulling the apartment door behind him.

He ran down the stairs, then out in to the snowy street, his boots skidding on the slippery cobbles. It was right then that he realised he had no idea where he was. But he remembered arriving from the right, and headed that way. He reached in to his greatcoat pocket for his side cap; he had not worn it when they'd walked through the streets together, but it was curfew now and safer to look like the soldier he was supposed to be. The cap was not there. He cursed softly, then ran on, to Kasper's, the square, then to Plac Zamkowy, where he had arranged to meet Pop – close to the ruins of the Royal Castle, which had been bombed by the Luftwaffe in September.

The snow-lined bare beams of the Royal Castle's once steep roofs glowed white like skeleton ribs in the moonlight. Pop sat in a cloud of smoke in the cab of the Polski Fiat 508, a car that had been converted into a small truck with a canvas cover over the rear. It was boxy, but it had stylish flowing wings at the front and back. It had previously belonged to the Polish army but had now been repainted in field grey with small 4th Panzer Division unit markings – propeller-like three-pointed stars – stencilled in yellow on its flanks. The snow beneath the door was scattered with cigarette butts. Ingo climbed into the cab, Pop was in the passenger seat. The engine was on, for the heater. Pop did not greet him, just kept smoking, and staring ahead, his chin angled upwards.

"We'd best get going, it's gone ten," Ingo said, the thick cigarette fumes causing him to cough.

"Five more minutes; I think she's going to bed."

"Who?" Ingo said, then followed Pop's gaze. There was a woman in a window, on the third floor of a building above a boarded-up restaurant on the other side of the square. She was staring out at the snow.

"No curtains, she'll be undressing soon."

"What. You're kidding?"

"No, wouldn't be surprised if she didn't know I was here, watching her. Some of them like that, you know?"

"Not sure Kroh will like it," Ingo said, and with that the woman stood up, moved away from the window and a second later the light went out.

"That's a shame," Pop said. "Once, back in Nuremberg, long time ago now, there was this redhead. She would undress in front of the window. Thought I'd better tell her I could see her; decent thing to do. Saw a lot more of her after that."

"You know, it's no wonder your marriage didn't last, Pop."

Pop opened the window and flicked the cigarette butt out. "Maybe you're right, Pup. Maybe. Best get to Wawer, eh? But tell me, did you?"

Ingo could not help grinning.

"Good lad," Pop said, quietly.

To his surprise Pop did not question him about it, and he was glad of that, he did not want to talk about what had happened. It was between him and Lidka. But he wondered if he had hurt his feelings, mentioning his ex-wife. Pop only ever joked about her, said she was frigid, barren, a nag, and ugly, too. Yet he had married her.

Ingo just drove. Drove fast. Pop had told him that the snow was a gift. In the snow you could learn everything there was to learn about driving, and a little Polski Fiat, under a litre, thirty-six horsepower, with a top speed of just eighty-five kilometres-per-hour, was as good as an Auto Union grand prix car – in the snow. Ingo had learnt plenty, since the snow had come to Warsaw. But Pop was not teaching him now, just sitting silently, puffing on another Reemtsma.

Ingo made the most of it. He loved to slide a car, and because of the curfew the streets were almost empty. Pop always told him it was slower; going sideways meant you were not going forwards. But Pop said nothing now. Ingo took the left off Nowy Świat and on to the wide Jerusalem Avenue. The snow had been cleared here but it was falling again now and the surface was slick, all four wheels skidding before the tail started to overtake the front. Ingo corrected, the skinny rear tyres scrabbled for grip like a dog on a frozen pond as he fed in the power. He crossed the Poniatowski Bridge over the Vistula flat in fourth, threading the little truck through the narrow gaps between the scaffolding in place to repair the damage the bridge had suffered in the fighting in September, and the car, its engine racing, sped on in to Praga, turning right on to Francuska, Ingo's smile as wide as the slide was wild. Memories of Lidka were fresh in his mind, he could almost feel her soft skin beneath the fingers that caressed the steering wheel … Things could not get much better.

They didn't.

There was a fast right-hand curve in the wide street before the junction with Francuska and Miedzeszynska, the road that followed the right bank of the river ... He was still thinking of her lying there, naked ... The rear of the car kicked out on the snow-dusted cobbles, and Ingo held it for a moment, but then a steepening of the camber increased the skid, and before he knew it the Polski was at a ninety-degree angle to the direction of travel, and looping into a spin. The headlights slashed the walls of apartment buildings, throwing the shadow of a tree into the snow-pocked sky like a propeller, the tyres swishing against the wet surface, as the Polski spun through one hundred and eighty degrees, twice, then mounted a sloping kerb, jumped half a metre in the air, before hurtling along the pavement, clipping a stone step with a loud pop of a tyre-burst that sounded just like a rifle shot, and finally slowing with a *thud-a-dud-dud* from the front wheel. Lights in the windows of the apartment blocks on both sides of the street were suddenly extinguished.

"That was bound to happen," Pop said, as they came to a stop, the little truck still on the pavement. He sounded annoyed, but it was difficult to see the expression on his face in the poor light.

"I thought I had it."

"Still a pup, Pup."

"What's that supposed to mean?"

"You were thinking of her, yes?"

"We haven't much time," Ingo said.

"You need to concentrate, always. Talent will only get you so far."

Ingo said nothing to that, just climbed out to inspect the damage. Pop did the same. There was a small dent on the wing, and the tyre was flat from where the wheel had hit the step.

"Never let emotion in ... Never," Pop said, shaking his head.

"It's just a puncture."

"Have you got that?"

"I've got it," Ingo said.

"Then let's get the spare on."

The spare was strapped on the side of the boxy engine cover, resting on the flowing wing. They swapped the pressed steel wheels and were on their way again within ten minutes. Ingo still drove very fast, but he did not think of Lidka now. They were sure to be late.

Wawer was on the edge of the city, a dormitory town. With the curfew this seemed a literal description. The whole place was draped in a thick duvet of snow, and the streets of single-storey little houses were carpeted in white from the fresh fall, which crunched softly under the wheels of the Polski Fiat, and took on a lemony tinge in the wash of its headlights. Pop had the money in his gasmask canister, looted zlotys, the promised payment for a large consignment of good Polish vodka, which Kroh planned to stow on a train going back to Germany, where it would fetch a good price, he had told them.

Pop directed Ingo to the inn in which the deal was to be done, following Kroh's scribbled instructions, which were on a small sheet of paper. The inn was a one-storey place that looked like it was sagging under the weight of the snow on its roof. There were no lights on, but wisps of smoke from the chimney could be seen against the speckled backdrop of the snowy night. They parked the little truck and got out, boots sinking into the fresh snow. There was a strong smell of wood-smoke on the icy air.

"Take this, put it in your greatcoat pocket," Pop said, his breath showing in frozen feathers in front of his face.

"What for?" Ingo said, taking the Luger automatic all the same.

"If Kroh told us to take irons, then there must be a reason, Pup. And if he was willing to trust us with his money rather than come himself, then the reason must be a good one."

Ingo shoved the pistol in the pocket of his greatcoat, as a snowflake tickled his nose. The tavern was a whitewashed building with a sign he could not read in the darkness. It did not appear to be open, no light showing, the windows shuttered; it was curfew, but Kroh had told them that didn't apply to this place, as the landlord had made a deal with the local cops. Yet it looked dead and buttoned up. Ingo walked up to the front door and tried the handle, it was locked.

"Looks like no one's home," he said. "Maybe they've given up on us?"

"There's smoke from the chimney – let's check around the back," Pop said. He pulled a small rectangular Daimon flashlight from his greatcoat pocket and turned it on.

Pop trudged through the snow and Ingo followed. They went up a dark alley between two buildings, one of them the tavern, the torch lighting their way. Around the corner of the building, at the rear of the inn, a rhomboid of light was thrown across the snow from what might have been a kitchen window.

In the centre of the bright carpet of light lay two men, wearing field grey greatcoats and trousers and glossy black jackboots, one with an impossibly bright red speech bubble blooming ever larger close to its head. They were not yet covered in snow, so they could not have been here long. Ingo noticed the pair of discarded wallets, one opened out to show a small photograph of a mother and child. It was clear that they had been shot, one in the chest, the other in the head, the end of his story marked with a bright full stop on his pale forehead. Pop stepped forward, checked for a pulse.

"Dead," Pop said, as flat and cold as the ground on which he now knelt beside the bodies. Pop pulled his Luger out of his coat pocket. The dead men wore idiot expressions of surprise, they both looked to be in their late twenties, and their greatcoats were ripped open to show the tunics underneath. Ingo could not see their sleeve flashes but they had the look of NCOs about them. These weren't the first corpses that he had seen, not even the first that were wearing the same uniform as he was, as the 4th had lost men in the fighting for Warsaw in September, and at Mokra and on the Bzura River, but they were the first he had seen so close up.

"Bastard treacherous Polaks; thought this pair of jokers were us, I bet. Going to take the money and run," Pop said. "And you can bet Kroh knew this was a chance." He shook his head. "Wrong place, wrong time, for these two, I'd say."

"But why has no-one come; someone must have heard the shots?"

"People have learnt to close their ears, and their shutters, to gunfire," Pop said. "But a good job we were late, after all, eh?"

"Not for them."

"No, not for them."

"Should we call the chained dogs?" Ingo asked.

"No. We're here to do Kroh's work; so I'd say we'd be better off if we *weren't* here, wouldn't you?"

They were back in the cab of the little truck a minute later, Ingo accelerating, then sliding it through the junction at the end of the street, a rooster tail of snow in the round mirror fixed to the edge of the windscreen feathering the dark night. They passed a small column of cars and motorcycle combinations going the other way, Feldgendarmerie, their wheels kicking up a snowstorm that looked like a swarm of angry white wasps.

"They're in for a busy night," Pop said, lighting up another Reemtsma R6, the flare from his match momentarily throwing his reflection on to the flat windscreen. There seemed to be worry in his eyes, in that moment, but Ingo did not ask him what he was thinking. He had learnt his lesson, earlier that night. And so instead he concentrated; concentrated on driving fast in the snow.

*

Ingo parked the little truck up close to the entrance to the barracks in Fort Piłsudski. The place had been hit hard in September and the fresh snow etched jagged lines in the darkness along the ragged ruins of some of the brick-built buildings within the walls. It was very quiet, almost silent, except for the hacking cough of a sentry on the gate and the faraway whine of a tortured violin. Kroh waited for them in the shadows of the deep doorway set into the battlements. Ingo smelt the raw onion at the same time as he heard Kroh crunch into it.

"All good?" he said, through a mouthful, his boots squeaking in the snow as he walked towards them.

"Well, we're still alive," Pop said, shutting the car door behind him.

"What's that supposed to mean?" Kroh said, at the very same time as he took out his flashlight and tossed back the unfastened flap of the canvas cover. "Empty?"

Pop took the thick wad of zloty notes out of his cylindrical metal gasmask canister and handed it to Kroh.

"No show?"

Pop shook his head. "Two dead soldiers. Took them for us, I'm guessing; lucky we were late."

"You were late?"

"My fault," Ingo said. "Accident."

"I thought I told you not to drive fast, Pup," Kroh said, breathing out white feathers of frozen breath.

"Good thing he did, or we would have been the ones turning the snow pink," Pop said, as he lit up a Reemtsma, the bright orange glow burning a hole in the darkness.

"No, I don't think so," Kroh said. "You had the money, right? They would have been happy with that."

"They would have had the money, and they would have killed us, it was a set up," Pop said.

"What're you saying, Pop? I'm not a good judge of character, that it?"

Pop shook his head, sucked on his cigarette, then blew out a thick cloud of smoke. The smell of the tobacco hung in the cold air.

"The way I see it, two German soldiers are dead, and a truck with 4th Panzer insignia was in the vicinity, right?" Kroh said. "There aren't so many of us here from the 4th now, are there?"

"But we had nothing to do with it," Ingo said,

"If you'd been on time those two poor bastards would still be alive."

"And we would be dead."

"It's not too late for that, Pup," Kroh said. "But first there's a little matter of compensation, right?"

"Compensation?" Pop said.

"Well, seems to me I'm out of pocket."

"I gave you back the money," Pop said.

"Polish money, that's next to worthless. The vodka was the prize; do you know how much that could have sold for in Berlin?"

"I think we're about to find out," Pop said.

Kroh shook his head. "It'll take you a while to pay off the debt, that I promise you."

"And how we're supposed to do that, on army pay?"

"Oh, there's always jobs to do, right? It's been a profitable little war, so far, maybe there'll be a little more business, eh?" Kroh said. He looked across the parade ground, where the falling snow was drifting in front of a floodlight that lit up one corner of the space; it seemed to freeze the snowflakes in their fall for an illusory moment or two.

"Look, we —"

"We can sort out the details later, Pop; first we have to get out of Warsaw."

"Leave, but why?" Ingo said. "We're not finished here."

"We're finished here alright, a fucking barrage is going to fall down on anyone involved in that little mess in Wawer, and that little fart-box Fiat has 4th Panzer all over it, right?"

"When will we go?" Ingo said, already thinking of how he could get a message for Lidka to Kasper's.

"Yesterday."

"You mean *now?*" Pop said.

"I mean *yesterday*. I'll have travel warrants for Bamberg backdated to yesterday afternoon, all it takes is a date stamp; Funk in the office owes me, and I own him. As far as anyone knows we've been gone for ages, and I'll make sure he gives me another set, in case we're stopped tonight; will sort out the gate log, too. It's about time we were out of this dump anyway, right? We'll take one of the other trucks; get your shit together and be back here in ten minutes."

"But I can't leave, not now!" Ingo said.

"Didn't you hear, Pup? Not *now*, *yesterday*, right? But you're not wearing a cap – in this weather?"

"Lost it, Feldwebel."

"Losing Heer property, is it? That'll be a fine. I'll put it on your account. Now get a move on!"

*

Warsaw. December 27, 1939

Sarah was reading a passage from a French-language edition of Voltaire's *Candide*, from Mr Paczkowski library downstairs – he had said it was right for the time. It was just two days after Christmas, but only Andrzej had complained about that. He was looking at Sarah now, as she read, but Lidka doubted he could really understand what she was saying, he was useless at French. The fact that he did not even smirk when Sarah read the part about the Old Woman's buttock seemed to confirm this.

There was no fire in the room, just large white ribbed-iron radiators, which gave off a faint smell of paint. This made it seem that the many art works hanging in the room were freshly finished, Lidka often thought. Outside it was cold and steely grey, and snow was falling again. But Lidka could not feel miserable, and she laughed with the others – all except Andrzej – at the Old Woman's story as Sarah read it out. Every now and then she would remember the night before. It had never been quite like *that* with Jósef, and she had never imagined it could ever have been like that, either. She felt her face grow hot, and she looked away from Sarah, glancing out of the full-length window.

A woman in a grey coat and fur hat walked along the pavement down below, in the narrow path where the snow had been cleared but was now beginning to stick once more, past an ornate lamp post, the clicks of her heels iron hard. Lidka returned her attention to Sarah, noticing Andrzej swiftly looking away, his face reddening. She wondered if not being able to understand the joke had hurt him. Good, if so. Maybe that would make him work harder, she thought. She then heard other footsteps outside, someone in a hurry.

A little later there was a knock at the double doors to the parlour, and then they creaked open before she had time to reply. Sarah stopped reading. The knock was a habitual courtesy, as it was Mr Paczkowski. He was still wearing his hat and coat, a dandruff of snow already melting on his shoulders. He looked a little out of breath, while his cheeks were setting suns above the ragged ridge of his beard, the skin the same shade as the scarlet tie he wore. His spectacles were beginning to steam up.

"What is it?" Lidka said straight away; it was unusual for him to interrupt a lesson.

"There's been trouble, two German soldiers were killed last night," Mr Paczkowski said, addressing the small class and using the tongue of his tie to wipe the fog from the lenses of his glasses as he spoke. "I have heard that the Nazis want revenge, it might be best to forget the lesson today, go home to your families, they will be worried."

"Soldiers killed, where?" Lidka said.

"Wawer."

She knew the place, a nothing settlement on the edge of the city the other side of the Vistula. Which was why it was surprising that she had now heard it mentioned twice in two days. The last time was just the night before. Ingo had said he was going there.

Sarah still held the book in front of her. "But we must finish the lesson first," she said.

"Not today, Sarah," Mr Paczkowski said.

"Yes, that's enough for today," Lidka said, and she was already reaching for her things, already heading for the door, fear like ice-cold fire raging within her.

"I will walk you home," she heard Andrzej say; to Sarah she presumed.

"No, you will stay here," Mr Paczkowski said.

Lidka changed trams at Plac Zbwiciela, then took the number 11 to the junction with Jerozolimskie and Nowy Świat. The snow had stopped falling now and she could not bear to wait for another tram and so instead she walked quickly down the elegant street, with its Art Nouveau architecture and fancy shops, and its bombed-out ugly gaps of rubble from September, until it seamlessly changed into Krakowskie Przedmieście, lined with Warsaw's grandest buildings and palaces. She walked on to the Old Town, fear hastening her pace. She was aware that there was more activity than usual, and most of it was field grey, as if the stone of the city had come to life. Once she heard and then caught sight of a motorcycle and sidecar, just like the one Ingo drove, and she stared at it as it passed, two passengers – one in the sidecar clutching the butt of a large machine gun, the other riding pillion on a sprung seat – staring back, with predatory grins. But it was not Ingo at the controls. She hurried on.

Kasper was at the café, but there were no customers. He was wrapping plates in newspaper and putting them in to a box, hunched over the work.

"Is there a message for me, from Ingo?" she said, through the cold grip of fear at her throat.

He merely shook his head, and did his thing of saluting with two fingers, like a Polish soldier, before turning it into a gun, puffing his cheeks then popping his mouth as he did so. Then he went back to wrapping plates in paper.

Lidka walked back to the old square. There were few Poles here today. A German soldier stood at its edge, a rifle slung over his shoulder, stamping his feet on the snow-coated cobbles and rubbing his gloved hands for warmth. Poles did not often talk to the soldiers, so he was surprised when she approached him, and spoke in German.

"Excuse me," she said.

He was young, with a mouth fringed with angry acne. He said nothing, just looked at her as if he did not know how to respond, one hand reaching for the leather strap of his slung rifle.

"The soldiers killed in Wawer, do you know their names?" she said.

"Why?" he said, still gripping the leather strap.

"I have a friend."

He smirked, then said: "Don't know their names, but two sergeants, from Bau battalion 538 – pioneer mob."

"Thank you," she said, as the fear within her dissolved into relief. She knew Ingo was not a sergeant, and she knew he was not a pioneer. He had told her, with just a hint of pride that had surprised her, that his unit was part of a panzer division. It could not be him.

Walking back to the apartment on Piwna she found herself thinking of the Stollen that awaited her. She had had some earlier, and cold roast goose, and it had been the best breakfast she had had in months. Her belly rumbled at the thought. The new snow had not been cleared on Piwna and she had to trudge through in her winter boots, before she reached the tall house her apartment was on the top floor of. She let herself in through the front door then, suddenly feeling very hungry, she almost ran up the stairs, her footfalls thunderous on the boards. On opening the door to her apartment she could smell cigarette smoke.

"Why the hurry?" Kassia said. She was sprawled on the chaise lounge that had come with the apartment, along with some varnished wooden furniture. There was also a large Ingelen radio set that belonged to Kassia, a record player, and a bookcase full of Lidka's books. Kassia looked like she was posing for a painting, but then she always looked like that. She wore a long black and red oriental style silk dressing gown, a present from a lover, and it was opened a little so that a smooth leg was showing.

"I didn't expect you to be home," Lidka said.

"No? Expecting someone else, then?" Kassia said, resting her lipstick smudged cigarette on the edge of a glass ashtray.

"What do you mean?" Lidka said, only then noticing the crumbs and the dusting of icing sugar on an otherwise empty plate on the floor at the foot of the chaise lounge.

"Had enough of the folks, too much nagging; and it's no fun in Wagrowiec these days – nice stollen, German, yes?"

"Mine," Lidka said, as she took off her coat and hung it on the stand that was by the door. She was still so relieved that Ingo was okay that she could not care too much about Kassia eating her cake – normally that would have sparked a furious row.

"It's not all *he* left," Kassia said. Although she was truly beautiful, film star looks many said, when she was scornful her top lip did ugly, snarly, things. Kassia stood up, the silk falling to hide her bare leg. There was some vodka on the table, a present from Ingo that Lidka had planned to trade for vegetables and perhaps a little meat. Beside the bottle there was a hat, lying flat. It was a grey German army side cap, with a small red, white and black cockade and a Nazi eagle at the front. Kassia picked it up, showed it to Lidka, and then tossed it back on the table. Then she poured herself a vodka, not her first, Lidka could see.

"You know what's happened?"

"You have come back to Warsaw, early."

"In Wawer?"

"Yes, I heard. Two German soldiers, they were killed."

"Two drunks I hear, crooks, too. Up to no good with two of our no-goods, they say."

"Did the Germans catch them?" Lidka said, the warmth of the room was spreading through her after the bitter cold outside. She did not want to talk about the hat, or Ingo.

Kassia shrugged. "I'm not sure. What I do know is that they have taken over a hundred men from Wawer, the first they could find. Some of them not even from there, some of them simply visiting for Christmas ..." Kassia trailed off, she was angry now, her hand shook a little. "Collective responsibility, they call it."

"What do you mean?" Lidka felt her voice was small as she asked the question, and dread was once again ballooning inside of her.

"Two of theirs is worth a hundred of ours, it seems."

"What will they do to them?"

"It's done. Most shot, some hanged. All dead. Everyone will know of it soon enough, but I have heard it from a friend, Jarek, the policeman. He swears it's true, and he has no reason to lie. Over one hundred men, dead." Kassia placed her small glass on the table a little too harshly on the final *d* of *dead*, and the crack of it made a fitting rifle shot of a full stop.

Lidka felt the shock of it as something physical, and she suddenly felt quite sick.

There was a long pause, measured by the drip of snow melt off the window ledge and the bark of a dog down in the street, before Kassia said: "You cannot have anything to do with these people, Lidka. No Pole can."

Lidka did not like taking lessons on morality from Kassia, but for now she said nothing. A sharp memory of the night before suddenly came to her. But she could not feel shame, only pleasure, at the thought of it.

"Besides, there will be revenge for this," Kassia added. "And those who are friends of our enemies, they will be the easiest targets."

There was a hint of vodka in that, but Lidka also knew that things would be very different now. Poles needed few excuses to fight back. Certainly not a hundred. Lidka did not reply, but went to her room, shutting the door firmly behind her.

*

Lidka had not set foot outside her apartment for three days. As the horror of what had happened in Wawer had gripped the city, dark rumours had seeped through the streets like noxious gas, and German soldiers were everywhere, some still bent on avenging their two dead comrades, Jarek, Kassia's policeman friend, had warned them. Like most, Lidka had been afraid. But now she could wait no longer. She needed to see Ingo. And that meant going to Kasper's, to check whether he had left a message, the way they had often arranged to meet over these past six weeks; for a German soldier turning up at a Polish girl's door, or that girl at the barracks, would mean trouble for both of them.

She walked to Krzywe Koło. Ahead of her a man in a long coat and a homburg entered the café. She was pleased that it seemed open; she had never been here this early in the morning before and she wasn't sure. Lidka could see the windows were steamed up, as always, but, closer now, she could also see that there was a small sign on the door.

Nur für Deutsche.

Only for Germans.

"Poor Kasper, he thought they'd forgotten about him, tucked away down here." The words were from a man in a peaked leather cap, smoking a pipe of evil-smelling tobacco. He was leaning against the door which was recessed into the wall of the house opposite, like a dejected sentry. He stared at the café, did not look at her. She recognised him as the one who had been there that second time she had heard Ingo play Chopin in Kasper's. He was a regular at the café. But now he was outside, in the cold.

"What's happened?"

"The Germans have forced Kasper out, given his business to a Volksdeutsche family."

Lidka had heard about this, it was happening all over the city, Kassia had told her. "Where has he gone?"

The man shrugged.

"Tell me, the German who played the piano; have you seen him?"

He shook his head. "Not for a while, no – and neither should you," he said, looking right at her now.

She moved towards the door.

"Wait, you mustn't —"

But she was already pushing the door open, the base of the frame squealing against the stone step as always. As she entered she felt the reddening of her skin as the warm air hit her cold face. The café smelt different inside now, of better tobacco, and of good coffee rather than tea, and of sizzling bratwurst – German Poles were always *so* German, even more German than Germans. There were few people inside; the man she had seen enter was taking off his coat and two German soldiers, their greatcoats hung on a new stand, were tucking into warm bread rolls and sausage, hot coffees at their elbows. The piano had gone, the space filled with a new table. She could not quite believe the old piano on which she had first heard Ingo play Chopin was no longer there, and she stared at the place where it had been.

"Yes?"

She turned to see a small man, who seemed as bent and wiry as the spectacles that were balanced on the end of his nose. He was behind the counter, in Kasper's place.

"I was wondering," she said, in German. "Has a message been left for me? My name is Lidka."

"But you are Polish?" this was as much accusation as question. Both the soldiers stopped chewing on their bratwurst.

"It is important, please, I only wanted to know if —"

"This is not your place now, girl," the man behind the counter interrupted, alternating his gaze from her to the soldiers.

"Please I am Volksdeutsche," she said, pulling back her headscarf, allowing her blonde hair to be seen.

He did not seem so sure now. He swallowed hard: "Your kennkarte then, please?" he said, referring to the folded cardboard, pictured and fingerprinted ID that everyone had to carry. The colour of the card alone would show she was lying.

"I ... I've not got it with me. Sorry. Please, I only want to know —"

"Get out; and stay out!"

***

Near Chillar. March 1950

When the rain had started he had been nowhere. But being nowhere was not a problem for Ingo Six. He'd been nowhere for years now, until Carlo Rossi had persuaded him to race, just one race, a nothing race in a nowhere place. Ingo hadn't minded that Sophia was old, and far too heavy for this sort of work, had not cared that she had no chance of winning. That suited him just fine. No one will want to know much about the man who finishes thirteenth. It was enough to simply race at last, not think too much about those who *should* be seeing this, nor those who *could* be seeing this, just race his race. It would be his first and his last race, after all, and it was a small race, an unimportant race. Ingo's first race.

Before the rain started the more than ten-year-old Chevrolet, which had been prepared for long-distance cross-country races, had been completely outclassed by the lightweight, stripped-down specials that ran at the front of the field. But when you learn your craft on Russian ice, a little rain is nothing. The first drops had carved narrow runnels in the dust that had coated his windscreen and raised curls of steam from the hot hood of the car. But as it fell heavier it cleared the screen of dust, and bounced like bright silver coins in the road ahead, splattered like starbursts on the windscreen, and hammered on the roof of the car like machine gun fire against the glacis plate of a Panzer IV, while the tyres swished against the road surface like harsh radio static.

The seven-kilometre circuit described a triangle, one leg of which was more or less straight, the other two undulating and serpentine. The road was both asphalt and dirt, but where it was paved it was also dusty and in places broken and crumbling at the edges. The first indication that the rain had changed the game came with the sight of a car in a ditch; the second a new Chevrolet on its roof, wheels still turning, so that it looked like a dog playing in the pampas grass, pawing at the sky. Ingo's senses were alive to everything, and he could smell the grass mown by the errant car on leaving the road above the earthiness of rain-awakened ground.

He had not slowed too much. Peering through a rainstorm, peering through a snowstorm, it amounted to the same thing; and driving on slick asphalt and mud was much easier than ice. He passed one car under braking for a corner, using the front tyres as a gauge for grip, and once they started to skid, lifting half way off the gas, quite sharply, to put the car into a tail-slide, and then driving the turn on the throttle, piano fingers on the wheel, making slight corrections, the engine purring to the small inputs from his foot, kissing-breeze light on the accelerator.

Ingo passed another car, a Ford with much of the bodywork stripped from it, around the outside of a long sweeping curve, finding grip out wide where others did not dare to look for it, allowing the car to slide just a little to help it turn, but not wasting time in big-angled skids. Just as he'd been taught.

When he passed his seventh car, ninth including the two off the road, a commando thought slipped through the bunkered defences of his concentration:

'I am *somewhere* in this race'. It was the last thing he wanted, and the easiest thing to rectify. He merely needed to slow down. And yet as he tried to ease his foot off the throttle on the straight, he could not; it was as if it was fused to the pedal which was in turn welded to the bulkhead. At the next corner, he slowed, of course, but only at the very last possible moment, his foot sweeping over to the brake pedal in a fluid, fast, yet smooth movement, the tap-dance of double-declutch, heel and toe, downchanges set in motion, before he was through the turn and flat on the gas as soon as the car had come out of its controlled slide. There was another car ahead, and he knew he would pass it in the next sequence of turns.

A little later he saw the chequered flag for the first time in his life, through the silver-beaded curtain of rain. He could see Carlo, too, punching the air, his hair sopping wet, his cheroot glowing in the murk. There was the sudden incendiary glare of a camera's flash bulb. People were standing out in the rain, clapping ...

Ingo just continued to drive, past the flag and on down the road. It was not that far to the Di Rossi garage in Chillar, and he thought there was just enough gas left in the tank to get him there.

***

Warsaw. March 1940

Lidka walked on to Plac Narutowicza from Filtrowa. In the open space of the square there was no protection from the icy wind, which chopped at her cheeks and mouth like a cold steel blade, causing her to wrap her scarf close to her face. The sky was mottled with scudding dark clouds that were tattered at the edges where the cutting wind hacked at them. There was a warning ding of a bell and she stopped for a moment to let a red and yellow tram clatter and rumble past, before getting on her way again, making for the junction with Słupecka, where she would be out of the wind, in the cover of the Church of the Immaculate Conception of the Blessed Virgin Mary, and close to the shop she was headed for. The shop where Mr Paczkowski's maid, Magda, had heard there was good, fresh pork for sale.

She wanted to get home, where it was warm, and where there might be a letter, or some word, somehow, from Ingo – though a small part of her was beginning to believe what Kassia said, that she would never hear from him again. She had tried to contact him; how many piano shops could there be in one city? she had thought, and so she had sent a letter to *Six Pianos, Munich*. She did not know if it had got there, she did not know if it had got past the German censors. She had had no reply yet. So, yes, she wanted to go home to see if a letter had come. But she was hungry, too. With the money Mr Paczkowski and the other parents paid her she was always able to buy food, usually potatoes, which was as much as most managed, but she was bored of spuds and she craved meat in a way she had never craved anything before – even makowiec or pierogi.

The shop she now approached was still owned by Poles. It had a glass front that had either been replaced or had survived the heavy fighting in Ochota in September; but either way there were few goods for it to show off, just a small triangular stack of various tins. The pork, she assumed, would be under the counter. She took the scarf from her face before she entered the shop and then sniffed at a hint of fresh paint in the cold air, which reminded her of the Paczkowski's parlour she had just come from. For some reason the smell of the paint made her feel a little nauseous.

Two doors down there was a shoe shop. It had once, she remembered, belonged to a Jewish family, but now it was run by German Poles, Volksdeutsche from the west, far from Ochota and Warsaw. The now sharper smell of paint was coming from that direction. The shoe shop was closed for lunch, it said so in a sign in the stencilled glass door. It also said *Nur für Deutsche*.

And now there was another sign on the door, too …

A boy in a cap was painting it. There was another boy with him, looking up and down the street, his eyes fixing on Lidka for a moment, before he decided she was not a threat. The boy in the cap had a pot of paint, red paint, she could see from the dribble traces down the outside of the tin, which reminded her of bloody claw marks. He was painting directly on to the glass, which made some of the letters translucent as the red paint smeared. He was just finishing the last word: *Wawer* …

The boy admired his work for a moment, then looked up. It was Andrzej Paczkowski.

He saw her, then. At first he looked afraid. But then he smiled, and nodded, but said nothing. He seemed older, quite suddenly – and so very proud. Andrzej picked up the pot, and then he and his young accomplice were gone, disappearing through the rubble of a building destroyed in the fighting.

Lidka looked at the sign he had painted: *We will avenge Wawer.*

It was stupid, dangerous. If he was caught he would be killed, she knew this. Recently a young girl had been executed for tearing down a Nazi poster. Suddenly she felt quite sick with fear, and that shocked her. She turned away and walked towards the tram stop on Plac Narutowicza, she could no longer even stomach the thought of pork. Fear could do that to a girl, she supposed.

***

Chillar. March 1950

The early autumn sun was ripening, heavy on the sky, and it would soon droop into the bruised fruit of the night. Deep orange light flooded the kitchen. Ingo allowed it to swim in the whisky, trying to concentrate on the beautiful effect of it as he swirled the shallow pool of bronze around the heavy based glass tumbler.

The kitchen smelt a little of the whisky, and a lot more of the steak he'd flash fried earlier, tanning it more than cooking it, before eating it with a bottle of pink Criolla Grande, the only wine he had. He wasn't quite drunk, maybe just a bit more than tipsy. Enough that it was difficult not to think of that which he knew he should not think of. Outside, the early evening was still; except for a distant chugging engine, a tractor, in one of the nearby fields. It almost sounded as if the sky was snoring as it began to doze off after a lazy, warm Sunday, even though it had hardly had a cloud to carry all day. Ingo had done much more than the sky, that day – the day after his first race – making himself busy with fixing the paddock fence that Zündapp had kicked down in a fit of hot-horse temper. But even that hard graft had not been enough to stop him thinking about the race.

Except for the distant noise from the tractor there was no other sound, and so he heard the engine of the truck, then its springs complaining and the deck on its back popping and clattering, long before he saw it slowly negotiate the rocky, deeply potholed track that led up to the farmhouse.

The truck was an old '38 Ford with a steel flat-bed on the back and a big oval chrome-toothed mouth of a grille, which made it look like it was always screaming, like a painting by some Norwegian he'd once seen a photograph of in a magazine. The cab of the truck was painted the exact same pale green with buttercup yellow detailing as the Chevrolet coupe race car of the same vintage that was now chiselled into the hardened surface of his consciousness, with the same sign adverting *Di Rossi Auto Repairs* stencilled on the door. Ingo had asked Carlo why the *di*, and Carlo had said he had thought it sounded more impressive, back when he had set up the workshop. The vehicle was badly battered, looking like it had seen as many long-distance cross-country races as Sophia.

A little later Carlo had parked up and was at the kitchen door, which was wide open. He was carrying a small trophy in one hand while a rolled-up tube of paper, about a metre long, was tucked under his arm. He knocked at the doorframe. Ingo simply nodded a come in and poured him a measure of Canadian Club. He pulled out a chair and sat opposite Ingo at the kitchen table.

"Ciao, Ingo," he said.

Ingo regretted telling Carlo his real name. That had been a moment of weakness, after he had been persuaded to drive the car that first time, been allowed to be himself for a little while. He should have taken it as a warning. He had also regretted telling him not to use it, for since then he had done so far more often; though thankfully not when others were around.

"It's Enrique, Carlo. Enrique."

"If you insist," Carlo said, grinning.

Ingo nodded, and took a deep slug of whisky.

"Here, this is yours." Carlo placed the tin cup on the table. "You came in third."

"Third, that's not bad – is it?"

"It's a goddamned miracle!"

Ingo felt the warmth of that spread through him as if it was another slug of whisky. He picked up the cup, it felt light, cheap, but when he held it to the low sunlight it seemed the most wonderful object he had ever laid eyes on. In its surface there was the distorted reflection of a man with a beard, a smiling man.

"You take it," Ingo said. "Please, put it in the garage." He offered it to Carlo, but he simply ignored him, looking away and making a play of taking time to light a cheroot.

"You know, my wife gave me hell over that, my friend? Because you drove on after the race, some people assumed it was me at the wheel. She got to hear of it, she gets to hear of everything. Last night I had to sleep in Sophia, but that's not the first time. I did not mind, though. I just wish it *had* been me, at the wheel yesterday."

"So, why not race it, it's your car?" Ingo said.

Now Carlo turned to him, and the angle of the light cast a shadow over his face, so he looked quite melancholy – and maybe was – as he said: "You know the answer to that, I have given my word. But you misunderstand me, my friend. It's not that I wish that I drove Sophia yesterday. No, I wish I still had the talent. You have it, you know? More than …" He trailed off, shook his head rather sadly.

Ingo wanted him to go on, but said nothing. The sun had dipped a little more now, the light was copper-coloured.

"Well, it doesn't matter, Mia from the shop at the train station saw me watching the race yesterday, she will vouch for me, I hope. I have to go now, though, my friend, I need to pick Aldo up from football – he's quite good, you know. But I wanted you to see this," Carlo said, draining the whisky and standing up, as Ingo looked at the cup again, before realising Carlo was talking about the rolled up tube of paper, which he tapped against the table twice, making a hollow popping sound, before putting it down alongside the empty dinner plate and empty wine glass, each pinkly spattered with drops of blood and wine.

"What is it?" Ingo said, picking up the tube.

"Just a dream."

Ingo put it back on the table.

"There's another race," Carlo said, his back turned to Ingo now as he walked out of the door. "In one month."

Ingo listened as the truck slowly rattled down the rocky driveway and then, after what seemed like an age, turned on to the road. He listened until he could hear it no more. And then he stared at the long tube of paper. The level of the whisky in the bottle went down, the light in the kitchen seeped away. He needed to turn the electric light on, a harsh unshaded bulb, when he finally slipped the elastic band from the roll of paper, then smoothed it out on to the kitchen table; the nearly empty bottle, his revolver, and two whisky glasses weighing down the corners.

What he saw brought a tear to Ingo's eye. Yes, it was just a dream. But it was the most beautiful dream.

***

Warsaw. March 1940

Someone else in the building was cooking up a stew for supper, and the siren smell of the boiling meat reminded Lidka of how hungry she still was, even though she had already eaten her evening meal. She wished she had bought the pork yesterday, after all, it might have filled her up so much better than a few vegetables, and she felt a stab of anger at her weakness. But what was more annoying was that, even though she ate very little and seemed to be hungry all of the time, she did not believe she had lost a gram of weight recently. Her skirt was even beginning to feel a little tight on her, and so she now fished around in the back of her wardrobe, looking for something that might be a little more comfortable in the morning, when she would teach at Mr Paczkowski's house.

Kassia walked in, without a knock, as was her way, and sat on the edge of Lidka's bed. She smelt strongly of her perfume – warm and spicy, and a little like balsamic. She always wore it, whether she was going out or staying in.

"Anything left to eat?" Kassia said.

"Nothing. We could try to buy some more potatoes, if there are any to be had?"

"Oh, I couldn't face another spud."

"It's more than many have," Lidka said, though this argument seldom worked with Kassia.

"But it's not more than *some* have, is it?" Kassia said, and there was enough venom in it for Lidka to turn and face her. But she was surprised to see that Kassia was not looking at her face, but at her belly.

"What's that supposed to mean?" Lidka said, her hand resting on her stomach now.

"This war has changed you, Lidka. First a secret boyfriend, and I can see why that one was a secret, all right. But I thought we always shared our food?"

"Do you really think I'm keeping any from you?"

"Well, you do seem to be putting on a little weight."

"I eat what you eat, Kassia."

"Well, unless you're ..." Kassia trailed off, and looked Lidka in the eye. Her pupils dilated, like spilt ink spreading on a flat surface, and her mouth matched them, opening in a silent exclamation.

Mathematics was one of the things Lidka taught at Mr Paczkowski's house. It was not her best subject, but she knew the basics. And this was not a difficult sum, after all. She wondered if she had been stupid not to see it, to feel it, to know it ... Or if a part of her had simply hidden away from the truth.

*

Andrzej shook his head, a very slight movement, almost imperceptible. But Lidka saw it, then ignored it. She was not about to tell Mr Paczkowski that his son had inherited his love of painting, but she would not tell Andrzej she was not about to tell him, either. He would be worried that she had come to the house earlier than normal, when the Paczkowskis were sat down to breakfast in the dining room, a place brittle with bone china and glass-fronted dressers, and just one picture, a portrait of Chopin – for this was Mrs Paczkowska's domain. It smelt of tea and cooked eggs, reminding Lidka that she had not been able to face breakfast that morning. Because of fear, because of nausea, because of shame. Because.

Mrs Paczkowska did not talk to Lidka often, just said hello, and this morning she merely nodded it, annoyed at the intrusion. The only thing they had in common, Lidka and Jadwiga Paczkowska, was the love of the long-dead man in the picture; a dark piece by an unknown artist that she thought Mr Paczkowski must hate, for its lack of colour – though she knew he loved Chopin. The maid, Magda, had answered the door and shown her through, just shrugging when she had said it was urgent – Lidka could not put this off for long, for if she did she might put it off forever.

"Miss Wadalowska, what is it?" Mr Paczkowski said.

"Could we go to your office, please?" Lidka asked. "I must speak to you."

"The parlour will be better," Mr Paczkowski said, and then finished his plate of scrambled eggs quickly, wasting eggs was not an option these days, if you were lucky enough to be able to find them. Then he led her into the hallway that met the first flight of stairs. He wore a yellow tie that was a shade brighter than the eggs he had just swallowed.

Someone was hurrying up the stairs, dainty feet tapping a quickstep. "Mr Paczkowski, Papa asked if we could move some more of the paintings into the library, it would ... Miss Wadalowska, I didn't see you."

Lidka had recognised Sarah's voice before she saw her. The girl looked a little embarrassed now. She was not wearing her coat, with its Star of David armband, just a simple blue dress.

"You're very early, Sarah?" Lidka said.

Sarah nodded, then glanced at Mr Paczkowski.

"I will talk to your father about it later," Mr Paczkowski said. Sarah nodded again, then hurried back down the stairs.

Mr Paczkowski coughed, and she realised she had been staring after Sarah. He led her across the spacious landing to the parlour, and had started to explain even before the door had shut behind them.

"You must not speak of them being here, Miss Wadalowska."

"Them?"

"We have taken Sarah and her family in. Her father, Sol, is a good man, and also a perceptive man. He sees the way things are going in the Jewish district, they are slowly turning it into a prison, squeezing the life out of it. He has told friends he intends to escape the city, but he knows that's impossible, and so he will hide with us. Until ..."

"Until?"

Mr Paczkowski shrugged. "I have known him for years. They will be safer here, I think."

"So Sarah and Leon now live here?"

"And their mother and father, the grown-up children left Warsaw some time ago. They are downstairs, in the storeroom, but there is my office and the library, too, so they have some space of their own, to live like a family, and they have the bedrooms at the back of the house, too."

"But it could be dangerous, couldn't it?"

"Perhaps, but we must all take risks these days, as you do yourself, with the lessons you teach. But then it is only really dangerous if the Germans find out, which is why you must tell no one."

Suddenly Andrzej painting a slogan on a wall seemed a small thing after all. But then she had not come here to discuss that.

She nodded, then dived straight in before she could change her mind. "I need your help," she said.

Mr Paczkowski said nothing, he just gestured towards the armchairs in the corner of the room. She did not feel like sitting down, but accepted the invitation. He remained standing. Her eyes were drawn to the Pleyel piano.

"It's about the German lad, isn't it?"

Lidka shook her head, then changed her mind and nodded. "I'm pregnant," she said, spitting it out before she could stop herself.

Mr Paczkowski did not look shocked, but he sighed, and then smoothed his beard with thumb and forefinger while he stared at the blue landscape by Zak on the wall. After a little while, he said: "Have you told your parents?"

"I have not written about it, no. My father worries, even as things are."

Mr Paczkowski nodded, then said: "There are other ways, you know?"

"Yes ... Other ways," she almost whispered, and again she looked at the piano. "But no, not that. I cannot. Not that."

"I understand," Mr Paczkowski said, and she knew he would not hint at abortions, illegal and dangerous as they were in Warsaw, again. "Things are different now, of course," he went on. "Many men have died, many are in England, or in Russian or German prisoner of war camps, there are ways we can concoct a story."

"You mean lie?"

"A story, I said. The German, he's a soldier, isn't he? And I take it he's no longer in Warsaw?"

"How do you know that?"

"Both guesses. Sarah says you don't seem so happy, Andrzej says the same." He stroked his beard against the grain of its growth, scuffing it up in a little brush of untidy spikes on his cheek.

"Andrzej said that?" Lidka said, surprised that he might have noticed.

Mr Paczkowski nodded. Then there was a long pause as he stared out of the window, perhaps at the horse and cart she could hear loudly clopping and clattering along the smooth cobbles of Mochnackiego. She heard a sharp voice from the other side of the parlour door, words indistinct, and then the fast thunder of boots on the wooden stairs.

"What do you want from me? Money?" Mr Paczkowski said. "There is very little, there is no call for art, now, but Sol Vogler might be able to help, part of the reason he has left Sienna Street – well perhaps most of the reason – is because they are already after his money, his stock, and he was careful to make sure they got very little. But despite all that people say, he's a generous man, is Sol – how do you think we were able to buy the eggs?"

"It's not money I need," she said. "Just advice. I don't know what to do, and there is no one else I can turn to."

He nodded, sharply, then he cleaned his spectacles with his tie while looking out on the street. She had noticed before that he often polished the lenses of his glasses when he was thinking.

"There are people in the Old Town who've seen you, with the German?"

"Not many."

"But some, then?" he said, as he turned to look at her again.

She nodded, remembering how popular Ingo's piano recitals in Kasper's were, and how they would always sit together after them.

"Will he be back, this German?"

"He said ..." she started, but then said: "I think he will."

"What *did* he say, when he left?"

"He did not say goodbye. I'm not sure why, something must have happened."

"So, when you say you think he will come back, you mean you *hope* he will come back?"

She did not reply, just took a deep breath. It was what she had not allowed herself to think.

"And he has not written?"

"I don't think he knows my address," she said. "When he came to the flat it was dark, and otherwise we always met in a café."

"And have you written to him?"

"I do not know his home address, and the German army is big. I have thought to, but where should I send it? Besides, I'm Polish, he's German, it could cause him trouble."

"I think he's the one that's caused trouble, don't you?"

"It wasn't like that."

"No, of course not, I'm sorry," Mr Paczkowski said. He started to clean his glasses with the tongue of his tie again and it was silent in the room for what seemed like a long time.

"I don't want to lose you, Miss Wadalowska," Mr Paczkowski finally said. "You are a good teacher, but perhaps it would be better if you returned home, Wagrowiec, I believe?"

"Yes, Wagrowiec," she said. "But I cannot go home."

He nodded sharply, then said. "Our maid, Magda, she's leaving us. She says she needs to look after her father in Kielce. He's ill, she says, but it was strange his illness coincided with the arrival of our new guests."

"Will she tell anyone, about Sarah and her family?" Lidka said.

"I doubt that, she owes us a little loyalty, I think. But she's just like many others. The Nazis are giving them someone easier than Germans to hate, that's all, they are saying the war is all the fault of the Jews. Nonsense, of course, but sadly anti-Semitism is not an exclusively German trait."

"So, you need a new maid?"

"We never needed a maid, that was Jadwiga's doing. What we need is a teacher, Miss Wadalowska."

"But how will I —"

"There is space for you here. Magda's room is small, and you will have to teach, to pay for your keep, but there will be just three pupils now; Andrzej and the Voglers, the others cannot be trusted with secrets, I'm afraid."

"I am grateful, but —"

"It is not a favour, Miss Wadalowska. They need education, everyone needs education — real education, not that Nazi nonsense — and this is the only way I can see they will get it. I am not making money now, to pay you, and although Sol Vogler has some, we may need that another time, for who knows what history has in store for us," he said. "It will be a suitable arrangement."

"But what about the baby? It will be ..." She didn't finish.

"We will say his father is away, in England, or Russia, or somewhere. But away. No one on Mochnackiego will know much about you, most will only have seen you in the street. We will say you are a friend who has now come to live with us, and yes, later, when we need to, that the father is away, like many fathers are these days."

"Jósef's away."

"Who is he?"

"He was my boyfriend."

"And he is Polish?"

She nodded.

"Then he is the father, that's what you must tell people — if they ask. It is better for you."

"But everyone here, in the house?"

"It's just one more secret for them to keep, Miss Wadalowska. And as sins go it is forgivable. A German soldier as a father is not, not now, so that must be our secret alone, yes?"

She nodded.

"Good, it's better for you, but more importantly, it is better for the child," Mr Paczkowski said.

"Yes, better for the child."

"What you have done is foolish, you know that, yes?"

"I know that."

Mr Paczkowski walked to the piano and lifted the fallboard. "Then you should also know that if it had been any other German then I may well have shown you the door and told you never to return. Do you understand?"

"Yes, I do."

"How long?"

"Three months now."

He hesitated before he added: "And you're certain?"

Lidka nodded. Once.

Mr Paczkowski played three dark notes on the Pleyel.

***

Marrakesh, Morocco. March 1950

He might have said he had no choice, or that he was merely following the orders of others, at the end of the war, when or if he had been asked why he had led his men in the Milice on the raids to round up the Jews. But he hadn't, this one had known he was guilty, and this one had fled. This one was not *the* one. But Sarah could not think of *him* now. She could never think of *him* when there was work to be done. But she always thought of him when there was not. One day, she would have her revenge.

But this day was for Jean-Martin Galliard. He used the name Julien Moreau now; the name of a quiet, respectable hotel keeper, who kept a quiet, respectable hotel in Marrakesh, an easy place for a Frenchman to hide. Galliard was a tall man who always wore a linen suit, a straw-coloured panama with a black silk band, a narrow black tie with a crisp white button-down shirt and American aviator sunglasses. He liked expensive things, and his shoes shone like wet seals in the sunlight. He had been sentenced to death in his absence for his work in Lyon during the war. Someone had told Gabriel the death sentence would be overturned, if Galliard returned to France; the French were too busy forgetting. He might see the inside of a prison cell, but for a few years, nothing more. This was the sort of injustice The Group had been formed for.

As with many evil men, Sarah now understood, he was quite ordinary. He also lacked imagination. That was dangerous for a man with blood on his hands, a man who had been personally responsible for shipping hundreds of Jews to the east, to their deaths. Because he was ordinary and lacked imagination, and because the war was now five years dead, he had allowed himself to slip into a routine. Every afternoon, after lunch had been served at the restaurant of his small hotel off the Djemaa el Fna – the suitably unimaginatively named Hotel de

Tourisme – he would cross the famous square and slip in to the labyrinth of alleyways beyond the souk and walk to the house of a friend, where he would smoke a little hashish and drink mint tea. He was following this routine now.

Sarah and the boys had spent a week watching him, planning and waiting for an opportunity, a time when there were no onlookers in that tight street in the Medina where they had set their trap. They had had to abort the hit twice. But Sarah believed today would be the day. She walked with Shlomo across the Djemaa el Fna, him taking pictures with his Kodak as she pointed things out. It would have looked out of place, a woman walking alone here, and she was used to pretending to be married to one of the boys. It was easier with Shlomo, as he was serious, more professional; but the main reason it was his turn to play husband this day was because he did not have Yitzhak's flair for killing. No one did.

It was a clear day, and the snowy peaks of the High Atlas were visible over the flat roofs of the pink-red buildings, looking like a theatrical backdrop behind the wrong play. She had been here before, but they had failed to find Galliard then. It had been summer and there had been no snow on the mountains; it had been as hot as an oven and the houses had seemed to be melting into a rust red sky. Then it really had seemed like a part of Africa. But now there was just a slight breeze bringing warm air from the Sahara; it was a more pleasant place to be, a pleasant place to hide. That always made it seem so much worse, she thought.

The dusty space of the Djemaa el Fna was dotted with carts piled with sun-bright fruit from which vendors sold orange juice; men with performing monkeys; dentists working in the open from little tables covered in gleaming sets of false teeth; jumbles of acrobats; bands of musicians playing the incessant jingling, drummy music of the square; and hissing snakes and their fluting charmers. It smelt of spices – cinnamon and cumin – and leather. It was a blitzkrieg on the senses, walking through the Djemaa el Fna, and sometimes difficult to concentrate on the man you were following. But they knew where he was going, so that did not matter too much. Shlomo took a snap with his Kodak then batted a persistent tout away with some earthy Arabic.

Galliard was not distracted by the sights of the Djemaa el Fna, he'd seen them many times before, and he never turned as he headed through the busy bus station in the corner of the square – where green and white buses were crammed with people and piled with luggage, boxes, and a goat or two – and then in to the souk. Sarah and Shlomo followed at a distance, not worrying if they lost sight of him too much, being there for the kill was the important thing. Their senses were ambushed every few metres or so: heavily minted tea; bright birds in shining cages; gleaming brass; dyed cloth in cobalt blue; the shouts of vendors. Soon they had twisted their way through the market and in to the alleys beyond it, where the riads hid behind pink walls, like veiled Moroccan women; the brightly-painted or intricately-carved doors henna hints of the beauty within.

In the tight alleyways the air carried a slight sweet-stale odour of rotting vegetables and it was cool after the warmth of the square. The route was a geometry lesson of 90-degree turns, a squeeze of rough stone and overladen donkeys; a rumble of heavy car-wheeled trolleys. She heard the muezzin cry begin, calling the faithful to prayer, and Galliard to his hashish, the narrow alleyways playing acoustic tricks as the calls from separate mosques overlapped in mystic music – but music Sarah would never enjoy, as Arab snipers on the minaret of the Hassan Bek Mosque in Tel Aviv two years before had taught her to be wary of such places. They could also hear the tap of Galliard's shoes on the stone paving, telling them he still walked ahead of them. But she did not expect him to stop, just yet.

Soon enough they were close to the place. A few men in long gowns hurried the other way in the direction of a mosque. She would not pray that there were none to see what must be done; God had died in Warsaw. But she would hope. It was hope – the hope for vengeance – that had kept her alive when God had died.

They walked quicker now until they were once again on the tail of Galliard. He did not turn, he was completely relaxed in his daily routine. He was approaching a wider street, which led to the Bab Agnaou, one of the Medina's gates. There was also a junction ahead of him. Yitzhak would be ready now. She could hear the rattle of the idling truck. Yitzhak was at the wheel. It was an old blue and rust Latil that they had bought through a Moroccan go-between in Tangiers. It was packed with broken stone and just about fitted in to the tight passage that butted on to the equally narrow byway Galliard had to walk along.

Galliard was alone in the street, except for them, and he did not turn to see whose footfalls echoed his. The muezzin chant continued in the background, and a cat passed before them like a sliding shadow, but there was nobody else. He came to the junction and was suddenly bathed in bright light from the wider street, it reminded Sarah of searchlights, and her voice was harsh as she called out his name, a name he had not been known by for five years:

"Galliard!"

It echoed down the narrow street and as he turned his face was a mask of shock – shock which froze him for the instant they needed. Yitzhak had heard her shout, too, and rough engine revs cut through the quiet afternoon. She heard the heavy rumble of the truck's tyres on the cobbles, the rattle of its chassis, and then saw it in the blue-blurred moment before the flat rear of the truck sandwiched Galliard between its tailgate and the stone wall, Yitzhak steering by looking in the wing mirror.

The hit shook the stone of the Medina like an earthquake and Sarah felt the impact through her shoes. Galliard's chest imploded with the weight of the truck and Sarah had no doubt that he was instantly dead, as the loaded Latil had to weigh about four tonnes. No one could have survived that. He was squashed between the truck and the wall, the stone of which was bowed in, and he looked like pale meat in an untidy sandwich. His eyes still showed the surprise of hearing his real name, again. For the very last time. The truck's engine had stalled and Yitzhak, his head hidden in the drooping hood of a dark brown djellaba, jumped from the cab and disappeared in to the maze of the Medina.

Just two tourists, Shlomo and Sarah, looked on, as others rushed out of the heavy doors of nearby riads in response to the earth-shaking din of the crash. A wedge of white masonry, like a slab of icy snow on a Warsaw rooftop, was teetering from the impact. It creaked in submission to gravity and fell; smashing Galliard's dead head, the chalky stone dust mixing with the dark blood. Sarah clutched Shlomo's arm and covered her mouth with faked shock; with her headscarf and sunglasses it was her own disguise, and they turned and left the scene of the *accident*. No one would question that, for in many cultures a woman should not witness such things.

Accident. Yes, that was how it had been planned, a runaway truck, a runaway driver, panicked in to fleeing the scene. Accident. That was also how it would be reported, if it was indeed reported. It suddenly occurred to her, some minutes later as they walked back in to the sunlight and bustle of the Djemaa el Fna, just how impotent this revenge was. Yet revenge it was, and justice too, and so she would not stop killing them. But she would admit that it only really made sense when she thought of *him*.

She had to find *him*.

***

Maastricht, Netherlands. May 1940

Of course it was a race. It was always a race.

Feldwebel Kroh's section of the reconnaissance group had been ordered ahead. Most of the Dutch bridges had been blown up, but Divisional HQ thought there was a small chance one still stood. This was not a time for stealth, this was a time for speed. This was a time for Ingo Six.

The road was mostly straight, piercing a tapestry of soft green fields pinned in place by the odd sturdy oak or poplar along the roadside. The trees threw brief capes of shadow across the helmetless Ingo – his stahlhelm was tied to the bike as it often was, rattling like a cowbell whenever they hit a bump. Pop was smoking, as usual, while he also held the pistol grip of the MG 34 that was mounted on the sidecar, ready for action.

The BMW was much faster than the heavy armoured car, and with Ingo at the handlebars a good bit quicker than the other two combinations, too, which also tended to stick close to the Sd.KFZ 222 'Horch Wagon' and Kroh. And so Ingo and Pop had quickly broken clear of the small formation. They could hear the guns of the 4th Panzer Division booming in the distance over the rasp of the bike's engine, and every now and then the stutter of machine guns. In the distance Stukas dived on an unseen target, their 'Jericho trumpet' sirens tearing the smoke-smudged grey sky. Ingo could just about detect the burnt metallic smell of battle, but mostly he smelt the hot bike beneath him, sucking greedily at the fuel he fed it, his wrist bent back to full throttle, nothing left to give, the vibrations of the machine singing through him like tingling nerves.

The road kinked left a little, and Ingo took the curve flat in top. The bike skidded a bit at the exit, and Ingo corrected for it. As soon as they were out of the curve Pop held out his hand in front of him so that it was in Ingo's field of vision and pointed to the roadside, then held up a finger; there had been more room at the edge of the road on the exit, the hand signal told Ingo, the slide, though fun, was unnecessary. Pop was always teaching; Ingo always learning.

There were houses now, a farm or two, a street, but no sign of Dutch soldiers. Ingo hoped they really were all retreating on the far side of the Meuse, as Kroh believed. But despite the slight worry on that score Ingo was in a good mood. He always was when he was riding fast, and when he was getting ever further away from Kroh. Problem was, he was also speeding ever further from Lidka, and ever closer to battle. But he was speeding, and that was the main thing. They were also getting closer to Belgium, and France beyond it, by the heartbeat – and the heart beat fast when Ingo Six was at the controls of a motorbike.

They now raced between tall red-brick houses with mansard roofs, then through a brick funnel of terraces, the houses buttoned up with shutters, as if they were pretending to sleep. At the end of this street was the bridge itself, seeming to rise up before them as they sped towards it. Pop reached up with his left arm, tapped Ingo on his right leg, the signal to slow. Ingo did not slow, so Pop reached up again, punched him in the leg this time.

Ingo laughed and applied the brakes and slowed the bike down through the gears with the H-pattern selector, the mass of the sidecar twisting the BMW to the left, so that he had to counter steer to keep the machine straight as it decelerated. He stopped close to the bridge, but still partly in the cover of the houses. There was no sign of life.

The steel bridge spanned the wide Meuse, the river canalised here between concrete walls. It was suspended from huge stone abutments and the roadway it carried was pinched in with sheet iron parapets to a tiny point at the furthest end. On the far side of the river a phalanx of red-brick factories kept the Meuse from spilling into the town, their chimneys like sentries, tall and rigid against the pale grey sky.

"Well, that's a surprise," Pop said, as he checked the belt feed to the MG 34.

"The bridge?"

"Yes, thought it would be blown to tinsel by now."

"What should we do?"

"Guess we should wait for the others," Pop said. He took a pair of Dienstglas binoculars out of the well of the sidecar, pressed them to his face and studied the far side of the bridge for a little while.

"Looks like they've scarpered," he said. "But then why's the bridge still standing? Maybe they think we've outflanked them already? Perhaps we have, maybe we've chucked a pontoon bridge over the river further down?"

"It's possible," Ingo said. "Those engineers work fast."

"Which would mean the door's wide open."

"What should we do?"

"Not sure, I suppose we should leave it to Kroh to decide," Pop said, rubbing his chin with thumb and forefinger. "But then again …" He did not finish the sentence, just shrugged, and took another puff on his cigarette instead. They could just about hear the sound of the other bikes and the armoured car, seemingly still locked in a whining formation.

"Then again?"

Pop exhaled a thick cloud of smoke, shook his head, and then said: "They ran the Mille Miglia last month, you know?"

"The Mille what?"

"Mille Miglia; a sports car race. A thousand miles through Italy, perhaps the greatest race there is. Though what with the war and all that it was a bit different this year, I hear, not quite the real thing. But it means racing's back already; good news that."

"Yes, good news."

"Won by an SS fellow in a BMW 328; they pull a lot of useful strings, those two little *esses*, you might need to get involved with them, or the NSKK, if we're to go further when this is all over, Pup."

"Really, Nazis?"

"Sacrifices, Pup, it's not just about speed; you should know that by now."

Ingo nodded, he would deal with all that when he had to.

"I never said, did I? I've written to an old pal of mine, at DKW, told him about you."

"You did, what did you say?"

"Said you were a bit raw, but you might have something; if only you'd use your head as much as you use the throttle."

Ingo laughed, and reached down to rap a sharp tattoo on Pop's helmet. The sound of the other bikes and Kroh's armoured car was clearer now.

"France should be good, Pup, eh?" Pop said, once again scanning the far side of the river with the field glasses. "French girls. You know what they say about French girls?"

"They speak French?"

"I had a French girl once …" Pop started. But Ingo wasn't interested in French girls, he was only interested in one girl, and she was Polish. He had had very little leave since they had returned to Germany, Kroh had seen to that. Once he realised that Ingo intended to return to Warsaw he made sure there was always a reason – some fabricated misdemeanor, or some dodgy work to do – which would keep him in their new base near Bergheim. The dust from Wawer had not settled enough for him to return, Kroh sometimes said, but Ingo thought it was more to do with spite, and he wished Pop had never mentioned that Ingo had a girl in Warsaw. Sometimes Kroh had not even needed to intervene, as often leave was cancelled or restricted; in readiness for this, Ingo now realised. The war wasn't over after all. But Kroh couldn't keep him in barracks forever and Ingo had finally been given Pentecost leave, a full seven days. He was at the Köln Hauptbahnhof, waiting for a train, when a chained dog spotted the divisional flashes on his tunic. A few hours later he was back with the regiment. The order had gone out, all leave cancelled.

He had written to her, of course, the letter addressed to *Kasper's Café, Old Town, Warsaw*. But for some reason the first letter, the second and the third, had been returned with a message scrawled across the top in German: *Address unknown*. He often wished he had taken a note of her address, that night.

Pop said there was sure to be leave after this; and *this* could not last long. But in reality no one knew how long *this* would last. And everyone knew that the last time the German army had visited France through Belgium it had spent the next four years in a trench … He hoped Pop was right, and history was wrong.

"… Nice and firm," Pop finished with a sigh.

"You know, I reckon we'd get an Iron Cross if we took that bridge, on our own," Ingo said. "Just rode over it; easy as that."

"Since when have *you* been interested in medals?"

"Would have thought DKW would like a rider with an Iron Cross."

"Probably would."

"And it's better than joining the SS."

"Probably is."

"And it would piss Kroh off."

"Without a doubt."

The others were much closer now, Ingo could hear the motorbikes rasping, the light throb of the armoured car's V8, the heavy hum of its thick tyres and the rattle of its armour cladding.

"Seems a shame to let him get the glory," Ingo said. "And, as you say, there doesn't seem to be anyone around, does there?"

Pop took another look through the binoculars. "I don't know … I just don't know …"

"Well, you know what I always say: when in doubt …" With that Ingo pulled his goggles down over his eyes, clunked the bike into first and twisted the throttle, the engine noise almost drowning Pop's "Hold on …" as he let out the clutch, the rear wheel spinning and shrieking against the road surface, the intoxicating smell of burnt rubber flooding his nostrils. Ingo didn't need to tell Pop that it was he who should be holding on, and Pop shook his head sharply, made a quick sign of the cross – an old Pop joke – and then gripped the MG 34 rather than the grab rail.

The BMW rattled across the cobbles and then on to the smooth asphalt of the bridge, Ingo quickly clunking it up through the gears, counter steering a little to the left now to account for the twist of the machine, Pop pressing the butt of the machine gun to his shoulder, biting tightly on the glowing Reemtsma clamped between his lips. When they were halfway over it seemed clear to Ingo that the bridge was undefended …

… They were well over halfway across when the machine gun fire started.

Ingo saw it a moment before he heard it, sparks off the iron supports of the bridge, feathers of grey-white powder lifted from the road surface, then the *rat-a-tat-tat* of the gun. Just then he felt the ground beneath the bike jolt, as if the whole world hiccupped ...

... The BMW was lifted with the road for an instant, and then seemed to hang there, flying at speed, the rear wheel spinning and the engine screaming as it over-revved, before the machine landed with a thump, a twang of springs, and a heavy slosh of fuel in the tank an instant later. Right then a harsh whooshing sound filled Ingo's head, while the breath was sucked from his lungs and the air turned to dust. Then a thicker curtain of debris rose up right in front of them, so dense with stones and steel that it was halfway to being a wall.

The bike hit the rising curtain of dust and flying rubble at barely diminished speed, and Ingo was then aware of a sinking feeling, as if he was falling in a waking dream ... It was as a zinging piece of steel sliced through his tunic and into his shoulder, a sharply hot pain, that Ingo realised the bridge had been blown.

By then the combination, and the road itself, was falling within the thick cloud of dust and stones and steel, before the now steeply sloping roadway cracked apart like a snapped slab of chocolate in front of the BMW. The machine crashed into the rising edge of broken road and then flipped. Ingo was thrown from it, flew for a moment, and then hit the asphalt. He tasted blood in his mouth and sucked in a stench of burnt iron. He was dimly aware that the machine, obeying some demonic law of physics, had spun up and away from him ... And then it landed on his legs. Ingo heard the brittle snaps of breaking bones, before he felt the searing pain as a jagged bone stabbed out through his skin. He had no idea what had happened to Pop. The roadway pitched up a little more and Ingo slid from it like wet dung from a shovel.

He was suddenly beneath the dusty surface of the Meuse, cold and slick with oil, blood from his nose and shoulder unspinning like red silk strands in the water behind him as he sank, sank, sank; the still crumbling bridge above him, an image jellified through the dirty water, fading ... Deeper, deeper, fading, fading, deeper, fading ...

*

Warsaw. August 1940

This time one year ago the Germans had yet to invade and Lidka's life was uncomplicated. The only pressing issue she had had then was Jósef, how to let him down gently. She never had, in the end. She sat on a hard kitchen chair in the courtyard beyond the walled garden at the back of the house on Mochnackiego. She liked it here, on a hot day like today, sitting in the sun while the hard edge of the shade, which this late in the afternoon fell heavily from the tall house behind her, crept along the cobbles towards a washing line, weighed down with white sheets that were as still as iron in the breezeless space. The courtyard-like area was almost enclosed with four-storey apartment buildings and the Paczkowski house, with a gap beside the house, partly choked by the large oak tree, and another in the opposite corner, where vehicles could enter. The Paczkowski garden had been dug up and planted with potatoes, and so a green fletched L-shape traced two edges at the side and rear of the house, terminating at the blue-painted weatherboard garage where Mr Paczkowski kept his car. It wouldn't be very long until the spuds were ready for harvest and Lidka was proud of them; it had been her idea and she had planted them, though she doubted she would be much use when it came to picking them. The thought of it brought on another twinge in her lower back and she forced herself to sit a little straighter on the wooden chair.

In a far corner some children played a serious game that seemed to involve an invisible boat and a lot of whispering, while a bald man polished a car he probably rarely used now, as there was little fuel to be had, the chamois squeaking against the already gleaming red paintwork. She could hear the rumble and clatter of a tram on Filtrowa, then its sharp bell. The windows in many of the buildings of the apartments were flung open, but there was not much noise. She could smell the heat from the cobbles, and feel it through the soles of her shoes, while the familiar scent of the warm clean sheets made her drowsy. She pressed her spine to the back of the chair, which helped to take a little of the strain, and rested her hands on her distended stomach.

And she hummed. Nearly all the time she hummed, these days. Hummed softly to the baby inside her. Chopin. It was always Chopin. She felt herself melting in to sleep ...

"Sarah told me you were out here."

She started.

"Forgive me," Mr Paczkowski said. Despite the heat he was wearing one of his cardigans patched with suede at the elbows, and a bright green tie.

"That's alright, I didn't mean to drift off. I have chores —"

"Sarah's seeing to all your chores, as you know, you need to take it easy now."

"Sarah can hardly be seen taking in the washing, can she?" The Nazis had started to come down heavily on the Jews. Not many, in the apartments overlooking the courtyard, would know Sarah was Jewish, but one might know, another might guess, and it was not worth the risk. It was a shame, for Sarah and her brother Leon, to have to stay inside on a day like this and Lidka had felt guilty coming out with the chair. But she sensed her unborn child needed sunlight. He was going to love the sun, she thought. She had also sensed that he was going to be *he*.

"Jadwiga can bring in the sheets."

Lidka said nothing, just raised an eyebrow, and Mr Paczkowski laughed. She noticed he held something in his hand. "A letter?"

"For you."

"But the post came this morning?"

"A girl brought it, when you were teaching earlier. She was …" It was rare for Mr Paczkowski to be lost for words.

"Kassia," Lidka said, but it was not a question. Her heart seemed to freeze. A letter. For her. That had been sent to Piwna. Had Ingo noted the address that night, after all?

Mr Paczkowski passed her the envelope. "It's from Lisbon," he said

"Lisbon?"

The envelope was indeed addressed to her, at the flat on Piwna. She had not seen these postage stamps before, a row of them, three blue and one red, the size of fingernails and featuring a geometrical motif. They were franked with *Lisboa* postmarks. The address had been pencilled over obliquely in German with the word *Bedeutungslos*, 'of no importance'. There was also *München*, Munich, stamped in the corner of the envelope. For a moment there was a flinty spark of excitement, for that was Ingo's home, she knew. But she almost immediately saw that the return address typed on the rear of the envelope was *Thos. Cook, Box 506, Lisboa, Portugal*. It had obviously been opened, and then sealed with the official looking tape with red writing on it. She opened it, to find another envelope within. She recognised the tidy, upright, handwriting of Jósef Sczcepanski on the envelope; which had also been opened and resealed with the censor's tape.

Disappointment filled her, like hot lead pouring into a mould. But there was something else; anger, too. As irrational as it was, she felt that Ingo had played a cruel joke on her.

"I will leave you to it," Mr Paczkowski said.

"There's no need," she said, softly. The sender's name at the top of the letter was *Zwolakowski H*. The letter was very short and simply said: *I am alive and well, and in the same work, in England. I hope you are safe and well and I miss you very much. I am sorry I could not say goodbye. Please reply if you can.* There was no signature. She passed Mr Paczkowski the letter and he read it very quickly.

"You know this Zwolakowski?"

"No, but I know the handwriting."

"It's probably a pseudonym, for security reasons; that is why he cannot give details, too. But he's taking a risk, it's illegal to receive a letter from an enemy country, Miss Wadalowska, and like it or not Poland is now a part of Germany."

"He just wanted me to know he was safe."

"It's this Jósef, yes?"

"Yes."

"In England?"

He had noticed the stamps on the inner envelope, she nodded.

"There is an address, to reply to," he said, pointing out the Lisbon PO Box number on the outer envelope. "Will you?"

Lidka folded the short letter and put it back in the envelope. "I don't know," she said.

"I understand, but I must ask you, if you do, then please not use this address. We're taking enough of a risk, the arrival of letters from Portugal could bring unwanted attention," Mr Paczkowski said. "And I simply cannot afford attention."

"Yes, of course," Lidka said, remembering the Voglers, hiding in the house.

"But it's good that he's safe?" he said.

"Yes, it's good."

"You could still reply?"

"Perhaps, but not yet," she said, running her hand over the tight drum of her belly.

*

Wehrmacht Hospital Complex, Würzburg, Germany. September 1940

Ingo Six was not made for sitting still, but right now his body was not much good for anything else. When the bridge had blown he had broken many bones, some high in his legs, and those take the longest time to heal. He hadn't helped, he would admit, impatient to walk again, and that had set him back twice now. And then there had been that wheelchair, and those stairs ... Ingo sighed, picked up the tennis ball from its nest in the crumpled sheets beside him. One of his legs was still in a cast and the skin itched like fire, as if an army of biting ants was marching beneath it. His other was raised in a sling on a steel hoist.

The military hospital was only three or four years old, and it was massive, which made Ingo think that someone had always known there was a war on its way. But there were plenty of empty beds now and many did seem to think it was almost over, with France having fallen. He could be racing soon, if his legs would just hurry up and heal.

The tennis ball had been to help with someone's physiotherapy, something for a mending hand to squeeze, now it was helping with Ingo's psychotherapy, something for a bored mind to focus on. And so he concentrated on throwing the ball, bouncing it against the highly polished floor, before it hit the metre and a half space of wall between the tall windows and rebounded into his waiting hand. Outside of the closed windows, a flotilla of steel-grey clouds slowly floated through a porridge sky over hills verdantly corduroyed with vineyards the other side of the Main River, which was hidden from sight in the valley below. The ward smelt more of the floor polish than disinfectant. It was too warm, and the large radiator behind his bed ticked loudly, as if it tutted in frustration as it expanded and contracted in its indecision.

There were no nurses around right now so Ingo was able to do the one thing that kept him occupied, fought the boredom, kept his mind off Lidka, and the motorcycles he should have been riding. Heckmann, a clerk from an artillery unit who had had a haemorrhoids operation and, Ingo thought, envied his more heroic leg fractures and the Y-shaped scar the piece of steel had torn in his shoulder, read his book and pretended not to notice that Ingo had started throwing the ball again, pulling the pages closer to his face. It annoyed Heckmann, he knew, but that in itself was a release from the crushing tedium. There were other patients the other end of the ward, but not many.

He bounced the ball again, hitting the wall between the windows right on the scuff mark he'd hit so many times before it rebounded. Pop caught it in mid-air.

"Where did you come from?" Ingo said.

"Bamberg," Pop replied, pulling a chair close to Ingo's bed, its feet screeching against the polished floor. He carried a rolled up magazine and a brown paper bag, the latter lumpy with fruit.

"Took your time," Ingo said, though he was pleased to see him.

"Kroh's no more generous with the leave; even if it's just an afternoon off to hop on the train to Würzburg. But how are you?"

"Almost fixed, I'd say."

"And what do the doctors say?" Pop said, arching an eyebrow.

Ingo shrugged, the movement pulling at the slowly healing wound on his shoulder. "What about you?" he said.

"I'm used to falling off bikes, good as new, me."

"It was more about falling off the bridge, than the bike," Ingo said.

Pop grinned, tossed him the copy of *Motor und Sport*, which disappointingly bore a coloured picture of a Stuka on the cover; it had been a while since they'd featured photographs of racing cars. Pop had been thrown clear of the sidecar, but the combination had not landed on him as it had on Ingo and he had suffered nothing more than a broken arm and a sprained ankle. When Ingo was out cold he'd pulled him from the Meuse, literally single-handed, and dragged him up so he was partially on to the steep slope of the collapsed roadway. Saved his life. Ingo had thanked him for that, when he had last visited, but it had embarrassed Pop, he had thought, so he did not mention it again.

"I've some good news," Pop said.

"DKW?"

"Well no, not that. Everyone's still a bit too busy with the war, but how long can that last now, eh?"

"So we'll be racing soon, you think?"

"Yes, I think so. A matter of months and this war will be history; the English are not a worry now, good as beaten I'd say. You can count on it, Pup."

"Good; that is good news."

"That's not the good news," Pop said. "No, the good news is they're going to give you an Iron Cross, me too."

"A medal; will it mean more leave?"

"Doubt that, quite a few of the lads have been given one, though Kroh's not among them. Seems someone noticed he was more interested in looting than shooting."

"Good."

"Perhaps, but he has a wasp up his arse about it. Not sure it'll make him any easier to live with."

"No, I can imagine; and if there's no extra leave in it an Iron Cross is just extra weight," Ingo said

"But, as you said yourself, before pulling that dumb stunt in Maastricht, it could help you get on a racing bike, or even in a racing car, when this war is done. So it might not be such a heavy cross to bear, you know."

"Maybe," Ingo said. Pop had put the tennis ball on the edge of the bed and Ingo picked it up, bounced it again from the floor to the narrow piece of wall between the high windows. It bounced back and he caught it – *plunk-plunk-slap*. "I need to get out of here, it's driving me mad," he said.

"You need to be patient," Pop said. "There's a lot of mending to be done before you'll be on a bike again. You know, if you had been a little patient in the first place you might not be here with your feet up. A racer needs a little patience, sometimes."

"No time for patience," Ingo said, and threw the ball at the wall again, catching it just as a nurse pushed through the swing doors, which closed behind her with a woody flutter.

"Enough of that, soldier," she snapped.

Nurse Mader was young and pretty, with copper hair that glared in contrast to the stark white headpiece that was pinned to it, high and far back on her head. She had chestnut eyes and wore a long white apron over a slightly longer pale blue pin-striped dress, its sleeves rolled into stiff and precise bands just above her elbows. She did not have large breasts, but they were breasts, all the same, and that was enough to make Pop stare; and then look away when she glared at him. Nurse Mader shot out the searchlights of a hundred Pops each and every day.

"I wonder, Nurse Mader, it would be nice to get some fresh air, you know?" Ingo said.

"You know that's impossible."

"Impossible?" Pop said.

"Yes, impossible."

"He has an Iron Cross, you know," Pop said, his voice slightly higher. He glanced at Ingo.

"He has one, too," he said, taking the hint.

"Yes, and half the boys on Ludendorff Ward also have an Iron Cross. I'm sure I will get one myself, before the week is done."

"I'll give you mine, if you let me out – just for a little while," Ingo said.

"You know it's not as easy as that," she said.

"Why not, there's a wheelchair just out there?" Pop said. "I saw it on the way in."

"He's not allowed."

"Not allowed?"

"Will you tell him, or shall I?"

"The last one I borrowed broke," Ingo said, then looked at the tennis ball, decided not to throw it at the wall.

She cocked her head to one side, smiled a rare smile. "The last one he borrowed broke because he tried to ride it down the stairs, when there was a perfectly serviceable elevator."

"You did?" Pop said.

"It wasn't so bad, just a matter of balance really. Would have made it all the way if I hadn't been interrupted."

"Would have been a lot closer to walking now if you hadn't tried, I'd say." With that Nurse Mader walked over to Heckmann's bed. He was painfully shy and he pulled his book even tighter to his face.

"She's nice," Pop said.

"You think?"

"Looks nice, I mean."

"Suppose so," Ingo said.

"Seems to like you."

"You reckon?"

"Yes, no doubt about it."

"Well I doubt it, and I'm taken anyway," Ingo said

"Oh yes, and how many letters have we had from this Polish girl, then?" Pop said, only now noticing the small photograph of Lidka propped against a glass of water on the bedside table, the one Ingo had taken in December. Pop had seen it many times before, but he always studied it for a moment or two. Ingo did not answer his question, which was an answer in itself. But as he had told Pop a hundred times before, there was nowhere really for her to write to, as he had never given her his family address in Munich, because there had not been time, in the rush to leave Warsaw. Besides, even if he had he knew his father would not forward a letter on to him, especially one from a Polish girl.

"Tell me, how do you wash, down there?" Pop said, not quite changing the subject, and loosely pointing at the area below the waistband of Ingo's pyjamas. "She help out?" He nodded in the direction of Nurse Mader.

"Sometimes," Ingo said.

Pop smiled. "Christ, how can I break a leg or two?" he said, staring after the nurse, who walked on down the ward, her flat shoes softly clicking against the hard floor. He watched her until she stopped at another bed and started talking to a lad with bandaged eyes. Then he turned back to Ingo. "Here, I've brought you some apples." He placed the paper bag on the bed.

"Good, I think I'll teach myself how to juggle."

*

Warsaw. December 1940

She had finally registered the child's birth, and his father as Jósef Sczcepanski. It was just ink. It still meant Fryderyk was a bastard. But not a German bastard. It had been humiliating, but not as bad as she had feared – a knowing smirk could not hurt her now; because she had done this for her son. The Church would not issue a birth certificate for an illegitimate child, and so she had come to the magistrate. Feliks Paczkowski had waited in his Polski Fiat Mazur outside the office on Jerozolimskie. She was glad of the lift, as it was bitterly cold. It was warmer in the car than it was in the big house, so she had not hesitated in bringing the baby along.

"It's good you're beginning to be practical," Feliks said, as he drove them home.

"It's just words on paper, he is still not really Fryderyk's father."

"Words on paper start wars, sign death warrants, allow a baby to be a real person with real rations. Words on paper are powerful, Lidka."

They had been on first name terms since the baby had arrived. It had happened suddenly, just like his real father Fryderyk had been in a rush, and the baby had been delivered by Sarah and Feliks Paczkowski in the small bedroom at the top of the house. After that there was little room for formalities between the former art dealer and his son's tutor.

Feliks had never used the Mazur much, even before the war, and he seemed nervous of it, but more nervous of the German vehicles he shared the street with, and each time they passed one of these travelling in the opposite direction he would look away from it, and as is the way with nervous drivers the car would follow his eyes, and drift towards the kerb – and once dangerously close to a bell-clanging number 12 tram. It was not a new car, yet is still smelt of new leather, and now new life; the sleeping baby in her arms.

There was snow on the ground and on the high rooftops, though the streets had been cleared to reveal dark, damp, wide stripes of cobbles that whispered wetly beneath the tyres of the big car. The sky was plated with iron-like clouds and she thought the snow would fall again soon. The heater ticked as it emitted warm air, which slightly fogged Feliks' spectacles – he cleaned them quickly with the tongue of his bright green tie and the car weaved a little as he tried to steer it one-handed, the wheels thudding over shining tram tracks. The baby smiled as he slept, wrapped up in his blankets. He often did that, and she wondered what he dreamt of. He was a happy baby.

"They will call him Freddy, you know?"

"I know," she said. She had named him after Chopin, of course.

"They would have called him other things, so it's good you have done this."

"Yes, I know. Ink on paper."

Feliks nodded. He was gripping the rim of the steering wheel as if it was his hold on life itself, his knuckle bones through the stretched skin of his fingers as off-white as the dirty snow piles at the side of the road. He slowed the car in plenty of time for the junction with Marszałkowska, slightly gnashing a gear change as he turned left; being careful to let a German truck, which was the same dark grey as the clouds, through first. He drove very slowly between the town houses and office buildings that lined the street, some still ruined from the fighting and bombing of '39. He pulled a little too far to one side to let a German motorcycle rasp by; Lidka could not help but look at its rider, but it was not him, it never was.

"I'm worried about Andrzej," Feliks suddenly said.

Lidka had been ready for this. Andrzej had been strangely sullen and uncommunicative since she had moved into the house, and now he had stopped coming to her lessons. He had said he had a job; but had not said what it was.

"He will be seventeen, quite soon" she said. "These days that's quite old. Many leave school before they are seventeen."

"Yes, old enough. That's what I'm worried about. He no longer listens to what I say, or his mother, we simply can't get through to him. I don't suppose you have any idea what it is he does all all day, and even at night sometimes? He certainly has no money to show for it."

"No, he's said nothing to me; why would he?"

"He always seemed to respect you. I thought that maybe he had talked to you, that's all."

"He has only said he has a job, nothing more."

"But what job? Why the secrecy?"

"What does Sarah say?"

Feliks shook his head sharply, and the car weaved with it. "That one knows something, alright, but she's not telling."

Lidka was not surprised. She thought Sarah would know *exactly* what Andrzej was up to. She remembered the slogan he had painted on the shop that time, but she kept that to herself, as Feliks had enough to worry about as it was. He was risking everything to hide the Voglers. All the Jews in the city had been herded into a walled Ghetto, and to harbour any who were not within its barbed wire topped walls, surviving on its meagre rations, was punishable by death. She worried about it, often, but she also respected Feliks for what he was doing. Sol Vogler had once said to her that Feliks had saved his family's life. At the time she had thought that an exaggeration. But times were changing.

"It's a hard to be that age these days, Feliks."

He said nothing as he concentrated on passing one of the bicycle rickshaws that had taken the place of taxis and horse-drawn droshkas; for Poles. Two middle aged women sat on its bench seat, a blanket over their legs, feathers of frozen breath mingling in front of their faces as they gossiped.

"It's also hard to be a father too, Lidka," he finally said. "Very hard," he added with a sad little shake of the head. "Tell me, your German, the pianist; can you imagine him as a father?"

Lidka paused before answering. Because she had suddenly realised she had never even considered it. She tried to picture Ingo scolding a little version of himself, or helping him with sums, and simply couldn't. She smiled as she shook her head.

Feliks briefly took his eyes off the road and faced her. "Did you believe he loved you?" he said.

"I think so," she said, noticing the tense of the question.

"But he's gone," he said. "What about this other boy, Jósef? Does he love you?"

"He said he did, yes," she said, unsure. But then nodded, sharply: "Yes, I think he does."

"I won't ask if you love him, that's not so important, really. But I will ask this one question, Lidka: which one of these two boys is the most likely to return to Warsaw?"

"I suppose that depends, doesn't it?"

"Well, the way the war is now, it seems to me only one of them would even be able to return to Warsaw; wouldn't you say so?"

"I don't know if *one of them* is even alive," Lidka said.

"Yes, of course, I'm sorry. But if he is, then would you not expect him to have visited you, at least? He knew where you worked, after all. And even if he did not know the address, Mochnackiego is distinctive, anyone would remember it."

"There might be a hundred reasons why he's not come."

"There might be one reason," Feliks said. "You will have to face up to facts soon, Lidka, perhaps you should try to get word to this Jósef?"

"There is still time," she said.

"But the boy must have a father. People will want to know who that is, and before you know it even the boy will want to know who that is."

"Perhaps, but not yet," she said. "For now, words on paper will have to be enough."

***

RAF Swinderby, Lincolnshire, England. March 1941

The cold wind whistling between the hangars reminded Flight Sergeant Józef Sczcepanski of winter in Warsaw, while the heavy steel doors shaking in the wind sounded like the distant artillery that had chased him out of Poland almost eighteen months before. He had not heard from Lidka since then, but few had heard from home – very few. He wondered how she was and worried about her often. More than anything else he wished he had asked her, that last time they had been together. He wished he had had the courage to ask her; to ask her to marry him. Like everything else in his life – except him, ironically – that was all up in the air, now.

Józef and his men had worked on the Wellington for days, as it had returned from its last mission, bombing Bremen, in a desperate condition. The dope hardened fabric that covered the Duralumin skeleton of the aeroplane like a drum skin had been blown away by flak bursts in places, but not so much that it let out all the blood. Józef had been sick, when he had helped wash it out, after finding a pocket watch-sized piece of hairy scalp, like a segment of a coconut, in the glutinous soup of the congealed blood. But he had made sure none of the men under him had seen him vomit.

There had also been a fire within the fuselage, and two members of the crew had been badly burnt. There was still the smell of burnt flesh in the plane, Józef thought, but he did not want to ask any of the others if they also smelt it, just in case it was really only in his head. The hangar also smelt of rubber, grease, oil and the drying dope and paint. It was freezing cold, his breath a frozen lace in front of his face as he examined the handiwork of his men. The bomber looked pristine now, green and brown camouflage on top, night black along the flanks and underside, the harsh electric lighting of the hangar bringing a faint gleam to the matt finish. It would be ready for tomorrow night's op'.

The 'Wimpy' was a great improvement on the Fairey Battles with which the Polish 301 Squadron of RAF Bomber Command had started its war, which had been more like elongated fighters, but without the speed. He had been told then that his skills were of more value on the ground, after he had completed the air-gunner course he had initially been placed on. He had not argued otherwise, when he realised he would not be aircrew, because he had been relieved, as he had always regretted requesting the training. And then he had got on with the job, playing his part in the fight, fixing the aircraft shot up over Germany.

Despite its size, almost twenty metres in length with a wingspan of twenty-six, and the machine guns that bristled from its gun canopies at the nose and tail, the Wellington looked vulnerable, he always thought, like a fat old bird. Yet, in reality, it was tough, and through the strip of Perspex that ran down part of the fuselage he could see the aluminium frame that made up the geodesic skeleton of the aircraft. It was this that made it so robust; even if a huge piece of its skin was blown away it retained its rigidity. He had seen Wellingtons return with whole sections bitten out of them. It was a remarkable survivor, and he could admire that in a machine, and in a man.

"Good work, Sczcepanski."

Józef turned to see Flight Lieutenant Wysocki, the man who had led him out of Poland, walking towards him. He glanced at the officer's burnt hands, as he always did, then looked quickly away, his eyes swivelling to the cold concrete floor, and an oil stain in the shape of the Iberian Peninsula.

"Thank you, sir," he said.

"Any word?" Wysocki asked, but he knew the answer, Józef thought.

Józef shook his head. Wysocki had told him it was a waste of time, when he had sent the letter via Thomas Cook nearly six months before, but then everything other than bombing Germans was a waste of time for Wysocki. He had not sent another letter, because he had had no reply, but also because they had been made aware of the risk to those receiving the letters. The postal service had surprised him. It had been advertised in a newspaper. They were not supposed to correspond with enemy countries, and occupied Poland was that, now. But they were allowed to send very short messages with very little detail, through the Thomas Cook travel company, which sent them on via its office in neutral Portugal, after the brief message had been cleared by censors.

"I doubt they ever get through," Wysocki said. "You just need to be patient. Beat the Nazis first, I say, then we can all go home."

"I suppose you're right there, sir," Józef said, but he somehow could not see Wysocki without his war, it was like his hair, and the burns on his hands, a part of him now.

"It was a big job," Wysocki said, and Józef looked up to see that his gaze was playing along the length of the machine. He sniffed, and Józef wondered if he, too, could smell burnt flesh. Wysocki was wearing his Irvin flying jacket with its big woolly collar and lapels and an RAF peaked hat. Józef wore two sets of brown overalls, to try to keep the cold out.

"The bastards certainly chewed her up, sir," Józef said.

Wysocki nodded, then his eyes locked on the gun position at the tail, where a pair of .303 Browning machine guns poked through the Perspex compartment in which the vulnerable rear gunner sat. "Bet you'd like to get at those *bastards*, eh?" Wysocki said, at the same time swivelling to face Józef, just as the rear gunner might turn his turret to take aim at an enemy night fighter.

Józef shrugged. He did not like to lie, if he could help it, but: "That would be something, sir," he said, trying a smile with it.

"Yes?"

Józef nodded.

"We have a space tomorrow night, Antoni's broken his wrist, arsing around in the mess as usual. I'm short of a rear gunner."

Józef felt a nerve twitch in his cheek, as if he had been zapped by a bolt of electricity, and for a moment or two he could not speak. He knew what Wysocki meant. It was not so common now, as it had been at the start, when quite often ground crew would take the place of aircrew, even non-NCOs back then – AC2s, AC1s and LACs – and sometimes even without training. But it still happened, now and again, on the quiet. And, as Wysocki knew, Jósef had had the training.

"Thought you deserved first shot at it," Wysocki added, filling the void of Jósef's hesitation. "There's only a tiny chance you'll need to use the guns, of course."

"I think my place is here, sir," Jósef said, after another pause. His voice sounded small in the large hangar, he thought.

"It's just one mission, a milk run – something to tell the grandkids, eh?"

"There's a lot to be done, sir."

"You sure?"

"Yes, sir."

"We've been through a lot, me and you, Sczcepanski." Wysocki said. "Well, a bit," he added, and for a moment Jósef thought there was a hint of a sly smile, like a nasty pike, just below the surface of a dark pond. "I thought you'd bite my hand off for this?"

"As I said, my place is here, sir," Jósef said, with as much finality as he could muster.

"Very well, but you should know Sczcepanski, opportunities like this do not come along often. There might never be another chance."

Jósef nodded, but Wysocki was walking away. He might have told him he was tired; he might have told him that he was needed, as an English speaker – as most of those in the ground crews were British – and so he could not take the risk. He might have told him many things which would have been true, but he suspected Wysocki knew the real truth, and maybe he had even enjoyed revealing it. That was the sort of dark joke the man lived for. That and killing Germans.

Jósef could feel the fear seep from his body now, a physical thing, to be replaced with a soothing relief that was almost giddying in its intensity. Before it transformed again; into the burning acid of shame.

***

Chillar. March 1951

Ingo finished tightening the sump bolt, then unhooked the caged-bulb lamp from the steering arm. He was in the inspection pit in the Di Rossi Auto Repairs garage on Belgrano. The new Ford V8 that Carlo had bought had been transformed into a road racing car. They had raised the suspension to cope with the rough terrain, cut back the fenders and replaced them with horizontal slats level with the bonnet, and then done the same at the rear of the car. They had also added an extra long-range fuel tank, changed the transmission to a stick shift, moved the exhaust so it was high on the side of the car, where it traced the curves of the rear wheel arches and was out of harm's way, and taken out all the excess weight. The car had then been beefed up, and Argentina does beef well; tougher leaf springs, and crash protection, but not so much that it might make her overweight. Carlo had also worked on the V8 engine until it purred like a Tiger cub, roared like its mother, and Ingo had worked alongside him. Neither of them had once spoken about why they did this work; they just did it. But they both knew that racing cars were for one thing only. Racing.

There was the sharp clack of heels on the hard floor of the garage and from his place in the inspection pit beneath the car Ingo caught sight of a shapely pair of ankles balanced on fire engine red shoes, the sort that suited the tango. Those ankles wore no stockings, just a gleaming bronze tan. The feet were widely spaced.

"Hello!"

Ingo climbed the ladder out of the pit at the rear of the car. She was looking at the Ford. It was painted a deeper red than her shoes, with white signwriting to advertise the garage and a local tyre supplier called *Gonzalez Hermanos*. The name *Enrique Hohberg* was also painted in white above the driver's door. He had ignored this, not commented on it, as Carlo had grinned his grin. The woman did not seem impressed with their racing car, probably wondering why someone would throw out all the leather, but Ingo was impressed with her.

Those ankles he'd seen from below supported a fine pair of legs that were interrupted just above slightly dimpled knees by a cherry red A-line dress with chalky piping, fashionably tight at her slim waist. She carried a large leather handbag in her left hand, while her right hand was pressed against her waist, her arm angled like a coffee pot handle, so that it almost seemed as if it was a counterweight to her breasts. He knew enough about engineering to see that she needed the support. She was older than 'girl', maybe in her early thirties, perhaps a bit younger, and she was also quite something; though a slightly acquisitive curl at the end of her nose almost spoilt the effect, and made Ingo think a man would have to work for that beauty. She had her hair swept back and intricately plaited in a Gordian knot of a bun, like a picture he'd seen of Eva Peron. But Ingo thought that was a mistake, for it looked like wild hair that should be set free. She wore an aggressive perfume that smelt of cinnamon and juniper and sliced through the grease and paint smell of the 'shop. Her lipstick matched her shoes; precisely.

Her dark eyes flashed when she saw him, and for a moment he feared the worst. Recognition.

"Mother told me never to trust a man with a beard," she said, her accent sounding local.

"Your mother's wise."

"Said it means they're hiding something."

Ingo turned away from her and placed the adjustable spanner and the inspection lamp on to a workbench, above which there was a row of grainy old photographs of Carlo and Carlos racing Sophia. The old girl had now been sold.

"Or simply hiding," the woman added.

"I'm a bit busy, I'm afraid, and if you've a car that needs fixing you'll have to speak to the boss."

"En-ri-que Hoh-berg." She read it from the sign on the car, enunciating each syllable. "That's you, isn't it?"

He was about to deny it, but then thought being Enrique was always better than being Ingo these days. "That's me," he said.

"And you're to drive in the Mil Millas, I hear."

"Then your hearing's better than mine," Ingo said. The Mil Millas was a big race, the first event of the Turismo Carretera, the Argentinian road racing championship, and a race that took in one thousand miles of some of the country's toughest roads and attracted its best drivers, even Juan Manuel Fangio had been in the entry last year. Ingo had learned that from Carlo, who never seemed to stop talking about the Mil Millas these days, perhaps because it reminded him of the Mille Miglia he had dreamed of since he was a child and also talked of often, perhaps for other reasons.

"If you were to race in it, you would need a co-driver, I suppose?" she picked up a spanner as she said this, then put it down straight away, perhaps because it was a little greasy.

"I suppose I would," Ingo said. "I believe that's the way it's done, with these long distant races you need someone to point the way."

For a whimsical moment he thought she might offer her services, but instead she shook her head, tutted sharply, turned and walked out of the garage, as if she had suddenly realised she needed to be somewhere else very quickly indeed.

He shook his head and laughed to himself. Then he looked at the name, the name he now used, above the door of the red stock car.

***

Warsaw. March 1941

It was a crisp spring day, and warm in the sun. But it was iron cold in the deep ravine of Krzywe Koło and she made sure Freddy was well tucked in – Feliks had been right about that, everyone did call him Freddy, and even she had started to now. He was in the second-hand baby carriage she had bought, one of its wheels squeaking just out of time with her footfalls. Freddy's little face shivered to the vibration of the wheels on the cobbles, and he smiled. He often smiled, especially when he was in the pram. His eyes were big and blue, like her eyes, and always full of light when he was not asleep, wide open as if he was scared he might miss a single new thing. His fat little fingers seemed long to her, but no one else agreed. He slept well, and ate well, when he could, too. His wispy hair was blond, and thickening fast. She did not yet see much of Ingo in him; but in quiet moments she would sit him by the piano, and allow his long – yes, she was sure of it – fingers to touch the keys.

It had been a long time since she had gone to the café that had once belonged to Kasper. Two months, at least. The answer was always the same; she was not welcome: *Nur für Deutsche.* The bitter little man behind the counter always remembered her from the first time and he would just ask to see a kennkarte that would prove she was Volksdeutsche, the card he knew she did not possess. She hoped that maybe this time there might be someone else there. But this hope was coated in fear; for while she wanted a letter from Ingo, something to tell her it had meant more to him than one night, she also feared there would be nothing.

From outside, the green-framed windows were steamed up, as they always had been, and there was a homely smell of sour soup and sausage coming from within. There was now a sign above the door: *Distler's.* It seemed strange to name a small café with a surname, but then those with German surnames liked to show them off, these days. She opened the door and it squealed against the stone step as it always had, and then she pulled the pram in behind her. The wiry little Nazi with the wiry little Himmler specs was not behind the counter. Instead there was a fat woman with red cheeks. She was serving out a bowl of żur.

"Be with you in a moment, love," the woman said, in German, with a little hint of an accent. Lidka allowed her time to take the bowl of sour rye soup, in which floated pink rafts of sliced smoked sausage and pieces of hard-boiled egg, to a German soldier who sat at in the corner of the café, where the piano used to be, reading a copy of *Der Stürmer.*

There were two other men in the café, both sitting alone. One wore a brown Nazi uniform and smoked a cigar as he flicked through a sheaf of official looking papers. He was overweight in a contented, lazy way, but was quite handsome all the same. The other, who wore a suit, concentrated on his bowl of żur. She wished she was allowed to buy some of the soup, and her stomach rumbled its agreement, the Polish cafés seldom had such luxuries.

"Yes?" the fat woman said, her jowls quivering to the movement of her jaw.

"Please, can you help me? I have a friend, we used to meet here. I was wondering —"

"Ah yes, you're the girl," the woman said, with a smile. "With a baby, too?" She peered in to the baby carriage, Freddy smiled back. "Ahhh, what a sweetie," she said, shaking her head a little sadly. "A boy?"

Lidka nodded. "Please, I was —"

"Yes, yes. Herman has told me about you; you're asking about a letter, yes?"

"Or letters?"

"He's being cruel, but he has his reasons, you know, things were not so good for us in Warsaw, until everything changed. But I'm sorry, there have been no letters for a Polish girl, I'm sure of that. But what a lovely baby!" She beamed a fat grin that cloned her red chin.

Lidka swallowed her disappointment, and it tasted of bile. She no longer wanted rye soup, and she said: "What happened to Kasper, do you know?"

"Kasper?"

"He ran this place; before ..."

The woman quite suddenly stopped smiling, and then she looked up from the pram, shaking her head. "I have told you what I know, now I suggest you take heed of the sign." She cocked her head in the direction of the door, in which was hung the sign that Lidka could only see the reverse side of: *Nur für Deutsche.*

She said nothing more, simply manoeuvred the baby carriage with its squeaky wheel so that she was able to pull it out through the door, reaching back to push it open. None of the German men in the café offered to help her, but then someone outside reached forward to hold the door; a fur arm and a slightly vinegary and spicy smell of perfume on the in-rushing cold air. A familiar smell.

"Why Lidka, what a surprise!" Kassia said, just as Lidka recognised the perfume. Lidka turned to see her; she looked more shocked than surprised. Kassia glanced quickly inside the café, and then turned away, letting the door close behind the pram.

"You're not going in?"

"No, of course not, Nur für Deutsche," Kassia said.

"Yes, so it seems."

Lidka expected her to ask what she was doing there herself, but instead she said: "I was just passing, saw you ..." She shook her head. "So, this is little Freddy, eh?"

"Yes, meet Aunt Kassia, Freddy," Lidka said. She had sent a message to tell Kassia all about Freddy months ago, but she had received no reply, and she had seen very little of her since she had left the flat on Piwna.

Freddy was staring at her, gaping and drooling; she always had that effect on boys, Lidka remembered. Kassia was wearing a fur coat that was long enough to stretch to below the knees; it covered everything, in a way that suggested there was nothing to cover. She also wore a wide brimmed hat that dipped over her right eye, the crown of which was belted with a fur band, which might have been taken from the same darkly-striped animal as the coat, and glossy shoes with tall heels, which looked as expensive as the rest of the outfit. Her lipstick was bright red, and it seemed like a single brush-stoke, a vibrant beginning of a painting which sang out in the drab stone channel of the cold, tight street.

"Let's walk," Kassia said, "and you can tell me all about him."

Lidka nodded.

Kassia looked back over her shoulder once, at the door to the café, when they came to the end of the street and before they turned in to Nowomiejska. "I must be somewhere, soon, an appointment," she said.

"An appointment?"

Kassia nodded; "Work, I suppose."

"Really, for who?"

"He really is a cute little thing, isn't he?" Kassia said, then made a point of leaning under the canopy as she walked, hiding her face from Lidka as she added: "So, have you told your father, and the dragon?"

"I've not quite got around to that."

"Not quite?"

"I'll let them know, when it's time."

"He will be pleased to have a grandson," Kassia said. "Maybe not so pleased not to have a son-in-law."

"He'll get over it, times have changed."

"Not that much; though he'll probably prefer no son-in-law to a German soldier son-in-law," Kassia looked up now. "Have you heard from *him*, then?"

Lidka shook her head.

"Well, at least he left you more than just his cap, in the end, eh?"

"In that case, how can I regret it, then?" Lidka said.

"Yes, you're right, Lidka."

Lidka thought that might be the first time she had heard Kassia ever say she was right about anything. She stopped, quite suddenly, then reached inside the pram, taking out the small quivering, warm and chortling bundle that was Freddy. "Why don't you hold him?"

"No, they're not for me, babies," Kassia said. "And I must go, soon"

Lidka carefully put the still smiling baby back in the pram. "Tell me Kassia, have there been any more letters for me?"

"None; you had the one from Portugal; I have to ask —"

"Józef."

"Portugal?"

"England."

"Really? He did well to get away, maybe there's more to the boy after all?"

"Maybe there is," Lidka said, quietly, as she made sure Freddy was snugly tucked in.

"I should tell you, Lidka, I'm moving from the apartment soon, and a German couple is moving in, I believe. I doubt they will forward mail from England, or Portugal."

"That's a pity," Lidka said. She had never replied to Józef, she had, she now realised, still been waiting on word from Ingo. But that was over, now.

"Maybe they will send on mail from Germany, though?" Kassia said.

"He never knew the address, as far as I know," Lidka said, saying to Kassia what she had said to herself a thousand times. It had been dark, and she had always doubted that Ingo had had his mind on street names high on walls and faded house numbers on old stone that night. She hadn't. Now she also felt quite certain there would be no mail for her at the café, either.

"He might not have known the address, but he knows where Warsaw is, and as I remember it, he knew where you worked, yes?"

Lidka nodded, Kassia was right. It was what Feliks said, too. If he had wanted to see her, he would have found her. How hard would it be, for a German soldier? Down the street someone threw water from a high window and it slapped against the cold cobbles.

"Maybe it's too late for him, now," Lidka said. "Maybe Jósef will be Freddy's father."

"Well, you *sound* like you mean that."

"Perhaps I do mean it. Besides, isn't it for the best? It's hardly a good time for a Polish baby to have a German father, is it?"

"Oh, really? Some would say it's an excellent time."

"You've changed your tune. I thought you hated the Germans?"

Kassia shrugged. "Most of them, yes," she said.

"Most of them?"

"And if Freddy grows to look like your German?" Kassia said, ignoring the question.

Lidka had no answer to that, she had thought the same. "He has my eyes, and hair, it's a good start," she said.

Kassia laughed a high laugh. "Well, I suppose that's all for the future, anyway. And who knows what that will bring; we must make the best of things while we can, yes?" she said.

Lidka nodded. "Say, let's go to the flat now, it would be good to see the old place, and to get Freddy out of the cold."

"Sorry, not now Lidka. As I said, I need to get somewhere, it's … Well, it's …" she shrugged. Looked at Freddy again.

"Yes, sorry, you said, you have an appointment; but tell me Kassia; where are you moving to?"

Kassia hesitated, then said: "Nowy Świat."

"Nice," Lidka said. "Have you an address, a phone number?"

"I can't recall the numbers, never been one for numbers, unless they're on bank notes," Kassia said, laughing and kissing Lidka very lightly on the cheek, but not lightly enough that Lidka did not feel the slight tack of her heavy lipstick. "I will send them to you, I promise. But I really do have to go now, dear Lidka." With that she walked back in the direction they had come from, turning her head to shout: "We must get together soon – by the way, you've lost weight, you know?" Her words were punctuated by the sharp clack of her heels on the cold cobbles. She walked fast, Lidka thought; too fast for those heels.

***

Chillar. March 1951

Carlo appeared at the kitchen door. That was no surprise as Ingo had heard his truck's rattling approach. He held out a bottle of whisky.

"I hear you met my wife?"

For a moment Ingo was confused, but as the only women he'd talked to recently had been Maria last night and the moody beauty in the garage this morning it did not take him long to figure it out.

"Don't look surprised," Carlo said. "I'm considered quite a catch in these parts, my friend," he added, with a grin, placing the bottle of Glenlivet single malt on the table. "It's better than that piss you have – but don't worry, we'll finish that off, too."

"And you'll be able to drive back after that?"

"I'm assuming you have a couch, or a floor? I'm certain you have a floor. And for tonight, that's all I have to go back to anyway."

"Why? Not something I said, I hope."

"No, it is because I have now admitted to her that *we* are doing the Mil Millas."

"I think you'd best open the bottle, Carlo."

An hour or two later the sun had gone down, as had the level in the bottle, and Carlo had unrolled the plans; those plans Ingo had first seen a year ago now, and many times since. Carlo had not mentioned the Mil Millas again. The room was lit by the single electric bulb, which threw their images on to the curtain-less window in reflections that looked as wobbly as Ingo felt. Carlo had smoked two cheroots and the aroma of the smoke mixed well with the slightly fruity smell of the whisky. He had offered one to Ingo, but he no longer smoked, had only ever done so because he'd been bored.

"The Di Rossi Condor," Carlo read aloud the heading at the top of the large drawing, which almost covered the table and was weighted at each corner with Ingo's two trophies for the third places he'd picked up in local races driving Sophia – the two wet races of the seven he'd contested before Carlo sold the Chevy to buy the Ford – the large key to the back door, and the hubcap ashtray that was only used by Carlo and sometimes Maria, now. They both studied the plan like pirates staring at a treasure map of an island. An island that was the other side of the world. Such dreams only worked with whisky. Lots of whisky.

It was a sports car. One of Carlo's dreams was to build the Argentinian Ferrari. The other was for it to compete in the Mille Miglia, in Italy. Carlo had told him the car would be painted blue with a yellow bonnet, the racing colours of the Argentine, but here it was just fine lines in pencil. Yet even so it was beautiful, like a sketch by Raphael, those clouds of shade in which you can dream of the glory to come. The side elevation showed a low-slung two-seater with a scalloped middle, so that the front looked as if it was bursting with power, the rear like the muscles of an African cat; big and rounded haunches, but feminine. The wire wheels were picked out in watchmaker detail – Carlo had spent long evenings over the drawing, and this was by no means the first draft. From the top elevation the proportions seemed different, far more of the car given over to the engine space in front of the narrow-looking slot for driver and passenger. The tail was short, yet rounded from this viewpoint, too. From the front elevation it looked meaner, a snarl of a grille hooded by the overhang of the long bonnet, on the tip of which sat the badge of a flaming sun.

"It's wonderful," Ingo said.

"But it does not live."

"What will it take for it to live?"

"What it takes for all of us to live. Money."

"The way of the world."

"Well, not for some, my friend." Carlo looked up from the drawings, but Ingo did not meet his eyes, he was not about to let Carlo in on any other secrets. Good friend he might be, but friends could be temporary in a life like Ingo's. He had told him his real first name, but that was already too much, and now he regretted that every time Carlo used it. There was a moment of quiet before Carlo turned back to studying the plans, with a soft sigh.

"There's a man named Esteban Varela," Carlo said, brisk and business-like now. "He is a big man in these parts. Though not quite as big as he thinks he is. Still, he has money – from potatoes."

"It's an honest living."

"But not an *honourable* living, not for someone like Varela. He wants to be a bigger man, and is willing to pay for it. He tried to race, but was too slow, too old – frankly he was too scared, but we won't hold that against a man, will we?" Carlo said, with a little laugh.

"So, he stopped racing?"

"Yes, but Senor Varela is not *done* with racing. He wants his name to mean more than fried potatoes."

"And it would mean more if it was the name of the Argentine Ferrari?"

"As always, you are ahead of me, my friend."

"So will he put up the money, for the prototype?" Ingo asked. He knew the plan by now, a racing prototype would prove the car, then others would follow, until the marque was respected enough for road car versions to sell to the rich and maybe the famous. Just like Enzo Ferrari was doing in Italy.

"He's considering it. But ours is not the only avenue open to him. There are Argentinian drivers doing well, like Fangio – a friend of mine, you know?"

"So you've told me," Ingo said, not bothering to add 'many times'.

"Have I? Oh, well, anyway, drivers like Fangio are impressing in Europe, and that goes down well in Argentina. And now Varela thinks he has found a younger Fangio – and believe me, Juan has been around the block a few times, and ours is a young man's sport, so how many years has he left at the top?" Carlo said. "Varela feels that if he was to sponsor the boy, get him to Europe, he would be doing a service to Argentina – the sort of thing that gets you invited to cocktails with the Perons." Carlo finished his whisky and poured another one, then poured some into Ingo's tumbler, the bottle's neck clinking against the glass.

"So, he has a dilemma."

"Well, not really, my friend. It's much cheaper to sponsor a driver, even in Europe, than finance a car build. Besides, if the kid does well he might even make a profit out of his cut of the prize money and earnings, and in the end Varela's a businessman – and spuds are spuds."

"There's more spuds in selling cars."

"But it's a risk."

"So, he's not interested?"

"Oh, he's interested alright. But he's not convinced we can do it."

Ingo noticed the *we*, but said nothing, for now. "Well, it's big step, you've said so yourself," he said.

"A big step, but just a step, all the same."

"But costly. And you've spent all your money on the new Ford."

"No, invested. I've invested," Carlo said. "You see, this boy Varela sponsors, Hector Otero, is entered in the Mil Millas, in a good car. If a car I've prepared could beat him with an unknown driver ..."

"You're hardly unknown."

"I'm no longer a driver," Carlo said. Then he placed the tumbler on to the plan, the whisky he'd already downed causing him to misjudge the movement so it was sharper and harder than he had probably intended and Ingo saw a small dolphin splash of scotch jump out and end its life in a tiny dark cloud on the white sky in which the dream was drawn. "Besides, my friend, you are a much better driver than I am," Carlo added, with obvious regret, each word wrapped in a sigh. "Much better than I ever was, too."

Ingo knew what that had taken. Carlo was a proud man, particularly when it came to racing, when it came to what he was, who he was. "You can't drive anyway, Catalina won't let you!" He said it with a laugh.

Carlo smiled, and said: "I think you mean I have given my word, and that's true. But there was no word about co-driving; and a foreigner like you will need someone to show you where to go."

"What will she say?"

"She will say plenty, and I shall sleep here, and then in the garage, then on the couch, and then in my bed when she decides she needs money for clothes. The practical engineer in me realises that there's nothing so different in my relationship with Catalina to your arrangement with Maria. But she will come round, she has to. She loves our children, and she loves me. Do you know what that means, Ingo?"

"But this is a big race," Ingo said, dodging the question. "There will be reporters, cameras. You have forgotten Carlo, I'm very *shy*."

"Argentinian reporters, Argentinian photographers! That's all. And their pictures are shit!" Carlo said. "Anyway, only a German could worry about such things – do you really think you will do that well? As you said, a big race – Fangio raced in it last year! To get in the papers you will need to win it, and that's impossible."

"I suppose so," Ingo said.

"Besides, all we need do is show Varela what *is* possible. Beat that arrogant brat Otero in a Rossi prepared car. Because I'm sure Varela wants his name on a car like this," he nodded at the plan of the Condor again. "There's much more glory in that than potatoes, or in living life through a younger man's success."

"That's true," Ingo said.

"Also, he has seen this," Carlo added quite matter-of-factly. "So he is in love with it already."

"You think?"

"I saw it in his eyes; I see it in your eyes now, my friend."

"It's a fine looking machine," Ingo said, almost a whisper.

"So, you will drive the Mil Millas for me, for this?" He slapped the drawing, quite hard, so that the surface of the Glenlivet in Ingo's tumbler quivered.

Ingo said nothing, just picked up the glass and took a large gulp of whisky, finishing it, and then tipping the bottle to find it empty. He placed it back on the table, then stood up, stumbled a little as the kitchen tilted a bit, then went to the cupboard to get his bottle of Canadian Club.

"Picture it in blue, with a yellow bonnet, and a large number – I mean a big number – on the side," Carlo said, spreading his hands out above the picture to emphasise the space.

Ingo did not quite know what he meant, *big* not large, but that might have been the whisky talking, he supposed, or more likely the whisky listening.

* * *

Warsaw. May 1941

When the sun shone through the glass panels of the upper parts of the two brick-built Mirowska Hall indoor market buildings, as it did in this one now, it could make them seem magical places to be; suffused with shafts of yellow-white light chequered with the outlines of the frames of the glass panels, and striped with bolder slashes of shadow as hard-edged as the cast iron structure they were a projection of. Lidka was taking her time, easing rather than pushing the baby carriage along. Freddy was enjoying the market, laughing at the noise, while his pink fingers tinkled at the dappled light that splashed across his pram. Vendors competed for trade, their shouts echoing and overlapping in the high space, yet there was not really very much on sale. There was still the smell of vegetables and fish, as there had been before the war, but there was no scent of flowers now. She wondered if people even grew flowers these days, never mind bought them, as most garden space was used for planting things you could eat.

The stalls were white-painted panel-glassed little cabins, shops in themselves, with long tables outside; now scattered with wares, rather than stacked, but even if they had been it would be a waste, as the Poles of Warsaw were severely rationed. Only German Poles had adequate rations, Polish Poles had to make do with a fraction of what the Germans were allowed to buy. The Jews in the Ghetto a lot less, she had heard. A lot less. The rows of stalls were separated by wide streets and inter-connected with tight avenues. She had bought some fish, a small piece of bream from the Vistula, and torn the perforated square from her ration card and given it to the vendor.

Mrs Babczyńska came around the corner and stopped to let the baby carriage by. Lidka recognised her, but feigned a sudden interest in a small pile of cabbages outside a stall across the way. She knew Mrs Babczyńska from when she had lived in the Old Town. She didn't know her well, really, but then that would never stop a woman like Mrs Babczyńska.

"Why Lidka; and a baby!" Mrs Babczyńska said, poking her long face into the pram, but not without a sly glance at Lidka's right hand, the ring hand in Poland, and the silver wedding band she now wore, given to her by Sol Vogler.

"Oh, hello Mrs Babczyńska."

"He's a cheerful little chap, what's his name?"

"Fryderyk."

"They will call him Freddy."

"They already do," Lidka said.

"His father? Do I know him?"

"I don't know," Lidka started. "I mean, I don't know if you know him. He's abroad; the war." That, at least, she felt sure was not a lie.

"My nephew's abroad, too, my brother Clem's boy. The air force."

"Józef's air force, too," Lidka said.

"Józef ...?"

"Sczcepanski."

Mrs Babczyńska shook her head, rather absent-mindedly. Lidka could see she was concentrating much more on doing the mathematics in her head.

"He's just over a year and two months old," Lidka said, adding six months to his age.

"He looks younger," Mrs Babczyńska said, slightly closing one eye and cocking her head a little.

"The war, I suppose; so little food. It makes the babies look younger, the adults older," Lidka said with a little laugh.

"Perhaps, but what a happy smile he has!"

"Thank you, but I must be getting on," Lidka said, and she started to push the pram towards the large double doors and the iron gates beyond them that led out to Plac Mirowski. But Mrs Babczyńska was not greedy when it came to taking hints and she walked alongside Lidka, the wheel of the baby carriage squeaking in time to the clicks of their heels on the stony floor. As she walked Lidka realised this was the first time she had actually told anyone, other than the registrar and the others in the house, that Józef was Freddy's father. She thought she had taken a big step.

Once they were out in the sunshine Freddy shrieked and sat up, to watch a car drive by. It was a German staff car, most of the cars were German these days – there was little petrol for anyone else. The Germans had even commandeered Feliks' Mazur; he hadn't minded, had no fuel for it, and was just relieved that they had not come for those he hid in his house, or for him. Lidka wished Freddy was not so fascinated by cars, because it did not do to draw attention to yourself, but then he was his father's son. The SS officer in the rear seat of the shining black Mercedes ignored them.

"Well, it was nice to see you again, Lidka," Mrs Babczyńska said, quickly; like many she did not like to share the street with the SS, and with that she was gone. Freddy watched the car skip across the tram tracks and drive out of view, and then his interest switched to something else: a motorcycle and sidecar.

Her heart stopped.

The field grey combination sped past, the steely fluttering of its engine only broken for a moment when the rider changed gear. But that rider was not Ingo. And she felt, she was surprised to realise, a slight relief at that. They both watched it until it was out of sight. And then, when it had turned the corner, she thought she had turned a corner, too. Life was about Freddy now, and Freddy needed a Polish father.

She took a deep breath, looked at the simple silver ring Sol Vogler had given her, and then smiled at Freddy. He smiled back. She thought he would enjoy a stroll in Saski Park and so she pushed the squeaking pram down towards Plac Zelaznej Bramy and the crumbling colonnade of the old Lubomirski Palace. The wall of the ghetto was to her left and to her right, as she was in a passage that passed between both parts of it. The walls were three metres high, made of brick and capped with pieces of glass embedded in concrete which was then topped with double strands of barbed wire. Someone, bravely or stupidly, had painted a dribbling black *PW* on the wall, beyond which the majority of Warsaw's Jews were now forced to live. Everyone knew the graffiti was shorthand for *We shall avenge Wawer*, the slogan she had seen Andrzej daub on the wall of the shoe shop in Ochota a little over a year ago. She had seen little of Andrzej recently. He was rarely at the house now; busy with his *work*, he had told Feliks, and also busy avoiding being conscripted as forced labour for the Germans. He had found another teacher, he had also said. She wondered what it was he was now being taught, felt sure it was not languages, Polish history and a little mathematics.

The people of Warsaw, some of them, were beginning to fight back, mostly in small ways like the graffiti. But she would not get involved in that, not now there was Freddy to look after. She hated the Germans, though she could not yet bring herself to hate Ingo, even if he had run out on her; the truth she was beginning to accept. Maybe one day she would hate him for that, but she could not now.

Freddy was a strong boy, and he rarely cried, but she knew he was hungry. She had to feed him with what there was, mashed old carrots that morning. The fish she had bought would be a treat for later, but it would have to be shared with the others in the house; it had been bought with money Sol Vogler had provided. She worried when Freddy was hungry, and hardly noticed her own hunger these days. But she knew for others it was far worse, and again her eyes drifted across the square to the wall of the Ghetto, perhaps because the sunlight glinted off the broken glass embedded in the cement on the top of it.

A number 21 tram passed, rumbling and clanging, arousing Freddy's interest. As it trundled by it revealed a familiar figure in a neat blue dress, hurrying. She recognised the dress first. Then Sarah. This puzzled her, and she thought she must be mistaken. It was possible, as the girl was quite far away and getting further away, quickly. And Sarah was not stupid. She would surely never leave the safety of the house in Ochota?

*

"That's definitely Warsaw!" Ingo said. He could now see the eighteen-storey art deco Prudential building as the train rounded a curve; the second tallest skyscraper in Europe was as stark as a tombstone in the clear blue sky.

"Looks like your long wait for tumble number two will soon be over," Pop said, by the look on his face enjoying the thought of it as much as Ingo.

They were in a compartment in a railway carriage, not the usual stark and utilitarian troop train, but a smart and quite new civilian one. They were in their uniforms, their kit stowed in the racks above them, while the vehicles had been loaded on to another train. This train was packed with German soldiers, but you wouldn't know it from the outside, as the lower part of each window was covered in a lace curtain, of the sort you would usually find in first class only, and Ingo had to lift up a corner of cloth to look out of the window. Their compartment, which had a door on either side of the train and no connecting corridor, was comfortable, and Ingo thought it had to be a mistake that they had been assigned to it, though Pop believed it was because the generals did not want it known that so many German soldiers were on the move – they had seen other civilian trains packed with field grey this day.

Either way, Ingo wasn't complaining. He had rejoined the regiment, by then in Bordeaux, after his recovery was complete. His legs had mended nicely, he could even run now. The only leave was local, and he had had little of it, as Kroh made sure he was kept busy. Pop had been right, Kroh had not been impressed with the Iron Cross 2nd Class they both now had pinned to their chests. They had moved from France to the Warthe training grounds, and since they had been there, about three-hundred-and-fifty kilometres west of Warsaw, there had been no leave at all, only manoeuvres. It had been good to get back on a bike again, though. He had fallen asleep three times since they had boarded the train in Breslau that morning, lulled by the soft embrace of the upholstered seats and the soothing rhythm of the wheels on the expansion joints.

It smelt clean in the carriage, of wood polish and the cloth of their recently issued new uniforms. The uniform smell aside, it was a smell from before the war. Some of the men smoked, but most slept. Many had learned in France and on their previous visit to Poland to sleep when they could. Kroh whistled, in his almost a whistle way, the *Panzerlied*. It sounded like steam escaping from the dark engine three carriages ahead of them. Silver smoke from its funnel swept past the window, and through its cloud Ingo caught sight of another train, waiting in a siding, a soldier like him, peering through a triangle gap of lifted lace curtain.

"Don't see why they would need so many of us in Warsaw?" Kroh said, looking up from his camera, which he had been fiddling with. "The Polacks are well licked, right?" He sat opposite Ingo, and he could smell the raw onion on Kroh's breath.

"We're on the way to Russia, that's what I hear," Leutnant Schirmer said.

Kroh laughed out loud at that, laughed at the officer. It was a mocking laugh and it was clearly a challenge, and the youngster – even to Ingo he seemed young – just turned away, lifted the curtain on the other side of the compartment, and looked out of the window, where the houses and factories at the outer edge of Wola were beginning to clatter by. Schirmer had not taken the opportunity to assert his authority. Again. This was his sergeant's platoon, not his. And Ingo felt that the lieutenant would not be the only one to pay for that. Ingo felt for him, the kid had done no one any harm, had just made the mistake of being posted to Kroh's platoon.

"We're not even at war with Russia," Kroh said, shaking his head.

"So, we'll be staying in Warsaw?" Ingo said.

"I doubt that, Warsaw's a place to travel through, not to stay, right?" Kroh said.

"What's the big deal with Warsaw anyhow, Pup?" Eckhart, a tall locksmith from Augsburg who had joined them before France, said, as he came awake, yawning and stretching to the clatter of couplings, and the rattle and shunt of a now slowing train.

"Pup wants to get his end away," Pop said.

"I thought you were the chaste type?"

"Faithful, I think you'll find it's called," Ingo said.

"Faithful to a Polish slut, right?" Kroh said.

"Volksdeutsche slut," Pop said, lying for Ingo as he always did. "A Volksdeutsche slut who doesn't even keep in touch, too."

"Oh, the girl in the picture, is it?" Eckhart said, referring to the photograph Ingo had taken of Lidka on Grójecka, which he usually pinned close to his bed in the barracks, and which was now tucked close to his heart in the pocket of his tunic. Ingo nodded, while Kroh shook his head.

The train slowed, almost to a stop, then rumbled through a station; Zachodni. A little later it came to a halt in a large shunting yard, in a steely sigh of rattling couplings. Ingo realised Ochota was now just the far side of the main track and a fan of steel rails, which shone in silver seams on the blackened ground of the yard they were now parked in. He was perhaps twenty minutes from where Lidka taught her illegal lessons, if she still did so, he guessed. He thought he could find his way to that house on the crescent, thought he remembered just where it was. Kroh was right, there was no good reason why they would stay in Warsaw now, but knowing the army as he did Ingo felt sure they would be held in this shunting yard long enough. It was the way of the Heer, to keep men waiting, always waiting.

He stood up and opened the window, smelling the acrid issue of the nearby factories, a hot moth of ash from the black locomotive landed on his cheek and he brushed it away. The engine was being de-coupled, he thought. That made his decision for him; it was now obvious they would be here for ages. And Ingo was not the type to think long and hard on things. He reached out and twisted the door handle, the heavy, smoothly-lacquered door falling open.

"Where the fuck do you think you're going, Pup?" Kroh said.

"Stretch my legs, Feldwebel."

"You'll stay put; you can forget your Polack plum."

"I thought you said I needed a haircut? Know a great barber in Ochota."

"We've orders not to leave the train, right?"

"They always say that. Look, we're parked up without an engine, you know what that means – we'll be here for hours, isn't that right Pop?"

"Leave it Pup," Pop said, and Ingo caught the edge of warning. But ignored it.

"I'll be gone an hour; no more – you'll still be here, we'll still be here tonight I should think," he said, risking a smile. He took one step down. From further along the train there was a German shout answered by a German curse, but otherwise it was strangely quiet in the shunting yard. Which is why he heard it so clearly …

The working of the slide of Kroh's Walther as he put a bullet up the spout was like a clash of rapiers behind him.

"Stop!"

Ingo took another step, so he was now just a single step from the ashy ground, Lidka in his mind's eye, seemingly just that single step away. But a sensible part of him knew it was a step he could not take. He somehow felt the hot play of the pistol on the upper part of his back.

"I said stop."

Ingo turned to see the muzzle of the gun, now aimed downwards at him as he was almost off the steps of the carriage and half of him was below the level of its floor. Kroh's treacherous smile seemed to be precariously balanced on the notch of the foresight like a malignant seesaw. His face had reddened, a sure sign he was angry.

"I'll be half an hour, that's all." Ingo said.

"Get back in, Pup. Or I'll shoot, right?"

Ingo believed he would.

"Disobeying orders; right?"

Ingo looked at Leutnant Schirmer. "You heard the feldwebel," the young officer murmured.

Ingo climbed back into the compartment and closed the heavy door with a meaty *thunk*, then sat back down, alongside Pop. Kroh took the seat opposite him again, holstering his P38. They sat in silence for twenty minutes, Kroh stared at Ingo, Ingo smiled back. Then there was a lurch and the train began to move again, the steel wheels of the engine squealing as they spun against the rails. It was going in the opposite direction now, an engine having obviously been hitched to the other end of the train.

"Good job you didn't get off then, eh Pup?" Pop said, with a smile. But Ingo could see the worry, and relief, in his eyes. He nodded, lifted the curtain and looked out. The train was going around the long loop of railway at the edge of the city, passing the loading bays and shunting yards of Wola's factories, then Warsaw's huge cemeteries, where grey figures, as still as gravestones themselves, knelt amidst the slabs. He kept looking, for a chance sight of her, but he knew it was hopeless. They trundled through the main Danzig Station and Ingo was looking out at the depressing red-brick bulk of the Żoliborz Citadel, now flying a swastika flag, when his world turned pink.

It took him a moment to realise he had been hit in the back of the head, the living daylights bounced through his skull as his forehead struck the window with a crack that sounded like broken glass or broken bone. He was still figuring out which when the second punch landed. The side of his face this time, as he was turning in to it, his mouth filling with blood, metallic and warm like setting lead in a toy soldier mould. The next punch hit his nose and he felt the hot blood as it burst from it. He then heard Kroh's words, dimmed and fuddled by the punches, as if they were spoken underwater.

"You don't ever disobey me again, Pup. Right?"

*

"There's not enough to go around as it is!" It was unusual to hear a voice raised in the Paczkowski household, and it stopped Lidka dead.

"Quiet, she might hear you," Feliks hissed. They were in the parlour; Lidka had not realised before just how much you could hear of what was said within from outside the big double doors. There was sunlight seeping through the foot of the doors, the light blocked halfway across one of them by the swimming shadow of a person.

Jadwiga Paczkowska continued, her voice no lower. "I don't care if she hears me – she is stealing food!"

Lidka felt her breath freeze within her.

"How can you think such a thing?"

"Not *think*; know! Don't you think we have little enough, what with feeding your Jews?"

"They are not *my* Jews, Jadwiga. They are people; you sometimes seem to forget that – you speak of them as if they are animals!"

"I speak of them as if they are a danger to us all, which they are! It has gone on too long, Feliks, we can't afford it." There was pleading in her voice now.

"Sol pays their way."

"What use is his money and jewels, when we have ration cards? We are too many for what we get, and even with the black-market food and the vegetables from the garden it's not enough. Besides, I bet he has much more than he says – everyone knows what *they* are like."

"We need his help, you know this; there is no call for art now, without Sol there would be nothing. Besides, we cannot, I will not, betray them."

"But what about *her*, isn't it enough that we have taken her in? Now she is stealing our food!"

"You're sure of this?"

"I am sure, yes."

"Very well," Feliks said.

Lidka heard the tap of shoe soles on the parquetry the other side of the door, she turned and hurried up the stairs and out of sight.

Her box room was at the top of the house. Lidka and Freddy lived in this small cell of a place that had once been used by Magda, the maid. She had been on her way up here to fetch a toy for Freddy, a wheeled wooden train that long ago had belonged to Andrzej, and then she had heard the voices from the parlour. She felt guilty for listening in, but more than this she felt angry. *They think I am stealing food.*

Sarah was looking after Freddy; Lidka had still not had the chance to be alone with her, to speak to her about seeing her in Plac Zelaznej Bramy the day before, and she could not talk of it with the others around. Sarah was taking a stupid risk leaving the house, and she had to be stopped, before there was trouble for all of them. Sarah and Freddy were in the kitchen with Sarah's younger brother, Leon. They spent most of their time there now. Since the forming of the Ghetto Sol Vogler and Feliks – neither of them the most practical of men – had somehow managed to block off a portion of the basement, with just enough room for the family to hide. There was a tiny hatch entrance to it behind the bookshelves in Feliks' study and library. It was for emergencies, but Sol Vogler and his wife, also called Sarah, seemed to be spending more and more time down there now.

There was a soft knock at the door, the knock of someone who does not mind so much if there is no answer. Lidka waited for a moment or two, she still felt angry and did not want to talk about it yet. *Stealing food …*

"Lidka, it's me, Feliks."

"Yes?" she caught the small catch in her voice as she answered.

He opened the door a little. "I need to talk to you."

She nodded at the high-backed winged armchair that managed to be in the corner and almost the centre of the tiny room at the same time, and he folded himself in to it, his green cardigan almost the same shade of the faded upholstery of the chair, his bright red tie in vivid contrast to it. He took off his spectacles, started to clean them with the end of the tie.

She did not want him to say it – *stealing food* – and so she spoke first, and fast. "You're right, about Józef," she said. "It will be easier, if I say we were married before he left; I have already told people this, now. And there's the ring."

She glanced at the silver ring Sol Vogler had given her. Feliks nodded, though seemed a little startled, as he knew all this. She started speaking again before he could say anything. "I will use his name, Sczcepanska." This was the feminine form of Sczcepanski, as tradition dictated.

"Yes, we have discussed this. But —"

"His parents and sister are in the east, moved to stay with family in '39 – who knew then the Russians were coming, too? It will make it easier to explain, when I meet people from before all this. I can say we married in a hurry, at the start of the war, before he went away to his unit, many did just that."

"It's for the best, yes, I've told you —"

"I don't even know if he's still alive, of course, and ..." Lidka started, and then she heard an aeroplane, quite high above. She still remembered the Stukas from September '39 and the sound of the plane stopped her talking, her gaze drifting to the square of bright blue sky visible through the dormer window. This gave Feliks the chance to say what he had come to say.

*

RAF Swinderby. May 1941

It was as if a comet had been fixed to the port engine of the Wellington bomber. The flames burnt a bright hole in the inky night sky and it was impossible not to watch, even if that was the last thing Jósef Sczcepanski wanted to do, as the stricken aeroplane, its other engine fluttering and stuttering, dipped and twisted in lurching spasms.

Jósef stood with a number of other members of the squadron, some of them aircrew with tired eyes who had landed safely a little earlier. One said: "It's Wysocki."

The Wellington was close to the ground, wheels still up, when the starboard wing suddenly dipped, like a dark slate dropping from a dark roof, and then the plane simply slid out of the sky. The wing crunched in on itself as it hit the ground, but there was enough of it remaining to pivot and tip the plane into a series of somersaults, spinning the fire on its port engine into a swirling Catherine wheel, before the aircraft landed on its back, with what seemed like a loud sigh, followed almost instantly by the crump and whoosh of an explosion. Both the heat and the shockwave washed over those who looked on.

The engine on the Fordson crash tender revved and he heard the crunch as first gear was selected. Without thinking – because if he had thought he would never have done it – Jósef followed the lead of the others standing close to him and leapt on to the running board. The fire truck raced across the dark grass, a Morris ambulance chasing it, the water in the tank fixed to the Fordson's bed sloshing and banging, the vibrations through the chassis singing through the soles of Jósef's shoes. They were in a great hurry, but they all must have known there was no hope.

And yet ...

... Jósef somehow knew it was the plane's pilot, Wysocki, and not some other member of the six-man crew. There was something defiant about the man on fire. But there was no other way he would have been able to tell that this was the officer who had led him out of Poland. The two trucks had pulled up within 50 metres of the burning Wellington and Jósef jumped from the running board. The heat from the inferno whipped his face, and he held his arm out in front of him, to shield him from the worst of it. The air was saturated with the smell of burning fuel and rubber, and the fumes caught at Jósef's throat. There was another smell, too; burning flesh, a smell he knew from when he had helped to clean out this very bomber just weeks ago. It was a smell that lingered in a man, like regret and shame.

The yellow cones from the headlamps of the ambulance, and the bright white sweep of the Fordson's spot-lamp, picked out the detail as Wysocki staggered forward. It seemed to Jósef that he was coming for him, reaching out for him alone, and he wanted to run, wanted to get away, but he could not move. Wysocki was a torch of a man by now, nothing more, yet still he stumbled on towards Jósef, skin peeling off his face like melting candle wax. He was still fifteen metres away when he crumpled to the ground. One man played a hose on him for what seemed like long minutes, until steam hissed off the corpse. But it was a waste of water.

*

Warsaw. May 1941

The kitchen smelt of the cabbage and potatoes which were being boiled up into a thin soup in a large pot. The curtains were closed, as they often were these days – it was known that some Poles had betrayed Jews to the Germans, and while the garden wall was high, someone in an upper-storey apartment might possibly be able to see into the kitchen. They might not know they were watching a Jew, but they might, too. Feliks took no chances, which made the risk Sarah was taking so much more unforgivable, Lidka thought.

The kitchen was large and L-shaped, the walls were white and the cupboards were painted lime green. The floor was linoleum, in a green and white checked pattern. There was a white stove and a large stoneware sink, with a rack of white plates drying on a wooden draining board beside it. There was also an old glass-fronted wooden dresser stacked with good china, but not the best china, which was with Mrs Paczkowska's other treasures, in the dining room; her current guests never ate there. Because the curtains were closed the harsh electric lights were on. In the reflection thrown on to the old sagging glass of the dresser Lidka watched Sarah. She noticed again how skinny the girl was, and pale, too – she had pointed this out to Feliks, and he had agreed. But that had changed nothing. Sarah's brother Leon had just left the kitchen, bored as only a young lad not allowed out on a sunny day can be, and this was the first time Lidka had been alone with Sarah for two days. Freddy slept on Lidka's lap and she still hummed Chopin's *Berceuse*, which had lulled him to sleep, as Lidka watched …

… Watched as Sarah took two potatoes from the pantry and placed them in a small sackcloth bag that hung on the back of one of the chairs in the kitchen; and then as she did the same with a tin of something or other, Lidka could not quite see what it was in the distorted reflection. She doubted Sarah would suspect she watched her, because Lidka always looked in to Freddy's eyes when she hummed this particular lullaby. Sarah then sat at the table and started to study the book that was opened in front of her. It was as Mrs Paczkowska had said, as Feliks had told Lidka – he had not been wholly convinced that Sarah would do such a thing, knew his wife's opinion of their guests, and so had asked Lidka to find out for sure.

"I saw you, Sarah." Lidka said.

The girl looked up, shock prising her eyes wide. "You did?"

"Tuesday, on Plac Zelaznej Bramy."

"Sorry, Miss Wadalowska, you must be mistaken, I never leave the house."

"You should call me Mrs Sczcepanska." They all knew the truth, of course. Well, part of the truth, the house was not so big that many secrets could be kept. But only Feliks knew that Freddy's real father was a German soldier.

"Yes, Mrs Sczcepanska," Sarah said. "Mr Sczcepanski; was he the piano player?"

"No, that was not Jósef," Lidka said.

"And that makes you sad?"

Lidka shook her head, quickly: "He's a good man. He will be a good father."

"Where is he?"

Lidka shrugged, then realised how skilfully the girl had changed the subject. "What were you doing there?"

"Where?"

"Tuesday."

"I have not left the house, it's too risky, you know that," Sarah said. "You must be mistaken."

"And am I also mistaken about what you have in that bag?"

Sarah took a deep breath, then exhaled very slowly, so that she seemed to deflate, her shoulders sagging. Then she started to cry. Lidka wanted to hug her, comfort her, but she was holding Freddy. This reminded her of her priorities. The girl cried in grating sobs, and Lidka could see her clavicles move like sticks beneath her thin blouse. She was even thinner than Lidka had realised. She knew then for sure that she could not possibly be stealing food for herself.

Freddy slept through the crying, and Lidka waited for Sarah to finish, for she sensed these tears had been bottled up within her for some time.

"Tell me everything," Lidka said, when Sarah had finally stopped crying.

"I had to see it," Sarah said, between sniffs.

"What?"

"The Ghetto."

"Why?"

"They are my people, perhaps I should be there? I don't know. But I needed to see, and so I crept out of the house, it wasn't difficult."

"How; without someone seeing you?"

"It was easy; Andrzej showed me how, ages ago."

"He's involved in this?"

"No, he's involved in other things, I think."

"Other things?"

"I went to the wall, by the Chłodna gate, where they let them pass from the Large Ghetto to the Small Ghetto, and in the other direction," Sarah said, ignoring the question.

"I know it," Lidka said, she knew that the Germans opened the gates, so that Jews could move between the two parts of the Ghetto for a short time.

"There was a boy, the same age as Leon," Sarah said. "He was more like a skeleton. I could not just stand and watch."

"What did you do?"

"There was nothing I could do then, but I went the next day, the same time. I could not risk the evening, it would be noticed that I was not here. I took some bread and some cheese I had not eaten, and some potatoes, but not much. You have to understand, they are given a ration of under two hundred calories a day to live on. It is a starvation diet. It is murder."

Lidka did a quick sum; that was about 10 per cent of what German Poles were given, twenty-five per cent of her own ration as a Pole. She could not help but imagine Freddy in the situation of that boy, when he was older, and it filled her with a nauseating horror.

"Are you okay, Miss Wadalowska?"

"Sczcepanska, *Mrs* Sczcepanska," she said. "The boy?"

Sarah shook her head. "I did not see him. I went to the wall when the Ghetto police and the Germans were all watching the people going through the gates and crossing the road. No one paid any attention to me, and so I shouted."

"Shouted what?"

"For someone, anyone. And they answered. I said nothing else, I had wrapped the food in a bundle, in some newspaper, and I threw it over the wall. Then I walked away."

The kitchen went quiet then. Freddy snored softly on Lidka's lap, and she heard someone laugh, somewhere else in the house, Leon she supposed. It broke the spell of silence.

"I went again, the same time, the next day, then the next day, then the next ..."

"Every day?"

"Not every day. I could not get away every day. I haven't been for three days, now."

"Your father?"

"He doesn't know, he mustn't know!"

"I have to tell him," Lidka said. "You are taking a terrible risk, Sarah. You don't even have a kennkarte, what if they stop you? If you're caught they will kill you: no trial, no chance. If they know you are Jewish, they will —"

"I know what they will do, and I am not afraid!"

"Quiet, you will wake him," Lidka hissed, as Freddy stirred on her lap.

Sarah leant over the table, her face closer to Lidka's. "I have to do something," she said, in a sharp whisper. Her tears had dried but her eyes were still red, and there was anger there, too.

"It is finished, you're risking everything – can't you see that?"

"What is *everything*, when they have *nothing!*" Her voice was raised again. "They are relying on me, and I have not been there for days now."

"You cannot go now, Mrs Paczkowska knows you are stealing food."

"She does? Will she tell father?"

Lidka nodded.

"It's why you have not been left alone, Sarah."

Sarah sighed and sat back in her chair, crossing her arms tightly and sitting silent for a moment, looking in to Lidka's eyes for long seconds, so that Lidka finally had to look away. Outside Lidka could hear children playing in the courtyard, laughs floating free and bursting into shrieks. Sarah had been playing, not so very long ago. But now she was playing a more dangerous game.

"Just this last time, so I can tell them I will not return? They deserve to know that, at least."

"No, you must not go; it's too dangerous – for all of us."

"But I promised I would return. They will be waiting, and they will wait every day, for something that will not now come. Don't you think they are tortured enough, Miss Wadalowska?"

Lidka did not correct her this time. She thought of those waiting, of a promise made. Freddy was awake now, blinking his big eyes. She smiled at him and he smiled back. But Lidka was scared. If Sarah was caught she knew what would happen. The girl would be taken to the Gestapo headquarters on Szucha and tortured; and she would talk. Everyone talked, because everyone had their limit. Then they would all be in trouble, for being Jews, and for harbouring Jews. She could not imagine what would happen to Freddy if she was sent to prison, and she did not think she could bear to be parted from him. And so she lied.

"I will take the food, and I will take the message that there will be no more food."

"You? How?" Sarah said, with a wry laugh.

Lidka was taken aback by the tone. "I am no Jew, I have a kennkarte and I have a pram in which I can hide food, more food than you can possibly carry – though we cannot afford to take too much," she said.

"You will do it, really?"

Lidka nodded. She did not like to lie, and wanted to talk of it no longer, and so she was glad when Leon suddenly burst into the kitchen, asking when the soup would be ready before he was even fully through the door.

***

Lampeter, Wales. May 1951

They could not read his face, could not tell from his expression that he understood them, because he did not have enough face for expressions. They talked, in Welsh, never realising that he could speak the language, far better now having picked up more while working with Dai Twice and his son Huw at the garage. Because he never responded, and they rarely looked at him anyway – few people did, if they could help it – they thought he did not understand, they thought Joe the Pole could only speak Polish and English. And so they spoke as if he wasn't there.

He sat in the corner of the bar in the Black Lion Hotel. The walls were decorated with horse brasses and faded pictures of prize-winning cattle and ponies. The windows were opaque, yet while none of the early evening sunshine outside could find its way through, it lit up the panes like a high white cloud. Otherwise the place was dark and gloomy, and quiet. It smelt of Woodbine cigarettes, with a hint of cow dung or maybe sheep shit, probably from the boots of the three tweed-encased farmers who sat on the tall stools, crouched under flat caps, by the bar. One had a dog, a black and white border collie who lay with his chin on his paws far below the seat of the stool on which his master talked and drank bitter. The farmer reached down every now and then and the dog would get to his feet, with a lazy tail wag, to receive a comforting pat.

He had come straight from the garage when the bar opened, at seven, as he did every Monday, because that was not a popular night for others. He would drink three pints of Felinfoel and leave it at that.

"They say he was burnt when his Spitfire was shot down," one of the farmers said, in Welsh.

"Nah, a bomber, wasn't it?" a second farmer said.

That made the pain sing higher. It was always there, of course, but he had become used to it, to a small degree. Yet sometimes it was so bad he was in the fire again, at others it was the itching that was worse, an itching he could not scratch. Three pints of Felinfoel would not ease the pain or the itching, but there was always the whisky when he got back to the small room in his lodgings on Bridge Street.

"Thought they could fix them now; plastic surgery, isn't it?" said the second farmer.

"I'd heard that, too. Suppose there's only so much they can do," the first farmer said.

"Perhaps he thought it best to hide away; this is as good a place to hide as anywhere, see." The other two farmers nodded at this, from the third.

"I wonder why he doesn't go home; Poland isn't it?" the first added.

The coughing started, with little warning as always, and the dog's ears cupped in curiosity. He knew it was a strange sound, the wheezy edge to it, and he wished he could put out the fire with a bigger gulp of beer, but he also knew he had to let the fit run its course. Those at the bar ignored his coughs, or at least they did not turn around to look.

"Poor man," Gwen, the barmaid, said.

When she served him she sometimes looked in to his eyes, and he often wondered what she found there. She was dark, in that Welsh way that hinted at pirate pasts, and had eyes of treacle and a body that clung to the memory the way he would like to cling to its curves. He had not had a woman in many years, and he would not subject a prostitute – if one could be found in this pious town – to the sort of work that fed nightmares. He knew the damage that could do. He doubted he could now, anyway. Never again.

"Duw, but it's no way to live a life, is it?" the third farmer said.

The bar was quiet then, so he could hear the rattle of the bus outside, idling as it waited for passengers for Aberaeron and Aberystwyth. He knew the farmers were thinking of the shotguns they kept in their kitchens, and what they would do, if they were him. But he also knew he did not have the courage for that.

***

Warsaw. May 1941

Lidka knew exactly what to do. Where to find the place at the wall. Where to wait for the whistle that was the signal. But she would not do any of this. It was too great a risk. Yet still she took the small sack of food, and hid it in the baby carriage, wrapped up in the small blanket, close to Freddy's tiny feet. Sarah had watched her do this, and so she had gone along with it. Sarah had also trusted her. But she would not take the food to the Ghetto. She could not.

Yet she changed trams at Ulrychow, taking the number 16. Because of the baby carriage she stood in the open space at the back. Freddy loved the movement of the tram, the way it shivered, then jerked abruptly to the turns in the tracks, the squealing of the wheels in the steel channels, the scrape of the connector against the overhead wires; she could see it in his face. He always seemed so content when he was moving, so a tram ride was never a bad idea. On the other hand, she could never forget that the Germans had taken Warsaw's fine trams, which had been like railway carriages, replaced them with these old rattle-box things. She was not sure of it, but to her they almost smelt German, a chemical tang that was in the bones of them, perhaps the paint.

She rang the bell and the tram came to a clattering halt at a point just before Chłodna, pinched in between the high walls of the Large and the Small Ghettos. She did not know why she had come this far. Perhaps, she told herself, she wanted another look at the Ghetto, to try to understand why Sarah had taken such a risk. The day was not warm, not cold, not grey, nor blue; just a sort of nothing white. Like a canvas waiting for its first splash of colour. There were two German soldiers at the tram stop, they would get on the *Nur für Deutsche* section beyond the wooden barrier at the front. But one of them saw her, said something to his comrade, and they helped her with the pram. She did not thank them, because others were watching, and it did not do to be seen speaking to Germans. But they did not seem to mind, young men, laughing.

There were other Germans laughing, when she came close to the gates. She walked past, looking left to the Large Ghetto, the southern part where the poorer Jews lived, the pram juddering over the shiny old cobbles, the one wheel still squeaking. The gates were closed on either side of the street. But they were not high gates, and they were made of steel frames and wire, so she could see the people there clearly. The laughing Germans were teasing an old man, throwing his cap between them, the casual bullying of bored young men. He went along with the game, defeat in his eyes, and he floated between them like a sigh, making no real effort to catch his cap.

She walked past the double gates. One of the Jewish Ghetto policemen Sarah had told her about, a uniform of just a peaked cap and an armband, eyed her a little suspiciously. She thought of the girl again. Sarah had been brave, or rather foolish. It was a terrible risk she had taken. And it had not been her risk to take; and once again Lidka felt sick at the thought of what might have happened if she had been taken to Szucha, or Pawiak Prison. When Sarah had talked they would have come for them all. The Ghetto policeman unfastened his gaze, obviously judging that Lidka was harmless, and so she looked at those who waited to tread these *Aryan* cobbles, a tiny taste of their old freedom between the high walls of the two islands of the Ghetto.

Now she saw the children. Lidka had never seen hungry children before. Truly hungry children. Their eyes seemed swollen in sunken faces. Swollen with accusation. They did not stare at her, but they might as well have done. She looked at Freddy in the baby carriage. He *was* staring; staring back at her, the edge of the woollen cover that lay over his chest fluttering to the bounce of the hard rubber pram tyres on the iron-like cobbles.

She tried to smile, but he did not respond. He did not look upset, he looked confused, the way he was when he stared up at the blue landscape by Zak in the Paczkowski parlour when he was crawling along the parquet floor. She heard the twin gates creak and rattle open behind her, then the light wiry clash as they came up against their stops. Then the movement of people, a scraping of footwear and the sound of lightly relieved voices as they crossed through the channel between the two open gates to the other side. She realised then that Freddy could see the indecision in her eyes. The indecision she had been trying to pretend was not there.

She thought of Freddy with hungry eyes, not curious eyes, and she took a sharp turn to follow the wall around a right angle, resisting the burning temptation to look back, to see if anyone was watching. They would be waiting here soon, having crossed from the Large Ghetto. Not so many *needed* food quite so badly in the more affluent Small Ghetto; here life was a little closer to normal, with cafes and commerce, and so on. Sarah had told her they were from the Large Ghetto; she had twice risked a shouted conversation with them.

They would take three minutes to get to the place beyond the three-metre high brick wall topped with barbed wire. What sunlight there was did not shine in this corner at this hour of the day, but still Lidka sweated. She shushed Freddy but he had made no sound. There were buildings close by, but Sarah had said that those that overlooked this part of the wall were in the Ghetto, and this was a blind spot from the street, at least when the Ghetto police and the soldiers were busy with the gate. She had said that with confidence. Reckless confidence.

Lidka did not really know if she should trust Sarah's judgement, but then she realised that Sarah *had* trusted her. With that she reached in to the pram and took out the small sack, which now seemed much heavier, and then she waited for the whistle. The wait seemed to take a Stone Age of clunking heartbeats, and at each one, and each breath which caught in her throat, she very nearly changed her mind.

The whistle was high and fluting, a cheeky three-tone birdcall.

Lidka quickly checked to see if anyone was watching, then swung the bag behind her before throwing it. She misjudged the throw, it snagged on the wire, but then, after a metallic shiver of hesitation, it fell back to the cobbles at her feet with a *thud-clank* of potatoes and tinplate. She felt suddenly angry with herself, imagined Sarah – brave, resourceful Sarah – watching her, then picked up the small sack again. This time she made no mistake, and it sailed over the wire with a quarter of a metre to spare. She listened for its fall.

"Ouch!"

That was from the other side of the wall. Then there was laughter, a boy's laughter, then more laughter, from another boy, a higher laugh, so a younger boy, she thought – perhaps a girl? There was that whistle again, a whistle that a wall could never imprison, and then the sound of shoes on cobbles as the children ran.

She turned the baby carriage and pushed it in the direction of the Mirowska Hall markets, resisting the temptation to look back at the gates. She glanced down at Freddy in the pram. He was smiling, perhaps because the pram was moving, perhaps for some other reason. Then she realised that she was smiling, too. She also realised that the fear had gone, to be replaced with something else; the thrill of what she had done, yes, but also pride. It had been a long time since she had felt proud of anything, other than her baby.

Lidka suddenly thought that she had forgotten to shout to tell those children there would be no more food tossed over the wall. Maybe next time she would. But then, she reminded herself, there was not to be a next time.

*

RAF Swinderby. May 1941

Jósef sat alone in the Sergeants' Mess. It had just been a dream, that's all, a dream he had had when he had tried to catch a little shuteye in the cab of the Fordson tender as they waited for the last of the Wellingtons to return. It was the same dream as always now, he never dreamt of Lidka anymore, he only dreamt of Wysocki burning. Yet although it had been just a dream the smell of burning flesh was alive in his nostrils and the aroma of frying eggs and bacon could not wash it away. He could hardly face the bacon sandwich, sliced into two triangles on a white plate, even though he had been lucky to get it – bacon and fresh eggs were usually reserved for returning aircrew. He sipped his tea, hot and sweet, but it somehow almost seemed to taste of ash.

The mess was quiet, as most of the aircrew had turned in, just the odd clink and scrape of cutlery on china as those that remained finished their breakfasts. The sun was just coming up outside, casting long black shadows of the buildings across the parade ground. The wall with the windows in it was lined with tables, while on the opposite side of the room there was a bar with easy chairs and tall stools, where the insignia shields of the old Polish squadrons were fixed to the wood panelling.

"Sczcepanski, so there you are; I've been looking for you." It was Flight Sergeant Jankowski; aircrew. He came from the Żoliborz district, like Jósef, and they sometimes talked of Warsaw, but not often. He did not think Marek Jankowski liked him, but he didn't know why. Before all this Jósef had been well-liked, but that had changed. Jankowski, a tall man, did not sit, he was on his way out; to get some sleep, probably – he had grabbed a bacon sandwich to eat on the go. Jankowski's Wellington, *L- Lublin*, had returned late, a large and jagged hole in its fuselage, and then the crew had been in 'interrogation', as the RAF called debriefs, with the Intelligence Officer, all part of the dull routine that followed six or seven hours of the rather less dull routine of cheating death. Jankowski's eyes were red raw and he slouched as if he hardly had the strength to bear his bulky leather Irvin jacket.

"Looking for me?" Jósef replied.

"Uh-uh, all day yesterday."

"I was off station, yesterday."

"Well that explains it. I've had news, from Warsaw," Jankowski said.

"You have?" It was rare that anyone ever had news from Poland, but some of them sometimes had letters through Thomas Cook, or via friends and family in neutral countries like Spain, Sweden and the USA, some even through more official channels; the couriers that kept the Government in Exile in touch with the homeland.

"Your wife. Kept that quiet, eh?"

Jósef must have looked as baffled as he felt, because Jankowski gave a sly smile.

"Was Lidka Wadalowska, yes?"

"*Was*? What do you mean, *was*?" Jósef said.

"Now Mrs Sczcepanska, of course, though I can't see why that's such a secret."

"I don't understand?"

"I sometimes get a letter from my mother, through a pal of mine in London; just gossip, pages and pages and pages of gossip. I suppose she expects me to pass on news. But it's good to know they're all okay, yes?"

"Tell me!" Jósef said.

"Mama says my Auntie knows her, has seen her. In the Mirowska market," Jankowski said, then paused before adding: "She's fine, Auntie says, mentioned her husband was in the air force, mentioned his name, Mama thought to mention it to me. She's good like that, is Mama."

Jósef felt the relief surge through him, to hear that Lidka was well after all this time worrying, and he breathed out a breath he had been unaware he'd been holding.

"And the baby's well, too."

Jankowski's duties as a navigator included bomb aiming, and he had aimed this one well. He watched as it dropped on its target. Jósef could see he waited for the explosion.

"Baby?"

"Auntie says so. But you don't give much away, do you Sczcepanski? So, wasn't sure if you knew. Anyway …"

With that Jankowski walked out of the mess. Jósef remembered that last evening with Lidka and then wondered how long a child would be called a baby. He thought the dates added up, but he wasn't sure. And then, quite suddenly, he realised something obvious; why would Lidka tell people they were married if it *wasn't* his child?

He picked up the bacon sandwich and bit into it, then chewed it slowly. It did not taste too bad at all, and the smell of burning was no longer in his nostrils.

*

North of Propoisk, Soviet Union. July 1941

The path through the wood was just wide enough for the Zündapp KS 750 motorcycle and sidecar. Earlier they had taken this narrow track and then dismounted and crept up to the edge of the trees to spy out the town of Propoisk, to see if it was occupied by Russian soldiers and if the bridge over the Sozh was still intact. The answer to both questions had been yes. Now, Ingo and Pop were back on the Zündapp and far enough away from the town and the Ivans not to worry so much about the noise of the engine.

Ingo threaded the machine through the wood, as fast as he could of course, the gears whining, the engine rasping. The new Zündapp was an improvement on the BMW. It had a foot-operated gear change and a powered sidecar wheel, so it could be two-wheel-drive, more like a car, but this was only the case when it was off-road; like now, when its *gelände* low range gearbox was in use. The harsh midday sunlight was fractured by the high trees, tiger-striping the path ahead, which meandered languidly through the wood. Ingo's meanderings were not so languid and every now and then a tree seemed to step out in front of them, but he was always ready for the ambush and jinked the machine one way or the other, dodging through the trees like a soccer star side-stepping defenders. The air was rich with gnats and mosquitoes, so Ingo wore his red neckerchief over his mouth and nose, looking like a bandit in a cowboy film, yet still the heavy smell of pine grated his nostrils, while custard splatters that had once been bugs dappled his goggles.

The Zündapp took flight over a bulging tree root, landed some metres later with a thump that clattered the equipment fixed to the bike, including Ingo's helmet. Then, quite suddenly, there was a steep bank ahead, and Ingo slowed, took it down two gears with the kick shift, then accelerated up the bank, the rear wheel and sidecar wheel spinning in the mulch. They suddenly burst out into the bright light of a wider and much smoother dirt track, the front wheel lifting as they crested the bank. He looked to his right and back a little for directions from Pop.

Pop glanced at his compass and map, while Ingo allowed the bike to idle as he looked around, noticing another lane, leading to a bottle-green painted house. Pop tapped his knee, pointed to the right, and Ingo turned, pushed the lever forwards to select the high range *Strasse* gearing, and then let out the clutch and opened the throttle.

They were at the rendezvous with the rest of the platoon – the spearhead of the reconnaissance battalion – within minutes. It was only now, as Ingo brought the Zündapp to a stop, that he remembered how tired he was. They had been going hard for days and there had been little sleep – his chin was a rasp of stubble and they all smelt of stale sweat and bad breath. The platoon was parked up off the road, in the cover of a stand of birch trees.

Kroh and some of the others were gathered around Leutnant Schirmer's command armoured car, an Sd.Kfz 223, its two-part grenade mesh thrown open to cast a lattice shadow on to Schirmer's face as he looked down on the small group of men gathered around the Horch Wagon. The armoured car packed a 3.5-litre V8 engine and – this Ingo liked most of all – the chassis was built by Auto Union in Zwickau, where they had made the grand prix cars before the war. As this was a 223, and not a 222, it carried the big bedframe radio aerial, which made it look like someone had grafted a piece of gym equipment to it.

"Well?" Schirmer shouted down, as Ingo switched off the engine, then laid the palm of his hand on the Zündapp's warm petrol tank for some seconds, as he always did.

"Ivan's in town, alright," Pop said, not bothering to call him sir. No one did, now.

"The bridge?"

"Still standing."

"With you two around?" Kroh said. "Well, that's a first."

"Send the signal, Hendel," Schirmer told the wireless operator inside the armoured car.

"And what now?" Kroh said.

"Now we wait," Schirmer replied. "Anything else?" he added, looking at Pop.

"Bugs and trees, and more bugs," Pop said. "Oh, and did I mention the bugs?"

Kroh shook his head, and took a picture of the Horch Wagon with his Leica: "The only thing worth taking a photograph of in this fucking godforsaken place and we had to bring it ourselves, right?"

"There was something," Ingo said.

"Yes?" Schirmer said.

"Yes?" Pop repeated.

"A house, at the end of a track, a couple of Ks down the road."

"These peasants don't have houses, they have sheds," Kroh said. He was wearing the uniform of an armoured car crew member, similar to that of the Panzerwaffe, black so as not to show off the oil stains, with a short wrap jacket with golden-yellow piping around the lapels. He also wore his own un-matching field grey alpine soldier, or Gebirgsjäger, peaked cap – which he'd won in a game of Skat and now seemed to have become attached to – rather than the regulation black side cap Schirmer and the others crewing the Horch Wagons wore.

"It was bigger than normal, quite a bit bigger, and painted, too," Ingo continued, climbing off the Zündapp and stretching the fatigue from his limbs.

"We have our orders, we're to wait until the rest of the battalion arrives, it's not our concern," Schirmer said, from his perch in the shallow turret of the armoured car, which seemed to give him a just a little more confidence.

"I think we should check out that dacha," Kroh said.

"Our orders are clear, Feldwebel Kroh."

"Dacha?" Pop said, tossing Ingo an unlabelled can of tinned rations which he caught one-handed — it could be anything from beef goulash to sardines, there were hundreds of varieties, but unless you saw the carton the tins came in you never knew the contents. True Russian roulette.

"Yeah, dacha. Like a country house," Kroh started, in response to Pop's question. "Only these Bolsheviks aren't allowed such things, everybody's equally poor, right?"

"That seems to be the five-year plan," Pop said.

"Only some are more equal, and so on. Gunther in intelligence told me so, some of these Communist Party big wigs, if they're good to Uncle Joe, toe the party line in nasties, he's good to them. And often that means a house in the country; a dacha, right?"

"We have to wait," Schirmer said.

Kroh looked up at the officer in the turret of the Horch Wagon and sighed. Ingo knew what Kroh was thinking; there could be rich pickings in a place like that. And their greedy feldwebel had found nothing to his taste in the Soviet Union so far. Kroh smiled as he looked at Schirmer, the kid who had long ago, it now seemed, lost the most important battle a leader must fight: the war of wills.

"Still, I think I'll check out that dacha. Come on you two," he pointed at Ingo and Pop. "Lead the way."

"But —" Schirmer started.

"What, best take some support, right? Okay, you lot, bring that Hanomag along," Kroh interrupted, pointing at the armoured half-track, to which five men now rushed.

"I meant —" Schirmer started again.

"That's settled, then. Mount up boys!"

The others smirked as Schirmer's face filled with the claret of frustration, anger and embarrassment. But he knew he was beaten, and so he clanged shut the gates of the steel grenade mesh like the sulky schoolboy he perhaps still should have been. Ingo felt sorry for him; just a little. But more than that he wished he hadn't mentioned the house, as he was tired and hungry. He had opened the tin quickly, as this campaign had been all about eating on the go so far, and was glad it was the vinegary-smelling beef and pickles in gravy, one of his favourites. He quickly spooned as much of it as he could into his mouth as he climbed back on to the Zündapp. Pop had eaten nothing, just popped a Pervitin pill from its red and white tube — he had been taking them often, since the invasion had started, sometimes he seemed to be living off just cigarettes and those little 'Stuka tablets'.

Ingo and Pop led the way and Kroh's 222 armoured car and the Hanomag followed, the tracks of the latter clanking and squealing on the broken surface of the road through the wood. Soon, they turned off on to the slightly narrower lane Ingo had spotted. They could see the house; in a clearing, surrounded by long grass.

Pop slapped his leg. "Let them through!" he shouted up from the sidecar. Ingo didn't like the idea of letting anyone past and he shook his head, then gave the Zündapp a little more throttle.

The grass had grown long in the centre stripe between the packed dirt lines formed by earlier visitors over the years, but the length of the grass that now brushed the bottom of the sidecar was reassuring. He doubted anyone had driven this way for a while. There was also waist-high long grass either side of the track.

"Can't you see he's letting us to take all the risks?" Pop said, raising his voice so it could be heard over the clacking and clicking of the valves and the flutter of the engine.

"Better than eating his dust," Ingo said.

"You'd rather eat bullets?"

"You forget, I'm faster than a bullet."

"That's little use if it's coming the other way."

"Stop fretting, this place looks empty anyhow."

"A good racing driver knows when, and when *not*, to take risks," Pop said, loud and firm, as he checked the load of the belt in the MG 34, then snapped the top cover down and latched it back in place.

With that Ingo opened the throttle a little more and they stretched the distance between them and the Horch Wagon and half-track by about fifty metres. He studied the basil-green bungalow as they came closer. It had a dormer in the high roof and a rusting open veranda, sagging from it like an iron cobweb. The green had faded and it exuded an air of neglect, the grass all around it was very long and some of the windows were smashed, he now saw. As they drew closer he realised there was a break in the grass to the left of the house, filled with a stagnant pond, almost dried up, what water there was almost as green as the chipped paint that just about clung to the dacha. The air was still and hot and smelt of the pond; fetid.

"Ivans!" Pop shouted.

His shout was punctuated with the exclamation mark of a rifle shot, a sharp crack, and then the bang of the detonation slightly later. Two running and stumbling figures suddenly appeared in the long grass to the right and in front, the top of the grass up to their bellies. They wore brown uniforms and olive-green helmets and one of them stopped to aim a Papasha, the wooden-stocked sub machine gun with its drum magazine. He let off a juddering burst, but it went wide, the rounds scything the grass behind the Zündapp with a light buzzing noise.

This had all happened in less than a second, but Pop had been ready and he fired in to the long grass with the sidecar-mounted MG 34, a couple of short and ear-splitting bursts of mechanical chatter that cut through the two Russian soldiers, brightening their drab tunics with rosettes of blood before they sank beneath the whispering surface of the grass. Just then there was more rifle fire, from within the dacha now.

They were exposed on the narrow track, which was now being plucked with little fountains of dust from bullet hits, and there was not the space to turn – and while one of the clever features of the Zündapp was a reverse gear, this would not take them out of range quick enough, and it would mean stopping, too. And so Ingo did what Ingo always did; he accelerated, and then turned in to the long grass to the left.

The grass was so high he was almost in cover as he bent forward over the fuel tank. The big machine crushed the brittle growth, though it fought back by snagging at the steering and Ingo had to keep the throttle wide open to power his way through. Pop fired the machine gun ahead of them as they went, in case there were hidden Ivans, so that grass flew everywhere with a whipping noise so that it was as if they were inside a threshing machine, the air filled with the peppery-iron smell of the bullet propellant and also of cut grass, over which Ingo sniffed burning. He knew at once that tinder dry grass had wrapped itself around the red hot exhaust pipe.

They burst through the last of the grass, into the open space of the stagnant pool. Pop leapt from the sidecar even as Ingo was bringing the Zündapp to a skidding stop, and set up the machine gun on the edge of the pond on its barrel-mounted bipod attachment, right where the ground dipped into the bowl of the almost dried up pond, which gave him some cover. He lay down and pressed the butt of the gun to his shoulder, then raked the dacha with the MG 34. Meanwhile, Ingo sloshed water from his canteen to put out the small flames that danced from the curving exhaust, and then took another ammunition box from its mounting on the sidecar as well as the spare barrel for the machine gun from its rack; they soon got too hot and then they needed changing.

The thrown object appeared in Ingo's peripheral vision and the shock of it froze the image – like jammed cinema film – for the instant it took him to recognise it as a Russian stick grenade, with the cross-hatching of the fragmentation sleeve on its explosive head. It tumbled through the air and landed close to Pop with a thud, breaking the crust of dried mud and half burying itself in the ooze below. It was four metres from Pop, just out of his line of sight.

Ingo had been moving before the grenade had landed and, almost as soon as it did, he dropped the ammo box and spare gun barrel and made for it. He plucked it from the mud at the run, by its thick metal shaft, and it made a slurping noise as he pulled it clear; and then in the same movement he threw it into the muddy puddle-shallow remaining water of the pond some fifteen metres or so away. Because it had landed in the sludgy pond bed the explosion was muffled and smaller than might have been expected, but it still threw mud and rank water in to the air, which fell back on to Ingo and Pop in a thick slap that knocked Ingo on to his back and punched the wind from his lungs.

Ingo wiped the foul smelling mud from his face with his neckerchief and tried to get his breath back.

"Much obliged!" Pop shouted, then started firing again.

Just then the MG 34s in the armoured car and the Hanomag joined in the fight, the Horch Wagon making its way down the track, the half-track ploughing through the grass for a better field of fire. Russian bullets threw bright sparks off the armour of the Horch Wagon, playing a dull percussion of dings against the steel. There were some more very long bursts from the armoured car in return, wood chips flying like yellow sparks from the façade of the dacha, while the shielded machine gun on the half-track took care of those Ivans still in the grass on both sides of the track, making good use of its elevated position. Then there was a sudden lull. Two shorter bursts, and a scream.

Then quiet.

They waited for some time, before Pop nodded at Ingo and they carefully checked the long grass close by for Ivans, and then walked up to the dacha along a narrow path that led from the pond, while Kroh and some of the others entered the house. Some of the grass had caught fire now and the flames seemed to melt the air, giving it the look of scalding liquid. When they got close to the dacha Ingo could see it was leopard shot with yellow woody, wounds; glass still tinkling to the floor, acrid cordite fumes soaking the air he breathed.

From inside there was a burst from a sub machine gun, an MP 40, and a little later Kroh and another soldier came out of the house, the former's face painted with frustration, and reddening with anger. Despite his annoyance he was whistling, in his non-whistle way; *Watch on the Rhine*, Ingo thought, it was sometimes difficult to tell exactly what he hissed.

"Nothing, not even furniture!" Kroh shouted, between airy *pheeps*.

"What did you expect, Fabergé eggs?" Pop said.

By now the others had rounded up some prisoners. Kroh spat at one of them, a loud splat as it hit his forehead. All of the Russians were wounded to some extent, and two of the five were sitting on the floor leaning against the flaking green paint of the dacha's wall. Ingo could see the white of a jagged bone poking through a blood-blackened trouser leg. Another pressed his hand to a belly wound, blood oozing jam-like between his dirty fingers. Ingo started to regret bolting down that tin of beef and pickles in gravy.

"Pup saved my life, you know," Pop said. "Tossed a live grenade away."

"Saved his own skin, too. Besides, if you're going to chuck a grenade, then throw it at the enemy, right?" Kroh said. "About time he started earning that fucking Iron Cross, I'd say."

Ingo said nothing, just started to peel the tacky scabs of quickly drying mud from his face.

Kroh changed the long magazine on his MP 40 and then, as casually as he might close a door behind him as he left for work, he shot four of the prisoners with one rattling three-second sweep of the gun, spent bullets curling from the breech and tinkling on to the hard ground behind him. The last of the Russians ran just as Kroh used up his ammunition, so he switched the machine pistol to his left hand and then took his Walther from its leather holster, firing it as soon as his arm was raised, the bullet thumped in to the man's back with the sound of a pebble hitting a mudflat, knocking him down like a painted tin flap at a fairground shooting gallery.

It had all happened so quickly, and Kroh had done it so nonchalantly, that no one had said a word. Now he holstered the pistol and took his Leica from the canvas bag he sometimes carried it in.

"What are you doing?" Ingo said.

"Memories," Kroh said, taking a picture of one of the dead men, getting the lens in close to the wound. "You'd think the fuckers would at least smile," he laughed at that.

"I mean, they were prisoners ..."

"They're Popovs; now dead Popovs, right?" Kroh said. With that he took a few more snaps, then put the camera to one side on one of the steps to the veranda, and started to go through the pockets of the dead, one by one. He looked in their mouths, too. The last of them, lying in a widening puddle of his own bright blood wore fancy blue breaches and seemed to be an officer. Kroh stripped him of his watch, and then opened his mouth to check his teeth. The flies were already buzzing around and some were beginning to settle on the raw wounds on the dead bodies.

"Well, this is as close as you'll get to striking gold in this country, right?" Kroh said, reaching into his inside pocket and pulling out his pliers. Ingo had seen them before, seen his bag of gold teeth and fillings, too. But he had never seen him take the teeth out. He did not want to watch, but for some reason he could not stop himself, and neither could the others, seven soldiers gathered in a half circle around Kroh and the dead Russian officer, most trying hard to appear unconcerned, to look tough.

There was a crunching sound, as the tooth was loosened in its socket, and then a long groan, like creaking wood. For a while Ingo could not place the sound, but then he saw the man's bloodstained hands twitch, the fingers clawing at the air.

"My God, he's still alive," Ingo muttered.

"Shoot the poor bastard!" Pop said, as the Ivan's legs started to slowly move in a swimming motion, slipping in the blood that still pumped out of them. Ingo could see pain and fear and pleading fill the man's eyes.

"Good idea, why don't you put him out of his misery, Pup?" Kroh said. But Ingo did not unsling his rifle. The Ivan's tooth came out and Kroh wiped it on the brown sleeve of the officer's uniform, still almost-whistling, *Watch on the Rhine*, in his hissing way.

When Kroh had finished Pop made a quick sign of the cross and then aimed the MG 34 from the waist. He tugged at the top part of machine gun's dual trigger for a single metallic clack of a shot, and put a bullet in the Russian's head.

***

Chillar. August 1951

"I thought you said we needed fuel?" Ingo said. Carlo had parked his old Ford truck up beyond the solitary YPF pump and was walking towards the windowless bar, a single storey, flat-roofed building coated in cracked stucco that was next door to the petrol station; both places occupying a windswept location clinging to the very edge of the town. A sign in faded orange read *Bar el Descanso*, though Ingo had heard it was as much a cantina as a bar.

"I said *we* needed fuel."

"I'm not sure —"

"Look, just don't criticise the beer and no one will ever guess you're German, that I promise you. They will think you're from Patagonia, they're all a bit strange down there, they go for beards like yours there, too, my friend," Carlo said, his shoe splashing in the edge of one of the caramel-coloured puddles that marked the chalky forecourt like patches on a shaggy pinto. There were a number of car wrecks in a ragged line at one end of the space, a workshop that was firmly shut, and a goat that watched them from a muddy patch of ground. Behind the cantina the town's water tower was dripping from the recent rain, sounding like it was leaking as the drops softy dinged against the steel lattice of its supports, while the huge drum of its container creaked and pinged to the cold wind. The air smelt of petrol and frying onions, a mix Ingo enjoyed.

"Anyway, I'm starving," Carlo went on. "And between you and me – and I mean that, you're not the only one with secrets, my friend – Catalina does some things *very* well, but cooking is not one of them. She can turn the finest steak into a shoe; but here they could turn a shoe into a steak!"

"Sole food?".

"A joke, ha! Come on then."

Ingo did not like to go to places where others were, but then again replacing a clutch plate in a Ford V8 stock car after another successful local race is a big enough job, so he supposed they'd earned a beer and a steak.

Inside there was a bar, with a couple of bottles of spirits on it, while a rusting refrigerator stood in the corner, buzzing like a two-stroke fly. Carlo took off his coat and said hello to the barman, who touched his forehead in a half salute, but did not reply, engrossed in an article in a copy of *El Gráfico*. The kitchen was beyond the bar, through swing doors that looked like they belonged to a saloon in a western.

Carlo took two bottles of Quilmes out of the fridge and tossed some coins on the counter. The walls, above the eye-level wood panelling, were painted white, and the white was painted yellow, stained by the smoke of a million cigarettes. The ceiling was the same. On those walls there were some framed photographs of football elevens posing in two ranks, and an old picture of Sophia, Carlo standing by the old Chevy, with his now dead friend Carlos alongside him. It was warm in the cantina, and Ingo took off his jacket and hung it alongside Carlo's heavy leather coat – he felt the cold more than Ingo, but then Ingo had got used to it the hard way.

In the middle of the room a man was eating an early dinner alone, wholly focused on his steaming plate of puchero. There was a piano in the corner. It was dusty, and the stool had been taken by one of a group of young men playing Truco and smoking like Essen in the opposite corner.

"Do you play?"

Ingo had not realised he had been staring at the piano. "No. No," he said, shaking his head.

"What about chess?"

Ingo nodded, and took one of the cold rather than chilled beers.

"Good, I seldom get to play these days. Catalina says she enjoys it, it's the sort of thing modern women like to say, yes? But she is hopeless."

"Just what is she good at, Carlo?"

The twinkle in his eye answered the question, then he washed the smirk off his face with a slug from his bottle of Quilmes, and pulled a chessboard and a wooden box of pieces off a shelf. Ingo took a swig of beer, too. It was a very ordinary lager, he always thought, but that only ever reminded him that he was German; and so he drank some more.

Ingo won the first game in a matter of minutes, leaving Carlo looking a little annoyed. He gave him a chance in the next, but still won. Ingo played quickly, as always, and it seemed to goad Carlo to do the same, and then to make mistakes.

They stopped playing to have their steaks, served with fried potatoes. They did not talk about the car or the Mil Millas. Ingo did not know how the decision to drive the big race at the end of the year had been taken, but they both knew he would. He had never actually agreed to, in so many – or any – words. It was more of an unspoken understanding. An understanding between racers.

There was a shout from the other table, one of the two-player teams tasting success at Truco, and all of them tasting a little too much of the Fernet. As Carlo set up the chess pieces again with a "now I am no longer hungry I can concentrate", Ingo took two more beers from the fridge and placed some pesos on the counter. The barman did not take his eyes from the report on a match between Independiente and Boca Juniors he was reading in the magazine.

As he turned Ingo was greeted with a mist of liquorice-smelling spirit, and the man who was exhaling it. He was a wide man, with a wide mouth and wide bloodshot eyes. Thick curly hair sat on his head like a tight hat. He had the look of a labourer about him. He also had the look of a man who had had far too much to drink.

"I know you," he said, his tongue thick with alcohol.

"I doubt it," Ingo said, and went to pass him, but the wide man made himself wider. Ingo walked around him and the man laughed.

"What's got in to him?" Ingo asked, as he placed the two beers on the tin-topped table with a double dull ding.

"Fernet," Carlo said. "I've seen him here before, thinks the world's treated him bad; too good for picking spuds, but no good for anything else. Sad."

"Sad."

Ingo won the next game.

"Goddammit, man. Is it not enough that you drive like Fangio?"

"I do?"

Carlo smiled, and shook his head. But Ingo did not know whether he meant *no*, or perhaps *you know so.*

A peanut shell skipped across the board, toppling a bishop. There was some laughter from the card players, most of it from the wide man. Carlo ignored it, and continued to set up the pieces.

"Why don't you get us a couple more beers, while I try to figure out what you just did to me?" Carlo said.

Ingo nodded and, taking a couple of Quilmes from the fridge, he went to the counter and added money to a growing pile besides the barman's magazine. He smelt the aniseed on the wide man's breath before he turned to face him. The man was swaying.

"You're the German, aren't you?"

Ingo said nothing.

"So, what you hiding from?"

Ingo went to walk around him, but he half stepped, half slid to block him. In the mirror on the wall opposite he could see the barman had come alive, excited by the prospect of real sport rather than reports in black and white. Over the shoulder of the wide man he could see Carlo, looking on, his head cocked a little in curiosity. There was a hint of a smile tugging at the corners of his mouth, Ingo thought.

"A Nazi?" the wider man said, slurring the z so that it almost came out as a failed whistle, then he brushed back an errant curl that had slid over his eyes with a finger, its nail encrusted in rich, dark earth. "Yes, that's it," he added. "Nazi."

Ingo did not respond, just took a sip from one of the beers.

"You're not welcome here, you and your murdering friends. Why don't you go back to Germany?"

With that Ingo decided to push past him. The wide man stumbled, but not quite enough, and he recovered quickly. And then he punched Ingo in the mouth.

It was not a good punch, but the man wore a ring, and the edge of it caught Ingo's lip, and he tasted blood, metallic and warm. But he did not respond. He did not even put the beers down. He simply smiled.

With that an electric eel of anger sparked in the glazed dark depths of the drunk's eyes, and the next punch was a little better, to the belly, and it left Ingo slightly winded. But he stood his ground and held the bottles tight by their throats. The other card players were laughing now, and the wide man obviously thought the laugher was directed at him. It spoilt his aim, while Ingo stepped aside as he punched, so the fist just smoothed his beard and the drunk followed it past Ingo's shoulder and toppled in to the bar. This left the way open and Ingo simply walked to the table and put the bottles down beside the chessboard.

"Why don't you fight?" the wide man shouted, letting the bar support him. "Are you a coward? Yes, you're a coward, hiding in our country. Yes you're a coward. Just like that one," he pointed at Carlo. "Him who's scared to race again."

There was no change of expression. Carlo simply stood, and within three effortless strides – though deceptively quick – he had reached the man. Before he had a time to react Carlo had taken a thicket of his curls in his fist and wrenched him by the hair towards the closest wall, a brutal act, but one carried out with the fluid elegance of a series of tango steps. Then he slammed the wide man's face against the wall. He slid to the floor leaving a wobbly perpendicular trail of smeared blood on the yellowish wall. Then he lay there groaning.

Ingo had seen more than his fair share of casual violence, but he had rarely seen it carried off with such panache. "I just remembered," Carlo said, reaching for his coat. "I have to pick Anna up from a birthday party."

Ingo stood up, took a last gulp of beer, and followed Carlo out of the door.

*

Jaffa, Tel Aviv. September 1951

Sarah Malka's husband, David, still believed she worked as a translator. He knew nothing of her real work. No one outside of The Group did, and no one could. Sometimes he talked as if he thought she was having an affair. But she had no interest in affairs, in truth she had little interest in him, either. All she truly cared about was revenge. She had said she would meet David and Benjamin for lunch today, but Gabriel had sent a message. This was more important than husband and son. They could keep each other company.

Gabriel had another place he liked to meet, a café on the edge of Jaffa, the wrong side of the railway line that connected the port with Jerusalem, close to the level crossing at the end of Herzl Street that many thought of as the boundary between Jaffa and Tel Aviv. It was an Arab café, but that never stopped Gabriel, it was only the Nazis he hated. Sarah knew of few places like it. Here they served mud coffee that was strong enough to strip paint, and sticky cakes of the sort she dreamed of often when she was in the camp. Ironically, she rarely craved food like that now.

"You are looking too thin, Sarah," Gabriel said. This had become part of their ritual.

"I'm okay," she said.

There was a strong smell of coffee and sweet smoke from a hookah in the café. Two old men played backgammon at high speed, the counters clicking against the board like castanets. It was hot and the shutters were flung open. The traffic was heavy in the street, the sharp bellow of car horns mixing with the hollow clop of horse-drawn carts.

"How is David?"

"He's fine," Sarah said, automatically.

"The boy?"

"He is well."

Gabriel sat in the shade away from the window, protecting his pale, parchment-skinned face from the strong sunlight. A waiter placed a tiny glass of coffee on the table and he thanked him in Arabic. "Shukraan," he said.

Sarah nodded her thanks as a glass of fresh orange juice was placed in front of her.

"Tell me," she said, feeling the excitement in her chest.

"It is not another target, not yet," Gabriel said.

"Then what is it?"

"Do I need an excuse to have a cup of coffee with a friend; we are friends, are we not?"

Sarah was not sure about that, had not thought about it. Had not thought about friends for years. Not since 1944. She sipped the orange juice, a cube of ice floating on its pulpy surface clinking softly against her teeth.

Gabriel smiled, then said: "So, I do need an excuse, then?"

"Have you one?"

He waited before answering, his gleaming eyes locked to hers, as if he was trying to reach inside her before he told her this thing. Then he looked down, stared at the dark surface of his coffee, and did not hold her gaze as he said. "He is alive."

Sarah's hands started to shake so she placed the glass of orange juice on the table, spilling a little as she misjudged it. The rawest emotion flooded through her, almost climax-like in its intensity, and she did not know whether it was pleasure or pain.

"Are you all right?"

"Is it true?" she said, after a long pause.

"It's true."

"How do you know?"

"We have had word, a reliable source, on some who have flown. It was a while ago, but your man gave his own name to prove he was *worthy* of help. It is possible that he will still be using the name on his Red Cross passport."

"And what name was that?"

"That, we do not know. Yet."

"What else *do* we know?"

"Nothing."

"But a passport – South America?"

Gabriel nodded: "Possibly." He took a sip of his coffee, grimaced at the hit of it, and then took another sip. The adhan began nearby, seemingly answered by another distant muezzin, somewhere across Jaffa, a tiny fraction of time later.

"What now?" she said.

"We wait," he said. "We have friends in South America, but it's a big continent, and we cannot even be sure he's there. And if he is, then there is Uruguay, Paraguay, Argentina, Brazil, Chile, Bolivia, all big countries, in this big continent."

"But you will tell me, if —"

"*If* we hear anything, yes; I promise."

"And then?"

"And then someone will decide."

"I will kill him, whatever they decide," she said.

"You make it sound so easy, you know that?"

"It's not a problem; I have put money aside. I can fly anywhere in the world, and I can leave any time."

"That's not what I meant."

Sarah shrugged.

"He is one man, Sarah."

"They are all one man."

Gabriel nodded, then looked at his watch. Then he said: "War destroys in many ways, Sarah," he said. "Perhaps, so does revenge?"

"Perhaps," she said. "But you will tell me?"

"If we hear anything more, I will tell you. That I swear."

*

Buenos Aires, Argentina. December 1951

"There's someone I want you to meet, Ingo," Carlo said.

"You should know by now I'm not the sociable type, Carlo; and I really wish you would remember my name is Enrique," Ingo said, regretting having told him his real first name for the hundredth time. But Carlo just laughed, put his arm around his shoulders and led Ingo towards the entrance of the Automóvil Club Argentino building.

On the other side of the wide, wide boulevard of the recently renamed Avenida del Libertador – the sort of street the Nazis would like, broad enough for five-panzer-deep victory parades – the racing cars were arranged in a half-herringbone, their windscreens licked with dazzling sunlight. In the large green parkland space behind the cars temporary stalls sold empanadas and barbequed meat; the siren smell of sizzling sausages and steaks mixed with the equally enticing aroma – to Ingo – of Castrol R and drifted across the very wide road thanks to a breeze off the Plata, which gave some relief from the humid summer heat. Plenty of people had turned out to see the racing cars before the early start of the one-thousand mile race, the Mils Millas, the next day, and many of them watched as some of the V8s and sixes in the stock cars the other side of the road were revved, fuel fumes seeming to melt the air above the burbling engines.

Further along the boulevard a military band played the *President's March*, music that always seemed to be on the edge of dribbling out of tune.

Ingo thought the Nazis would have liked this building as much as the street it sat on; stark and official, in the Rationalist style, eight storeys of cold concrete and glass. Though he would admit there was a lightness to it, too, the way, because of the overhang of its wings, it seemed to be balanced on the eight columns that fronted its lower floor, and also the way the light danced on the segmented glass of its façade.

Carlo led him through a wood, brass and glass revolving door and in to a very high-ceilinged lobby with a polished marble floor that swam with the melted reflections of the many people; the babble of mixed and slightly echoed conversation adding to the watery illusion for a moment. Directly in front, through the throng of people and a line of squared marble pillars, brassy elevators were flanked by staircases, also marble, with brass banisters – this was a place of marble and brass. The air was cooler, now they were out of the harsh sun, and it smelt of floor polish and cigar smoke. There was a tall and wide reception desk where drivers and co-drivers were signing on for the race. Ingo had signed on earlier, and shown the racing licence that bore the same name that was on the Red Cross passport he had had since Genoa five years earlier: Enrique Hohberg.

"There he is," Carlo said, pointing. "With the girls."

"Who?"

"Hector Otero."

Ingo knew the name well, Carlo often spoke of Otero, because Varela's potato money was to be spent either on this man's career, or the Condor. He looked quite small, not too small, but short enough for it to bother him, for as he spoke to the pretty girls he held his head high like a tree-feeding antelope, and while he was not exactly on tip toes there was almost air beneath his heels. He had thick dark hair, and a tanned face, at the centre of which was a small nose with a slight, but somehow disdainful, upward curl to it. Because of this and his upturned head, he had the appearance of someone looking down on people when, physically at least, that was unlikely. He looked about 23, Ingo supposed. The girls were quite young, in their late teens, maybe a little older.

"Come on, I'll introduce you." Carlo did not wait for an answer, but led Ingo through the crowd, greeting some others he knew with his trademark grin as he did so, until they reached Otero. He had just finished signing his autograph for the girls and they left, giggling and blushing. Close up Otero exuded privilege and entitlement, Ingo could not say how; it wasn't a smell, and not really a thing of appearance, but it was something he had seen in men all his life. He wore his racing kit, even though the race did not start until the next morning – some of the drivers, Otero among them, had had press pictures taken earlier. This was a yellow polo shirt with a blue silk scarf tucked inside, and blue slacks with a thick brown leather kidney belt. Both the shirt and trousers bore creases that could draw blood on brushing past. Ingo and Carlo also wore polo shirts when they raced in the summer, though they had chosen the same red as the Ford.

"Hector, I have someone who would like to meet you."

Otero turned. "Carlo, good to see you."

Carlo nodded at that and introduced Ingo and Otero to each other. Ingo saw the recognition in Otero's eyes when he heard his name. That was beginning to worry him; he had won races now, in the Ford V8, small races, but people were starting to point him out. Otero did not offer his hand.

"Would you like me to sign something?" Otero said, pretending, it seemed to Ingo, not to know who he was. It was a calculated insult, but not a clever one.

"Enrique's my driver," Carlo said.

"Really?" Otero's forehead corrugated in overacted surprise. "Oh, I'm sorry, it's just that ..." He trailed off, smiled what he might have thought of as an embarrassed smile, but it seemed more mocking.

"Just that, what?" Ingo said.

"Oh, I'm sorry. But, well, you seem quite old to be starting out in this game."

"I'm not as old as Fangio."

"No? Well Juan's not getting any younger, either, is he?" Otero said. "Anyway, I must be off now, Carlo ... Sorry, I missed your name?"

"Enrique," Carlo said.

"Well, Enrique, if you need any advice, any help at all, in fact."

"Just give us plenty of room when we come past," Ingo said, turning away from Otero as he said it, and catching the grin that split Carlo's face.

They both marched out of the hall and Carlo chortled quietly to himself. As they spun out of the revolving door and back into the heat of the wide street Ingo was suddenly aware of the music. Not the martial music of the band, but the music inside him. Chopin's *Heroic*, as pure and clean as if he was playing it himself, which he had not done for many a year.

"There's Varela," Carlo said, suddenly serious. The man was the other side of the wide road standing by the line of slant-parked stock cars, right next to Carlo's shining red Ford. Even from this distance Ingo could see that he was a large man. He wore a cream suit and a Panama hat. Ingo could not tell whether the man was impressed with the workmanship on the car from here, but he knew there was nothing he could be unimpressed with, for they had spent months preparing, modifying and polishing that race car. When they reached the Ford Esteban Varela turned towards them.

"You have done a good job, Rossi," Varela said, with no pleasantries, not even a good afternoon, taking a white silk handkerchief from his pocket, lifting his hat a little, and dabbing beads of sweat from his forehead.

"Signor Varela," Carlo said with a slight nod.

"And this is your driver?"

"Enrique Hohberg," Carlo said.

Varela nodded, then turned to inspect the car again. He tapped the hood with fat fingers and Carlo unbuckled the leather bonnet straps. As Varela studied the V8 engine Ingo studied him. He was fat all over, but in a spread out way that made him seem large rather than obese. He was tall, too, so that he had to bend low to look beneath the curling lip of the bonnet. When he had finished he nodded and Carlo slammed shut the hood. He took a rag from Carlo and wiped his hands, though he had touched nothing under the hood, and the engine was as clean and as shiny as the Perons' silver in any case, and then he leant against the front fender. It was only now that Ingo noticed the cologne he wore, thick and pungent enough to cut through the smell of fuel, oil, hot steel and the cooking meat.

Varela's face was hanging with fat, dragging down his features so that it looked impossible that he might, one day, smile. He had eyes like olives, and pitted skin, and a habit of looking at the palms of his hands from time to time, Ingo now noticed, perhaps to remind himself of the hard work that had got him here; deciding the futures of the people who worked in his fields, packed his potatoes, or looked for his support.

"I cannot fault your preparation, Rossi," Varela finally said. "But this is no *concours d'elegance*."

"The car is quick," Carlo said.

"The deal stands," Varela said, nodding. "I've put my man Otero in the best car money can buy, and he's fast. If you can beat him, then I will invest in your project, as agreed."

"That's fair."

"It's a gamble, you understand? Otero has not much experience of this type of racing, but he is quick, young, hungry," Varela added, then turned his attention to Ingo. "You, what do you think?"

"You've seen the drawings of the Condor, isn't that enough?" Ingo said.

"A car is more than pencil on paper. And a car that does not finish a race is as good as a car that does not start a race – *if* it is bearing my name. And if a car is not fast, it is not a racing car, this is a simple fact."

"The Condor will be reliable *and* fast," Carlo said. "If we have the money to make it so."

"I do not spend my money unless I am assured of success. I need to be sure." With that Varela left them, without even a nod. A male secretary who had been so ordinary that Ingo had not even noticed him fell in by his side, making a note as Varela dictated while he walked.

"Yet he spends his money on Otero," Ingo said.

"He's already committed to Otero," Carlo said. "If Otero fails, *he* fails. Unless there's another way out, something bigger and better to back, than merely a driver."

"*Merely*, is it?"

"If the Condor is to fly then *mere* will not cut it, my friend." Despite his grin there was an edge to his voice that was almost as sharp as Otero's creases. Right then Ingo wondered just how much Carlo really had riding on this race.

***

Near Rudnevo, Soviet Union. December 1941

A tank rumbled by, shaking and cracking the frozen ground, tracks squeaking and clacking, engine roaring and rasping. In the deep furrows previous panzers had carved there was a pressing of a man; like a butterfly in a collection, though with the drab Russian tunic perhaps more like a moth. Ingo found it difficult to believe that the brown patch had once been a human being, before 22 tonnes of Panzer IV had stolen a dimension from him.

"It must be warmer in those tin cans than it is on this bloody sewing machine," Pop said from the sidecar.

"Warmer," Ingo said, though chattering teeth. "But so slow."

The Zündapp's engine was idling, the frame shaking a little as if it, too, shivered from the cold. It was so cold that even Ingo wore his coal scuttle helmet, with a woollen balaclava beneath it, while he had insulated the layers of his clothes with scrunched-up pages torn from discarded copies of both *Pravda* and *Der Angriff*. He also wore his rubberised motorcyclist's coat belted tightly over a woman's fur coat he'd found on a Russian soldier – this one had had all three dimensions, but there was no breath within them. The Ivan's blood was still on the fur, in frozen patches. There had been no issue of winter clothing, his uniform was the same one he'd worn when they'd crossed the Bug River in June, perhaps because no one thought Blitzkrieg could really last long enough to become Blitzfreeze.

The sky was like opaque frosted glass that would not let the sunlight through. The ground was white with snow. They were on the fringes of what had once been a village, but now looked like a cemetery, all that was left the tall tombstones of stone chimneys and shallow humps of ash. The smell of burnt thatch was heavy on the air, mixed with the tang of fuel fumes from the panzers.

"You still think the war will be over soon?" Ingo said.

"Of course, we're almost in Moscow," Pop said, his frozen breath fracturing the air in front of him. But he didn't sound so sure. Red Square was about sixty kilometres away. But they were long, cold kilometres; and now the panzers seemed to be going in the wrong direction anyway, as far as Ingo could tell. The 4th had been a part of a pincer movement, but had been beaten by the mud, then the cold, and mostly the Russians. German wheels and tracks had churned up the muddy roads, which had then frozen in to rutted, corrugated byways that shook and destroyed everything from trucks to bikes, and even tanks, and on which even Ingo did not wholly enjoy driving. The Russians? They just kept coming.

"We have to get in to panzers," Pop said, as he continued to watch the tanks rattle by.

"Kroh would never let us leave, anyway," Ingo said.

"That's the real problem; all he need do is veto it, say we can't be spared to go off for training, and that kid Schirmer will say nothing."

"How much do you think we still owe him, for Wawer?" Ingo said, an image of a naked Lidka in a warm Warsaw apartment leaping into his head as he remembered that night.

"I reckon we've paid that off ten times," Pop said. "And he's noted every dodgy deal we've done on his behalf since. A proper Nazi, Kroh, he knows the real meaning of collective responsibility."

"There's no way out?"

"An Ivan sniper's our best bet, I'd say."

Another Panzer IV clanked and rumbled past, its commander quickly popping his black-capped head through the hatch. These five tanks were the only ones working, now, as far as Ingo could see. The temperature had dropped like a bomb from a Stuka these last few days; gone through the roof, then three floors, and into the basement. Tanks would not start, while other vehicles had had to be abandoned simply because they could not make it up slopes, or had bogged down in snow and then been entombed in its frozen-iron grip overnight. It had taken him an age to start the Zündapp that morning, but he had managed it. He wondered how long it would last, though.

The tank commander shook his head, then quickly disappeared back inside the turret, loudly clanging the steel hatch behind him.

"Yes, much warmer in there, pal," Pop said.

Ingo hated the idea of driving a tank rather than the Zündapp, but on the other hand driving was not shooting. And he really could not believe he could be as cold in a panzer as he was now. Even beneath two pairs of gloves his fingers were like icicles and he imagined they would snap if he played a scale on a piano, while his feet were so cold they seemed to buzz like the tingling metal of the bike frame – all this despite the fact he rested them on the engine cylinders, while the Zündapp also had heated handgrips, which were fed with warm air from that same 750cc unit.

"And those black uniforms, too. Bet the plum love that sort of thing, eh Pup?"

"Don't you ever stop thinking about women?"

"Got the itch now, is it?" Pop said, with a laugh, and Ingo realised the image of a naked Lidka had not drifted from his consciousness, but was burned into it like a brand and he felt himself stiffen against the freezing, icy steel of the Zündapp fuel tank.

"Pup, Pop," shouted Eckhart over the din of the tanks. "Feldwebel Kroh wants you."

They reluctantly left the Zündapp and the little heat its warmed hand grips and sidecar floor heater gave and scrunched through the crisp snow to the nearby sawmill, the only structure in the village that remained standing. It was a long wooden building, encrusted in sparkling frost, with a steeply pitched black roof scarred with the claw marks of the snow that had fallen from it. An extremely short narrow-gauge railway ran through the building, the rails just about showing through the snow on the ground like tight sinews through white skin. The little railway led to an open double door, and Ingo assumed there was the same at the rear of the building, so that logs could be wheeled in and wheeled out as planks. There were in fact piles of planks outside the building, plus a scatter of wrecked vehicles; a ZIS-5 Soviet army truck and two cars, one he recognised as a GAZ. Both cars had been well perforated by machine gun fire, while the truck's propshaft was snapped and lying half in the snow like greased entrails hanging from a dying beast. There were bullet holes in the sawmill, too, with fringes of clean white-yellow wood like exposed bone in a wound. The only Horch Wagon armoured car that was right now of any use was parked up away from the sawmill, its engine running, its steel shivering as much as every man stood around it, as it puffed out frozen fumes which weaved a lace of scratchy smoke in the air.

When they had first seen the sawmill, and that it was still standing, Pop and Ingo had assumed it would be their billet for the night, but they had now heard they were moving on. Someone has said there was a house nearby they could use – such was the cold that the fighting quite naturally and wholly necessarily stopped most afternoons, so that soldiers on both sides could find a place to spend the night without freezing to death. It had been twenty-below yesterday, Ingo had been told, and it could only get colder. Perhaps Pop was right about tanks, he thought, again.

The sawmill was being used to house Russian prisoners, ten or so that had been brought in earlier; railway workers who had been given guns and asked to fight like soldiers. Ingo could hear them now inside, whispering and shuffling, trying to stamp icy blocks of feet back to life.

Kroh was with Leutnant Schirmer and a group of other soldiers. The officer was saying something, but Kroh was ignoring him, whistling in his non-whistle way – *Horst Wessel*, this time. Some of the others laughed and the lieutenant reddened. When they reached them Ingo smiled at Schirmer, a smile he had intended as friendly, but it was hidden by his itching balaclava. The young officer spun on his heel and walked away, back towards the road where shivering mechanics were trying to resurrect the command armoured car.

Kroh laughed. "Christ, you look cold Pup," he said. He was wearing his field grey Gebirgsjäger cap, its side flaps unbuttoned and pulled down to help protect his ears from the frigid air, but his face was exposed and pinkly-red. His Leica was slung around his neck, jostling with the square package of his gas cape across the front of his captured white Siberian snow smock. His black trousers disappeared into overlarge Russian felt boots.

Ingo's teeth still chattered, and that was answer enough. He could see inside the sawmill now, although it was just a glimpse, as the doors were closing. For a moment the cold, white faces of the Ivans within looked upturned, as if in the dark slot of a grave, before that image was pinched out with the rattle of the meeting doors. One of the others, a stout lad they all called Treacle, took a pickaxe handle and jammed it into the loop of the steel clasp on the doors, hammering it in with a half brick. It occurred to Ingo then that it would take a while to prise it free, when it came to letting them out.

"We haven't food, space or time, right?" Kroh said, to no one in particular. "Just Slavic monkeys anyhow," he added, in a mutter, as he took a pressed steel fuel can from a small stack on the floor, and then sloshed petrol over the door and on top of the piles of planks resting against the walls. Some of the others did the same.

"Why the waste of fuel?" Pop said.

"Well, we can't take it with us, haven't the trucks now; so better than leaving it for the Popovs, right?" Kroh said. "*Much* better."

Kroh emptied the can then tossed it aside. "This will warm you up, Pup." he said. "A light, someone?" Treacle gave Kroh a small brown Bakelite cylindrical lighter. There was a broom made of twigs leaning against the wall of the sawmill, and Kroh reversed it, holding it low on the shaft, then lit the bristles; the flame taking hold quickly. There was a light whoosh in the cold air as Kroh swished it in front of Ingo's face. "You've been having a free ride long enough, Pup. Time you did something useful, I reckon."

With that Ingo was handed the broom, its brush flaring flame. It was only when he had hold of it did he realise what Kroh meant. He dropped it in the snow, where it sizzled, but did not go out.

"Do it, Pup," Kroh said. "It's about time you realised we're all in this together, right?"

Ingo said nothing, did nothing, except look away.

Kroh unslung the MP 40 machine pistol that was hung over his shoulder and cocked it. Even with the background noise of the rumbling, squealing tanks, the sound of the machine pistol's mechanism was startling, like the snap of a mantrap in a dead forest.

"I can shoot you, if you refuse to obey an order."

"You can't order me to murder," Ingo said, the words muted through the wool of the balaclava, but as cold as the air, for he felt no fear – just an absolute certainty that he would not burn the wooden building.

"They're not even soldiers; it's not murder to kill partisans, it's our *duty*."

Ingo shook his head.

The others had gathered around, and Ingo realised there was no turning back for the feldwebel now. Prisoners had been killed before, and nothing had been done about it. No one would side with Ingo. He did not face Kroh, but he somehow sensed, and saw from the dilating pupils of the others, that the sergeant had levelled his MP 40.

"It's too cold to be arsing around here, let's get this fire going!" It was Pop, Ingo turned to see him walk between Kroh's sub machine gun and Ingo himself, scooping up the flaming brush. He watched as he lit the fuel doused planks, the deed done before Kroh had the chance to stop him.

Kroh said nothing, just made sure he took a photograph or two of Pop setting fire to the sawmill. Ingo turned to leave.

"No!" Kroh shouted. "You will stand here and get warm with the rest of us! Right?"

Ingo knew he had pushed him far enough, so he stood and watched the sawmill burn. He listened, too. First there was pleading, he did not know the words but true begging transcends language, and then there were the screams of panic and the crying. There was a thumping against the side of the sawmill walls and some of the planks shook and shivered, bulging out a little, as those inside tried to escape. The smell came before they were completely silent. At first it was like roasting meat; first pork, then beef, but that was gone very quickly to be replaced by something close to the smell of burning hair, bubbling fat, and earth, with a hint of charcoal. It was nothing like a cookhouse, nothing like anything else he had smelt before or wanted to smell again.

The flames were molten bright at the centre; billowing into clouds of sunset orange before they turned black at the boiling edges of the inferno. The fire was roaring hot, and they all did as they were told, warmed themselves in front of it, Ingo's limbs singing painfully as warmth returned to them, and he was soon able to remove the scratchy balaclava and his hated helmet. The snow around the sawmill melted in a widening corona. Kroh walked a little closer, to get a bit warmer, and take another picture. The screaming had stopped by now.

"They were partisans," Pop said now. "They had no chance."

"You didn't have to do it," Ingo said, the heat now licking painfully at his face, but he did not turn away from the fire to face Pop.

"If not me, then who? Eckhart, Treacle, Kroh himself? The Ivans were dead as soon as they were put in the sawmill. Besides, one of these days Kroh may very well follow through on one of his threats; so maybe I saved your life, eh?"

"Maybe you did."

"Again."

There was a huge double crack of beams letting go and the burning roof collapsed into the sawmill with a whoosh, and particles of hot ash floated towards them. He knew Pop was right. But he also knew this was wrong. Kroh whistled softly, in his strange non-whistle way, like steam escaping a kettle. Then stopped and shouted: "Pup, here!"

"Best go," Pop said, and Ingo walked over to Kroh, Pop followed him.

"You've a problem with me, right?"

"Not at all, feldwebel."

"Good, good," Kroh said. "Because I think we should get to know each other a little better."

Ingo had nothing to say to that, so merely nodded.

"Good lad. Tell you what I'll do, Pup; let's say we get you off that bike, bloody cold place to be that, and I put you in my Horch Wagon," Kroh said, holding out his hands to warm them in the heat of the blaze. "Not driving, mind; not fair on Treacle that. No, you can be gunner, on the autocannon and the MG 34 – maybe do a little shooting then, right?"

"I'd rather —"

"You and Pop have been angling for a nice warm panzer, haven't you?" Kroh cut in. "An armoured car's the next best thing; nice and toasty in there, especially when the guns are firing."

"But, he's the best rider we —"

"Good, that's settled, then," Kroh said, interrupting Pop, a grin spreading across his face like cracking ice. "Maybe you can show me how to win an Iron Cross, too, eh?"

Right then Ingo felt the rage burn within him, and he recognised it for what it was. He did not want that again. Ever. Ingo Six took a deep cold breath, then he turned and walked away from the burning building.

**

Near Coronel Pringles, Buenos Aires Province. December 1951

He kept his foot flat to the floor. There was a bend to the right approaching, more of a kink really, lined on either side with brutal dry stone walls, jagged with menace. They had practised on this stretch before and Ingo remembered it. It was like music, play it once or twice and it would stick, the same with a piece of road. He knew that Carlo would be flexing his leg in the passenger seat, looking for a brake that wasn't there, but he also knew he could take this corner without lifting his right foot. It was just a matter of stealing a little space from the inside of the turn ...

He had no idea how they were doing in this race. Carlo said he didn't need to know, but also said there was no way they could win the Mil Millas, and it was unlikely they would place highly. All that mattered was that they beat Otero. Ingo had kept his foot hard down for the first part of the race, on the asphalt south from Buenos Aires; through and past towns like Las Flores, Cachari, Azul, Chillar – where the whole town had come out to watch and cheer as the local car came through – Benito Juárez, and Tres Arroyos, the sun rising to their left and half-baking them through the morning. Some way beyond Tres Arroyos they had reached the second section of the one-thousand mile course, where the road turned north east. They were now somewhere near a place called Coronel Pringles, sheep country, the grasslands scattered with the animals, little maggots munching on the green lettuce of the land.

The surface was not paved here, they had left that far behind them, but it was not as rough as it was in other places and Ingo had kept the speedometer needle nailed to one-hundred-and-twenty kilometres-per-hour for a little while now, checking the other gauges, water temperature and oil pressure, every minute or so. He guided the car with his fingertips, in tune with it as it floated across the surface of the rattle-top road, which etched a caramel-coloured groove in this land of pale fields. The engine roared strong and true, the stripped-out body reverberated to it and the road surface, buzzing electrically. He could feel it through his piano fingers, through his seat, through his right foot, which sang with the pins and needles of the speeding, and living, machine. The car smelt of hot oil and hot steel, and the sweat from its two occupants, because with the afternoon sun beating down on them it was like an oven inside the Ford. The kink was closer, now; but Ingo kept his foot pressed firmly on the accelerator.

He caught the nervous movement of Carlo's right leg in his peripheral vision, as he had expected, but now he was at the turn, a caress of fingers on the leather-covered rim of the wheel, pinching a little from the inside of the road, feeling the kick of a small stone – nothing that could do damage – and taking a deep, deep breath. He did not drive the car through on the throttle, for there was no throttle left. It was all used up. Instead he flicked the steering slightly, and he felt the grip go in each tyre, the rears just before the fronts, so there was a minute correction on the wheel, and then the car was in a four wheel skid, drifting through the turn like a gull cutting through a breeze. He felt the brush of the tyres over the loose surface through his fingers, the thrill of it like pure music in his soul.

They were out of the turn in an instant, and Ingo let go of the breath he had held, sensing Carlo do the same, then seeing his right leg unstiffen through the corner of his eye, before he let out a wild *whoop* that Ingo could clearly hear over the racing engine and the shaking chassis. Ingo knew that it was in turns like these that he would make up the time. Never let the momentum drop, that's what Pop had always said, whether it's by lifting off the gas or sliding around too much, you must not lose momentum, every pfennig of it counts – for the interest from those saved pennies builds on the next straight.

The cars had been sent out at 15-second intervals, and without really counting them off Ingo was aware that they had passed many, some on the road, some by the side of the road, a black Buick far from the road, lying on its roof, one wheel still slowly spinning. The starting times were decided by past results, and so Otero had started just a little way ahead of them, because he had not taken part in many Turismo Carretera races. Carlo was leaning forward now, peering through the dust cloud kicked up by the car ahead. Ingo could see it was a blue Chevrolet, the same make and colour as the car Otero drove.

They could not tell for sure, and on such straight and flat – if broken – roads, there was little that Ingo could do to reel the other car in. But an old soldier knows patience – the lesson that had been the hardest for Ingo Six to learn – and so he settled in, the accelerator still jammed to the bulkhead as the car kicked and bucked, buzzed and shook, and roared and rattled. There were some corners, though, like a long S-bend near the village of Santa Maria, where he was able to push the Ford to its very limit in a pair of four-wheel drifts, shaving the dry and grassy, swishing, edge of the roadway at the exit of each of the two turns, before changing up to top in a smooth Swiss watch tick of a gearshift.

Even though there were few corners like these on this stretch, Ingo made each one count, and soon they seemed closer. The sun was to the right of them now, high in the sky, washing out the green of the pampas, turning it silver-white. Ingo saw Carlo take a time check with his wristwatch as the car in front passed a squat white kilometre post – it was now undoubtedly blue, they could see – and then he held up a hand and spread his fingers three times, showing a gap of fifteen seconds. A little later, as they passed the turnoff for Pasman, he did the same; the dust was not so bad on this stretch and they had the distant blue Chevy in view all the time now. The gap was now thirteen seconds. The other driver was quick. But then, as Pop had often told him, anyone can be quick when the roads are straight.

It went on like this for an hour or so. They passed some other cars as they continued to head north-west, one of which had crashed and was now ablaze, its crew safe. It smelt like Kursk, burning paint, rubber and steel, and for a moment Ingo felt the bile rise within him, and his tinnitus intensify, but they were soon past it and he once again concentrated on the blue car ahead of him.

At Trenque Lauquen the route turned hard right, and beyond that it started to snake a little, and they closed up a bit more. When the car in front was forced to slow for a tight corner, so that its right flank was in view, Ingo could see clearly it really was Otero, as the Chevrolet was sign-written in the big white letters of one of Argentina's largest potato exporters: *Varela*. Carlo punched the air in delight. They had beaten him, for the simple reason that they had caught him, after starting behind. The race was against the clock, as much as it was against the other drivers, and Ingo knew he would have maybe a minute or more over the other man now. But he also knew that that would not be enough, not for him, not for Carlo. Racers race.

They began to eat slowly into the blue Chevy's lead. Taking a second from him every two kilometres, the lowering sun and the dust making vision a problem, so that sometimes Ingo would have to hold his right hand up to shield his eyes from the glare. Soon they were so close that the cars seemed to be drawn together, as if they were giant magnets, and Ingo sensed the moment when Otero recognised the Rossi car in the mirror, for at that very second, as the car was being pitched into a medium turn, Otero overdid it, his car sliding wildly, before snapping back in line as he recovered it. It was a good save, but it would have cost him time.

Over the next few kilometres Ingo inched closer, never getting a corner even slightly wrong, keeping it clean and sliding only when he needed to; like in to the tighter corners, where he would flick the car away from the direction of travel, kicking the tail out, then the other way, so that it seemed to swim like a pike in the shallows. It helped to slow the car, and he found that it also helped him turn in. *Sometimes* spectacular is the right way, as Pop had also once told him.

Otero did not know this technique. Most of his racing had been on the European-style asphalt park tracks and street circuits, in single seat racing cars bought by his father, and when Dad's money had run out, by Varela himself. It was where his hopes and dreams lay. He had not driven fast on Russian snow and ice; how many had? Here that gave Ingo an advantage, he realised. Ingo followed the other car through a ford, slowing just enough, so that waves of water rushed by on either side of the car, before he chased Otero's Chevy out of the crossing, rear wheels spinning, the tail kicking out in the muddy ground on the other side of the ford. They gained a couple more seconds here as Otero's car had fishtailed for longer – just perhaps because his mirror was turning red with the Ford V8 that was beginning to fill it.

Now Ingo was close. Very close. In the dust it was not always easy to see a car behind, so the accepted way to let someone know you wanted to get by was a gentle tap on the rear bumper. Ingo allowed the round front of the Ford to close up with the trunk of the Chevy, and then the bumpers, made from old leaf springs, kissed softly; a dull ding, but nothing more, as Ingo had judged it perfectly – Otero would feel it as a polite tap on the back. But Otero did not politely move aside; also the accepted way.

Ingo tried again, then again, a little harder the third time, so that the hit of it caused an optical illusion, making it look like both cars had bounced apart – the blue Chevrolet shimmying on the loose surface a little as Otero deftly held it. On the next attempt Otero was ready; he braked suddenly, forcing Ingo to lift off the throttle sharply, the abrupt shift of the weight to the front of the car causing the back end to go light, then snap out. Ingo corrected the vicious kick of the tail with an armful of opposite lock, then a rapid squeeze of half throttle to drive out of the skid.

He was soon on the rear of the Chevy again, keeping back 20 metres so as to give him space to accelerate should he spot a way through. Ingo glanced at Carlo, who shook his head, then patted the air with an open hand, making it clear that Ingo should slow. If they kept Otero in sight they had him. Time for cool heads. But it was also clear now that Ingo and the Ford were faster than Otero and the Chevy. It did not take all his concentration, all his being, to drive now that he was stuck behind Otero, and Ingo wanted to – needed to – feel that again. He had been dead a long time. Now he just had to live life when he could.

Both cars were now closing on another racing car, a yellow Chevrolet sedan with bold red signwriting, its body golden in the lowering sunlight. It was not so dusty here, and as they approached it Ingo could see that the car was crabbing, its rear suspension damaged, its race over, the back of the car swinging out to overtake its front, as if it was on castors. The driver would be trying to limp to the next town, La Dorita, to fix it. He would be concentrating hard on keeping his car as straight as possible. Ingo had looked well ahead, saw that the road turned sharp right and cut down a bank into another ford. The Ford and Chevy were closing quickly on the crippled yellow car. Ingo saw a chance.

As the three cars approached the sharp right hand turn the yellow car pulled to the right to let the other two through before the corner. Otero went for the gap on the left, which would give him a clean line in to the tight turn, from the left of the approaching road. But Ingo stayed right as he braked and double-declutched down the 'box at the same time as blipping the throttle, using the heel and toe technique. Then, as the yellow Chevrolet directly in front of his car slowed, he eased off his brake. There was a tinny crunch, not much of a hit. But then Ingo put on a little more power, enough to push the yellow car on, on past the entrance to the corner – and to block the way into the turn for Otero, who was forced to suddenly turn left, overshooting the entrance to the sharp right-hander.

The yellow car skidded to a standstill at the entrance to the turn, but there was just room for Ingo to nip by on the inside as he had planned, snagging his wing mirror against the fender of the yellow Chevy and shattering the glass as he did so. He powered down the slippery slope, slowed a little for the ford, and then eased the car through, great curls of water rising up on either side of it, waves of silver-flecked chocolate that lapped and splashed against the side windows. In the rear view mirror he could see that Otero was reversing the blue Chevy from behind the yellow Chevy that blocked its way. Carlo's laughter was almost as loud as the roaring engine as Ingo accelerated out the other side of the ford, the rear wheels spinning arabesques on to the muddy ground.

An hour later and they were alone. Alone with the throaty gnash of the V8, and the road that sang its song through the shuddering steering wheel, the drumming beat of the loose gravel against the floorpan its accompaniment. There was a sign for a Mil Millas fuel stop ahead, which meant this must be Bragado, and Ingo soon saw the blue, white and black YPF branding above the petrol station. There was a checkpoint here, too, and he slowed the car to a halt by the shelter that was made from what looked like an unfinished tent, one of its sides missing. The sun was red and low now, its rays painting the pampas grass a shimmering silver. There were plenty of spectators here, all shouting and cheering, much more than anywhere before, and Ingo assumed they had had lots of wine and Quilmes as they had watched the cars check in and out through the late afternoon. He could use a cold beer himself, he thought, as he brought the Ford V8 stock car to a stop.

Carlo opened the side window, letting in a strong smell of sun-hot grass and just a little dust, and handed the race official the timing card. Then he started to talk to him. In Italian. The man looked a little surprised, but then he answered in Italian, too. The man was grinning manically, a grin that was mirrored on Carlo's face for a moment, before he saw that Ingo was watching him and then it dropped, as if his lips had turned to stone.

"What was that all about?" Ingo said, as he drove the car in to the refuelling area.

"Oh, know him from way back. Best to laugh it out when you can't remember a man's name, eh?" Carlo said.

"Why Italian?"

"Good to practice, when one gets the chance."

Ingo parked the car up close to their fuel dump and they set to their well drilled procedure, Carlo filling the tanks with an unlit cheroot in his mouth – the air was heavy with the reek of spilled gasoline – as Ingo checked over the Ford. There was a little time as it took a while to refuel, and so he drank some water and then placed the palms of his hands against the warm steel of the machine, feeling it breathe as it ticked and pinged while the hard-worked panels contracted. He saw Otero also arrive for refuelling, but the other driver made a point of not looking his way.

There were quite a few spectators here, penned back by a rope cordon which was guarded by local policemen. Ingo was surprised by how enthusiastically they had been welcomed. Bragado seemed like a friendly place, and he made a note to perhaps look at moving here should he ever need to change addresses fast. But then he realised that a friendly place might be the last thing he needed in those circumstances.

"Signor Hohberg," someone shouted, "an autograph?"

Ingo ignored it, then spotted a photographer with a press armband and turned away just as the flash lit up the dusk.

"Carlo!" someone else shouted.

"Ingo, take this, please," Carlo said, almost ordered. Ingo took over filling the tank as Carlo walked towards the other man, out of earshot. There was talk, laughter; Carlo seemed popular in Bragado. The last of the petrol glugged in to the second fuel tank. He was beginning to feel the effects of so long at the wheel now, a dead, lead-like weight in his arms and shoulders, a treacherous back-stabbing ache at the base of his spine. His tinnitus sang and was giving him a headache. That was the problem with stopping.

Carlo was back, climbing in to the passenger seat.

"He seemed in good spirits," Ingo said.

"Who?"

"Your friend."

"Oh," Carlo said, after a moment's hesitation. "A mutual acquaintance has put his car on its back; he's okay, but his pride is bruised. He has a lot of pride, so it must have been a lot of crash." Carlo paid a little more attention than usual to checking the timing card while Ingo fired the Ford up.

As Ingo left the fuel stop the spectators cheered and clapped. He was not sure that that had been the case at other stops. In fact, he could not really remember anyone cheering that much for them during this long race, even when they had driven through Chillar. He took second crisply and quickly, and wound the V8 up into third as they drove out of Bragado.

Ingo drove five kilometres or so out of the town, then slowed, changing down a gear. He was off the throttle now and so he could hear Carlo as he said, his voice still raised because the body of the car still sounded like a percussion section as it flexed and popped: "What is it; engine?"

Ingo did not answer, just brought the car to a crunching halt in the deeper gravel by the side of the road. As he did so another car flashed by, kicking up small stones which peppered the bodywork like a volley of rifle fire on the armour of a Panzer IV. He switched off and the movement of the fuel in the full tanks as it settled sounded like a sigh.

"What is it, Ingo?"

"You're as bad at lying as Catalina is at cooking, Carlo."

Carlo blew out breath sharply, then seemed to melt back into his seat. "That's true," he said.

"Tell me."

Carlo faced him, smiled broadly, and then laughed as he said: "We're leading the race!"

Ingo felt the thrill of the words like electricity, coursing through his fingertips then the rest of him, but even as he enjoyed it it was turning to lead in his veins. Winning was the thing he craved, but the last thing he could allow. He could not have his picture in the newspapers. Carlo knew this.

"So, what now?" Carlo said, after some long seconds of silence.

"How far ahead are we?"

"I doubt we are ahead, not now," Carlo said. "It was not a big lead." Then he was quiet, staring out over the pampas. Another car flashed by, and Ingo watched as it shrunk in size with distance, listened to the dwindling rip of its V8.

"I have never asked you what you're hiding from, my friend," Carlo said. "And I will not ask you. But I know you have not hurt anyone; you could not even find it in you to smack that idiot in the cantina. I know people, Ingo, and you're a good man – and a great racing driver, goddammit!"

"That ape, in Bar el Descanso? He just didn't push hard enough," Ingo said. "I will tell you something; like every car, like every corner, every man has his limit."

"Not you. Not now!"

"I will tell Varela I slowed," Ingo said.

"You think he'll believe that? He will think my car has broken."

"I'm sorry, Carlo," Ingo said. "I can't help that."

"Just drive, my friend, please – you were born for it! My God, you're faster than a bullet!"

"No-one is faster than a bullet, Carlo," Ingo said, as another car passed. He watched it go by, smelt the fumes from its exhaust over the flinty tang of baked ground. Then he said: "People must not know that I'm alive, Carlo, it is as simple as that. I am dead, and I must stay dead. This was a mistake."

"You know that last car that passed us?"

"I know, Otero." With that Ingo turned the engine over again, it caught almost at once, and then he selected first and accelerated away.

"It was good, my friend. While it lasted," Carlo shouted over the gathering rumble of the engine, shaking his head, and because his voice was raised Ingo could not tell if he was angry or sad, or simply being stoic.

Ingo said nothing, just concentrated on shifting early, and driving well within himself. It left space in his head for memories, for pain. This was the second hardest thing he had done in his entire life.

*

Chillar. December 1951

El Gráfico came with the groceries. It seemed absurd to Ingo, now, that he had ever arranged to have his shopping delivered. He now saw that he had long lost sight of who he was, and who he could not be. The artificially coloured picture on the front of the magazine was the head and shoulders of a football player, in the blue and white stripes of the national team, with a pencil moustache like Carlo's. Ingo dumped the brown paper bag on the table and an apple rolled out of it, rumbling softly along the table-top before it fell on the floor with a bump. He left it there, as he quickly flicked through the pages to the report on the Mil Millas, the noise of the delivery van rattling and bumping down the rough track in the background. The low morning sun threw a hard-edged crucifix of window-frame shadow across the kitchen.

In the race report there were pictures of Juan Gálvez in his winning Ford V8 and a photograph of the second-placed driver, Hector Otero, being congratulated by his sponsor, Esteban Varela. That result had twisted the knife for Carlo, and they had driven back from Buenos Aries in silence. Ingo had not seen him for a week now. Otero had done much better than expected in the race, no one had thought a circuit racer would show so well on the Mil Millas. Ingo turned to the next page.

It was what he had feared. For so long.

The picture was from just before the start of the race. He leant against the car, looking happy and relaxed. Looking like he had looked before; anyone who knew him then would know him now, even with the beard that, with his head bowed as it was in the picture, almost brushed the top of his chest. Ingo was sure of it.

There was a caption beneath the picture: *Enrique Hohberg starred in a Ford V8 prepared and co-driven by past Gran Premio del Sur winner Carlo Rossi, even leading the race for one hour before a stop to fix a puncture.* The puncture had been Carlo's idea. Varela could not blame his car, and perhaps not his driver, for that; though the fact that they had been sitting in the red Ford and not changing a wheel when Otero had passed them would not have helped. Varela had not come to see Carlo after the race.

Ingo put the magazine on the table. Maria walked through from the bedroom. She was in her work uniform, a pair of white French knickers and cheap perfume – the slightly citrus smell of which Ingo liked, but only because it reminded him of her. She stopped to pick up the apple from the floor, the silk stretching tight across her behind. He almost forgot about the picture in *El Gráfico* for a moment.

"What's this," she said, putting the apple on the table and looking at the black and white image in the magazine. "You're famous!"

"You think so?"

She nodded. "Eggs?"

Maria had told him once that she had a hard face and a soft body, and that's why she had become a whore. But he liked her for her soft heart, really. It was true, that her face was a little too chiselled for her to ever be thought beautiful, and it was lined with the long nights of her profession now, too, but her body was firm, rather than soft, though her breasts were just beginning to sag after a long life of staying up late looking perky. He had only ever wanted two things from Maria, the obvious, and lessons in Castellano Spanish. She had only ever wanted his cash. They had both, he thought, got so much more.

"No, I have to go," he said.

"Into town?" she said, still looking at the picture in the magazine. But he knew she understood.

"You can stay here, if you want," he said. "There's no rent to pay; the house belongs to me." With that he went through to the bedroom and pulled the small suitcase he had bought long ago in Genoa from under the bed.

"The picture's not clear, you know," Maria shouted from the kitchen. "It's all beard, and you cannot really see your eyes."

He flicked open the latches and started to pack the case with a few shirts and some underwear. Then he took his thirty-eight from the bedside cabinet and placed it in the case.

"What's that for?" She had come through from the kitchen and was leaning against the door frame, her breasts hanging at a slight angle to her body; something about it appealed to him, a part of him at least. He wondered if he had time to say goodbye properly, decided not, and went back to packing. He did not answer the question.

He took his Red Cross passport from the drawer in which he kept it. It would be out of date very soon, and useless for travel outside of Argentina anyway, but it was all he had to prove that he was who he wasn't. Then he stood on one of the chairs to reach the box on top of the cupboards. It was coated with dust and as he took it down some of it was disturbed, causing him to sneeze. He took the hat from the box; it still smelt a little of that time, he thought, of ash and death, but he ignored that. He ran his finger along the seam inside the fedora to feel for the small stones.

"I've never seen you wear a hat?"

"I never wear a hat," Ingo said, putting it on. "You'll look after Zündapp, yes?"

"That evil thing? No way I'm going anywhere near that damned horse!" she said.

He laughed.

"What will I tell Carlo?" she said.

"I shouldn't think you'll see much of him, I've rather let him down, I'm afraid. But if you do, just say I've gone to a place where my beard will fit in; think he'll understand."

"How long, Enrique?" she said, and he saw that tears were brimming in her eyes; her hard face suddenly soft and vulnerable. He felt an iron fist of doubt expand within his chest. But he turned away without answering, walking out of the bedroom and through to the kitchen, then out of the door, throwing the suitcase into the rear of the Jeep.

***

Warsaw. February 1942

Lidka pushed the baby carriage under the new wooden footbridge, its body rattling as it bumped along the smooth cobbles. She could hear the thumps of boots on the boards high above her – the bridge was wide and more than double the height of the walls and was reached by two stairways, one in the Small Ghetto and one in the Large Ghetto. The Jews who used the footbridge were fenced in and were not allowed to stop on the bridge. The bridge had replaced the gates that had connected Żelazna Street at the junction with Chłodna.

The children had stopped coming, for the food she had continued to take to them, and she supposed they had died. She had heard there was typhus in the Ghetto; it had been the Nazi's lying excuse for it in the first place, so she thought that sickly ironic. But most, she knew, died from starvation. Some were simply killed. So the children had stopped coming for the food, but people had not stopped coming for Lidka. There was a new organization, called Żegota, part of the underground, set up to help the Jews in the Ghetto. How they had known where to find her she did not know. How they had persuaded her to help them she also – still – did not really know. All she knew was that there were those that could find other uses for a woman who was so often seen with a pram, and so she had other work now, heart-breaking work. And terrifying work.

The baby in the pram was crying. It would not be crying for what it should be crying for – even Lidka felt like crying for that – it would be crying because of the cold, the bumpy ride, but also hunger. Lidka could not imagine what it took for those women to give up their babies. They knew it was the only way they could save the lives of their children, but they also must have known they would almost certainly never see them again.

She pushed the pram along Chłodna, one wheel squeaked and another one, which now had a chunk missing from its solid rubber tyre, made a thumpity-thump sound as it rolled across the iron-like cobbles. The Ghetto stank like a rubbish dump. A pall of decay hung over it and the wind would often lift the stench of disease and death over the high barbed wire-topped brick walls. It was bitterly cold, and the gusts that carried the odious smells of the Ghetto funnelled down the wide street like chilled water filling a conduit. The wind carried tiny daggers of icy snow, which chipped at the skin on Lidka's face. Older snow sat in dirty piles where it had been cleared, like crouching corpses in grubby shrouds. A number 16 tram rattled past and the baby cried a little louder.

The baby had been asleep, with the help of a little phenobarbital, when she had met the carpenter in what they called the evangelical enclave, a little isthmus of 'Aryan' buildings, like the Calvinist church and parish house, the Evangelical Hospital, the Działyński Palace and some others, that overlooked the misery beyond the wall, bulging in to the boundary of the Ghetto. The carpenter was allowed into the Ghetto, he had official work to do, was employed by the Germans. He went in with tools in his long box, came back with a baby in the same. It was fear of the diseases rife within the Ghetto that stopped the Jewish Ghetto Police thoroughly searching those who had to work there when they left, and also the simple fact that they were leaving and not arriving and would therefore not be smuggling in food. Still, it was an extremely risky undertaking, for the carpenter; the penalty for helping Jews was death. It was the risk Lidka also took.

They managed to keep the babies quiet when they smuggled them out, with the drug, but they could not give them too high a dose, or that in itself would kill them. So it was then up to Lidka to take over, and she had been a calming mother to twenty-eight babies now. It was her job to take the infant to a Żegota safe house in the Old Town, then the Ursuline Sisters would take it and its uncertain new life would begin. A certain death avoided.

She had not spoken to the carpenter, the fewer connections made the better for everyone. He had merely placed the baby in the pram and she had walked up Okopowa and turned in to Chłodna and now the baby carriage was rattling away from the footbridge as she pushed it towards Mirowski Square. She had never been inside the Ghetto, so she did not know what drove mothers to give up their children. Sarah said she wanted to visit the Ghetto. She had no fear, that one, and Lidka worried that one day she would go too far. She also envied her, for having no fear, because for Lidka fear felt like being pregnant again; it was a part of her, a living thing. But while there was fear, there was also pride.

And, now that she saw what the Germans were doing, she also felt shame, for her naivety, with Ingo. But if it had been a mistake to sleep with a German, she could not regret that – even when she heard the worst of their crimes in the Ghetto and elsewhere – because without that there would have been no Freddy. She no longer believed Ingo would return, wondered if she truly ever had, and she no longer believed she wanted him to return. Jósef was Freddy's father now.

She had planned to send an anonymous message to the PO Box in Lisbon, addressed to the pseudonym on the letter she had received from Jósef, but the nameless Żegota woman who passed on her instructions had told her this way was no longer reliable, or safe, from Warsaw at least. She hoped that there might be some other way to get word to him. It now seemed more important than ever that he should know as soon as possible. Now that she was sure that this was the right – the only – path she and Freddy could take.

"Halt!"

He was SS. Bored, possibly. Dangerous, probably. He looked in the pram at the crying baby, then at her. She felt her fear squirm within her. The SS man, in a field grey greatcoat and cap, once again looked in to the pram.

"It's cold, for a baby to be outside?" he said.

"There is no one I can leave ... um, him ... with, and we need to buy our food ration," she said, hoping he had not picked up on the pause when she had realised she did not know whether the baby was a boy or a girl. Luckily, a kennkarte was only issued at the age of 15, so he would not ask for that.

"He has red hair?" he said, looking up at the blonde tresses that strayed from beneath Lidka's scarf.

"His father has red hair."

"Yes?" the man said. She expected he would now ask where his father was, but he did not; there were many missing fathers in Warsaw these days.

"You speak good German, Volksdeutsche?"

"No, not Volksdeutsche. Polish," she said, deliberately clumsy this time. He seemed disappointed with that, disappointed that she was sub-human. Disgusted even. Perhaps he had been hoping for more from her. But he said nothing more, as he took one last look at the Jewish baby, who had now stopped crying, then walked on towards the footbridge over Chłodna.

She pushed the pram on, its thumpity-thumping tyre mocking her heartbeat as she pushed faster, far too fast, she knew, but she could not help it, she pushed on until she was close to the big Mirowska Hall market buildings. A tram rang its bell, as if it was an alarm, and clattered down the middle of the square. Fear played its vilest trick then, and she was sick before she could find an alley to throw up in, acidy bile burning her throat, sweat soaking her forehead despite the icy air. It took her some long moments to collect herself. No one had come to help her, they had just walked past. Some looked the other way. Then she heard sharp footsteps.

"Hello, Miss Wadalowska."

*

Near Zhizdra, Soviet Union. February 1942

Ingo juggled the stick grenades. The people whose home this was sat on the floor in the corner. They did not complain, they just kept quiet. They were like discarded ornaments, Ingo thought. It was easy to forget about them after a little while. Kroh did not even think of them as people, and in a way that was their good fortune. Ingo hoped they had the good sense to keep still, to keep quiet. The rare order from Divisional HQ was that they should not – this time – be turfed out of their homes; and even Kroh would think twice about disobeying a command from the top.

Kroh had found vodka, lots of it. There had been a deal at the railyard in Zhizdra. Ingo and Pop had – as always – taken the risks, and taken the Panje horse and sleigh into town. Kroh had traded morphine for the vodka. Not their morphine, not even he was that greedy, but some that had fallen from the back of a Hanomag, as the saying went. He had sold most of the vodka on, but had kept some back. He was in a good mood now, because of the vodka.

The last armoured car had broken down, and had had to be abandoned, almost as soon as Ingo had taken his place at the gun. That would have to wait until spring now – which wasn't so far away, Kroh liked to remind him – and the melting of the snow, when the front would become fluid again. They had been put to work protecting the railway line and they had only fought partisans, mostly from a distance. Ingo had finally fired his rifle; but it had just made a noise, nothing more. There was a small child in the cuddle of civilians in the corner; Ingo winked at her, as he juggled, and she smiled back.

Kroh sat on one of the rickety wooden beds and half-whistled *Erika*, stopping every now and then to chew on a raw onion or take a swig of vodka, his mountain infantry cap with its edelweiss badge pushed back high on his head. Ingo concentrated on juggling the three stick grenades, it was a trick of his when he was bored, which was all the time in Russia he was finding. They were not primed, and he rarely dropped one anyway, so nobody cared. Ingo had not drunk so much. He did not enjoy drinking with Kroh. The child was mesmerised by the juggling, and her eyes were no longer swimming with fear.

The single room house was in a tiny settlement near one of the lakes to the south east of the town. It had a fire in one wall, but the chimney was inadequate and the air was smoky, the ceiling black. No one minded the smoke, for it was burning cold outside, and to most of them the fire was even more welcome than the vodka. There were few possessions in the rickety hut, just the row of four skeletal beds, and a rough table, on which there was a clutter of German issue mess tins, from which they had eaten tinned beef and barley with carrots, along with some crispbreads. The single window looked like a piece of ice, and let in little light, but there was a lamp that burnt a rancid-smelling oil which sat above the fireplace.

There was a sharp knock at the door, and Eckhart and Treacle reached for their rifles – those two always the most jumpy – while the others hid the vodka bottles under coats and chairs and Ingo stopped juggling the grenades. Pop opened the door to reveal Leutnant Schirmer, shivering and stamping snow off his boots. There was another officer too, and although his insignia and rank badges were hidden beneath a long leather coat and a fur gilet on top of that, he had the air of brass about him and so they all stood to attention, and saluted. There was a Totenkopf badge, skull and crossbones, on his high peaked cap.

"Stand easy," Schirmer said, and the other man nodded, as they both walked in. They all relaxed a little, though Ingo noticed that the peasants seemed to push themselves further into the corner of the room, trying to merge with the darkness, squashing themselves into shadow. The child looked scared once again.

"Feldwebel Kroh, this is Standartenführer Richter of the Waffen SS," Schirmer said. Kroh seemed impressed with that, and he puffed out his chest a little. "He has a task for you and your men; it's … important." The way Schirmer said it made it sound as if he wasn't so sure it was, but Ingo could see he was also enjoying being able to order Kroh about without fear of insubordination. "His car has run out of petrol, a few kilometres up the road to the railway. It's a Horch, here are the keys." He put them on the table. "Take some men, and bring it back to Major Brack's billet, you know it? In the large house at the top of the village by the junction with the Suchinitschi road. Standartenführer Richter will be Major Brack's guest tonight, so just park it in the barn behind the house."

Kroh nodded, then after a pause said: "Yes, sir."

"I want *you* to see it is done, personally, understood?" Schirmer added, a malicious little smirk briefly snaking across his lips.

"Understood, sir," Kroh said, but he looked at Standartenführer Richter as he said it. "I'll get on to it right away."

"Very good, Feldwebel," Richter said. "I'm relying on you."

"Oh, you can always rely on Feldwebel Kroh, Sir," Schirmer said, as he led the SS officer out and Pop closed the door behind them.

"Arse!" spat Kroh. "Well, you heard the little prick, right? Pop, Pup; get a can of petrol and go find the good standartenführer's car."

"But he said you were to do it," Pop said, though there was already resignation in his voice. Ingo didn't mind so much, the inactivity was almost as numbing as the cold, to him.

"I'm busy," Kroh said, then took a pull on the vodka bottle, gasping ecstatically at the hit of it. He laughed at that, and Eckhart and Treacle laughed with him, though the latter was out of the line of sight of Kroh and so shrugged as he did so. Ingo understood.

Ingo took the photograph of Lidka that had been propped up against a gasmask canister and slipped it in to the breast pocket of his tunic. Him and Pop then stuffed their tunics with old newspaper then pulled on jumpers and civilian coats, then Pop his greatcoat and Ingo his motorcyclist coat; then gloves, woollen hats and helmets on top of that.

"How about a bottle, for the road?" Pop said, as Ingo took the keys off the table. Kroh tossed a half-full bottle of vodka at him, which Pop caught, although it almost slipped out of his gloved hands. Ingo realised that Kroh had regretted giving Pop the bottle as soon as he'd thrown it, but it was too late now, he would not go back on a decision. That would show weakness. Pop and Ingo went to leave.

"Aren't we forgetting something, Pup?" Kroh said, glancing at the rifle Ingo had left barrel down by the window. Ingo nodded, to a little laughter from the others, then slung the Kar 98 over his shoulder. Pop was already carrying his MP 40, he was seldom without it.

A little later they trudged through fresh snow. They had taken a shortcut which they thought should lead them to the newly cleared road a little further along. They carried a petrol can between them, of the sort Ingo had heard the Tommies called a jerrycan. It was designed with thee handles, so that by using the one in the middle a single soldier could carry the can when it was empty, while if it was full two soldiers could take an outer handle each. But even between them it was hard work carrying the half-full can through the deep snow, and beneath the many dirty layers he wore Ingo was sweating, while they both gasped for breath, though that did not stop Pop from sucking on a Reemtsma.

It was afternoon, and it would be dark in three hours or so, so they did not stop often, just once or twice to take a breather. The sky was a very pale grey that almost seemed to merge with the snow. There was nothing else, just silence, an iron silence, cold and hard. There had been no word of partisans in this area for a while, but there was often no word before they hit, and Pop kept one hand on the pistol grip of his sub machine gun.

"You still think we're winning?" Ingo asked; it was not the sort of question to pose when Kroh was around.

"No doubt about that," Pop said, between panting breaths. "But then again, now that the Americans are involved, well maybe it'll take just a little bit longer."

"That's a pity," Ingo said.

"Don't worry, you're still young, there's plenty of racing left in you."

"Not much patience, though," Ingo said.

"No, you've never had much of that,' Pop said. "But you've self-control, I'll give you that."

"You reckon?"

"Sure I do. I've never, ever, ever, seen you lose your cool. Not once, however hard that bastard Kroh pushes you, even when I think he's gone too far, when I can see it in your eyes that he's gone too far, you never, ever snap."

"I just try to avoid confrontation, makes life easier," Ingo said, with a smile.

"You try to avoid confrontation, you say? And yet here you are in the middle of the biggest bloody confrontation in history," Pop laughed.

"Well, I hadn't banked on this when I joined up."

"What had you banked on?"

"Motorcycles."

There was a sharp cry of a crow, seeming to mock Ingo.

"And now you're to be a gunner in an armoured car, with our pal Kroh, eh? Might need a little rage then, Pup."

"Never seen the point in rage," Ingo said.

"Well, everyone loses their temper, at some time," Pop said.

"I don't," Ingo said. "Not ..."

"Not?"

"Nothing."

Pop nodded, sagely: "Long fuse, that's what it is. Long fuse."

"You think so?"

"You know what they say about a long fuse?"

"No."

"A fuse is long so as to give people the time to get away from the bang. Because the bang is big." Pop was panting between his words and Ingo could not tell how serious he was, so he merely shook his head, and laughed. "But never mind eh? At least it will be warmer in an armoured car."

He did not like to think about the armoured car and the spring that would soon be here. He remembered the day near Rudnevo, when Kroh had made the decision.

"Since we're talking psychology," Ingo said.

"We are?"

"Tell me, the saw-mill. You didn't have to?"

Pop said nothing, just trudged on, his cigarette clamped between his lips. He was silent as he walked. And then he stopped suddenly, forcing Ingo to stop too, the fuel sloshing inside in the can they held between them. They put the steel container down and it sank into the snow.

"Someone has to," Pop now said.

"You've said that before. But why you?"

"Because I'm someone. Though I will admit this; it's not easy. But then I have help."

"Help?"

"The Stuka tablets," Pop said. "They can help make you see things clearer, I find."

"Clearer?"

"Some things just need to be done, no point worrying about it. Get them done and the war will be over sooner, I reckon. A little bit of Pervitin makes it easier, that's all. Makes me feel braver, too, and sometimes you only really need to *feel* brave to kid yourself you are."

"I thought they only kept you awake?"

"There is that, too," Pop said. "And I don't doubt they'll always keep me awake, one way or another."

Ingo yawned. "Maybe I should take them, too?" he said.

"No, I don't think they're for you," Pop said.

"I'd rather sleep, anyway."

Pop laughed, then said. "Look Ingo, I know it was wrong. But the way I see it, I'll save it all up, go to church and confess it all in the end, eh?" he said, with a laugh. "Then that's me sorted."

"That easy?"

Pop shrugged.

"I thought the sign of the cross thing was just a joke?"

"It's all just a joke," Pop said. "C'mon, let's find this bloody car."

They scrunched on until they came to a tall snowbank which marked where a panzer fitted with a snow plough had cleared the road the day before – this road was one of the few which had escaped being chewed up in the autumn mud and it was in quite good condition. More snow had fallen since, but as they slithered down the bank Ingo could see that it was not too deep, and it would be easy and – more to the point – fun, to drive on this road, even in a Horch 901, the most common model from that manufacturer to be found here, but more of a truck than a car. They walked on a little further, their boots squeaking in the fresh snow, before they came around a bend. They both stopped. And stared.

Even with a thin coating of snow, which made it look like a piece of exquisite confectionary, it was clear that this was something very special indeed. The car was long and low, and was made of swoops and curves.

"That's an 853," Pop said, in an almost reverential near whisper. Then he laughed, very loud, the sort of laugh that would have started an avalanche if they had been up a mountain. "What sort of an idiot would bring a car like that to Russia?" he said, shaking his head slowly. They both knew they had come for a Horch, but no one would have expected a Horch like this here.

Despite the heavy can of petrol and the fact that they were tired from the hike across the snow they both ran, and slithered on the slippery surface, to get closer to the Horch. Pop scraped a parabola in the snow that covered the long bonnet when they reached the car to reveal a crescent of bright candy red paint that was dazzling in the bland white of their world.

"What sort of an idiot ...?" Pop said again, but he laughed too. "I suppose he must have shipped it out here by train, maybe he thought he'd be able to drive it through Red Square when the summer comes." He shook his head.

"Must be a big man; to get room on the train to Zhizdra."

"What sort of an idiot ...?" Pop repeated, and then they both started scraping the snow off the car with the excitement of kids unwrapping presents at Christmas. As they worked at this, Pop talked: "Five litres ... One-hundred and twenty horsepower ... Eight cylinders ... This is some car, Pup. Some car."

"Shame we have to take it back to him," Ingo said, staring at the car's beautiful lines; to him it also seemed a shame that such an object should ever be still. This was made for speed, just like Ingo Six.

"No one ever said anything about taking it back straight away, Pup. Besides, there are only so many things I can teach you about driving on a Zündapp or in a Kübelwagen. Let's get this thing fuelled up, then take it for a little spin, shall we?"

Half an hour later and Ingo was alive. It was if he had never been cold, as if he had never been bored. The heater in the car helped with the first, but the second was all down to the pulsating, crackling straight-eight that answered to the soft touch of his right foot on the *H*-embossed steel accelerator pedal. There was little grip, and his every movement had to be delicate. And so he drove the Horch with the nerve endings in his feet and his piano fingers, with which he softly caressed the smooth Bakelite steering wheel.

There was a frozen lake south of Zhizdra, covered in snow, so that it looked like a luxurious white carpet. The cleared road ran alongside it and Pop quickly found a way on to it, through a wood that sheltered a track from snowfalls and then down a shallow, icy bank. He took a slug of vodka and grinned broadly as Ingo drove the Horch on to the lake's surface, the tyres squeaking on the packed snow.

"Don't worry, I've seen a Panzer IV drive across Russian ice, it will hold," Pop said.

But Ingo was not worried about that. Ingo was worried about nothing now, as he got to work carving grand arabesques in the snow covered lake, allowing the car to dance a waltz, controlling it with his fingertips, letting it slide sideways, but never letting it spin, the snow slushing beneath the tyres, the engine purring to Ingo's gentle inputs. He felt as if he was driving a cloud.

"Wonderful, bloody wonderful," Pop said, taking another gulp of vodka. "There is not much more I can teach you pal, so best we get on and win this war and put you in a racing car, eh?" He laughed out loud at that and Ingo laughed with him, the compliment snatching a little at his concentration, so the car looped into a long and lazy spin.

"Come on Ingo, I think that's enough, let's get this beauty back to that idiot standartenführer, shall we? Because I can guarantee one thing; a man will love a car like this more than he will ever love his wife, and I have a feeling he's the jealous type."

"You called me Ingo."

Pop nodded, and smiled.

After a bit of wheel-spin and effort Ingo managed to coax the big car off the ice and back on to the track through the woods and then to the road.

"You know," Pop said. "I've always hankered after one of these. Don't suppose you'd mind if I drove it back, would you?

Ingo did mind. He did not want to stop driving this car. Ever. But he owed his friend much, and so he brought the Horch to a stop and allowed Pop to slide over in to the driver's seat while he jumped out and ran around the front of the car to sit in the passenger seat, taking just a little time to lay his hands on the long bonnet.

It had been a while since Pop had driven anything. He was always willing to let Ingo take the wheel. Ingo thought now that he was a little rusty; and he'd also had quite a bit of vodka. He skimmed a couple of snowbanks with the flowing rear fenders, but the snow was soft and it did no damage. Pop laughed it off.

The road now curved right, then tightened a little. This was the portion they had not walked earlier, because they had cut the long loop of the corner by going through the deep snow.

"See, still got it," Pop said, as the rear stepped out, and then he overcorrected, so it stepped out the other way, then the other, in a lazy fishtail which he *just* about managed to control. The tighter part of the corner was approaching and Pop went in a little too quickly, the front wheels skidding and the front fender filing chips of snow off the bank. But again no damage was done.

"Maybe I should take over," Ingo ventured. "I mean, the vodka ..."

Pop sniffed, shook his head, and turned in to the next bend.

Then Ingo saw it. And he knew they would hit it before Pop had even come off the gas. It was the wreck of a Russian BA-20 armoured car, burnt an oxidised red, only its rear end showing, its nose deep in the snow, sniffing at the depths of a ditch – a bit more solid than a snowbank. Pop was off the throttle now, the car thrown in to a slide, but it was too late.

The Horch hit the rear of the old fashioned fighting machine with a rending crash that was of an altogether different variety to the sugary crunch of snow; this the crunch of soft steel on hard steel, then an almost animal shriek as the long and languid fender on the left of the car was curled back, while the ugly edge of the armoured car's rear wheel-cover cut into the red paintwork with envious malice. The Horch bounced clear of the armoured car, and planted its nose in the opposite snowbank. The engine stalled. Then all was quiet, except for the mocking creak of the badly crinkled fender, which flexed up and down.

"Christ, who put that there!" Pop said, looking in the rear view mirror at the burnt out Russian armoured car.

"Do you think the standartenführer will notice?" Ingo said, as he stepped out of the Horch to look at the damage, but it was more of an ironic statement than a question, and the enormity of the trouble they were in slowly started to dawn on him.

"I said he was an idiot to bring a car like this out here, didn't I?" Pop said, taking a swig from the vodka bottle.

"I suppose he'll understand; I mean, it's slippery?"

Pop rolled his eyes at that. "He's SS, top brass, and I'm guessing this car's his pride and joy." Pop suddenly sounded very sober.

"Do you think it might be warmer, in jail?" Ingo said.

*

Warsaw. February 1942

"You're to call me 'Bullet' now," Andrzej Paczkowski said.

"Bullet?" Lidka shook her head, laughed a little laugh.

"We all have *nom de guerres*. It is safer that way, for family and friends," he said, sharply enough for Lidka to know she had stung him.

"I see you're still painting." She was looking at the black *PW* on the side of a news stand at the edge of the park, the *P* growing out of the middle ascender of the *W*, so that it looked like an anchor. She knew it was already called the *Kotwica*, the anchor, and that it had developed from the *W* that had stood for Wawer. She also knew that it was the mark of the Armia Krajowa, the Home Army, and the symbol of resistance.

"We are still painting, but not me," he said. She had suspected he was in the Home Army, or would be soon, they all had. They had not seen him at the house for some time now and it had been a surprise when he had approached her near the Mirowska Hall market buildings just ten minutes or so ago.

They were in the Saski Garden now. He walked alongside her as if he was the father of the Jewish baby, now asleep in the pram, and with that thought she realised Andrzej now looked rather older than his age of nineteen. She wondered where the years had gone, where the boy had gone. He seemed bigger, too, and looked well fed. The ground here was white and frozen, but someone had cleared the pathways. The naked trees shivered to the cold wind, and she pulled the collar of her winter coat up to shield her cheeks from the icy blast of air that swept through the colonnade of the old Saski Palace at the eastern end of the park. Despite the cold there were other people in the garden, but none sat on the ornate iron benches by the swan lake, probably because they feared they would freeze to them. At the far end of the large garden there was a group of German armoured cars, hatches closed tight, their chugging exhausts almost seeming the reason for the hard, grey sky the fumes bled in to. They walked quickly, Lidka and Andrzej, the squeak and thumpity-thump of the faulty wheel in time to their step.

"Your mother is worried about you, and your father," Lidka said.

"There are many worried parents in Warsaw."

"Sarah, too," Lidka said.

"Sarah? She's a child."

"She's not that much younger than you."

"Age is no longer counted in years, Miss Wadalowska. But you can tell Sarah from me that she needs to stay in the house, it is not only her own life she puts at risk when she strays."

"Shall I tell her something else?"

Andrzej did not answer, and when she turned to look for his reply she saw no change in his hard, proud expression.

"I should be going soon, I need to get this little one to ... well, somewhere safe."

He smiled, at last. "Yes, you're right not to tell me where; you know what you're about, eh teacher?"

"What's that supposed to mean?"

"We've heard of your work with Żegota," Andrzej said. "Have seen it, too. The Nazis might not have noticed you and your pram, but it's our city; we see everything."

"They are starving the Jews, murdering them too, the children need to be saved, those that we can save."

"And you speak German very well, teacher."

"You might speak it better, Andrzej, if you had paid more attention at lessons."

"Bullet, not Andrzej; but yes, that boy was a fool."

A German soldier on a creaking bicycle pedalled past and Andrzej made a show of looking in at the baby and smiling.

"What an ugly baby," he said, once the German had passed, then added: "We need people like you, teacher."

"I'm busy, I still teach, you know? And then there's this." She nodded at the baby.

"Education can wait until after the war, and the Jews are doomed anyway. There is more useful work you can do. We have runners, messengers, boy scouts mostly; they are called the Grey Ranks, but they cannot carry much, and cannot deal with Germans, and do not look German, like you. You're an older woman, with a pram —"

"I do not consider myself so old. But I do consider myself too busy," she said. "*Grey Ranks*; Jesus, Andrzej, it's like a child's game."

"You're old enough to be a mother, and it's no game. But I will tell you about games I have played, teacher. In the house I liked to play a game I called *Spies*. I played it one time because and I wanted to know if you were going to tell Father about the slogan I painted, on the shoe shop; but you remember that. There are few secrets in that house, you see – have you ever noticed how much you can hear of a conversation from outside those parlour doors, eh?"

"What do you mean?" Lidka said.

"It's not a good time to be a child of a German soldier, or the mother of that child. We can make things awkward for you teacher, and you can be helpful to us. Still think it's all a game, eh?"

Fear now swelled within Lidka's chest. Without her really noticing they had walked in a long circle and they were now back on the edge of the park, at Królewska. A dog barked at a red and yellow tram that rattled past the grand buildings, there was the smell of roasted chestnuts on the cold air. A group of German soldiers blocked the pavement, smoking in a huddle, as if to gain warmth from each other's cigarettes. They all carried rifles over their shoulders, but they did not seem as dangerous as the young Pole now walking by her side.

"What do you want me to do?" she said.

"Much the same as now; but not babies."

"Then what?"

"Guns."

*

Near Zhizdra, Soviet Union. February 1942

The banging on the door sounded like a grenade attack, and the soldiers in the hut reached for their rifles and machine pistols, a reflex action. But not Ingo. He had been awake anyway, thinking about army prison, realising he could not even imagine just how grim and boring that would be, and so he had seen the all too obvious silhouette of German officers through the iced window. Pop looked at him, stretching, as the loud thumping on the planked door continued.

"Best let them in, eh?" he said, and Ingo, who was closest to the door, pulled himself up from his place on a pile of blankets under the table. The cabin smelt stale, and the fire had been allowed to dwindle to smouldering ash as the others had slept their vodka sleep, so that Ingo's breath now froze in front of his face.

He unbolted the door and opened it to bright winter light that made him lift his arm to shield his eyes, which was close to the salute the shadowy figures in the glare would be expecting. He had been expecting them, too:

Leutnant Schirmer and Standartenführer Richter, with an SS soldier, carrying an MP 40, escorting them.

"Where's Kroh?" Schirmer said, real steel in his voice, but with an edge of triumph, too, while there was also a new gleam in his eyes. Richter stared at Ingo, his cheeks hot with fury. Ingo suddenly thought they all might be shot there and then, and he hesitated long enough that Kroh answered before he could say a thing.

"I'm here, what's all the noise about arse-wipe?" Kroh shouted, having heard Schirmer but not seen either him or Richter from his bed near the fireplace.

With that Richter pushed past Ingo and slammed the door back against its hinges, causing a slab of snow to slide off the sloping thatched roof and land a metre from where the SS soldier stood with a window-rattling thump. Richter ignored it, marched inside, the steel heel-plates of his gleaming jackboots like sabre strikes on the frozen-hard dirt floor.

Kroh was sat up on the bed, fully dressed including belt and holster, covered with blankets, the large felt boots on his feet sticking out the bottom of the covers. Fully dressed except for the Alpine peaked cap he always wore ...

"Is that the way to speak to an officer?" Richter snapped.

"Sir, I —"

"Quiet!" With that Richter noticed the slaughtered platoon of 'dead soldiers' on the table, which seemed to trip something within him, and he swiped the table clean of the empty red star-labelled vodka bottles which shattered and smashed with such a noise it was if the cold, brittle sky was finally snapping. The peasants in the corner of the cabin looked on, fear swelling their eyes. Ingo looked over at the little girl, tried to smile her a reassuring smile, but he was far from sure that he had carried that off.

Kroh tossed aside his grubby bedsheets and stood to attention beside the bed, as if it was time for kit inspection. The others, Ingo and Pop included, followed his lead.

"This cap," Schirmer said, holding up the Gebirgsjäger cap. "It belongs to you, Kroh?" Ingo knew he asked the question for Richter's benefit, as everyone else in the room was well aware of whose hat it was. Schirmer had once ordered Kroh not to wear it, as it was not regulation issue, and he was perhaps enjoying that memory now. Schirmer handed Kroh the soft peaked cap, as the sergeant touched his head, surprised that it indeed was not there; he often wore it when he slept.

Kroh looked confused, and merely nodded.

"My orders were that you were to bring the Horch to Major Brack's billet and park it in the barn, Kroh, were they not?"

"Yes sir. And it was done."

"It was not done, Feldwebel," Richter said.

"But I told these two to do it, sir." With that he glanced at Ingo and Pop.

"Feldwebel Kroh's right sir," Pop said. "We did as ordered."

"Quiet!" Richter snapped. "You were ordered to *personally* see to this, Feldwebel."

"It was not brought to Major Brack's billet anyway," Schirmer said.

"We were told to bring it here, to Feldwebel Kroh, first," Pop said, another interruption.

"I said *quiet!*" Richter said, then added: "Is that true, Feldwebel?"

"No sir, I told them to —.""

"It was your responsibility, Feldwebel Kroh," Schirmer said.

"But I had been drinking and — "

"You were drunk?" Richter interrupted.

Kroh nodded, the empty vodka bottles were all too obvious.

"You were drunk, and then you disobeyed a direct order," Schirmer added.

Kroh said nothing now, just stared at the iced up window.

"And then you crashed my car," Richter said.

"Crashed your car, sir?"

Richter nodded at Schirmer, like a detective in a denouement, handing over to his deputy to fill in in with the details. Schirmer spoke, and spoke with a quiet authority, though it was spoilt a little by the hint of a vengeful smirk tugging at the corner of his mouth.

"We found the car this morning, Kroh. It's severely damaged. Inside there were two empty vodka bottles, Red Army issue like these, in fact. Your cap was in the footwell, and your pay book was on the seat."

"But I was here all night, isn't that so, lads?" Kroh was pleading now, and Ingo thought of the Russians he had killed, how they had pleaded. "Treacle?"

"I was asleep all night," the man who had once been quite fat, and now wore an oversized uniform, said.

"Eckhart?"

The tall man shook his head, gingerly, as he was the most obviously hungover. No one would be sorry to see Kroh go, Pop and Ingo had known that. Ingo stole a quick glance at Pop now. He stood to rigid attention like an SS Liebenstarte guard at the Chancellery, wearing no expression at all.

Ingo hoped he looked the same, though that would be a first. Most of all he hoped he did not look like a man who had taken a cap and pay book off a man in the deep sleep of a vodka coma, then taken another bottle of vodka, all of which they had put in the crippled but just driveable Horch. They had poured vodka on the carpet and then parked the car against a tree close to the village, nose first. And they had almost been shot by a jumpy sentry for their trouble.

"Put this man under arrest Schirmer," Richter said. "And I want to see him punished properly, so make sure he's handed over to the Feldgendarmerie: disobeying orders, destruction of SS property, drunk on duty, improper uniform, and whatever else you can come up with."

"Yes sir," Schirmer said, and it somehow sounded like *with pleasure.*

Ingo glanced at Kroh, who was slowly and resignedly sliding his Walther from its holster, placing it on the upturned wooden crate beside the bed. He knew the game was up, but as he put his incriminating cap on his head he stared at Pop, who kept looking the other way, stiffly at attention. And then – quite suddenly – Kroh's eyes fixed on Ingo. He did not look away, for he was surprised at what he saw there. It was, he thought, a grudging respect. Kroh knew he had been fixed up good and proper. It was the tiny nod, hardly noticeable, that carried the promise of vengeance, though.

"Sure we'll bump into each other again soon enough, Pup, Pop," Kroh said, and with that he pulled his Siberian snow smock over his uniform, grabbed his kit, and then walked out, whistling the *Panzerlied* in his near-whistle hiss as he did so.

*

Warsaw. February 1942

It didn't take much sunlight to get the people of Warsaw out in the winter, and so Lidka was even happier that today the sun was shining. Because when there are many people out walking on Nowy Świat, who would take too much notice of one woman with a baby carriage?

Andrzej had provided her with detailed instructions, which he had ordered her to memorise and not commit to paper – she thought he had enjoyed that, lecturing his former teacher. She had followed the instructions to the letter. She had picked up the sack of grenades from a flat above the Rzymska bakery and café on the corner of Nowogrodska and Marszałkowską in the city centre.

"What should I say if they ask where the baby is?" she had said, as the sack was placed in the pram by a nervous man who called himself Lightning – though that did not suit his lazy eye, nor the fat that hung from him; an ever-rarer thing in Warsaw.

"Say they are potatoes; spuds are far more precious than babies these days," Lightning had joked. But that hadn't suited him either, and he had then told her to be careful, and above all not to touch the grenades, as he almost lovingly tucked the small sack into the bedding as if it was indeed a baby.

She had pushed the pram down Jerozolimskie and then turned left on to Nowy Świat and walked along to the shop where she had been told to wait, on the opposite side of the street as instructed; to wait for whoever was to make contact and take the sack of grenades. It had not seemed far for her to go at all, but she sensed she should not question these men; these boys. Fear had walked with her all the way. It had walked with her often lately, and she had almost grown used to the tightness in her chest, the nausea, the burning bile that always seemed just a cough away from vomit, and the sweat that greased the palms of her hands, even on the coldest of days. Fear was like pregnancy, she thought once again, all about the future. She did this thing for Freddy, for his future, to keep him safe. And, she knew, she did this thing *because* of Freddy.

There was a boy, maybe twelve or thirteen, cycling in the middle of the street, in aimless circles, the tyres of his bicycle thudding over the tram tracks. A basket was fixed to the front of the bike. Everyone else walked as if they had somewhere to go, except for two men in long coats and hats who talked as they shared a cigarette close to the entrance to the shop.

The shop sold clothes, but the sign on the door said it only sold them to Germans, which was not unusual. The newly painted sign that was above the shop said it was owned by Germans, too: *Hoffmann's*. In the gleaming window straight-faced manikins tantalised passing Poles by wearing warm-looking mink stoles and fur coats. The building next door, to the right, was clad in rust-edged corrugated iron across its ground floor while the ragged brick of ruin rose above this, the property not yet rebuilt after the bombing of '39. On the corrugated iron someone had painted the Kotwica, and grey patches of fresh paint further along showed where other AK anchor signs had been covered over. The bombing at the start of the war seemed a lifetime ago, but Lidka still thought the air tasted and smelt a little of ash on Nowy Świat. She believed it always would.

The door to the clothes shop swung open and Lidka heard the dull ding of a bell from within. For a moment she thought the bell was in her head, for it went with the sudden recognition of the young woman with the large cream-coloured box stepping out of the shop.

"Kassia," she said, under her breath.

Lidka had not seen her for almost a year now, heard nothing, either, and Kassia had never passed on her new address after all. She looked well, very well. But then Kassia always had.

Kassia had recognised her at the same moment. For a second she seemed to panic, and Lidka thought she would turn away and pretend she had not seen her. But then she smiled, and mouthed: "Lidka," her glossy lipstick bright in the sunlight. Kassia walked towards Lidka, and as she came halfway across the street she looked at the pram, her forehead corrugating slightly in puzzlement, as she obviously wondered whether this was yet another baby. And then Lidka realised she would want to look inside …

There was a sharp and very loud crack, and Kassia's head snapped left, she stumbled, breaking a heel and dropping the box which fell to the floor with a *plop*, the lid coming off to reveal fur and a red silk lining. Then she twisted and fell. The two men in the long coats ran to her, their coats unbuttoned and flapping like capes. Lidka could see that now they carried pistols. Kassia looked at Lidka from where she lay on the cobbles, her eyes pleading, painted mouth wide open in a silent scream. Another woman took up the scream for her, but this was then lost in a ragged volley of gunfire as both men shot Kassia twice at very close range. Lidka saw the precise moment when Kassia turned ugly, a bullet smashing though her teeth and bright blood erupting from the back of her head, splashing wetly against the cobbles.

All this had taken a moment. Now the men tossed the pistols into the basket on the front of the boy's bicycle, and then both walked off quickly in opposite directions. The boy stood high on his pedals and sprinted away, the frame and chain of the bike rattling as it clattered along the cobbles.

The Germans were never far away in Warsaw and now a group of them burst out of a nearby café, each bareheaded and without their greatcoats, but not one of them had forgotten his gun. It was now that Lidka remembered the pram. And the sack of grenades within it.

She started to walk away quickly, somehow resisting the temptation to run.

"You!"

She kept walking, until a large hand clamped upon her shoulder, spinning her around.

"Do you speak German?"

She shook her head, thinking it best not to have to explain. Another of the soldiers peered into the pram, looked a little puzzled, and then whipped the blanket away to reveal the lumpy sack of grenades. Then the first of the German soldiers kicked over the pram which crashed down into the street, landing on to its side.

The sack tumbled out on to the cobbles, and then split. Potatoes spilled on to the road, one rolling awkwardly into the gutter.

*

"This is not the place to make a scene, teacher," Andrzej said.

She had boarded the tram at Narutowicza as instructed. Andrzej sat cheekily close to the *Nur für Deutsche* section, just a few rows back from two German officers who were engrossed in conversation and enveloped in the smoke from a pipe one of them smoked – it filled the carriage with a warm, peaty smell. This was not a busy time and the tram was not full, just a few Poles towards the back – as far from the German section as possible – one of them coughing and snivelling. The tram windows were steamed up. Andrzej drew a quick Kotwica in the condensation, then grinned as he just as quickly rubbed it away with the sleeve of his coat. It was a stupid risk, but he seemed to thrive on such things. And he'd just told *her* not to make a scene.

He was right, though. She would not make a scene. It would not help anyone. Kassia was dead. "I'm done with your games," she said, quietly.

"They are not games, the whore was a traitor. Traitors die. It is so the world over."

"You tricked me."

"And would you have pointed her out for our men otherwise?"

"I don't know," she answered, truthfully.

"There are few Polish women who sleep with Germans. But we have to make sure that everyone knows what will happen if others are tempted, by nice things, even by love – if such a thing exists, now."

"Sarah was asking after you," Lidka said. "She misses you."

"The kid has too much time on her hands," Andrzej said, sharply, as the tram lurched over points, the contact rails above it swishing and crackling. "Did they question you?"

"Yes, but not for long. A German in the street saw the shooting; I suppose they make better witnesses," she said, and Andrzej nodded.

Once the Germans had realised that Kassia was Polish they had been more concerned that she had shopped in Hoffmann's than that she had been shot dead, Lidka had heard. But then a note was found on her person, from a senior German officer who worked in the office of the Chief of the Warsaw District, which was based in the Hotel Bristol, not very far from where Kassia had been killed. Or executed, as Andrzej would undoubtedly have put it. Kassia had been seeing the German officer, and it had given her certain privileges, and money. The officer would be in trouble now, not for getting a Polish girl killed, but for getting into bed with an untermensch Slav. Lidka had been questioned in the street, but like everyone there, she had seen nothing, she said, just heard the shots, saw the men running. She did not mention the boy on the bicycle, but it had occurred to her that getting the pistols away from the scene very quickly had been important, as if they were more valuable than the men who had used them. No one questioned the care she had taken for her potatoes; the lazy-eyed Lightning had been right about that.

"Why me?"

"We knew her name, and we knew she was once your flat mate – a patriot at your old place on Piwna told us that," Andrzej said, keeping his voice low so that the Germans would not hear him, even though it was unlikely they spoke Polish. "We just did not know what she looked like, and a popular army needs to be careful when it comes to killing the wrong whore, teacher. We had heard she shopped there, every Wednesday at three, though that was just gossip. But we knew she would recognise you, if she was there, and in doing so she would give herself away."

Through the porthole made in the condensation on the window by Andrzej's sleeve she could see the Prudential Building, the top of it lost in the thick cloud.

"So, it was all about Kassia?" she said.

"No, there were other ways we could have killed her, but it is important these things are done in public. People need to learn, yes teacher? But your part in it? Think of it as passing a test, eh?"

"Then it's not finished?"

He nodded in the direction of the two Germans. "It's not finished until they are gone. You are now one of us."

She was not surprised at that, it had seemed inevitable. And she could get no more scared than she already was. All she could do was sigh, as Andrzej continued: "You have skills, and as a teacher you might know how to control the kids that make up the Grey Ranks, that will be useful. There will be extra food, for you and the kid, too. Being in the AK has its advantages."

"That's something, then."

"But what happened to the whore should remind you, too, teacher. Best no one ever knows about Freddy's dad, eh? I hope for your sake the father has the good sense to stay in the Fatherland."

"I've not seen or heard from him for over two years."

"Do you want to?" Andrzej said.

"No," she said. "It's too late. Now."

"Good."

"But I need to get word to Jósef."

"Jósef? He really exists?"

"Yes, and he will be Freddy's father, when this is over," she said. "Is it possible, a single message? He's in England, I think?"

"It might be possible," Andrzej said, but then changed the subject abruptly: "You will need a *nom de guerre*, teacher?"

"French, Andrzej? You are flourishing in this killing business."

"Perhaps *Teacher*, will do, eh, Miss Wadalowska?" Andrzej said.

"No, Bullet. My name will be Chopin."

*

Warsaw. March 1942

"What's a German soldier doing with a Polish girl, anyway?"

"What's a Pole doing with a German name?" Ingo had replied. He hadn't liked that, the bent and wiry little Volksdeutsche with the bent and wiry little glasses, the man who now ran Café Kasper, his name above the door: *Distler's*. He had been no help, though at least Ingo now knew why his letters had been returned; it had not been *Kasper's* since the end of 1939, he was told. After the café he had then tried to find the house in which her apartment had been. That had been very difficult, and it had gobbled up precious hours of his leave. It had been over two years ago, she had taken him there in the dark, and he had had other things on his mind. In the end he thought he had found the right place, on a street called Piwna. He tried two houses that looked likely, one he felt might well be it, but no one there had heard of Lidka Wadalowska, they said.

He realised now, riding the rattling, swaying tram to Ochota, that the uniform he wore did not make it easy for people to trust him. While his long *kradmantel,* a rubberised motorcyclist's coat, kept out the cold, field grey was not a popular colour in Warsaw and most had looked nervous, even frightened, when he spoke to them. But he had no other clothes, and so very little time. Just twenty-four hours leave on his way through Warsaw, before he needed to get to Gross Glienicke for the first part of panzer training. He could not be late; Pop would kill him. Leutnant Schirmer had been quick to accept their request, once Kroh had gone, even added a recommendation, grateful for the part in Kroh's downfall he suspected they had played. Kroh would be in Fort Zinna now, or some other military prison hellhole, but Ingo wasn't going to worry about that. He was just pleased that it was unlikely he would ever see him again. Ingo had been anxious that he might spill some dirt on them, but as Pop had said at the time, that would only mean digging the hole he was already in a bit deeper. That's the thing about collective responsibility, Pop had added, it cuts both ways.

Ingo jumped off the red and yellow tram on Filtrowa, before it had quite stopped, as he was in a hurry – though he would probably have done the same if he had a month's leave – and his boot guards scraped and slithered on the greasy cobbles. There was a bunch of kids riding free on the back of the tram, for kicks rather than trips, and they scattered like pigeons as it came to a stop. It looked fun, and he laughed, but none of them laughed with him. He blamed the coat, the hat, and the belt that clinched the kradmantel to his waist, complete with its holstered P38 sidearm. That was not the sort of thing he could leave in the Wehrmacht luggage store at the Danzig Station with his kitbag, and he had been told by a chained dog to carry it as there had been trouble with the resistance in the city. The wind was biting cold and it blasted shotgun-pellet particles of ice up Filtrowa from the east – everything bad came from the east these days, he thought, as he jogged across the street.

He could never remember the name of the street on which she had worked – *Mochnackiego* he now read, one of those complicated Polish names – and even back in 1939 he had relied on Lidka's instructions; to get off the tram two junctions on from where the tracks split into two, then take the next left; a little way in, the house with the oak tree in the garden space to its right. The oak, skeletal and shivering in the icy wind, its top branches creaking, flayed tips clawing at the swirling grey sky like the fingers of a drowning man, led him to the house. There was grey-white smoke, like the essence of the day, issuing from one of the two chimneys and an electric light was on inside, on the first floor. From the street he could see bright pictures hung on a yellow wall. He recognised the room as that in which he had played the piano. He went through the gate, its hinges squeaking loudly, and on to the main entrance that was at the side of the house. He took off his side cap and stuffed it in the pocket of his coat – that same chained dog had warned him about being improperly dressed once already today, but there did not seem to be any field police here, and he did not want to scare the maid.

Ingo rapped out a little tune on the iron knocker, from the start of Chopin's Scherzo No.2: *clack, clack; cla-cla-cla-clack*. Lidka would like that, he thought. There was no answer. He decided to try again, but as he went to knock the door it opened inwards, though not all the way.

It was not a maid, but the bearded man he remembered from his previous visit over two years ago. He wore a cardigan with suede elbow patches, round spectacles with thick lenses, and a bright green tie. His pupils spread like spilt oil on seeing Ingo and his eyes flicked up and down the long, glossy coat with its large dark green fabric collar facings, and the holster attached to Ingo's leather army belt.

"Yes?"

"Nice tie," Ingo said, grinning. He could smell potatoes boiling, and a wood fire, from within the house.

The man tilted his head a little and recognition seemed to topple within it, a pfennig dropping. But the door was not opened any further, and there was no smile, instead his nostrils flared slightly and his head tipped back, just a little.

"What do you want?"

"Don't you remember me – I played your piano?"

He shook his head sharply. "You're a soldier."

Ingo glanced at the pistol on his belt, then shrugged. "There are a few who would argue the point," he said, still smiling. He heard the laughter of a small child from within.

"I've no time for small talk," the man said – Ingo could still not remember his name, *Pac*-something-or-other. He was freezing cold, and he rubbed his hands and blew into them to make a point, but the man in the bright tie did not take the hint, shut the door a fraction more, looked set to close it fully.

"I'm looking for Lidka."

"There's no Lidka here," he said, without hesitation.

"Lidka Wadalowska, she used to teach here?"

"This is not a school," he said, his forehead creasing in concern. Ingo then remembered that it was illegal, the teaching she did.

"No, of course not," he said. "But you do know her, don't you? She asked me to play piano, for you and your friends, remember?"

He shook his head and Ingo felt the familiar sludge of disappointment begin to ooze through his core.

The man sighed, perhaps because Ingo had stopped smiling now, and then said: "I've not seen her for a very long time, she no longer comes here."

"But she's still in Warsaw?"

He went to speak, hesitated for a moment, and then shrugged as he said: "Perhaps."

"Where?"

"Sorry, I don't know." He closed the door, not quite slamming it, but shutting it firmly enough that Ingo knew there was little point in knocking again. He waited, and felt sure the man also waited, the other side of the door. Then he turned, put his side cap on, and started to walk back to the tram stop.

He still had the rest of the afternoon and the evening to search for her. He would go to the Old Town. He would find her there, of that he was sure. He had waited too long, come too far, endured too much, to be wrong about that.

***

Chillar. May 1952

Ingo parked his Jeep by the side of the road. Its yellow paintwork was now battered, and chipped in places to reveal some of the olive drab beneath. He reached back for his small suitcase from the rear compartment. The hat was stuffed between the steel seat frame and the padded driver's seat, where it would not be caught by the airstream – he liked to drive the Jeep with the windscreen folded down flat against the bonnet. He pulled the fedora out of its tight space, punched it straight, and put it on his head. Large dark clouds were scudding across the pampas, like the hulls of battleships carving through a milky-grey sea. It would rain soon, he thought. He could not see the farmhouse from here, and could not be seen from it, as it was over a rise. There was a way to the house around the back, what had been his escape route, and he took it now, approaching the rear of the building through Zündapp's paddock. He greeted the horse, patted its nose, but could not tell if the beast had missed him these past five months or so. Zündapp looked healthy, though, his coat glossy and his eyes bright, and it was clear someone had been looking after him.

Ingo walked up to the side of the house, careful not to make too much noise, to the top of the driveway, close to the kitchen door, with the rough space outside that made it a natural spot to park a car – but there were no automobiles or trucks here. Through the window he could see there was no one in the kitchen, either. He tried the door. It was unlocked.

The kitchen smelt of maté, which reminded him a little of Russian cigarettes, and Maria's distinctive, lemony perfume, which didn't. It was brighter than he remembered it, and he realised it had been decorated, the same shade of yellow he had painted the Jeep three years before – he remembered there was, or had been, plenty of it left in the old shed down by the paddock. On the kitchen table, which was now partly covered by a chick-yellow checked tablecloth, there was a cooling calabash gourd of maté with a metal straw. Carlo had once told Ingo it was not quite the done thing to drink the slightly bitter, grassy, infusion alone – then that was one of the things Ingo had always liked about Maria, she didn't care about the rules. There was also a single plate, flecked with crumbs from medialunas. He suddenly felt hungry, and looked to see if there were any more of the little croissants in the pantry, but could not find any. He had been driving since well before dawn and had not stopped. Had hardly stopped at all since the decision had been made to return to Chillar, three days and 1270 bumpy kilometres away in a lonely hotel room with pictures of Welsh mountains on the walls, in Trelew, Patagonia.

In the hall that led down to the bedroom, and the living room he had never done much living in, he could see that a framed picture of Julio Martel, the tango singer, had been hung.

"Enrique!"

They caught up, in the bedroom. Then they dressed and went into the kitchen to talk. The rain had come and it hammered off the corrugated iron roof, while silver beads raced down the window panes. Maria scrambled some eggs for him as he sat at the table. There was a pot of coffee, too.

"I like what you've done to the place," Ingo said, but he wasn't so sure he did.

"Where have you been, Enrique?"

"South, mostly," he said.

"South is big."

"Yes, it is."

"I've a feeling you're not going to bore me with vacation stories, Enrique?"

"Boredom was all there was, and a little bit of sea, lots of sky. In a way it was like ..."

"Like?" Maria said, placing the plate of eggs in front of him. He did not elaborate, just dashed some Tabasco on them and took a forkful. She poured him some coffee.

"Tell me, Maria," he said, after a few mouthfuls of scrambled eggs. "Did anyone come looking for me?"

"No," she shook her head. "No one, and nothing, except the deliveries, they still came."

"You sure?"

"Yes, every Thursday, as always. Oh, and Carlo. But just once, I told him you had gone."

"What did he say to that?"

"Nothing. He has not been back since, and that was months ago, just after you left. I have seen him in town, though, and that fancy wife of his – but, you know, she seems to wear the same old clothes these days," Maria said, with a little relish, Ingo thought.

"You go into town often?"

"I have a job now, a real job. In the Bar el Descanso by the petrol station; you know it?"

"I know it."

"It's been easier for me, you know. I feel settled here," she said, now taking a seat herself. "And a girl cannot be a girl forever."

"You can stay here," he said. "Until you find a new home." He scooped up another forkful of egg.

Maria nodded her head, a little sadly, and he pretended not to notice. She looked at the clock above the basin, the clock that had always seemed to tick so slowly, and said: "I need to go soon, to get the bus into town. I start at eleven."

"Don't worry, I'll take you into town."

*

He dropped Maria off at Bar el Descanso. It was not raining quite as heavily as it had been earlier but it was always difficult to keep dry in a Jeep, even with the canvas top in place. She did not thank him for the lift, but he thought that was more to do with other things than wet clothes. He was surprised that she had still been there, waiting for him. He thought she would have grown bored and moved on by now. The job was a surprise, too. It worried him. A little.

The Jeep splashed through the pitted streets of Chillar until he reached the Di Rossi Auto Repairs garage on Belgrano. He parked up outside. The metal roller shutter door was half open and so he ducked under it and entered the garage; enjoying the familiar smell of grease, oil and scorched steel. There was the bright gleam of an inspection lamp from beneath an Oldsmobile, like an electric eel glowing in the dark depths of a deep sea. The car was being worked on and there was the sound of hammering, interspersed with soft Italian curses – Carlo nearly always did his swearing in Italian. There was no sign of the red Ford V8 stock car.

"I will be with you in a moment!" Carlo yelled.

"I was expecting to see a blue sports car here, by now."

"Ingo!" Carlo shouted, dropping a tool which clanged in the bottom of the pit.

Moments after his shout the door to the tiny adjoining office was flung open. Catalina was in grey slacks and a beige sweater, no makeup. She looked tired and puzzled, and she wore spectacles and held a pencil as if it were a hypodermic needle.

"You," she said, surprised. "So, you're back, Enrique."

"Seems so."

By now Carlo had climbed the steps out of the pit. He hugged Ingo, held him by his shoulders to look at him closely, and then said: "A hat, eh? Suits you. But you look like you could use a drink, my friend?"

"You know that Dr Guzmon is expecting his car to be ready by the end of the day, Carlo."

"Just an hour, Catalina, please, an early lunch. God knows I deserve a break," Carlo said, rubbing the grease off his hands with some cleaning gel and a rag and then peeling off his work overalls. Catalina said nothing, just went back into the small office, not quite slamming the door behind her.

"Sorry, it's been difficult for her," Carlo said.

"What has? And where's the V8?"

"I'll tell you over that drink, my friend," Carlo said. "But it will have to be on you, I'm afraid – Bar el Descanso?"

"Maybe not, how about the hotel?"

It was not a long walk to the desperately ambitiously named Hotel Internacional; which was opposite the flat-roofed and utilitarian train station and close to a general store. The hotel was Art Deco in design, but Great Depression in character. It was tapered in shape, the thin end of its wedge marking the point where two streets met in the ragged square in front of the station. It was a whitewashed building which needed more white, and maybe more wash, too. As they entered a train rumbled by, the boxcars packed with beef heading for slaughter, some lowing, but most stoic in their ignorance of what was to come. It reminded Ingo of other trains he had seen.

"You okay?"

Ingo nodded. "Quilmes?"

"Something stronger, I think."

They sat close to the pinch of the building, where they could see the streets on both sides of the hotel and also the train station. Ingo had chosen the table. It was the ideal place for someone waiting and watching out for a train, or for other things. For some reason the hotel bar had recently been decorated with an aeronautical theme, and there were framed photographs of aeroplanes on the walls. He recognised a Convair, in the livery of Aerolíneas Argentinas, plus an Aeroposta Argentina DC-3. Ingo thought it must have been quite a tease for someone awaiting the late train to Azul and beyond, looking at aeroplanes that could whisk them away at speed. He had a sudden thought of home, like a signal flare burning within his consciousness. He doused it with that other memory, as always. That was easy; like pain masking pain. His beard started to itch, and he run his fingers through it.

"Carlo, I need to know. Did anyone come looking for me?" he said.

"No one," Carlo said, as he sipped his scotch, grimaced, then took a large gulp of the same. "That's better." He lit a single cigarette he had taken from the top pocket of his shirt, a cheap brand, the smoke pungent.

"Nobody?"

"Not a soul, my friend," Carlo said. "And if they were looking for you on account of the picture in *El Gráfico* then you can be sure they would have come to me first, as the garage name was all over the Ford. What about you, did you find that people were stopping you in the street to ask for your autograph?" He grinned at that.

Ingo shook his head. Once, he thought, a teenage boy in Puerto Madryn had looked at him as if he recognised him but could not place him. But that had been it. He relaxed a little, took a sip of whisky. Then asked the question that burnt within him with the same intensity as the taste of the scotch.

"Carlo, the V8?"

"Gone."

"Why?"

Carlo sighed. "I had to sell it. I never told you, but I could never afford it in the first place. I told the bank in Tandil that I needed money to extend the garage, true enough; and they gave me a loan. I had hoped to pay it off later by selling the race car once it had done its job, my friend; and maybe with part of what Varela might invest in the Condor. As it turned out, I needed to sell it quickly, and cheaply, just to keep the wolves from the door."

"I didn't know."

Carlo shrugged. "But I knew, my friend. You told me often, and I should have listened. I asked too much of you, I see that now. But it doesn't really matter, that brat Otero did well. He's in Europe now, you know? Varela has bought a Maserati for him to race. I have not had the time, nor the heart, to find out just how well he is doing."

"What about the Condor?"

"The dream is dead, my friend. It's work enough to put food on the table for my family and to start to pay off my debts."

"I don't suppose Catalina has taken this well?"

"She has stood by me, and in truth that's surprised me. Divorce is illegal here, and of course there's the children. But still, she has stayed with me, and worked with me, too."

Ingo said nothing, took another sip of whisky. A truck splashed through the puddles outside, Carlo puffed on his cigarette, staring into the smoke for a moment. "Tell me, where did you go?" he said.

"South; Patagonia."

"I was right about the beard, yes?"

"No."

Carlo laughed, drained his whisky. "I can hear the wheezy call of Dr Guzman's asthmatic Oldsmobile, my friend."

"Dreams should not be allowed to die, Carlo."

"Many things should not be allowed to happen. But a little man has no control over events."

"What would it take, Carlo? To see the Condor fly?"

"That's simple. Money."

Ingo took his hat off, felt for the remaining small stones sewn in to the seam, then tossed it on the table. "Make me a list Carlo, everything you need to build a prototype, and the costs of each and every item, and the costs for your time and the time of anyone else we might need to use; coachbuilders, engine men — anyone."

"Why would I waste my time doing that?"

"How much it would cost to build it; and then how much it would cost to race it."

***

Near RAF Hemswell, Lincolnshire, England. May 1942

Wysocki was coming towards him, staggering, his skin melting from his face, his eyes boiling liquid. He was reaching out for him, his fingers fire, flames, touching his hand …

Jósef awoke with a start, to find himself still staring at fire. He shuddered, as he heard their laughter. The spaniel sleeping by the fire was close enough to it for its wet coat to steam. It took Jósef a moment or two to realise he was in The Crown in Glentham, that he had fallen asleep. He was not surprised, he had worked 30 hours, non-stop, and had not really wanted to come to the pub. He had drifted off with his half-empty pint gripped tightly, and had not split a drop.

But why were they laughing? Why were they laughing at him?

"What is it?" he asked.

"Nothing, you slept through a good joke, that's all," Jankowski said. There were four of them altogether, and some locals at other tables, plus a man in British army battledress, who drank alone in the corner. The pub smelt of the coal burning on the fire – it was a cold, wet evening – and cigarettes. Jósef's Woodbine had half-smoked itself into a column of ash in the tin ashtray.

"Tell me it; the joke," he said.

"Would take too long – anyway, your round."

Jósef realised he was thirsty, his throat raw. He could still smell Wysocki, burning in the dream, but he knew that could not be so. He thought it could be the dog, too close to the fire, hair singeing. The spaniel awoke, right then, without a whimper, and moved a little further away from the fireplace. Jósef wondered if he had awoken without a whimper, hoped so. But there was something in the way people looked at him, some hiding grins, some laughing behind their hands … He sank the rest of his Bass and went up to the bar. There was more laughter, and a sharp *shhhhh* from Jankowski.

"Same again, please."

The barmaid was pretty, red hair and pale skin, dusted with freckles. She was not laughing, and her horse-chestnut eyes dripped with what Jósef took as pity.

"Look in the mirror, duck," she said, with a sad smile, and the others booed and laughed louder. The mirror was to his side, below a black leather strap displaying horse brasses. It was etched with an advert for Gilbey's Gin. He looked at himself in it. While he had been asleep they, Jankowski probably because he laughed the loudest now, had taken some soot from the edge of the fire and blackened a little toothbrush moustache beneath his nose. It made him look a bit like Hitler.

"Just a joke," she said, handing him a bar towel.

"Yes, a joke." He dabbed away the ash while she took the top off a bottled Guinness and pumped the first pint of draught Bass.

"I've seen you here before," she said, as the beer sloshed and foamed into the pint pot. "But not for a while."

"We've been busy."

He wondered if she thought him a pilot, or aircrew, hoped that she did. But thought it unlikely that a barmaid in a pub so close to an RAF station would not know that aircrew wore wings on their breasts – and did not fall asleep by the fire after just half a pint, as a rule.

"I suppose it's difficult for you to get time off," she said, clunking the pint on the bar top.

"It can be," he admitted.

"This war's no fun, is it?" she said.

He didn't reply to that immediately. He found he was thinking of Wysocki again. He could barely remember the man as he had been, only the man in flames, and that bothered him. The others had started a game of darts, and he could hear the steel points thud into the cork of the board.

"No fun at all," he agreed, finally.

She finished pulling the second pint. "I'm free, Saturday afternoon?"

It surprised him, and it must have shown, for her head dipped, in embarrassment, he thought.

"I'm sorry, there is someone," he said, after a pause. "At home."

"Back in Poland?"

"Yes, Warsaw," he said.

"A wife?"

He did not answer directly, but instead said: "And a son."

He had had the confirmation in a letter a week ago, though typewritten and with an envelope franked in Northolt, London. It had told him he really was a father; and that Lidka was well. It was all it said. But it was all he had wanted to hear. There was no way he could see to reply to it.

"They must be very proud of you," she said, with a sigh. "Coming all this way, to fight."

He nodded, slightly, but said nothing, as she poured the third pint of Bass.

*

Warsaw. June 1942

Something was different. It wasn't the weather, because it had been hot for days now. Hot and still. Poles were allowed only 699 calories of rations a day – the Jews in the Ghetto just 180, as Sarah always reminded them – so those who had not been taken for forced labour had little energy to do so much when it was hot like this. Hot and still, and quiet, then. So, if not the weather, then what was different? Lidka suddenly realised what it was. She felt at ease with herself. And, she felt proud. And, she did not feel scared. But most of all she no longer felt guilty. She was in a good mood. It had been so long since she had felt like this that she had hardly recognised it for what it was.

Bullet, Lidka was getting used to the name now, had told her that morning that he was pleased with the work she was doing with the AK. It occurred to her with a slight jolt that it was also this that had put her in such a contented frame of mind. This work, carrying arms and messages mostly, had been frightening at first. But with Bullet's encouragement she had grown into the role. He had *taught her* things; and that would have seemed absurd not so very long ago. But then they had both changed. She had at first scoffed at his lack of fear; then she had slowly begun to envy it, and now, sometimes, she could almost admire it – if not the rashness that sometimes went with it.

She had opened all the windows in the parlour, including the full-length double glass doors to the little balcony, but the breeze was lazy, didn't even have the energy to stir the light lace curtains, through which the sun spun webs of shadow on the gleaming parquet floor. Some of the heavier curtains were closed because Sarah was in the room. The leaves and branches of the oak outside the un-curtained side window stood still, like intricate sculpture, and a deluge of tree-fractured light spattered the paintings on the far wall.

Freddy was naked except for a pair of tiny shorts, and happy, and he sat on Lidka's lap while she sat on the broad piano stool. Sarah sat close to them, but hidden from the outside by the curtains, so she could not be seen from the upper floors of the buildings opposite. In the corner of the room Feliks was in an armchair, reading Bergson's *Laughter*.

Lidka opened the fallboard of the Pleyel and Freddy's chubby little fingers immediately darted to the keys, jabbing three plinking, glassy high notes, as sharp as the lemon sunlight. Then he wriggled in her lap, and stretched, with Lidka's help, to reach a deeper key, a dramatic low G.

"It's almost a tune," Lidka said, as Freddy chortled. She said it as a joke, of course, but everybody knew that great pianists and composers start young. Chopin was performing in public at the age of seven.

"Almost," Sarah said, with a smile and a soft clap.

Freddy beamed at Sarah and played the same again.

"Well now it's definitely a tune," Sarah said, and they all laughed, Feliks included. Freddy jabbed at a few more keys, he never tired of this, to Lidka's delight, but now it was all noise, no melody.

"Have you seen Andrzej lately, Mrs Sczcepanska?"

Lidka had been waiting for the question. She always asked it. She shook her head.

"It's just, I was wondering; the kennkarte?" she said this quietly, but Feliks would have heard. They now all knew that Andrzej was with the AK.

Sarah had heard the AK could supply forged kennkartes; Andrzej had one with an occupation on it that meant he could avoid conscription for forced labour. With an identity card Sarah would be able to leave the house in relative safety. Lidka had asked Andrzej, but he had refused. It was too risky, he had said. They are expensive and not handed out like candy, he had said. Better she stays hidden, he had said. And who else would look after Freddy when you're here with us? He had also said. Lidka just shook her head, now, not looking at Sarah.

"And again Freddy," she said.

"Mama!" the toddler cried – it had been his first and so far only word – and his fingers once more crushed down on to the keys, while he laughed at the noise of it. She did not look at her, but she could sense Sarah's frustration.

"You know, I've often wondered," Sarah said, quite suddenly. "Whatever happened to the man who played Chopin for us?"

Lidka feigned bewilderment for a moment, and for some reason glanced over at Feliks, who was watching them now, though his gaze dived back into the book as soon as she saw him. He looked troubled, she thought. His eyes, magnified by his thick lenses, were not now following the text, she could see, just staring at the page.

"He played wonderfully, it was Christmas Eve, you let me stay and listen, remember?" Sarah said.

"Oh, yes, I remember," Lidka said. "I suppose he went away."

"The war?"

"Yes, the war. Everything's the war."

"So, it was not so serious, you and him?"

Lidka did not answer the question immediately, just smiled at Freddy as he plonked the keys once again. She could not look at this piano without thinking of Ingo, and she could not look at Freddy without thinking of Ingo, either. In between she also thought of Ingo, of where he was, if he was safe. But that made her unhappy again. And sometimes, these days, it made her angry, too. It had taken her a long time to accept that he had run out on her. And it would take a much longer time to get over it. It was better to think of other things. She knew she had to forget Ingo Six. Jósef was Freddy's father now.

"No, there was nothing between us, Sarah," she finally said, holding in a sigh.

"I think I will go outside, for some air," Feliks suddenly said, putting down the book and polishing his specs with the tongue of his bright blue tie. "I will not be long."

Sarah frowned as he left the room but said nothing. It was unlike Feliks to go outside these days, even in good weather. Lidka wondered where he might go. Most of his friends had disappeared long ago, taken away by the Nazis for no other reason than being intellectuals. They heard the door close as he left. Freddy went back to jabbing at the keys on the piano, but there was nothing close to a tune now.

Around ten minutes after Feliks had left Lidka heard the quiet tap of shoe soles on the pavement through the open windows, and then the gate set in to the iron railings squeaked loudly, as it was meant to – it was left un-oiled to provide an early warning. Lidka lifted Freddy from her lap and sat him on the piano stool, and then went to the window. Down below, now closing the gate behind him, there was a man in a dove grey suit and a black hat with a silk band around it. He was carrying a flat parcel, wrapped in brown paper. At this time of day his shadow was iron-hard, but short. He walked up the path that led up to the main door at the side of the building.

The man did not look threatening, he wore no uniform and he came alone. But they could not take a risk with visitors. There was a well-practiced routine to follow. It was a game to Freddy and he loved it, and he laughed as always as Lidka took him in her arms and Sarah went on ahead. They hurried down the second staircase at the rear of the house, then through the storeroom and into the library. Mrs Paczkowska would always take her time in answering the door; Lidka believed she would do so even if they did not have Jews hiding in the basement.

The library was walled with book spines, mostly in green, blue, red and black, though some had bright paper covers. It smelt of old books and new books and Lidka loved it here. Sol Vogler had heard the knock at the door and had waited for Sarah. Mrs Vogler and Leon were already in the basement, Lidka guessed.

Sol Vogler would have been unremarkable had he not been so pale from spending so much time in the cellar, unlike Sarah he had never risked a step outside the Paczkowski home since they had come here to hide, more than two years ago now – but then even Sarah was beginning to look a little pasty. Sol Vogler had a way of looking at people which could be disconcerting, Lidka thought, as if he searched for their worth in their eyes, like he had looked for faults in a diamond when he had worked as a jeweller. It was the jewels he still owned, and the money he had, which was just about keeping them all alive, for Mr Paczkowski had not worked as an art dealer since the Germans had come. There was no room for art in Warsaw now.

"What is it?" Sol Vogler asked.

"Just a visitor," Sarah said, calmly. Then Sol Vogler knelt down in front of the part of the bookcase which had been slid away to reveal the hatch. The hatch was usually hidden beneath works by Goethe and Schopenhauer and some other German writers and philosophers – a touch Feliks had enjoyed – and stretched back in to a hidden recess in the wall. It was still a narrow entrance, and at other times it might have been difficult to fit inside, but everyone was thin now.

Mr Vogler and Sarah crawled through the tight opening behind the bookshelves, feet first and backwards, and Lidka could hear the sound of their feet clunking on the wooden ladder that led to the walled off section of the basement. She could also hear Mrs Vogler and Leon questioning them, and Sarah replying with urgent *shushes*. Lidka placed the books back on the shelves while Sarah sealed the entrance to the hiding place from behind. The last book was Volume II of Schopenhauer's *World as Will and Idea*, which slipped in between Volume III and Volume I with a soft clunk.

She then picked up Freddy again and went through to the kitchen via the storeroom, with its clutter of stacked paintings, and then through to the hallway that led to the main door. Now she could hear voices. Mrs Paczkowska was explaining to the man that Feliks was not at home. He was an old man, Lidka now realised, his stoop had not been obvious from the upstairs window. The man had a painting he wanted to sell, that much Lidka quickly gathered.

"I have told you, my husband is no longer in that business," Mrs Paczkowska said.

"But please, we have nothing. If he could just take a look?"

"We cannot help you," Mrs Paczkowska said. Then her gossamer mask of civility slipped and she closed the door on the man. She did not slam it shut, but it still seemed a brutal act, closing like a trap. Lidka just caught sight of the despair filling the man's eyes before his face was lost behind the wood of the closing door.

She thought Mrs Paczkowska smiled slightly as she turned away from the door.

"Shall I tell them it's all clear?" Lidka said.

Mrs Paczkowska looked surprised to see her there. "No," she said, collecting herself. "We should be certain. Give it another hour, or two."

"But there's no danger now," Lidka said.

"This is still my house," Mrs Paczkowska said, then she walked up the stairs.

*

Panzer school, near Lyck, East Prussia. June 1942

Flying a tank. As it was with most things in Ingo's life, the secret was speed. The Panzer I was light for a tank, at five and a bit tonnes. This training version was lighter still, as it had no turret, so in a sense was like a cabriolet tank. But it was still a huge hunk of iron. The secret to keeping up the speed in a panzer was fast and smooth gear changes. A missed change, a hesitation, and momentum gave way to inertia. It was all about momentum then, driving a tank, just like it was in a racing car, Pop had told him.

The Waves of the Danube – no one had any idea why they were called this as they were very far from that river – stretched for kilometres east of Lyck. It was undulating ground that called for the slickest of gear changes to keep the panzer going, never allowing it to get bogged down in its own weight. Ingo had quite quickly found a *wave* which he believed would help him fly the tank.

Without a turret, or hat, the summer sun beat down on Ingo as he pressed his foot hard on the throttle, only easing off to make a quick change in to fifth and top gear, clutching and moving the stick swiftly – just like a car, except for the steering levers rather than a wheel. He had the engine buzzing, and the tank was clattering along at its maximum off-road speed of around 37km/h, the steel around him shaking. He spied the ground ahead through the narrow vision slit in the steel windshield that made it seem a little more like a real panzer. It was track-hammered, rutted ground, but he kept his foot hard down as the tank hit the low slope and sped to its crest, where it then seemed to stretch itself on its suspension like a hesitant diver for a moment, before lifting slightly in to the empty space above the steep back slope.

The Panzer I flew for around five metres, at an altitude of about a metre. Then its nose dipped, before it hit the ground with a cymbal smash of tracks and a body-shaking, clanging, boom, the crunch of it snapping through the control levers and buzzing up Ingo's arms, while the force of it bounced him out of his seat for a moment. Great curtains of stone-laced dry dirt were thrown up on either side of the machine, a little of it raining down on its interior, pinging and plonking against the steel surfaces.

Ingo glanced at Pop in the commander's seat – the Mk1 was built for two, a machine-gunner and commander, and a driver. They had both qualified as drivers the week before, but Pop had managed to persuade one of the instructors, with the help of a donation of a bottle of Mackenstedter korn to the mess, to let them have one last joyride in a Krupp Sports Car, as the Mk 1 was known throughout the Panzerwaffe. Pop grinned, then signalled for Ingo to pull up. He braked smoothly and brought the open-topped panzer to a halt very close to the road back to the camp, which was lined with close-cropped trees that looked like they had been planted upside down. The land smelt of baked, dry earth and the tank smelt of oil, rubber and gasoline.

They climbed out of the Panzer I and Pop lit an Atikah, even he had been finding Reemtsmas hard to come by for a while now. Other stuff was easier to find though and, with Kroh now far out of the way, Pop had started to make a little real cash from this war. Ingo had never realised just what a businessman he was, and in the last few months he'd almost doubled the money they had been saving with his buying and selling on the black market; mostly alcohol and cigarettes, but also, sometimes, stuff he *found*. It wasn't really looting, Pop always said, it was more about making sure things didn't go to the Ivans; for that would be a terrible waste. From Pop this sort of thing always seemed more reasonable than it had from Kroh. Besides, one day they would need that money.

Pop offered Ingo a cigarette, but he shook his head, he had given up long ago and Pop only offered out of habit now. He had read that smoking was not good for an athlete, and a racing driver was most surely that, and while Pop had said that was just Nazi guff – because they hated smoking and most good things – Ingo wasn't so sure. Even Nazis could be right about *some* things.

Like uniforms.

Pop was pleased with his new black Panzerwaffe uniform, and so he was now a little annoyed to find a splodge of dried dirt on the sleeve, from the messy landing. He rubbed it away. Ingo sat down on the ground, back against one of the stunted trees. Pop seemed to think about sitting, too, then decided he did not want to get his new uniform dirty – he had already told Ingo that the new threads would get him in the knickers of every fräulein from Hamburg to Vienna. The short, black, double-breasted uniform jacket was wraparound, and buttoned to the right, leaving a triangular flap of woollen cloth that spoke of hussars of old, as did the silver death's head, or *Totenkopf*, shining on the lapel. Trousers were black and laced with drawstrings at the cuffs to fit inside boots which were short and rubber-soled, to help with grip on the steel slopes of a tank's interior. Pop also wore a black side cap, while Ingo's was stuffed inside his belt, with its silver-coloured *Gott mit uns* buckle.

"That's one reichsmark, Pop; a bet's a bet."

Pop laughed: "Fly a tank ..." He shook his head, then reached into a pocket in his new black uniform trousers for his wallet and pulled out a pale pink banknote. He was tapping his foot quickly as he stood, a new habit of his, Ingo had noticed.

"It flew well," Ingo said, taking the money.

"Like a Messerschmitt."

Ingo laughed. "You know, Warsaw's less than two-hundred and fifty kilometres, that way," he said, nodding to the south-west.

"You're not still thinking of her, are you?"

"It's not that far, really."

"Tell me Ingo. Has she tried to get in touch with you, in any way?"

"It's difficult, she's Polish, and —"

"Yes, she's Polish. *And,* that my friend, means she's out of bounds to good clean Germans like you."

"The whores are Polish, some of them," Ingo said.

With that Pop turned away, stared to the east. It was the direction all of them stared, if there was staring to be done. Ingo put the banknote in his pocket and his fingers brushed against the ragged edge of the photograph. He did not need to take it from his pocket to remember her, he had looked at it so often the image had burnt its way on to his consciousness, like a brand.

"Besides, she promised me. Said she would wait," Ingo said.

"Well she wasn't waiting for you the last time you were in Warsaw, pal; was she?"

"I just didn't find her, that's all. She's there, still waiting – I'm sure of it."

Pop shook his head, and then was quiet for a little while, puffing on his cigarette, so that all that Ingo could hear was the breeze whispering in the dry grass, and the distant rattle of an air-cooled four-cylinder Krupp engine in another Panzer I training tank, about half a kilometre away.

Pop turned around, spoke: "Listen Ingo, you're not planning on going there, are you?"

"I'm due leave."

"But Warsaw's not on your travel warrant, is it?"

Ingo had told Pop this earlier. "No, but what's one more German soldier in that city, eh?"

Pop took a long drag on his cigarette. "You will end up in jail, Ingo. And DKW or Auto Union won't look at you them, you know that."

"Are they looking now?"

Pop shook his head. "It's the war; but how long can that last?"

"You used to tell me."

"Maybe a year, say two at most."

"Long time."

"Long time to be in Fort Zinna," Pop said.

"Chained dogs won't catch me anyway, Pop; I'm faster than a bullet, remember?"

"They're everywhere, lad, they won't need to catch you," Pop said. "Listen, you know I've signed up to be a gunner?"

"Sure, I know."

"Thought why, though?"

Ingo had, but he shrugged.

"The reason is so that we can stay together," Pop said. "We're going back to the 4th, but there's no room for two drivers in one panzer. But they like a tank crew to be thick, and with the lads I know at Division HQ it should be easy for us to get assigned to the same tank, eh?"

"You think so?"

"Well, not if you're in jail."

Just then the other training tank Ingo had heard came over the closest rise, not flying, its tracks squeaking and clattering.

"Listen, when was the last time you saw your mother?"

Ingo shrugged, but he knew it was over a year. Almost every week he had another letter telling him how long it had been. He felt guilty, sure, but he also felt guilty about Lidka.

"And your father?"

"Well, that can wait."

"It can?"

"We don't get on so well."

"Really?" Pop said. "You never said."

"Long story."

"Got time."

"Boring story."

Pop shook his head. "Well, anyway, listen; I'm not going on leave. I'm going back to the depot, to swat up on blasting Ivan." There was no formal training for a tank gunner, it was something a driver moved on to, usually; these days few got to waste shells at the Panzer Gunnery School in Putlos. "It will be a good drive, all that way, with some fast roads once we're back in Germany," Pop added, turning away to unsuccessfully hide the crinkled smirk that spread across his face.

"Drive?"

"The CO here, old Shovel Face," Pop said. "Being moved east in a hurry, Ivan's making panzer officers a rare breed, eh?"

"And?"

"Has an Opel Admiral."

"3.6-litre, straight six?"

"Ah, I see you're acquainted."

"He comes from Würzburg, was in the 4th himself for a time. Wants someone to take the car home. Nice coincidence, yes? Munich's an easy train ride from Würzburg; much better than sitting on troop trains for days and days, eh?"

"You offered to take the car home for him?"

"Yes, but it's a long way for a man to drive all by himself."

"But fuel?"

"There's no shortage of fuel here, not when it comes to an officer's car, any rate."

"We can go through Warsaw?"

Pop shook his head. "No, north of Warsaw, through Kutno then Łódź. There are dispatches and parcels to deliver, and I have some business to attend to as well, and it's the only route the travel warrant allows anyway. In a swell car like that you can bet the chained dogs will stop us every-time they see us, and I for one am not willing to go to prison just so you can taste Polish plum, Ingo."

"But it's so close ..."

"It's a fast enough car, that Admiral," Pop said. "And we're sure to go through Warsaw again soon, it's on the way to Russia, see; and you can bet they didn't train us as tank crew to sip champagne in Paris. We'll be going east again; count on it."

Ingo thought it through, as the smoke from Pop's cigarette tickled at his nostrils and the other training tank rattled closer. He did not want to go to military jail, and he did not want to be sent to a penal battalion. Then he remembered his fruitless visit to Warsaw in the winter. Then he thought about the car.

"You sure you're not missing Mama?" Pop said.

*

Warsaw. September 1942

Lidka had seen them as soon as she had turned on to Mochnackiego from Filtrowa, and her heart had almost stopped. But she *had not* stopped, because these days she knew not to stop. The truck was a dark green Opel Blitz, with a canvas cover over the rear, and there was also a Polski panel van that had been painted in field grey. A black Mercedes 260D was next in line, right outside the Paczkowski's house on the outer curve towards the end of the crescent, one of its front wheels cocked up on to the sloping cobbled kerb as if it had been parked in a hurry. The 260D was the favoured car of the Gestapo, everyone knew that. It was raining, and she had an umbrella, which she dipped to help hide her face a little. She walked past the small truck, the van and the Mercedes. She could hear nothing but the thrum of the rain on her brolly and the cover of the Opel, the tinny splash of it on the top of the van and the car, and its wet slap on the cobbles.

Bullet had told her how to react in a situation like this: *Do not look. Do not change direction. Do not speed up or slow down. Do not panic.*

It was difficult not to panic, and it was impossible not to look. The main door on the side of the house was open, but there was no one there. She walked on. But the open door was like a powerful magnet, the draw of it a physical thing, and she had to fight it, almost straining her neck, as she tried not to look again. She wanted to rush within, but knew that could not help. But she also knew that if they had come for Sarah and her family, then they would be sure to take everyone else in the house, too, Freddy included.

She almost turned back, but somehow she forced herself to carry on walking down the pavement, past the oak and the next building along, the effort of it such that she bit her lip, tasting steely blood. She walked on around the curve in the street, turning in to Adama Pługa, where she found a doorway to an apartment block in which she could pretend to shelter from the rain. For the first time in a long while she was sick. Physically sick from the fear.

Lidka forced herself to wait, there was not much to show that she had vomited in the porch in which she stood, as she had eaten little that day. There was just the acid stench of it on her laboured breath. If anyone watched from inside they kept quiet. The rain continued to fall on to the cobbles, like silver whip cracks on the stone.

She allowed enough time, she thought, that she might have been visiting someone, should the vehicles still be there, and she did not know how she had managed to wait those fifteen minutes or so, for they had seemed like fifteen weeks. She walked the short way back to the house, and as she did so the rain slackened then stopped. When Lidka saw that the car, the truck and the van had gone she almost broke in to a run, yet again she was able to stop herself. But she walked quickly now, her heels sharp clacks on the wet paving stones of the sidewalk. The gate shrieked loudly, as always, when she pushed it open. The door was still ajar, creaking softly in the breeze. She could hear nothing from inside the house.

Lidka walked inside, then halfway up the stairs. She stopped and listened, but did not call out. Still, she could not hear a thing, other than the drip of rainwater from the guttering over the hall window. She took another step and felt something beneath the sole of her shoe just before there was the firm crunch of thick glass breaking. She looked down and lifted her foot. It was a single thick, round lens from a pair of spectacles, now a starburst of splintered glass, which still held a scallop of light, reflected from the shaded bulb above her. She recognised the lens.

Then she heard sobbing. It came from the parlour, and she rushed up the final few stairs and pushed open the double doors. At first she hardly recognised the place. There was no furniture in the room now.

Mrs Paczkowska sat on the floor in the corner, her legs stretched out straight and stiff in front of her, her head bowed, shoulders shaking to her sobs. Then Lidka suddenly realised there was something else about the room. All the pictures had been taken. In their place there were brighter squares of yellow against the slightly paler wall, and ugly nails that it hurt to look at, almost as if they had been driven in to her flesh. The piano had also gone.

"They have taken Feliks," Mrs Paczkowska said, with a loud sniff.

"Freddy?"

Mrs Paczkowska did not answer.

Right then Lidka heard quiet footsteps behind her. She spun around quickly.

"Sarah, you're still here!"

Sarah nodded.

"Fre —"

"He's safe, with my family, in the hideaway."

"It's your fault," Mrs Paczkowska said. "Damn you Jews, I told him you would be nothing but trouble – and now he's gone!" she shouted the last four words.

"Mr Paczkowski?" Sarah said.

"Get out of my house, Jew!"

"Come Sarah, we should leave Mrs Paczkowska be for a moment."

Lidka took Sarah by her elbow and led her out of the parlour, closing the doors behind them. The click of the catch was like a switch for Mrs Paczkowska and she screamed her husband's name out loud, three times, before resuming her sobbing.

"He was an intellectual, we always knew there was a chance," Lidka said, quietly. He had been lucky to avoid being rounded up at the beginning. They had taken all the writers, the journalists, the theatre directors, the lecturers, the artists, anyone of cultural worth, and they had not been seen again. Now they had come for the art dealer.

"I must go and find Andrzej, he will need to know," Sarah said.

"No, it would be stupid for you to go out now," Lidka said. "Besides, you will not know where to find him."

"But —"

"Take me to Freddy, Sarah."

Mrs Paczkowska still sobbed behind the door. But Lidka did not know what she could do for her. Then she shouted once more: "Get out of my house, Jewish bitch, and take your dirty family with you!"

"What will we do?" Sarah asked, as they made their way down the stairs.

"You will stay here, she would not survive without the money from your father, it's all we have. She will calm down, in a day or two, and then she will realise that if the Nazis were made aware that you were hiding here, it would be the end for her, too."

"Mr Paczkowski; is there a way? Perhaps Andrzej?"

Lidka said nothing.

"But we must do *something!*" Sarah said, louder now.

"I will get word to Andrzej. There is nothing more we can do."

*

Lidka knew where to find Bullet at this time. She was one of the few people in Warsaw who did. He was staying in an apartment on Opaczewska, less than half an hour's walk away from the house on Mochnackiego, though he would not stay in this place, or any one place, for long. They had told neighbours on

189

Mochnackiego that he had been conscripted into forced labour in Germany, as many had, and so he seldom visited his family now. That, it had been decided, would be safer for everyone, for there were prying eyes everywhere in Warsaw.

The modernist apartment building, with its tall windows and steel-railed balconies, had been badly damaged in the fighting in '39. There were huge holes in its outer walls, so that it looked like a loaf that had been eaten through by giant mice, while its skin was dotted with acne-like scars of machine gun hits, which revealed the shattered brickwork beneath the cream rendering. She let herself in, knowing that someone watched from above. Bullet was on the third floor.

When she reached flat 33 she knocked twice, then paused, then knocked four more times. It was a sequence that changed every three days. Then she said through the door: "It's Chopin."

The door opened.

Cat did not greet her. Cat was not one for pleasantries. She thought there might have been a tiny switch at the corner of her mouth, which lit a dim light – off and on – in her eyes. But it might also have been the change of light, as Lidka stepped out of the dark corridor and into the main room of the apartment. Cat was a *nom de guerre,* Lidka did not know her real name, doubted she ever would. Cat did not give much away. Even when she was naked.

Cat stepped into a long skirt, her small but weighty-looking fruit-like breasts pointing at the floor as she bent down. She did not rush to dress. It was slow and deliberate, perhaps deliberately slow. She was pretty, although she always looked bored, which spoilt the effect a little. But now her face was flushed, and a few strands of her brunette hair were wetly pasted against her forehead. Lidka felt a knife of sharp emotion within her, something she had not experienced for a long time. It surprised and annoyed her.

Bullet sat at a rectangular dining table with four chairs around it; he wore dark-blue trousers and a grey vest, was barefoot and breathing slightly heavily. He watched the girl dress and did not greet Lidka, except for a quick nod. On the table in front of him was a pistol and two hand grenades, like dangerous salt and pepper, plus a copy of the *Biuletyn Informacyjny*, the AK's underground newspaper. The girl finished dressing, lacing up deliberately clumsy-looking boots and pulling a simple sweater over her naked breasts.

Lidka thought she should perhaps wait outside, but instead she just looked away from him, and the dressing girl, angry at the blush that seared her throat. There was a single picture on the wall, a photograph of a horse race in a wood and glass frame. Lidka read the caption, which told her it was the Warsaw Derby at Mokotów Field in 1935. It seemed so distant it might have been Venus, she thought. There was a small camp bed on the far side of the room, on which a single blanket had been twisted into the shape of a ragged S, a corner of it licking at the bare tiled floor. The bedroom would be still used by whoever lived here, she knew, though she guessed they were probably out now.

The light was milky grey, but strong enough to throw a hard-edged shadow across the room. She could smell gooseberry jam. Her sense of smell had become as keen as a spaniel's since the start of this war, and through the door to the small galley kitchen she could see the open jar of the tart smelling preserve, and half a loaf of bread on a cutting board. The AK always managed to find a little more food than most. Some resented that, but for Lidka it had been just another reason to join – though most of the extra food she was given went to Freddy, some to the others in the house.

Cat limped towards the door. It was not a disability, it was a stone she placed in her boot. She had discovered early that the Germans did not look twice at limping girls, would not force them into their field brothels. This and the scruffy clothes she wore made her almost invisible – in the way things are when a person looks away – and it also made Cat one of the best the AK had when it came to moving guns, taking messages. Almost as good as Lidka.

"It was good," Cat said, as she left, closing the door firmly behind her. It was about as much as Lidka had ever heard her say, but Bullet did not respond.

"I didn't know."

"Know what?"

"Cat and you"

Bullet shrugged: "It's nothing; do you disapprove?"

"Your business."

"I'm surprised to see you so soon," he said, as he picked up one of the egg-shaped pre-war Polish army hand grenades, ran his thumb over its smooth surface.

"She's young," Lidka said. "But then I forget sometimes, you're just a boy yourself."

"You were told not to visit unless it was import —"

"It's your father," Lidka cut in, then walked to the window where there was a view, between apartment blocks, of the railway sidings in the vast stock yard for the Warsaw-Vienna railway and the surrounding foundry and factories, one of which drizzled scratchy pencil-scribble smoke from a slender redbrick chimney. The low sun was an ash-burning glower through a fissure in the cloud-blotted sky. Down below the broken ground was dappled with glossy caramel-coloured puddles from the earlier rain. She waited for him to say something, but he did not.

"He's been taken, by the Gestapo," Lidka added.

Bullet still said nothing, but she heard the heavy tap of the grenade being softly placed on the table. She turned.

"What do you want me to do, cry?" he said. There was no sign of emotion, he wore the very same expression as when he had not acknowledged Cat as she left. Lidka felt a sudden chill in the room.

"He's your father."

"Just another father, one of many fathers they have taken."

"But *your* father"

"There's nothing that can be done."

"What will happen?"

"A camp, like the rest of them."

"Then?"

Bullet shrugged. Then he stood up, walked across the room, his bare feet squidging across the tiles, he reached for a thin brown sweater that was on a stool next to the low camp bed. He pulled it on, and she watched as his muscles bulged to the movement. She suddenly realised she was staring, and when his hair showed through the hole in the sweater she turned away again. She thought of her own father. She had visited him in Wagrowiec, a year ago, but without Freddy. She had argued with her stepmother and left after just a day. The letters from him had still come, though even fewer. Now they no longer came, and she had been told her father, an engineer, had been taken to Germany to work. She had not told him about Freddy, there had not been the right opportunity, and she wondered if that would have to wait until after the war, now. Thinking of her father reminded her of why she was here.

"So, you will do nothing?" she said.

Bullet did not answer, and now she picked up one of the hand grenades on the table. It was much heavier than she expected. It would take strength to throw one far, she thought.

"Be careful with that, teacher" Bullet said. "It's dangerous."

She put it down. "Your father, Andrzej?"

"I must forget him. Life goes on. It's war."

"That's awful," she said, facing him again.

He stared back at her, and paused before replying. Then said: "No, it's wonderful." For the first time since she had arrived there was a light in his eyes. "Don't you see, teacher, there are no rules now? Just survival. It's good to be alive at this time, if you're strong."

"That's a stupid thing to say."

"Is it, why? I can do what I like, now."

"And sleep with who you like?" she spat that, regretted it instantly.

"If you want." He smiled as he said it, but it was a mocking smile, she thought. "Better than waiting for Jósef, eh?"

She made for the door, not looking at him but saying as she went: "Your mother is still well; upset, of course, but she's stronger than you might think."

"The Jews?"

"As well as can be expected."

He did not ask about Sarah specifically, never did these days. Lidka left, annoyed that she had slammed the door behind her.

***

Mar del Plata, Argentina. February 1953

When Ingo was racing there was no room for doubt, no room for memories. All that mattered was the corner he was in, and then hitting the straight beyond as cleanly and quickly as possible. Sometimes, in the days when he had played piano, it had also been like this. A transcendent state of being, when all there was was the music.

The Condor slid in to the tight turn and he balanced it on a trailing throttle, before feeding in the power, the tail sliding a little more, but Ingo making sure the car was straight as he almost shaved the straw bale at the exit of the corner, before arriving at the start-line at the top of the serpentine and undulating street circuit to start his final lap. He had driven the race the way he had those two others he had competed in in the Condor; carefully to begin with, when the fuel load was heavy, saving the brakes and the tyres, then close to the limit for the final twenty laps. There had been little real competition here, a couple of Cisitalias and a Healey Silverstone, other than that it was mostly local drivers in sedans.

But there had also been Otero, in Varela's new Ferrari 225 Sport Berlinetta. Ingo had passed him on the brakes into the same tight corner he had just exited twelve laps ago, Otero having overheated his brake linings, judging by the smoke, in his efforts to keep Ingo behind him. The kid had tried to stick with Ingo, but had now dropped back to a vivid red insect bite on his mirror's surface on the straighter parts of the winding course. He would be busy trying to find an excuse now, Ingo thought, perhaps those brakes? It could not be his fault; that was for sure.

Ingo hit the downward slope, catching a peripheral glimpse of the Atlantic below, then took the left-handed first corner, and the series of turns that led to the seashore that followed it, in the same flowing manner he had on each and every lap before, cutting apices with precise surgeon strokes, and balancing the car in a light slide in each and every corner. Then he hit the section of the circuit that ran alongside the seashore; hotels clinging to the cliffs to his right, while to his left there was frothing surf and glossy black rocks, or dazzling sand, while the sun threw shining scallops of light on the water, on which bobbed nodding yellow fishing boats. The road was not straight here, but he ironed it with speed, almost skimming the high blue and white painted kerb stones as he threaded the needle, the V8 engine, a well-prepared Cadillac unit, still roaring sweetly. The airstream pushed Ingo's goggles tight to his face, while the smell of hot oil, finely baked brake linings, and the scorch of a well-worked clutch washed back over him, mixing with salty snatches of sea air.

There were people lining the street course along almost its entire length. Many were very close to the action, straw bales and ropes their only protection, their faces an olive and pink blur at this speed, against the blinding white of the buildings in the harsh sunlight. Sometimes, in this state of utter concentration, the world would seem to slow, as if he had beaten time into submission, and he would pick out a stark detail: a pretty girl in a prettier hat; a small boy with a melting ice cream, tracks of white painting skeletal patterns on his hand; a gull slicing through the sun-bleached sky. But they would never distract him.

Another corner ... Ingo positioned the car to the left of the track, almost brushing the bales once more, then let it slow a little on engine braking to save the linings, the V8 grumbling and crackling. Then he braked, and took it down a cog, double declutching and making the change as the clutch was out and the car was in neutral, blipping the throttle with the side of his right foot, the ball of it still firmly on the brake at the same time, this whole process the work of a part of a second. The engine sang a wonderful, steely high note to the blip, then burbled – a thoroughbred taking a breath – as Ingo finished the braking. The braking and downchange had settled the nose of the car in to the corner, the weight shifting to the front so that the steered wheels bit in to the asphalt. Ingo was still coming off the brake as he turned in.

He switched his right foot from brake to throttle, smoothly yet at the speed of thought, and floated the car through the turn. For a while all four tyres slid and he balanced it on the throttle, making tiny corrections with hands which sang with the shaking of the big, dimpled steering wheel, feeling the car through his fingertips – those piano fingers. The Condor kicked a little on a new patch of oil or fuel as he exited the turn, and he instinctively wound on a little opposite lock, easing the throttle very slightly, before pushing it to the floor for the straight that followed.

Soon he was flat out again, racing through a short tunnel now, the engine barking back at itself from the curved brick walls. He felt the camber in the road switch through his fingers, his right foot pushed firmly to the floor, the car's life transmitted through it, through his leg, through his entire being – shaking, pulsing, screaming – foot hard down, so that it almost hurt, wringing every last thrill of speed from the machine. He passed a smaller car, an old Ford sedan, as if it was standing still; just an acrid snatch of its burning clutch in his nostrils and a smear of bright green paint on his retinas.

No, there was no room for doubt at times like these, no room for memories. But times like these cannot last forever. The sight that saddened him most these days, even when it was being waved to show him he had won the race, was the chequered flag.

*

There were often photographers now. But they were usually content to take pictures of Ingo in the Condor. He would keep his helmet, now painted yellow and blue like the car, and goggles on for a little while, so there was not much to him other than that and a beard. But he knew from his past life that camouflage is not really about hiding, it's about deception and distraction, and there could not be many things quite as distracting as this beautiful sports racing car. Everyone wanted to take photographs of the Condor.

Ingo's arms now felt as heavy as wet sandbags from the effort of steering the Condor through the streets of Mar del Plata, his right leg ached from the braking, a little, while his left leg ached, a lot, from bracing himself in the seat in the turns. The heat radiated back from the engine and sweat ran down his face. He was tired and thirsty, and more down that the race was over than he was up that he had won it. It was always this way, finishing a race was like a little death.

Ingo climbed out of the mostly blue machine. There were no seatbelts to undo. Some thought them safer, most thought it better to be flung clear in a crash, but with the jury undecided on that, weight was the final judge – as always when building a racing car – and it had ruled that the Condor could do without belts. He stretched some of the stiffness from his limbs, and then he thanked the beautiful car, pressing his hand against the hot metal of the yellow bonnet and holding it there for some long seconds as the engine and body ticked and pinged as it cooled.

"I've never seen such love," Carlo said, patting him firmly on the back.

"I would marry her at the drop of a clutch," Ingo said.

"But first you need her father's permission."

The photographers were now taking pictures of Otero in the Ferrari. He had just parked up two pit stalls along. Ingo unbuckled his helmet and took it off. It was made of layers of hardened fabric stretched over a cork inner. There were leather earflaps attached to a chinstrap, and Ingo would usually fix a leather eye-shield, like a peak, to the front of the helmet. His goggles were glass, and he carried a spare pair in the car, while on the back of one of his thin leather driving gloves he had sewn a patch of chamois to quickly clean them during races – when it was wet he used a visor attached to the peak of the helmet. He knew of the damage loud noise could do, and so he always used rubber ear plugs. He wore a pale blue polo shirt, with a velvet strip sewn inside the collar to stop his neck chafing in long races, and trousers with elasticated cuffs, so they would not snag on the pedals. He also wore a wide kidney belt, to keep everything in place when the car bucked and jolted on badly surfaced roads, while his racing shoes had been made specially for him, here in Mar del Plata; leather with thin soles, but with an extra layer of asbestos beneath the soles on each shoe to stop his feet burning due to heat conducted through the steel pedals.

"We have a visitor," Carlo said.

Varela was walking towards them, his fat face quivering as he shook his head sharply. Ingo guessed that he had been talking to his driver, Otero. Varela's tan was deeper than when he had last seen him, muddy going to leather, and Ingo smelt his strong cologne before he had come within three metres of them.

"You would think *that* one would have learnt how to lose, by now," Varela said to Carlo.

"In Europe he had his arse handed to him so many times it now has more fingerprints than the Federal Police," Carlos said, laughing.

"But the speed is there," Varela said.

"You're a patient man, Signor Varela."

"Some say stubborn."

"I didn't."

"No, but they might be right. On occasion." He looked over his shoulder, down the pit road a little way, to where Otero glowered at the fine-looking red Ferrari coupe, like a thrown polo player admonishing his pony.

"Brakes?" Ingo said.

Varela did not answer the question, but said: "The speed is here, too." He was looking at the Condor, not Ingo. He could not blame him for that. It was parked in the temporary pit area amidst a cluster of fuel cans and spare wheels in front of wooden tables and outside one of the garages made of scaffolding stretched with canvas, a place smelling strongly of spilled petrol. Some said it looked like the new Maserati A6GCS, but Ingo knew that was just coincidental, as he had seen the drawings for this car long before the Italian car had been conceived. Its fenders, front and back, were large and rounded, bulging proud of the bodywork like muscles, and, even when coated in the dust from a hard race, the tops of them shone as if the sun was favouring them. They covered wire wheels, now caked in grime. The grille was a snarl, but rounded a little so that anger did not spoil its beauty. The front of the car was long, so that it would take a variety of engines, while the bonnet bulged in to the driver's eye-line to accommodate the V8's height. There was a single small windscreen, and in this race version – the only type yet produced – a canvas cover was stretched over the space where a passenger seat would normally be. The doors were small, and it was almost as easy to step over them as to open them to get in. The rear of the car was rounded, and there was a shining fuel cap behind the cockpit and in front of the small trunk-lid, which marked where the tank was located. The Condor bore the number 57 and was a shade deeper blue than the Argentinian flag, with a yellow bonnet. It also had a badge of a blazing sun set within the radiator grille. There was no mistaking this for anything other than an Argentinian car.

There was also no mistaking Ingo for anything other than an Argentinian driver, everyone now simply took him for a German Argentinian, of which there were very many – and had been even before the rats had escaped the sinking pocket battleship of the Third Reich.

"I will be in Buenos Aires on Wednesday, before I fly to New York," Varela said. "There will be time for lunch."

"Lunch?" Carlo said.

"There are things we should discuss."

"Why not here?" Ingo said.

"I'll be staying at the Alvear Palace," Varela said, addressing Carlo and ignoring Ingo. "Bring your driver, if you wish."

Ingo turned away, to see a photographer taking a snap of the Condor with his Graflex Speed Graphic. Otero stood some way behind the photographer, up the pit lane, his arms folded tightly to his chest. He was staring at Ingo, looking like a kid who had had his toy smashed. But even as Ingo acknowledged him with a slight nod, that look morphed into hard, grown up, anger, and Otero turned his back on Ingo and walked away.

***

Oryol, Soviet Union. February 1943

"Every brothel has a piano."

"Even a field brothel? Seems a lot of effort, to lug a piano around Russia," Ingo said.

"Well, if you don't think there'll be a piano, why you coming then, eh?" Pop said. He seemed irritable. Had been all day.

"Just saying … Lot of effort."

"Yeah, lot of effort to play the piano."

It had been a lot of effort. First they had had to go to the medic to check they were clear of pox, clap, crabs and whatever else; then they were given a date-stamped pass to say so, plus an Odilei rubber in a little white and red packet and a small green can of disinfectant. All this because he wanted to play piano. For, as Pop said, there was always a piano in a brothel.

This was the first time Ingo had agreed to go with Pop to one of the military brothels. They were queuing in a frozen space between two apartment blocks on Moskovskaya. The wind whistling past the entrance to the alley carried a buckshot of snowy pellets that hurt the face, so Ingo was glad of the shelter, but still shivered uncontrollably from the cold that now resided in his bones.

The queue of well wrapped-up German soldiers, each one in an ironic hurry to get out of his uniform, stretched for twenty foot-stamping metres, a double line between brick walls blistered with patches of dirty ice. Not many of them spoke as they stood in line. There was not much to say, no one wants to talk about the weather when it's always way below freezing, and no one wants to talk about the news when it's always way beyond bad. Stalingrad had fallen, an entire army gone, thrown away some said; quietly. When an army is destroyed it makes a single soldier feel vulnerable. Pop reckoned it might take another two years to win the war now. At this rate Ingo would be an old man of 26 before he raced his first race.

While others stamped their felt-boot clad feet for warmth Pop's right foot did its now-usual thing, as if he was tapping time to some unseen drummer. He placed his thickly-gloved hand on the shoulder of the man in front of him, and asked as the snow-smock wearing soldier turned: "Say pal; got any Stuka tablets?"

The man looked numb with the cold, his lips parted slowly, but nothing came out except a cloud of white breath.

"Panzer chocolate?" Pop added; there seemed to be almost as many nicknames for Pervitin as there were soldiers who had developed a taste for it.

Pop had already asked others in the line, but with no luck. It was getting harder and harder to find it now, since the Heer had stopped issuing it. Even for Pop, who could usually get his hands on most things, one way or an another. The man shook his head.

"I'll pay good money for it," Pop said, but the man did not answer, just turned away.

"I thought we were keeping the good money for racing?" Ingo said, through chattering teeth – he seemed to be always shivering these days, as if he was still sitting on a vibrating motorcycle.

"Just to help get me through the cold, Ingo, that's all," Pop said, risking taking his gloves off to light up an Atikah.

They queued a little while longer, until the line shuffled through a steel door that clanged shut behind each pair of men and led into a corridor stained and slippery with the snow melting off the boots of the soldiers. This led to another door, where two chained dogs were stationed. Beyond the two military policemen there was another inside, sat at a table, checking the health passes and then adding the Feldgendarmerie stamp to them. Pop and Ingo were next in line.

"Is there a piano?" Ingo asked the chained dog.

"Comedian, eh?"

"Come on Ingo, stop arsing around; you know why we're here," Pop said.

"I'm not sure, what about Lidka?"

"You could be dead tomorrow, she could be dead now, or more likely married with children. Just live, Ingo," Pop said, pushing his way through a swing door and taking the stairs on the direction of the chained dog, who was still shaking his head. Ingo followed him. The place looked as if it had once been a hostel for workers, and the corridor on the third floor they were directed to was lined with small rooms. It was a depressing building, the paint was peeling from the walls and only a few of the unshaded bulbs down the corridor were working, and what light there was had a sick yellow tinge to it; it all somehow reminded Ingo of severe bruising.

An old woman swaddled in about five layers of clothes checked their cards and took their money, then showed Ingo to a room, leaving him by the door, before leading Pop further down the corridor. Ingo knocked, but there was no reply. Then he pushed open the door. The naked girl lay on the bed. She was young, and she had breasts where there were supposed to be breasts and a clump of wiry hair where there was supposed to be hair, and the whitest skin. He felt the beginnings of arousal. It was cold in the room, though nowhere near as cold as it was outside. There was a heavy smell of heated metal and a radiator ticked against one of the walls, there was also a strong smell of disinfectant. There was a window, which let in grey light and rattled to the strong wind, while beads of icy snow dashed against the glass, like a brush on a cymbal.

He smiled at her, said "hello" but she did not smile, or reply. She just opened her legs, mechanically.

He knew this was when he was supposed to spray her with the disinfectant. He aimed it at her vagina, which looked red and sore in contrast to the pale skin of her thighs, and then emptied the small can. To not use it and the condom would mean trouble, if he caught anything from a whore it could mean a spell in jail and a transfer to a penal battalion, but as soon as he had sprayed it at her, in her, he knew he could not do this.

The last time – the first time – had been somehow magical, special. But what he had just done had felt like oiling a machine. That small spray can had shrivelled all the aching hope he had had that he would be able to do it, and for the first time that day he honestly wished there had been a piano in the field brothel. But he also felt a little relieved.

He took off his black side cap and then his reversible camouflage coat, now showing its white side, which he lay over the girl, who closed her legs as he did so, then he sat on the end of the bed, looking at his Helma Heer-issue wristwatch and wishing his fifteen minutes would finish.

The minute hand moved slowly. He could hear the sounds of beds creaking and headboards banging and men panting. There was laughter, too, from somewhere, a woman – a whore he supposed – cackling loud.

"Well, at least someone's having a good time," he said to himself.

"I don't think so," the girl said, in German but with a peculiar accent. He turned to face her. She had wrapped the coat around her, and it made her look small and vulnerable. He realised he had hardly noticed her face when he had come in to the room, and he felt bad about that now. She wasn't pretty, nor ugly, and her mousy hair was cut short with a stark fringe that formed a triangle with the sharp cheekbones of her thin face. Her eyes seemed older than the rest of her, he thought. He knew that many of the whores were forced into this work.

"There is still time," she said. "If you want?"

He shook his head. "Where're you from?"

"It no longer matters," she said. "Why not?"

"There's a girl."

"But she is far away?"

He nodded. Then he heard that laugh again, then a sound he did not recognise at first, sharp, yet wet-like.

"It doesn't pay to laugh," she said, and as she said it he realised the laughing woman was being beaten. He heard another slap, or punch, then a few more, and then men's voices, raised; more punches. One of those voices was unmistakable: Pop.

Ingo stood up, the bed creaking, and made for the door.

"Your coat?" she said

"Thank you," he said, as she threw it to him.

"No, thank you," she said, and almost smiled.

He opened the door and looked up the corridor. Other doors had opened, too. In the wash of one of the yellowish lights Ingo saw that Pop, naked from the waist down, had a man by the throat. Because Pop was far shorter than the other man and had to look up at him it almost seemed as if he was holding him in the air, the muscles in his right arm bulging. The man's nose was a ripe cherry explosion of blood, a drop of which dripped and splashed against Pop's upturned face. There was a big-breasted woman, a whore, of course, naked except for a pair of lace drawers, she was crying, and the skin around one of her eyes was reddening. She was jabbering on in Russian. Other doors had opened because of the noise of the fight, but some ignored it and he could still hear the rhythmic squeak of bedsprings. He could also hear steel heel guards dinging up the stairs and the jangle of Feldgendarmerie gorgets.

Pop saw Ingo; looked surprised, then said: "That'll teach the bastard, eh?"

"Chained dogs!" Ingo shouted.

"Come on," Pop shouted back. "There must be another way out down the corridor." With that he let go of the naked soldier and the man slid down the wall to the floor, clutching his throat. Pop quickly gathered his things from one of the rooms and they ran, disappearing through a door at the bottom of the corridor just as they heard the Feldgendarmarie arrive – it was always best to run rather than reason with the chained dogs, even if you were in the right. Soon they were down another staircase, stopping quickly in a stairwell for Pop to hurriedly dress in the rest of his black Panzerwaffe uniform, plus his large felt boots, side cap and winter coat, and then they were through a steel door and out in to the snowy street, emerging behind the long queue for the brothel. They walked on for a while without talking, the ice-laced wind stinging their faces.

"Do you reckon there'll be trouble, for that?" Ingo said.

"Doubt it. It's a brothel. There are always fights in a brothel."

"You said that about pianos," Ingo said.

"It's a pity, she was nicely stacked, all right," Pop said.

"So, you didn't?" Ingo said.

"No, no time," Pop said. "What about you?"

"Same, I heard you going to the rescue; and that was that."

"Looks like that thug spoilt the fun for both of us, pal, eh?" Pop said, and there was an edge of anger to his voice.

"I only came along to play the piano, anyway."

"Sure you did," Pop said. "Like you only came to war to ride a motorcycle."

***

Buenos Aires. February 1953

Catalina had said she wanted to see inside the Alvear Palace, Buenos Aires' fanciest hotel, but Ingo thought there was more to it than that. She trusted Carlo, he knew, just not where racing cars were concerned. This was probably the real reason she had decided to join them on the long drive to the capital – a *very* long drive in Carlo's rattling old Ford truck – and leave the children with a friend. Well, that and the chance to spend some of the prize money they had started to rake in shopping in the swanky boutiques on Florida. Either way, now it seemed that they were not to see so much of the Alvear Palace after all …

It wasn't much of a walk to La Biela, just around the corner and a little up the hill from the Alvear, maybe 250 metres at most. Not much of a walk, but then Varela was not much of a walker, and so they took a black and yellow city cab. The French style corner café, where Quintana meets Junín, overlooked a pleasant green space between it and the high white walls of the Recoleta Cemetery, where the great and the good of the gone and the dead of Argentina lay in tombs of granite and marble that were grander and costlier than most of the houses in San Telmo and La Boca.

Ingo had heard of this place, many in the racing business had. Biela meant 'connecting rod', a new name the café had acquired recently from its clientele; for this was where the racers connected in Buenos Aires. When Fangio was in town he would come here for a drink, as would the Gálvez brothers. Jorge Luis Borges was also a regular. But there were no writers nor racing drivers – Ingo aside – here now, and he caught the disappointment in Varela's eyes when he could find no one of note he could make a scene of greeting. But then BA could be like that this time of the year, when it was stifling hot, and those who could afford it got out of town. Most of the customers here today sat outside on the terrace, beneath a huge rubber tree that dripped dappled shade, or under the green and white striped canopy which fringed the café and seemed to change aspect as you looked at it, from green stripes on white to white stripes on green.

Because of the heat the large windows had been slid up and bunched white cotton curtains moved a little to the slight breeze. The café was quite large, with a bar space backed with glistening bottle of spirits. Square wooden tables with stark linen cloths sat beneath black ceiling fans that spun slowly, like feathered propellers on a Heinkel. In common with many Argentinian bars and cafés the walls were panelled in dark wood to head height, and then painted a milky white to the high ceiling. There were pictures here, too: Ingo recognised Fangio in an Alfa Romeo 159 and there was González, bullying a Ferrari 375 through a turn. The café smelt of freshly brewed coffee and frying onions and the high ceiling amplified the clash of cutlery on crockery, and the laughter from those few other groups of diners.

The waiter, dressed in a green waistcoat and bow tie, made a fuss of the big man with the sheen of sweat on his forehead and Ingo thought that cheered Varela a little, made up for the lack of a famous face to greet. They were shown to a table close to one of the open windows and Varela ordered Cubano cocktails all-round. Ingo was glad of the ice-clunking drink, for he was as hot as Varela looked, but that was because Carlo had persuaded him to wear a suit. It was something he had picked up at Gath & Chaves on his last visit to Buenos Aires, for the sports car race here a few weeks earlier. A big beard and a suit always seemed a strange combination to Ingo, but he knew it was best to do what was expected of him – these days. Carlo, too, wore a suit. But Ingo thought it was worry that made him sweat a little, not the heat. He could not recall seeing him quite so nervous ever before. Catalina was in a light red summer dress, while Varela wore a linen suit.

"The last time I was here it was with El Cheuco," Varela said.

"El Cheuco?" Catalina said.

"Fangio's nickname," Carlo said.

"Many Argentinian drivers have nicknames," Varela continued. "Fangio is El Cheuco, and Froilán González is El Cabezon. Though I hear the English call him The Pampas Bull."

"Pampas Bull is right, the man can be unstoppable when he's in the mood," Carlo said.

"You have one, too," Varela said, looking at Ingo.

"I do?"

"El Tímido."

The shy one, Ingo translated it in his head.

"Well, that's true," Catalina said.

"You do not need to be a braggart to win races," Carlo put in.

Varela looked at Ingo, and said: "But who wins these races, the driver or the car?"

"What do you think?" Ingo said.

Varela did not answer him, but instead he turned to Carlo: "Have you thought how that car might go with a better engine?"

"I think of this all the time."

"*That* is also true," Catalina said.

Varela laughed at that, then said: "But here's lunch, at last," though they had not waited long for their food. Ingo thought Varela seldom waited long for anything.

They ate starters of fried calamari and Ingo chose a steak for his main – that was a sure way to show you were 100 per cent Argentinian, he had found. Varela went for something even more Argentinian than beef, though, parrillada, a mixed grill of sausages, lamb, chitterlings, testicles, kidneys and some other lumps of bleeding offal that reminded Ingo a little too much of things he had seen falling out of bodies on battlefields. They wouldn't normally do parrillada, that was usually the sort of thing you'd only find in a parilla, naturally, but Varela tended to get what he wanted, and paid for the privilege.

Varela did not talk too much during the meal, he concentrated on chewing, however much Carlo tried to turn the conversation around to the Condor, but once he had hastily dispatched his dessert of pancakes and dulce de leche he lit a Romeo y Julieta, without waiting for the others to finish, and then stared out of the open window, in the direction of the grand cemetery. He looked at its walls through the smoke of his cigar for long moments, perhaps wondering if he might ever buy his way into it, one day, then he studied the palm of his left hand for a moment before finally saying: "Next year there is to be a world championship sports car race, here in Buenos Aires."

"I've heard," Carlo said, as Varela sucked on his Havana.

Varela puffed out some cedar smelling cigar smoke, then added: "Your car could go well there, with a new engine; a thoroughbred racing engine, rather than that Caddy lump you're carting around now."

"We have no new engine."

"There's a new engine in my Ferrari."

Carlo dropped his fork in his dessert dish and it clanged dully, then sat with his mouth wide open.

"Oh, and I have money, too, of course," Varela added, over-casually.

Carlo shook himself, literally, pushed his plate away and – without asking – took one of Varela's Havanas.

"And my driver?" He glanced at Ingo.

"We will need two drivers, it's a long distance race. And we have two drivers."

"Yes, that's true," Carlo said, holding the cigar between his fingers, but not yet attempting to light it.

"So, we are in agreement?" Varela said. "I will come in as partner, put up the money to race this car, *these* cars perhaps, eventually."

"You have changed your mind, then?" Carlo said.

"No, the Condor has changed my mind."

Carlo looked at Ingo. It had been his money that had built the car, but they always knew they could only go so far on that. But the real issue was that that was pretty much as far as Ingo wanted to go. He said nothing, just swallowed some of the sweet Malbec dessert wine, and looked out of the window in the direction of the Plata and thought of the sea beyond it, the huge Atlantic Ocean, across aching miles of which lay Europe, and the past. But the ocean did not seem quite so vast to Ingo at that very moment.

*

Nice, France. February 1953

Sarah gazed past her reflection and watched the activity on the Promenade des Anglais three floors below her room in the Hotel Negresco. The seafront road was busy with noise and light. She opened the window a little, letting a little of the fresh, cold sea air in to help wash away the fug from Yitzhak's cigarettes. He had been smoking all day, Gauloises. It was what he did while they waited. In the reflection she could see him now, cool and calm, as always. To look at Yitzhak no one would guess he packed a double-edged British Commando dagger, the tool of his trade, and that tonight he would use it. He wore a black Brioni suit that was as sharp as his knife, and a thin grey snake of a silk tie.

Sarah went to the dressing table, checked her makeup one last time; as much a tool of her trade as Yitzhak's dagger was of his. She added a dab of Fracas by Robert Piguet, it worked well in the night, disarming with its swirl of flowery top and heart notes with orangey hints, then the sandalwood and cedar dark forest smells at its base. When a man thinks for a moment about what he is smelling, it's another moment he is vulnerable.

"You look good, as always," Yitzhak said, matter-of-factly, sniffing the perfume.

"You're ready?"

"Been ready for hours," he said.

She looked at her watch, there was a little time left, and it was no use being early – walking too slow could look as bad as walking too fast, people wanted to get somewhere at this time on a winter's evening.

"Five minutes," she said.

"Time, if you want?" Yitzhak said with a leery grin, throwing a sideways nod at the huge double bed. "Won't take me longer than four minutes with you looking like that."

She was about to tell him to shut up when the phone rang. It was so unexpected they both froze for a moment, before Sarah shook herself and answered it.

"Mrs Burrows?" the hotel telephone operator said.

"Yes," Sarah said. Yitzhak and Sarah had travelled as a married couple on US passports. For the plan they had he needed to be the husband this time, and Shlomo had already gone on ahead to the Vieille Ville. Yitzhak was a soldier, could sleep anywhere he always boasted, and so he had slept on the floor.

"There is a call for you." With that it was put through.

"Hello, can you talk?" Gabriel said hello in English, then switched to Hebrew, but did not say her or his name. She glanced at Yitzhak and he nodded and left the room, pointing at his watch to remind her to be careful of the time.

"What is it?" she said, it was unusual for Gabriel to call when they were on a mission.

"I know you have work to do, so I will be brief. I always promised you that as soon as I knew anything, then I would tell you straight away."

"It's him, you've found him?" The thrill of it was like an electric shock.

"Not quite, but the net is closing. We know which country he is in."

Sarah was silent for a moment, the only sound the static hiss of the line, and a horn from a car on the wide boulevard below.

"You still there?" he said.

"Yes, sorry. Is it where we thought?" Even though they spoke in Hebrew she knew it would not do to talk in detail over the telephone.

"It is."

Argentina.

"Anything else?"

"Not much, but as I said, we're closing in."

Yitzhak opened the door and pointed at his watch.

"I have to go," she said.

"Yes, of course."

"Thank you," she said.

With that Gabriel hung up and the line went dead.

"Good news?" Yitzhak asked.

She said nothing, shrugged the fur coat over her sleeveless bottle green silk dress, took a last look in the mirror, and then they left the room, Yitzhak locking the door behind them.

They walked along the promenade overlooking the Plage Beau Rivage, watching the lights on the yachts offshore twinkle and dip in the soft swell, which shushed against the beach like soothing bedtimes she only half remembered. The sea smelt like it should do, finally loosening the odour of Gauloises from her nasal passages.

It would take almost 15 minutes before they crossed the road and headed in to the Vieille Ville. They had chosen the place where they would meet up with the Doctor carefully. Ten years before the Doctor had worked in Buchenwald, alongside Waldemar Hoven, experimenting on the inmates, or finding more efficient ways of killing them. Dr Kurt Braun had disappeared at the end of the war. It was an American, a former airman and POW who had been held in Buchenwald for a while, who had spotted him in Nice. Word soon reached Gabriel. Now Braun was selling morphine to the many who would buy it – some came out of the war with medals, most with nightmares, others with addictions. War changes everyone, in some way.

She did not know if war had changed *him*.

... They had not operated in South America yet, it might be tricky, she thought. The cost would be an issue, too, but their backers were generous, they had even started to pay for good hotels and fine clothes ...

"Shlomo is in place," Yitzhak said, and it startled Sarah. Without her really realising they had crossed into the Vieille Ville and were now in the alleyways. She had not been concentrating, she had been thinking of *him*. It was unforgivable.

"You okay?" Yitzhak said.

"Of course."

Thinking of *him* ... As always ... Gabriel was right, an obsession. She wondered what he now did, in that far off land. She knew little of it – tango and gauchos, that's all – she would have to buy a book. Many books ...

"He's here," Yitzhak said, a sharp whisper from the corner of his mouth. She shook herself from within and tried to shake the image of *him* from her head. Shlomo would be ready at the other end of the alley, with a Browning 9mm in case Yitzhak messed up. But Yitzhak never messed up. There were no windows overlooking the alleyway. It was perfect for buying drugs – or killing Nazis. The man leant against a wall, one leg bent back, a shoe sole pressed flat against the stone, the other leg stiff. He smoked, and he wore the peaked leather stevedore's cap that was his trademark.

It was time for her to play her part.

"You're the doctor," she said.

"Tonight, I am the doctor."

That *tonight*, snagged within, but there was no time for hesitation. She had one of Yitzhak's cigarettes ready, in the long holder that fitted her furs and fine green dress so well. She asked the Doctor for a light; it was the signal. He stood up straight, yet he was somehow a little shorter than she expected ... then he stepped and leant forward and spun the wheel on his Zippo lighter as Yitzhak moved behind him. There was a sharp sniff of lighter fuel, and then a hazy patch of light burnt through the alley's dark cloak.

She saw his face as she heard the steel sink into his side; once, twice, Yitzhak's hand over his mouth in the same instant, then the blade passed across his throat, a dark gash of bubbling blood, as the lighter dropped from a dying hand.

By now Sarah knew they had killed the wrong man.

***

Ivot, east of Novgorod-Seversky, Soviet Union. March 1943

Being in a tank was like being in an oven in summer, and a refrigerator in winter. Today their Panzer IV was a fridge. Pop had been wrong about that, it was not really an escape from the cold, the IV had no heater, but Ingo supposed it was still much warmer than sitting on the Zündapp. He glanced at his photograph of Lidka, which he had affixed to the steel plate alongside the vision slit, it flickered to the vibrations of the steel. He wondered what she was up to now; and then wondered if she wondered what he was up to ...

Their panzer was the first of the three-tank platoon to enter the village. Ingo was still only along for the ride, but it was also still a race. Panzers were slow, compared to the Zündapp, but when there was ice and snow on the ground, or a little mud, Ingo could sometimes get it to slide, and today there was a mix of all three. He double declutched, blipping the throttle to match the engine speed of the lower gear, and changed down in to second; clutching and braking the right track with the right-hand lever, wrenching the heavy control back two thirds of the way, the tank squirming a little in the porridge of snow and mud, its nose dipping as the right track snatched. The turret above and behind him was traversing, and he could feel the weight of the long 75mm calibre gun hanging out to the right through the levers as he steered around the tight turn, driving the left track in first gear – which gave the panzer a turning circle of just under six metres. All the while the inside of the tank filled with the deafening noise and the choking cordite from the coaxial MG 34 machine gun, mounted alongside the main gun. Even when the machine gun stopped firing the noise was oppressive; what with the clanking of the tracks and the leaf-spring suspension, and the roar of the 300bhp V12 Maybach engine in the large rear compartment.

Ingo could not see much through the thick block of layered ballistic glass in his rectangular vision slit, it was as if he was looking at the world from far inside a letterbox, but with the addition of smudges and a dim reflection of his own face. This heightened his other senses, overstretching them as they reached out for grenade bangs, rattling gunfire, the crackle of burning wood and the snatched smells of fire, fuel and the pepper-iron of propellent; the feel of ice cold steel – even through his padded seat – the clattering movement of the panzer tracks through his quivering, firm grip on the controls; and the dry, acid taste of battle in his mouth. He caught glimpses of the village as they went through it, much of it was in flames already.

He straightened the tank and then accelerated, made a very fast but ultra-smooth gear-change through the double-H pattern six-speed gate, the tank not quite hiccupping in its progress as he kept its twenty-four tonnes moving forward with barely diminished speed, never giving the heavy tracks the chance to smother the panzer's progress with their high rolling resistance.

The Russians had counter attacked, and the Germans were now counter attacking the counter attack. The village had simply chosen the wrong place to be a village, but Ingo doubted it would be a village for too much longer. The Russian soldiers, aided by partisans, were fighting for every inch of it, but most of them were dead, many in the road ahead, like fallen brown leaves in autumn. The panzers had destroyed the outlying buildings and moved in slowly, but now they were in the centre of the burning settlement, trusting the panzer grenadiers to protect them as much as the panzer grenadiers trusted them to clear the way forward.

One hundred metres ahead the heart of the village was framed in the glassy oblong that was Ingo's world. It was a tight patch between the houses – some burning, some not yet burning – rather than a town square, with three rough streets radiating out from it. In the foreground the white-wrapped crouched backs of panzer grenadiers rushed up the street ahead of them, some tossing stick grenades in to houses.

Their tank was now being hit by small arms fire, pinging and ringing against the armour, noisy but harmless, mosquitoes teasing a rhino. Even sealed in the panzer he could smell the reek of death in the air, stronger now, and fires, always burning. He was looking far ahead, out of habit from driving fast, ahead to where a bright flower of machine gun fire burst from a point beyond the square. To his right side, his head just visible over the steel bulkhead between them, the radio operator, Roth, was raking the front of a house with the hull-mounted MG 34, aiming through its long sight and swivelling it with its pistol grip, bright yellow flashes blooming in the dirty wood, the machine gun so close to Ingo that the noise of it seemed to be hammering inside his head, behind his eyes.

Just then something closer caught Ingo's eye; on the ground ahead, right in front of the tank's left track. The Russian soldier was dragging himself through the slushy mud with his arms. There was nothing of him from the thighs down, and he looked like a crawling paintbrush, turning the mud and snow bright red behind him. But he was still obviously alive, and his eyes, as he looked at the approaching tank, were ablaze with fear, and hatred.

Ingo stood on the main clutch and brake, and the heavy machine slithered in the mud, the sudden slowing throwing the four others in the tank forward. They came to a halt just a metre or so from the mutilated Russian.

"What's the problem, driver?" The commander's voice was tinny over the intercom, and breathless. It was Leutnant Graf's first action.

"He's stopped to save an Ivan!" Roth snapped back, the sneer in his voice crackling over the intercom. He then pivoted the hull machine gun hard-left and down, at its extreme minimum elevation, and aimed at the half-man's head, the only thing he could see from his seat because the Ivan was now mostly hidden by the front of the tank. He pulled the trigger on the MG 34, taking the top off the man's skull as if he was slicing open a boiled egg.

Just then there was a clunk from behind, dull but heavy, like a bell in a submerged church, and Ingo felt the tank slide a little to one side on the slick mud. The following panzer was barging past, he realised, probably assuming they had a mechanical problem, and he now heard it scraping down the side of their tank as it found a way through on the narrow street. Ingo selected first gear, gunned the engine and let out the clutch, the tracks crushing what was left of the dead Russian. The other tank rattled on in to the small village square, ahead of them now.

The shell hit the other tank from close range, smashing its track, which flailed out and beat the ground around it, the dry bark of the enemy gun heard the same time as the hit. "Halt!" Graf's voice was brittle over the intercom, and Ingo once more stepped on the brake, seeing the barrel of the main gun dip in front of him through his slot as the tank bowed on its suspension. Ahead of him the other panzer's turret was traversing, but before it had gone through forty-five degrees it was hit again, this time in the engine compartment. The tank exploded with a hollow crump, bright flames rising from its rear deck. Its hatch then popped open and clanged against the top of the turret. Then a man appeared amidst the flames, his arms raised like a puppet, but his strings were quickly snipped with a scissors of enfilading machine gun fire, while at the same time an Ivan lobbed a grenade through the hatch. There was another, more muted, explosion.

"What was it?" There as an edge of panic in Graf's voice, accentuated by the static.

"Yellow-painted house at two-o'-clock!" Pop's voice came over the intercom, clear and sure, and Ingo heard the turret's motor whirr as it traversed, saw the shadow of the gun like a watch hand ticking off time on the muddy dial of the street in front of him. He selected reverse ready for a quick getaway, but held the tank steady for Pop to take his shot.

The panzer rocked to the recoil of the big gun, the gases hot and acrid within the tight space, choking Ingo and causing him to cough. The HE shell ripped through the wooden walls of the house, sending a tin bath high in to the air, well out of the scope of Ingo's view so that he never saw it land. Then he heard the loader, Krause, ejecting a hot shell case and loading a replacement, a noise of steel and gas, while the smoke in front of Ingo cleared to reveal a squat grey and white painted wheeled anti-tank gun with a shield that scraped the floor in what had been a living room – a Pak 38, a captured piece, then. It sat right inside what was left of the house Pop's high explosive shell had all but destroyed. Its crew were dazed and staggering, but somehow alive, and also managing to move the gun, now trying to get it to bear on Ingo's tank. It had been a clever ambush, using surprise and close range to knock out the other tank, and they had done well to hold fire until the first panzer grenadiers had passed them by.

But now there was nowhere to hide. Both machine guns opened up and the gun crew were cut to rare mince, while other rounds sparked off the Pak's shield.

"Forward driver," Graf said, and Ingo selected first and let out the clutch.

"Christ Ingo, we would have been tinned meat if you hadn't have stopped for that soggy Ivan," Pop said over the intercom.

"Quiet!" Graf ordered.

It did not take long for the panzer grenadiers to clear the village and then they all moved on to a wood the other side. Ingo parked the panzer up in a clearing and the crew swapped the misery of confinement for the misery of even colder air. Krause had built a fire and was heating up five mess tins, each hanging from a spit over the flames, the lids placed loosely so as not to stick. In one he boiled potatoes they had scavenged, the others contained a mix of tinned rations: beef goulash; bacon and peas; and liver sausage. Krause would normally add a fresh onion if he could, or whatever he had. It was hot, and sometimes tasty – either way, mixing the food helped to disguise the awful texture of the hated bacon and peas. A good fire also gave warmth, so when possible they would always heat their food this way, rather than using the folding Esbit field stoves and trioxane tablets.

They sat around the fire, warming their hands in front of it like supplicants at the altar of heat. They wore white winter coats and trousers over their black panzer uniforms, the hoods covering their side caps. Graf wore a peaked hat; as was the fashion with many of the young officers he had removed the wire stiffener from the crown, so that it looked like a crusher cap.

Their position was guarded from any remaining Russians by panzer grenadiers, but they could not guard against the biting wind which – despite the shelter of the tank and a heavy, stiff, tarpaulin that was over it and them – still stirred the flames under the mess tins into a flickering dance. Graf was writing in a notebook. The other panzer, still smouldering in the village, was part of his platoon, and he would have to explain its loss; the third tank was parked a hundred metres away, also under a camouflaged tarpaulin to help hide it from Ivan aircraft. Ingo's eyes feasted on the relatively unrestricted views as much as his nose feasted on the smell of the warming mess tins – spicy goulash the dominant aroma. He could still see the burning village, and the burning tank when the wind tugged at the pall of black smoke that lay over the place, but otherwise, they were hemmed in by trees, except for a dirt road, which the wind was using as an autobahn. The tall pines nodded and fidgeted, and some dumped slabs of built up snow every now and then, the resulting crunches causing the nearby group of panzer grenadiers to reach for their weapons.

Graf snapped shut the notebook.

"Ingo, I need to speak to you," Graf said; tank crews were supposed to be tight, first names would often do, in one direction at least.

"Sir?"

"Alone."

"It's too cold to go wandering off now, sir," Pop put in. "And what've you got to hide? We all saw what happened, Ingo stood on the brakes – a rare thing in itself," he grinned at that, "and pretty much saved our bacon."

"I didn't see it like that Unterfeldwebel," Graf used Pop's NCO rank to show him he was annoyed. "He stopped because he was not able to run over that man."

"And if he hadn't stopped we would have been the first tank in, sir – and we know what happened to that."

"Six did not know —"

"Combat instinct, sir," Pop cut in.

"What's that supposed to mean?" Graf said, looking at Ingo.

Ingo shrugged, as the camouflaged tarpaulin above them cracked in the wind.

"It comes, sir, with time," Pop said.

Graf looked puzzled. Then he yawned, and Ingo yawned with him. They had been on the go for days before they had finally gone into action earlier today, and none of them had had much sleep, beyond nodding off at their stations.

"Leutnant Graf!" a panzer grenadier hauptmann shouted from a position behind some fallen trees one hundred metres away, the rest of his words were whipped away by the wind, but he beckoned, too. Graf stuffed his notebook in the pocket of his winter smock, then jogged towards the captain.

"Combat instinct!" Krause said, laughing and shivering at the same time. "What's the real story, Ingo? Why didn't you juice that Ivan?"

"Pop's right, instinct it was," Ingo said.

"That's bullshit," Roth said.

"Maybe not combat instinct, granted," Ingo said. "But instinct, all the same."

"And what the fuck's that supposed to mean?" Roth said.

"Forget it, Bernd," Pop said to Roth, with just a little NCO edge to it. "How long until grub, Hans?"

"About done," Krause said, lifting a lid on one of the tins and stirring the contents with a fork.

Pop glanced over at Ingo, a bemused look on his face, but he said nothing. Ingo yawned again, then Pop reached into the pocket of his snow smock and took out his red and blue tube of Stuka tablets.

"Maybe I should have one of them; help keep me awake?" Ingo said.

Pop was about to say something when there was a distant crack, a rifle, which was then answered by the distinctive buzz of an MG 42. Then he simply shook his head, and popped a single Pervitin pill into his mouth.

***

Chillar. March 1953

Maria traced the smooth and shiny scar of the old Y-shaped wound on Ingo's right shoulder, his souvenir from Maastricht in 1940, with her finger.

"I've always wondered; where did you get this?"

They lay on their backs on top of the bed, their naked skin glistening with sweat. It was hot for an early autumn day and the window was open, but the light curtain was as still as iron, as there was no breeze to stir the air. The corrugated iron roof creaked and pinged as it expanded in the midday sunlight and the warm air smelt of sex, wine and Maria's lemony scent.

"Questions? That's not so professional."

"I'm not so professional, not now," she said.

"No? You still do a pretty good job."

She sighed, and turned away from him. But he did not overly care, not today. Maria had soon given up her work at the Bar el Descanso, it had never really suited her. She had gone back to her old profession; too many knew of her past to let her forget it anyway. Ingo had understood that, and although he no longer needed the Spanish lessons he still paid her well for what she was best at. These days, though, he seemed to be her only customer.

"You know, I'm here a lot now. I was —"

"Don't worry about it, I can afford it," he said.

She suddenly sat up and swivelled off the bed. There was a bottle of red wine open on the dressing table, a dressing table that had slowly been colonised by her tiny bottles of perfume and bigger jars of cosmetics. She took her glass from the bedside table and her bare feet padded against the floorboards. The neck of the bottle clashed against the rim of the tumbler like sharp swordplay. She did not ask him if he wanted more wine. He did.

She came back to bed, sat on it with her legs jack-knifed in front of her breasts, the tumbler resting on her right knee.

"You didn't have to say that, Enrique."

He swung himself off the bed. "What?" he said, as he stood up and then took his own glass to the bottle, filled the glass, emptied the bottle. She was, he knew, a little drunk. He was, too.

"You know what," she said. "What's wrong with you today?"

He shook his head, took the glass to the window, shifting the curtain to one side. Zündapp was in the paddock out the back, as still as sculpture, the sunshine glistening on his smooth chestnut coat so that he looked like a polished wooden ornament.

"Why don't you let me in, Enrique?"

Ingo sipped the wine, said nothing.

"In the town they say you're hiding, because of something you did, in the war," she said. "I tell them that's not so, yet that's all I can say."

"You talk about me?"

"If I'm asked about you, then I answer."

Ingo turned away from the window to face Maria. She looked vulnerable, with her knees drawn up close to her face.

"They're wrong, aren't they?" she said.

"Small town, small people, small talk," he said.

"Yes," she said. "I never did believe you could hurt someone."

"Really? Then you don't know me."

"I know you."

He shook his head.

She nodded. "I know you, and I know you're not capable of hurting anyone. When I worked at Bar el Descanso, Diego the barman told me what happened that time there, with that drunken idiot."

"What time?"

"He punched you, you did not respond; but then Carlo did."

"Oh, that time," he said. "Well, there you have it, I'm a coward – that's why I'm still alive, you know."

"No, I don't believe that. A coward does not race cars; and a coward for sure does not ride Zündapp." she smiled, slightly, at that.

"Well, I'm also a fool, then."

"You're no fool, you're … I'm not sure what you are, really," she said, the last words dripping softly from her.

"As I said, there's a lot to me you've not seen."

Maria flicked her eyes up and down the naked length of him. "I've seen plenty," she said, with another slight smile. "And I know you well enough to be certain that what you hide from is not something you have done. You, Enrique, are incapable of evil. It's why I …" she trailed off.

Ingo turned away from her, quite sharply, and took a gulp of wine. "Anyone is capable of anything when they reach their limits," he said. "And everybody has a limit."

"Not you," she said.

He paused for what seemed like a long time, seconds filled with the soft drip of water in a trough outside. Then he said: "I have a limit, alright, as I said, everyone has. And I've reached my limit. Not just once, either."

"Tell me, please."

He was about to say no; was about to walk out of the bedroom and close the door behind him. But he was sick of closing the door behind him. Sick of running from it. And he was a little drunk. And a little sad, too.

"I always told people I joined the army to ride motorcycles, and there was truth in that," he said. "But there was another reason. Father."

She sipped her wine, nodded for him to go on.

"He took a business from a Jew; well the shop at least. It was on Wagmüllerstrasse, in Munich, should have been much better than our old place in Schwabing. But the piano shop never thrived there. Father blamed the Jews for that – how he figured that out I never understood – but while he blamed them, he took it out on Mother."

"That's often the way," Maria said, a slight twitch in her cheek.

"She would pretend it was accidents at first; then she would make excuses for him. Then, one day, I came back from a piano recital I had, I forget where —"

"You play piano?"

"No, I did. But not now," he said, waving the question away. "Mother was lying unconscious on the kitchen floor; he had knocked her out. I thought she was dead." The tinnitus started to sing higher at the memory of it.

"What did you do?"

"I lost control, completely. There was a heavy pan, I almost killed him," he said. "Then it was Mother saying *he* had fallen down the stairs. But I'd broken the family, there and then, shattered it. Mother went to live with her sister, but soon returned; I never understood that, either."

"It's what women do," Maria said.

"Maybe," he said, wondering now how Mother was, if she still was. "Anyway," he added, shaking the thought from his head, as always. "For me there was nowhere to go, except into the army, which would have happened soon enough anyway. I saw a poster, it showed motorcycles. That was it."

"There's nothing wrong in what you did," she said. "You were protecting your mother."

"It's like I said, everyone has their limit."

There was the sound of a car rattling up the rough drive. He reached for his denims, which were draped across a chair, and then stepped into them.

"But you said it was not just once?" she said.

"Yes."

She tilted her head a little as she heard the car's rattling approach. "Visitor?"

"Get dressed, Maria, that's a taxi. It will take you in to Chillar," he said as he fastened the leather belt.

"But why?" She placed her tumbler on the bedside table and swung herself off the bed, her breasts jiggling to the movement, almost making him go back on the decision he'd made the day before in town.

"Things are moving on. Varela is a man of principle."

"Varela, what has he to do with us?"

"Varela has much to do with *me*."

"Varela has a tiny dick!"

"He has?" Ingo said. "I thought you didn't talk of clients?"

"That fatso was never a client of mine; but others talk. And I know that Varela has no principles!"

"Maybe not, but he has money; enough for me to race the Condor," Ingo said. And then he told the lie. "And if he says he's not happy for me to be living with a whore, then —"

"Am I still just a whore to you, Enrique?" Her eyes brimmed with shining tears, and that hard face could not look softer, or more hurt. But Ingo could ignore it; he had learned a long time ago that some things needed to be ignored, if you were to live. But more to the point, if those you cared for were to live. He wondered if she wanted to live more than she wanted him to say he cared for her, but he could not ask that question. Even though he knew it hurt her, sometimes this was the easier way. Things were moving quickly, and he felt that he might have to leave again soon, and fast. And he did not want to leave a trace, did not want to leave someone who might be hurt in other ways.

And so he took the roll of banknotes from the drawer in the dressing table and tossed it on to the bed. There were 22,000 pesos in all, around a thousand dollars. She had always been expensive, for Spanish lessons. "There's enough there to set you up nicely; maybe in Mar del Plata. You always said you liked it there, lots of trade, too, I should think."

The tumbler spun across the room and unfurled a pink ribbon of wine behind it that spattered on the bed and the money like blood before the glass missed Ingo's head by a finger then smashed against the bedroom wall with a high crack and a shivering tinkle.

"You'd best pack," Ingo said, as he walked out of the bedroom, and closed the door behind him.

*

Lampeter. March 1953

He did not understand why the pain did not wake him. He knew he was dreaming, and he knew he was burning again, in that dream; that nightmare – as they were the only kind he had it was enough to call them dreams. When it had happened the pain had been at its worst a while after he had been pulled from the fire. The body can ignore it at first, as it fights with the need to survive, to get away from the blaze. It had been when he realised that his skin had hung from him like sheets that it had begun to sing its song of agony. That song had never stopped. Sometimes pain sang softer, but pain never stopped singing.

When pain sang in his dreams it often woke him. But not now. Even though he knew it was in a dream, it did not wake him, and he could not wake himself. He panicked, and shouted out loud. Then felt the gentle shake of a hand on his shoulder.

It was Gwen, the barmaid. "Are you alright," she said in English, the words lilting, caring.

"Yes, sorry, I ..."

"You fell asleep, Joe," she said.

His eyes focussed, solidifying the melted mess of the air; the surrounding world was always like pork pie jelly in his nightmares. Now he could see the others, staring at him, as if they had been taking the opportunity to have a damned good look at the freak show. They turned away, the three farmers at the Black Lion bar, and dipped their faces to their pints. The sheepdog had grown old, all of a sudden it seemed, and slept a peaceful sleep at the foot of the stools. The dog would know how to die well, he thought. Outside he could hear the rain lash the street while the windows shook to the wind. He suddenly wanted to be naked, in the cooling rain and wind. But he knew that would not help.

"Did I shout out?" he asked Gwen, and tried to imagine her outside, naked in the rain.

"Yes," she said.

"I'm sorry."

"It was foreign, Joe," Gwen said, with a caring smile. "We didn't know the words." Then she turned away from him, crossing the room to pick up the coal scuttle to feed what looked and smelt and sounded to him like a healthy and crackling fire. He started to cough, and as always he could not stop it until the painful, lung heaving, fit had run its course. He sipped some of his bitter.

"You should go to the doctors about that cough, love," Gwen said.

He nodded. He would. Soon. He liked it when she called him love. But he knew it meant nothing. Sometimes he wondered if it had ever meant much.

*

Tel Aviv. April 1953

Their apartment was in a gleaming white Bauhaus building on Dizengoff Street. The balcony faced west, jutting out over a wide sidewalk. At this time in the afternoon the sun found the balcony and it could be pleasant to sit outside. Benjamin played happily at her feet as she sat in the deckchair, struggling to concentrate on a novel, *Martha Quest*. Thinking of *him*. It was Saturday and there was little traffic, the shops on the street below were closed, and the lingering smell of a lunch of lamb cholent, cooked by David's mother the day before, hung like ivy on the balcony. The child rolled a diecast toy fire engine into the smooth concrete balustrade, a rattling crash.

"Play quietly, Benjamin," Sarah said.

David smiled.

"What?"

"Nothing. Just, well, it's been good to have you around."

"Has it?" she said. She had not thought so.

"He needs a mother," David said, again with a smile. It was a salesman's smile in a film star's face. She had once overheard a woman say he looked like Cesar Romero. But he'd put a little weight on since then. David Malka was still a handsome man, though. The radio was on in the living room, playing the folk song, *Shepherd*.

"You were working too hard, it was taking you away from us," he said. "It's good you can spend more time at home, with Benjamin."

"Yes," she said, turning back to her book, rereading a paragraph but still not taking it in.

He turned his attention back to the financial pages of *Maariv*. There was a bottle of Goldstar on the table next to his chair, sweating a fever chill from their new refrigerator. David was doing well at work, at the Bank Leumi Le-Israel.

Since Nice, she had had no work.

The Group had escaped, just as if they had killed the man they had come for, and not the wrong man. It was meant to look like a drugs deal gone wrong rather than a hit – as was The Group's way – and it still had. But Gabriel had needed to report their failure, her failure, as he was always scrupulously correct about such things. There had been no word from him since then and he had not responded to her messages. And she knew better than to go to his office and apartment on Montefiore Street; that would only make matters worse.

"Perhaps now," David started, from behind his newspaper, which rustled a little as he spoke. "Now that you have more time ..." He trailed off.

"What?"

"Benjamin is almost six. He should have a brother," he said, lowering the paper.

"You sound like your mother," she said, knowing he hated that.

"Is it really so unreasonable, to want another child?"

The music on the radio changed. It was Chopin; *The Minute Waltz*. She threw aside the novel and stormed in to the room, viciously twisting the knob on the walnut radio set as if it was a knife in a heart.

"Hey, I was listening to that!" David shouted, and Benjamin started to cry, as he always did when they raised their voices.

"I hate Chopin!" she shouted back.

"Just what don't you hate, Sarah?" David said.

"I'm going for a swim," she said, suddenly deciding it was close enough to the time she would take her exercise. She hurried through to the bedroom and put her bathing costume on, and then a long white and blue dress over it. David made no attempt to stop her, he was too busy trying to get Benjamin to cease his wailing with promises of cookies; he was better at that than Sarah had ever been, ever would be. She thought they would probably have their row later, as usual, which would give her an excuse not to sleep with him. She did not want another child. Did not really want the one she had. She only wanted revenge.

Sarah walked the short way down to the beach and slipped off her dress, leaving it bundled with her towel close to a piss-smelling old British concrete pillbox that was already showing rusty ribs where the sea had eaten through to the reinforcing steel cables.

Then she swam. She swam to escape the prison of the apartment. She swam because she was bored. She swam so the sound of the sea would wash the music which reminded her of so much she could never forget from her head. She swam hard, until she was exhausted, that was always the way. The low late-afternoon sun was behind her now as she headed back to the shore, the swell of the waves lifting her, before she sank back in to the shallow troughs, losing sight of the white Art Deco buildings which were a dazzling smile beyond the beach. The water was cold and her muscles ached, she had swam fast for an hour, but it was a good, honest ache; a cleansing pain. It told her she had done something – something worthwhile – in a way that was beyond argument. But then she realised there was someone watching her, on the beach, close to where she had dumped her things near the pillbox. It was a man in a short jacket.

She did not recognise Yitzhak until she was quite near, he had a way of never looking out of place, would strike a pose like a chameleon would take on hue. He held her orange towel, bright as a flare against his dark trousers. She swam in to the shallows and stood, walking over wet sand that was elastic beneath her feet. Yitzhak watched her as she came out of the sea, the bathing costume clinging tight to her skin, her heavy, laboured breathing pulsing her breasts.

"It's been a little while," he said, as he handed her the towel. She said nothing, took the towel then started to dry her limbs. "I was hoping I would find you here – in a bathing suit," he added. She had always kept fit by swimming in the sea, Yitzhak knew that.

"Argentina?"

"Well, let's not waste time with pleasantries, now," Yitzhak said, grinning.

"I don't have much time."

"You have plenty of time."

"So, it's true," she said, and he nodded. "I thought Gabriel might tell me himself?"

"He's fighting the fires you've lit. Wouldn't do to seem too close to you now, he's waiting until it all blows over; trying to protect you, seems to me."

"You were there, too?"

"As our friends always say; I was merely following orders."

She felt the cold in her bones and her nipples pushed out through the cloth of her bathing suit. Yitzhak stared, as he always would, but she made no effort to cover them with the towel. A gull shrieked overhead.

"We were on a short leash, you know, not so long ago the death of a drug dealer would have been chalked up as collateral damage, but those days are gone," he said, looking in her eyes again. "The Institute has more power now; they're jealous of our success, want to shut us down."

"Why would the Mossad want that, we're on the same side?"

"No, they're on the politicians' side; and some say they're the future." He shrugged: "Who knows, maybe this country's out of the vengeance business?"

"This country was built on vengeance."

"You reckon? The prime minister does not go in for revenge, says 'how will killing six million bring six million back?'"

"Ben-Gurion doesn't understand revenge, not like me and you," Sarah said.

"Not me, I'm in it for other things."

"You are? What?"

"Maybe I enjoy it?" He shifted his attention to her breasts again. The waves sighed against the shore and the sun started to warm her skin. A briny-smelling wet dog padded by, its nose close to the sand.

"Why are you here, Yitzhak?"

"Gabriel, he told me to tell you something."

"Yes?"

"We know where your man is," he said, his eyes on hers again now, as he waited for a reaction. He smiled, so she knew the electric thrill that had shot through her body and soul had sparked in her eyes.

"Where?" she said.

"We're going in," Yitzhak said, ignoring the question.

"To eliminate him?"

"Yes."

"We?"

He paused for a moment before saying: "Not you. But I will not miss, that I promise."

Even though she had expected it the disappointment surged within her like the roll of the surf on the sand. She understood why, yet still she asked: "Why not?"

"Gabriel says you were distracted in Nice. Says you're too tied up with this one, liable to make a mistake."

"And you?"

"I agree, you're not a messy killer. Something was not right there," Yitzhak said. "It could only have been that phone call. And right now we can't afford any more mistakes; they'll shut us down. Serious business, killing. No room for emotion."

"Revenge is all emotion."

"Well, I wouldn't know about that," he said.

"And I was not distracted."

"Then you simply made a bad mistake; and that's worse."

"Okay, I was distracted. But it was *him*. Don't you see? I need this! Tell me, where is he?"

"You know I can't tell you that. But he will die, and that's all that matters," Yitzhak said, half turning to walk away.

What she knew was honey, it was her job, how she killed. And so she also knew exactly how to stand and how to hold herself, her body turned to show the curve of her breast and a cold, hard bullet of a nipple tight against the wet cloth of the swimsuit, as she said: "Yitzhak, you keep in touch, yes?"

He laughed, and said: "Sure, a soldier never minds paying for it," before walking back up the beach, leaving her alone on the sand.

*

Chillar. April 1953

With Varela's money coming in Catalina didn't really have to work in the small office in the increasingly cramped Di Rossi Auto Repairs garage. But she did; because she had got used to it, she said. And because she liked to know what was going on, Ingo thought. They had taken the Condor for a quick test run along some local roads. It had taken a little while to modify the engine bay to fit the Ferrari 2.7-litre unit, but not as long as expected. It was as though the V12 had been built specifically for the Condor. Just like Ingo, Carlo had joked.

Ingo threaded the sports car into the tight space in the garage, between the workbench and the office, its wheels straddling the inspection pit. There was very little room to work on the Condor, for while the engine fitted the car the car, and all the paraphernalia of a racing team, hardly fitted the garage. Varela was working on that, turning an old potato store in nearby López Camelo into a race 'shop. Ingo revved the Ferrari motor one last time, the sound from the open racing exhaust ear-splitting in the tight space, a deep, sharp rasp that shook the corrugated iron roof. He caught Catalina's annoyance as she kicked the door of the office shut; she was trying to talk on the telephone. Carlo smiled broadly. Ingo cut the engine and after a burble it seemed terribly quiet, except for the mild tinnitus between his ears. The sudden stillness seemed to emphasise the smell of paint, lingering from when they had applied a grey undercoat to one of the new bonnets – they had arrived from the body-shop in Balcarce the day before. They were no longer to be yellow, but blue; Varela had not liked the yellow hood, and so they had decided to paint a yellow band around the nose of the car instead.

"She doesn't look happy," Ingo said, too loud after the roar of the car, and with that Catalina opened the office door.

"She's after some new Di Tella refrigerator, never lets up about —"

"It's Signor Varela," Catalina said. "He wants to talk to you about the new workshop."

Carlo nodded and climbed over the low passenger-side door. He would not keep Varela waiting for long.

"How did it go?" Catalina said to Ingo, leaning against the car's front fender with her hands turned out – her curves didn't quite match the car's curves, but it was a close run thing.

"You really want to know?"

She nodded.

"Understeers quite a bit with a full fuel load, but otherwise, perfect."

"Good," she said. "You know, I've not seen Maria for a while?"

"She's gone."

"Gone? I thought —?"

"She thought so, too," he said.

"You're a cold one, aren't you, Enrique?"

"I always thought you two didn't get along?"

She shrugged, and Ingo climbed out of the Condor, stepping over the low door.

"Oh, but I almost forgot," Catalina said. "Seems you're famous."

"Famous?" It was a word that twisted within him, like a bayonet.

"Had a photographer call in earlier," she said. "I told him you wouldn't be gone long, but he said he couldn't wait. Strange man. Told him I doubted you would be interested in having your photo taken anyway, what with you being so shy."

"Why me?" Ingo asked, the tinnitus singing a little higher. "Why not Carlo, he's far more well-known than I am?"

"Maybe because Carlo is no longer a racing driver?" she said. "Maybe he just wants to make sure he has pictures of drivers in case … Well, you know. The newspapers will need pictures then." She smiled a slick smile. "His card is on the bench," she added, nodding towards a little bright white rectangle which was propped up against a blue vice.

Ingo picked up the business card: *Pedro Gruber, Commercial Photographer*, it read. There was an address on Guatemala, in the Palermo district of Buenos Aires, and a telephone number. He could sense that Catalina was watching him, looking for a reaction.

"I don't understand, why didn't he wait?" Ingo said.

Catalina shrugged, lifting her palms from the shining blue fender and holding them open as if checking for rain.

Ingo held up the card in front of him. "Tell me about him, Catalina."

*

Buenos Aires. April 1953

The cold notch of the sight on the tip of the snub-nosed Colt .38 was digging in to Ingo's lower spine. He wore a short sleeved blue cotton shirt, not tucked inside the waist of his trousers, so it was draped over the butt of the revolver. It had been warm enough when he had arrived in the afternoon, but now darkness had come it was much cooler. He had believed he would never use it, the Colt. But now he thought he would have to.

Gruber's studio was part of a small, very square house with a flat roof, typical of the other houses Ingo had seen here in the Palermo district. One lower window was blocked off, maybe to make a darkroom. The other was a shopfront with a blanked out half-white background which showed off portrait photography; some graduation pictures and one of a naval officer with a sword, plus a colour picture of a modern factory. There were no photographs of racing drivers, or any other sportsmen. There were wrought iron bars over each of the windows, which was not unusual here, and the house opened straight on to the street, like all the others. There was an upstairs, whitewashed walls gleaming a sickly yellow in the wash of the street lighting. The windows were barred on the first floor, too, and the slatted wooden blinds were closed. There was no sign of light, or life, from inside the house. Ingo had knocked the varnished wooden door earlier in the day, but there had been no answer. He knew that he might have walked in to a trap. But this time running was not an option. And so now he waited. The tinnitus was insistent, and beginning to take on its steelier tone.

Guatemala was quite narrow, and tree-lined like all the streets in Palermo, its London planes now shivering to a sharp breeze, as if they grew colder as their rusty leaves fell from them. Ingo shivered, too, but he did not put his jacket on – he needed to be unencumbered, when the time to kill came. Again.

It was quiet, but the noise of the city was always there, a little muffled, as if the street wore the rubber earplugs he used when racing. Someone, somewhere, was frying mince and onion, preparing for dinner. There was another smell, too, though so faint Ingo could not quite place it.

He sat in his Jeep, opposite but eight houses up from Gruber's house and studio, in a place where the lemony light from the street lamps that bracketed the Jeep didn't quite reach him. The *El Laborista* newspaper he had pretended to read as he had waited all afternoon was now folded on the passenger seat. He watched the studio through the rear view mirror he'd fixed to the top of the windshield; it reminded him of looking out the oblong vision slit of a panzer. He was glad of the scant cover the plane trees, and now the darkness, offered.

The Mercedes came down the street from behind him and he watched it pull up and park against the yellow-painted kerb in the mirror, swaying a little on its soft suspension as it stopped. It was a bright blue 170V, its vivid colour startling in the wash of the street lights. Gruber stepped out of the car through the rear-hinged driver's door. He was wearing a Tyrolean hat with a small feather sticking out of its band. That was all Ingo could see of him from where he sat in the poor light, yet it was enough. Catalina had told him Gruber wore such a hat, drove such a car. Gruber walked to his front door, his silhouette dissolving into darker shadow as he stepped out of the lamplight. Ingo climbed out of the Jeep, checking the gun was still securely stuck in the back of his belt. As Gruber let himself in to the studio Ingo crossed the road and walked up the street.

He approached the front door, his heart hammering now, a film of sweat forming on the palms of his hands. But he was angry, too, and the tinnitus grew louder, sharper, like cutting steel. He put his right hand behind his back so he would be ready to use the Colt. He paused for a racing heartbeat or three, took a deep breath, then with his free hand he reached out to knock the door ...

The sharp dash of his knuckles on the varnished wood coincided with the explosion, so that it almost seemed to have caused it, Ingo thought in that fraction of a second when the air shattered into shards of glass around him. His heart froze and his lungs seemed to squeeze themselves empty, and he knew instantly it was an explosion, seen and felt too many in his time to be mistaken, and he was waiting for the ear-splitting noise that always came a moment later as the shock wave lifted him over the blue Mercedes, his feet banging against its roof ... But the world turned dark and quiet first ...

*

Tel Aviv. April 1953

Yitzhak handed Sarah a copy of an Argentinian German-language newspaper: the *Argentisches Tageblatt*.

"Page five," he said.

She was in the sitting room, wrapped in her short, white towelling robe. David had already left for the bank, and Benjamin was at school. She guessed that Yitzhak would have waited outside for David to leave before coming up. He was carrying a small khaki backpack, which he placed on the floor.

"Hope you don't think you're staying?" she said.

Yitzhak grinned, his eyes flicking to her bare legs, then to the backpack. "Oh that, tell you later," he said. Then he nodded at a framed photograph of Benjamin on the coffee table, which was also scattered with a massacre of grey plastic soldiers around a potted cactus bastion. "Your son likes soldiers?"

"More than I do," she said, then turned to page five of the newspaper. There was a story, and a head and shoulders picture.

Yitzhak sniffed deeply, then said: "Coffee?"

"Kitchen's through there, there's a fresh brew in the finjan."

"Cardamom?"

"In the small white jar."

She could speak German fluently, so reading the news story in the Argentinian paper was not a problem. But first she dwelt a while on the photograph. It was him, all right.

Sarah read the story. Read of how a gas explosion had claimed a life. It was a short piece, and Yitzhak had poured himself a mug of black coffee and was back in the sitting room by the time she had read it through, twice.

"Telephone?"

"Yes," Yitzhak said, sitting on the low sofa. "I waited in a house over the street; owner was away. I knew when he was out, when he was due back. He was a little bit early, so the blast might have been a little bigger. But seems he was cooked well enough."

Sarah nodded. They had done something similar before, in Koln. Yitzhak would create a gas leak, then set up the telephone to spark when it rang. There was always the risk it would ring beforehand, but then there was always Yitzhak's knife when things went wrong. They seldom did go wrong. Nice was an aberration.

"What I don't quite understand is what happened to his visitor," Yitzhak said, slurping a full stop.

"Visitor?"

"Not even mentioned in the paper, but I saw him. Took a hell of a flight, cleared a Mercedes and landed the other side of the street."

"Dead?"

Yitzhak shrugged: "Well, like I said, nothing in the paper."

"That's good then. I don't think Gabriel would be happy with more collateral damage."

"I was more worried about what *you* would do if we messed this one up, so wasn't about to hold back on the dialling. Anyway, he was probably another Nazi, there's one on every street corner in BA these days. But tell me, I know he was a no-good, they all are, but what exactly was this man to you, you've never said?"

"No, I've never said."

She looked at the picture again.

She had never met Christian Kroh, but he had been a part of her life for so long she could now hardly imagine it without him.

Yitzhak reached for the backpack, knowing her well enough not to press for an answer. He unstrapped it and plunged his hand inside, pulling out a fan of glossy black and white photographs. "I found these in that bastard's studio. Seems he was taking snaps right through the war."

"Tourist pictures?" It was what the German soldiers called the photographs they took of the dead, and the dying, the killing and torturing. There had seemed to be a real need for some to record their crimes. This had helped The Group many times in the past.

"Yep, they were just lying around – careless of him, eh?"

"What's it to me?"

"Gabriel wants you to go through them, sure you'll recognise someone from the files. You're good at that."

"So, I'm just a clerk now, is it?"

"It's called intelligence."

With that he drained his coffee, glanced at her legs once more, and then left. She looked at the small backpack. Then she looked at the picture of Kroh in the newspaper.

"It's over," she said aloud. She did not feel especially happy, nor sad. But she thought that both would surely come. For now, she just felt empty.

*

Chillar. April 1953

"Stupid horse."

"Stupid Enrique," Carlo said. "For riding the goddamned thing."

Catalina dabbed at one of the abrasions on Ingo's arm with a little cotton wool cluster soaked in iodine. The pain sang out like his tinnitus, which was worse than ever after the explosion. He dimly realised both pain and tinnitus were in perfect tune. The wounds had already been cleaned once, some of them dressed for a few days, but not well enough, Catalina had suddenly decided.

"Yes, stupid Enrique." With that she shook her head then went through to the hallway of their house on Pellegrini, just a couple of blocks away from the Di Rossi Auto Repairs workshop on Belgrano.

The kitchen smelt of iodine, smoke from Carlo's cheroot, and the remnants of a lunch of locro which Ingo had interrupted, then joined – the spiced stew of corn kernels, diced pork and sweet potatoes hadn't been the best he'd tasted, Carlo was right about Catalina's cooking, but it had done much to revive him after his long drive from Buenos Aires, though he still felt a little nauseous from the concussion. The children had gobbled down their food quickly, then rushed outside. A maté gourd, with a silver sipper, sat on the checked tablecloth like a forgotten chess piece. They had shared it, passing it anti-clockwise, which Catalina had insisted was the proper, and only, way to drink the infusion. The refrigerator rattled and buzzed, then clunked every so often; Ingo remembered that Catalina was after a new one. The floor was tiled, the table and chairs lacquered pine, while gleaming black saucepans hung from hooks on the wall like helmets in a Leibstandarte barrack room.

"But this is not Zündapp's doing, is it, my friend?" Carlo said, once he judged Catalina was out of earshot, cocking his head as he studied the cuts and bruises down Ingo's left arm.

"Has a hell of a temper, that horse."

Carlo slowly jacked up an eyebrow then pulled his chair closer to the table with a screech of wooden legs against the tiles; he sat opposite Ingo and looked him in the eye as he said: "So, are you going to tell me?"

Ingo shrugged, which hurt – his whole body was bruised and he was still amazed nothing was broken. There were a few small cuts from glass on his face and larger cuts all over his arms, with which he had shielded his face; a reflex action. "Not much to tell," he said, as he remembered how he had come to, soon after the explosion, and then fled the scene on wobbly legs. He had made his way to Zum Edelweiss, a German-run beer house on Libertad, just off Corrientes. No one asked questions; he was German, he looked as if he'd been beaten up; a barmaid helped clean and dress his wounds. Another German, a customer at the beer house, then helped him find a hotel room nearby where he could rest for a while.

The street in Palermo had been cordoned off, there had been a fatality, the police manning the barrier told him, when he had gone back the next day. He thought it best not to mention he wanted to retrieve his Jeep, as he had left the thirty-eight somewhere in the street, too, he had realised. He waited for two days before he went back for the car, giving himself some time to recover a little, and then he drove it back to Chillar. In that time he'd read all about the gas explosion on Guatemala in the papers. There had been no mention at all of a bearded man, or of a revolver being found in the street.

"Not much to tell, eh?" Carlo said, taking a puff of his cheroot before adding: "Catalina says we had a visitor? She told you about him right before you disappeared. Says you looked like death, when she mentioned the photographer."

"I'm camera shy, you know that, Carlo."

"Says you seemed more afraid of his whistle than his camera – or, what was it? 'His whistle that was not a whistle'. Another strange German, eh?"

Ingo remembered exactly what she had said, how it had hit him like the explosion that it had led to. Catalina had also told him he had been eating a raw onion. That had been the clincher. He shrugged, but said nothing, and the kitchen was silent for a moment or two.

"Never mind," Carlo then quite suddenly said. "I have some good news."

"You have?"

"You can now be a true Argentinian, more or less," he said, with a grin.

"Which; *more* or *less*?

"More, I'd say."

"How?"

"Signor Varela is an important man," Carlo said. "I'm assuming your Red Cross passport run out long ago?"

Ingo nodded. He had had nothing other than his racing licence to prove who he was, or wasn't, for some time now, and he had been putting off applying for an Argentinian passport for fear of refusal and then, perhaps, deportation.

"Which means you are a man with no country."

"Suits me."

"Maybe it does, but you should have gone to the Federal Police to apply for an Argentinian passport to replace it. And to get this you need to prove you have been a good boy while you have been living in our fine country. You need someone to vouch for this, my friend. Signor Varela will do this for you, and Varela's word is worth its weight in potatoes."

"And this is good news?"

"Means we can race in Brazil."

Ingo thought on that. There weren't so many races for sports cars in Argentina, and they had missed an event in Rio this year already.

"Well, what do you think?" A wisp of cheroot smoke almost formed a question mark above Carlo's head.

Brazil was still a long way from Europe. And Kroh was dead. That was for sure. The newspaper said so, though not quite as convincingly as the bang had. Ingo was not sure about it being a gas explosion, but he was sure Kroh would have had plenty of enemies, he had always collected them like others collect pressed butterflies. Should it be such a surprise that someone got there first? He felt no satisfaction that Kroh was gone, just relief that it was now done. There was still danger, but Brazil was still far away from Europe – and every day he was getting further away from his past.

Catalina came back through to the kitchen, her heels clacking like castanets on the tiles. She was carrying a roll of bandages which she placed on the table.

"It's just Brazil, it will give us more time to test the car in proper race conditions before the Buenos Aires race," Carlo said. "It's not as though we'll be doing the Mille Miglia, my friend."

"No, that's true."

"Though that would be something, eh?" he added, with a sigh.

"Ouch!" Ingo said, as Catalina viciously applied burning iodine to a cut.

***

Warsaw. April 1943

It was strange how Lidka almost noticed the paintings even more, now they were gone. Where each had hung there was an ever so slightly brighter rectangle on the yellow walls, edged in grime that had accumulated over the years. Absence can be a very present thing. The absence of Feliks Paczkowski filled the house like a bad smell, but they rarely spoke of it. Mrs Paczkowska hardly spoke at all now, she just quietly waited for him to come back. But Lidka did not think he would ever return.

Andrzej *had* returned, but only to visit. It had been Lidka's idea, and it had taken persuasion, as it was risky for him; people knew his true identity on

Mochnackiego. Sarah had been leaving the house, trying to reach the Ghetto, but she had never even come close to it. There was a tightening noose of steel around that place now, steel and hate. It was a stupid risk, and there was no one who could stop her, now Feliks had gone. But she might listen to Andrzej.

Lidka and Andrzej waited in the quiet, achingly empty parlour. They stood in exactly the same space the piano had once filled. He stood close to her. Freddy played with a toy car and Andrzej watched him. She thought the chipped and dented toy had once belonged to Andrzej. It was a fine April evening, some birds were singing, but every now and then they would hear a muffled explosion from the north. The double doors to the parlour swung open with a soft creak.

"Andrzej!" Mrs Paczkowska's voice had a trace of echo in the large and empty room, a trace of emotion, and a trace of uncertainty, too, as her heels tapped against the parquet. "You've grown, you're ..." She smothered the sentence she could not finish by hugging him. Andrzej hugged her back. It had been six months since he had last risked coming to the house – a few weeks after his father had been taken – six months since he had last seen his mother, but his hug was mechanical.

The room wasn't quite empty. They had moved the table up from the kitchen and now they would move the Jews from the basement – Mrs Paczkowska would not allow *those Jews* to eat in her dining room, which remained intact, there had been nothing in there the Nazis had wanted. But she would eat with *those Jews* because Andrzej had insisted.

Leon Vogler, Sarah's brother, was first in. He did not run now, as he always had, but almost crept. Even filtered through the lace curtains the evening light was sharp, for a boy who lived in a cellar, and he blinked as he saw Andrzej, blinked twice more before he recognised him, then breathed out in relief – strangers were dangerous. By now Sol Vogler and his wife had caught up. Neither Sol Vogler nor his wife, the older Sarah, looked well, as pale as a winter sky and as crooked and bent as leafless trees beneath it. Since Feliks had been taken they stayed in the hiding place in the basement almost all of the time.

Sarah came in last of all, carrying the large hand-painted soup tureen, the handle of its matching ladle sticking through a slot in the shallow dome of the lid so that it looked a little like a blue and white tank turret. She too was pale, but not as pale as her parents, and there was a hint of colour at her cheeks, from the heat of the pot, or from seeing Andrzej.

"Andrzej, it's really you!" she said.

"Hello," he said, with a curt nod, then instantly turned to Lidka. "Hope this is good, chicken's hard to come by." But she knew it had not been particularly hard to come by, for him. The large pot seemed to double in weight in Sarah's hands and she placed it on the table with a thump.

Mrs Paczkowska's *tut* snapped like braking ice in the large room. Sarah ignored it and started to serve out the rosół she had made, with the pieces of chicken plus the carrots and onions Andrzej had supplied. The simple aroma of boiled chicken was more delicious than Lidka would ever have imagined, before the war. Andrzej did not look at Sarah, or thank her, when she ladled the soup in to his bowl with a slight slop, and spilled a little on to Mrs Paczkowska's third best table cloth as she did so, her hands shaking a little.

"I thought we might be able to hear it, up here?" Sol Vogler said.

"Gunfire doesn't always carry that far, in a city; and its three kilometres, as the crow flies," Andrzej said, and he looked at Lidka as he said it, as if for confirmation. He sat next to her, Sarah was down the other end of the table, squeezed up close to her father so that they ate with their elbows tucked in close to their bodies. The table was not quite big enough for all eight of them, but eating like this was a rare luxury for the Voglers and they would not complain. Mrs Paczkowska sat the other end, with Andrzej and Lidka. *She* had insisted on that.

"Artillery, now that carries." As Andrzej said it there was the familiar rumbling boom in the distance, and he smiled. Andrzej was wrong about the gunfire, though, often they heard it from this room.

Lidka helped Freddy with his rosół, cutting up the bigger pieces of chicken, then she ate some herself. She rarely craved the delicacies she once loved now, just simple sustenance for her child and herself. They had no bread to soak up the juices – what they had bought as rations and from the black market, with money from Sol Vogler, would be used for other meals – and so they sipped and slurped at the thin broth, all eating quickly. Except for Sarah, who had eaten some of the chicken pieces, but now grasped her spoon tight in front of her, so that the bones of her knuckles showed alabaster through the pale skin of her slim hand. A snub is a heavy hand with the salt, even if you're hungry. Especially if it's from one you care for, one you've missed.

For a moment Lidka remembered how she had felt when she had finally realised Ingo would not be coming back, and then she understood how the girl would be hurting now. She glanced at Freddy then, as she always did when she thought of his father. His hair was thick now, thick and blond, and a bit too long, but she liked it like that and did not want to cut it just yet. The hair was Lidka's, as were his eyes. Everyone still said he looked like her. He was talking well now, in his own way, and he was interested in everything.

"Got a gun?" Freddy suddenly said. He had been staring at Andrzej since he had started to talk about guns and explosions.

Andrzej grinned, then reached behind his back and pulled an automatic pistol from his belt. It was German, a Sauer 38H – Lidka was learning plenty about weapons, it had been a long time since she had believed a bag of spuds was a sack of grenades. Freddy's pupils inflated like little balloons, Mrs Paczkowska went white and started to tremble.

"That is not for the dinner table, Andrzej," she said.

"*That* belongs three kilometres away," Sarah said. "As the crow flies."

Andrzej laughed, shook his head; didn't even look at Sarah. "It's easy to be brave when you can't even hear the gunfire, isn't that right, Lidka?"

He had used her first name as he might pull a dagger. Sarah was staring at her now, a slight frown creasing her pale forehead.

"I have heard the gunfire," Sarah said, now looking at Andrzej again.

They all knew what gunfire they spoke of.

The Jews were being killed. Many of the Ghetto Jews had already been taken to a place called Treblinka in a forest eighty kilometres northeast of the city, the AK had discovered, where they were being executed in gas chambers. It had taken Lidka a little while to believe it, that it had come to this. The Nazis had now decided to finish off those few Jews still left in the Ghetto. They had sent in 2000 men a week or so ago, but the Jews – who knew the fate that awaited them – fought back. Some were still fighting back, three kilometres away, as the crow flies. Others wanted to fight …

"Why is the AK doing nothing?" Sarah said, standing up quickly, the foot of the chair leg squealing against the parquet. She still held her spoon tightly, as if was a weapon.

"We are doing plenty," Andrzej said, calmly, again deliberately glancing at Lidka as he said *we*, before spooning a piece of chicken into his mouth.

"Sit down, Sarah, please," Sol Vogler said. But she remained standing.

"They need help in the Ghetto, Andrzej, they need the AK's help now!"

"There's nothing that can be done for the Ghetto, sit down child," Mrs Paczkowska said.

This seemed to make Sarah even angrier; she was now nineteen, just a year younger than Andrzej, and Lidka knew she hated to be called *child*; she suspected Mrs Paczkowska knew this, too. Sarah breathed in deeply, running her hand through her dark hair.

"Mother is right," Andrzej said.

"Is it because they are Jews, is that why the AK won't help them?"

"You are Jews, too," Mrs Paczkowska said. "You have been helped."

"Helped to hide, but not to fight – where is the AK, Andrzej?"

"It's not time," Andrzej said.

"I will fight them, give me your pistol!"

"You will get yourself killed," Andrzej said, not taking his eyes off his meal. "You're a child, Sarah, you have no idea what it takes to fight. You have no idea of the realities of this war."

Sol Vogler reached up, tugged her arm gently. "Sit down Sarah, Andrzej is right."

"You will do nothing?"

"There is nothing we can do."

She slumped back on to her chair.

"Bottle the anger," Sol Vogler said. "Let it ferment. There will be a time for revenge, and you should be ready for that, Sarah."

"If you all live that long," Andrzej said, casually, then took another spoon of broth, slurped it.

"What do you mean?" Sol Vogler said.

"*She*," Andrzej looked at Sarah for just the second time, "has to learn to stay put. She is risking everything. If I find out she has left this house once more, then I have no choice. You will all have to leave."

There was silence then, not even a clink of spoon on china.

"But they will kill us?" Mrs Vogler finally said, and it was the first thing she had uttered since 'hello'. Lidka glanced at Mrs Paczkowska, who was looking down at her bowl of rosół. She thought she saw the tug of a thin smile at the corner of her mouth.

"You wouldn't, Andrzej?" Lidka said. Sarah was staring at him, diamond points of tears sparkling at the rim of her eyes.

"Yes, I would. She risks the life of my mother ... She risks your life, and Freddy's too, Lidka."

There was another distant explosion, from the Ghetto. It shook Sarah out of her shock, and she dropped her spoon into her soup plate and left without saying another word, her meal unfinished.

"Best not let that go to waste, eh?" Andrzej said, nodding at Leon, who passed the bowl of soup up the table.

The meal would have passed in silence after that, but Freddy chattered away and Andrzej indulged him. She was glad they got on so well. Once the others had left, Lidka and Andrzej sat at the table alone, while Freddy played with the toy car in the corner of the room.

"Why did you treat Sarah like that, Andrzej?"

"It's Bullet again, now, Chopin."

She nodded. "Why?"

"You wanted me to warn her. I warned her."

"You hurt her, too."

"As hurt goes, it hardly makes a mark in this city, I'd say."

"It might make a mark on her."

"Then she will have to live with it, we all have to live with things, eh teacher?"

"What you said, you wouldn't, would you?"

"Turf them out? Of course not," he said. "Old Vogler has a packet of dollars with him down there, you know, as well as his zlotys, maybe even diamonds. I heard Papa say he had sold some, once. Probably has much more stashed away elsewhere, too. Once this is all over, then I'll be making sure he pays his rental arrears and more, you can bank on that."

"Is that the only reason?"

He smirked. "It's reason enough, there's not much of a pension in the AK, and he seems to be a generous type, despite what they say," he said, glancing at the ring on her finger.

Lidka touched the silver ring Sol Vogler had given her, the silver wedding ring that had never seen a wedding, and she twisted it slightly on her finger. It was a loose fit.

"Heard from the hero, have we?"

She shook her head, she had not heard from Jósef and she did not expect to until the war was over, as it had been too risky to send the address of this house with the few letters she'd sent through the AK; and there was no way now he could reply anyway. But Andrzej knew all that. There was another dull boom from the direction of the Ghetto.

"You know, I always thought you liked Sarah," she said, changing the subject. "I always thought —"

Andrzej laughed, cutting her short. "It was never the pupil I had eyes for, Miss Wadalowska."

"Mrs Sczcepanska," Lidka said.

"If you insist, Chopin."

***

Tel Aviv. May 1953

The door slammed behind them, and a nearby shutter rattled its applause. Sarah did not know if the door had slammed because David had his hands full with Benjamin and the toys he was taking to his mother's for Friday night dinner, or because he was angry that she was not going with them. Either way, it was not like him to slam the door.

She had said she was not well. That had been a lie; an easy lie as she did not want to spend the evening with the widow Malka and her grinding nagging, her greed for grandchildren. As soon as Sarah heard the engine of David's new Kaiser Manhattan rumble into life in the street below she went to the little wooden locker, which doubled as her bedside table. It was always securely locked, and it was where she kept the things to do with The Group. She hesitated before opening it. She knew Kroh had taken pictures, that day. She did not want to see *those* pictures. But Gabriel had passed on a message via Yitzhak. The Institute was putting The Group under pressure, trying to close it down. They were jealous of The Group's success, and they had made much of its – her – failure in Nice. They talked of a new way of doing things, the Mossad, bringing Nazis to court; proper, fair trials. But it had not been like that in Warsaw, or the camps, there had been nothing fair about those places. Gabriel knew how to play the game, though. Find something in the photographs, the message had said, something we can give them. To show there is more to us than killing.

She had told Yitzhak she would not look at them, and she had left it three weeks now, she had said it was all behind her. But he knew she would look at the photographs, and she knew she would look at the photographs too, even though she was still afraid of what she might find. She had always known she would look at them. Eventually.

The shutters and the windows in the bedroom were open and she looked out to see David's big and curvaceous American car drive away down a busy Dizengoff Street, slotting into the slow stream of traffic. The early evening sun was hard and stark, toppling a white tombstone of brittle light on to the cream-tiled floor. The air carried a gritty citrus smell from the street.

It was right that Sarah should look at the photographs. Her feelings should mean nothing, that was all over. Now. There were always more war crimes, and war criminals to track down, and she had a knack of recognising those who were still hunted; slowly building up their dossiers of death. This had been a part of it all since the start. Now that Christian Kroh was dead it had been easy for her to put off this important work, but with an empty apartment she could allow herself no excuse. But the apartment was not the only thing that seemed empty. With the death of Kroh, something had died within her, too. Revenge is fuel, she thought, without it it can be difficult to find the strength to rise in the morning.

She sighed, crouched down and unlocked the little door. She pulled it open a bit then heard the scraping slide of the canvas against the wood inside the locker, then the weight of the photograph-stuffed small backpack forced the door fully open, and it fell out on to its side, a fan of musty-smelling black and white photographs whispering against each other as they spilled out on to the floor and in to the hard and stark shaft of sunlight. There was dust, too, and she sneezed.

Sarah started to sort through the stiff black and white squares, some of them tacky in her fingers. The subjects were the sort of thing she was used to: a naked woman in a ruined street, forcing a smile to save her life, the picture cracked and crinkled where it had been handled many times; an old man hanging; the corpse – or maybe not – of a Russian soldier with his nose and ears sliced away; dead women lying in a row in the snow, their skirts lifted and panties torn off to show rough triangles of pubic hair. These were all common themes in the tourist picture genre and Sarah had long ceased to be shocked by such images. Another fan of photographs, some blurred, showed Waffen SS soldiers in combat in a street she recognised – Wolska Street in Wola, she was sure of that. She put these to one side and shifted the toppled backpack, some more photographs slid from its mouth and one fell into the bright light. On seeing it her heart seemed to tighten into a hard steel ball within her chest, time turned to cold stone and she felt as if she might never breathe again. Yes, this was what she had feared she might find … But more than that, far worse than that …

It was him.

***

Teploe, Soviet Union. The Battle of Kursk. July 1943

Flat out. It's the only way, even in a twenty-four tonne panzer that will do just 40km/h at best, much less on rough ground like this, and so Ingo's foot was jammed to the floor. They had raced ahead of the other Panzer IVs, the IIIs and the handful of old IIs, and they were far ahead of the panzer grenadier support. Right now the Panzer IV he drove was at the very spearhead of 4th Panzer's full-division, 101-tank assault on Teploe. He was winning the race. But they were racing into Hell.

Through the crazed thick glass of Ingo's vision slit the ever-shaking, ever-bouncing, picture was one of smoke and fire. Ivan was throwing everything at them: mortars, machine guns, then those shrieking, fizzing Stalin Organ rockets, scraping the smoke-blotched iron sky like claws on a blackboard, trailing comet tails before laying forests of dark explosions like slung rugs of destruction. Artillery, too; shells whistling through the air, each whistle finishing with a crump that was a relief to all in the tank – because it had not hit them. Now there were so many whistles they were overlapping, intertwined, like a great net of noise. More worrying were the hull-down tanks, KV-1s and T-34s, half buried in trenches so only the turrets showed, and worse still were the anti-tank pieces, the well dug in field guns that hunted the panzers over open sights, those could hit before you even heard them … Yes, it was best to go as fast as possible, a moving target is harder to hit, and yes he knew no other way, but the faster he went the sooner they would get to Teploe. And who knew what awaited them there?

Their panzer was a tiny part of what Graf reckoned was the biggest tank battle in history. It had been going on for three days already, the 4th had been held in reserve until now, the 8th of July. Its objective was the higher ground beyond Teploe, which the officers called Hill 240. Ingo's objective was to stay alive.

He sometimes thought that being inside a tank was like being a component in an engine. A mere cog in the machine, oiled by sweat and ground by steel parts, plugged in to the intercom, shaken like a loose bolt, gassed and baked. His body buzzed with it, too, and he pressed the accelerator so hard, as the tank bucked and bounced on the uneven ground, that he seemed to be forcing himself even deeper into the pulsating steel of the panzer.

The tank was gouging a channel through long, pale yellow grass, but he could not hear the swish of it against the lower front plate and the floor over the roar of the racing Maybach engine and the clatter of the steel tracks, or the fall of shells outside – one fell close by, throwing a scatter of earth and stones against the panzer, sounding like sleet dashed against a window. Ingo glanced at his instruments, a quick check of oil pressure and temperature, then caught Lidka's quivering smile in the picture on the shivering armour as he shifted his gaze to the vision slit again; seeing just a tiny oblong of the expansive battlefield through the thick block of glass in the tight slot and a slight reflection of his own eyes.

As Pop had taught him, he tried to look far ahead – like a racing driver would and should. But it was close to impossible with the restricted view he had, and usually he would rely on Graf and his better view high in the turret, and then his directions over the intercom or via the small signal lights, especially in the confusion of battle. Either that or trust to the feel of the ground beneath the rattling tracks through his shaking steering levers.

"T-34s!"

The shout over the comms was from Graf, combat drill forgotten.

"They're left of us!" There was panic in Graf's voice.

Now Ingo could also see them, a jellified mass in the top left corner of his vision slit. It was the way Ivan often used his tanks, counter attack in force.

Ingo rapidly slowed, not waiting for the order, knowing what had to be done, down through the gears so he could use the engine braking to help arrest the huge machine.

"Nine-o'clock, one-thousand metres," Pop put in, much calmer, calling his own direction and range, then shell: "Armour piercing."

Ingo had the panzer down in first now, so could do a tight spin turn to face the threat with the thicker frontal armour, yanking the heavy left steering lever right the way back to brake the track fully. Now he saw all the T-34s. Many of them, more than he could count, massed together like a green and thick noxious gas drifting across the battlefield, some of them firing on the move – Ivan's bad habit – dirty smoke from guns and exhausts further blotting air already grey-brown with the smog of battle, as if the uniforms of each side's foot soldiers had bled in to it.

He stopped the panzer, its body swaying on the suspension, and then, as it settled, he waited. He ached to select reverse and accelerate away from the advance, his foot twitching over the vibrating throttle pedal, the gear lever shaking in his hand. But he knew that Pop could not shoot accurately, precisely, when the panzer was moving – shooting on the move was just for *Die Deutsche Wochenschau* newsreels. Through his slot he could see the Russian tanks coming towards them through the long grass, which reached to the bellies of the brown-jacketed infantrymen advancing with them. Other soldiers clung to the bodies of the T-34s like shipwrecked sailors hanging on to flotsam. He knew he should work the lever to close the thick armoured shield over the vision slot, but he wanted to see what would happen next, wanted to be ready to make his own decisions rather than be guided by Graf.

Roth was working the hull-mounted machine gun hard, and the pepper-iron propellant fumes filled the tank. There were more shouts of range and direction over the intercom, Graf getting his act together, and then a huge bang that rung in Ingo's ears, while the tank rocked from the recoil. The machine gun stopped. Ingo heard the strange whirr of the shell, saw the flash of tracer, then there was the peculiar *plunk* of a hit far away, but no sign of an explosion; all this in a fraction of a second during which time the panzer filled with choking blue-grey gases from the gun that stung his eyes. Then there was a loud rasp of metal on metal as the breech block opened in the turret behind and above him, a clang of a spent case, and the smooth slide of a new shell into the block, then the mechanism snapped shut.

"Ready!" the loader, Kraus, shouted over the intercom, and the electric motor hummed as the turret traversed a little. Then the hull machine gun opened up again, adding to the din of enemy small arms pinging against the panzer. The tank rocked once more to the action of the main gun and this time the distant clonk of its hit was followed by a huge *whooomf*. They'd struck the T-34's ammunition hold. Through the slot Ingo witnessed the aftermath, as the force of the explosion sent the tank's turret high into the battle-fogged air, gyrating and wobbling in flight like a duck with a wing shot away, while shells and ammunition boomed and zinged from the decapitated chassis far beneath it. The turret landed a second or so later, 100 metres from the T-34, with a dull clang, looking like the crown of a boiled egg which had been sliced off with the dash of a spoon and left on the side of a plate. Inky smoke seeped into the sky from the remaining lower part of the T-34.

Kraus had already loaded another shell and the turret was traversing to snapped orders from Graf, Ingo saw the long gun barrel moving in front of him, on to a target approaching very quickly from the left.

Then they were hit.

The panzer shook, and Ingo heard the scab of detached steel zinging round the inside of the tank, and felt the flash of burning heat. Kraus screamed, an animal shriek, as he was hit by the flake of white-hot metal. But the armour piercing shell had not penetrated the turret. Pop fired again, and this time the shell simply bounced off a KV-1 heavy, that Ingo could just see at the edge of his vision slit, like a pea flicked at a church bell. Then they were targeted by a machine gun, thwacking against the front of the panzer, its slugs splatting liquidly against the steel ...

... There was a whiter than white flash of light, the air seemed to be sucked from his lungs. Lidka's photograph became unstuck and was blown away by the hot blast that beat down on him. Yet he could hear nothing. The tank was filling with choking smoke. Something landed on his back, heavy and warm, and then slid silently to the floor. A detached arm, still quivering with life. He recognised the silver wedding ring that belonged to Kraus on one of the fingers. This galvanised him; everyone knew that a tank would shoot another tank until it was finished, and it was clear they had been hit hard. Ingo looked for Roth to his right, but he was already gone, up and out of his hatch.

Ingo unfastened the driver's hatch and started to push it up, ignoring the bullets that still spurted, now strangely silently, against the tank, sparking bright orange chips on the camouflaged panzer paint; green and rust-brown blotches on a mustard background. He then felt, rather than heard, a dull clang, the jar of it travelling down his arm. The hatch had stopped dead, with just twenty centimetres or so of a gap.

He was trapped.

The gun was aiming over the left corner of the tank and was blocking the hatch. It was something they tried to avoid, aiming over a corner of the panzer, but in the heat of the battle Pop would have been thinking of saving the tank. By now Ingo could hardly breathe for the fumes, and so he took a deep gulp of the outside air, a tease of life. Behind him there was no way out, just a near full load of over eighty shells, many in the rack to the rear of his seat – and there was every chance that these would explode soon, too.

Through the Tantalus gap between the hatch and the big gun barrel he watched as Roth was hit, machine gun fire undoing his belly, blood wet daubs like shining oil against the black of his Panzerwaffe uniform. Just then the tank was struck again. It rocked to the impact, but the shell did not penetrate. He could feel the heat of the fire above and behind him on the back of his neck, scorching and toasting.

The main gun moved.

Ingo realised with some surprise that he had been pressing the hatch up all these long seconds of death, as it suddenly burst open like a Jack-in-the-box lid. He was out like Jack, too, but in the rush he forgot to unplug his intercom and this snagged, pulling his head back and wrenching his neck just as he was about to jump clear of the burning tank. It was only over the one ear – as a driver needs to hear the engine to help judge the gear shifts – and so it then ripped itself away from his head, while he yanked his throat microphone free, too.

Pop was there now, clambering down from the top of the tank, carrying the MP 40 sub machine gun that was kept on a bracket in the turret. Ingo could now see that the engine compartment aft of the turret was cloaked in black-shot flames; there was a body too, now burning, which he assumed must be Graff. He realised Pop had saved his life, climbing back in to the turret and traversing the gun a little way so that it unblocked the hatch; his face bore small black scorch marks and the black panzer uniform he was so proud of smouldered, but he did not seem to be badly burnt.

Pop mouthed words. There was no sound, except for a buzzing in Ingo's head. Pop turned away and jumped from the tank, the space taken by the soundless firecracker sparks of machine gun fire on the hull almost at the same instant. Ingo jumped, too, feeling the pass of a bullet close to his face, its swift caress, and a tug at his sleeve, like pinching fingers, as another round passed through the slightly flapping cloth of his buff-coloured overalls.

They ran. Ingo did not know where they were running to. He could hear nothing, except for the buzz in his head. The battlefield was a chaos of smoke and fire and rumbling tanks, which he felt through his boots, the ground quivering to German and Russian armour. The long grass was burning in many places, and Pop used these fires and the drifting smoke from them as cover as they tried to avoid the Russian infantry. After a little while, the buzzing in Ingo's head louder now, fumes from the fire still burning his throat and the inside of his nose, Pop sank to the ground, and started to crawl through the long grass, which was welcomingly wet and cold from the earlier rain. It was then that Ingo realised the others had not made it …

And that he had left Lidka's photograph in the tank.

He stopped. Pop continued to crawl ahead of him, holding the MP 40 in front of him and moving on his elbows and knees. Then he seemed to realise Ingo was not following and stopped, too. He turned, said something, but Ingo only knew this because his lips moved. It suddenly occurred to him that he was deaf. *Could a deaf man drive a racing car?* he thought, almost at once.

Pop crawled back to him, his lips still moving, but there was no noise except for the steely buzz in his head. Ingo remembered that Beethoven had been deaf, but now Pop was shaking his shoulders. Ingo shook his head, pointed to his ears, and said: "I can't …" the words tore at his dry throat like barbs and he was not sure any noise came out.

The grass in front of them was suddenly shredded; for a second or two, no more. Then Pop propped himself up on one knee and let off a sharp burst from the MP 40, a juddering silence for Ingo, pepper-iron cordite snatching at his nostrils. Then they were up and running again, Ingo not knowing if the Ivan had been hit or not, the tall grass swishing silently against his legs, the buzz in his head constant and solid.

Soon enough they were out of the long grass. He sensed they were on the edge of the fighting. Behind them there was smoke and fire, through which a confusion of tanks and soldiers moved; but he could see nothing of Teploe. The air here was smoky, too, and smelt of burning. The buzz in his head seemed to soften, slightly. Pop pointed to a wall, which had once been a small building, but now stood like a solitary jagged, rotten tooth. They approached it cautiously, Ingo feeling the crunch of pulverised brick beneath his rubber-soled Panzerwaffe boots.

When they got to the wall Pop peered around the edge of it. He watched for a little while, and as the minutes crept by Ingo felt the dryness tighten within his throat like a garrotte and his breathing was like the rasps of a file on steel. This was mostly because of the fumes and the fire in the tank, and the smoke of the battlefield – the sky had been obliterated, blown to tattered streamers to be replaced by brown smog – but also from the raging thirst that comes with battle; while it was a warm day, too. He needed water, and their canteens were still in the panzer.

But now the buzz had quietened, and with cautious relief he thought he could hear the battle, soft plopping explosions, like stones tossed in to a deep, deep well.

Pop turned: "... ... ... Yes?"

Ingo heard the last word quite clearly, and with it came the sound of gunfire, the clacking of the Russian machine guns, then the more familiar zip of an MG 42; and the thunderous boom-booming of the tank battle behind them. But the buzzing was still there, too. He felt the grin tight on his face, as Pop shook his head, smiled, then reached for Ingo's holster, on the belt buckled around his overalls, and took out the P38, slapping it coldly in to Ingo's palm.

"We need water," Pop said.

Ingo nodded, his mouth and throat too parched for him to talk.

Pop slowly walked around the edge of the ragged wall. Ingo followed, the pistol held loosely at his side. There was a burnt-out T-34 sitting in the centre of a large circular patch of scorched ground about seventy metres away. There seemed no other chance of finding water for miles around, and so they walked carefully towards it, until they came up close to the smoking husk of the Russian tank, which still radiated a harsh heat and glowed a dull orange around the pushed-in steel of the hole where the shell had penetrated. The rear of it was completely scorched, and there was a blackened body halfway out of the turret, stiffened and twisted, baked in the agonies of death, teeth bright and silently screaming in the shrunken skin of a charcoal face, glazed eyeballs shining white. The smell of burnt flesh was almost overpowering; Ingo did not think anyone could ever get used to that particular smell. It was mixed with the equally familiar, equally unpleasant, stink of a cooked-up tank: hot metal and bubbling paint, burnt rubber and leather, sizzling electrics, cordite and diesel. Behind the tank lay another dead Ivan, part of his face missing, as if it had become unstuck and fallen away, like a shard from a pot.

Pop walked carefully towards the front of the tank. There was another fallen figure on the ground about five metres in front of the T-34. Ingo could feel the heat of the burnt grass through his boot soles, and hear it crackle beneath Pop's boots.

The relief of not being deaf suddenly swam through him, mixed with the relief of being alive, and so he just stood there, did not move.

Pop approached the figure on the ground. It was a woman, Ingo could now see, more girl than woman, he thought. He had heard that the Ivans used women as tank drivers, the crew had often joked about that, but it was still a shock to see a girl, and a pretty girl at that, lying dead on the floor on her back in the middle of a battlefield. Pop had stopped and was staring at her. He seemed to be breathing heavily, as if he sobbed. Ingo had never seen him like this before, and he felt the urge to go to him, as Pop knelt beside the girl, but he did not move. Her brown tunic was undone, her shirt ripped open too, and her white, rosy tipped breasts were showing, a red stained bandage at her belly marking where someone had tried to save her. Her padded leather driver's helmet lay on the ground beside her and her glossy raven hair was spread around her head like a dark halo. Ingo supposed she would have been taken by a machine gun after she'd escaped from the driver's hatch when the turret caught fire. He watched as Pop made a quick sign of the cross, then reached down, to close her eyes to this world, he thought.

Ingo suddenly remembered there was a crew of four in a T-34 – this at the very time he saw the other Russian. He was the other side of the tank, which was at the centre of a triangle, the points of which were Ingo, Pop and the Ivan. He was standing, swaying, coated in sticky blood and black burns, a Papasha sub machine gun, a wooden-stocked device with a Tommy Gun-like drum, in his blood-painted hands, fiery hatred in his eyes. The gun was aimed at Pop, ten metres away, crouching over the body of the dead girl …

The Ivan had not seen Ingo. He tried to shout, as he saw the man's bloody finger tense on the trigger of the Papasha, but there was a just a burning, wheezy creak, and he knew no real sound could come out of his parched, dry throat.

Then the buzzing noise filled his head, as the frustration fed his anger like petrol on a fire. The noise was steely, but grating, a messed up gear shift, but constant. He did not want to kill. But knew he had to. He let the rage win …

Everything he had been taught on the ranges came back to him, and his was a cold – yet quick – action as he flicked off the safety and straightened his arm. He squeezed off four shots, stopping the Ivan with hits to his body, all four rounds making the sound of a well-thrown stone hitting sodden dirt, before the man fell. Then Ingo walked forward, firing as he went, aiming for the head of the Ivan on the burnt grass, and hitting it with every bullet, turning it to a black-red pulp, unable to stop himself now as the anger took hold, and the steely noise screamed within. He used all nine rounds – eight in the mag, one in the chamber – the Walther twitching like a living thing in his hand, the sharp cracks of the shots cutting through the steel din in his head, spent shells clinking softly on to the burnt ground at his feet. The slide shot back with a slick clashing noise when the magazine was empty.

He stared at the man he had killed. The first man he had killed.

The anger seeped from him and he felt light-headed. The steely noise inside his head calmed a little, to a high-pitched whistling whine.

Pop walked over to the body, just a few metres in front of Ingo now. He knelt down beside it and took something from the dead man. Then he walked over to Ingo.

"Thanks, Ingo," he said.

There was still a strange look on Pop's face; and Ingo thought it had more to do with the dead girl than nearly being killed – that had happened plenty of times. Ingo could say nothing, because of the burning dryness in his throat, and Pop tossed him the water bottle he had taken from the body of the man Ingo had killed. The contents were blood warm, but he drank gratefully from the aluminium canteen, all the while staring at the man with no face, the man he had shot dead.

"That's the first time I've killed," he croaked, when he had finished drinking.

"You're kidding, right?"

Ingo shook his head.

"Well, you certainly made sure if it," Pop said, glancing at the obviously empty Walther hanging heavy in Ingo's hand, pointing at the earth.

"It's a pity," Ingo said.

"For him; perhaps."

"I wonder what he was like?"

"Just another Ivan, they have millions more."

"And her?" Ingo said, cranking his head in the direction of the dead driver. Other than the now steady and steely noise in his head, everything was back to normal. He had killed, but the world was still here. For the second time in his life he had let the rage win. And it meant Pop was still alive.

Pop did not answer, but turned away from him, waiting a little while before saying: "Welcome to the war, Ingo."

***

Warsaw. August 1943

The Kozłowski Brothers Beach was made of sand, the sea was made of river. On a hot day like today it was a nice place to be, and this had been a popular place to cool off since the '20s. They had wooden pavilions with changing rooms and everything else you might expect by the 'seaside'. Before the war there had also been ice cream, little sailing boats, many more people, and much more laughter. Still, Freddy was laughing, and paddling and splashing in the rippling shallows at the frayed edge of the Vistula, just metres from where Lidka and Cat sat. In the *Nur für Deutsche* area.

There were few others here, just a scattering of family groups sat around picnic baskets, and four German soldiers further along the beach, who had stripped down to bathing trunks. They had snow-white torsos and arms tanned to a nut brown, so that they appeared to be wearing pale vests. It was hot, the sky was clear, and chips of bright light seemed to float in the Vistula as the water lapped lightly against the shore, while the sunlight felt good on the bare skin of Lidka's arms and legs.

Lidka sat with Cat on towels laid out on the coarse sand, she wore a buttercup-yellow bathing suit that she had borrowed; her own was a little loose on her these days. The beach was on the right bank of the Vistula, just upstream of the Poniatowski Bridge. Across the wide river the Czerniakowski port was visible, as were the factories and apartment blocks behind it, while a little further along she could see the ruins of Fort Czerniakowksi. There were also many barges, on the other side, shrugging to the lazy lap of the river. The air seemed cleaner here than in the city, yet it still seemed to taste a little of the ash of the now destroyed Ghetto. They had been given fake kennkartes that said they were Volksdeutsche, which meant they were able to sit in this part of the beach. As this was the only bit of it that gave them such good views of the bridge and its defences that had been vital. It was a risk, but they were far from Ochota, where people might know them – and she doubted anyone would recognise Cat anyway, her transformation had been complete. Besides, there was always a risk when there was work to be done for the AK.

"Your tits are good," Cat suddenly said. She had a habit of saying exactly what she was thinking, on the few occasions she spoke.

"Be careful Freddy," Lidka said.

"Do they get bigger, when you have a child?"

"Of course, but I had him nearly three years ago now."

"You've been a mother a long time."

"Three years is not so long."

Cat shrugged. To these kids of war, and only war, three years was a lifetime, Lidka knew. "I think Bullet likes your tits," she said.

"Is that what he said?"

The girl shook her head. "Tell me about his father."

"Mr Paczkowski?"

"Freddy's father."

"Jósef? Not much to tell."

"Then you do not love him," Cat said, concern ever so slightly creasing her forehead.

"I didn't say that."

"If you loved him, there would be much to tell."

Lidka smiled shook her head, tried to remember Jósef, the last time she had seen him. "He's kind," she said after the pause. "Nice."

"Bullet's not nice," Cat said.

"I thought we were talking about Jósef?"

"I suppose he is much closer to your age, Jósef?"

"He is."

Cat nodded, then said: "You work hard, harder than most. Why?"

"Isn't that obvious?"

"No, it's not," Cat said. "If I was a mother, I would stay with my child. No, I think you are after something, Chopin."

"Maybe I'm just patriotic?"

"Bullet says you have a point to prove."

"He does?"

"I don't think that's it, though."

"Then what do you think?"

Cat shook her head, then she stood up, quite quickly. She glanced at the group of soldiers along the beach. The old wooden changing rooms were no longer open so their field grey uniforms were stacked up like furry rocks on the sand. Her figure, pressing through the pale blue cloth of her swimming costume, was slim and athletic, yet delicately curved. Her breasts were not big, but they were round, firm-looking fruits.

"The camera's in my bag. I'll walk to the water, they will watch me," Cat said. "Go further along the beach, take some pictures of Freddy, and make sure the defences of the bridge are in the background."

Cat walked down to the water's edge, moving her hips just enough so that it seemed natural. For a girl who spent most her time dressing like a tramp and limping like a cripple to avoid the attention of German soldiers she did a good job now of holding their gaze.

Lidka did as asked, though the asking had been unnecessary, because they had been briefed fully by Bullet earlier. She took six photographs of Freddy, and he pulled a face in each one, but in the background of each photo she managed to include every part of the bridge and its surrounding fortifications, by getting Freddy to move into different positions each time she took a snap. She did not know why this was important, she perhaps never would, but she knew the time to fight was coming. And soon, some said, so would the Russians, maybe via the Poniatowski Bridge.

When she had finished she lay on her back on the towel. Cat also came back from the water's edge and sat down beside her.

"We will wait a little while," the girl said, as Lidka closed her eyes and let the sunlight play on her face, pulsing bright orange-pink behind her eyelids. The soldiers had moved closer, and were now skimming stones on the river. She could hear them laughing and joking, and the soft splashes and plops of the flat projectiles. They did not realise how much their voices carried, or perhaps they did not care, but Lidka could just about hear them. One of them said: "I prefer the other one; better tits."

She tried to shut out the German voices. She tried to picture her life, her and Freddy's life, when all this was done. An ordinary life, with Jósef. But she sighed, as she always did, when she thought of that. It seemed so dull, after all this. Yet she hated herself for thinking it.

"Probably more experienced," one of the Germans said. "*Yours* is like a boy!"

"Perhaps Franz prefers boys?" They laughed at that, those Germans.

She unconsciously brushed the swell of her left breast with her right hand; they weren't as big as they once were – when she had had Freddy, or before the war – but they were firm and taut now, like the rest of her body. She suddenly imagined someone caressing it; that was the sort of thing that jumped into her head all too often of late, because these days Lidka thought about sex like she used to think about pierogi. It was a different sort of hunger, but insistent. Again, she tried to remember what it had been like, with Jósef, and her mind played its trick once more, as she knew it must, and she was in her room in the apartment on Piwna, with Ingo. "Your tits are good," the Ingo in her head said, just as Cat had ten minutes or so ago, but then – as quickly and surely as Jósef's face had changed to Ingo's – his then turned into Bullet's.

She woke with a start, instantly relieved to realise she had drifted off to sleep. Cat was shaking her shoulder.

"It's best we were going, those boys are forgetting their shyness," Cat said, and she was already letting the red and white cotton summer dress she'd worn for this mission fall over her long limbs then cascade down her body.

Freddy was by the river still, a little further along now. It was not dangerous, there, the water was very shallow, but now he was taking an interest in the game the soldiers played with the stones. He had been told often never to talk to Germans or strangers, especially Germans. But he was a curious child. Lidka knew she should not have slept, even if it was just for a moment.

"Freddy!" she shouted.

"He's been fine, I watched him," Cat said.

"We should never have brought him," Lidka said, as she stood, the sand warm beneath her feet.

"Bullet thought it better cover; they would take you for a wife with a child, maybe a soldier's wife."

"He had no right."

"It's a little late to think of that, isn't it?" Cat said.

"Freddy!" Lidka shouted, again.

***

Buenos Aires. January 1954

There was something soothing about a racetrack at night, Ingo always thought. There was noise, sure, but comforting noise; the soft clink of spanners, the dull drip of oil into a pan, the monk-like murmur of quiet problem solving. Here, there was also music. Varela had laid on a party, the other side of the paddock, and had invited many of his porteño friends; and where there was a party in Argentina there was tango. The distant music just added to the mood. It was a good place to be, and it felt like the right place to be.

During the war Ingo had been responsible for looking after the tank. Panzerwaffe drivers were excused watch as they checked the machine over, or made repairs, and he hated now to leave the car to Carlo and the growing band of mechanics Varela had hired. But they were good, experienced men, proud racers all, and there was nothing he could do other than watch, as they worked on the propshaft links – a precautionary move as it was a possible weak point and Ingo had felt a little slack in the transmission as he shifted to third out of one of the turns – while also checking and rechecking every bolt, fastener and hose clip on the Varela Condor CR1. Carlo had not thought much of the change of name, but dreams are never cheap, and for Carlo and Varela's dreams to merge, that had been a condition.

There was also a dent to knock out. Otero's doing, that. It was a long-distance race, and so Ingo would share the driving with Varela's man, though he believed he could drive the 1000 kilometres alone. Otero had over-drove, trying to match Ingo, and now the mechanics had the extra job of knocking out the ding in the fender – Otero had not explained how it had got there, just shook his head, as if it was the car's fault. As for Ingo, he had already done his job that day, putting the Condor fifth on the grid, in amongst the works cars from Ferrari and Maserati and the very quick Allard-Cadillac.

Under the arc lights the Condor shone so bright the car seemed almost unreal, like a blue jewel glowing in a glass case. It was easy to imagine that if the bubble of bright light around it should burst, then it too would disappear. The mechanics seemed somehow frozen in the stark light, even as they moved, as if it was a series of perfect pictures rather than a movie in glorious Technicolor.

There were other glowing snow globes of light across the paddock, each with a sharp gem of a racing sports car at its centre; in the bright red of Ferrari, the deeper red of Maserati, the forest green of Aston Martin, the dark blue of an Ecurie Ecosse Jaguar, the pale blue of a Gordini, the white and blue of Rayforth … The Buenos Aries 1000km was the biggest event the team had entered yet, and it was the first race in the 1954 World Sports Car Championship.

A small wooden trolley rattled along the concrete floor and Carlo appeared from beneath the CR1 like a doll in a drawer. "About done," he said, smiling up from the trolley, the curved smear of axle grease on his forehead almost a mirror image of his moustache. Ingo smiled back, then sucked in the rich, warm air of the paddock, enjoying the aroma of Castrol R20, gasoline, and the lingering smell of baked brake linings and cooked clutches, like some might savour the bouquet of a good Malbec. "Best we show our faces at the party, my friend," Carlo said.

Ingo nodded. He would rather be with the car, but they had promised Varela they would be there. He would stay half an hour, no longer. He had promised himself that.

"You go ahead," Carlo said, lifting himself from the trolley. "I need to get cleaned up." He looked at his watch. "Tell Catalina I'm right behind you."

"Will do," Ingo said, before saying good night to the mechanics and leaving.

Varela had supplied them with a car transporter, a Chevrolet which was part box van and part flat bed, painted in Argentine blue with a yellow stripe, and *Varela*, also in yellow, along its side in a font that would not look out of place on a billboard for a Hollywood movie. Once Ingo was in the lee of this truck the darkness settled on him suddenly, like a cloak, and it took his eyes a moment or so to adjust to the gloom. The party was at the edge of the paddock, most of the light from it blocked off by the hulk of another, much bigger, truck, but the sound of the tango music and the smell of sizzling beef steak both intensified as he walked towards it. He was suddenly quite hungry.

White light.

Ingo raised his hand to his face instinctively – in his life sudden light had often meant sudden death. He kept it there when he realised that it was a camera flash.

"Sorry, signor," the photographer said, but he didn't sound sorry.

Ingo was still blinking the light from his eyes, big yellow-green parrot-coloured chips of it, when there was another voice, coming from the direction of a glowing cigarette that floated like a tiny flare, burning a bright hole in the velvet darkness.

"You know something, Enrique, I've never seen you scared. Not even worried, now I come to think of it." A man's face took a soft form around the glowing light of the cigarette, and then he stepped to one side, out beyond the dark mass of the truck and into the light cast from the party. It was Otero.

"Hector, I didn't see you."

"Except when there are photographers," Otero added. "You always seem nervous of them?"

"The flash, it startled me," Ingo said.

"Maybe it did, but I've seen it before, in daytime too," Otero said.

"I'm just shy, didn't you hear?"

"El Tímido? No, I don't buy that."

"We were wondering where you were, we needed to discuss the car, after practice?" Ingo said.

"Had things to do."

Otero had been almost a second down on Ingo in practice, had said the car did not feel right, and that had been the last the Varela team had seen of him.

"We've a race, tomorrow."

"Needed to think it through," Otero said. "I'm used to more sophisticated equipment; maybe I need to change my driving style, to get the most out of that pampas tractor, eh?"

"That might be a good idea," Ingo said.

Otero shrugged: "Maybe."

Ingo nodded, said "goodnight then", then he too walked into the light, and across the paddock to the party.

The orquesta típica was dressed in tuxedoes with black bows; there was a string section with violins, a viola and a cello, a piano and double bass, and three bandoneon players, which gave the music that decadent, dreamy, rusty edge that made it sound so much better at night. On the dancefloor pairs moved like single creatures, pacing out territory. Others stood at the edge of the floor; drinking, eating, talking, the latter leaning in to each other so as to be heard over the music, with what looked like abandoned kisses. Almost everyone smoked and the issue from their cigarettes and cigars seemed to tangle above them, the strong artificial light shining through it, so that it looked like the very silver of a dark cloud's lining. His tinnitus sang a little higher as he joined the press of people.

Ingo spent a moment or two avoiding conversations and ignoring shouts of his name, and then found a juicy steak and a glass of wine. He sat at a trestle table covered with a linen cloth and tucked into the excellent beef. He smelt the cinnamon and juniper of her perfume before he realised she was taking the seat beside him.

"Catalina," he said. "Carlo's on his way."

"Carlo's always on his way," she said.

"Good party?"

"A lonely party."

"I thought you liked this sort of thing?"

"So did I."

"Missing the children?"

"More than they are missing me, I expect," she said. Ingo knew that they were at her sister's house in Tres Arroyos, where they always spent time during the long summer holidays.

Across the dancefloor and the press of people at its edges Ingo saw Carlo arrive. He nodded in their direction, then went the other way, towards Varela.

"I've been jealous of a car, and other things," Catalina said, glancing at Ingo. "Jealousy is a good thing, a healthy thing. But …"

"Carlo has to keep him sweet. He buys the wine, the steaks, the music, the fuel, the parts, without Varela …" Ingo let it trail off.

"He's bought my husband."

"No, it's a partnership," Ingo said. "Carlo has what Varela needs, Varela has what Carlo needs."

"Looks like he's given him a little more of it," Catalina said.

Ingo saw what she meant. Carlo's grin was seldom sheathed, but now it seemed to slash through the partygoers with its scimitar sweep as he made his way through the throng towards them, then sidestepped through the dancers like a rugby outside-half. Then Ingo realised Varela was following him; like a breathless prop in the eightieth minute, a sheen of sweat shining on his forehead.

"You look pleased with yourself?" Ingo said, as Carlo took a seat opposite them. He said nothing until Varela also sat down, with a little stumble as he did so, tipsy perhaps.

"I am drunk," Varela confirmed, around his thick Havana.

"You are?" Ingo said.

"I must be, I only ever agree business deals quickly when I am drunk," he said, now resting the cigar on the edge of an ashtray. "But you know, they are always the best of deals."

"Tell them what the deal is," Carlo said.

"See that man over there," Varela started, obviously annoyed at the interruption. They looked to see a short man with a crewcut and a cigar that was so long it made his fuzzy grey head look like a mildewed lollipop. "He comes from Akron, in the States; he's in rubber."

"Well, each to his own," Ingo said.

"His name is Huck Buchanan."

"Buchanan Tyres?"

"The very same."

"They're with Rayforth, aren't they?"

"They were," Varela said. "Until Huck saw this local *two-bit* car of ours, that's what he called it, saw it blow the works Rayforth into the weeds today. Seems he had a performance clause, and Rayforth didn't perform."

"It's just one race," Ingo said.

"One too many, Huck says."

"He was impressed with our car, Enrique," Carlo said.

"Yes, he was most impressed with *my* car," Varela said.

"Impressed enough to make us an offer," Carlo said.

"Are you saying we now have a tyre contract?"

Varela looked at Carlo, and Carlo took the cue. "And the Mille Miglia, my friend." It landed in the conversation like a flaming Molotov through the hatch of a Panzer IV. Even the orchestra stopped for a moment, though that was just a coincidence. Ingo could see that Buchanan watched from afar, his round head split with a satisfied grin.

"The Mille Miglia? Won't that mean a passenger?" Catalina said.

"Of course," Carlo said, waving her quiet.

"Why the Mille Miglia?" Ingo said.

"Huck needs to prove his tyres in a high profile race, on roads. Is there any better, my friend?"

"You know I can't do the Mille Miglia, Carlo," Ingo said, suddenly losing his appetite and pushing the plate away.

"Then Hector will drive," Varela said, without hesitation. "But you, Carlo, will sit beside him, yes?"

Carlo hesitated, glanced at Ingo, thought for a moment then said: "Of course, an Argentinian will need an Italian beside him, it's the only way; the way it's always done."

"When were you last in Italy, Carlo?" Catalina snapped.

"You never forget the Mille Miglia," he said, his smile falling away.

"It's time I turned in," Ingo said. "It's a long race tomorrow."

"I also need to go back to the hotel, I have a headache," Catalina said. "Could you give me a lift, Enrique?"

"I think that's a good idea," Carlo said, then quickly turned to talk to Varela just as the band struck up another number.

Ingo's Jeep was parked by the paddock gate, which was crowned with a very big and very wide white-painted concrete arch with struts within it, which made it look a little like a giant car radiator. There was also a gleaming white obelisk reaching for the moon to its left. The Autódromo lay on flat land in the south of the city, and it was a half-hour or so drive to Catalina's hotel – Varela had put the Rossis up in the Alvear Palace, but Ingo had refused the offer and had found a more modest place on Esmeralda.

Now they were away from the party he could smell the booze on her breath. They climbed in to the Jeep. Her skirt had rucked up to show her knees. He put the key in and switched the ignition on, pulled out the choke and the throttle knob, and then turned the engine over by pressing the starter button on the floor with his right foot. It clattered into life and he closed the choke and balanced the throttle knob until it idled nicely, then he took it up on the accelerator pedal.

"I saw you talking to him before you came to the party, Enrique," she said, as he took the Jeep through the main gate and turned north towards the city centre. He glanced at her; the streetlights striped her face in strobing champagne-coloured bands as they passed them. The meaty tyres hummed on the asphalt and the transmission whined above the low-revving engine – Ingo drove slowly because she was talking, and it was difficult to hear in the open Jeep otherwise.

"Who, Otero?"

"Yes. I don't think I've ever seen you talk with him before. What did he want?"

"He's sore about something, I think," Ingo said.

"You were faster." It was a statement, not a question, and Ingo said nothing. "He scares me, that one," she added, and shivered – maybe because of the cooler air spilling over the moving Jeep.

"He does?"

"He has no fear, and if Carlo is to sit beside him for the Mille Miglia. Well, that frightens me."

Ingo said nothing, made a show of concentrating on overtaking a Rastrojero pickup truck that was overloaded with melons, its rear suspension compressed so that its nose sniffed at the night sky.

"I would feel better if you were driving the Mille Miglia, Enrique," Catalina said.

"You would?"

"Yes."

"I thought you …Well."

"Things are different now, I cannot turn back the clock," she said, then nodded sharply before continuing. "Carlo says you have never crashed?"

"It's true."

"I'm not sure he believes you, but I do."

"I cannot drive the Mille Miglia, Catalina."

"Why not?"

"I do not wish to return to Europe, there's nothing there for me. I've made my home here."

"So, you're still hiding," she said, then seemed to notice that her skirt had rucked up, tugged it forward.

"Otero will do fine, Carlo will keep him under control."

"Do you believe that?"

Ingo did not answer, just drove past the French Embassy and turned on to Alvear, the street lighting tiger-striping the dark asphalt ahead of the Jeep as it rattled down the avenue between the grand houses. The Belle Époque-styled edifice of the hotel was lit up like a liner and Ingo jinked right into the main entrance, which was tucked under a colonnaded gallery bathed in soft golden-white light. He brought the Jeep to halt with a squeak of brakes.

"Do you really still fear it, Ingo?"

"Ingo?"

"Why pretend? I've heard Carlo and you talk, many times," she said. "It's nicer than Enrique, suits you. Perhaps I will always call you Ingo?"

"Do I fear what?" he said, wishing for the thousandth time he'd never told Carlo his real name.

"Whatever you're hiding from."

"I've never said I was hiding."

A smartly dressed doorman in snow-white gloves was walking towards the scruffy Jeep, shaking his head, like an oberfeldwebel appraising a new recruit. Ingo held up a finger to indicate 'one minute' and the man gave a sharp nod, making a point of looking at his watch.

"You know, if anyone was looking for you, then I think they would have come for you by now."

"Why would you think that?"

She shrugged. "It's been a long time, hasn't it?"

"It doesn't seem so very long; it never will."

"It's history."

"History's a process, it never ends."

"Yet lines are drawn"

"And lines are crossed."

"But then, if you're not hiding, what is there to be afraid of?"

Ingo sighed, and the doorman pointed at his watch as a Rolls Royce Silver Wraith pulled in behind them.

"Please, drive the Mille Miglia; for Carlo – for me," Catalina said. He shook his head. She swung her legs over the low side of the Jeep and then walked up the stripe of patterned red carpet that hugged the shallow marble staircase, and then in through the bright-brass revolving doors, the harsh light in the lobby beyond spinning her giddy reflection in the glass.

Ingo clunked the Jeep into first gear and accelerated away.

*

Tel Aviv. January 1954

It was the first time he had spoken to her since Nice, nearly a year ago.

"How is David?"

"He's fine," Sarah said.

"The boy?"

"He is well."

There was a long pause, then Gabriel said: "So, for all that time you hated the wrong man?"

They were speaking on the telephone, David had had one put in when his latest pay-rise had come through, so Gabriel would not have seen the sharp nod, nor that she was biting her lower lip. She stood in the hallway, the floor was scattered with toys and the laundry basket she had been carrying when the phone had rung was now at her feet. She hated dirty clothes in a pile, it reminded her of those piles of the dead in Warsaw the Germans tried so hard to make neat; but a bloody arm, like a loose sleeve stained with sauce, would always mess it up.

It had taken Gabriel over seven months to respond to the messages she had passed via Yitzhak, messages about *him*. Just like Sarah, Gabriel was not good at forgiveness. The Group had taken all she had discovered in the photographs – far more crimes committed by far more criminals than they could ever hope to track down – and they had passed on some of the information to Mossad, Yitzhak had told her. But the pressure on The Group had not subsided. She thought that maybe the Institute now wanted a monopoly on revenge.

Gabriel would no longer meet with her in Bendel's on Allenby Street, or the café on the edge of Jaffa, so she had to be content with this call. It was raining hard outside, the fall of it against the road surface sounding like a fresher version of the static on the line. The windows had been closed all day and the air smelt stale.

"Kroh still deserved to die," she said.

"Of that there is no doubt. But from what Yitzhak tells me this other one is small fry; in the scheme of things?"

249

"But still *in* the scheme of things."

"Yes, that is true."

"Please, put out the word, that's all I ask."

There was another long pause, then Gabriel said: "Things have changed, since Nice."

"I know," she said.

"We do not have the friends we once did."

"I know," she repeated.

The line went quiet, but she knew he was still there.

"His name is Ingo Six," she said. Then she placed the Bakelite handset back on to its cradle.

*

Buenos Aires. January 1954

The Condor rasped by, its 2.7-litre Ferrari V12 engine howling through the open exhaust, the noise tearing at the bleached summer sky. A ticking hand on one of the large Heuer watches affixed to the clipboard Carlo held clicked to a stop.

Carlo looked up at Ingo, his eyes wide in surprise. "He's just half a second down on you."

Ingo nodded. He didn't need to tell Carlo that it was one lap, and that the last time around he had been a second down, the one before that three seconds, nor that the next lap would almost certainly be slow, as Hector Otero had another adventure, more close calls.

"He's pushing," Carlo said, raising his voice as another car, a Jaguar C-Type, thundered past the pits.

Carlo had not added *too hard*, but they both knew it. They were standing in front of the Varela pit stall, the last garage in the row, which gave them a view of part of the first corner, but little else of the nine and half kilometre course on which the Buenos Aires 1000 Kilometre race was now taking place. Varela stood alongside, sucking on an unlit Havana; it didn't matter how important you were, no one could light up in the pits. Even over the familiar smells of the pit stall – oil and grease – and the track – baked brakes and hot rubber – Ingo could smell his pungent cologne. The Condor was in fifth place.

The track consisted of the new grand prix circuit, but before completing the lap it turned left and out on to the Avenue General Paz, which the cars raced up, then down the other side, with sections of roundabouts at either end of these long straights to connect them. By combining the new circuit with the flat out blasts along General Paz they had come up with a close to six-mile course – and half a second over that distance was getting close, that was true. But Ingo knew this game was about consistency, too, and that was the key: his times were the same, a tenth or two either side, each and every lap, when he was pushing and not saving the car. Otero did not even understand the concept of saving the car, all he cared about was beating Ingo's times.

But Varela only saw the lap time, and nodded thoughtfully, then turned back to the conversation he was having with Huck Buchanan; the latter wiping blisters of sweat from his pale forehead with a handkerchief. Ingo watched as Otero lined up for the first corner, a challenging right-hand fast sweep that lassoed the track around in the other direction. There was a much slower car in front, a thing of sports car competition where cars from various classes compete in races within races. It was a pale green Osca 1100 coupe and it was already turning in to the curve, shrugging its weight over to the left, the inside wheel lifting and now just brushing the surface of the asphalt.

This will slow Otero, Ingo thought, surprised – and a little annoyed – that it pleased him. It seemed clear he would have to wait to pass after the turn now, or go around the outside through the corner. But as he was thinking this Ingo realised that the yellow-ringed nose of the mostly-blue Condor was already ducking inside the little Osca. Contact was inevitable.

Ingo heard the hit, a dull *doof*, then saw the front left fender of the Condor crumple a little, felt it, too, like a jab to the heart. Already at its limit of adhesion the little coupe was instantly tipped into a spin by the impact with its rear, looping off the circuit. Ingo heard the gasps of spectators over the shriek of its tortured tyres. The Osca spun completely once and then hit the bumpy ground at the edge of the track. For a moment it dug in and stood on two wheels, on the tip-toe-toppling edge of a rollover, so that Ingo could clearly see the routing of its exhaust and its grimy floorpan. Then it crashed back down onto four wheels and the driver was able to return to the track, weaving to check his steering, and shaking his head.

"That was close," Varela said.

"Too close," Carlo replied.

"But Hector held it well, no?"

Ingo shook his head, but Varela had turned to say something to Buchanan, who was also chewing on an unlit cigar.

Two laps later and it was time for the stop. Ingo pulled on his helmet and his leather driving gloves, buckled up his wide kidney belt, and strung his goggles around his neck. The Condor drove on to the pit apron and Otero pulled up outside the team's stall, vaulting over the low door as the mechanics set about changing the wheels and refuelling the car.

Before he climbed into the car Ingo looked at the tell-tale at the rear of the rev counter. It was as he had suspected, down the long straights of General Paz Otero had stolen a few too many revolutions, had put too much strain on the engine. There was a carbon-ish smell issuing from the bonnet vents, too, and the tyres that came off were down to the canvas at the rear. The crumpled fender, where it had hit the Osca, somehow reminded Ingo of a sad face he had once seen, on a dead girl in Warsaw. Then he felt a sudden flare of anger, like a throttle blip, matched by a steely surge of tinnitus.

"Signor Varela wants Otero to take another stint," Carlo said, shaking his head slowly, his nostrils twitching at the smell of overworked steel coming from the engine. "He thinks he's doing well; is getting quicker, and that he needs the experience with the car." With that he handed the clipboard with the lap chart and the watches fixed to it to the chief mechanic.

"The engine won't take much more abuse," Ingo said, almost shouting to be heard over the roar of passing racing cars, looking over at Varela, who simply turned away and continued to talk to Buchanan – though Ingo knew for a fact he had been watching when Carlo had given him the news. Carlo shrugged. The tinnitus now seemed to drill in to the inside of Ingo's head.

Ingo took his helmet off and ducked under the pit stall counter. The door at the back of the workshop space was open to allow a breeze to come through, and Catalina sat on a deckchair in the shade of the concrete garage reading a copy of *Atlántida* magazine. The Condor left the pit in a wreath of tyre smoke, the burn of it tugging at Ingo's nostrils. Carlo followed him in to the work space, also ducking under the counter. Ingo let a Ferrari 375 MM, a Rayforth Hawk and an Allard special pass by outside before he spoke.

"I'll do it," Ingo said, and he was aware of the edge to his voice.

Carlo paused for a moment, a space filled with the sudden echoed, tinny jabbering of a commentator, talking about Farina in the Ferrari.

"What?" Carlo said.

"The Mille Miglia."

Two laps later the Varela Condor CR1 was retired from the race, its engine blown.

***

Brindisi, Italy. March 1944

Józef Sczcepanski was helping to load the canisters into the bomb bay of the Liberator. It was spring and the sun was out, and across the aerodrome someone was doing an engine test on one of the flight's Halifax bombers. The B-24 Liberator was painted black, except for the upper part, which was in brown-on-green camouflage, as if it had been held by its wheels and lightly dipped upside down in an algae-coated pond. The black paint of the fuselage and underwings was because most of their flying was still done at night – the Polish resistance did not take daytime deliveries. On its nose, below and in front of the cockpit and behind the greenhouse-style observation pod, there was the square red and white chequerboard insignia of the Polish Air Force, and the plane's personal nose art; a flying, flaming sword – always reminding Józef just how much flying and flaming seemed to go together.

The cigar-shaped canisters lay on the floor in a row, like a line of limbless and headless steel corpses, bundled colour-coded small parachutes were in a separate pile close by. The air was saturated with the stench of highly flammable aviation fuel, a smell he had grown to hate, but every now and then a medicinal breeze off the Adriatic would bring in a snatch of cooling briny sea air and sometimes he caught a whiff of the wild thyme that grew around the scruffy fenced fringes of the base.

The squadron was no more, because 301 had been unable to find the Polish crews to replace those that had been lost, so now the remnants had been turned over to other work, no longer bombing Germany. Jósef was now part of what was called 1586 Special Duties Flight – though they all still referred to it as 301, because sometimes a number is more than a number. Some said they wished they were still loading bombs to kill Germans, but they all believed their work was vital. That work was dropping supplies in to Poland for the AK, the Armia Krajowa, the Home Army.

Bosko was talking as he worked loading the canisters. Bosko was always talking, unless he was smoking, and he wasn't allowed to smoke near the aircraft. This was not Jósef's rule, but it would have been if it was not already in place. He had seen too many aircraft in flames in this long war, still saw them in his nightmares, too. Any risk of fire was a risk too great, however much he sometimes fancied a Woodbine himself.

"Jankowski says they're dropping a Cichociemni in, too," he said. The 'Silent Unseen' were the British-trained experts who were parachuted into Poland for special work, or to teach others the art of dealing death.

"Jankowski should know better than to talk of such things," Jósef said.

"Maybe, but they're brave men, those Cichociemni, eh Joe?" Bosko never called him by his rank, few did, after they had been with 301 for a little while. He didn't mind, did not really know how to mind without causing a scene. And it wasn't worth that.

"I suppose so," Jósef said. They both pushed up on the bottom of the heavy canister, stuffed with weapons and equipment, its steel skin warm from the afternoon sun, and from within the fuselage others pulled it through the roll-up bomb doors of the Liberator, metal clanking and screeching against metal.

"Heroes, really."

"What we're doing is important, too," Jósef said.

"I never said it wasn't," Bosko said, wiping the sweat from his brow. "But it must be good to get back at them – to have a real go at them, eh?"

"We're having a go at them, sending these," Jósef said, nodding at the next canister waiting to be loaded into the plane.

"Perhaps, but when my son asks what I did in the war, I would rather say I was Cichociemni – maybe I will anyway," with that Bosko laughed.

"I think we'd all be a little happier if you were silent and unseen," Jósef said, and Bosko laughed louder – Jósef rarely made jokes, wasn't even sure if he had meant it as one, but he smiled anyway. "You have a son?" he added.

"Well, one day, perhaps," Bosko said.

Jósef thought of Lidka, and the son he had never seen. He had had two more letters since the first one, one to tell him his son's name was Fryderyk. He would not have chosen it himself, but he had grown used to it now. There had been no photograph, perhaps because that would have been risky, and no address to write back to, also understandable, if deeply disappointing. Once he had very briefly toyed with the idea of putting a message in one of the containers in the hope it might get to Lidka, somehow, but he knew that would be stupid – if the container was found by the Germans it would incriminate her. It would mean death; for her, and their son. The test of the Halifax's engine the other side of the field finished with a long flutter, and then quite suddenly it seemed unnaturally quiet, except for the scratchy rendition of *Paper Doll* Jósef could just about hear coming from the overworked gramophone in the officer's mess.

He tried to imagine what Fryderyk looked like again. Pictured a boy with Lidka's face, that was always so, and how he might look maybe in a year or two, when all this was over, hopefully. Then, in his mind's eye, the child asked him a question: "What did you do in the war, Daddy?"

*

Tilburg, Netherlands. July 1944

Sardine had tried not to seem so keen, but by the fourth glass of the local La Trappe beer he could not help himself: "So, we will be going to Normandy soon, eh?" he said.

Sardine had a real name; but no one used it. He was their new loader, a tall lad; too tall for a tank, really, kept banging his head. But then sardines belong in cans.

"Didn't have you down for the hero type, Sardine?" Pop said, though he didn't take his eyes off the barmaid as he said it. She was tall, had long legs, but was plain. She was also making a point of ignoring them, a lot of the Dutch had done so since the Allies had landed in France a few weeks earlier.

"Just saying," Sardine just said.

Café Havenzicht was on Piushaven, overlooking the canal basin, where heavily laden barges ticked and creaked in the setting sun, the dirty canal water too lazy to lap at the hulls. In the Dutch way, there were large and tall windows in the brick built café, with a band of off-white netting suspended from a brass rail which covered the lower parts and hid sitting drinkers from the street. The ceiling was high and the floor was of varnished planks, which amplified the noise the soldiers, the crews of three panzers, made as they talked and drank at the long wooden table that ran down the centre of the room. The walls were panelled in lacquered dark wood to eye level, and stained a dirty brown from cigarette smoke above that. The low evening sunlight pinkly lit up the cloud of cigarette smoke over their heads so that it shone like candy floss, while through a small gap in the low band of the lace curtain the light was extruded in to a long and slender orange-yellow shaft, shot through with volleys of lazy dust motes. The place smelt of sweat-soaked army wool and panzer oil, spilt beer and the smoke from their cigarettes. They were the only customers.

The 19th Panzer Division was stationed a little way out of town. It had had few tanks left after it had broken out of Hube's Pocket, and not many men to fill them, and so it had been sent to Holland to refit. It was short of experience now – that leaks like thin oil from panzers – and so a few old sweats from other divisions had been transferred to help rebuild it.

Pop and Ingo had been among them; and they had picked up their new Panther at the start of the week. At close to 45 tonnes it was much heavier than a IV, but it was also a little quicker thanks to its 700bhp Maybach engine – which Ingo liked – it had a good 75mm gun – which Pop liked – while the armour was sloped and much thicker – which everyone liked. It was their sixth tank, the other five were burnt out wrecks in Russia, four the victims of Soviet fire, one blown up by the one kilogram demolition charge inside the panzer when the gun had been put out of action during a Sturmovik attack; the Panzwerwaffe would not feed toothless tanks with precious fuel.

It had been sad to leave the 4th, but then there were few of the originals there now – they had lost far more friends than tanks – and, besides, the 4th was still on the Eastern Front. A hot day's training in the new Panthers near Tilburg – getting used to that tricky shift from first to second – with cool monk-brewed beer in the evening, was better than fighting Ivans. Most things were better than fighting Ivans; even fighting Amis and Tommies, some said.

"I see no reason to hurry back to the war," Woof, their new wireless operator, said. Woof had been in one of the few tanks to have been knocked out by a Soviet anti-tank dog at Kursk.

"Once bitten, eh Woof?"

They all laughed; *they* being other old soaks of the 19th, most just 21 or 22. Sardine looked confused, Ingo took pity.

"Woof's tank was attacked by a *hundminen*; they're Bolshevik dogs packed with pouches of explosives, trained to run under tanks, tickle their bellies," he said. "There's a long wooden handle on their backs and when they go under a panzer it's flicked like a switch and, well ... *Woof!*"

"Oh, and that's why it's *Woof?*"

"No," Pop said. "That's because his breath stinks."

The others laughed again, Woof included. He was quite small, a terrier of a man, with wiry hair and a facial tick that was, they all knew, a souvenir of Russia. Once, when asked about it, he had said that it was not a tick; just a way of cursing people, mostly officers, in Morse code. Ingo had tried to read his face since then, but all Woof's SOSs, for they were clearly that, were in a dark cipher.

"You know why the German army has so few dogs?" Ingo said.

Sardine shook his head.

"Stick grenades."

Sardine thought for a moment, then laughed, a little after the rest of them.

"We have some dogs, though," Woof said. "I saw one set on an Ivan partisan; chewed his face off – the nose was really crunchy. We thought that funny, all right."

"Funny?" Sardine said, then took a deep swig of his beer.

"Light relief," Woof said, his tick stuttering a garbled message as a memory flashed bright in his eyes. "We had just found one of our own with used shell casings hammered into his hands and feet, and one in his forehead – you can be sure they did the head last, though it hadn't killed him."

"He lived?"

"He died. Eventually," Woof said, an especially pronounced twitch his full stop.

This was a great game. Every soldier played it, when there was a keen one among them, one who might be looking for an Iron Cross, or a wooden one.

"Shell cases, yeah – seen that all right," Pop said, he was tapping his foot beneath the table, a shaft of sunlight was lighting up his face, his pupils shining big and bright in the crazing of his bloodshot whites. Ingo quite suddenly realised Pop was beginning to look much older, his skin harshly scored in the ruthless wash of the light. "Worse was the group of lads we found in a cabin near Mzensk a couple of years ago. Panzer grenadiers from our division." Pop was still looking at the barmaid as he talked; and now he raised his voice a little. "The bastards had nailed their tongues to the table."

"What? But that's ... How?"

"I will let you figure out the details when you can't sleep tonight, eh Sardine?" Pop said, taking a long puff on his vile smelling Jan Maat cigarette; he had managed to get hold of a load of them, to sell on once they were back in a German city, but Ingo thought that his nose for business, or just his nose, had let him down this time.

"There are animals on both sides, though," Woof said. "We were put on one of those anti-partisan operations once. Working alongside an SS unit, headed by a maniac called Dirlewanger. I heard it started out as a bunch of poachers, released from prison to track partisans."

"That's not such a bad idea, actually," Pop said.

"It was *actually* the Führer's idea, they say. He was having a lot of good ideas back then. But then they started taking convicts from prisons, and the camps, even some Ivan traitors."

"Russians?" Sardine said.

"Russians, Ukrainians, Martians, whatever. Sometimes I think we have more Ivans fighting for our side than they have on theirs. Any road, our panzer grenadiers said they couldn't move forward, on account there were mines laid. Know what this SS bunch did?"

Sardine shook his head.

"Walked a whole village in to the minefield to clear it, everyone in the village, blown to bits, or shot if they survived the walk," Woof said.

"Everyone?"

'Well, everyone except the girls, of course."

"What happened to the girls?" Pop said, giving up on the aloof and lofty barmaid and taking his beer from the long wooden table, which was scattered with an archipelago of optimistic and pessimistic glasses, and three smoking ashtrays.

"Well, they might have taken them home to meet their mothers …" Woof said with a grin, and Pop sniffed a little laugh, then sank a deep slug of La Trappe. "But say, now I come to think of it, one of those SS lads, he wanted to be all chummy, reckoned he'd been in a panzer division, reconnaissance, with the 4th — that's your old lot, isn't it?"

"Yes," Pop said. "What was the name?"

"Didn't say. Friendly enough, though, unless you were a partisan. Wore a Gebirgsjäger cap and whistled a lot, only —"

"It wasn't much of a whistle?" Ingo said

"No, it wasn't really a whistle at all. You know him?"

"The cap fits," Pop said, looking at Ingo.

"As does his new outfit, by the sounds of it," Ingo said. He hadn't thought of Kroh for ages, made a mental note of that other name, *Dirlewanger*, always good to know the word for danger, in every language.

"He always wanted to get back in the SS," Pop says. "Seems he owes us one, eh Ingo?"

"I doubt he would see it that way," Ingo said.

"Well, I hear that mob is still out east, so I doubt you'll bump into him any day soon," Woof said. "I'm just glad we'll be fighting the Amis next. I'm sick of Russia and Russians."

"The Americans? So, we *will* be going to Normandy?" Sardine said.

"Bollocks!" shouted a gunner from one of the other panzers, a prematurely greying man named Günther who sat at the other end of the long table, where the conversation had withered and someone had produced a deck of cards for a game of Doppelkopf. Günther was the type who liked to think he knew it all, the type every platoon had at least one of. What made him such a pain in the arse was that so far he had been mostly right.

"We're off east in a week or so," he said. "Warsaw first, I hear."

"That's shit," Woof said, but he could not hide the disappointment in his voice, and his facial tick tapped out a prayer in indecent haste, while the others hid their reactions behind upturned beer mugs.

But not Ingo. He could not help smiling, as he fixed an image of Lidka in his consciousness; all he had since he had lost the photograph when their panzer was hit in Teploe.

"You'll never find her," Pop said, guessing where his thoughts had taken him.

"This time I will," Ingo said. "I know it."

***

Lampeter. April 1954

Joe had come to the green-doored surgery on Bryn Road for his results. But he knew the outcome, had known deep down for a while and he – almost – welcomed it, because it took the future out of his hands. It was raining heavily outside, the fall of it sizzling against the slates, but it was hot in the waiting room, where a bar heater emitted a buzz and a nauseating slightly burnt-electric smell, and the windows were steamed up. A boy drew an aeroplane in the condensation with a fingertip. He drew it at an angle, so that it looked like it was crashing; then melting, as the minutes dripped by.

There were five others in the surgery's hard chair-lined square waiting room, but they all sat the other side, away from him, as if they might catch his dreadful and obvious affliction. But it was not the burns that had brought him here, they had only served to mask it. The others, a skinny woman with an annoying cough, who was the mother of the boy who drew the aeroplane, and a recently arrived farmer with a bandaged hand – steaming like a race horse in the hot room and loosening the top button of his shirt – did all they could so as not to look at him. All of them, that is, except for the younger sister of the boy who had drawn the aeroplane. She was maybe six or seven, and she stared. He thought she was about to speak, ask her mother what was wrong with that man. It embarrassed people, when kids did that, but he could see why they did, saw it in the one mirror he owned every morning. So he reached across to the low table in the centre of the room and picked up the first magazine which came to hand. Just something to hide his burnt face behind.

The masthead of the magazine announced that it was *Autosport*. It was a three-month old copy. He enjoyed the pictures of the cars. But then racing cars can burn, too, he thought, as he turned a page to a report on the Buenos Aires 1000 Kilometre race. There was a photograph that drew his eye immediately. And almost stopped his heart.

The sports car was beautiful, but that was not why he stared at the black and white image which showed a man in a big beard, googles around his neck, standing in front of the car and pressing the palms of his hands against the bonnet. The caption read: *Argentine sensation Enrique 'El Timido' Hohberg seems to thank his Varela Condor CR1 after putting the locally-built car fifth on the grid in Buenos Aires.* He searched for the name in the body text, found it, and something else: *El Timido, the shy one, is to drive the Varela in the Mille Miglia at the beginning of May, the new Argentinian marque having signed a tyre deal with Buchanan ...*

Right then the receptionist called his name, almost pronouncing it right, and so he put the magazine back on the table and went through to the doctor's office, hearing the horrified and loudly whispered Welsh of the little girl as he went: "What happened to him, Mam?"

He did not wait for Doctor Howells to greet him and the door had not quite closed behind him as Joe said: "Just tell me how long I have."

***

Warsaw. August 1, 1944

The way Andrzej paced the room reminded Lidka of a tiger she'd seen in the City Zoo, long before the Nazis had sent the animals they were interested in to Germany, and then killed the rest – that had been a foretaste of it all, in a way. Every time Andrzej turned, his shoe soles squeaking against the parquet, he glanced at his watch. He was agitated, but she knew it was not fear, not nerves. It was, she thought, a kind of lust ...

"They will call it off, again. I know it!" he said, stopping suddenly.

"I doubt it," Lightning said. "There are just hours to go now, it would be impossible to get the message out, to tell even a tiny few of those who wait, like us. Warsaw's ready."

Andrzej nodded sharply at that, then started to pace again. Like all of them, except for Freddy, he wore the red and white armband of the AK, his over the sleeve of an old crazed leather jacket he had taken to wearing. Yes, they were ready, as were thousands of others across the city, close to five long years of waiting was almost at an end.

They were in the upstairs parlour of the Paczkowski house on Mochnackiego. Freddy sat in the corner on a stool. He was in awe of Andrzej and did everything Bullet asked of him. Andrzej – who seemed very fond of Freddy – had told him to sit still, and to sit quiet. Freddy now looked and acted like a carved cherub. There was a sudden roll of thunder, though they all knew it was not thunder, but the big guns of the Russians, east of the Vistula. Some said the Soviets were already in Praga, within the city itself. The sky was bruised with darkening clouds and the curtains over the floor-length doors to the narrow Juliet balcony were almost fully closed, with just a gap of half a metre to allow the milky light in. Some of the other windows were also covered with drapes, though the side window had just a net curtain in place, so the light in the room was dim, but sufficient enough that they did not have to switch on the electric lamps. Lidka wore lightly paint-spattered light brown overalls she'd found in the house, the legs and sleeves turned up, pinched tight at her waist with a leather belt, yet they were still baggy on her. She also wore stout boots. It all seemed more practical than a skirt and blouse. For war.

This was the second time the cell had been told to be ready, the second time they had come together here. On the last occasion, just three days before, it had all come to nothing.

"The Russians are just over the river," Andrzej said, not for the first time that day. "We need to fight before *they* get in to Warsaw, otherwise we will have no stake in our own future; we will be swapping like for like." A burst of far-off artillery both punctuated and emphasised his sentence.

"But there are also panzer divisions to the north, and the word is some are even detraining in the Gdansk Station right now," Lightning said, he probably did not disagree with Bullet, but he was naturally pessimistic.

"Monter says they are poor units, nothing to worry about," Cat said, it was unusual for her to say very much, but she never missed a chance to side with Bullet. Monter was the *nom de guerre* used by one of the men at the top of the AK in Warsaw; an old soldier unsuited to this new war, Lidka thought. She also thought he lacked imagination, and that could be dangerous, but she kept that to herself.

"Tanks are always something to worry about," Lightning said.

Cat shook her head. She wore overalls, like Lidka, only hers were blue.

Mrs Paczkowska pushed her way, back-first, through the doors, carrying a tray crowded with cups of German acorn coffee which rattled in her hands – her hands shook all the time these days, Lidka had noticed. There were eight cups, for the AK members in the room, and a glass of water for Freddy. The ersatz coffee smelt nutty, which cut through the metallic tang of gun oil and the musty atmosphere of the now seldom-used room.

Mrs Paczkowska placed the tray on the table in between the tangle of weapons: Andrzej's Sten, a captured Schmeisser machine pistol and a Mauser rifle, a brace of revolvers and a half-dozen grenades. There were not enough guns to go round and Lidka knew there were few bullets for some of those guns, too, and that this was an issue right across the AK. Also on the table was a map of Warsaw, as it had been in 1939, so it did not show the desolated space where the Ghetto had stood; was from a time before the Ghetto had even existed. Someone had very lightly shaded the main Nazi areas in red crayon, including the Dom Akademicki. The Paczkowski house was just a block away from the SS Police headquarters based there, and it was their target for the first day of the uprising, along with other fighters of the Ochota AK, and the reason Bullet had chosen the house as the place they should meet. Mrs Paczkowska left the room.

"I hope we have not left it too late," Andrzej muttered.

Right then Lidka heard a car's engine. It was being driven hard, and it was a note she recognised, the distinctive fluttery clatter of a German Kübelwagen. They all froze for a stretched moment, then Andrzej reached for his Sten as the vehicle came along the curve of Mochnackiego from the left, its tyres buzzing against the cobbles. He moved the cocking handle from the safety notch. The car drew up in a long scuffing skid just as the others also took up their weapons. Lidka did not have a gun, as a messenger she was searched often, and to carry a pistol would be too much of a risk. Besides, she did not think she could kill.

Andrzej kept in the shadow as he went to the side window that overlooked the main door and peeked through the lace curtains. Those who had weapons cocked them. He held a finger to his lips, for despite the gathering clouds it was a warm day and the side window was partially open. Then he signalled with his hands for two of them, young lads who had taken the names Badger and Raven, to cover the rear door of the building that led into the kitchen. They seeped out like smoke.

"Just one." Andrzej whispered, and she heard the squidge of shoes or boots on the pavement down below, but not the clack of steel heel guards. Cat was close to the window, and she looked out, too.

"Gestapo?" Lightning asked.

Andrzej shook his head sharply: "No, a black uniform; maybe SS?" He raised his Sten, pressing its simple metal butt into his shoulder, holding the long side-entry magazine like a handle, as he looked down the length of the stubby sub machine gun.

Then Lidka heard whistling, beautifully tuneful whistling. She recognised it instantly; *Heroic*. Andrzej paused, smiled.

"I hate to let a German die happy," he said, with a sour grin.

Lidka crept close and looked over Andrzej's shoulder. The mottled green and brown painted car was parked by the kerb; not a Kübelwagen but obviously a cousin of it, though rounded and boat-shaped, with a spare wheel on its bonnet looking like a black lifebuoy, and a propeller hinged up like a bee's sting on the rounded rear. There was even a wooden paddle clipped to its side.

Lidka saw him.

He wore no hat, his hair was still too long for a soldier, and he was whistling through a smile. His uniform was a black jacket, unbuttoned to show a grey shirt beneath it, and black trousers tucked into short boots. She blinked, twice. Shook her head. He placed the palms of his hands on the front of the car and stood there for a moment or two. She did not think he had aged much at all, he looked just how she had remembered him, placing his hands on the Pleyel piano in this very room in that very same way four and half years before, as if he felt the life in it, and thanked it. In a matter of a moment Lidka first felt relief swim within her, and then a bursting joy, but then fear, and then a burning desire to shout out ...

"What's wrong?" Lightning whispered.

"Nothing," Andrzej said, obviously puzzled by the question.

Lidka stopped herself shouting to Ingo, bit her bottom lip hard, and then saw a muscle twitch in Andrzej's right arm as he took up the first pressure on the trigger.

"Do it, Bullet!" Cat said, quiet but assertive.

"Wait!" Lidka whispered, sharply.

Andrzej's trigger finger froze, and down below in the street Ingo opened and walked through the creaking gate, before rapping at the door with the iron knocker, making it a percussion section to the whistled *Heroic*.

"What is it?" Andrzej said, quietly, after he had slowly moved his torso to allow the slender barrel of the sub machine gun to follow its target.

"It's not time, we have to wait!" Lidka hosed out the whispered words, unable to slow her speech.

"What's an hour or two?" Cat said.

"What's one man?" she said. "There will be plenty of Germans to kill at the Dom Akademicki, Bullet – we should not give them a warning by firing early!"

"Chopin's right," Lightning whispered. "We should be careful, Bullet."

Cat was looking at Lidka now, her head tilted to one side, slight ripples on her forehead, but not quite a frown.

Andrzej said nothing, but he too looked at Lidka, then shook his head, while down below Ingo knocked again. They waited. He knocked once more, then walked back in to the road to get a better view, and they all stepped back so they could be doubly sure they would not be seen though the gap in the curtains over the floor-length windows.

"Anyone in?" Ingo shouted, in German. His voice was still so full of life, it was like a song, she thought. She looked over at Freddy, pressing his lips tight shut, his eyes bursting with the excitement of it. He had only ever known this sort of thing, and it was just a game to him. Then it suddenly occurred to her that Ingo might shout her name. Her heart seemed to freeze at the thought.

But he did not call out her name. Instead, there were more knocks at the door, and then, a little later, they heard the car start, then pull away with a rattle of its engine and the squeal of tyres spinning on cobbles, then the howling skid of it turning right into Filtrowa. They all listened until they could no longer hear the car. Badger returned, cradling the Schmeisser.

"Any others?" Andrzej asked.

Badger shook his head.

"I wonder what that one wanted?" Andrzej said.

"Who was it?" Freddy suddenly blurted out.

Right then Lidka wished she could have told him.

*

Ingo was in hurry. Not because someone had taken a pot shot at him as he sped down Jerusalem Avenue – these days that almost seemed normal – but simply because he was at the wheel of a car. Also, perhaps, because he was late. He took the left turn in to Nowy Świat flat in third gear, using an apex kissing line that made the right-angled junction of the two wide streets into a sweeping curve. The fat, knobbly tyres on the front of the boat-shaped Schwimmwagen squirmed then slipped half way through the corner, Ingo lifting off the accelerator to bring the tail around a touch, correcting the small slide then planting his foot once more as the flat-four buzzed through the high-mounted exhaust pipes, the folded-up propeller on the back rattling along with it. He dimly realised the streets of Warsaw seemed much quieter than he remembered them being.

Ingo had spent too much time looking for Lidka, and by now they might have detrained the entire regiment. He had promised Pop he would not be late – and Pop had also promised him she would not be there. The tinnitus that was his souvenir from Kursk had kicked in with the disappointment. He crisply changed into fourth, pressed the throttle harder, so that he was almost squeezing it in to the water-tight bulkhead of the little amphibious vehicle – he had daydreamed of taking Lidka for a cruise on the Vistula in the Schwimmwagen, after other things. All that would now have to wait.

There had been no one at the small apartment building on Piwna in the Old Town when he had gone there earlier, or at least no one had answered the door – he was not certain it was the same building, and so he had tried another two, with the same result. The café that had once belonged to Kasper had been boarded up and was obviously empty, and there had been no answer when he had knocked at the door of the house in Ochota where she had worked, either, then that had been a long shot as he knew from two and a half years before that she no longer taught there. Still, he had sensed it had not been empty. He had decided that if he should get another chance to slip away then he would try to find some civilian clothes first. But Ingo doubted he would get another chance, the 19th would be out of the city soon, he could even hear the German guns from the battle they would be joining at Wołomin. He could only hope they would be back in Warsaw when it was finished.

By the time he arrived at the railway yards close to the Danzig Station it was clear the division was well into the process of moving out. The large space was a chaos of tanks and other vehicles, capped with a fug of blue-grey exhaust fumes. The last of the panzers were being driven off their low flat railcars one at a time. Ingo had already done this with the Panther – his new tank commander, Klein, was a keen one, always wanted to be first. The air was thick with the smell of petrol and the roar of Maybach V12s, which he loved, and the deceptively frenetic atmosphere of a panzer unit about to go in to battle, which he hated. A train chuffed, and somewhere close by the wheels of another squealed as they spun, steel on steel. The soft ground vibrated like a drum skin to the movement of the panzers upon it, and the rails sang like tuning forks.

He threaded the Schwimmwagen through the tanks, like a baby elephant picking its way through a restless herd, and then pulled up in a sharp skid on the ashy ground once he had found the spot where he had left the Panther, close to where a wheeled gantry crane, a strabokran, was hoisting a repaired engine into a Panzer IV. Pop, Sardine and Woof leaned against the Panther, smoking. Pop shook his head and flashed Ingo a wry smile. The tank was painted in a sandy dark yellow colour, with wispy, wavy, green tiger stripes on top of that.

Ingo climbed out of the Schwimmwagen. He would leave it here, he thought, better that than explain to the Danzig Station transport officer how and why he had borrowed it. Once all the tanks had gone it would be easy for the officer to find, sitting on its own like a beached boat on a black beach.

"Judging by the look on your face, I'm guessing she's not around, eh?" Pop said.

"She?" Sardine said. "Who's she?"

"Local girl; old flame," Pop said.

"Oh, Volksdeutsche," Woof said, with a sharp facial twitch; neither Ingo nor Pop made an effort to correct him. "Klein is after your head, Ingo. We should have been out of here by now," he added, twitching a little more.

"The war will still be there, what's the rush?" Ingo said. Just then Leutnant Klein arrived, sidestepping another Panther that rumbled and clanked and squeaked past them, Woof and Sardine stood up straight, but Pop kept leaning against the tank, his boot tapping out a sharp tattoo on the black earth, the movement so quick it was as if it shook to the vibrations of the panzers. Klein was young, had never seen action, was in a hurry to get his head taken off by a shell. They had already lost four commanders who had been just like him, back in the 4th. When Klein had joined them in Tilburg Ingo had sensed his envy, when he had seen on the left breasts of Pop and Ingo's black panzer tunics the Iron Cross, second class, and under that the silver Panzer badge, with 50 tank combats marked, and the Wound Badge in black beneath that. Ingo had done nothing to deserve any of these, he knew. Other than survive.

"Where have you been, Six?" Klein snapped. He was about 19, and his hair was that blond turned mousy colour that broke the heart of any aging Hitler Youth, while he had grey-blue eyes that had a speck of brown in them, like a tiny turd trapped in dirty ice. His skin looked like the side of a half-track after it had been hosed by one of the turntable Ivan machine guns. He made up for all that with zeal. Klein was full of zeal.

"Ingo was asked to take a dispatch to the lads in the depot in Mokotow," Pop said. "Oberst Winter's orders." Ingo guessed the colonel had already gone up to the front, Pop was a master of the real soldier's art.

"Dispatch? But we were to be part of the spearhead?" As Klein said that a rumble of artillery fire came from far across the Vistula. His eyes drifted in that direction, as did Sardine's.

"Ivan?" Sardine said.

"Ours," Pop said. "We're hitting back."

"About bloody time," Woof said.

Klein nodded at that, then spotted something on the Schwimmwagen. "A bullet hole?"

"Oh yes, someone shot at me," Ingo said.

"They did?"

"I was driving a German army car, you get used to such things, sir."

"Driving it bloody fast, yes?" Pop said.

"Faster than a bullet, Pop," Ingo replied, the old joke.

"Evidently not," Klein said. "Is this usual, to be shot at here?"

As he said it there was a burst of small arms fire from the northeast.

"Ours?" Sardine said.

Pop shrugged, and took a long drag on the dwindling stub of his Atikah, and then discarded it, treading it into the ashy black ground. Ingo knew he was running low on cigarettes, and Pervitin tablets. He now had a new thing of grinding his teeth when there was no fag to prise them apart, Ingo had noticed.

Hauptmann Schulte suddenly arrived. Schulte was a pleasant man who treated the war like an inconvenience to be endured, a rare and sensible officer. "You're running late Klein?" he said.

"Yes sir. Sorry sir, I ... My driver, sir, he —"

"Not to worry, we have a job here for you. A little local difficulty in Żoliborz, just over there." Schulte pointed in the direction of the main Danzig Station and the huge red brick fortress of the Warsaw Citadel beyond it. "Shouldn't take you long, just support the infantry, eh?"

"But sir, we —"

"Knew you'd understand, Klein, good man." With that Schulte was gone.

"So, we're stuck in Warsaw," Ingo said.

"No need to look so damned happy about it, Six," Klein said. "How do we get to Żoliborz, anyway?"

"I know a shortcut," Ingo said.

"Not even you can take a Panther through the Old Town, Ingo," Pop said, with a grin. "Besides, it's in the other direction." Just then there was more gunfire, but this time actually from the Old Town.

"Let's get this damned errand out of the way," Klein said, as he climbed up on to the Panther's body, his rubber soles squeaking against the armour. "And hope to God we don't miss the *real* battle."

*

Lidka had taken Freddy and Mrs Paczkowska down to the cellar where they would be safe, when the shooting had started ten minutes ago. They now had half an hour before it was the time they had agreed to move up to where the cells of the Ochota AK were to muster for the attack on the Dom Akademicki SS barracks. But now Bullet and Cat wanted to leave earlier, because of the sound of battle, machine guns and rifles, some of it close by. It had been inevitable some young, over-excited kid would start firing ahead of time, Lidka thought. The artillery fire they still heard seemed a little more distant now, which was strange, if the Russians were advancing to liberate the city, but now was not the time to worry about that.

Nor was it the time to worry about Ingo. *Why now, Ingo ...?*

He had come from nowhere, and he was in the city. She could hardly believe it, *why now, Ingo?* It had been a long time, she had changed, and perhaps he had, too. And yet he had seemed the very same Ingo, as he whistled Chopin, and waited for her to open the door to him. She hoped she might see him again soon, and then hoped not, for if she did see him again soon, he would be the enemy. But more than that, it would complicate everything. She had somehow come to terms with a future with Jósef, for Freddy's sake she had done this, just another sacrifice. But now he was back ... *why now, Ingo?* She tried not to think of it, but it was like trying not to think about toothache.

They had decided to leave through the rear of the house, as there would be other AK fighters to link up with on Filtrowa. To get to the potato garden and the yard beyond it, they needed to go through the kitchen. Their boots and shoes seemed to make a new sound as they thumped down the corridor. They were no longer creeping around, they were coming out of the silent shadows. As always Bullet led the way, somehow seeming to fill the corridor, as if he wanted to burst free of the house, with Cat right behind him and then the four others, then Lightning just ahead of Lidka, who was the last in the line.

Sarah stood in the door to the kitchen. She was dressed in her blue dress as she often was, but with her father's coat over it. It was unbuttoned and her legs were apart and her arms akimbo; she seemed like a paper-chain cut-out figure, standing in their way. In the dim light of the back corridor her pale cheeks glowed like moons.

Bullet said: "What are you doing?"

"I'm coming with you, Andrzej," Sarah said.

"Out of the way."

"I need to fight them!"

"You need to stay here, to look after your family, and Mother and Freddy. Like we have looked after you!"

"Stay here and look after Father's money and jewels, you mean."

"Yes, let's not forget that," Andrzej said.

"Andrzej, please I need —"

He slapped Sarah's face with the back of his hand, the hit of it cracking like a pistol shot in the tight space. But she did not move, did not even flinch.

"Get back in the cellar, girl, where you belong!" Andrzej said, and this time he roughly pushed her back and she stumbled into the kitchen table, its legs shrieking against the floor. He led the others through, when Cat passed Sarah she sneered, but Lightning and the others were more sympathetic. Lidka could hear the crunch of their footfalls on the gravel path through the potato patch by the time she was with Sarah.

"I will not be gone long," Lidka said. "Please, Sarah, I need you to look after Freddy."

"And when will I get my time?"

"There will be time, for revenge. After this. Please, Sarah?"

Sarah paused for a moment, time filled with distant gunfire. Then she said, as she looked deep in to Lidka's eyes: "You seem different?"

"I do?" Lidka said, then added, too quickly she thought, as she spoke: "I am afraid, like everyone is afraid."

"No, it's something else, you seem ..."

"It's nothing."

"It's Andrzej, isn't it?"

"No Sarah. Not Andrzej."

"Then Bullet, if you must play games!"

Lightning called from the yard beyond the gate in the wall: "Chopin! Quickly, please!"

"I will be back as soon as I can. I will explain then."

"I do not care about that now, I only care for revenge; for the Ghetto."

"There will be time for that, I promise."

"When?"

"Chopin!"

Lidka left the kitchen, running to catch the others.

***

Tel Aviv. April 1954

There was a fissure between two buildings the other side of the street which meant that at a certain time in the evening, as the sun was dipping to extinguish itself in the sea, blood orange light would flood the apartment. David Malka had arrived home from work five minutes ago, to find Sarah packing her small pale blue suitcase. The message had arrived ten minutes before her husband, delivered by a young man in a crisp open-necked white shirt. She had never seen him before, and he said nothing to her as he handed her the note in its unaddressed manila envelope.

It was a fiery sun, and its light, sliced through the slats of the blinds, daubed the white walls of their bedroom with vivid, bloody claw marks. The room was quite bare, just their bed on the tiles, the short locker beside it, a chair and dressing table, and the wardrobe from which she pulled clothes with half a thought to what the weather would be like in the spring, in the country she would soon be visiting. Outside car horns mixed with the brays of donkeys; the ripping of impatient engines with the clops of steady horses. It was the music of this new yet ancient land. In the room the warm air smelt slightly of burning, and the ashes that were once the note were now in the trash can, the information it contained carved into her memory, as if it was chiselled into the inside of her skull like an epitaph on a headstone.

"I thought this *work* away from home was over?" David said.

"It soon will be," she said.

"You said it was."

"Did I? I don't remember saying that." There was a dress she had not worn for two years, green and tight. But she was not sure it would fit the situation this time, and so she discarded it, allowing it to fall to the floor as she picked out a sweater and a skirt; there was only so much she could take as she intended on travelling light. David was staring out of the window, a Noblese cigarette smouldering in his fingers.

He turned, and said: "I don't want you to go."

"I have to go."

"If you go, I don't want you to come back."

She stopped packing for a moment. Then she nodded, and picked out a stout pair of shoes, something suitable for rugged country.

"Is that it, then?" he said.

She heard what he said, and yet the words in her head were not his, they were Gabriel's, as they had been written on the note, in his spidery hand.

It is over. We have to accept the new ways. The Group is no more. But I have a parting gift for you. I believe you are absolutely sure this is the man. I do not believe you would make the same mistake twice. We have been lucky; he has left Argentina. You need to be in Rome, by Wednesday. There is a reservation in the name of Mrs Deborah Burrows at the Gabriella Hotel, near the Termini station. There will be a letter waiting for you, with further instructions. But then you're on your own. It was the name she had used often, and the US passport that bore it and Sarah's picture was still valid, and now in her handbag. He did not add *good luck*, or *goodbye*, but she believed that this note, now destroyed, would be the last she would ever hear from Saul Gabriel.

Sarah fastened the small suitcase and walked out of the room and into the corridor, then she left the apartment, not even pausing to look in on Benjamin as he played a clattering game with building blocks in his bedroom.

*

Just north of Argenta, Italy. April 1954

The Milan office of one of Varela's importers had provided them with a sedan; a navy-blue Alfa Romeo 1900 Super. It would have to do for now, as the Condor was still somewhere in the Atlantic, or perhaps by now the Mediterranean, aboard a freighter. Someone would meet it in Naples later in the week and drive it to Brescia.

Ingo drove quickly, but not at ten-tenths. The route was fast along this stretch, between Ferrara and Ravenna, but would soon get much quicker when it hit the long flat out blast alongside the Adriatic. There were some quick turns along the part of the course they now drove, though, and kinks that would take on another dimension in the Condor at race speeds; a wrinkle in the road can become a corner at 150 miles per hour and more. But they were not at race speeds now, and not in the racing car either, and there were other things to think about, like dawdling Fiats, wayward buses, daydreaming pedestrians, dogs sleeping in the road and puffing trucks.

They had left Brescia in the darkness, arrived in Padua as the streets were beginning to fill. Parts of the course were already growing familiar to Ingo, which was a good thing, for he had soon realised that Carlo knew as much of the 1000 miles of the Mille Miglia as he did, something he would never have admitted to Catalina, or even Varela. Carlo had not been to Italy since he was a child, and that had been the wrong part of Italy anyway. Ingo didn't mind, Carlo deserved his Mille Miglia – Carlo's Mille Miglia in Carlo's car. Besides, they had a plan.

The only way was to learn as much of the course as possible, making notes as they went, and rather than talking in the quiet of the saloon car –

something that would be impossible in the sports car during the race — they practised the hand signals they had perfected, based on those they had used on the Mils Millas. Carlo would make these close to the steering wheel, so that Ingo could see them in his peripheral vision. Sometimes they would stop, and if it was a particularly challenging piece of road, they would go through it again, getting the line just right. They had been driving the route for five days now and this was their second time around, checking the notes, improving on them, before translating it all to a neater master copy in another notebook in the evenings.

Carlo was just finishing scrawling a new note now, as Ingo brought the car down through the gears, braking gently, slowing it for the obstruction ahead.

"Train coming," Carlo said, looking up and voicing the obvious, as the double red and white barber poles dropped to block the road in front of them and in the distance a dirty belch of smoke was dragged along the ground like a tethered rain cloud. They both took the opportunity to get out of the car and stretch their legs. For a moment Ingo rested the palms of his hands against the roof of the Alfa, its steel warm, as this was the first dry day since they had arrived in the country — they both wore Ray Ban Aviator sunglasses to shield their eyes from the strong sunlight that slanted in as they cut through the thigh of Italy. The air smelt of wild herbs, rich earth and the warm steel heat from the briskly worked 1975cc twin-carb, twin-cam engine. Ingo breathed deeply of it all, but mostly the engine, it was a smell he never tired of.

They leant against the Alfa sedan, which ticked as it cooled, and Carlo lit his cheroot. On the other side of the twin tracks of the railway there was a dirty brick hut, crusty old red tiles clinging to its roof like scabs. The land was flat and the earth was dark, with rugged, gnarly, arthritic olive trees poking through it in places. The surface of the road was weathered and smooth, and Ingo felt it through the thin soles of his driving shoes, getting to know it, the grip it would give, the grip it would take away — a road like this gave a nervous handshake. It would be like glass in the wet, he thought. But the road surface was poor everywhere, they had discovered, especially in the mountains, for it had been a hard winter in Italy. Ingo could hear the train approaching, the breath of the engine and the clatter of its wheels on the expansion joints.

"Do they stop the trains, during the race?" Ingo said.

"No. There will be a man, with a red flag, if a train comes, then he stops the cars. You just have to wait."

"You could lose a lot of time?"

"Could lose the race," Carlo said. "But then that's the way the biscotti crumbles, eh?"

The train thundered by, tarnished silver smoke pouring from its funnel. The pole of the barrier juddered and bounced as the weight of the passing carriages shook the ground in which it was set. Ingo stared at the red and white pole for a few moments after it had passed, the rails still singing a steely song.

"What is it?" Carlo said.

"Nothing, just thinking."

"About what?"

"Contingencies ... They used to say Mussolini made the trains run on time?"

"Mussolini only made one train run on time; it's a myth."

"Thought it might be, there used to be a lot of that," Ingo said, then opened the door to the Alfa as a man in a leather cap that matched his weather-beaten face lifted the barriers.

Three hours later they sat on hard chairs in a small trattoria on the outskirts of Roseto, just north of Pescara, where the course would soon, finally, turn away from the sea and head up into the Apennines. The trattoria was right on the outside edge of a fast left-hand bend that rose slightly towards a flat steel-railed bridge. Here the railway and the rocky shore separated the road from the sighing surf of the Adriatic. It would be a challenging turn during the race, Ingo thought. The trattoria was painted in a faded pastel yellow, with green shutters, and there was a vertical sign that read from top to bottom and said that it was also a *Tabacchi* – there was a short counter at the entrance stacked with cartons of cigarettes. The place smelt of onions and garlic and roasting pork; and if they hadn't already been hungry they would have been as soon as they had come within fifty metres of it.

They each had a dish of maccheroni alla chitarra, pasta in a pork and tomato sauce which tasted of garlic, meat and sweet peppers, while there was a bottle of Montepulciano opened on the table, though they would both only take a glass of it; there was still much work to be done before their day was finished. There was one other diner, who also sat with a plate of the local spaghetti and a basket of bread, a shiny-headed old man who concentrated on his lunch as if it was a chess problem, never taking his eyes from his plate. The tables were bare wood and the window at which they sat was open, so that a breeze brought in gusts of sea air that was seasoned with the iron smell of the sun-warm railway line, detectable for an instant before being smothered by the aromas of the trattoria. Over the railway Ingo could just see the waves break on dark rocks, and a small blue and white fishing boat nodding in agreement with the white-flecked swell. The sun was high now, and it painted faceless Dali clocks on the flatter water further out to sea.

"I still can't quite believe Scuderia Verde has taken on Otero," Ingo said. It was the third time he had said it since he had read the news in *La Gazzetta dello Sport* when they had stopped in Padua for breakfast.

"Most only saw the lap times from Buenos Aires, not the damage to the engine," Carlo said. "When Necci was killed at Syracuse, well he was the obvious choice, everyone else – *El Tímido* included – was already signed up for the Mille Miglia. Besides, he has some experience, he raced here last year; and experience counts for a lot in this race."

Ingo knew that Carlo had had to insist that he should drive the Mille Miglia, for Varela was amongst those who only saw the lap times from Buenos Aires, while he still had a stake in Otero. But, for once, Carlo had stood firm with Varela, and had demanded that Ingo should drive the Condor.

"I guarantee that particular Ferrari will end up embedded in a house, flattened like a nameplate," Ingo said.

"You might be right," Carlo said, taking a sip of the wine. "Which is just one of the reasons I'm glad you're by my side." Then he looked pensive, for a moment, before he added: "Tell me Ingo, are you never scared?"

"I've been scared," Ingo replied, without hesitation.

"In a racing car?"

"No, never in a racing car."

"But you see there is danger?"

"There's no danger; some idiots, perhaps. But no *real* danger."

"Yet Wimille, and Varzi, and —"

"Only because they crashed."

"Well, I can't argue with that."

Ingo smiled and wound some of the stringy pasta on to his fork. There was a snarl from outside, an elephantine blast of indignation that marked a downchange throttle blip, and neither of them could resist looking out of the narrow window on hearing the clarion call of the open exhaust. A slightly dated blood-red Ferrari 212, dusty from the road, with just the driver in it and no co-driver, was soon in to the fast turn on which the trattoria was set. It was understeering, and then the rear kicked out as the driver overdid his corrective lift off the throttle; he fought the ensuing slide, almost clipping a white kilometre post at the exit of the corner. Then it was out of the turn, the air quivering to the steely shock of its unsilenced 2.6-litre V12. It wasn't unusual to see a racing car out on the course at this time. Many of the other cars in the race were on the road already, and Ingo and Carlo also planned to take the Condor around the thousand-mile course once, maybe twice, when it arrived.

They were both smiling when they turned away from the window. If you can't enjoy a car on the limit, even if it's driven a little clumsily, then you can't enjoy wine, air and love.

"You know," Carlo started. "I don't remember you ever crashing, I mean through fault of your own."

"Why would I want to do that?"

"Even Fangio crashes, sometimes."

"Fangio did not learn his trade where I did."

"He learnt his trade in the mountains, on the big city to city races. I don't think there's much you can add to that."

"Ice and snow," Ingo said.

Carlo thought on that for a moment, tilting his head to listen to the diminishing rip of the Ferrari as it made its way up the road towards Pescara.

"I have spun, though, on the ice. Once I even hit a kerb, blew a tyre," Ingo said, before adding, rather quietly: "That was because I let emotion in, shouldn't do that when you're driving. But I was Pup, back then."

"Pup?"

"It's what someone once called me."

"A friend?"

"It was long ago," Ingo said, and he took a mouthful of pasta, sucking up the slippery tails of it, to give him an excuse not to have to go on.

"How long have we known each other, Ingo?" Carlo said, once the Maranello music had faded, to be replaced by the sound of an argument between a woman and a man, which was just catching fire in the kitchen.

"Nearly five years, I suppose," Ingo said, when he had finished his mouthful of spaghetti.

"I've never asked you what you're hiding from, in all that time."

"No," Ingo said. "You haven't."

"Maybe now, my friend?" Carlo said.

A pot clanged to the floor in the kitchen and the argument dissolved into laughter.

"Not yet, Carlo," Ingo said.

***

Wola, Warsaw. August 1944

Ingo clanged opened the driver's hatch and sucked in the fresh air – only to find it was not so fresh. He choked on the acrid smelling fumes of the fires, and was still coughing when he'd climbed out and joined Pop the other side of the tank, the broken glass that coated the cobbles of the side street they had parked the Panther on crunching beneath the soles of his boots.

A number of the red-brick apartment buildings were burning, some were smashed in, ragged holes showing furniture, and wallpapers that seemed overly bright in the smoke-filled air. A few dead bodies, all of them civilian, also lay on the cobbles, one with a speech bubble of blood slowly expanding alongside his head, the scream that might have filled it silent on his dead lips. The battle, if it could be called that, raged on a block away, on what the Poles called Wolska Street, the Germans Litzmannstadtstrasse; Ingo could hear the rifle and sub machine gun fire, and the odd-sounding hollow percussions of grenades exploding on a hard surface.

"One of these will sort your cough out," Pop said, offering him an Atikah from an opened yellow carton, but Pop did not look at him as he did so, because he was staring at the wall that was ten metres in front of him. Ingo declined the offer of the cigarette, as always, which was maybe why Pop still offered even though his precious stock was dwindling. They were in the Wola district, an area of factories, and tenements that housed those who worked in the factories. It was now burning in many places, and although Ingo knew it was sunny, had even seen the sun earlier as they made their way here, the sky was shrouded with a tattered cloth of smoke which made it seem like dusk. It was around 10am.

Pop still stared at the high wall, red brick and pocked in two intersecting lines of bullet marks that formed a squashed-up cross. On the top of the wall there was a line of hands, and some wrists. For a moment Ingo fostered the grisly illusion they had been placed there, but then he saw that they were moving, some of them shaking, and that they obviously belonged to people, held up in surrender. When he looked closer he also saw, in the gaps between the floating hands, that there were some pinkly glowing fingers. Children. There were women's hands, too, and hands that had lived long lives; tired hands on sagging upstretched arms.

Then there was the familiar rattle of an MP 40, and the hands fluttered, and fell, like shot birds. The magazine was emptied in about three seconds. Ingo then heard the crack of pistol shots.

They had both seen enough of this war to know what had just happened.

"Bastard SS," Pop said, as Woof and Sardine joined them. Ingo's tinnitus sang a little higher. He thought of Lidka, wondered if he'd recognise her hands, floating above a brick wall.

"Jesus, who were they?" Sardine said.

"Insurgents, I suppose," Woof said. "*Banditen.*"

Pop and Ingo looked at him, but said nothing. Nothing about the women, old ones, the children. They knew there was nothing to be done, nothing they could do.

Klein hadn't realised what had happened. He was some ten metres from them, busy talking to a bareheaded soldier in a field grey tunic with no rank badges or insignia, the sleeves rolled up. They had not yet been told why they had been sent to Wola, Klein liked to keep them in the dark – it was all he had – and so they listened with interest.

"We're looking for the Dirlewanger Brigade, I have been specifically requested to report for special duties," the young lieutenant said, emphasising *special.*

The man laughed, then said in German, but with a Russian accent: "Special duties – you don't say." He did not add 'sir'. He nodded in the direction of a staff car, fifty metres down the street, a field grey Skoda Superb. It was being loaded with silver; candelabras and a dinner set. And a large gilt framed mirror that reflected the dancing flames from one of the buildings, so that it looked like a hatch into Hell.

"Dirlewanger? I've heard that name," Pop said, and Ingo thought the same.

"Sure you have," Woof started. "I —"

The sight of a naked girl running from one of the apartment buildings cut Woof short. She held a patch of cloth that looked like the remnants of underwear, and slick blood painted the inside of her thighs. She looked young, perhaps 16. Her face was dirty, and the grime that covered it was tiger striped with the tracks of tears. Her bare feet tinkled in the broken glass, which cut her soles, so that bright dabs of blood marked her passage across the cobbles. There was a gunshot, from the building she had run from. The bullet entered the back of her head then tore away a piece of her face as it exited. Ingo thought that in that sliver of a second before her face exploded into a black-red pulp she had perhaps looked relieved.

The echo of the shot had still not died when an SS man came to the door of the building, holding a Kar 98 rifle like a pistol in one hand, a clear glass bottle of vodka in the other. He was laughing. Ingo could see his pupils were dilated, oily pools glistening in spidery bloodshot eyes. He said something, in Russian, and there was more laughter from behind him. His sleeves were also rolled up and his wrists and forearms were striped in wristwatches.

Something made Ingo look over at Pop. He was staring at the dead, naked girl, his lip was slightly curled, and it quivered a little, too. His right foot tapped against the cobbles. The girl had fallen on her front, her legs apart. The blood on her inner thighs shone fresh and was in stark contrast to her round milk-white buttocks. It was too obvious she had been raped. The scrap of clothing was still held tight in her dead hand. Pop shook his head, slowly.

"Evil," he said. Then again: "Evil."

"But there's nothing we can do, Pop, you know that, you've told me a thousand times," Ingo said. "Please, look away." As he said it the tinnitus drilled through his head just as the bullet had drilled through the head of the girl.

The group of SS men who had been loading the staff car with loot approached the dead girl. One was an officer. He carried an MP 40 in one hand, a Leica camera in the other. He was whistling *In München steht ein Hofbräuhaus*. Only it wasn't much of a whistle …

***

London. April 1954

Joe had a compartment to himself on the 16.45 British Railways service to Dover. He doubted there was anyone else in such a privileged position on the train. One or two other passengers had almost come through the sliding door, had opened it halfway, but had changed their mind on seeing him there, and it was now left ajar, sliding a little to the movement of the train, the grating noise it made at one with his burning breath. He didn't mind that they did not want to sit with him, he was used to being alone.

The thick-as-gruel London air had almost killed him. There was none of the killer smog of December '52 now, but the air still had a metallic solidity to it, to him at least. But no one had come to his aid as he coughed up bloody phlegm and clung to the railings outside Victoria Station. He had thought he had been dying, there and then, but he had been wrong. There was still time …

The air in the compartment smelt of stale cigarette smoke. He stared out of the window with his nose close to the glass; that way it was less likely he would chance upon his reflection. The wheels beat a tune against the cross ties and the carriage creaked as the elevated track curved and cut through the gleaming slate rooftops of grimy terraces. Every now and then there was a gap in one of the streets, like one or two of the rotten teeth had been yanked out, leaving a mess of decayed debris. There were much larger bombsites, too, and some modern buildings throwing sharp reflections off new glass, a sign that London was rebuilding. But he knew London had not had it so very bad, he knew what real destruction meant, and what it looked like. The train crossed some points with a clatter of steel on steel and the sliding door suddenly slammed shut. He jumped, twisting to see what the noise was, pain flaring within from the sudden movement – it took little to fan the flames of the fire that never died.

His journey so far, by train to Carmarthen, then another to Swansea, and then on to Paddington, had been hell. And there was still a chunk of Europe to cover. But Joe knew he had to do this one last thing.

***

Wola, Warsaw. August 1944

"Small war, Pop. Right?"

"Herr Hauptsturmführer I was told to report to —"

Kroh waved a hand, cutting Klein short; he had hardly looked at him.

"Don't suppose you expected to see me again, eh Pop; eh Pup?"

Ingo could not remember the last time someone had looked so pleased to see him; but the pleasure was that of a poacher, with a crippled rabbit in the snare. They stood around the dead girl, it seemed as natural and as comforting to these men – Kroh and two other SS soldiers – as standing around a campfire. Kroh took a few snaps of the corpse with his Leica. Pop's expression was rapidly morphing between what looked like the deepest disgust and complete surprise, as his gaze switched between the dead girl and the officer – former feldwebel of the 4th Panzer Division, Christian Kroh, now a captain in the Waffen SS.

"But I have orders —"

"Wait over there, would you Leutnant – by your tin can."

Klein looked about to protest, but Pop threw him a warning glance that was as subtle as a massed Sturmovik attack. The young lieutenant hesitated, stared at Kroh, who was wearing a field grey SS uniform and that old Gebirgsjäger hat of his, now even more battered, faded and stained.

"Yes, Sir," Klein finally said, then he turned on his heels, scrunching broken glass beneath his boots, and marched back to the Panther. Woof and Sardine went with him, having also caught Pop's warning.

"Keen one, right?"

"Green one, too," Pop said.

"Lucky to land up with you then. You pair know how to keep alive, I reckon."

Pop grunted, then looked at the dead girl again. The heat from the burning buildings washed over them, making the hot day hotter, and the sweat was starting to bead on Ingo's forehead. The roar of flames and the crackle of the infernos mixed with the stutter of machine gun fire and the cracks and pops of rifles and pistols. The girl's bowels had voided when she had died, and the smell hung in the thick, gritty, smoky air. There was nowhere for the stink to go, for this part of Warsaw was draped in a heavy, dirty grey blanket of dust, and shit likes blankets.

"You've gone up in the world," Pop said, switching his attention back to Kroh, nodding at the ribbon for the Iron Cross on his tunic and then glancing at the two pips of a Hauptsturmführer on his silver shoulder board.

"Yes, I suppose you did me a favour, in a way."

"Always happy to oblige."

"Of course, I didn't see it quite like that at the time. Smart move, that stunt with the Horch. Your idea, Pop?"

"My idea," Ingo said, but Pop nodded at the same time.

"With that and the stuff that prick Schirmer had saved up I was put away for six months. Still, never mind. In the end it got me where I am today, where I belong, back in the SS, right?" Kroh said.

"So, no hard feelings then?" Pop said.

Kroh smiled, a whiplash of lips, then pushed his cap to the back of his head. "You know, I look back fondly on my time in the 4th, good days, right?"

"Had their moments," Pop said.

"I was talking about all that just yesterday, as it happens. We needed tank support. Spoke to your boss, got chatting about the old days, when I was with a panzer division – some of these Heer types look down their noses at SS, you know, so it pays to talk on their terms. Told him I was once in the 4th."

"And I suppose he told you he had a couple of lads from the 4th in his mob," Pop said.

"You got it; asked if I knew them."

"Well, Klein did say we were specially requested, so that explains that," Ingo said.

"He would be heartbroken if he knew the reason why," Pop said.

Kroh laughed, then turned to one of the men with him, said something. In Russian.

"Russian?" Pop asked

"I've had to learn a little."

"Are all these men Russian?" Ingo asked.

"There are some Ivan traitors, and then some are Ukrainians. They're touchy about that, all right, so best not call *them* Russian. Some Muslims from the Caucasus, a few Germans, too; ex-prisoners like yours truly; some of these because they have special talents."

"Special talents?" Ingo said.

"You'll soon see, you're to work with us."

"Surely, you mean fight?" Pop said, and once again he glanced at the dead naked girl.

"You know something, this entire battle is being controlled by the SS," Kroh said, ignoring Pop's remark.

"Yes, we've heard the happy news," Pop said.

"Happy news, *sir.*"

Pop nodded, said "Sir," he knew when and where to play the game.

"Maybe they'll see that if we'd been in charge since the start this war might have gone a bit better, right?"

"I thought we were still winning," Ingo said.

Kroh ignored that, too. "You know, Reichsführer Himmler himself has issued an order. We are to destroy everything in Warsaw; every building, every street, and mostly every fucking living thing in this shitty city. Now that's something, right?"

"It's murder," Pop said, glancing at the girl again, before adding: "Sir."

"It's war," Kroh said. "But I wonder, Pup. How's the killing going? Must have killed a few Ivans by now, eh? To get this far and still be alive."

Ingo said nothing.

"Hope so, because there's lots of honest work ahead of us. Big machine like that," Kroh said, looking at the Panther now, "could juice hundreds of these bandits; save plenty of bullets. And I'm guessing you're the driver, right?"

"Yes."

"Yes?"

"Yes, Sir."

"Of course you are, always the driver, our Pup." With that he turned away from them, as did the Ivans in German uniform with him, and he started to whistle again, as he walked towards the tank to brief Klein. Ingo had a sudden vision of Lidka, framed in the oblong of the Panther's vision slot, lying on the floor, naked and dead like the girl.

"You know something, Pop?" Ingo said. "His whistling's no better."

"True. But I wish I could believe he was no worse."

***

Rome. April 1954

Sarah had little time for history, she had lived through too much of it. Besides, the Pantheon reminded her of the Nazis, because even though it was a church now, and had been for centuries, it was still a place that shouted *power*. She had been surprised that she was to pick up the weapon here, as Gabriel had never been one for theatrics. They had always met in ordinary cafés where he had eaten ordinary food, with a relish that perhaps only a survivor of the camps would ever understand. But, then again, her cover was a tourist, so perhaps it fitted.

The instructions had been in a sealed letter that she had picked up when she checked in to the Gabriella Hotel, a new place on Via Palestro near the Termini Station. They had been in code, as always, and she used a memorised mathematical key to access the words of the message in an English edition of the New Testament, printed in Glasgow in 1938. Every member of The Group had had a copy – Gabriel rarely did jokes, but when he did it was with a certain class. The instructions had also made it clear that once she had picked up the weapon, she was on her own. But she knew that; The Group was no more.

It was raining outside, raining inside, too. For the great dome of the Pantheon was pieced with a circular roof-light, an oculus, that let in the rain in a soft and sparkling column that splashed down on a large circle of slick marble in the centre of the space, before draining away through small brass-rimmed holes in the floor. That aspect of the Pantheon reminded her of Warsaw, rather than Nazis; many of the buildings had let in water in '44, though there hadn't been much rain during that hot summer, she remembered – except for the steel kind.

The fall of the water on the marble was loud and slappy. It was midweek so there were few tourists, and their conversations were muffled by the rain; muffled by their reverence for the holy, and for the past, too, but now and then the odd raised voice echoed in the space. She could also hear the buzz of Vespa scooters and the honk of car horns outside, the heartbeat of the city. There was a slight smell of incense, and also of the smoke from the candles that burned in the niches.

It was a little chilly in the Pantheon, a stony, old cold, and so she drew the collar of her woollen coat close to her face, the rough material tickling her cheeks. The space was immense. She allowed her gaze to float up to the dome, taking in the niches and the columns that lined the vast circular interior and then the fine frescos as she did so. Then the coffered underside of the dome itself, a grid of creamy sunken Roman concrete squares, like massed cohorts, surrounding the white smooth space around the eye of God that let in the rain. Somewhere a door slammed, its boom-a-boom echo like gunfire, causing her to look down again.

Through the insubstantial indoor column of rain, which stretched to the ocular like a glassy, silvery, prop holding up the dome, a man now watched her. He was leaning on a dripping, loosely furled umbrella.

Sarah walked around the space where the rain fell and stood next to him, a little closer to the column of water now, so that tiny cold drops splashed on to her legs.

"You know something? This was built close to 2000 years ago, and it's still the largest unreinforced concrete dome in the world," Yitzhak said, glancing up.

"You don't say. I'm surprised to see you."

"Nice surprise?"

"Hope so. Never had you down as the tourist type, so I'm guessing you have the weapon?"

"I am the weapon."

Sarah nodded, accepted it; there were few weapons more effective. "He tell you who the target is?" she said, they rarely used names.

"Just a name, some background. It's him, isn't it?"

"It's him."

"The right one; this time?"

"Definitely."

"Then for you, they've saved the best till last."

"The worst."

"I doubt that. He's small fry. But we can make the big fish take notice."

"How?"

"I'll tell you over coffee, the Sant Eustachio café is just around the corner. It's about time you started to enjoy the good things in life, and I guarantee you will not find a better cup of coffee in Rome."

"Was this your idea, or his?"

He smiled. "It's regular soldiering for me when I get back, and I reckon I'll miss all this. So, I intend to go out with a bang." He paused for a moment, and then looked her up and down, as was his way.

Then Yitzhak took Sarah's arm, unfurled the umbrella, and led her out of the Pantheon and in to the rain.

***

Wola, Warsaw. August 1944

The machine gun bullets plucked a long line of dusty spurts from the road before taking down the running insurgent, who fell neatly between the gleaming tram rails. Ingo drove on, the tracks of the forty-five tonne panzer crunching in to the smooth cobbles beneath them; rifle and pistol fire pinging and ringing off the body of the tank. Klein had had the top hatch open; not because of the heat, but because he was an idiot. It was closed now. Even idiots learn fast, in a battle. Ingo looked out of the inches-thick ballistic glass in the vision slit, made from cheaper glass these days, which gave everything a nauseous greenish tinge.

Every now and then Klein would tell Ingo to stop the tank and Pop would lay the gun on a piece of building, that soon became many pieces of rubble, amidst which Ingo would see the dead. Or pieces of the dead. The day was hot, and the sky was burning, but it was much hotter in the tank. Woof fired the hull machine gun again from his seat to Ingo's right, the fumes from the propellant of the MG 34's bullets stinging Ingo's eyes. Thirst scored his throat.

Sweat bathed him. The tinnitus sang in his head, always a little louder than the battle, it seemed.

They were advancing down Wolska Street, supporting Dirlewanger's men who were clearing the buildings, some throwing stick grenades and incendiary powder in to basements through smashed pavement-level windows. Ingo thought of Lidka, all the time; hoped she still lived somewhere in the Old Town, and not in Wola.

Most of the enemy fire was coming from a brick-built factory building to their right, its roof holed and its huge windows already shattered into creaking teeth of broken glass, across which the jagged reflections of the battle slid. Clusters of Dirlewanger men, and the Azerbaijanis that were attached to the unit, fired back with MP 40s and rifles from the doorways of the tenements that were opposite and up the road a little way, while there was gunfire from within these apartment buildings, too. And screaming. Klein called a halt so that they could fire the gun, his voice high over the intercom, words coming out fast. Muzzle flashes brightly pinpricked the big, shattered windows of the factory as Pop lay the gun, Ingo revving to 3000rpm which boosted the hydraulic mechanism so that the turret was turned through forty-five degrees, and the gun was elevated, in just five seconds; Pop making the final adjustments with the hand traverse wheel, Sardine loading a high explosive shell.

Then the big 75mm gun fired, filling the inside of the panzer with choking fumes, the chassis rocking to the recoil. Ingo did not see the shell hit, but as the ejected shell case bonged against the steel floor behind him, he did see the front of the building as it first crumpled like a rapidly aging face, then bulged outwards, and then peeled away and fell forward in to the street, leaving dazzling white-painted doll's house spaces, as the outer walls crumbled into individual bricks and cascaded on to the floor like a spitefully spoilt game of building blocks.

Suddenly there was a flash, and a ball of fire burst against the front of the Panzer, a Molotov cocktail, a tongue of its flame looking liquid as it licked at the thick glass of Ingo's vision slit, scorching its outer surface slightly. He drove around the fire, the co-axial machine gun took out another partisan, and the fallen bricks, in a snake's tongue-shaped isthmus across the roadway, crunched like sugar beneath the tracks of the Panther. Ingo could hear the rattle of MP 40s over the roar of the big Maybach V12 and the grinding clatter of the tank, and he imagined the Dirlewangers rushing the factory. They were brave. Because they were drunk. They all seemed to be drunk; he didn't know where they got it, and he didn't know where they put it. But as drunk as they were they could run, and fire, and it did not affect their ability to kill. The tinnitus sang a little higher; a steel mosquito in his head. And now he tried hard not to think of Lidka.

There was a great clang of a hit against the hull, and the Panther rang like a bell for a moment, while Ingo saw the steel projectile bounce off the sloping front armour and land in the road with a noise like a dropped manhole cover.

"PIAT!" Pop shouted over the intercom. "The next one might not be a dud."

Klein said nothing, and Ingo thought it was because he had nothing to say. The PIAT was not the best anti-tank weapon, but it *was* an anti-tank weapon. So, without orders from Klein, Ingo trod on the brakes, the tank dipping to the sudden deceleration, Sardine swearing as he hit his head on something hard – fighting a tank is a learning process. Then Ingo put the Panther into reverse, dropped the clutch and accelerated.

"Yes, yes ... Driver; back, back!" Klein shouted over the intercom, ordering Ingo to do what he was already doing, Ingo only too pleased to obey.

When the tank was much further back up Wolska, Klein told him to stop. Ingo heard the hatch pop open above and behind him, and he clanged open his own hatch so that he had marginally cleaner air to breath. He choked on the smoke and wondered then if Warsaw would ever stop burning. He then caught the almost fruity smell of decomposing bodies – flesh putrefies quickly in the heat, he knew. He looked to find where the smell was coming from. There was a pile of corpses to one side of the street, where they had been executed, their gunshot wounds already clotted with fat blue flies.

"What's the problem, Leutnant?" Kroh shouted; Ingo could not see him, he was the other side of the tank, but he would recognise that voice anywhere.

"They have an anti-tank gun!"

That was stretching it a bit, and Kroh laughed, as he walked in front of the tank, looked at the bullet pocks and the scuff mark where the PIAT shell had ricocheted. He grinned at Ingo, shaking his head. He held his MP 40 and it was obvious he had been doing his share of the work; his cap was pushed back on his head, his camera was slung around his neck, and sweat had carved runnels in a face caked with brick dust. "Killed anything yet, Pup?" he said.

Ingo dipped the clutch, selected first, revved the engine a little. It would be so easy for his foot to *slip* off the clutch pedal; but that was not his way, and it would mean death to him, too, one way or another.

Kroh winked, then called out to Klein in the turret hatch: "Better armour, that's what you need, right?" Then he shouted something else – to someone else – this time in Russian.

Kroh ordered them to move down Wolska again, then to stop on the edge of the fight; he had hitched a lift back to the battle on the rear of the Panther. In the near distance grenades shattered the cobbles into stony fountains of destruction, while a petrol bomb smashed and erupted in a cockscomb of flame between the tram tracks. Ingo allowed the panzer to shiver at the idle, as if it was scared of what was to come, the resonance of it vibrating through his hands, which gripped the steering levers lightly.

He could hear Klein clearly, he had left his intercom on *transmit*; a beginner's error. He was now arguing, with Kroh.

"I won't do it, Sir. I can't!"

Ingo had not heard what Kroh had said, nor his reply, but wondered if the latter was simply a pointed weapon, because Klein then said: "Jesus, no …"

"What is it?" Woof said, over the comms.

"The bastards," Pop said, and Ingo could now hear the sound of feet on the hull of the tank above him, but not army boots, rather shoes, he thought, clanging lightly and scraping. He could hear sobs, too, and the crying of children, and then there were people, civilians, obscuring his vision slit, some standing and holding on to the gun for balance, others sitting on the sloping glacis plate in front of him, partly obscuring his view: children, women, and an old man who shook as much as the idling tank.

"Like I said," Kroh shouted, from the front of the tank now, so that Ingo could hear. "Better armour, right?"

More civilians, women and children mostly, were lined up in three files in front of the Panther, while others, Ingo guessed, would be standing alongside it, out of his line of sight.

"Forward," Klein said, and Ingo thought he was choking back tears; they don't train officers in the use of human shields at their panzer school in Munster. Ingo hesitated. A young face, a kid of about nine, turned to peer through the thick glass shield of his vision slot, its greenish tinge making him look sick, as did the fear that painted his face. The tinnitus sang a little higher.

"Forward!" Much louder now.

"Best do as he says, Ingo," Pop said over the intercom. "These lads don't strike me as patient types."

As he said it one of the Dirlewanger men walked in front of the tank, raised his machine pistol, pointed it at a young woman with a trickle of urine running down her leg who was with those who stood in front of the Panther. He shot her with a brief burst. Ingo got the message. He selected first gear and let out the clutch as carefully as possible, but the painted, sloping, glacis plate gave little purchase and the young boy fell from the tank. Ingo only saw a flash of his red shirt, but he knew the child had gone under the tracks. The scream, from the boy's mother, cut through the clamour of the shaking machine and its churning engine, and Ingo stopped the Panther. The woman's screaming continued, until there was the tap-tap of pistol shots, then laughter.

"Forward." Klein was sobbing now. Ingo almost said, *welcome to the war*, but there was no room for even a dark joke, the world was overstuffed with darkness right now; darkness and anger, and always the piercing steel in his head. But he knew he had to concentrate; for once he had to concentrate on driving as slowly as possible.

Again Ingo nosed the tank forwards, as carefully as he could, as slowly as he could, peering through the gap between two quivering bodies, both women, thin and vulnerable in their summer clothing, clinging to the steel plate on the outside that could be swung into place to protect the vision slit in action. The Panther had gone just a little way when there were a few rifle shots, and two of the civilians in front of it fell, as if the thin strings on which their lives danced were snipped. He thought he heard shouts, in Polish, above the clatter of the tank and the crying of its passengers, and then the firing stopped.

They drove on: slowly, slowly, slowly; slower than walking pace. They passed the burning factory and headed towards a barricade that had been built to block the street, and Ingo could imagine the cluster of SS men following them, ready to pounce on the enemy once the tank with its armour of dilemma had brought them close enough to the makeshift ramparts.

The partisans weren't firing now, for fear of hitting their own. And the tank drew ever closer to the barricade, which was made from an overturned red and yellow tram, built up with blocks of masonry, steel beams, and huge cable reels. As they crawled ever closer Ingo could see that the Poles had placed a couple of portraits of Hitler on the barricade, probably taken from German offices, so that SS bullets would hit them. Nice touch, he thought. He could also see the insurgents peeking over the top of the barricade, and he could hear the distinctive chatter of MP 40s and the pops of rifles as the Dirlewangers tried to keep their heads down.

Then there was a sharper crack, just audible over the clamour of the tank, followed by a choking "*Uggh*" over the intercom. He became aware of commotion behind him, and turned back to see Klein sliding down from his post at the top of the turret and in to the belly of the Panther, a red full-stop in the centre of his forehead. Ingo guessed Klein had had his head out of the hatch again, and had been taken by a sniper sited in one of the tall buildings. Klein knew the danger, had learned it just that morning, so he wondered if he had chosen this way out. It was not one Ingo would choose … Ingo Six still wanted to live.

Right then, with the sudden killing of Klein the catalyst, the human shield dissolved in panic. Those in front of the tank ran towards the barricade, only to be shot in the back by the Dirlewanger men who came on behind the Panther; an old man, a boy and a woman were folded into bloody rags in the landscape frame of Ingo's viewing slot. Then those on the tank peeled themselves off it, toppling down on to the street; he did not see them die, but he knew they would have no chance. Other Dirlewanger men had rushed from the cover of the tank and were at the barricade now, tossing potato mashers over its parapet. The partisans were retreating, leaving the explosions of the stick grenades in their wake.

Ingo stood on the brake and the panzer rocked a little on its suspension as he turned the engine off.

"What is it, Ingo?" Pop said over the intercom.

"Kaput! Get out!"

No one ever hesitated in getting out of a panzer when someone said they should; there was never time to enquire or argue, a fire could take hold all too quickly, and as Pop and Sardine climbed through the circle-shaped rear escape hatch in the turret, Woof through the hull hatch above him, Ingo reached for the *kiloladungen*, a one kilogram demolition charge, about the size of a brick, which he armed and placed on the driver's seat. He looked back to see Pop watching him from the open escape hatch.

"It's a way out of this," Ingo said, though he hardly heard himself over the screaming steel in his head. "If we don't have a tank, they won't have a use for us – and I can't do that again!"

Pop shook his head sharply, then cursed, and Ingo opened and climbed out of the driver's hatch. He stared down the street, now blistered with ragged humps of dead and dying, civilians and Dirlewangers, and a tattoo of machine gun fire rapped at the sloping steel besides him, throwing up dancing sparks, and chips of mustard-yellow paint. They had sixty seconds before the charge would blow. They were well clear by the time it detonated.

They heard the blast, then the secondary explosions of unused shells, but they did not look back to see their Panther die.

"Smart move, Ingo," Pop gasped, as they ran.

Ingo guessed that was sarcasm.

Pop seemed to judge they were out of danger and slowed to a walk, wheezing and coughing after the effort of the sprint. He walked with his arms akimbo, hands pressing his sides, and gulped in the dirty, smoky air. "This could mean jail," he finally said. "You know that, don't you?"

"I don't care," Ingo said, but that was a lie. "What does that mean anyway; it used to be that DKW wouldn't look at me if I'd gone to jail, but now – after this?" He looked at a dead Polish woman lying on scorched cobbles, a corona of broken glass around her body. Her eyes had been burned from her face by incendiary powder. "There will be no racing for us, for any German, when all this is over. No nothing."

"It could also mean death," Pop added, as he caught sight of Woof and Sardine, who were catching their breath, sitting on the floor with their backs against a bullet-pocked red brick wall.

"What was it, Ingo?" Woof shouted over the gunfire. His facial twitch was jumping to the beat of an MG 42 a couple of Dirlewangers had set up in a window high above them.

"Final drive," Pop said, still catching his breath, and Woof raised an eyebrow, while a facial muscle twitched three times.

The battle was still all around them, confused, as if there were many battles going on at once; pops of pistols and rifles being met with the unmistakable zipping chatter of MG 42s. The burning buildings seemed to roar in pain, and Wola stank of smoke and the unmistakeable smell of death.

"Guess they'll have to send us back to our lot," Sardine said. "No use here without a tank, are we?"

Pop looked at Ingo, shook his head and said: "No use at all."

There was a command half-track parked across the street; the field grey paint of its armoured bonnet had been scorched black. In the cover of the vehicle a gathering of SS officers leant over an open street map. One of them, a man in a long leather coat despite the heat of the day, and of the battle, was using a pencil to shade in areas, as if he was colouring in the cloud of smoke that hung over the city.

"Nothing sadder than a panzer man without a panzer, right?" It was Kroh, on his way to join the other officers. He had a violin case under his arm, which made him look like a gangster, and his Leica was slung around his neck. His machine pistol dangled from his shoulder by its leather strap. Woof and Sardine stood up.

"*C'est la guerre,*" Pop said. Then, changing the subject, he nodded in the direction of the half-track. "That him, then?"

The man in the long leather coat, and a peaked officer's hat, was now stabbing at the map of the city with a skeletal finger. Kroh nodded. The man had the look of an ascetic about him, sunken cheeks, and as thin as a refugee. It was easy to imagine him in the habit of a monk. But he was no monk, they knew that already.

"That's him alright; probably mad, definitely bad, but a damned fine soldier all the same."

"Soldier?" Pop said. "You call this soldiering?"

"Let me tell you a story, right," Kroh said, a little annoyed.

"Let me guess, a horror story?"

"It's the only kind I know. But at least Oskar Dirlewanger's story is not a dull one," Kroh said. "He was in the last show, the trenches. Damaged him some say; made him fearless, crazy too, right? But that sort of thing depends on the time you're living in, your point of view, and I'm just glad he's on our side." Kroh dropped his voice a little now, though Dirlewanger was not in earshot, not even close. They had heard a bit about the man already; had heard he had a thing for drugs and drink, and young girls, too young. Some even reckoned he was both a paedophile and a necrophile. But that seemed a bit too much bad for one man alone, even a Nazi, Ingo had thought.

"Anyhow, that was not the end of the soldiering for him; he then fought in all those messy little scraps just after the war with the Freikorps, and then, in the '30s he was in Spain, with the Spanish Foreign Legion at first, then our Condor Legion. He was wounded three times there, to add to his scars from the First War. So, like I said, a soldier, right?"

"And what about the rape?"

"Ah, just like Pop, always looking for the romantic angle," Kroh said. "She was just a BdM tart; no doubt she was gagging for it anyway, that's always the way, right?"

"A fourteen-year old BdM tart, I hear," Pop said.

"Old enough, Pop. Old enough ... Besides, he served his time. And we all make mistakes, right?"

Pop shook his head.

"Oh, and he's not just a soldier, you know, he also has a doctorate in political science," Kroh added.

"It's been a while since there's been much science in politics," Pop said.

"Best be careful Pop, right?" Kroh said. "Anyway, enough of that. What about your tin can?"

"Bloody Panthers, always breaking down, wish we were still in IVs," Pop said. "The final drive, as usual – isn't that right Ingo?"

"Yep, final drive. Always the final drive."

"So, you decided to blow the fucking thing up, right?"

"Couldn't leave it to the Poles," Pop said.

"Why not, what could they do with it – the final drive was kaput?"

"Fix it, or they could use the gun," Ingo said. "Would be more effective than that barricade, I would think."

"By the time you set off the charge we'd already overrun the barricade," Kroh said.

"Hard to see details, from where I sit," Ingo said. "Besides, why would I blow up my own panzer, otherwise?" The noise in his head was diminishing, but the noise of the battle wasn't. A stray shot ricocheted off a nearby wall, and the MG 42 in the window above them let out a loud burst in reply.

"I suppose you think you should go back to your unit now, perhaps pick up another panzer, get sent somewhere else? That the plan, right?" Kroh said, once the machine gun had stopped firing.

"Well, we're no use without a panzer," Pop said.

Kroh thought on that for a little while. Looking up the street just as an explosion filled it. He whistled a few bars of the *Panzerlied*, like air escaping from a tyre, then stopped and looked at Sardine and Woof. "You two, find your way back to your unit," he said, and they both gratefully rushed away, with an apologetic glance back at Pop and Ingo as they went.

"What about us?" Ingo said.

"The bandits have taken some of your outfit's tanks, a couple of Jagdpanthers, I hear."

"Yes, so they say," Pop said. Woof had heard the news over the divisional radio net, had passed it on to the rest of them. The tank destroyers had been stopped with grenades and petrol bombs, and the Poles had captured them. No one yet knew the extent of the damage, or whether they could be used again.

"And that's exactly why Ingo was right to set off the demo charge."

Kroh ignored that. "So now we need experts, panzer experts."

"And we need a panzer," Pop said.

"No, for now you're attached to my company, as advisers, in case we come across these Polish Panthers, right?" Kroh said. "You'll be like poachers turned gamekeepers; very apt for this outfit. I'll clear it with your lot; it's an SS show this, so sure they'll understand. And we'll sort out what really happened with that tin can of yours when this is over; love a nice inquiry, us SS."

Kroh shouted an order in Russian to an SS soldier who was drinking from a bottle – Kroh called him *scharführer,* but the man wore no rank badges to show he was the SS equivalent of a feldwebel; none of the Dirlewanger men wore rank badges, except for the officers. He came running, the clear liquid in the bottle sloshing as his boots crunched against the shattered cobbles.

Kroh came up close to Ingo's face, so that he could smell the raw onion on his breath, as he said: "This is Sunshine; he will see you're given proper weapons, and he will also see to it that you use them; right, Pup?"

Kroh said something to the scharführer in Russian. He seemed very young. Ingo had seen him earlier, smiling, he was always smiling. Ingo had thought he was German, as he looked like he'd stepped off an SS recruiting poster, except for the smile. He wore a forage cap; few of Dirlewanger's men seemed to bother with helmets, partly so as not to be mistaken for the insurgents – many of the Poles had taken to wearing captured stahlhelms – and partly because they were always too drunk to care. Once Kroh had finished giving Sunshine his instructions he smiled a little wider. The only thing that spoilt the effect of his grin was his eyes. His pupils were black and small and matt and dead. Ingo thought they were eyes that had seen too much, and had now stopped seeing things for what they really were.

"Sunshine here speaks little German; only really the words he needs to know: *vodka, pussy, money, rape*; right?" Kroh said.

Sunshine nodded, still smiling.

"This means he will not be reasoned with. If either of you step out of line – our line that is – if either of you doesn't pull his weight, then he knows what to do. And don't let that angelic smile fool you, he will do it." Kroh grinned, then walked over to the half-track, the looted violin still tucked under his arm.

"You'll need a thick skin from now on, Ingo; 80mm of face-hardened steel, coated in Zimmaret paste," Pop said. "Because I have a feeling if we don't do exactly what these bastards want us to do then we won't be getting out of Warsaw alive." With that he took out a new red and blue tube of Pirvitin tablets, unscrewed the lid and then popped one in his mouth. "One good thing about this mob, though, they seem to be able to get their mitts on plenty of panzer chocolate," he said, after swallowing the pill.

"Maybe it's about time I tried one?"

Pop nodded, and offered him a Pirvitin. "Right now, it can only help."

***

Brescia, Italy. April 1954

They had eaten a main of beef in oil with polenta, washed down with a couple of bottles of an honest Groppelo red, and then they had finished off with some local Franciacorta white. Ingo and Carlo had spent the day on part of the Mille Miglia route in the Alfa, concentrating on the Futa and the Ratticosa passes, and then the evening with Buchanan and Varela in a small place down an alley off the Piazza del Loggia. The Condor had arrived in Naples earlier in the day and had now cleared customs and was being driven through the night by the two mechanics who had been sent down to collect it. It would be ready for Ingo to take it out on the course in the morning. The race was less than a week away.

It was a long time since Ingo had felt so good, and it was not just the wine. Varela had *somehow* managed to find them rooms in the popular Hotel Vittoria, the rear of which overlooked the square of the same name where the cars would be scrutineered during the three days before the race – an event itself in the week of the Mille Miglia. The *somehow* was probably *some* money, that was always the somehow with Varela; he had hinted that that had got the Condor through customs quickly, too. Tonight, even he had been good company, as excited as Carlo and Ingo about their prospects for the race, as they devised a fuel and tyre stop strategy that would play to their strengths. The Condor was on its way and Ingo could not wait to take it out on the course. This new life was working for him, at last. Ingo was happy. A little drunk, perhaps, but happy.

Ingo took the wide stairs from the marble and brass lobby, as was his long-held habit, rather than the elevator – but then his room was only on the second floor, anyway. The hotel had been put up in the 1930s when the square it helped form was built by the Fascists, after they had first levelled a historic neighbourhood of alleyways and tottering old buildings, some of them mediaeval, Ingo had been told. The hotel, like the square with its grand post office and its telescopic-looking tower-block, was both classical and modernist; they liked chariots *and* dive bombers, those Fascists.

He snorted a little laugh at that thought, as his shoes sank in to the soft, wine-red carpet that lay in a broad stripe down the centre of the marble staircase. He came to his floor and walked down the high-ceilinged, wide corridor. There was a window open at the top of the stairs and he could hear the night. Nowhere in Brescia was quite quiet in the week of the Mille Miglia, and even now, at 11.30pm, as the strange brass clock told him – like one in a railway station, fixed high on the corridor wall – there was the bark of an open exhaust on a racing car echoing through the tight streets, like a trapped beast in a stone labyrinth; someone tweaking at a throttle intake, tuning it, or just to make nice noise. Ingo didn't care, he liked it, and he had slept through far worse. He smiled to himself as he turned the key in the lock.

Ingo walked in, switched on the light in the narrow anteroom and hung up his coat. There was a connecting door, to an adjoining room, and he heard the giggles of intimacy, and a gasp. He stopped and listened for a moment, keeping silent and still, then realised what he was doing, and quietly told himself off for being such a dirty old man.

Was he so old? He thought, as he turned the brass knob to the door to his room – just thirty-four, not so very old. And then he suddenly thought of Lidka, for the first time in a long while …

… Long dead Lidka …

He thought of her as the walnut door swung open with a soft creak. Because he had drunk so much wine he had been distracted, so he was a second or so late in remembering he had left that door ajar when he'd gone out earlier.

The window was open, and the languid breeze played with the edge of the curtain, as a scooter rasped by outside. He could make out the broad band of the picture rail, nearly a metre below the ceiling in this high room, and he used it to help him get his bearings in his tipsy fumble to find the light switch. He could smell drink; whisky. He stopped still, his finger on the Bakelite switch.

In the street light that spilled through the window he could see there was someone there, in the low armchair, the glass he was holding twinkling softly. There was a soft hiss. No, it was a whistle, he realised, as a cold hand seemed to clutch his heart, and his breath froze within him.

Ingo did not recognise the tune. But he did recognise the whistle. He turned on the light.

***

Wola, Warsaw. August 1944

The tiled floors and the high ceilings amplified the horror. As did the drug. Screams and gunshots echoed down the corridors and through the wards. This was a place of blood, by design, but no one could have ever envisaged such things would take place here. If anyone had, in that time before all this, they would have been in possession of an imagination that would have consigned them to a very different type of hospital.

Ingo was still dazed from what he had already witnessed, yet buzzing from the Pervitin Pop had given him, too. He had told himself he did not need it, needed sleep now, not the utter wakefulness of the Stuka tablets; needed soothing fog now, not the complete clarity the pill also gave. But he had taken it all the same. He could feel his heart thumping fast in his chest, like machine gun fire; this too was the drug. The rest of it was pure evil …

They were with a group of Dirlewanger's men, though the word *group* did not fit, and neither did *platoon* or *squad*. This was a *pack*. Russians, Ukrainians, Azerbaijanis, a few Germans and Pop and Ingo, with Sunshine usually keeping very close to them. So far Ingo had fired high when told to shoot, but he did not know how long he could not kill, without being killed himself. Most of the SS men were well and truly liquored up and they had drunk a bit of vodka themselves, Pop and him, though for them it had been as an anaesthetic to the horror. But it had not worked, and he felt completely sober. A sort of heightened sobriety even, where he saw and heard and smelt every tiny detail of what was happening with a hyper lucidity, so clear he could not miss a thing; and he knew he would never stop experiencing this. The tinnitus was also solid within him now, like steel; but steel which still expanded within his head. He did not think he could take it much longer, but he had no idea how to stop it.

Kroh was walking along the length of the ward, like a consultant checking charts. He was stopping at some beds, examining the female patients with an almost comic tilt of the head, then sometimes shooting them dead, as he whistled. With some, he took their pictures with his Leica, too, once they were dead. The only patients he did not shoot were those healthy enough to inflame the ardour of his men. To Ingo's right a Dirlewanger man had his trousers around his ankles and was pinning a woman to the edge of a bed, a hospital gown rucked up around her neck. A nurse who had stayed with her patients stared at the body of a doctor, lying silent in his white coat, an expanding pool of blood by his head. She stared at the dead doctor while they took her. They had completely ripped her uniform and underwear from her, and it hung like streamers from her lower legs. They took it in turns with her. It did not seem to take any of them long, and Ingo thought the screams and the crying added to it for them; perhaps it was the only way they knew? Pop just stared; wide eyed in revulsion.

Ingo looked away from the nurse. On the other side of the ward a Dirlewanger man, a Ukrainian, had dragged a middle-aged patient from her iron-framed bed and was now pulling the dressings from her body, revealing operation wounds the colour of spoilt banana and vivid puckered stitches. She was too scared to cry or scream, and she could not fight him off when he forced himself on her, the tip of his bayonet pressed against the bottom of her jaw, blood dribbling down her neck. The woman suddenly saw Ingo and her pleading, animal eyes – staring and filled with pain and hurt, so they seemed they might burst – snared him.

Ingo ran to the Ukrainian and grabbed him by the shoulders, but before he could pull him clear of the woman he felt the jab of something hard at the base of his back. He spun to see Sunshine, the snout of his MP 40 now level with Ingo's gut. For some reason he hesitated and did not shoot him there and then; perhaps the vodka had made him indecisive, or maybe there was a tiny trace of the human he had once been in there, somewhere. He flicked his head to one side, still smiling, as if to say 'stand clear', and then Sunshine just watched as the Ukrainian raped the woman.

"We can do nothing here, Ingo," Pop said, his voice high, his eyes bulging, with fear, with anger, Ingo cold not tell which. He had never seen him like this before.

Just then there was a shriek, a wilder scream amongst a purgatory of screams. A young child, maybe six. Where she had run from, he could not say, but she was in a nightdress, and her bare feet slapping against the hard floor of the ward made the very same noise as the SS man now taking his turn raping the nurse.

Someone raised a machine pistol.

"Waste of ammo man – you know the drill, right?" Kroh shouted, and the soldier dropped the snout of his MP 40 and ran after the girl, then grabbed her by the throat, cutting the scream with a big handed grip. Then he turned her upside down, swung her by the ankles, round once, then twice, and dashed her head against the ward's wall.

Not one of them stopped, nor commented. It was clear they had all seen children killed, and in this casually inhuman way, before. But it seemed to galvanise Pop, shake him out of his shock.

"Go ahead, Ingo. To the next floor, warn them what's about to hit them!"

"Yes, come on Pop, we must!"

"No, Sunshine will follow us, then. Listen, he will stay with me if we split up, down here, with this," Pop let his eyes pass over the scene of rape and death. "We must separate, if we are to help!"

Ingo nodded, Pop was right. He did not waste any more time, just ran to the nearer exit from the ward, the opposite end from where Kroh was now taking a snap of the dead child. He barged through the double swing doors, the Kar 98 rifle he had been issued with feeling awkward in his hands, and tumbled through into the stairwell. Gunfire echoed up from the floors below. The Dirlewanger platoons had been leapfrogging each other, floor by floor, ward by ward, but now it was more of a free for all. He added to the clamour with the high squeal of his rubber-soled panzer boots against the stone steps.

As soon as he made it to the next floor he knew he was the first. There was no gunfire here, no screams, just the sound of sobbing behind the doors. He pushed his way through. He was met with a pungent smell of iodine; and by three nurses, standing in a straight line, which seemed to curve back like a drawn bow at either end as he came closer. The one in the middle was clearly in charge; one of the others was crying, the other trembling like the surface of an ersatz coffee during a bombardment. The nurse in the middle was handsome, rather than pretty, with the stern look of a matron not used to be being told what to do.

"You must escape, is there a way out?" Ingo said, but he was answered in Polish by the matron, something that seemed to have been prepared, like a funeral oration. But he did not know enough of the language to be able make any of it out. Through the paper doll barrier of the three nurses he could see the ward was full, each bed with a sick or injured man tucked in bright white sheets. He thought he would be able do little for most of them.

"Please, leave here, take who you can with you!"

The matron said nothing, just tilted her chin a little higher.

"Go!" He shouted, in Polish, a word he knew, and then he repeated it: "*iść!*" pointing to the other end of the ward as he did so, where there might, he thought, be the chance of escape, or somewhere to hide at least. Just then he heard steel heel plates clacking loudly on the stairs.

"Please!" he said, "*proszę!*" and then he reached for the matron.

She had the scalpel reversed, hidden in the palm of her hand. The light caught it as she struck, flashing like a signal mirror. Ingo was too fast for her, but the blade still scratched the back of his hand, a thin line that beaded with instant blood; the sting of it delayed, as the matron stood back, dropping the scalpel with the shock of what she had done.

The swing doors seemed to gulp as they were swept open, and Ingo knew he was too late as two Dirlewanger men burst in. They laughed on seeing the nurses and the first of them, a Russian, wasted no time in taking the matron and ripping the top part of her apron away. She slapped him. He simply shot her in the mouth, the bullet coming out of the back of her head in a fountain of blood and bone.

The other man held a stick grenade, and he clubbed one of the other nurses with it and she staggered back. The third nurse ran, and the grenade man felled her with a single one-handed burst from his MP 40, which hosed as he fired it, an errant slug smashing the skull of a bedbound old man, the shade of his passing pinky red on the white walls above him.

The tinnitus stopped then. Right then. To be replaced with a sudden crystal clarity. Everything seemed as pure and strong and clear as the vodka he could not feel in his veins. This was not rage, like it had been when he had shot the Ivan near Teploe, like the time with his father in the kitchen in Munich, it was much, much colder than that. Ingo Six knew exactly what he needed to do.

He lifted his rifle to his shoulder and shot the Dirlewanger man in the head, the pepper-iron cordite fumes mixing with the smell of iodine, the bang echoing down the ward like rolling thunder. He worked the bolt as the other SS man recovered from the shock of what Ingo had done, the smoking spent shell falling on the tiles with a dull clink. Ingo had another round in the breech by the time the second soldier had lifted his sub machine gun. He finished him with a shot to the heart, then another to make sure.

The swing doors *thwuck-a-wucked* open and he felt the breeze of their movement on the back of his neck as he waited for the bullet that would end his life.

The nurse who had been clubbed with the stick grenade ran, blood pouring from the deep gash in her forehead, a treacherous trail of red starbursts splatting the clean ward floor. Ingo's tinnitus had returned, drilling through him.

"Christ, Ingo!" It was Pop. He had already started to drag one of the bodies of the Dirlewanger men away from the centre of the ward, and Ingo dropped his rifle which clattered on the hard floor, then he did the same with the other body.

Some of the patients now saw their chance, their only hope, and they jumped or rolled from their beds; then some ran, some hobbled, some crawled. Some escaped, for now. But for those who could not it was too late, and very soon the Dirlewanger were among them, killing them quickly. If anyone noticed the two SS-unformed dead bodies beneath the first bed in the ward they said nothing, too intent on their work, or more likely hardly caring … Sunshine, who must have been held up downstairs as he arrived a little later than Pop, looked at Ingo, then the dead nurses, and his grin widened as he nodded his congratulations, obviously assuming this was Ingo's work. Then he slit the throat of a shaking man with a bandage over both his eyes, laughing as he did so.

It was no surprise when one of the windows of the ward suddenly shattered into crystal confetti, nothing could surprise Ingo this day now, certainly not a partisan sniper firing at them from a nearby building.

Pop and Ingo took cover under the beds, lying alongside the two men Ingo had killed. He looked at one of them, a man with such an ordinary peasant face that the only thing that could possibly make him stand out in a crowd was the neat red hole Ingo had put in his forehead. Ingo felt no regret for that. Further down the ward the Dirlewanger men were returning fire, they never seemed to take cover. That was a part of the madness.

Pop was lying on his side. He had to speak up to be heard over the gunfire as he said: "I'm going to have a word with one of Dirlewanger's signals lads; give him a little present, maybe – most of these crooks will do anything for money. I'll ask him to contact Hauptmann Schulte, get him to demand that we're sent back; ask him to take it higher than Kroh. They always need good drivers and gunners. I'm thinking he can get us back where we belong, in a panzer, in the 19th, SS orders or not."

"You think so?"

"Hope so," Pop said, then started to say something else, but his words were lost in a sustained burst from an MG 42 two Dirlewanger men had set up on a window ledge. He then made a quick sign of the cross, more habit than joke now, and awkward to do, on his side under the bed.

"Maybe we can do more good here, in the meantime, anyway?" Ingo said, once the machine gun had dealt with the Polish sniper. He was still looking at the corpse of the man with the ordinary face.

"Perhaps," Pop said, and Ingo thought there was just the light tug of a tiny smile at the corner of his mouth. He was glad Pop understood. But then he knew he would.

***

Brescia. April 1954

Ingo switched on the light.

"Turn it off, Pup," Kroh said. He was holding a Luger in one hand, the tumbler in the other, the whisky within catching the light; like a crucible of molten bronze. The pistol was pointed at Ingo's belly. "And close the door."

Ingo did as he was told, catching sight of the shock on his own gaping face in the reflection in the partially opened window just before the light went out. He also noticed the room had been completely turned over, as if a small tornado had passed through it. Over the smell of the whisky Ingo caught a whiff of onion – Kroh hadn't changed so very much. Outside, in the street below, a man was speaking Italian and a woman laughed at what he had said, a giggle that floated into the night as her shoes clicked on the marble beneath the colonnade that fronted the hotel.

"You look like you've seen a ghost, Pup."

"I thought …" Ingo started, but did not finish.

"That was the idea. Then again, Christian Kroh is dead enough, as is Pedro Gruber. I'm on to my third life, you see. Good value, right?"

"A better deal than you gave most."

"You didn't do so bad yourself, Pup, in the end."

Ingo sighed, then sat on the edge of the big brass bed, the mattress springs seeming to echo the sigh. A minute before he had been drunk and happy. But it seemed an aeon had passed since then; an ice age of frozen fear, a dozen millennia of re-stoked hatred. There was enough lemony light from the street seeping through the window for Ingo to make out Kroh's features. He had made little real effort to change his appearance, although he did wear spectacles now – perhaps because he needed them, perhaps not – while he had also put on weight since the last time Ingo had seen him almost ten years before, fat which had cloned his chin and filled out his face.

"My whisky?"

"Help yourself," Kroh said, and Ingo reached over to the opened bottle of Black & White that sat on the bedside table. There was not another glass to hand, so he took a swig from the neck.

"What do you want?" Ingo said, after he had swallowed the slug of whisky.

"I'm here to help you, *Enrique*."

Ingo snorted a little wry laugh, shook his head. "It's all gone, Kroh. How else do you think I've been able to race, it's a rich man's game, you know?"

"You have a rich man, Varela, and you are also rather good, good enough for him to pay you – but we always knew that, right? Pop never shut up about how you two were going to conquer the world."

"Yes, Pop."

"It was a long time ago, Pup. Same day you cheated me, it seems. Same day —"

"Yes, I remember," Ingo said, cutting him short.

"You were never one for hats, were you?" With that Kroh put his glass on the arm of the chair and reached down to the floor and picked up the fedora, always keeping the Luger trained on Ingo. He made a point of feeling at the small lump within its lining so that Ingo could see he knew there was something there. "You should have found a new hiding place," he said.

"Thought I had."

"Diamond?"

Ingo nodded, there was little point in denying it now. It had been a risk, bringing his last stone, but coming here in the first place had also been a risk, and there had always been the chance he might have to move on quickly, to hide again. "So, you've got what you came for; now you can go," he said.

"Oh, but I didn't come for this," Kroh said, holding the hat up then placing it on the arm of the chair, swapping it for the whisky in the hand that didn't hold the gun.

"Then best get on with it, then," Ingo said, nodding at the Luger, while wondering if he could throw a bottle quicker than Kroh could tug a trigger.

"Nor that."

"Then what?"

"Should have realised there was something in the hat when you took it, right? But then we never quite had the chance to talk things through, did we Pup?"

"So that's why you came to Chillar, for a chat?"

Kroh sniggered, shook his head. "No, not that," he said, then glanced at the hat. "But if I had known about this, I would definitely have come visiting earlier, you can be sure of that."

"How did you know I was there, who told you?"

"No one, I was just told that there was another Dirlewanger man hiding out there – never would have called you that myself, mind, and would never have thought you would, either."

"It opened doors, not all of them to Hell."

Kroh snorted a little laugh, raised the glass, as if making a toast, and then continued. "I had a payment to pick up for a photographic job I'd done, in Tandil. Had to work fast, right, as I'd been tipped off that the Yids were coming for me. That same time I was told there was an old comrade from my mob, in Chillar; our people tend to keep tabs on those who are hiding, you know. Naturally, I was curious, stopped there on the way back to BA. Asked around, and I was told this Hohberg fella was a racing driver, and might be found in some local garage, so that's where I went. You were out. Couldn't wait all day. Had places to go, back then, and didn't know it was you, did I? Maybe I should have guessed, what with the racing, but then I always kind of assumed you were dead. Told the doll in the garage a story about wanting pics of racers, not really my line of work, as it was, but better than announcing a Dirlewanger reunion. You know, I would have said I was an old friend; but they're seldom welcome, for people like us, right?"

"I'm not like you."

"If you say so. Anyway, left my card. Thought this Hohberg fella might ring, right? By the time I'd figured out it might be you, well I was far from Argentina by then, far from you, far from this." He looked at the hat, sitting on the arm of the chair. "Tell me, the doll, yours?"

"No," Ingo said, realising he was referring to Catalina.

"Pity. Still, she passed on the message, didn't she? You were the joker outside my place in BA, I'm guessing?"

Ingo nodded. "Gas explosion?"

"That was real enough, but then you know that; bad timing, eh? Tell me, the police found a thirty-eight; yours?"

"Mine."

"Revenge?"

"Not just that; survival, too."

"Well, both are reason enough, right? That's why I came here with the iron," Kroh said, waving the Luger slightly.

"Thought the job had been done for me," Ingo said. "That was a big bang?"

"Wasn't even there."

"Then who?"

"Some nobody who thought he'd lucked in," Kroh said. "He was due a flight over the River Plate, they're one-way tickets, those. The Argentinian secret police are pretty good at getting rid of those who don't play ball, right? They drop them from high up. He was given the chance to live, then the Argentinian secret police are pretty good at lying, too. The condition was he did what I would do; he looked a little like me, and with the hat, the Merc, and the darkness, well … We knew they were coming for me, we even knew what day, and we made it easy for them."

"We?"

"The Brotherhood. I work for them now; here in Europe. It's the price I paid for their help with the death of the former me." Ingo knew all about the Brotherhood. It was the organisation that helped those who fled Germany, helped them to disappear; Nazis like Kroh, people like Ingo. Kroh continued: "Though to be fair it's the Argentinians who really deserve my gratitude; they filled in all the forms, and Pedro Gruber the dead man is more real than the living Pedro Gruber had ever been. Which means Christian Kroh is also dead. So no one is looking for that fine fellow now, which in turn means I'm pretty safe, even in Germany." He took a gulp of whisky, then exhaled softly, as he glanced at his gun. "Now it's my job to help keep other old comrades safe."

"And am I safe?"

Kroh laughed. "Let's say *yes* … And, *no*. As far as I'm concerned, it's forgive and forget. You ran out on me, deprived me of my spoils I now know, but I've been paid for that." He glanced at the hat again. "But our Yid friends are not so *Christian*, right? They were after me, now they're after you."

"What do you mean?"

"The Argentinians have someone inside the Israeli Embassy in BA, and the Argentinians are friendly; that's how I found out they were after me, you see; and also how we knew where and when. Now they've been getting different intelligence. Seems you've made an enemy, Pup. Someone told them everything they knew about you. It wasn't much. But, eventually, it was enough."

"An enemy?" Ingo took another hit of whisky. "I hardly know anyone; I tend to keep myself to myself since … well, since."

"Admirable strategy," Kroh said. "Except for this racing business; living in the shadows involves an element of shade, right? Anyway, from what I understand a link was made, someone in the embassy had a name on file, maybe two names – that's often the way, some of the lads can't quite believe they're someone else, they'll often blurt out an old name by mistake, or some other secret. Anyhow, whatever it was it wasn't much to go on, and it had been sat on for a while. But when this Enrique Hohberg fella was in a newspaper, this same someone thought it worth digging out the file, being a sneaky Yid. Sent a message to Tel Aviv, even included some newspaper cuttings; with pictures."

"Pictures of me?"

"No, of fucking Lolita Torres!" He grinned and finished his whisky, putting the tumbler on the small table. "I imagine they have an album stuffed with pictures of you, by now."

"Meaning?

"The Yids took a stash of tourist photos from my place before they rigged the gas to blow. I thought they might, so took out the ones that would incriminate my friends, and the more important old comrades, of course. But I had to leave them something, right? We had to have our patsy looking the part now, didn't we?"

"Pictures? You mean ...?"

"Yes."

Ingo took a deeper gulp of whisky, as if to extinguish the acid-sweet bile that rose in his throat with that flaring memory of the thing he would never forget.

"What now?"

"Guess you'll hear from them, soon enough."

Ingo squeezed the bottle's neck tightly. "Who are they?" he said.

"Hit squad. They're the best. So good, in fact, we've only vaguely been aware of their work. But there have been many accidents, suicides —"

"Gas explosions."

"Stay away from the stuff, Pup. It's dangerous, only has one good use as far as I'm concerned, and we all know what that is, right?"

Ingo shook his head, slowly.

"You know, they've not been so active lately. We thought they were finished. And it seems strange they're after you, of all people," Kroh sniffed an ironic little laugh at that.

"And how do you know they are after me, Kroh?"

"There's no Kroh here, *Enrique*," Kroh said, standing up now and putting the Luger in the pocket of his long mac, though he made sure that Ingo could see he was still holding it, and that it was aimed at him through the taut material. Then he continued: "The mole in the Israeli Embassy again. It had all seemed like nothing much to the Yids, just small fry. I must admit, I would have agreed. But a little while after the Embassy sent the cuttings to Tel Aviv the heat came on like a fucking Flammenwerfer. Someone there wanted to know everything about this Enrique Hohberg fella, right?"

A small car rattled down the street outside, the cone of its headlights lighting up the room a little more; enough that Ingo could see that Kroh's smile was as barbed as it ever was.

"What now?" Ingo said.

"I think they'll be here, I'm sure of it. It's difficult for them to work in Argentina. But they will know you're in Italy for this race, you can bet on that. Yes, they will kill you here. And note that word well: *kill*. These people do not take a man, put him in front of a judge and jury; they kill him, right? They will kill you. Here."

With that Kroh placed the fedora on his head; it was a good fit. The hat he had arrived with sat on the low table. As he walked to the door Kroh added: "I would have thought a thank you was in order?"

"Why should I believe this?"

Kroh shrugged. "That's up to you, I don't care. But the funniest thing of all is that because these Yids are after you some of our lads think you might be pretty damned special after all, doesn't matter what I tell them. Now doesn't that take the fucking biscuit, eh killer? As for my part in all this, well, this is the last place I want to be right now, why do you think we're talking in the dark? But – and this might make you smile – I am, in fact, just following orders."

"Get out, Kroh."

"Make sure you lock the door behind me, and fuck off out of Brescia in the morning, if you want to live." With that he opened the door, throwing a carpet of light from the anteroom on to the floor of the main bedroom. "Oh, and forget about any thoughts of revenge, that's for the Yids. The girl's gone. Rough times, they were. Right?"

"You killed her, I'll never forget that," Ingo said, for the second time that night remembering Lidka.

"You won't see me again, Pup."

Kroh closed the door behind him, and Ingo could just hear that leaking air whistle of his. This time he recognised the tune; *Rags to Riches*.

As soon as he heard the outer door close Ingo shut the windows and the shutters, and only then switched on the light. Suddenly a screaming steel wall of tinnitus closed off the rest of the world. Most of Ingo's clothes and things were strewn across the floor after Kroh's search of the room. Ten seconds later much of it was stuffed inside his leather holdall.

***

Powązki Cemetery, Warsaw. August 1944

The bullets hammered against the other side of the small but thick tombstone Lidka hid behind, her back tight to it, her knees tucked up close to her chin, her elbows digging in to her sides and her hands pressed to her face to give her some protection from the flying chips of white stone. She could feel the thump of the rounds against the gravestone through her spine; it was as if the dead person nearly two metres below her was coming back to life, knocking hard in an entombed panic. If Lidka believed such a horror could be so – and after nine days of this she believed in many horrors – she would tell the dead person not to bother. They were in a better place.

Andrzej had taken cover behind another stone, where he was now inserting a fresh magazine into the slot on the side of his Sten, while Cat huddled behind the next gravestone along. Neither Lidka nor Cat had had many messages to deliver these past days; they had been too busy simply surviving. Raven lay in the long grass between the stones, his jaw three metres away, where it had been whipped away by a sniper's bullet. The German snipers were at home in this place of death. Lightning had held a cigarette for Raven to smoke, for a moment, because he had no lower jaw to clamp it in his mouth, his hand shaking as he helped the boy do this last thing in his short life.

The German machine gun took a breath, and Andrzej popped up over the narrow parapet of his gravestone cover, selected a target and fired a single shot. They were short on ammunition. Short on hope. Short on time. She remembered what she had said to Sarah, nine days ago: *I will be back as soon as I can.* She did not know what had happened in Ochota since they had left. But she *did* know what had happened in Wola. She needed to get back to the house. Somehow. She had to know that Freddy was safe.

A mortar bomb dropped close by, raising a plume of dust and stones which fell amongst the graves with a rattle like hail dashing roof tiles. Bombs had dropped on the same spot on three occasions in the space of a minute, churning up the dirt, churning up the dead. There was a skeletal hand, like a dirty chalk spider, lying on the floor between the grave which Lidka used as a shield and Raven's now dead body. It jumped and clattered to the fall of bullets and grenades, as if death was bringing it back to life. She had to look away. She caught Cat's eye; the girl smiled, a rare thing. But it was a mocking smile.

Lidka heard bigger guns, further away, and the rattle of tanks. She knew the sound of German guns by now. And now they all also knew that the guns they had heard, on that seemingly distant first day of the uprising, had not been Russian artillery, but the Germans counter attacking the Soviets to the north. The Germans chose the right time to hit back against the Russians. And the AK had chosen the wrong time for insurrection …

Yet it had gone well to start with, in some parts of the city at least. The Ochota rising had failed, but Andrzej had led his small group, and some others, in to the nearby neighbourhood of Wola, where the AK had been more successful – they had even found a warehouse full of Waffen SS jackets, which many of them had adopted as a uniform, with the AK armband over the sleeves of the green leopard-like pea-dot camouflaged smocks. Andrzej still wore his leather jacket and Lidka preferred the baggy overalls that now smelt bad, were coated in dirt and brick dust, and were ripped at the right knee. She did not want to look like a soldier. Particularly a German soldier. She suddenly thought of Ingo, then tried not to. Because she could not bear the idea that he might be the other side of this gravestone that barely kept her alive. Or at the wheel, or whatever steered those monsters, of one of the tanks that were now forming up behind the red brick wall of the large cemetery. She ached to see him, but she hoped to God she would not.

For a while, in those almost carefree early days of the uprising, they were happy and proud. It was then just a matter of waiting for the Russians to come and finish off what the AK had started, they had thought. Only the Russians didn't come. Ochota was in German hands, as was most of Wola now. She hoped and she prayed that Sarah had kept Freddy safe in the cellar. But she also knew that they would be very short of food by now.

There was a very loud creak, snap and crunch, followed by the rattle and roar of a tank, and she knew before the shout went up that a panzer had broken through the cemetery wall.

"That's it!" Andrzej shouted. "Pull back!" No one questioned him, he had won his authority on the battlefield, and they all knew that if Bullet said they should run, they should run. Cat went first, as quick and agile as the animal she was named after. Lidka ran, too, sticking as close to Andrzej as she could, as they dodged through the gravestones and the fresher dead, the air thick with bullets that whipped past her body and head with lethal little *phutts*, and struck the stones with loud cracks and bursts of white powder.

The machine gun on the tank opened up, and Andrzej dived to the ground, sliding on his belly before rolling in to cover behind a tomb the size of half a car. Lidka did the same, and they lay face to face as the air above them was ripped to tatters, and the stone tomb shook to the hits, the bronze cross on its lid sparking and then snapping with a high ping, under the sheer weight of shot.

Andrzej's breath smelt stale, as he shouted: "You okay?"

"I have to go to the house; Freddy!"

"No, you stay here, you're a soldier now."

"I'm no soldier."

"No? Then the Germans *are*; and there are thousands of them between here and Ochota."

"I need to know he's alright!"

"He's safe, with Mother and the Jews and old Vogler's diamonds — surely that's better than here? I, for one, am banking on it." He actually smiled as he shouted that. She wondered if Andrzej truly understood fear.

"I am his mother!"

"You cannot be a mother if you're not alive. And there is no way back through that!" Andrzej shouted, above the racket of the machine gun fire, cocking his head to indicate the oncoming tank, which was slowly moving towards them, snapping the brittle teeth of the graves and churning up the dead and dying. There was a sudden *plonk* on the top of the hollow tomb and then a soft rattle before a German stick grenade dropped into the small gap between their faces, the priming cord dangling loosely from its base. Andrzej did not hesitate; he picked it up, threw it back over the tomb with an awkward twist of his elbow. A hail of broken stone fell upon them just a moment later.

Suddenly the machine gunner in the tank found another target, picking out a running boy and severing his legs at the knees.

"It's our chance!" Andrzej shouted, and they both run, bent over, and Lidka waited for the bullet to hit her back. Andrzej was right, there was no way she could get through all that; there was not a way to Ochota, to Freddy, through the lines. *But* … Her thought was snatched away by a bullet that was so close she felt its passage through the air as a caress on her cheek, before it ripped in to a beech tree and tore off its bark to leave a flash that reminded her of clean bone, and the gravestones through which she ducked and dodged.

*

Wola, Warsaw. August 1944

There was a line of people, standing close to the smoke-blackened inner wall of the fire-lit large courtyard. Some days before – it was difficult to remember how many days he'd been in this hell, what with the relentless horror, what with the Pervitin – those in the line would take a step back, against that wall, and they would all then be shot. Maybe it would never have even got to be a line in the first place. It often depended on whether those doing the shooting, lobbing grenades, or bayoneting, preferred straight lines or messy piles. But tidy minds had now prevailed. Walking them out, as live prisoners, and then executing them was neater than killing them where they were found and did not slow up the advance – the macaroni factory at Wolska 60; the tram depot on Młynarska Street; the railway viaduct at Górczewska; the Ursus factory, all of these favourite human abattoirs.

They would still be killed, most of them; children and old people included, and the women – again, most of them – would still be raped. Their bodies would be carefully stacked, to be burnt. It had been harder to burn the dead than many had foreseen, but they already had experts for that, it had turned out. The air was often thick with the smell of burning bodies now.

This line of people in front of him would die, that was almost certain; they might even be shot right now, as the Dirlewanger men still killed when the mood took them, as did many in other units across the city. Ingo could do nothing for these people. But others would live, he had seen to that. Some of Dirlewanger's men would not, he had also seen to that.

An aircraft roared overhead, so low Ingo could feel the beat of its passage through the burning night air, so low he could see the detail within the black belly of its bomb-bay – from where supplies would have just been dropped to the insurgents – so low its bellowing engines shut-out the constant roar and crackle of the burning streets. It was gone a moment later, before any of the soldiers in the courtyard had even managed to take a pot shot at it. There was a slight smell of high-octane fuel, a smell he liked, but it was soon washed away by the fumes of the burning, and the sickly-sweet decay of the dead.

"Supply drop," Pop said. Sunshine would not understand the German, but smiled, as he always did. The three of them stood at the edge of the courtyard, close to an unnecessary brazier – on this warm and burning night – which threw stretched toffee shadows of them on to the wall behind. Despite the fact that Sunshine had been ordered by Kroh to shoot Pop and Ingo if they stepped out of line, anyone looking at Pop and Sunshine would think they got on like a house on fire – which ironically enough was where they spent most of their time. They shared a love of Pervitin, a dependence even, and Sunshine could always get the Stuka tablets. Sunshine had shown Pop a new way to take them, crushing the pills into powder and sniffing it up like snuff. Ingo, too, had taken the pills, but not that way. It meant he had not slept in days, now, but it also helped. The drug seemed to clear his head; made him feel more energetic and bolder. He could not save them all, but he could save some, if he himself stayed alive. So, what he had done was all cold calculation, not decisions made in the heat of rage. A block or so away a machine gun chattered, a grenade exploded.

A wave of tiredness passed over him, as suddenly as the aircraft had. He thought the drug might be wearing off. He sat down against the brick wall and closed his eyes, tight; so tight he could feel the skin scrunch into the hollows of his sockets, and he could see nothing but a pale orange blob, the afterimage of the brazier. He could hear the shooting, and the shouts and laughter of the SS men, but it faded, as the steely whine of the tinnitus filled his head.

Then he remembered.

The Orthodox Children's Home on Wolska. When was that? Two days ago; three? They had been small children, and Dirlewanger had ordered that no bullets should be wasted, so his men had used the butts of their rifles, or daggers and bayonets. Kroh had told Ingo, with pride, they had killed 351 children there – Kroh was responsible for keeping the tally, and taking the photographs. He had asked Ingo how many he had killed at the Children's Home. Ingo had admitted he had killed; did not tell Kroh it had been as SS man, who he had shot dead with his rifle as Ingo helped six children escape through the back door … But he had killed none when they raped the girl, over and over, in the basement of a house – where was that? When was that? He could not recall. He only remembered the way the Dirlewanger man gutted her, from stomach to throat, and how they had all laughed. They would have killed him if he had tried anything then; but the mercury that flowed through his veins was cool … He got one of them later. In the back, a little too late to save the old man he was shooting, and too easy a death for him. Pop had not been there, as usual he had lured Sunshine away, in the hope that Ingo could save one or two innocent people …

… When had the Dirlewanger men killed the nuns; on Górczewska? He was not sure, he only remembered the well in the garden of that place of death, not full of water, but choked with bodies … He recalled the stench of it, believed it was still on him, in the fibres of his uniform … But he had hidden two nuns in a cupboard, and he hoped they still lived … He had killed another of the SS men there … Then there was the church on Chłodna. Another child, swung by the ankles, his head dashed against the edge of a stone altar; accusing dead eyes staring at the helpless man on the crucifix above him …

Ingo could take it no longer. He opened his eyes.

"You okay?" Pop asked.

Ingo hauled himself back onto his feet. "Any word from your signals friend?" he said, a question he asked from habit more than hope now. He did not worry too much about Sunshine hearing, he would not understand, and besides, he now seemed to be completely absorbed in watching the play of searchlight beams on the night sky, a broad smile upon his upturned face.

"Nope. Seems two highly trained panzer men are not a high priority," Pop said. "Or maybe Schulte's too scared of Dirlewanger to rock the boat? He's a practical man, knows when to be cautious. It might get more difficult, too, I've heard that all the 19th are out of Warsaw now, just a rumour of course."

Ingo nodded, he knew to expect nothing more by now. His eyes then rested on the line of prisoners again. They were about to be marched off. Ingo looked at them, these unfortunates, one by one. The flickering flames lit their faces. It would have been easier for him to turn away, but he always looked at the people in these lines of the damned, in the hope – and, yes, the fear – that he might see her. He often looked at the faces in the piles of the dead, too, but never then with hope. This line of people, about twenty of them, were mostly men, some quite elderly. But there were some women, just a couple who were too old to be raped. Lidka was not among them; and he felt both relief and disappointment, as his attention was drawn to one man, slouching, something about the way he stood seemed familiar …

… There was sudden burst of loud laughter from diagonally across the courtyard. It came from a group off to one side of the main body of Dirlewanger men. There was another brazier near the laughing soldiers and it gave off plenty of light. The men were drinking vodka, which was not unusual; some of them had their tunic sleeves rolled up to show wrists and lower arms striped with looted watches – badges of rank in this outfit. Ingo knew them, they were all Germans, and they liked to stick together. He had seen them kill, and rape, torture for the fun of it, and burn and defile their way through Wola. He had seen them earn the crossed stick grenade patch that some in the Dirlewanger Brigade had started to proudly sew on to their collars. But he had also seen something else. A trace of humanity.

It wasn't much humanity. But it burnt bright as a flare in the smoke-knitted sky of Warsaw. There was a boy, a cripple, a simpleton, a Pole. They had found him in the ruins of a house on Płocka, adopted him as their mascot. The lad was maybe twelve, with a simple trusting way, a benign smile, and a lack of awareness of the horror around him that had to be a gift in times like these. He had one leg, the other had been amputated high up, perhaps after or during the bombing in '39, and there was now just a heavy-looking knot of tied up trouser leg in its place. But he could use his good leg very well, could hop incredibly fast, and impressively high. This small group of Dirlewanger men had saved him from the others, saved him from a certain and ugly death, and now delighted in using him to send their messages, collect their vodka. And he delighted in doing so. They called him Rabbit.

One of these Germans was nicknamed Spud; a thick-set Frankfurt man who had a peculiarly smooth and ruddy complexion, like the skin on the sausage that was a more useful product of his city. He always looked too hot; boiled, and he seemed to sweat all the time. Ingo had seen him kill civilians, many times. He liked to use grenades, throwing them in to basements. He talked of it as if it was a hobby, and it was because of his prowess with the potato mashers that he had been given his nickname. Ingo had heard that Spud had rammed a stick grenade up one woman, then pulled the cord at its base and ran. He wouldn't have believed that, just a few weeks ago. Now he did. But Spud seemed fond of Rabbit. The kid was jumping for them now, he liked to show off, how high he could hop.

"I can make him jump higher," Spud shouted, staggering from drink, wiping sweat from his brow with the sleeve of his tunic. Then he pointed to the space in the middle of the large courtyard, where an old couch with bullet-holed red velvet cushions had been set, for some reason that probably had something to do with vodka.

"Hop!" Spud shouted, and Rabbit took off, knowing the word well now, hopping a metre in the air, and making good ground forward, his speed quite remarkable.

But as he set off Ingo had seen Spud drop a stick grenade into the beaten-up old shopping bag Rabbit always carried, tugging the cord first. A few seconds later and Rabbit had hopped halfway across the courtyard, was close to the couch. Then the grenade went off with a high cracking sound, throwing Rabbit more than three metres into the air. The body, the blood and the bits of boy slapped back on to the cobbles, the explosion reverberating around the square, shuddering what windows remained unbroken. "Told you; much higher!" Spud shouted.

The others laughed, as did Sunshine. Ingo thought that even Pop smiled a little; it was easy to grow cold in the heat of this Warsaw summer. The steely tinnitus in Ingo's head changed pitch, a little sharper; louder too, and he looked away, seeing the line of people again.

All the prisoners stared at Rabbit's remains. One of them, the slouching man, seemed to salute the surviving pieces of the lad, in the old Polish way, with two fingers to his temple; and then he cocked out a thumb to make a pistol of it, and ballooned his cheeks, before making a popping sound.

Pop and Sunshine were still distracted by the aftermath of Rabbit's final hop, looking in the same direction as the slouching man faced. Ingo unhitched his rifle from his shoulder and quickly covered the few metres to the line of Poles. He pointed it at the man, whose lower jaw then seemed to turn to iron, his mouth suddenly wide open in silent shock.

"You, out!" Ingo snapped.

"Hey, what you doing?" the Ukrainian SS man who was guarding the group slurred, in halting and drunken German.

"Hauptsturmführer Kroh wants to speak to this one," Ingo said, then he grabbed him by the collar and hauled him away from the group, the man's feet slipping on the cobbles, but Ingo gave him no time to dawdle. He dragged him, half walking, half falling, to the nearest doorway, which was lacking a door, then pulled him along a narrow corridor. He tried a door, it opened, and Ingo pushed the man inside, where he tripped and fell onto the floor. There was no light, and Ingo took the square Daimon flashlight from his pocket. The small room smelt of paint and paraffin. He closed the door behind them and then pressed his ear against it for a moment or two, to check if Sunshine, or anyone, had followed. He turned on the torch, flashed it around the space, then into the man's face.

"Good to see you, too, Ingo," the man said, rubbing his shoulder where he had knocked it on the hard floor with one hand, shielding his eyes from the glare of the torchlight with the other. The narrow room was some kind of store, a clatter of tyre-less broken bicycles at one end, some smashed up furniture, dribble-clawed paint pots, and cleaning equipment nearer to the door.

"Hardly recognised you, Kasper, lost the moustache, eh?" Ingo pointed the light to the corner of the room, which gave them enough illumination without dazzling Kasper.

"Someone said it made me look like Stalin. I was thinking of re-growing it, a couple of weeks ago, but ..." he shrugged. Kasper had not only lost his moustache, he had lost weight, was skinny, and his clothes hung loose on him now. Ingo had only recognised him because of that habit of his, making a two-fingered salute into a pistol.

"I didn't see you out there, Ingo, wasn't looking I suppose," Kasper said, running his eyes up and down Ingo's black Panzerwaffe uniform. His German was much better than it had been in '39. "You're in the SS now, then?"

"No, not SS; long story."

Right then there was a shout from outside and Ingo heard the shuffle of feet as the line of prisoners were led out of the courtyard.

"Where are they taking them?" Kasper said.

Ingo shrugged. "Probably the tram depot on Młynarska."

"And from there?"

"That's the terminal, Kasper; the end of the line."

"So, it's true," Kasper said, shaking his head. "Seems like I owe you my life, Ingo."

"Well, you're not safe yet."

"No, but thanks, all the same. Say, you still play piano?"

"Not for a while," Ingo said. "So, you moved to Wola, when they took over your place?" he added, reminded of the café.

Kasper nodded. "Should have got clean out of Warsaw when there was a chance."

"That's true; that's still true. We're moving on from here soon, wait until then, then get out of the city."

"Out of the city, how? Shouldn't I just hide?"

"No, Warsaw's finished – they aim to destroy it."

"What, all of it?"

Ingo did not answer. Kasper looked at him for a moment or two, and then nodded. He seemed about to make that same old gesture again, but curled his fingers up before they reached his temple.

"Tell me Kasper," Ingo said. "Have you seen Lidka?"

"Lidka?"

"You remember, the girl I used to meet in the café?"

"Ah yes, I'd forgotten her name," Kasper said. "It seems such a long time ago, now. But, yes, I've seen her alright."

"You have; where?" Ingo said, his heart beginning to race.

"Here; Wola."

"Is she okay?"

"I think so, I didn't speak to her."

"Was she alone?"

"No, she was ..."

"Tell me, Kasper"

"She was with the AK."

"A fighter?"

"Well, she had no gun, but many of them don't; then again a lot of the women with the AK are nurses, I hear."

Ingo nodded, he could imagine Lidka as a nurse. "And she's here, you say?"

"Not now. If she still lives, then she'll be in the Old Town, I should think, that's where they'll fight next, I'm sure of it."

"How did she seem?"

"I was quite far away, in my apartment, looking down on the street; but she looked well; a bit skinny perhaps, but then that's been the fashion in Warsaw for a while now," Kasper said.

There was a shout from outside and Ingo realised he'd been a little while, would soon be missed. "Keep your head down, Kasper," he said, and with that he turned off the torch and opened the door, checking the corridor and then leaving the room, closing the door behind him.

As he walked back out into the courtyard he saw that Pop was looking worried and Sunshine, although still smiling, had his MP 40 to hand. Ingo pretended to finish belting up his trousers and doing up his fly.

Someone shouted something in Russian and Sunshine answered, then trotted over to the other side of the square, skirting Rabbit's torn and twisted body.

"Jesus, Ingo; that was pushing it a bit," Pop said. "You were lucky I was able to keep Sunshine distracted."

"It was someone I knew, from before."

"Stupid risk; could get us both killed," Pop said. "Well at least you didn't kill one of ours this time, eh?"

"I only wish I'd had the chance, when Spud pulled that trick."

Pop shook his head. "You know what, not so very long ago killing anyone was beyond you, Ingo," he said.

"I only kill to prevent more murder, and I can live with that."

"Yet you know, if you think about it, in the eyes of the law – whatever that means these days – you're the only murderer here."

"It's not murder; it's pest control."

"Talking of which, I can only keep our pal out of your hair for so long," Pop said, nodding in the direction of Sunshine, who was now sharing some vodka with an old comrade. "Say, doesn't that make me an accomplice?" Sunshine held the bottle up, as if toasting Pop.

"He seems to like you," Ingo said, ignoring the question.

"Well, I've always got along with idiots, haven't I?" Pop said. "But, you know, by my reckoning you have now killed four men, Ingo. Three of ours, and one Ivan, at Kursk. The score is three-one, you've done for three times as many of ours as theirs."

"The score is five-one, Pop."

"Five! Maybe you should think of joining the other side."

"Maybe that's not a bad idea," Ingo said.

"I knew you'd lose it one day, Ingo," Pop said. "Long fuse, big bang. Didn't I say?"

"I've never lost it, not here," Ingo said.

"You've lost it, alright. You know, there's one lesson I never felt the need to teach you, Ingo," Pop said. "But maybe I was wrong."

"And what's that?"

"Never take rage into a racing car, a sure way to get yourself killed, that."

"Racing car? First time you've mentioned racing in ages."

"Well, perhaps I thought there was nothing more to teach."

There was the stutter of a machine gun, from the east. The Old Town was also to the east, Ingo remembered. Kroh walked into the courtyard and started to bellow a series of orders and the Dirlewanger men, Ingo and Pop included, gathered their kit and prepared to move out.

"Kasper told me something," Ingo said, as Pop slung his MP 40 over his shoulder.

"Kasper?"

"Said he'd seen Lidka, not long ago. Said she was alive."

Pop shook his head, and sighed. "And she will not be the only one in this cursed city that *was* alive," he said.

*

Brindisi. August 1944

There was always spare kit around; always more kit than flight crew. And he wouldn't be the first to hitch a ride. It had stopped for a while, but now the war, finally, seemed to be coming to an end, with the Americans and the British in France, the Russians close to Warsaw, a few of the ground crew had once again talked their way on to a mission, before it was too late.

Jósef had always been against this sort of thing, and he would threaten to report any man under him who tried it; though he never had reported anyone. But when he heard that the flight was to drop supplies to Partisans in the forests outside Warsaw, rather than into the city itself, he thought suddenly of the son he had never seen. He wanted to one day tell Fryderyk that he had at least tried. And now he sweated in a flying suit and long silk underwear, with a submariner's jumper tied around his waist, and his feet were sticky with perspiration under four pairs of socks beneath his fur-lined flying boots, and there would be even more clothing to put on once he was at the storeroom close to the runway where the Liberator waited – he knew it got bitterly cold up there. But it was not the cold he was worried about. The warm gear made him perspire heavily on such a hot day, yet right now he was glad of the excuse for his sweat.

The hot air was shot through with the tang of aviation fuel; one of the Liberators had been started, its four 1200bhp engines ripping and roaring. The Bedford came out of the fireball of a setting sun to the west. Jósef made a peak with his hand to shield his eyes from the sunlight. The truck, which he knew was carrying Kapitan Dabrowski and his crew, was hurtling towards him, its transmission whining loudly, the men within and on top of it laughing and joking, as they always did, to hide their fear, or because they had no fear; Jósef was never entirely sure which. He did not understand these men, never had. He fought with himself, but did not allow himself to win, and he stepped in front of the truck, holding up his other hand, showing the men on the Bedford a palm glistening with sweat.

The truck, which had an open cab and no cover over the framework above its deck, braked to a halt just in front of him, casting a very long slightly slanted shadow which allowed Jósef to take his hand from his eyes. The crew members were hanging off the frame like buccaneers silhouetted in the rigging of a pirate ship. There were eight men in the crew of the Liberator. He hoped, but also feared, there would soon be nine.

"What is it, Sczcepanski?" Dabrowski said, but it was obvious what it was, a man doesn't rig himself out in gear for 12,000 feet and higher in August in the south of Italy unless he's hitching a ride.

"I want to go with you, sir."

The Bedford idled roughly as Dabrowski thought for a moment. He was a big man, with the broad, strong shoulders all good bomber pilots seemed to have, and a brow permanently ploughed with thought. Jankowski, now standing on the rattling deck of the truck, was the beam gunner – they had no need for another navigator and so he had volunteered to man the machine guns, nothing would keep that one out of the war. He looked surprised, his head cocked, fingers kneading his chin.

"Impossible," Dabrowski said, shaking his head. "You surprise me, Sczcepanski; you of all people. You know the rules, man."

Jósef said nothing. He was more ashamed that he felt relief than he was of the dressing down, and he dipped his head in what the others might take as disappointment. Dabrowski hit the driver of the Bedford on the arm and pointed to his B-24, waiting on the other side of the field. The driver revved the truck then took off with a lurch. Jósef watched them go. At least he had tried, and one day he would tell Fryderyk that, perhaps. That would have to be enough. He noticed Jankowski was leaning forward, shouting something in Dabrowski's ear from the back of the Bedford as they drove on.

The brakes on the truck suddenly squealed and it once again came to a halt. Dabrowski shouted back: "Sczcepanski!"

"Yes, sir?"

"Jankowski tells me you're from Warsaw?"

"Yes, sir."

"And that you can you handle the guns'?"

Jósef merely nodded, for fear choked him now, as suddenly as an assassin.

"There are night fighters, in Kraków and Tarnów; they've been busy. We could use another beam gunner, and there's space – as you know." Jósef did know. Most of the Libs had been flying with one waist gunner for a while, it was all they needed, normally. He said nothing. "You're welcome to come along," Dabrowski shouted. "Be something to tell the grandkids, eh?"

For some reason Jankowski found that very funny, and he was still chortling as the others in the crew hauled Jósef and his kit aboard the Bedford, which took off with another lurch, the thick tyres humming on the concrete surface of the apron as it drove to the gear store close to the crew's bomber. He clung to the sun-warmed frame above the truck's deck and the Liberator with the nose art of a flaming and flying sword grew very large as they sped towards it. Flaming and flying … He hated that particular patch of that particular B-24.

***

Brescia. April 1954

The gleaming blue car, bathed in the light that spilled from the opened garage doors, seemed impossibly bright in the murk of the dawn, reminding Ingo of skies far brighter than that which lay upon the city this morning. There was a mist which licked at the rust red roof tiles, and crypt-cold air that gnawed at the bones, but the broad yellow stripe around the nose of the Condor was like a beam of sunlight in the blue, and just looking at this racing car warmed Ingo – it was going to be very hard to walk away. An aroma of bread baking, somewhere close by, mingled with the oily smell of the garage and the whiff of petrol. Carlo stood beside the car, on the street outside the garage. Ingo came from a different direction to the one that Carlo would have been expecting, and he caught him glancing at his watch.

"I need to talk to you," Ingo said.

One of Carlo's eyebrows arched.

"Later," Ingo added, as he vaulted over the low door and into the cockpit; the leather bucket seats were cold from the night but it felt good to be sitting in the Condor again. Too good.

Ingo had not been able to leave without saying goodbye. More to the point, the night before, when he was about to get out of Brescia, he had realised he simply could not go without trying the car out on at least a small part of the Mille Miglia course, even if only for a few hours – and then this life would be over. He had decided as soon as Kroh had left that if Kroh had found him, *they* would find him. And so Ingo had checked out. Immediately. He had then found a room in an apartment on a narrow street, not much more than an alleyway really, off Corso Martiri della Libertà, near the grand-looking Banca San Paolo. The apartment was not so grand, above a small butcher's shop, with a sign in the shop window that offered one room for rent. He had seen the seams of light through the shutters and heard a piano playing, quite badly, and had knocked at the door, which was within the tight street.

The widow, who said she hated the race and was awake because of the noise it created even before it started, had shown him the room. The previous occupant had broken his legs practising out on the course after hitting a truck in his Gordini and was now in hospital, which meant this was a rare thing in Brescia right now, a vacancy. It would do, for one sleepless night. He still had money to pay for it, he had long made a habit of carrying lots of cash. Though once that had gone, he would now have nothing.

"You're late?" Carlo said.

"Yes, best get going then, eh?"

"Where have you been? I waited for you in the lobby, then asked reception to ring your room. They said you've checked out?" He looked worried.

"The hotel was too noisy," Ingo said, as Carlo climbed into the Condor beside him. "Found a quieter place."

Carlo cocked his head. "You told me you could sleep in a battle?"

"That was the younger me, I need quiet now."

"Is there something I need to know, my friend?" Carlo said.

Ingo was as good at lying to Carlo as he had been at lying to Pop. "A woman; her husband's away," he said, and left it at that. Which at least was true; in a way. Carlo responded with a wolfish grin.

"Full?" Ingo asked, sniffing at the fuel on the air while also changing the subject.

Carlo shook his head. "Just three quarters, I want to make sure we're right about this," he said.

They had discussed it the night before. For some reason the Buchanan tyres did not work well when the car was full of fuel; they had discovered this when testing them on the grand prix layout of the Autódromo in Buenos Aires before leaving for Italy. It was to do with the weight over the rear, where the tank was, this levered the front of the car up a little. Because of this it understeered quite badly, the front skidding, wearing out the front tyres, which then made the understeer even worse. But on three quarters of a tank and below the tyres were excellent and wore well. Last night they had come up with a solution. Extra tyre and fuel stops; and not filling the tank at those stops. Carlo had done the sums, they would still have to start with a full tank for the first part of the race, where there was a lot of straight-line running and too much time to lose in stopping, but then they would put in less than a full load at most of the control stops – at Pescara, Rome, Florence and Bologna – and take on fresh tyres, too, making the car ideal for the mountain passes. It would mean they would not need to hold back where it mattered. They would lose time with the stops, but gain more in the long run. It was a quicker way, Carlo's calculations seemed to prove; and so a better way. But now Ingo would not be there to find out if Carlo's sums had been correct.

The Varela team's race 'shop was in a garage on Via 25 Aprille, a little way to the southwest of the Mille Miglia start ramp on Via Rebuffone. Varela had paid its owner a small fortune for him to close his business for a week or so. Many of the teams did this; Ingo had wondered where the people of Brescia had their cars fixed in the lead up to the Mille Miglia. The garage took up the space of two houses, and was flanked and attached to a residential property, where the garage owner lived, and a flower shop that Ingo had never seen open. But then, to get used to their start time in the race they had left Brescia in the dark every time they had set off to cover the route in the Alfa, and they had returned late, too. It was important to know when the sun would be in their eyes during the race – not that there had been much of that. They were starting later, today, but with the mist it made little difference.

The garage was a mustardy yellow and had large blue-painted steel doors, with iron bars over the frosted windows in the upper part of them. There was also a smaller entry set in to one of the large doors. Above the big doors there was a sign, the name of the owner: *Corsetti*, flanked by two adverts for Pirelli. The blue of the doors was not quite as bright as the Condor. There were some old fortifications across the road, overgrown and neglected, with a deep ditch around them. It was the perfect place for a sniper to hide, Ingo realised. And the lit up Condor was the perfect target. Though from what Kroh had said he did not think that was their way; far too obvious a killing, that ... Still ...

"Best get going," Ingo said.

Varela had hired the best Italian mechanics available, to add to the crew who had come over from Argentina and to help man the fuel and tyre stops. One of these, a comfortably corpulent-looking ex-Maserati man called Guido, who always looked as if he had just got up, especially at this time of the morning when he really had, opened the bonnet. Ingo switched the car on, then pushed the starter button as Guido tweaked the linkage to the three Weber carburettors. The roar of the motor seemed to crack the frigid air, then shake it as Guido's fat fingers worked the throttle, the Ferrari 2.7-litre V12 engine spluttering at first, then warming to a ripping music that trumpeted though its open exhaust – people did not sleep well in Brescia in the week leading up to the Mille Miglia, that much had been true enough. Guido gave Ingo the thumbs up, and he then took up the tune on the accelerator pedal, watching the gauges, as oil pressure settled, and temperature creeped up. He waited impatiently; he did not want to stay here long, it was one of the few places where those people Kroh had spoken of might be able to track him down – it would not take too much digging to find out where the Varela team was based.

The gauge nudged towards the engine's optimum operating temperature and Ingo stretched his fingers, flexed them – just as if he was sitting at a piano – and then he gripped the dimpled steering wheel.

A little later and the Condor was slithering through the curve where Via Castellini met Via Venezia, onto the Mille Miglia route, cold tyres on greasy cobbles, Ingo holding the car in a third gear tail slide, the thudding road surface buzzing through his piano fingers, the headlamps slashing at the buildings through the dark dawn, then seeming to startle the chestnut trees that lined the road into a strange hyper-solidness that lasted a second, before they melted in to the gloom behind the car, its passing shown by a brief red taillight glow on the bark that Ingo caught in the wing mirror. Two policemen stood at a junction, hats like admirals; they smiled and waved him on, warmed by the sight of the racing car at the end of a long nightshift. Ingo took the road out of town, on the weather-cracked asphalt now, racing into the widening cones of his headlights.

There were few other cars on the road at this time in the morning, and Ingo savoured the freedom of it. It was good to be on an open road like this, at close to racing speeds, in the Condor. He knew this section of the course well already, but still Carlo went through the hand signals; holding his left hand up close to the steering wheel so that it was just in Ingo's line of sight: fingers to show which gear; a fist to show danger; fingers on an upturned hand to show the severity of a turn. Simple, but it worked. There was a fast section halfway to Verona, mostly straight, and Ingo wound the car up. They did not have a speedometer, as this was a racing car, but Ingo knew that at 7000rpm in fifth it was going close to 155mph; and he reckoned he could get 160 and maybe more out of it at the max of 7200 – it was not just beautiful, the Condor, it was also slippery. The accelerator pedal was jammed to the floor as he tried to squeeze more revs from the machine, so the vibrations from the bodyshell travelled through the pedal and up his leg, tingling through him, and taking him back, to another time: flat out in Poland, on the BMW motorcycle and sidecar. *Faster than a bullet*, he had thought, back then.

Carlo held up his fist; then three fingers; then four fingers on an upturned hand; all in a second or two, and Ingo started to slow the car as the curve came in sight; braking gently for a moment, then easing more pressure on the pedal; a downchange to fourth, two swift pumps of the clutch, between each a blip of the throttle with the side of his right foot, pivoting from the brake, while he was still slowing the car. It was like playing the piano, the action and the music of this, as he went into third with another crisp blip of the accelerator and double

declutch. He turned the car in, a small turn, then almost immediately a larger turn, and felt the weight of the Condor shift, and then the front tyres beginning to bite in to the road. There was a little understeer, but not much, just the right amount; which meant he could lift off, allow the rear to step out, helping tuck the nose in to the turn, then balance the car on the throttle in a four wheel drift as it took its set in the corner. He eased on the gas as it approached the exit, millimetre by millimetre, then more, and more, until he was on full throttle at the end of the turn and the car came out of the corner like a bullet from a gun ...
Faster than a bullet ...

Then Ingo slowed.

The roadway was raised a metre or so here, as if on a causeway, but there was enough of a shoulder to park up, and he pulled the car over, the tyres crunching the gravel at the edge of the road. He switched off and the body of the Condor ticked and pinged in the sudden silence. The land was flat, and green, though one field was ploughed. In the distance, to the north, the mountains beyond Lake Garda were hidden in the grey. The air smelt of dewy ground and hot steel. It was light now, in a porridge-grey way, and Ingo turned off the headlamps.

Carlo spoke first: "Understeer?"

"Just a little. But it works a treat, Carlo; that's the sweet spot all right, and we know it's perfect on lighter loads."

"Tyre pressures?"

"Fine, but they will have to be adjusted through the day, if it gets hotter, colder, or wetter."

Carlo nodded, then sighed, and said: "But this was not what you wanted to talk to me about, was it, my friend?"

Ingo said nothing, just stared ahead, down the road to Verona, where the crusty grey asphalt seemed to merge with the smudgy grey sky at the vanishing point. The car had seemed even better on the open road than it was on the race track or the tight streets of city and park circuits. It was as if it was born for this race; and Ingo felt the same was true of him. He wanted nothing more than to go on driving the route of the Mille Miglia; maybe another hour, maybe another two. But he had made his decision.

Ingo turned to face Carlo, and saw the concern in his eyes.

Just then he picked up the distinctive howl of a racing engine, a V12, coming from the direction of Brescia, a racing car driven hard. Carlo turned in the bucket seat: "Red," he said, as the car came closer until Ingo could see it clearly in the wing mirror, growing ever larger as if someone was pumping air into it. Then it flashed by, the air that it displaced washing over them, the sound changing as it dopplered into the near distance, hurtling east.

"Otero," Carlo said.

Then the sound coming from the Ferrari 375 MM Coupe altered again, its intensity diminishing a little, then dying. There were the sharp throttle blips of downchanges, and there was tyre squeal, too. Otero turned the car, using the gravel verge to unstick the rear and bringing it around on the power, an instant cloud of white smoke like a chalky patch on a horse's grey coat: Hector Otero was not the type to save tyres when he could make a noise. He accelerated back up the road towards the Condor.

Otero skidded to a halt alongside the Condor, the red car now just an inch or so from the blue car, with the Ferrari facing in the other direction, driver's door to driver's door, the window of the closed-top Ferrari now wound down. It was close enough that Ingo could pat him on the shoulder; or knock his boyish grin upside down. The air was flooded with the smell of melted rubber and there was a wobbly number eleven on the road behind the Ferrari. Otero's co-driver was a short man in spectacles and a yellow helmet, clutching a notebook in one hand – and the top edge of the dash in the other; knuckles white, eyes wide.

"Broken down?" Otero said. "You haven't got far, have you?"

"Car's fine," Carlo answered.

"Well, there's the high speed section to come, that should do for it – never thought that engine was up to much, you know, even in a proper car, like Varela's Ferrari."

"Well, it's been abused in its time, that's for sure," Carlo said.

Ingo laughed. The 375 MM was a beauty, though nowhere near as beautiful as the Condor, more voluptuous than svelte, but then it packed four and half litres of engine, a little less than two whole litres up on the Condor's own Ferrari motor. In deference to the team name, Scuderia Verde, it sported a forest green nose band on its headshot-red bodywork, behind its howling-wide radiator grille, in almost the same place where the Condor's nose band was yellow.

Otero turned his attention to Ingo. "Will be tough, taking that tractor through the passes, eh?"

"Can't think of a better car for it," Ingo said.

Otero laughed. "If you say so." With that his grin spread like an oil slick across his face. "Well, see you out there then, Ingo."

Otero revved harshly and dropped the clutch and spun the Ferrari on the throttle again, and Carlo had to wait for the engine noise and tyre screech to fade before he could speak about the quiet hand grenade Otero had just lobbed in to the Condor.

"He knows your name," Carlo said, once the din of the coupe's open exhaust had diminished and the car had become a red smudge in the distance.

"Seems so."

"I guess he must have heard me say it, some time. For that, I'm truly sorry, my friend. I don't know how, when —"

"It doesn't matter, Carlo. Not now, forget it."

It was then that Ingo realised. Realised who would have benefitted most from betraying him. He wondered when Otero had done it, maybe at Buenos Aires, in January? If Ingo was out of the way back then, then there would have been no one to humiliate Otero, to take his seat in the Condor for the Mille Miglia. Then he remembered that Kroh had said they had not acted at once on the information. He had the spite to do it, too. Men like Otero – spoilt children like Otero – cannot bear to be beaten. If he had betrayed him because he simply believed he was a Nazi, hiding from his past, then Ingo would understand. But he knew that was not the reason.

What Ingo had to do was now clear; even through the singing steel of the tinnitus that was swelling inside his skull. But what of *them*? He remembered what Kroh had said; how they made it look like accidents, like gas explosions, or suicides. If that was so, then all he would need to do was keep his head down and make sure they didn't find him, until the race. There would be hundreds of thousands watching the Mille Miglia. During the race he should be protected, as there would be far too many witnesses. He would be safe, hiding in the most dangerous race of them all …

Ingo started the car, revved it. He was not a vengeful man, but there were limits. Besides, it was easy to get back at Otero. You merely needed to beat him.

"But you said you wanted to tell me something?" Carlo said, as the revs dipped and Ingo crisply slotted the gear leaver into first.

"Oh, I was going to ask you to change the pedal set-up, move the brake to the right a whisker. But I think it'll do fine. For the race."

"I'm glad it will do, my friend … For the race."

***

Over the Carpathian Mountains. August 1944

Jósef had been told that fighters should not be a problem until much later in the mission, and even then it was rare; but that had not stopped him searching the vast, dusk sky for them; had not stopped every chip of light becoming a Messerschmitt; every candy floss strand of sun-pinked cloud the wings of a Focke-Wulf, guns blazing. They had gained height as they crossed the Adriatic, and the sun had hung on the horizon, as if time stood still, as they ascended. They had then flown the length of Yugoslavia, the fifth in the strung-out flight of three Halifax bombers and then three Liberators.

It had been dark for a while now, and they were over the Carpathians, he estimated. The Lib' had climbed to its ceiling for this mission, 12,000 feet, which would easily prevent it snagging a peak. But he could see nothing of the mountains from his open window on to the night; nothing except for the dark sky and the double gun that was fixed to the bracket on the lower sill in fact – he manned the guns on the starboard side, Jankowski the port, so that they stood back to back within the fuselage in the middle of the plane. One time, Jósef thought he saw another bomber, but he realised it was the Liberator's moon shadow cast on a cloud and just stopped himself before he reported it over the intercom. It seemed strangely calm, the night outside, even with the constant, deafening roar of the four engines, 4800 horsepower in all and all he could hear apart from the gentle hiss of the oxygen through his mask. Strangely calm even with the vibration of the plane that shook through him, too, despite the many layers of clothing he wore. But Jósef felt far from calm.

As soon as he had climbed aboard the B-24 he had regretted his decision. A little later he had hated himself for it. The target for tonight was not the forests outside Warsaw, as he had believed, as he had understood from the gossip in the mess. The target for tonight was to drop supplies into Warsaw itself. He had not expected that, the same gossip said they were done with such suicide missions. He did not attend the aircrew briefings, that was not his place, and the fuel load was the same as it would be for other drops, and so the plane was in the air by the time Jósef realised that this mission was far from the milk run he had expected.

He had had the oxygen mask on since 7000 feet – it wasn't needed at that altitude but it had been proven the brain was sharper with it and so this was operational practice. The oxygen tasted and smelt strongly of rubber, but he could always smell the aviation fuel over that. You could never get away from that in a bomber. He wished he didn't know that it was the smell of two thousand gallons of highly flammable 100 octane petroleum.

Jósef had tested the twin .303 Brownings soon after they had taken off, all he had learnt on the course he had taken at RAF Penrhos back in February of 1940 had come back to him quickly enough, in a rush of cordite; the glints in the sky that might be Messerschmitts an aide-memoire. Penrhos had been in that time before he had happily, guiltily, allowed them to persuade him that his engineering skills were of more value. He had liked it, in Penrhos. It had been peaceful in Wales, despite the gunfire. One day he might go back, he thought. He remembered that it had also been pretty cold there, during that hard winter, which was good training in itself for air gunners.

He had seen many gunners come home with frostbitten fingers over the past years, and while it was summer, and they would not be flying at the very high altitudes the Americans did, he had taken no chances. Jósef now wore most of the kit of a beam gunner: long sleeve vest; long johns; layers of socks; battledress jacket and trousers; an electrically heated waistcoat which plugged in to the vitals of the B-24 by means of a lead; heated slippers; heated gloves; a padded inner flying suit; a thin outer flying suit; fur-lined flying jacket; flying boots; leather gauntlets; Mae West life jacket; parachute harness; leather flying helmet; and goggles … He was glad of the layers, as the hatch was open for the guns to protrude out of, and the wind howled through it. In the mess the gunners would argue over whether the beam or the tail was the coldest place, it had been an amusing argument to listen in on, with a steaming mug of tea.

Despite all the gear Jósef shivered, but he knew that was not because of the cold. Jankowski clapped him on the shoulder, and he turned. Even with his oxygen mask and goggles on Jósef could see that he was grinning. He managed a stiff smile in return; before realising it was hidden by his own mask and all that Jankowski would see would be the fear in his treacherous eyes. He turned away, stared back in to the darkness. The plane seemed to twist and flex slightly as each of the propellers on the large engines bit at the sky, Jósef fancied, and the fuselage shivered like a living, cold, beast. The engineer in him marvelled that it could shake so much without falling apart, and he felt both pride, then fear – more fear – at the thought. He felt the plane dip, and he realised it was beginning to slowly sink, like a deep sigh, in to the lowlands of Poland.

Flying over Poland, gradually descending. It was five years, almost, since he was last in his home country, but he felt nothing now; for there was room for nothing, for nothing but fear. They had taken a detour to the east to avoid the night fighters known to be operating out of Kraków and Tarnów and as they turned back to line up for their approach he momentarily caught sight of a red ball on the horizon, glowing like a hot coal. He realised what it was just as Dabrowski came on the intercom. His voice was high and light, they all sounded younger over the comms, but also crackling with static, and maybe emotion.

"Warsaw," the skipper said. "It's burning."

No one replied, there was nothing else to say. Jósef thought of Lidka and the son he had never seen. It did not help. Fear was alive in him; fear was a flame. They flew on; to Warsaw. Home. Fire. Death.

When they drew closer to the city he took off his oxygen mask, as they were flying low now. So low; 150 metres. So slow, too, with the flaps down, just 140km/h. Even without a scale of reference it felt like walking pace to him. But he knew it was the only way they would have even a slim chance of dropping the canisters on target. Yet he also knew it made them easy prey for the German guns. He tried to pick out features on the ground, not to think of the fear which clutched his chest, his belly, and shook his limbs. The Liberator banked a little to follow the river and he caught a brief glimpse of below. He spotted the shining silver-lead vein of the Vistula, saw burning buildings reflected in it, but then the plane levelled and all he could see was the night sky, now suffused with the orange of the burning city which Jankowski would have a better view of from the port side – Jósef had no urge to see it, did not want to move, and so he stayed at his post.

The first flak burst was quite far from the plane, a magna-veined inky blotch of smoke, stark against the background of a cloud, that caused him to jump back from his position, letting go of the guns, and then bump into Jankowski, who laughed, silently – nothing could be heard in the plane above the roar of the motors but he could see his mocking laugh now that his mask dangled loose. He could also see that coloured beads of anti-aircraft fire were now strung like deadly jewels, draped in drooping arcs across the dark sky. The next explosion was closer, a tinny scatter of shrapnel against the fuselage, and he briefly sniffed the peppery-iron stink of it.

Then the inside of the Lib' suddenly turned bright silver-white, as if a light switch had been flicked, and he covered his eyes to shade them from the harsh flash. He quickly realised they had been caught in the bright snare of a searchlight; but as they were flying low they were soon through it – at this sped and height the Germans would not need a light anyway, he thought, just as he heard the hit of machine gun rounds against the airframe, even over the engines, an untuneful percussion of metal piecing metal: *ka-plonk, ka-plonk, ka-plonk, ka-plonk*. Long lances of light shafted through the new holes in the aluminium. Jósef made himself small, crouched down, curled up. And he sobbed.

The bombardier called out over the intercom; "Bridge one!" Jósef knew that they were to turn hard left at bridge three, the steel Kierbedzia Bridge, the skipper had reminded the crew of the instructions earlier on. It had been then that he had realised the mission was over Warsaw itself. The bombardier's words were given an ellipsis of *ka-plonks* as the plane was hit by more ground fire, and then there was a larger hit, shrapnel clanging against the rear of the fuselage, and the Liberator seemed to swivel, then drop abruptly for a few metres, before recovering a wobbling poise. Then a high scream came over the intercom.

"I've been hit!" It was Zajonc, the rear gunner, Jósef recognised his voice.

"How bad?" Dabrowski responded.

"Bad … I can't operate the turret …"

"Bridge two!" the bombardier called out.

"Sczcepanski, take his place, we will need a rear gunner when we get out the other side."

"Not me; Jankowski!" Jósef almost screamed it.

"He's too tall for the turret; you do it!"

But Jósef could not move, he was frozen in a foetal position on the shuddering deck of the bomber, it was as if all the fear he felt within him – like electricity and bubbling lava – had suddenly solidified, like concrete. He looked at Jankowski, and the scorn in his eyes. But he did not care about that now. He wanted to live.

Jankowski kicked him, hard, then lifted him and shoved him towards the rear of the plane, so that Jósef stumbled, just as a bullet whipped through the fuselage, striking sparks that spat hot against his cheek. There was a sudden burst of steaming red liquid across the floor; hydraulic fluid, the tiny calm engineer that lived in a small cave in his mind instantly realised.

Jósef made his way along the very narrow catwalk that ran to the tail of the plane. He had disconnected the jack-plug of his intercom so did not hear the bombardier call out 'bridge three', but knew they were there when the plane turned. The Liberator handled like a whale, and Jósef had to cling to the ammunition rail that led to the turret while the plane banked; a hail of smaller bullets now hitting it. Zajonc had crawled out of the tiny space of the turret and was lying in a bleeding heap to the right of the catwalk, in a ball in the curve of the fuselage, draped over the ribs of the airframe. He was covered in blood, like a freshly skinned rabbit. But Zajonc said nothing, just nodded towards the tight entry to the turret, the steel flaps of its doors both wide open.

Jósef had sat in the rear turret before. But not when the plane was flying. Dabrowski was right, it was not the place for a tall man. He was not an especially small man, but Jankowski was much bigger; and he hated him for that. He slid feet-first in to the little space, which contained the Perspex-covered revolving gun position, reaching back to close the heavy steel doors, which were there to stop cannon shells ripping through the length of the fuselage, once they had ripped through the rear gunner.

Once in he had the best – or worst – view in the plane; though it was filtered through a film of Zajonc's blood that made the Perspex seem like stained glass. There were also crown-edged holes in the steel to his left, where the rounds that had hit him had entered the turret. The guns pointed high either side of him, and he felt for the trigger control, assuming they were armed, for a tail gunner like Zajonc is always ready. Warsaw burned beneath him. He was sweating heavily, as he still wore much of the altitude gear, and he would have sworn that he could also feel the heat of the inferno beneath him. Some of the flames seemed to reach out for him, as they flew over the Old Town, like a drowning man's fingers grasping for a lifeboat. He recognised the shape of the Rynek Starego Miasta, fringed with gleaming red roofs, but mostly he saw the fires.

Then there were the parachutes from the plane, mushrooming briefly before falling – some into flames, some into streets – and he felt the Lib' lift slightly as it lost its load. He knew this sort of thing could only be so precise, and they seemed hopelessly spaced out as he watched them fall. He wondered how much of it would land with the AK, how much with the Germans. But he did not care. Survival was his only concern. He tried to make himself small; but he was already squashed in like an egg in its shell. He felt just as vulnerable, too.

The flashing pearl strings of white tracer criss-crossed the sky behind him, one pulsing by the turret, less than a metre away, a lance of fire like a lightning bolt thrown by an angry god. A searchlight found him, and he squeezed his eyes tight shut in the blinding glare and covered his goggles with a thick gauntlet, but then it was gone, slashing across the sky to latch on to another plane, crippled and smoking, climbing and slowing, he now saw on opening his eyes; the last of their flight perhaps, or one of the South African B-24s. The bright sword of the searchlight beam seemed to stun the plane into stillness, so that it was as if it floated on its tail at an acute angle, like a balloon rather an aeroplane, then an instant later it writhed in the cone of white light, but could not escape it. He saw bullets and shells strike it in sparks, and flames suddenly burst from its outer port engine. Jósef looked away.

Down below, in the firelight, he spotted a German tank, stopped in the centre of a street. He thought of depressing the guns and firing a burst at it, to hit back, even if it was useless. He wanted to be able to say he had shot at the Nazis. Yet by the time he thought this it was gone, far behind him, and he suddenly realised the Lib' was speeding up, Dabrowski putting the flaps down and the plane on to full power.

Another big hit, on the port wing, he thought. He plugged in his intercom, but there was nothing, and he could not get his throat mic to work. They were beyond the burning part of the city now – maybe that had been just seconds, but it had felt like hours. Yet the streets felt closer, somehow. He could see individuals down there, German soldiers, bright flashes from muzzles. He thought he could smell the city burning, then he realised, with a rush of panic, that it was the Liberator, and the sky to his right was blotted with swirling, thick black smoke swimming with bright chips of fire. He sensed and heard the change in the notes of the engines, one of the four had stopped, and the plane seemed to twitch to the unequal torque across its wingspan.

The Liberator lost what little height it had; slowly, steadily, twitching to the left and then to the right as Dabrowski made corrections. They were above the outskirts of the city now, sparsely spaced dark-roofed buildings giving way to trees and fields. They were so low, maybe just fifty metres, that his view of Warsaw itself was gone, but he could see the tops of trees bowing to the wind of the plane's burning passage, and he could see the bright slash of the fire in the air behind them.

Jósef realised he was gripping the turret control column tightly, but he could not relax his hold. He had never been told what to do in a crash landing. He had seen some, too many, and he knew that they often ended in flames and he supposed, with another flash of panic, that was even more likely with half a load of fuel still onboard. He knew it was too low to bail out; had been for a while. He also knew that the hydraulics were shot to hell, had seen the plane's blood spill from the hoses, and that there was not the time to lower the undercarriage manually now.

Quite suddenly they seemed to be hardly three metres above the ground. A field of quite long grass scuffing behind him at what seemed to be an impossible speed. The image of Wysocki burning came to mind, as it often did in his nightmares. He had thought he had known fear, but this was something more. It screamed within him, and yet he knew he could not utter a sound; it clamoured for action, for escape, and yet he knew he could not move. So he sat there, in the turret at the tail of the Liberator, as the huge aeroplane landed, wheels up, in a field some kilometres west of Warsaw. He tried to close his eyes again, but fear held him tight, and he could not even do this one simple, cowardly thing.

Brush of grass against the underside; a whisper as the earth says to the great steel bird: can you trust me? But it ignores it, settles on to its belly with a crunch and screech, tearing at the ground, so that Jósef could see chunks of dark soil thrown like spinning footballs behind the plane as it flattened a wide furrow in the long grass. The turret, like an eye in a socket, shook violently – his own eyes did the same – and the guns clattered as if they were firing.

Then a huge bang. He is lifted high as the tail kicks up, his view just the night sky once more; he hears the squeal of deforming metal and feels the plane twist to the left. He seems to hang in the air for an age, on his back looking up into the darkness, as if the Lib' is balanced on its nose, but then it drops and hits the earth like Californian timber, shaking the airframe, shaking the ground, the impact of the hit jarring his spine like a train crash.

There was dust. There was smoke. Then Jósef heard the unmistakable roar of the flames, and felt the heat behind him, radiating through the steel doors. He turned and tried them, but they were hot to touch, even through his gloves, and it was clear there was fire beyond them now. He tried the turret control column, in the hope of turning it through ninety degrees, so that the entry hatch would be at an angle to the fuselage, a clear way out. But the mechanism was not working. He could not move it manually either, as the fuselage had buckled in the crash, the tail now dipping to touch the ground, which had, he now saw, jammed the turret. Jósef suddenly knew the awful truth.

He was trapped. Trapped in a burning plane.

***

Brescia. April 1954

Dai Twice had once taken Joe to a rugby match, up at the club on North Road. Dai had not been comfortable, and Joe had wondered why he had done it; maybe Mrs Davies had put him up to it? He knew she felt sorry for him. Joe had not enjoyed the experience. The sport was fine, it was the people staring he could not stand, or rather trying so damned hard not to stare. That was always the worst. This reminded him of that now, the same old not-staring – but also the scrum. Only this time he was a part of it.

He had not thought so many people would turn up simply to watch the cars go through their technical inspection, but the enthusiasm for all things to do with this race was fanatical. They were being scrutineered in the Piazza Della Vittoria. The rain had stopped, but the sun was still in a sulk, hiding behind the heavy curtains of the clouds. The only brightness came from the racing cars, in their fresh coats of paint, and the yellow and red Pirelli banners that hung from the wet marble of the walls, or the red arrow signs that were the logo of this race and were to be seen everywhere in Brescia.

He could not remember the last time he had been in such close-proximity to people, other than doctors and those nurses with their innocent, supposedly soothing, cream-applying tortures; the painful bliss of it. It was hard to compete with the others in the crowd for what damp air there was. What he could suck in – like a man on a balcony drinking porridge through a very long straw – tasted of the exhaust fumes of the racing cars above all else, but it was as thin as light, and his lungs burnt as brightly as his skin.

As the people pressed against him they squeezed him like an accordion, only the tune that came from the hole in his burnt face sounded like tearing sandpaper. Joe suddenly thought that if he should pass out now then he would not fall, the crush of bodies would hold him upright. And he would die standing up. A girl, smelling of cheap perfume, garlic and cigarettes looked back at him, annoyed at being jostled by the acne-strafed youth to his right. She started to give Joe her Medusa stare as she turned, thinking he was to blame for the jostle, but it melted into shock as she saw him, and she turned back to look at the cars, her shoulders stiffening.

Maybe she would think him an injured racing driver, with burns likes these? But he doubted that even a toasted racer would smell like a dying man who had spent three of the last four days and nights living on trains, and last night sleeping out of the rain in a cold corner of the Loggia, after arriving far too late to find a room.

Just then, through heads that bobbed lightly like dark dandelions, he caught sight of the Condor, being pushed through the crowd and into the fenced off space where the scrutineers awaited with their white coats and clipboards; in front of the colonnaded walkway behind the Hotel Vittoria. The racing car was far more beautiful in the shining steel than it had looked in the black and white picture in the magazine he had seen in Doctor Howell's waiting room. It had its Mille Miglia number painted on its side in white, 532, so there was no doubt it was the right car. The driver was at the wheel, but from this angle he could not see his face. He was bareheaded, his hair slicked back with brilliantine. He started to turn, to answer a shout from the crowd, something in Italian. Joe could not afford to hold a breath, but he did, and his heart almost stopped in that moment when the driver faced him …

… There was a moustache and a broad buccaneer smile. This was clearly not the man he had come all this way for.

He sighed, a painful thing for him, and the crowd seemed to crush him tighter. He wondered why Ingo Six was not here, at scrutineering. Hoped that he had not made this journey, his last journey, for nothing.

***

West of Warsaw. August 1944

The glare of the bright light forced him to close his eyes tight shut. The air was soaked with the sulphurous smell of red-hot metals. He could hear shouting above the beat of the flames and the hiss and splutter of burning aluminium. The shouting was from outside, was in Polish: "Sczcepanski, take out the truck, aim at the searchlight!"

He understood the words, and yet they meant nothing to him. He was dead. He would be burnt to death. He had known it would end this way, and he had been an idiot to come …

"Leave him, he's done for!" That was Jankowski's voice.

"He's alive! Look, he's trembling." The next sound was a loud crunch, and chunks of Perspex hit his face. The light that was trained on him was strong and even with his eyes shut everything was pinky-orange. He could hear the engine of a truck, and the wheeze of its suspension as it bumped along the uneven field. There was another crunch, as he began to feel the scorch of the fire behind the steel doors. The light went out. He opened his eyes again, and saw

322

Dabrowski, one of the escape axes that were attached to the inside of the fuselage in his hands. Jankowski stood beside him, it was him who said: "Quick, their searchlight has failed, it's our chance; we can escape into the darkness!" There were more shouts, further away, in German.

Just then bright green tracer unzipped the sky, and there was the metallic burr of a machine gun. At the very same moment the intensity of the heat increased, singeing his neck painfully, and the panic started to grip him again. But now Dabrowski was pulling him clear of the shattered turret, the axe thrown on the ground.

"Leave him!" shouted Jankowski again, as the machine gun opened up once more, slashing at the long grass to the right of the Liberator, its aim obviously spoilt by the truck's jolting progress over the rough ground. Jósef tumbled out and fell on the floor, quickly rolling to his feet and running in to the night after the other crew members. The Liberator was almost completely in flames now, and he turned to see the place he had been sitting swallowed by the inferno, and beyond that the shrouded headlamps of the truck, pissy yellow gashes of light, bouncing over the rough ground.

The clatter of the truck grew closer, and Jósef ran. The light from the fire lit the way, and he could see the other crew members clearly, his tall inferno-thrown shadow reaching for them, racing them. He was dimly aware of the Lib's machine gun belts igniting, a crackle of small explosions. He ran fast, not knowing what else to do, and soon he was level with the others; he had never suspected he could run so quickly. By now they were approaching the edge of a wood and the gun on the truck had ceased firing. The wood meant safety, he knew that, something deep within him told him so, and he ran so hard he felt his lungs would burst. Then he was in the trees, welcoming the painful rip of branches against his face. It was once that he was in the shelter of the wood that he suddenly realised he had escaped the fire with nothing worse than a small burn on his neck. A miracle ...

Relief was already flowing through him when another machine gun opened up. Bright flashes of white suddenly appeared on some of the trees, there was a cry of pain from someone, and then Jósef was kicked in the behind, as if a horse had lashed out at him, catching him in the lower part of the arse, on his right buttock, the knock of it instantly turning from hit to heat, like a rivet through plate. It floored him, and as the fungi-tasting mulchy earth filled his mouth and nose, he knew he had been shot.

*

Ochota, Warsaw. August 1944

It smelt of what it was. A river of shit. But this was the only way to reach Ochota now. Lidka was on her knees, which were sunk in to the slimy, silty muck that thickly coated the smooth, curved floor of the sewer. She held a stout stick in front of her, which she used for support and to help pull herself along in painstaking little slides, the only way to make progress here. The tunnel was less than a metre high at this point, and the level of effluent was over halfway up, so that her face was close to the filthy liquid. She gagged, but there was nothing left to vomit. She carried her pack on her chest, strapped tightly so that it squashed her breasts, and yet still her back scraped against the slippery, lichen-coated bricks of the oval vaulted sewer, while her knees slipped in the shitty sludge.

She had a Daimon flashlight, fastened by its steel clip to the collar of her overalls. She'd taken it off a dead German. The AK was getting most of its equipment that way, it was more reliable than those few brave but mostly ineffective Allied airdrops. The yellow light the torch emitted seemed to slide over the greasy bricks and the dark water, everything seemed to slide in this evil place. Here the flow was slow. Earlier, near the place she had entered the sewer in the Old Town, the effluent had run fast, the current strong enough to carry pieces of debris and other things, including an arm in a field grey sleeve today. She had often feared she might be swept away there.

Her face was hardly a finger's length from the slow dark flow now, so Lidka saw its surface shake an instant before she heard the noise. She stopped. She could feel the vibrations in her body. The noise was metallic. Tank tracks, she realised, and soon the machine passed some metres above her head: loudly clattering and squealing, the noise interspersed with the sharp gunshot-like sounds of cobbles cracking. A piece of faecal matter shook on the vibrating surface of the effluent, close to her mouth, as she tried not to think about whether the sewer had been built to withstand 45-tonne tanks.

The rumble diminished and she moved on, trying not to hit the bricks with her stick; because the Germans knew the AK used the sewers, and some would stand at drains or manholes, ready to toss in grenades if the slightest sound was heard. She had found two corpses, floating face down in the river of shit, already this day. She sometimes tried to picture Ingo standing above a drain with a stick grenade, listening out for Poles in the sewers. But she couldn't. Or perhaps a part of her wouldn't? That, she did not know for sure.

Lidka knew the Warsaw sewer system quite well now – all the messengers did, it was how they passed between the various areas of the city still held by the AK – but she was not so familiar with this part of it. She had counted the junctions memorised from the map of the underground passages, but she was not completely confident she had taken the right path. It had been a long way, underground, sometimes through water, sometimes just shitty sludge. She had delivered her message to the AK HQ in Śródmieście, the city centre outside of the Old Town, and only then had she decided to carry on, walking west above ground first in the AK held areas before taking to the sewer again. She had been in the sewers for five more hours since then, sometimes able to walk, but also sometimes having to make progress like this, on her knees, the sewage close to her face. Rats squeaked and pattered somewhere ahead, which might mean a dry shelf, somewhere to rest. She had learnt to trust rats since they had started to use the sewers. But she would also have to trust to luck. It was daytime up above, sunny some said – somewhere beyond the smoke – and she knew that when she lifted the manhole cover she might find herself in a street full of RONA soldiers. Worse than rats, RONA, worse than any creature known to man. Some said worse than Dirlewanger's lot, and for those that believed the stories coming out of Wola and Ochota – and many did not, could not – that was a grim debate to have over an acorn coffee.

There were some in the AK who were regular army and worked as intelligence officers, and they knew a little of their enemy. Part of Lidka's important work – work she was shirking now – was to take their messages through the sewers. One of these men had told her of RONA. They were Russians, but SS, he had said. They were commanded by a man named Bronislav Kaminski. They had joined the Germans when the war was going well for the Nazis, killed a lot of partisans and even more innocent civilians, and now they were doomed. They knew the Soviets would execute them. They had nothing to lose, for they had lost everything; all it was to be human. They lived for drink, for rape, and for murder. Lidka did not tell the officer she had a son in Ochota. She did not tell him that she hoped to God she *still* had a son in Ochota.

RONA had hit Ochota like a hurricane. They had killed and raped their way across the district and burnt everything in their path. She had spoken to a nurse who had survived their attack on the Marie Curie hospital, the Radium Institute. They had shot their way in, drank the medical alcohol and the ether, and then raped the nurses and the patients – even women with terminal cancer – before killing them. And these men had probably also murdered their way, burnt their way, along Mochnackiego. She did not know if Freddy had survived, and she could only pray – though God had gone up in smoke with the Ghetto a year ago, and it was a prayer of habit – pray that they were all okay, that the hiding place had proved secure; that Sarah had not tried to be brave, not tried to fight them. That was one of her biggest fears.

She pulled herself through into a wider, higher part of the sewer, where she was able to stand upright again, feeling the little nudges of the larger pieces of sewage against her hands and trying not to think of it, as she tried not to think of other things; like Ingo, like Freddy lying dead. The yellow cone of light from the flashlight fell on a vertical row of rusty climbing irons, and she thought she might have finally arrived at the catchment chamber she was looking for. When she reached the row of rails she climbed the few rungs until her hair brushed against the bottom of the iron cover. She stayed still, for long minutes, and listened for noises in the street, even though she was desperate to breathe cleaner air. She could hear nothing.

The manhole cover was circular and heavy, and it took all of Lidka's strength to shift it while she wedged herself against the sides of the access shaft. She slid it to one side, the rumbling noise as it scraped across the cobbles sounded very loud to her, like steely thunder. But she knew she could not hesitate, and as she lifted her head in to the street she looked around, her eyes level with the cracked and scorched stones, squinting through the harsh light after so many hours underground. When she had turned through ninety degrees her eyes met those of a young girl five or so metres away, eyes prised open in fear and surprise. She was as still as iron, and her skin had already begun to bloat and corrupt. There was no blood, dry or otherwise, just a strange dent in her forehead, like a little crater. Lidka stared at the dead girl, stared for too long. Then she focused on the job at hand, heaved herself out of the manhole, replaced the cover, which wobbled into its hole with a *wocka-wocka-clang*, and ran to the cover of a burnt-out house, its open door framed with charcoal. She ducked inside then searched the street from one of the glassless windows to make sure no-one had seen her. She breathed deeply now, for the air here seemed sweet after the sewer; although it dripped with the rotten apple and bad meat smell of the decaying dead. But then that was a smell she had grown used to.

Lidka tried to figure out where she was. She had hoped to come out on Filtrowa, and she had, but too soon, just before Park Wielkopolski. She realised she had not gone far enough along, she was on the junction with Orzechowska, with its fine villas, most looking a little less than fine now. She could hear gunfire, both near and far, and the sound of the artillery dropping shells on the Old Town.

In normal times it would not take her long to walk from here to Mochnackiego, but normal times had been a dream. She thought about returning to the sewer, but that was an even slower route, and she was already neglecting her duties – as the soldier she would never be, if not as a mother. Also, the fear was alive in her, like a wriggling prisoner inside her skin: fear for her son, fear for herself. She shifted her pack on to her back and moved on, keeping in the shadows as much as she could. At the next junction she heard voices and ducked behind a low wall pockmarked with bullet holes that marked the boundary for a once-smart pastel yellow villa which had now been holed by German guns. She unhitched her backpack and sank close to the ground, brick dust quietly crunching beneath her body. The wall supported twisted railings and had a cross-shaped hole in it where bricks had been blown away. Through this she could watch the men as they came around the corner and then approached her hiding place, walking in the centre of the street.

They were clearly Russians, she could hear them; she knew a little of the language. They wore a sort of German uniform, a mixture of many types plus some civilian clothing, and they were very scruffy, all unshaven. One of them had a length of string rather than a leather strap for his rifle. They also wore white armbands with a black cross on a red and white shield; and the letters *POHA* above it, which she quickly translated as RONA. They were clearly drunk, staggering and laughing. She ducked down and allowed them to pass by, just metres from her. They stank of stale sweat and alcohol. She looked through the gap in the wall once they had passed. One turned and fired a Luger at one of the few unbroken windows in the house behind her, and Lidka jumped at the sound if it. He missed the window, and the others laughed. He fired again, this time the glass broke with a crack. They moved on. Lidka's heart bounced within her chest.

She took an hour to get to the house, through the shot-withered park, and then using the side streets and crossing gardens, making short, sharp runs when she needed to cover clear ground. All of the houses looked uninhabited, some had been burnt; most seemed to have had their windows broken, just a handful had obviously been fought over, died for. She approached the house that had become her home from the rear, crossing the courtyard quickly, her boot falls on the iron hard cobbles tapping too loudly in the echoing space. She saw immediately that the door-like gate was no longer in the high garden wall, it lay flat on the gravel path behind it, while there were yellow wounds of splintered wood in the gate post. Her fear was strung like a violin bow within her, she had thought it could not get tauter, yet it tightened at this sight. She walked along the door then scrunched across the gravel path to the back of the house.

There was no sign of life. The curtains were closed and she could not see into the kitchen, but the windows were not broken and the house looked untouched, from here. For a moment the thinnest filament of hope burnt bright within her. But then it was extinguished with a sudden thought – what if the Germans, or RONA, had taken over the house? She stopped dead. Then she shook the notion away – she had to know if Freddy was safe. Lidka tried the doorknob, it was locked. That, she thought, might be a good sign. She took her keys out of the pocket of her overalls and unlocked the door.

The door opened and she walked inside. It was dark, smelt musty in the kitchen. She reached for the switch on her flashlight.

There was a loud shuddering thump, the heavy door slamming behind her, and even in the near darkness the blade shone silver as it shaved close to her cheek and cleaved the stale air with a sharp *swoosh*.

***

South of Brescia. April 1954

Yitzhak drove the tiny off-white car just like an Italian would drive it. He puffed at a Nazionali, too, and the pungent smoke filled the tight compartment. Getting into character was as easy as putting on a pair of slippers, for Yitzhak. Sarah wondered if he would make an actor, when he finally got bored of killing. But people like Yitzhak never get bored of killing. Driving the little Iso Isetta just like an Italian meant driving it as fast as it would go. Which was not so very fast. But it still made a noise; enough that she had to almost shout to be heard over the rasping engine and the rattle of the chassis as it bounced down the rutted farm track.

"Where are we going?"
"Somewhere quiet."
"Why?"

"So I can make a noise," Yitzhak said, glancing at her knee, bare where the vibrating car body had rucked up the hem of her skirt. She did not tug it straight, and he did not tug his grin straight, either. She would sleep with him; soon. She had decided. Maybe before it was done, maybe after. That was still a decision she would have to make, but it would probably be before. She did not know what she would feel like later. But she had had a preview, when Kroh had been killed last year, when she had believed she had had her revenge. She had felt empty, then. And that had scared her.

They had driven down the road towards Cremona, which was bracketed by flat land; a patchwork sea of green and brown with little islands of boxy farmhouses, biscuit coloured with red roofs, and trees dotted across it like pins on a war map. The sky was blotched with grey cloud. The rain had stopped falling five minutes ago, just before they had turned off the main road.

The track took them between wire fences that dripped raindrops towards a farm building. The car bucked up over a bump, the rear tyres – very close together so the egg-shaped Isetta looked like a three-wheeler – bouncing over the crown of the road, buzzing against the stony track as they went light. A front wheel dropped in to a rain-filled pothole and *café au lait*-coloured water splashed against the bubble windscreen. Sarah felt as if she was inside a tin can which was being kicked down the street.

They finally arrived at a wide farmyard, dappled with puddles, which was in front of the half-derelict brick building, and Yitzhak brought the Isetta to a skidding halt – fluent Italian. He switched off the engine and it fluttered to a stop.

"So, now we can talk, yes?" she said.

"He's checked out of his hotel," Yitzhak said, as he pushed open the door, which was also the entire front of the car, hinged on one side. The steering wheel and column moved outwards with it.

"Gone?" She felt the disappointment solid within her; as though her soul had turned to cold, grey stone.

Yitzhak motioned for her to get out, so that he could slide across and do the same. She did so. The muddy ground was slippery under her shoes. He stepped out, too, stretched, and made a point of deeply breathing in the country air – even though it smelt of nothing but the steaming heap of manure in the corner of the farmyard.

"Not gone. He's still in Brescia," he said.

"Where?"

"I don't know."

"He's on to us," Sarah said.

"Might be, but if he's going to drive the race …" Yitzhak said, as he reached back in to the car and over the back of the seat to the wide parcel shelf, taking a sack that bulged angularly as it swung heavy in his hands.

"You think he will; drive the race?"

"He's still practising, in the blue car," Yitzhak said. "I've seen him. Though he's taking precautions, being picked up from different locations. Never the garage, now. But why practise, why learn the route, if you are not going to race?"

"I hope you're right," Sarah said, and a crow squawked.

"I am right."

"We should strike soon, we must find out where he is staying, and then finish this."

"No, we will wait," Yitzhak said. And with that he reached in to the sack.

***

Ochota, Warsaw. August 1944

Lidka was still shaking. The blade had come so very close, and she kept touching the part of her cheek where she had felt the air from the knife's swooshing swipe, as if it had actually scarred her. Sarah sat on the other side of the kitchen table, as calm as a cup of water, though her nostrils twitched a little because Lidka smelt strongly of the sewer. It did not seem to Lidka that Sarah had realised how close she had come to cutting her with the large kitchen knife she still held. Lidka was shaking from the shock of that. She was also shaking with relief. Freddy was safe.

He sat on Lidka's lap, wriggling and chuckling. He had eaten a few triangles of the captured, quite bitter, Wehrmacht-issue Scho-ka-kola chocolate and some of the bread she had brought with her, wrapped up very tight in paper then canvas, which was then stuffed within a rubber bag that was inside her pack, to protect it in the sewer. He had had more than his share and she felt a little guilty about that. But not too guilty. There was very little room for more self-reproach within her; it already played an iron-taut tug of war, between a duty born of guilt itself, and the more natural call of her child. A literal tug of war.

Sarah had taken the rest of the bread and the chocolate, which she would distribute to the others later. Sol Vogler, his wife and Mrs Paczkowska never left the basement hideaway now, Sarah had told Lidka, with just a little scorn in her voice. She had also explained how the RONA had gone through the house like locusts, coming in through the rear gate and then the side door – the heavy back door proved too sturdy – while they listened in silence from the hidden space below. They had broken most things, taken some. But they had not lingered in the library as there was nothing to interest them there; Feliks Paczkowski had been right about that. They had been lucky they had not burnt that room and the house with it, Lidka thought, thinking back on all she had seen since the uprising had started – she looked at her son's smiling face and shuddered when she realised just how fortunate they had been.

They still had some tinned food, though Sarah had said there was little of it left. They also had water, as the Germans had no reason to turn off the supply in this part of the city. Sarah had opened the curtains a little, so there was some light, on which motes hung like a tantalising parachute drop. Leon stood guard at that rear window, looking out at the wall with its flattened door and the courtyard beyond, constantly fidgeting, coughing often. There was a distant background noise of the continuing battle. It had become so familiar it was as inconsequential as the clatter of a tram out on Filtrowa had once been.

"Will we go back with you, to the Old Town?" Sarah said.

"It's safer here, believe me," Lidka said, and tousled Freddy's hair. One of the first things he had said on seeing her was 'you stink!' But that hadn't stopped him hugging her and holding her tight.

"I'm sick of hiding," Sarah said, raising her voice now so that Leon turned and shushed her, holding a finger to his lips.

Earlier, Sarah had heard Lidka outside, thought the worst, as she was certainly not expecting visitors. A millimetre more and she would have sliced into Lidka's cheek. Yet Sarah had still not even mentioned that.

"Have you stayed in the house, Sarah?" Lidka asked, but she thought she knew the answer to that.

"Mostly, but sometimes I have searched for extra food," Sarah said, cocking her head slightly and studying her reflection in the shining blade of the kitchen knife.

"That's a stupid risk."

"The Old Town, why not?" Sarah ignored the rebuke.

"I need you to look after Freddy."

"We can bring him, and the others."

"Through the sewers?" Now Lidka had raised her voice, too, and Leon shot her a sharp look. He seemed to have changed in these past two weeks, and now he had even more of the manner of a startled deer about him. She lowered her voice, and calmly explained. "It's not just the smell, Sarah. They are waiting, with grenades, at many of the drains. And what about when you get there?"

"I can help, like you."

"You don't understand. You have escaped capture here; that cannot be guaranteed in the Old Town.

"But we are winning, aren't we?" Leon said, turning to face Lidka so she could see the fear in his eyes. He coughed again; he seemed ill.

"We are still holding," Lidka said. "So there is a chance; if the Russians …" she trailed off. Like many now she wondered if the Soviets would ever come. Some even believed they had deliberately left the AK, and the people of Warsaw, to their fate. It had been a long time since a Russian plane had been seen over the city.

"They will come, yes?" Leon said, then coughed four times.

"Yes, they are coming; they must come. But until they arrive it is safer here."

"If it's safer here, why don't you stay – with your son?" Sarah said.

Lidka shook her head. "I know the sewers well; I wish I didn't," she wrinkled her nose, tried a smile. "But I do, as I know other ways to carry messages through this city, and so I'm needed."

"I don't mind the smell, and I could learn."

"Freddy is safer here and your family is safer here. It's as you say, they have come through, taken what they wanted, destroyed houses, but not this one. You must sit still, and wait. Remember, you're Jews, there will be no mercy for you."

"I have seen no mercy for anyone, Jews and Poles are all alike, now" Sarah said.

Lidka nodded, slowly, then added: "Please, a little more patience, that's all.'

"Always waiting," Sarah said.

"I must go now," Lidka said. She knew she had to leave fast, or she would never go, and she kissed Freddy on the forehead, before saying: "I will bring more food when I can, try to stay in the hiding place. Please Sarah."

"More chocolate?" Freddy said.

"Yes, more chocolate, Freddy."

"Revenge is sweeter than chocolate," Sarah said.

"Yes, and after this you will not be the only one who believes that, Sarah. That I promise you. The time for revenge – for the Ghetto, for Wola, for Ochota – the time for revenge will come."

Sarah nodded, sharply, then said: "Andrzej?"

"He's alive, and well," Lidka said. "Have you a message, for him?"

Sarah shrugged, and once again stared at the blade of the knife, glinting in the dull light. Then said: "Andrzej never really cared about what I said or thought. There was always someone else. But you know that."

Lidka sighed. "It's not what you think, Sarah. When this is over, I will explain it all, I promise."

"You are making a lot of promises – are you sure you will be able to keep them all?"

"I have kept tougher promises than that."

Sarah glanced at the wedding ring on Lidka's finger, but that had not been what Lidka had meant. She nodded, anyway, and then put the now empty canvas pack on her back and slipped through the back door, closing it behind her, not trusting herself to look one last time at Freddy or to kiss him again. She heard him start to cry, and Sarah soothing him. It almost made her turn back, but she knew she could not stay, she had important work to do for the AK. There were few who knew the sewers quite like she did now, Andrzej had told her that himself. They would also need more food soon, and who else would bring it here, if not her? Yet she could not bear the guilt, as heavy as a panzer, as sharp as a bayonet, as she crunched along the gravel path, clattered over the fallen wooden gate, and then ran out into the courtyard.

*

The southern edge of the Old Town, Warsaw. August 1944

"Oh, so you're following fashion, are you?" Pop said. "I've seen a lot of those recently. Most with holes in them."

Ingo was wearing a camouflaged Waffen SS jacket over his Panzerwaffe uniform; in the pockets of which he had stuffed a ribbon and an armband, all taken from a corpse. They were in the ruins of the Royal Castle, ruined pretty well in '39, ruined a little more thoroughly in more recent times. The room might once have had a fine chandelier, but now it didn't even have a ceiling. Pop was sat on the floor alongside a huge glassless window that was shaped like a wide *u*, because the floor above was no longer a floor. Much of upstairs had been piled in the corners of this large room in jagged ski slopes of debris.

Ingo heard the roar of an engine and looked up to see a Stuka, flying low over the Old Town like a flitting shadow. The role of the Junkers Ju 87s had changed at Kursk, becoming tank busters with cannons fitted under their creased wings, but they were still as good at wrecking towns as they had been when they were used solely as dive bombers earlier in the war; some were now used in the earlier role here, too. The Stukas had feasted on the Old Town and the area around it, as had Heinkel bombers and strafing Messerschmitts. And there was nothing to stop them. Once again, Ingo wondered what had happened to the Yaks, as Soviet fighters were nowhere to be seen.

The gunfire never really stopped here now; German artillery and MG 42s mostly, and they could now also hear tanks outside, crunching the cobbles, their motors revving impatiently, a clear sign of a nervous driver. Sunshine had gone for a crap, and probably also to find vodka, both a call of nature for Dirlewanger's men. Ingo had just pulled the green-brown camouflage Waffen SS jacket on. He risked a look out of the space where the window had been, hoping the tanks might be from the 19th, but he instantly saw they were Hetzer Jagdpanzer 38s, low-profile tank destroyers, sleekly ugly turretless self-propelled 75mm guns that looked a little like flattened panzers – and they were not in the camouflage of the 19th. He guessed Dirlewanger had been given some for support, and they were now getting in position. It would soon be time to attack, again. Black smoke boiled over the Old Town and the air crackled and smelt of burnt iron. Every breath Ingo took tasted of ash.

Seeing the Hetzers reminded Ingo: "Any news from our lot?"

"I've tried again, but I think that maybe they've been moved out of Warsaw; either way there's been no reply," Pop said, with an air of resignation. "Hurts, not to be missed, eh?"

Ingo nodded, deep down he had become resigned to this. If the 19th had wanted them back, they would have heard something by now; Pop had sent enough messages through his Dirlewanger signals chum, and had also spent enough of his dwindling stock of Atikah cigarettes, and some cash, to persuade him to pass them on, he had told Ingo. But he still held out hope that they might bump into some tanks from their outfit, somewhere, sometime, in this mess of a city. He would still prefer to bump into Lidka first, though – preferably before anyone in the Dirlewanger Brigade did.

Ingo stepped back from the windowless window, he had tempted a sniper for too long. Kroh had told him that the Hetzer was a favourite of Hitler. He had also told him, once again and with some glee, that the Führer wanted Warsaw destroyed. Completely levelled, then turned into a lake. Which was why some of Hitler's special toys had arrived lately, not just Hetzers, but stuff that had only one use: annihilation.

They had seen a Grisly Bear – a Sturm Panzer IV – earlier that day, one of ten in the city, some said. These top-heavy, square-turreted self-propelled guns packed 150mm ordnance and could take down a house. Even better at destruction was the Sturm Tiger Rocket Mortar; which looked like a fat tank with a dustbin fitted to its bulky turret; but this dustbin could fire 38cm rocket-propelled shells. It had been designed after Stalingrad; to blow buildings apart. There were just two of these, but two Sturm Tigers could do more damage to a city than a regiment of regular Tigers.

There was also every type of artillery piece and siege gun imaginable trained on the Old Town, and soon the unimaginable would be involved, too: a Karl-Gerät self-propelled siege mortar, weighing 124 tonnes and shooting a shell the size of a sidecar. It was one of only seven Karls in existence, they were so rare they had names – the one coming to Warsaw was called Ziu – and it could only be used because the Soviets weren't in the air. Again, Ingo thought of the Sturmoviks which had chased Pop and him out of bastard Russia – where were they now? The Karl was to be positioned in the Sowinski Park to the south, when it arrived. They took a while to set up, he'd heard, but not so very long to level a town.

All in all it was like using a Panther as a nutcracker. But then again, a nut had a hard shell. And so too did the Old Town, layers of thick old concentric defences that made it a fortress in its own right. The only way in was to fight through the narrow streets. Or maybe over the rubble once the Karl mortar had finished its work.

Ingo stopped thinking of the utter destruction that was about to rain down on Lidka – she had to be there, he knew it – and straightened out the camouflaged jacket while Pop watched him, his forehead creased in curiosity. The AK had captured a storehouse full of Waffen SS jackets in Wola, identical to those some of the Dirlewanger men wore, and they had taken others off dead SS soldiers once it had become their unofficial uniform, along with German helmets. Ingo put on his coalscuttle helmet; he had never liked to wear these things, or hats. But when needs must …

"A helmet, you?"

"Haven't you noticed, the streets are in a frightful state, a fellow could trip and hurt his head," Ingo said.

"And the leopard skin blouse?"

"Goes with my eyes, don't you think?"

Pop was silent for a moment, time measured by the fizzing flight of a rocket in the distance, and then its detonation. Then he said: "You weren't serious, were you?"

"About what?"

"About joining the other side."

"You know me, I'm never serious."

Pop cocked his head to one side, held his eyes steadily. "The girl? It's the girl, isn't it?"

Ingo shrugged, the grey helmet was a loose fit and it bobbed a bit, so he tightened the chin strap. It was a hot day, and he would have rather not worn it anyway. But it was part of his plan. "Kasper said she might be in the Old Town, it's all I have to go on," he said.

"And you believed him?"

"Why not? He had no reason to lie, and I'd just saved his life."

"And he's probably dead all over again, by now, as she might be, too. Or soon will be at any rate, and that is for damned sure, pal," Pop said. "Haven't you seen what they've got to throw at these bandits now? Forget her, please, Ingo. You don't even know she'll be there."

"She'll be there," Ingo said.

"But you can't get *there*. We can't get *there*. Which is why we're eventually going to flatten *there* and pulverise everything that lives and breathes *there*. Possibly lovesick panzer drivers included, as shells are no judge of character, Ingo. They will take an idiot as readily as a bandit."

Sunshine walked in right then, on the idiot cue, smiling as always, smiling wider when he saw Ingo in his SS combat jacket and coalscuttle helmet. He had found vodka, some Estonian stuff labelled *Viin*. He offered them a swig, which they took. Both Ingo and Pop had worked hard to befriend him, especially Pop, and it had made their lives easier; he wasn't watching their every move now, it seemed, although it was difficult to know for sure what he was thinking as he had no real German and he smiled in any and every situation. He now made a clicking noise and jerked his head to one side, which meant they were to follow him.

They were soon on the edge of Plac Zamkowy where the Dirlewanger men were massing for their next attack, the usual chaos of soldiers looking for their loose units, and taking on more vodka, fuelling up for the fight. MG 42 machine guns on mounts were now constantly firing at the tight entrance to Piwna, across the square, so that the edges of the corner walls of the first houses in the street now looked like chewed toffee.

Other units were coming at the Old Town from all directions, Dirlewanger came from the south. His men were almost all fighting pissed already. That meant much the same as 'bayonets fixed', for this lot.

Pop offered Sunshine a Pervitin tablet, which tumbled from its red and blue tube into his grime-caked hand, 'panzer chocolate' one of the few German phrases he understood, and then Pop said: "Ingo?"

"Sure, why not?" Ingo said. He was not sleeping anyway, who could in this hell, except Sunshine, and the drug could help, he knew. He took a tablet from Pop and swallowed it, taking a swig of the Viin vodka to help wash it down. Pop and Sunshine crushed two pills each, and snorted the powder off the edge of a bayonet; eyes bulging to the instant hit of it. Pop went to make the sign of the cross, that old joke of his. But for some reason he did not finish it, had hardly even started when he gave up, his hand slipping down by his side.

Ingo heard Kroh's shouted orders, in a mix of Russian and German, and then the Hetzers began to creak and clatter, their engines howling, and the tank destroyers moved forward, to form up around the narrow entrance to Piwna – the street on which Lidka had once lived.

*

Kampinos Forest, Poland. August 1944

They had been in the forest for two days and two nights. The Germans had not immediately followed them on the night they had been shot down. Dabrowski had fired his revolver from the edge of the wood, and that, while it had probably done no damage, had dissuaded their pursuers for ten minutes or so. Only Dabrowski and the co-pilot, Wojciechowski, had been issued with Enfield .38s. Wojciechowski had been killed at the edge of the wood and Jankowski had claimed the other revolver. The small time Dabrowski had bought them with his pistol shooting had saved them from capture or worse.

Dabrowski, Jankowski, Nowak – the navigator – and Jósef were the only survivors. While the co-pilot had been shot dead, the others had died in the burning Liberator, or when it had hit the ground, or were hit by shrapnel, or … There were far too many *ors* when it came to dying in a bomber, Jósef thought. But, somehow, he had not been burnt alive; he could at least be thankful for that. He did have some burns on the back of his neck and his shoulder, they sang with sting, but they were not serious, both the doctor and – especially – Jankowski had told him.

They had been lucky. Extremely lucky, Dabrowski reckoned. Nowak and Dabrowksi had dragged Jósef away from the edge of the wood, Jankowski had thought he would have received better treatment as a prisoner, had said so, but Dabrowski ignored him. A poacher, alerted by the gunfire, had found them, taken them to a doctor in a nearby village – he had a son with the army in the west and he had seemed pleased to be able to help them. But the doctor had said he wanted nothing to do with them; Dabrowski's pistol had persuaded him to help. The doctor had said Jósef's wound was not so serious, a small calibre round from a sub machine gun, and perhaps a ricochet, but then the doctor did not have a German bullet in his arse. After that Jósef was under some sort of anaesthetic, chloroform he thought, and he had awoken in the back of a small truck, stinking of iodine.

It had still been dark when they had been brought to the Kampinos Forest. Jósef remembered picnics here from before the war, and the smell of the place, pines and marshy water, brought back memories. He also recalled coming here once with Lidka, and then he remembered why he had been aboard that plane in the first place. He thought himself a fool; but he also thought he did not deserve this.

They had been told where they could find the old cabin – Jósef had been unconscious so he did not know who had given them the instructions but assumed it was the poacher – and Nowak and Dabrowksi had carried Jósef between them to begin with. The anaesthetic had worn off after a while, and the wound grew a little painful, yet he had thought he might be able to walk on it; though in the end he did not believe he should risk making it worse, so he said nothing. Jankowski had refused to help carry him, until Dabrowski ordered him to do so.

It had taken three hours to get to the shack, as they lost the path through the forest many times. It was morning by the time they arrived; a low, harsh light was fractured by the spruces amongst which the cabin sat. There was swampy ground nearby, a lake with trees growing from it, and tufts of rough grass poking through the shining surface of the dark water, looking like the crowns of submerged pineapples. The water smelt stagnant, and there was the steely buzz of mosquitoes zipping between the trees. The door to the cabin had not been locked, and they had been told to wait here. There were partisans in the forest, they would come for them soon, went the promise. But there were also sometimes Germans, so they had to be quiet, and careful, went the warning.

There was little food. They had eaten most of what was in their small RAF-issue emergency ration tins. These had contained barley sugars, chewing gum, malted milk tablets and energy pills, and now only the latter were left. There had also been a couple of almost stale loafs of bread the poacher had given them. There was a rainwater barrel and they had been told the water in this was okay to drink. It was hot and humid in the forest, so that was welcome, and as they did not trust the water in the pond – this did not look clean or safe – they had decided to ration the water from the barrel.

The windows were filthy dirty but Dabrowski had rubbed a roundel in one of them and they had a little thin light, filtered through the trees, in which to sit. And wait. The cabin was made of overlapping planks with a simple board roof, and it too seemed to be waiting; marking the passage of time by growing mould and collecting dust. It smelt of festering decay, and Jósef kept sniffing at the air, gradually persuading himself that the smell was coming from his wound. Even though they had told him the bullet had been removed he would have sworn that it was still in there, burning hot, and throbbing like a bad tooth. He constantly worried that the wound might turn gangrenous. He lay on one side on the hard, dirty floor, being careful not to put weight on his wounded buttock.

It was hot in the cabin, hot outside, too, and there was no breeze to relieve them. They had long since abandoned their heavy flying gear so that they wore just their itchy RAF-issue battledress trousers, while the short jackets that went with them were piled on some sacks in the corner and they were all in shirtsleeves. Jósef mopped his brow with his sodden handkerchief again. He wanted water, needed it, but he would not dare to ask for more than his share when Jankowski was in the cabin. Jankowski did not even talk to Jósef now. He was nothing to him. Jósef understood that, but he hated him all the same.

"Look at him, he's like a child," Jankowski said, not at all bothered that Jósef could hear him.

"Leave him be, Jankowski," Dabrowski said.

"Leave him here, more like; and then clear off ourselves."

"The crew sticks together."

"I'm sick of this place, sick of waiting and doing nothing." With that Jankowski slapped his neck, killing a bug.

"The decision's been made. We have to stay together, and hope the partisans come soon."

"But can't you see, we've been abandoned. There are no partisans here, nothing but flies and mosquitoes!"

"It's been just two days, and it's a big forest."

"What if I go?" Jankowski said. "Just one of us could find them, maybe; bring the partisans here and —"

"Enough!" Dabrowskwi shouted, standing quickly, so that the rough low stool he was sat upon was knocked over and clattered on to the hard-packed ground. "My turn on watch, I think," he added, looking at his wristwatch, calmer now. He walked outside through the wedged-open door, his boots crunching the dry grass. A little later Nowak came back, having been relieved by Dabrowski. Nowak picked the roughly hewn stool that Dabrowski had upturned off the packed dirt floor, then sat on it.

"Been arguing with the Skipper again, Jankowski?"

"Just trying to make him see sense, that's all."

Nowak tutted and shook his head.

"It is no use sitting here waiting, surely you can see that?" Jankowski said. "One of us needs to get help, find these partisans, or some food, at least."

"The Kapitan doesn't want to split the crew up," Nowak said, making a point of referring to Dabrowski's rank.

"The crew is mostly dead, and we could be too, if we don't find the partisans."

They were quiet for a moment, the only noise the rattle of a woodpecker, and the sound of Dabrowski pacing around the perimeter they had set.

"We could surrender," Jósef said. They both looked at him now. Stared at him, with the intensity of hot rivets piercing steel. "I mean ... I need treatment ... my wound ..."

"That's not a wound, that's not even a bee sting!" Jankowski said. "And you could walk well enough, if you had the guts. You make me sick, Sczcepanski."

Just then Dabrowski hurried back in, running his fingers over the stubble on his chin. "I've been thinking about what you said, Jankowski," he said. "Maybe it's worth a try."

*

Old Town, Warsaw. August 1944

The control cables of the Goliath unwound like long snakes behind it as the motorcycle-engined tracked mine bumped and twitched its way along the broken road surface of Piwna Street. It was like a tiny remote-controlled panzer without a turret and it looked a little like the original British First World War tank, but was much smaller. It was around a metre and a half long, less than a metre wide, and about half a metre high. The ironically-named machine would have seemed like a comical toy – if you didn't know it contained 100kg of high explosives.

The combat engineer controlling the little tank, with stuttering little steering corrections, was taking cover behind one of the Hetzers, which had parked up at an angle in Plac Zamkowy with a view in to the street. He was using the parallel white stripes on the rear of the Goliath to help line it up with its target, the barricade some way down Piwna. Clumps of Dirlewanger men were amassed on both sides of the entrance to the street, in tapered wedges – the end houses had been secured so they were safe enough, for the moment – as they awaited the signal to attack, which would be the detonation of the Goliath when it reached or was close enough to the barricade. This was typical of Dirlewanger tactics. They rushed in aggressively, to overwhelm the often lightly armed AK with force of numbers, even if the numbers in the force were well down at the end of the action. They might be many things, but the Dirlewangers were often brave under fire – or perhaps suicidal, maybe psychotic – and Ingo had heard Kroh boast that they had not only killed more Poles but had also lost more men than any other German unit in Warsaw. He seemed equally proud of both claims.

Kroh was now with Dirlewanger himself, the latter in his long leather coat as always despite the heat of the day, which seemed to hang thick in the dusty, choking air – perhaps his long-dead heart chilled him from the inside, Ingo sometimes thought. They were with the men at the mouth of the tight street. Dirlewanger led by example, and Kroh wasn't afraid of a fight either. Ingo could see that Kroh was whistling, his lips kissing the dirty air, but he could not hear it from where he crouched, tucked in behind a Hetzer. Ingo, Pop and Sunshine, along with some others, were ready to go in under the cover of one of the brown, sandy-yellow and green dappled tank-like machines. The familiar smell of the panzer grease and heated engines made Ingo a little homesick; he would rather go into combat driving a tank, if he had to go into combat, any day. Most of the others wore caps rather than helmets, so as not be taken for insurgents. It was an irony not lost on Ingo, and he chuckled. But he knew that was the drug.

The Pervitin was beginning to take effect. He could feel his heart rate was up, sense the blood coursing through his veins, the thump of his pulse like the machine gun fire that was the constant panicking heartbeat of this dying city. But he also felt invincible.

The Goliath shuffled towards the barricade, at the speed of a small dog running for a ball, and from there and the houses above the Poles fired on it, the bullets ricocheting off the armoured shell of the little remote-controlled tank with bright ticks of sparks. Then they threw Filipinkas, the AK's homemade grenades, from the houses above. One bounced off harmlessly, two more detonated in the street, churning up fountains of cobbles and grit. Another was right on target, exploding behind the baby tank, ripping its umbilical away and leaving it stranded in the centre of Piwna: an abandoned toy.

There was a mighty silence then, as the Poles stopped shooting at the Goliath. It was a silence that seemed to fill the air as much as the expected explosion would have. But that was an illusion, of course, for the battle continued in other parts of the Old Town: planes strafing; rockets shrieking; people screaming … The false silence seemed to last an age, but it could only have been a stretched second before some unheard radioed order caused the first of the three Hetzers to jerk forward, its steel tracks squealing on the cobbles, while the Praga sixes in all three of the tank destroyers ripped ferociously as the drivers revved them unnecessarily.

Hannibal would have recognised the way the Dirlewanger Brigade stormed the tight conduit of Piwna: the elephantine Hetzers with their 75mm calibre trunks; the charging war-lusting infantrymen; and the utter carnage and confusion …

In a matter of minutes the Hetzers could go no further; they were already caught in a trap. Filipinkas fell upon them, exploding and causing the driver of the first to step on the brake and hook reverse – tanks, like elephants, don't like narrow streets. Meanwhile, the Dirlewanger soldiers broke from behind their cover and ran into a swarm of *thsipping* hot-wasp bullets from in front and above, the gunfire amplified and echoing in the tight street. Ingo and Pop instinctively ran for the haven of a doorway while soldiers fell around them, the bullets splatting into soft flesh, *poinking* off hard steel and sparking on cobbles. The yellow façade of the house was pockmarked with bullet strikes, so that it looked like careless polka-dotting, while the front door was blown open, hanging from the hinge like a drunkard reaching for the support of the door frame. Ingo ducked in to the doorway just as a bullet buried itself in to the door with a drilling thump. Another took a bite from the step, lifting a fragment of stone which clanged against his helmet.

This building had not been cleared yet, but that was part of his plan. He took a position at the base of the narrow wooden stairs, looking up, while Pop,

Sunshine and two others tumbled in after him. One of these was Spud, a stick grenade held like a truncheon, the other man was clutching at his wounded leg, bright blood seeping through his fingers.

Sunshine started to fire from the doorway, aiming up the street, his MP 40 shuddering as he let off a full magazine, the spent shell cases curling from the gun and tinkling against the old stone floor. Ingo could hear the sound of running men above him, thumping boots shaking floorboards, and he guessed the AK were retreating in to the next house along, through cut holes or along the attics. They had seen this before.

"I'll clear the other floors," Ingo shouted.

Pop looked at him, curious at the keenness, then nodding as he suddenly understood. "Careful, Ingo," he shouted, over the gunfire. "Careful!"

Ingo nodded.

He rushed up the first flight of stairs, his rifle held before him – hurrying because he needed to find space and time; space and time for what he had to do. The house was old, the walls wood panelled and the stairway tight. There was gunfire from the top floor and boot clumps on the wooden stairs behind him, and the stick-on-stick clatter he recognised as Spud's bulging bag of grenades. Then another noise: *thump; thump, thump, rumble* ... A Filipinka, tossed from above, rolling on to the tight first floor landing. It was trundling in an elliptical arc just a metre from Ingo. He grabbed the grenade, kicked open a door off the landing and tossed it in the room, slamming the door shut and diving into the lee of the stairs, Spud breaking his fall just as the Filipinka exploded; an ear-bashing bang in the confined space, followed by a shower of wood splinters and larger chunks which clunked off Ingo's helmet, and then tinkling bits of glass from the frames of pictures that lined the stairway.

Spud was enraged, he did not appreciate being on the wrong side of a grenade attack, but more than that a jagged piece of glass had pierced his cheek, and was lodged there like reckless jewellery, a thin, perpendicular trail of blood trickling down his sausage red skin. He pushed Ingo to one side, out of his way, and started to charge upstairs. Ingo saw his chance. He took the red and white pre-tied ribbon from his pocket and placed it around his helmet, sliding it down until it was tight where the steel dome widened, slipping the armband on in the next instant. Then he followed Spud up the stairs.

Around the corner of the next stairway, which led to the second floor, Spud had stopped. It was one of those moments in battle when everything seemed to freeze around an instant, and all could be seen with an eye-burning clarity, moments the drug accentuated. At the top of the stairs a teenaged insurgent in an ill-fitting German helmet stared disbelievingly at the Sten gun that had jammed in his hands. Between him and Ingo Spud was raising his MP 40, having allowed his grenade to drop on a stair without pulling the cord.

Ingo felt the tinnitus swell his head from the inside, but then settle, and without the time to take aim he fired his rifle from the hip. The bullet hit Spud in his lower spine, and he crashed down the flight of wooden stairs like a sack of the root vegetables he was named after. Ingo then worked the bolt of the Mauser, the spent cartridge bouncing off the hard stair, and put another bullet in Spud; to make sure – and to bolster his credentials. As he did so he remembered the hopping cripple, Rabbit, and all those other frightened innocents killed by Spud's stick grenades.

The boy at the top of the stairs said something in Polish, Ingo did not understand, so he just nodded. There were now other AK fighters passing behind him, heading up the stairs, and then moving along the upper floors of the houses, retreating for now. It was not as Ingo had planned it. He had hoped to play dead, and then blend in with the AK when they counter-attacked, as they always seemed to do, but the boy was motioning for Ingo to follow him.

He ran up the rest of the stairs, then tagged on to the last of the line of fleeing AK fighters as the boy still smiled his thanks. Ingo knew he could not stay with them for long without discovery, the fog of war could disperse quickly in a small group. And so he slipped away as soon as they had crawled through a hole in the thick old stone – which would have taken an age of work to cut – that led in to a neighbouring house. This was then plugged with a team manning a Bren gun. He hoped that Pop had the sense not to follow.

There was a fire escape ladder at the rear of this other house. Ingo climbed out on to it, checking that he was not seen first, and then slung his rifle on to his back. He reached up to the gutter that ran the length of the building, then tried it for strength. It held his weight, with just a nervous creak, and so he pulled himself up on to the roof.

Ingo had a good view from here, and through a gap in the buildings he could even see the Panzer Train on the railway at the edge of the Old Town on the Danzig Station side, moving every now and then to bombard the houses from a new position with its 105mm guns. It looked like a cross between a battleship and an armoured slug, every millimetre of it sheathed in steel, its turrets spouting death with absolute impunity. Elsewhere he could see smoke and fires; too much of both. In the heart of the Old Town the shells kept falling, while rockets seemed to tear the sky on their way to dropping fiery death on some Pole, any Pole. He remembered what Pop had said: *Shells are no judge of character, Ingo. They will take an idiot as readily as a bandit ...*

He smiled at the thought, then started to move along the rooftops, aiming to pass the point where the barricade was in the street, the other side of the buildings, keeping clear of the crest where he would be silhouetted against the sooty sky, and sliding his hand along the warm tiles to steady himself, the treads of his rubber-soled panzer boots helping his feet to grip the weather-worn old slate. Through the thick strands of the smoke he could just make out the blue sky above, and see and hear the Stukas racing through it – one so low he felt its airstream on his back. One of the houses was all but destroyed, and he had to balance across shaky timbers like a tightrope walker, unslinging his rifle and holding it flat in front of him in two hands as if it was a balancing pole.

Soon he found a roof with two large holes in it, probably made by an artillery shell that had gone through the apex but not fallen within, and he was able to drop down into the attic space below. The light from the gaps in the roof above allowed him to locate an attic hatch, which he opened, then he dropped down again, to find himself on a landing, his knees jarring as he hit the floor. To his right, stood by a window, was a boy. He wore the armband of the AK over the sleeve of a red shirt, and a German helmet, with the red and white band painted on it. He held a revolver, it looked like a Nagant. He could have been no older than fifteen, angry acne was scattered across his face. He said something that Ingo did not understand. Then he raised the pistol, which shook in his hand.

Ingo did what he often did in situations like this: he laughed. The boy's finger relaxed on the trigger, and a confused little smile tugged at the corner of his mouth. Ingo walked to him and tapped three times on the top of his helmet, as if he was knocking at a door. Now they were both laughing.

Leaving the laughing boy behind him Ingo went down the stairs of the house, walking casually, passing other AK fighters, few of who gave him a second glance, probably because he looked just like them in his SS jacket, black trousers and AK armband and helmet ribbon. When he went out on to the street he saw, as expected, that he was now far beyond the barricade. Now all he had to do was to continue to exude confidence, which was seldom really a problem. And find Lidka.

He soon realised he was close to what he thought might be the building which had contained her flat, but also that it was now just a crumbling gap in the dying grimace of the street. So he headed towards the centre of the Old Town, into the market square. Some of the buildings here were no longer buildings but slopes of rubble, while the square itself was filled with running insurgents and stretcher bearers taking wounded people, some screaming, to field stations. Every now and then the poisonous grey-brown mushrooms of exploding shells erupted within the square. He did not know how or where to start his search, but he did know the way to Krzywe Koło from here and he decided that the café that had once belonged to Kasper was as good a place to begin as any.

It was not far from the square and he was there soon enough. But the building which had once housed Café Kasper had now been all but destroyed. The front of the block had been peeled off in an explosion, exposing all the bright walls within, while the café itself was choked with broken bricks and wreckage. Ingo had not really expected to find her here, it was just the first place he thought of to look, but he was surprised at the depth of his disappointment. Further along, the street was blocked with sloping debris, through which a buckled pram poked poignantly. Even as he looked on another shell landed on the roof of a building down the row, and he heard it rip through wooden floor after wooden floor, stopping with a dull clang when it hit ground level. A dud.

Ingo did not know where he should search next. He could not ask people about Lidka; he did not speak Polish. And he doubted that enquiring whether anyone might speak German would be the most sensible thing to do in the circumstances. He would have to wander the Old Town in the hope that he would find her. There was no other option …

His gaze drifted up to the first floor of the naked building. One of the exposed rooms, with powder blue-painted walls and a white picture rail, caught his eye. In the corner of this room, sugary-white from the plaster dust that coated it, was an upright piano.

*

If there was anything as valuable as water right now it was privacy. Perhaps only ammunition would be more welcome to a denizen of the Old Town at this time. But Lidka did not have a gun anyway, so water and privacy would do. It was not much water, and the soap she had was German Unity soap; the best soap there was, but not really soap. It was hard to get it to lather, but when you've spent most of yesterday and then hours this morning in a sewer it's easy to find the energy to squeeze a sud or two from a brick. It gave off no scent, and all she could smell was the shit that caked her overalls, lying in a pile in the corner of the little room, and the burning of the buildings. Always that.

Lidka had almost become used to the smell. It was the wrinkled noses of others that had told her she needed a wash, and this was also the only reason she had been given the water and soap; it was water that had already been used for other things and was not drinkable. It was a hot day, the heat trapped in the net of smoke that was draped over the Old Town. Shells exploded with lethal monotony outside. But she had soap, water, and privacy. If it wasn't for worrying about Freddy, thinking of Ingo, she might have enjoyed it.

She stood naked in front of a large enamelled bowl which sat on a low stool. The space had once been a storeroom of some sort, but someone had found a use for whatever was kept here and now it was empty. It was on the ground floor at the back of a building on Kiliński Street, where the command post of the AK leader, Tadeusz Komorowski – now known simply as Bór, the Forest – was located. This room had a small barred window of clouded glass that let some light in. She had found some other clothes, and she thought that later she might try to clean her stinking overalls and her headscarf.

She bent down and soaked up some of the water in a rag, with which she wet her skin. Then she forced the bristles of the stiff brush in to the rock-hard brick of soap, before hurting herself clean with the brush. An explosion close by shook the bowl on the low stool and it thrummed a little, the surface of the shallow water within it quivering. She faced the thick frosted glass window, so as to make the most of the dead-tooth light that squeezed itself through it, so she was only aware that someone had entered the little room because she heard the door creak open.

"Nice."

She turned.

"Nicer."

"Get out!"

Andrzej laughed, made a show of licking her with his eyes. "Yes, very nice," he said.

There was nothing within reach to cover herself with, and so she turned her back on him and continued to scrub herself with the hard brush. He walked around her, the Sten gun that hung around his neck clinking against the British Mills Bomb grenades attached to the webbing belts slung over the short leather jacket he never now seemed to be without.

"I said; get out," she repeated, calmer now.

"We're soldiers Chopin, no secrets between comrades – especially such pretty secrets."

"What do you want?" Lidka said.

"You were gone a long time, yesterday. A problem?"

"No problem," she said. Then added quickly: "Some Germans were covering a drain, there was no way through. I had to wait for them to go."

"A long wait," he said. "Too long …"

He then reached out for her breast, then stopped, a finger hovering just millimetres from her left nipple, which hardened treacherously. His finger almost seemed to spark with energy, the energy of not touching, like the space between the hands of God and Adam in the Sistine Chapel, an emptiness full of everything. "What a waste," Andrzej said, and his hand dropped. "He's probably with his English sweetheart right now," he added.

"No, not Jósef," she said after a pause, and she could not help the catch in her throat.

"So you always say," Andrzej said.

"When he comes home —"

"*If*, teacher. *If.*" He tore his eyes from her body, looked at the wedding ring she wore.

Lidka made busy with the scrubbing brush, the bristles burning her skin.

"This will be over soon," he said. "We should live, while we can … Anything might happen."

"Is that what you say to all of them?"

He shook his head: "There's only ever been one, really, Chopin – don't you know that?"

There was a long pause, and she stopped scrubbing, so the only noise was the brutal orchestra of the bombardment outside. One shell dropped nearby, shaking the stone around them.

"I'm married."

"You *almost* sound like you believe it."

"I have to believe it."

"Yet it didn't stop you before, did it?" Andrzej said.

"That was different, there was no Freddy, then."

"A German," he said.

She said nothing.

"The German, yes … If a German, why not me?"

"Get out, Andrzej."

"No, the time for games is over," he said, and he slowly reached out for her again.

"Bullet!" someone shouted down the corridor, a young voice, but tearing with the dust and smoke of battle.

"Shit!" Andrzej snapped. "What now?" he shouted back.

"Bór is asking for you; come quickly!"

"Later, teacher," Andrzej said, then left the room, slamming the door behind him. Lidka found she was suddenly shaking. But she was not scared, she knew the feeling of fear all too well, and it wasn't that. She finished washing and dressed in the clothes she had found in a bombed-out house. She wore a checked skirt and a cream blouse, and she tied her hair back. She also wore her boots, which still stank of the sewer, but she was sick of overalls, did not want a uniform, and needed to feel like a woman again. She almost had, for a moment.

Once Lidka had dressed she went down in to the command centre in the basement of the building; safe there from some of the bombs, at least. There was a small door-less room where the messengers could rest between tasks; a bare place except for the graffiti of the younger girls; messages of love for boys with ridiculous *nom de guerres* like Eagle, Iron and Kite. It smelt a little of the sewers they crawled through. She was enjoying the feel of the clean clothes she wore instead of her stinking overalls. She could not pretend the war was not happening, she would need to be dead to shut out the sounds of it and the shaking of the walls — she had ceased to be amazed that the buildings seemed afraid — but she could pretend that one day there would not be a war. If only the Russians would come.

"Bullet is pissed off with you," Cat said, as she entered the room, unable to hide a slight smile. "You were gone a long time, yesterday." She was wearing her blue overalls and her hair was bunched up in a head scarf, tied at the front, in a turban. She was carrying a brown leather dispatch case.

"There were Germans, covering the drain."

"Where?"

"I'm not sure, near the Bankowy junction, I think," Lidka said.

"You can get past them, if you're quiet enough, good enough. If you trust to feel, and don't use the flashlight."

"Not this time."

Cat shook her head, then left.

Lidka tried to doze; it had been weeks since her sleep had amounted to anything more than pilfered naps. There was an old green sofa, too short to stretch out on, and so she curled into a foetal position that suited the situation. But as exhausted as she was she could not drop off, because it was difficult to ignore the screaming of the aeroplanes, the crump of the guns on the armoured train, the thump of the howitzers, the rip of machine gun fire, and — worst of all — the ghostly howling of the Nebelwerfer rockets they all called *Krowas*, bellowing cows. She scrunched her eyes tight shut, but there was no soft darkness, just images exploding in her head in time with the barrage: sometimes Freddy, sometimes Ingo, and then Andrzej, his finger outstretched, her nipple thrusting to meet it. She tore the thought from her mind as if it was a page of bad work to be thrown in the litter basket.

Again she tried to shut out the barrage and the bombing, concentrated on the other noise, the business-like bustle of the command centre, rather than the sounds of death, in the hope that the coolness of the AK leaders would reassure her. Somewhere beyond the much larger adjoining room someone was cooking a stew, and the smell of it was slowly taking over from the taint of the sewer in the small room. She had seen the dead horse outside, pieces being hacked from it as the bombs fell, she had wondered how it had stayed alive so long. She suddenly felt hungry, realised she had eaten nothing for over twenty-four hours, and she hoped she would be offered some of the food.

Outside the room she heard someone coming down the stairs and in to the vaulted main area of the basement that the door-less doorway opened out on to, hobnails on boots clicking against the stone steps. He was laughing.

"What's so funny?" someone else said.

"Takes all sorts, they say," the new voice said, still laughing.

"Do they?" the someone replied.

For some reason, maybe it was because she had not heard much laughter recently, she opened her eyes. The one who had spoken first was an AK fighter with a completely bandaged head that looked like a tight helmet with a bright red rosette of soaked-through blood on its side. He was a lanky lad, no more than nineteen. His bandaged head brushed the sweeping low curve of the vaulted ceiling, and he stooped a little. He carried one of the AK-produced MP 40-style sub machine guns, called a Błyskawic, which they had been making in secret workshops since before the uprising. They had manufactured many of these, but there were still never enough guns.

"You know the old café on Krzywe Koło?" the lad with the bandaged head continued. "It was once called Kasper's, I think."

"I know it," Lidka said, her interruption from the side room taking them both by surprise. "I often went there, in Kasper's time, before it was taken over," she added, standing up and walking through.

"I went there once or twice, too," the other AK soldier, an older man who wore a Red Cross band on one arm, a red-soaked bandage on the other, said. "Small and stuffy sort of place, wasn't it?"

"Well, it's a well-ventilated sort of place now, you'll be pleased to hear," the lad said.

"Where isn't?"

"The sewers," Lidka said.

The second man smirked at that, then said: "And what's so funny about this well-ventilated café anyway?"

"At this very moment there's a soldier – one of ours, of course – on the bombed-out first floor above what was that café, playing a piano; in the middle of all this!" A shell landed close by, which helped emphasise his point.

"Chopin?" Lidka said, and her heart seemed to stop.

"No, I doubt that. There are plenty of ghosts in this city right now, but you would think *he* would have more sense."

"I mean —"

"I know, yes, Chopin."

"Is he playing well?"

"Well, the percussion section's rather lively, so a little hard to tell."

The man with the bandaged arm laughed at that, but the soldier must have sensed something in Lidka's expression, something she was perhaps not aware of herself, for he added, quite gently: "Yes, the parts I heard. Very well."

"What does he look like?"

"He's playing a piano in the middle of the biggest bombardment to hit the Old Town yet; so he looks like a bloody idiot!"

Lidka knew it could not be true … Yet … And he said an AK soldier … Yet … And that it was impossible … Yet … It would be good to hear Chopin played well again, she told herself. To hear something beautiful, rather than the bombs and the guns and the screams of people in pain. No, it could not be true, but then again, why there of all the places someone might play a piano? For the first time in over three years she took off the silver wedding ring that Sol Vogler had given her so that people might believe she really was married to Jósef Sczcepanski. She put it on a shelf alongside a withered flower that someone had left there a while ago now – no one knew who, and no one had thought to remove it.

The lad with the bandaged head had moved on to report to an officer at a desk in the corner of the larger room while the other man went back to reading a copy of the *Biuletyn Informacyjny*, now one of many newspapers printed in the Polish held areas of the city. On the other side of the room AK officers were leaning over a table on which a map of the city was spread out. Lidka slipped out of the command centre and made her way up the stone stairway, squeezing past those who sat there, sheltering from the guns and the planes.

"Where are you going sister?" said a soldier near the top of the stairs. "Don't you know it's hot up there?"

"I have a message to deliver," she lied. "I will be safe in the sewer soon enough."

"Still in the shit, though; eh?" he laughed at his own joke, but no one else did. "Seems a shame to spoil the skirt," he added, wistfully.

At the front door to the building an AK soldier wearing a Polish army helmet, who was on guard, recognised her as a messenger, and let her out. As soon as she was out of the building and in to the broken street – broad for the Old Town, and roughly scabbed where slabs of cobbles had been lifted by explosions – a shell landed about thirty metres or so away, throwing rubble skywards, and more dust in to the air. She crouched into a ball and allowed the gravel-laced blast to pass over her. She waited for some seconds, and then she ran.

The air was thick with dust so that the high sun seemed to be trapped behind a dirty glass dome, and she tasted the dying city with each harsh breath.

She tried not to think of the shells and rockets that seemed to be falling all around her, and by now she had learnt, from the noise they made when they fell, whether she should duck in to a doorway for cover – although doorways were becoming rarer by the hour. The streets were covered with debris and the dead, and she had to clamber over a pile of smouldering rubble on one occasion, where the front of a house had collapsed and blocked the way.

It did not take her long to reach Krzywe Koło. There was fighting nearby, short bursts from a machine gun and the sharp cracks of pistol fire. For a moment there was a pause in the shellfire. Then she heard it, washing the noise of the guns and explosions from her head. Cleansing music.

It was *The Raindrop Prelude*, and it was beautiful. Perfect. A shell must have fallen a little while before because ash and dust hung in the air in little clouds and she could not yet see from where the music came. Another shell fell, two streets away: crunching brick and wood, tinkling glass, but no explosion. A dud, there were many; the AK would tap it for its explosives later, to make bullets and Filapinkas. The sound of another shell, an explosion some streets away, drowned out the music for some seconds, and for a moment she thought it had stopped, and she was relieved when she could hear it once more. She moved closer, walking, not running now, until she was near the place where Café Kasper had once been. Then, quite suddenly, there was a break in the dust and the smoke and she saw him, in a room one floor up, a room without an outside wall, so that it looked like a theatre set.

He wore the SS jacket in green camouflage that the AK had made their own. But she could only really tell that from the cut of it. For the light coat, and the man who wore it, was covered in a creamy white plaster dust, dust that was still falling on him from the badly cracked ceiling, like snow. She thought about what the tall soldier had said to her about ghosts, and it might have been easy to believe this was an apparition of Chopin. The shells kept falling. But the ghost of Chopin took no notice.

She was dimly aware of the roar of a Stuka, its sharply creased wings scything through the smoking sky, then the howls of a barrage of a group of six consecutive incendiary Krowas, which fell close by, to burn something already burnt, yet all that she could really hear was the music. She stood still, and watched and listened, and ignored the sounds of destruction and death ... Just Chopin ...

He played until he came to the end of the piece, and when he stopped the air was full of dust and ash and smoke once more and now she could no longer see the ghost of Chopin. But from beyond the murk, high on the stage created when the outer wall had been peeled from the building, she heard his voice.

"I hoped you would come, when you heard the music."

*

Kampinos Forest. August 1944

They were talking about him. Jósef knew it. There had been gunfire in the forest. Sporadic rifle shots, the pop of a pistol, and then a quick burst of a machine gun; the fast rattle of a German weapon – an MG 42, Jankowski had said – like a steel woodpecker in the trees. Nowak had gone off in that direction and they supposed that now he was either a prisoner, or dead. The shooting had now stopped.

Dabrowski and Jankowski were outside the cabin, they were talking quietly, but not whispering, and Jósef had heard his name mentioned. Twice. His wound still hurt, but there was no sign of infection, Dabrowski had told him, when he had inspected it earlier. "No sign, yet," Jósef had added.

Dabrowski punched the palm of his hand and stomped back in to the cabin, his boots booming on the root-veined ground. "We have to move; you can walk with the stick, and we will carry you between us if it gets too much," he said, as he pulled on his short blue battledress jacket. In the background Jankowski stared in to the forest, making a point of looking the other way, it seemed to Jósef. It was hot and Dabrowski's forehead shone with sweat. A mosquito zipped around his face, but he ignored it. Jósef had been bitten a hundred times, and could not ignore it.

"We should surrender," Jósef said.

"No, it is our duty to escape, to fight on."

"What, with a single pistol – are you mad?" Dabrowski stared at him, and he realised he had overstepped the mark. "It's my wound, sir, it needs attention."

"Your wound's fine," Dabrowski said. "We will go in the other direction, away from the gunfire. Hopefully we will find the AK, they have men in the forest, I've made drops to them – we drop medical supplies, so they must have doctors." He was trying to sound encouraging, Jósef thought.

"The Germans have doctors," Jósef said.

"The Germans have been shooting – didn't you hear?"

"Perhaps it's the partisans, maybe they have German weapons?"

"Nowak went that way, Sczcepanski. He has not returned," Dabrowski said, sharply now. "It's time we moved." He checked the load in his Enfield .38, smoothly braking it open and examining the small rounds in the cylinder chambers. The other revolver had gone with Nowak – Jankowski had not liked that, and he had not liked it that Nowak had been told to leave and find help when it had been his idea, either.

"The Germans will take us prisoner; is that so bad, sir?"

"It's worse than death!" Jankowski spat. He had walked in without them noticing.

"You are both not thinking straight," Jósef said. "My wound, it's — "

"Get up, that's an order, Sczcepanski."

Jósef stayed put, on his side, supporting his upper body on an elbow on the dirty, hard floor, to take the weight off the wound in his buttock. While it was still painful, the intensity had dulled. He did not want the hot pain to return, and he feared that walking, even with the stick Dabrowski had made for him, could only make it worse.

"Perhaps there are no partisans?" he said. "Perhaps it was a lie?"

"There are partisans," Jankowski said. "*Most* Poles fight!"

"I cannot fight, I am wounded."

"No, you will *not* fight," Jankowski said.

Jósef shook his head, his eyes filled with burning tears, but he could not help it. He was not air crew. "I have had enough … I will surrender," he said.

"You heard the coward," Jankowski said. "C'mon sir, we will be able to go further and faster without him."

"Yes, leave me; please … sir."

Dabrowski looked him in the eyes, his expression a mix of disgust and pity, and Jósef looked away, staring at the iron-still spruces through the open door instead. There was a long pause of solid silence, in which he heard Jankowski's belly rumble. POWs got food, too, Jósef thought.

"Let's go!" Dabrowski finally said, and Jankowski picked up his jacket and they left without saying another word, their flying boots crunching the tinder dry undergrowth.

It was what he had wanted, but he had not expected it. He listened until he could hear them no more. Until he could hear nothing but his own quickening heartbeat. It was a little while until he realised how utterly alone he now was. And then the panic took hold, like a raging fire within him.

"Help!" Jósef shouted, and his voice sounded small. He knew they would not hear him now. But he hoped that others might.

***

Brescia. May 2, 1954

Ingo walked from the apartment off Corso Martiri della Libertà to the start ramp on Via Rebuffone. It was a cold and foggy Sunday morning, and behind the woolly murk the sun was not yet up. He wore a flat cap and an overcoat, both borrowed from the widow; once her husband's clothes, Ingo supposed. Beneath the grey coat he wore his racing slacks, a short flying jacket, and his polo shirt, plus his wide kidney belt. The crack of the thin leather soles of his driving shoes on the cold paving stones echoed in the tight street. He had left his helmet and gloves with the car, when they had completed their final practice run – concentrating on the stretch between Florence and Bologna – two days before.

It was a long walk, yet he didn't mind that, and he made sure to check there was no one following him every so often. But he felt safe enough, now. If they had known about the apartment he was staying in he felt he would have been paid a visit already; would maybe be dead already. The race had started many hours ago, and Brescia did not sleep during it, so the streets were far from empty, even at this hour, and there were others walking in the same direction as Ingo, to catch a glimpse of the faster cars before they set off on their race around Italy. He felt anonymous, and safe, this dark and foggy morning.

Sounds travels far in fog, he had noticed that on the Eastern Front, and every minute he heard the roar from the open exhaust of a racing car as it started its one-thousand mile odyssey, and every minute he walked a little faster; down the canyon way of Via Tosio – where the engine noises echoed like gunshot – and through the open ended square at Piazzale Arnaldo, until he was on to the wider Via Venezia, where the crowd was still large and excited despite the early hour. Via Rebuffone was off Venezia, kinking abruptly before feeding back on to it, and the start ramp was located in the space that filled the triangle formed by the two streets, which was a small park. Crowds were pressed in to the area, some in stands on Via Venezia overlooking the yellow start ramp – the advertising hoardings behind them made ragged-topped by the fog – others standing amongst the trees, the cigarettes they smoked burning bright pinholes in the gossamer mist.

Nearly all the cars that were yet to start now waited in line on Via Rebuffone, penned in by sturdy wooden rails which the crowd pressed against, to get a glimpse of a star driver, or even an autograph – Enrique Hohberg was unknown here, and so no one asked for his signature as he elbowed his way through the scrum of spectators. He showed the Carabinieri his pass and was let through, and then he walked down the line of cars, passing those of Collins, Farina and Ascari, and other names he had often read in *El Gráfico*, until he reached the Condor. Carlo saw him before he arrived and his grin shone through the fog of the morning like a tipped up crescent moon. Seldom had someone been so pleased to see him, Ingo thought.

"I was beginning to think ..." Carlo shook his head, and didn't finish his sentence.

"I would not miss this, Carlo," Ingo said, pleased to see that his helmet and goggles sat in the bucket of his seat, waiting for him.

The sound of another racing engine cracked down the street, and he turned to see a car, a scarlet Osca, leaving the floodlit start ramp. The cars had been doing this for nearly eight and a half hours now. The first, a tiny Iso Isetta, had set out at nine the previous evening, and wore the number 2100, its time of departure. There were 378 cars in the race in all, but those early competitors last night were the slowest, small cars – more Isettas, Citroen 2CVs, Fiat 500s, Renault 4CVs – departing at thirty-second intervals. From midnight the cars were released at minute intervals – Peugeot 203s, Lancia Appias and a swarm of Fiat 1100s; then the quicker sedans – Alfa Romeo 1900s, Lancia Aurelias, the smaller-engined Porsche sports cars; then the under two-litre sports cars – Frazer Nash,

Gordini, Triumph – and soon the big cars would be leaving; those with engines over 2000cc, the cars that had a chance of winning the Mille Miglia outright. The Condor was in this group, though no one except Carlo, Varela and Ingo thought this largely unheard of Argentinian sports car had a hope of taking the fight to the Lancia D24s and the Ferraris.

There was a delicious mélange of aromas around the start ramp area, smells sharpened by the fog: Castrol R20 and gasoline, fresh bread and brewing coffee. Ingo breathed deeply of it, placed the palms of his hands on the dew-spattered cold bonnet of the Condor for a few seconds, and then he started to walk around the car. On the bonnet and doors a number had been painted in white some days ago: *532*. It was their race number, and also the time they would start – just gone half-past-five.

Catalina arrived, carrying a tray of espressos. She wore a dark headscarf and a shapeless thick coat, yet she shivered, the little cups clinking on the tray. She looked tired and – in an instant that was burned away in the very spark of it – Ingo believed he saw her as she might look as an old woman. The children had come over with Catalina, a little later than Carlo; he wanted them to see the land of his birth. Ingo assumed they were watching the cars depart somewhere; Aldo at least, that one already had the passion for it.

"We were beginning to worry," she said.

Ingo smiled, then took a tiny cup of coffee and stared into its dark eye for a moment, the steam rising from it tickling his face. Another car, a TR2, number 517, trundled down then rasped away from the well-lit ramp. *Fifteen minutes.*

Carlo was now deep in conversation with Varela now, who did not greet Ingo. He knew that Varela was unhappy with him. He had not seen him for a week and Varela was the sort of boss that needed to boss. Ingo didn't care, he knew this would have to be Enrique Hohberg's last race.

"You will be careful, yes?" Catalina said.

"I'll be careful."

"It's a long race, it's better to —"

"I'll be careful, Catalina, I promise."

Three cars in front, beyond an Aston Martin DB2 and a Maserati A6GCS, was Otero's Ferrari, number 529. The one who had betrayed him. Ingo was sure of it. And, with a child like that, there was only one way to get revenge, Ingo knew. He needed to do what he would have done anyway; beat him. Otero was stood by the car, arguing with one of his mechanics, stabbing his finger close to the man's face. The mechanic hurried off, and Otero looked back along the line of cars to where Ingo stood. But he did not meet Ingo's eyes, just turned away.

It would be enough to beat him, Ingo thought, but better to pass him, too. But that would mean closing the three-minute gap first. He thought it could be done. Knew it. And in doing so they would surely be high up in the race, too.

The mechanics pushed the car forward in the queue a little, the tyres creaking against the asphalt. Then Guido opened the bonnet of the Condor and they went through the routine of starting the engine. Ingo gave his coffee to Catalina, took off the cap and coat and then slid in to the bucket seat, thrilling to the feel of it. The engine was fired up with a bark then a roar, and Catalina handed Ingo the tiny cup, before putting her fingers in her ears. As Guido tweaked the throttle linkage on the carburettors, the dark surface of the coffee shook. It reminded Ingo of explosions, the way the blasts would raise circles of dust, as if a stone was thrown in a pond. He remembered the last explosion he had experienced, in Buenos Aires, and with that the warning from Kroh.

He wondered where they were, those who had come for him. But sat here now, in this racing car, taking up the throttle on the thumbs-up from Guido, he felt safe. There were thousands of people, newsmen and cameras, and he doubted they would strike now. Yet it was not just that. He realised that he had always felt safe at the controls of a car, or on a motorcycle in those early days. But then he had also always known he was faster than a bullet. He smiled at the thought, and then he remembered Pop.

*

"There is time," Sarah had said.

Yitzhak had looked at her, took a drag on his Noblese – an Israeli brand and part of his plan. Then said, with a sharply cocked eyebrow: "Time for what?"

"What you have always wanted, from me," she had said. She had been sitting on the edge of the narrow bed and she had parted her legs, very slightly, as she had said it.

Then he had laughed, before quietly getting on with his preparations, shaking his head and chuckling once, or twice, but saying nothing more.

Now there was no longer time.

It was 5.27am. What light there was this dawn was not good, the fog saw to that, but Yitzhak was not concerned. It had angered her, she realised, him laughing. She had misjudged the situation, and that had been foolish. But she also realised she was disappointed; and that it had been the first time she had felt disappointed about anything in life not to do with Christian Kroh, Ingo Six, or some other bastard Nazi for a very long time. She would say no more about his rejection. She knew that in five minutes time it would all be done, and then she doubted she would ever see Yitzhak again.

Yitzhak's little hire car was now parked north of here, away from the race, where it would be easier for him to get out of town once the mission was completed. She would take the train to Rome; The Group had always split up after an operation, and they would not change their ways for the last, even if this was by no mean a regular, and even less a sanctioned, mission.

With the fog hanging in the grey dawn it was dark enough for the street lamps to still shine, while the yellow start ramp was bathed in white light from powerful floodlights so the spectators could clearly see the bright cars; which looked like glossy toys, frozen in the stark light, sitting between red and white painted kerbs that traced the plank-built arch of the ramp on both sides. The fog around the start ramp was shot through with the illumination, and it almost made the cars seem like they were trapped within a lightbulb.

The car now on the ramp was an Austin-Healey, Yitzhak told her, and it bore the number 528 in white. It had a driver and a co-driver; some of the cars, mostly those painted red, had just a driver. The men in the Austin-Healey both wore windcheaters to keep out the morning chill. A man in a long coat and bowler hat dropped a flag and the driver eased the gleaming green car down the wooden start ramp, which was plastered with Pirelli signs, and then brutally accelerated once the car was off the ramp, its rear end squirming as the tyres spun against the damp paving stones. The headlamps were switched on, and it scooped yellow cones out of the gloom once it was out of the glare of the floodlights, lighting up faces in the packed ranks of people either side of the road. The crowd was still large, and tightly packed around the start ramp and the fork of the two streets, and despite the fact that most had been there all night, they still cheered the Austin-Healey. Another car, with a roof this time and in the red of Italy with a forest-green nose band, and bearing the number 529 in white, took its place on the ramp.

"That's Hector Otero," Yitzhak said, from memory, as the light was off so he could not read the programme on the low table by his chair.

They had an excellent outlook on the proceedings from here, and that was all down to Yitzhak. His cover meant it was natural he would want a very good view of the start ramp on Via Rebuffone, and this room, high in a house on Via Venezia, close to the Missionari Combaniani building, just two hundred metres from the ramp with a clear view of it through a gap in the towering chestnut trees, gave him just that. He had talked to the man who had rented this room, an American racing driver, and had been told it had cost a fortune – many rented out rooms this close to the start for lots of lira. It was not much of a room, a bed, a framed picture of the Rotonda of the Duomo Vecchio on one wall, and a few items of practical furniture, including a chair, which Yitzhak now sat astride, backwards, looking out of the window towards the start ramp. The chair was a metre or so away from the window, to the right of it, and at an angle to face the ramp, so that with the room's light switched off he could not be seen from outside. The window and shutters were open and the beginnings of a lazy dawn breeze licked at light lace curtains, which were pulled back a little way to offer a better view. Cold dawn air carrying the smell of hot engine oil and petrol drifted in, as did ghostly tentacles of fog, only to evaporate as soon as they touched the warmer air within.

The American drove a Jaguar, number 411. He would not need the room for a while before 4.11am, and a long time after. And if a photographer – Yitzhak could be convincing about such things – needed a good place to shoot the bigger cars at the start, and had lira enough to help him pay the bill, well … The American driver had left the keys under a flowerpot that hung in an iron basket near the back door of the building.

Yitzhak had brought a camera, an expensive looking thing with a large flash, which would not be used. But that was not the sort of detail he would forget. He had also brought the rifle he had zeroed in on the farm on the road to Cremona earlier in the week. How had he explained it?

"At 5.32am we will know precisely where he will be: on the ramp, lit up in the bright lights. We know it will be him and it will be an easy shot. We will escape in the confusion. But we will leave the rifle. It's not the way we usually do things, but it will send a message to those that are still living. The Group might no longer be active, but after this many Nazis will live in fear."

That was why this time he smoked Israeli cigarettes and was using a Mauser Kar 98 sniper rifle with his country's stamps visible upon its steel surfaces; this time Yitzhak and Sarah wanted everyone to know it was revenge. It would not take long for Enrique Hohberg's true identity to be discovered, once he was dead. There were letters, already posted, to newspapers and embassies in Rome, they would see to that. There would be little doubt who had killed him; killed him in front of thousands of people and the world's press. The Group would be gone, but many Nazis – even those who thought themselves unimportant in the evil scheme of things – would not know that and they would live in fear of it and believe they would be safe nowhere. Mossad might pretend to be put out for a little while, but Yitzhak and Sarah would not care about that, and they would deny they had anything to do with it anyway; Yitzhak had even constructed a solid alibi for them both.

It was a good plan.

The Ferrari with the number 529 painted on its bonnet and doors eased off the ramp, then accelerated away towards the east, its taillights dwindling, glowing red dots in the fog, but soon snuffed out. There was now less than three minutes left.

***

Old Town, Warsaw. August 1944

They were naked, except for a fine coating of plaster dust, shaken from the ceiling every time a shell fell close by. Earlier Ingo had discovered that playing Chopin on a piano during a barrage of Nebelwerfers and big guns was a sublime experience. Tonight, he was discovering that making love during the same was even better. The only time he had felt more alive was at speed at the controls of a motorbike or car. But this came very close.

They had found an empty flat. It was on the third floor of a tottering, narrow, four-storey place on Nowomiejska. The building had not been locked, but then there is little point in locking a house with a hole in it. The apartment, too, had been unlocked; and there was a ragged hole in the ceiling and floor of the living room where a bomb, probably another dud, had passed through. The bedroom they were in had a dressing table, an empty wardrobe with its doors flung open, a large brass bed – on which Ingo was now putting nearly five years of frustration behind him – and a family picture, the glass of which had cracked in the same lightning-like S as an SS rune, slashing through the proud smile of a mother. The only illumination was from the explosions and the fires outside, which threw boomerangs of fractured red and orange light through the splintered windows and across their dusty bodies. An ashy throat-catching smell of burning was heavy on the air.

Nebelwerfer rockets, or Krowas as Lidka called them, howled from their launchers and she tensed around him, and he knew she was afraid. They came in sixes, clawing fire across the dark sky; the rending, shrieking, moan of one; then a small gap, then another, then another ... Then there was the wait until they landed: six explosions – a longer wait if they had been incendiaries, filled with sticky, jellified petrol, for they needed to crash through roofs and floors to inflict their evil damage. The night sky shuddered to them, shook to the big guns of the Panzer Train, and shivered to the rattle of machine guns.

She had lost weight since he had last been with her, and her breasts were not as big as they had been, but they were firm. He liked her breasts, the way they were now, he liked her slimmer body, too. This time it felt, somehow, different from the last time, he thought, but that had been a long time ago now, and while he had recalled that night often, too often, he had never been able to recapture just how it had been in his memory. It didn't matter so much, as he could not now imagine it could be any better than this, anyway. This was perfect. Except for the missing ring ...

More Nebelwerfers landed close by, one after the other, and the floor on which the bed sat shook, six times, and he felt her clench around him to each detonation, and for a moment he thought that would finish him. One blast took out what remained of one of the windows, and a small shard of glass cut Ingo's back, but he ignored it. He had waited too long for a sliver of glass to spoil this. He could ignore most things now ...

Most things, but not all things ... The invisible ring; just a faint white mark on a slightly tanned hand, and it might easily be something else, for it was not clear. She moaned a soft moan, velvet warm, the antidote to the howling moan of the Nebelwerfers.

When they had finished he softened within her, and they melted together, as if fused painlessly. Their heartbeats were as one for a few moments, before they slipped out of step, and their bodies were pasted together with sweat and dust, her breasts squashed beneath his chest. She shivered to someone's screams outside, and he stroked her cheek. The bombardment slackened a little, the kettle drums and symbols making way for the glockenspiels of the machine guns, the chorus of suffering people, and triangle tinkles of glass falling on to the cobbles three floors below. The firelight threw the shadow of her arm and hand, which was draped over the end of the bed, on to the far wall. He thought of the ring, again. But it was Lidka who said: "Has there been anyone else?"

"No," he said, and paused before adding: "And you?"

"No," she said, without hesitation; her mouth was close to his and her breath smelt just a little sour, as if she had not eaten for a while. There was a single crack of a rifle shot, close by.

He could not see her clearly now, it was too dark, and for a moment there were no explosions to light up the room, so her face was just a dim alabaster glow of white skin. He waited for her to say something else. Both wanting to know, and not wanting to know.

"Ingo ..."

"Yes?"

"I promised I would wait," she said. "I waited for a long time, Ingo."

"I waited, too."

"But you never came?"

"It was difficult, believe me – but I did come looking for you, I swear it."

"I saw you, on the day all this started, but I had already waited a long time by then."

"You saw me?"

"Yes, outside the house on Mochnackiego."

"Then why — "

"I could not."

"Why not?"

"You seem to forget; you're a German soldier, Ingo."

"Then you were not alone?"

"I'm with the AK, you know that; there was a gun pointed at you the entire time you were there."

"That's not very welcoming."

"It was all I could do to persuade him not to pull the trigger."

"Him?"

She hesitated, for a heartbeat, then said: "Just a boy; but a solider, too."

Ingo nodded, there were a lot of lads lying dead in Warsaw. "But that was not the time I meant; there was another time I came looking for you," he said.

"There was?"

"Yes, over two years ago; I tried Kasper's, where I had sent letters before, too, and then your old place – I saw it again earlier, you know; at least I think I did, I was never sure which house it was."

"You came in through Piwna?" she said, and he felt her heartbeat quicken, felt it through his own chest.

"Yes. Not a route I'd recommend, though. But back in '42 I found nothing; so I went to the place on Mochnackiego, I remembered it from that Christmas, when I'd played piano."

"But I was living there then?"

"I was told you didn't even work there anymore."

"Feliks," she said, and he felt the sigh as she said it. "He would have thought he was doing the right thing, saying that."

"Was it? Was it the right thing?" Ingo said, and then another salvo of Nebelwerfers shrieked across the night sky.

"I don't know," she said. Then, when the last of the rockets had exploded, some blocks away, she added. "But I do know that it would have been difficult, for everyone."

He peeled himself from her, the sweat and dust that pasted them together tacky as they came apart, and then lay on his back by her side.

"I wrote to you, too," she said.

"You did?"

"Well, I tried; I sent a letter to *Six Pianos, Munich*. There was no reply."

"It's not called that; called Wagner's, or it was last time I was there. Anyway, even if it got there my father would never send it on, we don't talk, fell out long ago. And he's a proper Nazi, that old bastard, so just reading your name and a Polish address would have given him a heart attack," Ingo said.

She was quiet for a moment, and he wondered if it had shocked her, the way he had spoken about his father. Then she suddenly said: "Ingo, you told me something once. You said you had never killed?"

He remembered saying that. Then he remembered Teploe, where the rage had taken him and he had had no choice but to kill, if Pop was to live, and much more recently here in Warsaw, where he had killed for other reasons.

"Well?"

He had not been aware he had taken so long to answer. "It's war, Lidka," he said, as he did now want to lie to her now. "Sometimes ..."

"Sometimes?"

"Let's not talk about that; not now – eh?"

She said nothing and they lay there in silence for a little while, while the noise of the battle continued around them. Pop had once told him that Pervitin was not only good for keeping you awake; it was also good for keeping you up. He had been right. They made love again soon after, and then she slept in his arms, while the bombs and the shells still fell. He did not sleep; not because of the Nebelwerfers, not even because of the Pervitin, but because of the doubt. He could not see the light band of a ring on the skin of her finger now; but he knew it was there.

*

The Stukas always made their first attack on the Old Town at just after six.

"It's our alarm call," Lidka said.

She had slept a little during the night. Ingo had not slept. They had lain on their sides, cuddled together like spoons in a drawer, and they both smelt of their love making, a heady smell that was an antidote to the smoulder and decay that also filled the air. She rolled away from him and stood up beside the bed, stretching out the stiffness of the night, her breasts jiggling playfully as she shivered a little in the morning air; he watched her, from the bed. Some of the Stukas had reverted to type, as there were no Yaks to worry about over Warsaw, and they were divebombing again. One started its dive and the scream of its siren seemed to rip the sky apart. Its bomb dropped some blocks away.

"I can bear them a little better than the Krowas," Lidka said, as she pulled on her underwear. "But I wonder why the Russians aren't attacking them. Have they no planes?"

Ingo shrugged. "They have plenty; too many! Some of our men think the Ivans have left you to your fate," he said.

"Some of our men think the same," she said, swiftly stepping in to her skirt and then reaching for her blouse.

"I believe it," he said. "Why are you dressing?"

"I have work to do."

"What about me?"

She shrugged. "The war has not ended, and I'm needed."

"You promised me, Lidka. You said there had been no one else, yes?" The lighter band on her finger looked less vivid than it had, now, almost invisible, he thought. But he could not stop thinking about it.

"There is no one; there has never been anyone else, Ingo."

"I would understand if —"

"No one, Ingo. I swear it."

He said nothing for a little while, time filled with a pistol pop answered by the distinctive buzz of an MG 42, as the one-sided argument continued in the Old Town. Then he nodded: "Then you have to come with me," he said, standing up now, still naked. "Warsaw is finished, you will have no chance if you stay here, but we will have a chance if we go; go now. Right now!"

"Warsaw's not finished yet," she said. "We're still fighting."

"You have no chance, and there will be no help from the Russians."

"So, you think we should simply surrender? I might have trouble persuading the others, you know?" she said, smiling now.

Ingo shook his head, sharply. "Surrender will save no one anyway. They will kill you all; you saw what they did in Wola," he said. He had felt sick to think what might have happened to her if she had been found by Dirlewanger's men there. That danger had not yet passed.

"There is still a chance," she said. "There must be."

"There's no chance; they will kill you all, destroy the city. I know it!"

"I'm needed here," she repeated, busying herself with buttoning up the blouse front.

"I need you more! Don't you see? It's our only chance. Come with me, we can escape to the forests, we can live there! This war cannot last much longer."

"I must stay," she said, firmly, then reached for her holed socks and the boots which looked too big for her.

"You have to know something, Lidka," he said. "There is an order, from Himmler himself, some say it's from Hitler himself. They intend to completely destroy Warsaw – and kill every living thing within it."

She laughed at that, but it was a nervous laugh. "Not even they could think of such a thing," she said.

"Couldn't they? Didn't it occur to you that these guns they are using would be of better use killing Ivan soldiers, rather than innocent civilians? It's occurred to us, alright."

"The AK is an army, not civilians."

"The AK is a nut in a nutcracker. And they are bringing up a Karl, Lidka. Do you know what that is?"

She shook her head.

"It's the biggest of guns, a mortar really. It throws shells the size of dustbins. It has one purpose; to destroy towns, cities even. There is no hope for anyone left in Warsaw – that is the truth, I swear it."

"The Russians might still come —"

"And flamethrowers, Lidka," Ingo interrupted. "I've never seen so many, trucks full of them, and they have only one use. I do not know what Warsaw has done to Hitler, but he intends to utterly destroy it. I've seen how these people work, and I know they will not rest until every building in the city is rubble, and every living being in Warsaw is dead, and —"

"Everyone?" she said, almost in a whisper. "Even children?"

"Yes, children. I have seen it myself, the way they kill them, they never waste a bullet on a child, it's ..." He let the sentence fade away, for she was looking away from him now, staring out of the broken window to the southwest, though any view would be blocked by other buildings. She waited for a minute or so, saying nothing. A shell whistled through the smoky air and then crunched through a roof some blocks away, before exploding seconds later.

"Ingo," she said, not turning to face him. "I will come with you."

"You will?"

"Of course, I have been waiting for years," she said, then sighed, before adding: "But it's not that simple; first you must do something for me."

*

Lidka talked as they walked. She spoke to Ingo in German and only switched to Polish when others were in earshot, talking about food, as everybody always talked about food or the lack of it, while Ingo nodded as if he understood what she said.

She had not told him he had a son.

Lidka had shown him a way out of the Old Town, now she had to make sure he knew precisely what she needed him to do. The rubble filled the streets, and often they had to pick their way through it or clatter over it, but at least, for now, there was a rare break in the shelling and the bombing. Many were making the most of the lemony sunlight that peeked through a ragged tear in the cloth of ash and cinders which lay like a shroud over the Old Town. Ingo was a German amongst the enemy, but he was dressed like them in his SS smock with its red and white armband, and even though he did not wear his helmet with the AK band around it, swinging it by its strap instead, with his longish hair he looked every inch the cheerful and dashing insurgent; an important one, too, for he had two guns, a rifle and the pistol in the buttoned-down leather holster on the belt worn over the light camouflaged jacket. One of the Polish girls smiled at him and being Ingo – still Ingo – he smiled back. Lidka felt a small stab of jealousy, reminding her of the girl she had once been herself, and also of the girl she could no longer afford to be.

For a while, in the year or so after Freddy was born, she had rehearsed and worried about what to say, and what he might say, about the child. But since then, until she had seen Ingo on the day the uprising had started outside the house on Mochnackiego, she had become used to the idea that he would not return; used to the idea of an ordinary, safe, life with Józef.

Lidka had changed since they had last been together. Grown up, she supposed. At first she had thought Ingo had not changed. Before all this she had never been able to imagine Ingo ever changing, but now she was not so sure. He had admitted he had killed – yet she knew now a soldier had to, sometimes, simply to survive, so that she could understand. But then he had also told her that he had come into the Old Town through Piwna; wearing an SS jacket. She knew the name of the SS unit that was attacking from the south, working in headquarters you heard such things. It was Dirlewanger. She had seen what they had done in Wola – this was why a part of her had no trouble believing Ingo when he said that Warsaw, and everyone in it, was finished. She did not want to believe he was a part of all that. Yet this was not what had stopped her from telling Ingo about his son. That had more to do with Freddy's future.

They walked along Kiliński. Soon he would need to leave the Old Town, the way she had shown him. She knew of a blind spot in the lines, a drain beneath Mostowa, where sometimes Andrzej had slipped out to kill Germans, and take their weapons. For one or two men this was just possible, but no more than that. The AK snipers covering the opening would not shoot at Ingo as they would think him one of theirs; if he waved and appeared confident, and once he was close to the Germans he only needed to lose his armband and helmet ribbon and shout to them in his own language. It would be safer in the day, she thought, as no one hesitated to shoot in the night.

It might have been better for him to use the sewer, as she intended to tomorrow, but that was impossible, as there were AK military police guards stationed by the entrance at Krasiński Square and without a message to deliver – which she was sure to get at some point tomorrow morning – there was no way anyone else could use the sewers. The guards were there, and at other manholes, because people were beginning to realise that this might be the only way to escape. To realise that the Old Town was surrounded. And, also, that the Russians just might have abandoned them to their fate.

"These people are dear to me," Lidka said to him, in German, now that they were well past the Polish girl. "They have been holed up in Ochota, hiding, since 1940."

"That's a long time; why?"

"They are Jews, Ingo. Is that a problem?"

"Not for me, no. You know that. But it might make it more difficult."

Some lads in AK armbands, maybe no older than 15 or 16, had put down their guns – the few of them that had them – and were using the lull in the barrage and bombing to kick a football around in a patch of street almost clear of debris; the leather scuffing against the broken cobbles a strangely comforting sound, she thought. The ball bounced in front of Ingo, with a thump, and rather than leave it go he stretched his leg, trapped it with the side of his right foot, brought it down, then kicked it past the goalie, who was standing between two German helmets placed on the ground. The lads laughed; one of them shouted: "Nice goal mister!"

Ingo bowed, although he could not have understood what the kid had said.

"You are drawing attention to yourself."

"I'm blending in – but a good goal, eh?" He grinned, and it was impossible not to grin with him. "Why are they so important to you, these people?" he then asked.

"Tell me first, can it be done?"

"It's possible," Ingo said, as they wound their way through a snaking pathway which cut through great mounds of rubble formed by the collapsed façade of a building. Ahead of them there was a commotion, people cheering, and Lidka could hear the now familiar high-pitched squeal and rattle of tank tracks on cobbles and smell the acrid fumes of an exhaust. For a moment she was confused. Two lads in AK armbands pushed past them.

"We've captured a German tank!" one of them shouted.

"They seem pleased; have the Ivans come?" Ingo said, calmly.

"They say they have taken a German tank."

"Really? Well done them," Ingo said.

"What will you need?"

"I will need you to be there."

"I'll be there," she said. "I will come through the sewers, I promise."

"Then we'll need a truck. There are too many police; well they call themselves police. Warsaw's full of these clowns, so we will get nowhere on foot. And this forest; it's far?"

"Kampinos? An hour's drive from Ochota at the very least. Can you get a truck?"

"No, I can't. But I know a man who can."

The street was wider now. Ahead of them she could hear the tracks of the tank crunching the already broken cobbles. It was hidden from sight by the great mass of people who had gathered to see it and to celebrate its capture, but she was surprised she could not see its turret from here. The noise of the tank and the excited babble and cheering of the crowd forced Ingo to talk louder, which in turn made Lidka glance over her shoulder to check no one could hear him speaking German.

"You remember I told you about my pal, Pop?"

"He's still around?"

"They can't kill Pop," Ingo said, almost sounding like he believed it. "Anyway, he can get his hands on anything – well, almost anything – a truck for certain, though, maybe even the right documents. But he will take some persuading."

"Because they are Jews?"

"Because it could get us killed."

"Of course, I'm sorry," she said, yet Ingo had said it with a grin. "And how might Pop be persuaded."

"Money."

"Oh, is that all. Not a problem."

"I mean real money, not German or Polish money."

Lidka smiled. "You know, there are some who are sleeping on piles of złotys in the Polski Bank; they say it doesn't even make good bedding. But you needn't worry, Sol Vogler is a jeweller; he has dollars – he even has diamonds, I think."

"Diamonds, eh? That should help persuade Pop."

"But he'll do it?"

"If we are to be together, he will have to do it, so I will make sure he will – tell me, just how many diamonds does this Jew jeweller have?"

"I'm not sure; but some," Lidka said, although she did not really know if he had any now. Some had been sold earlier on in the occupation, when there was still a market for such things, but that's all she knew. Yet Andrzej, for one, was convinced that Sol Vogler had squirrelled the very best of his stones away, for when the war was over.

People were now rushing out of the buildings, cheering and shouting, everybody wanted to see the captured tank.

"Can you trust him? A man who will do things only for money is —"

"I can trust him, trust him more than anyone," he said, and, for a moment, he seemed to glance at her hand.

"What about them being Jews?" she asked.

"That, we have never discussed. But all he is interested in is women and racing, and I've never known him to have a woman he didn't have to buy," he laughed as he said that. "And he says racing is even more expensive than women!"

Some children rushed past, running to see the tank, their soles slapping noisily against the cobbles.

"Racing? You still have your plans, then?"

Ingo shrugged. "We never really talk about it these days; haven't for a while," he said, shaking his head. "It's not just people that die in war, Lidka."

"No, but not everyone, or everything, has to die, Ingo."

He nodded, smiled. Then said: "You're right, the future will be better; it has to be – but tell me about your Jews."

"There are four Jews, and two others, an adult and a child; but they must be helped too, if what you say is true. Three of them are middle-aged, and not so fit. There's a lad, in his teens, he's a nervous type. And then there is Sarah; you will have to be careful with that one, when she sees you in a German uniform she will try to kill you, I swear it. She has more fight in her than most of these AK boys, that's for sure. But then she may know you from before; remember the girl, that time when you played the piano?"

Ingo shook his head.

"It doesn't matter. Just say I sent you, and then give her this note, it will explain everything," Lidka said, handing him a folded piece of paper. He took a quick look at it, but it was in Polish. He did not ask her what it said, and so she didn't have to lie to him. He folded the note and put it in the pocket of his black trousers.

"And the child?"

"An orphan," she said quickly. "We took him in, he had no one else, but he deserves to be saved." She had written this in the note; as she did not want Sarah to let on Freddy was her son. Not to begin with, at least.

"Fine, the more the merrier, eh?"

"So, we meet at the house, as agreed?" she added.

"I'll be there," he said.

She stopped walking then, and he stopped too.

"What is it?" he said.

"There is something I need to ask you, Ingo."

"Then ask."

"Are you with Dirlewanger?"

He shook his head, grinned. "You thought that?"

"The jacket, and Piwna?"

"Now you come to mention it, I can see how it might look that way," he said. Then he laughed; laughed softly at first, then louder, and louder, until others were looking at him, smiling to see him laughing. She laughed, too. It had always been impossible not to join in, when Ingo was laughing; and in that very instant she was transported back Kasper's café in 1939. Ingo had not changed. She was sure of it. Now.

"I'm nothing to do with Dirlewanger, I promise, but it's complicated. I will tell you everything, tomorrow," he said. "Right now, I think this would be good time for me to leave, while everyone's busy with the tank, eh?"

They were around a hundred metres from the crowd that was pressed up tight to the captured tank now. Whoever was driving it gunned the engine and it must have lurched forward, as the crowd parted quickly.

"Before you go, Ingo. There's something I should tell you," she said, having made the decision that very moment.

"Yes?"

It was a strange looking tank, smaller than most she had seen, and open at the top with a thick rectangular and perpendicular windshield behind which the grinning AK driver sat. It also had what looked like a huge square box on the front. But in between them and the weird tank something else also caught Lidka's eye: a girl in blue overalls, her hair in a red head scarf, tied at the front, in a turban. She recognised the leather dispatch case slung over her shoulders before she recognised the girl.

At that very instant Cat turned. And Lidka saw the exact moment that she realised the man she was with was the very same German who had knocked at the door of the house on Mochnackiego on the day the uprising started.

"Borgward!" Ingo said.

The word seemed to trigger the explosion. It sucked the air from the street and Lidka felt her lungs compress, before the grit-laced blast knocked her down, and Ingo, too – as if they had been hit by a grey tram. For a moment the sky turned to jelly and she could hear nothing, and then the noises came back; sharp screams first, that pieced through the fog of dust and befuddlement. An arm landed with a thud close by, a watch still attached to the wrist. The fingers twitched against the cobbles, as if playing a piano, but only for a moment. Lidka reached for Ingo, and tried to talk to him, but she found her mouth was clogged with dust, her tongue pasted to her palette. He nodded, signalled that he was okay, but she saw there was a bright gash on his forehead and his face was speckled, measle-like, with someone else's blood. She suddenly remembered Cat and looked around for her, but she was lost in the dust and the smoke. From somewhere above a great slab of masonry dislodged in the explosion fell in to the street with a crash, adding to the dust.

"Go, now!" she managed to say, as they helped each other back on to their feet.

He shook his head, coughed, then spluttered: "You were going to tell me something?"

"Tomorrow, Ingo," she said. "You have to get out of here, now!"

With that he hesitated for a moment, but then nodded, briskly, kissed her, his mouth tasting of grit and ash, and then he was gone, disappearing into the cloud of dust that was slowly sweeping up the street like a lazy tidal wave.

*

"Were you worried?"

"Hardly noticed you'd gone," Pop said. His eyes looked watery and bloodshot, and his words were just a little slurred. Ingo doubted he had slept for days. He was sat against a brick wall pockmarked with bullet strikes, his legs splayed out in front of him. Sunshine sat some way off leaning against the same wall, eyes closed, sleeping soundly and noiselessly despite the howling whooshes from a Neberlwerfer battery, the steady barrage from the Panzer Train, and the wail of the Stukas. There was a dead body, a girl, perhaps thirteen, maybe a little older. She was naked from the waist down, her summer dress torn at the front like an open tent flap. Her legs were coated in sticky looking blood, on which the fat blue flies feasted; her throat was cut and her dead eyes were bulging with frozen fear, her face was a purple bruise. There was a broken vodka bottle at her feet.

Ingo glanced at the body.

Pop slowly shook his head. "Wrong place, wrong time," he said, looking away from the dead girl, focussing instead on a StuG III that was rattling across Plac Zamkowy.

"Wrong place, wrong time. That's Warsaw, alright," Ingo said.

"Kroh thinks you're dead, or you've deserted."

"Then why disappoint him?"

"But you're back, aren't you?"

Ingo did not answer.

The battery fired off a salvo of six rockets and Pop waited until the noise had passed before he said: "Your face?"

Ingo ran his finger over the cut on his forehead, which wasn't so deep. "Borgward," he said.

"We heard it. Big bang."

Ingo nodded. The Borgward was the Goliath's bigger brother. A turretless panzer which was abandoned by its driver before delivering a huge box of explosives by remote control. It seemed to Ingo now that this one had been taken by an AK soldier who believed he had captured a tank, but the 450kg charge in its detachable rectangular steel box had still been fixed to its front. It was a Trojan Horse, with a big kick, the Borgward. Ingo had quickly got out of the Old Town after that. The way Lidka had shown him worked well, in one direction at least, and, by shouting, he had managed to persuade the SS on the other side that he was German before they started shooting.

The smell of corruption and burning in the air was tinged with a slight aroma of spice, and he looked down to where Pop was seated to see a mess tin half full of Wehrmacht-issue tinned goulash. He suddenly realised he was hungry and his stomach growled in agreement.

"Help yourself," Pop said. "I've lost my appetite."

Ingo took the mess tin and ate quickly. "Business has not been so good here, has it?" he said, between mouthfuls of the lukewarm goulash.

"Not for us, no, but I dare say Kroh is prospering," Pop said. "He's been taking truckloads of loot, from what I can see."

Ingo glanced at Sunshine. "Let's go somewhere where we can talk," he said.

"Let's stay, a sniper's bullet won't find us here — and that makes this a good place to talk."

Ingo looked at Sunshine again.

"If he can sleep through this, then a few words will hardly wake him. He only knows three words in German anyway: *schnapps*, *Fräulein* and *wurst*. I think we'd be in the shit, well deeper shit, if he knew anymore, the things we've been talking about lately – don't you? Besides, he's not so bad … If you can look past the rape and the murder."

Ingo nodded, and batted a fat fly from his face. "I know where there's money; dollars."

Pop leaned forward: "How much?"

"And diamonds."

Pop's eyes lit up, a little, at that. "How many?"

"That I don't know, all that I know is that there are dollars and diamonds. It all belongs to a jeweller – a jeweller who wants to get out of Warsaw."

"How do you know this?"

"I was told."

"That's not enough."

"Lidka."

"Really? You *really* found her?"

"I found her"

"And?"

"And," Ingo said, with a wink.

Pop grinned at that, but it was not the old grin, it was somehow a sad grin, Ingo thought, like a painted smile on a ruined clown. Ingo glanced over at the smoking, burning Old Town, just as a Stuka pulled out of its screaming dive. They both remained silent until the bomb exploded.

"So, what do you think?"

"I think you're crazy," Pop said.

"It would be crazy not to take something from this hell – do you want just bad dreams from it all?"

"I just want to live; and anyhow, since when have you been interested in money? It's not as though you can use it to buy a racing car, all that's finished, Ingo," Pop said, then dropped his voice a little as he added: "Germany's finished."

"I'm doing it for her."

"Doing what?"

Ingo told him as he finished off the goulash and Pop listened quietly, puffing away at a pungent smelling Russian Belomorkanal cigarette through its little grey cardboard holder, which he had squashed flat in the middle with his fingers, just as an Ivan soldier would – he was out of German fags, everyone was.

"These people, why are they so important to her?" Pop said, after Ingo had finished the tale and the food.

"That, I don't know," Ingo said, putting the empty mess tin to one side, and he remembered the very slightly paler band of skin around her finger. Pop coughed; a harsh, rattling cough – the strong Ivan cigarettes did not seem to agree with him – and Ingo repeated, softly now: "That, I don't know ..."

"We'll need papers," Pop said, pulling some reichsmarks out of his pocket.

"Then you'll do it?"

"I'll take this to Beck, the guy with the glasses at HQ, he's always after cash," Pop continued, not answering Ingo's question. "That's the great thing about Dirlewanger, bunch of crooks."

"The truck?"

"That'll be easy."

"Thought so," Ingo said. "About the only thing you can't arrange is getting us back in the 19th," he laughed as he said it.

"Well, that's Kroh's doing," Pop muttered. "But listen Ingo, you need to steer clear of that bastard, right?"

"Yes, you're right. I'll make my way to the house and hide out there, you meet me with the truck and the papers tomorrow, late afternoon, it will look wrong transporting prisoners at night; you sure you can find it?"

"Yes, the crescent off Grójecka, south of Plac Narutowicza. I'll find it."

"Come from that direction and drive around until you can see the end of the street; then rev the engine loud, three times, yes?"

Pop nodded: "Ingo music, eh?"

"Yep, Ingo music."

Sunshine suddenly snorted a loud snore, which seemed to wake him up with a start, and he reflexively reached for the MP 40 that was slung around his neck. Ingo cocked his head in his direction.

"Don't worry, he trusts me now – and he's easily distracted, anyway," Pop said.

"Thank you, Pop," Ingo said. "I'll never forget this."

Pop turned away from Ingo, looked at Sunshine, and said: "Get going Ingo, before this one tells Kroh you're back from the dead."

*

Lidka had spent the last few hours helping with the many wounded, only stopping when the Stukas came, every half an hour, deadly clockwork. Now she was clearing the dead, and the bits of the dead. Everyone was, as they had been ordered to, because on a hot day like this there was a risk of disease.

She had almost told him.

She had almost told Ingo that he had a son. It was not because she thought he was more likely to help her if he knew; she believed that he would help, if he could, for her, and because she said she would leave Warsaw with him – or maybe for Sol Vogler's money, and diamonds if he had them, if she had been wrong about Ingo. Almost telling him was not because that would be the right thing to do, either. Freddy could not have a German father now, not after all this, and she had long come to terms with the idea that Jósef should take

Ingo's place. Even if he had been killed, a dead Polish father would be a better lie to live with. It was not because Ingo had a right to know, either; she had not heard from him for years – though she had been happy to hear he had tried to contact her, see her, after all – and he had played no part in Freddy's life, while she could still not see Ingo as a father. He might have killed, but Ingo Six was still a boy. No. Now that he had left the Old Town she could see clearly that she had almost told him he had a son for some reason that had nothing to do with *reason*. It had been a madness that tasted like love, how she had remembered love, and how she had relived it the night before. A dangerous thing.

But then fate had intervened. The tank-like vehicle had exploded. It had perhaps saved her from making a mistake; but it had killed many. She believed Ingo would still help her, and hoped the lure of money and the chance of diamonds would persuade his friend to help, too. She hoped that they would help because she knew Ingo was not exaggerating. Lidka had seen what the Germans had done in Wola, and she believed what he had told her, that they would destroy everything in Warsaw. And everyone. She now wondered why she hadn't seen it before. The Russians would not be coming. Warsaw was doomed.

What would become of them, Ingo and her, once they were out of Warsaw, would be down to fate. If the explosion of the tank had been fate, if fate was so decisive, she would trust in it to make other decisions, too. But right now there was work to be done.

There were bodies piled on a handcart, dreadfully lacerated bodies, some already putrefying in the heat. The stink of it all, thick and sticky in the air, made her gag. The dust coated her nasal passages and her throat, and she desperately needed water, but there was none to be had. And there was still so much work to be done. The street was a shambles of broken stone, twisted steel; flesh and blood. She lifted her head to look for the sun in the dust, and she saw limbs, hanging from the guttering like hams in a butcher's shop. A fat crow took a strip of red-pink flesh from a rooftop, peeling it off the tiles like bacon from a frying pan.

She turned away and forced herself to pick up a leg, a leg wearing a torn stocking and a bottle green shoe with a broken heel. It had lain in its own little patch for a while, while all the others who helped stack the dead on the handcart worked silently around it. Lidka picked it up, surprised at the weight of it; weight that made it seem alive, weight that made it twitch in her hands. She tried not to look at the bony, red-black severed end of the leg, as she threw it on to the pile of bodies. It hit with a slapping thud, then slipped off and landed on the cobbles.

Lidka sighed, then wondered if this latest tragedy, in which more than three-hundred must have died, would be the end for the Old Town. People looked defeated now; *capturing* the tank had been the cruellest of jokes. The barrage had started again, and she heard the high moan of the Krowas, scoring the smoky sky like fingernails on a blackboard. She picked up the leg once more and took more care as she placed it on the pile of dead bodies and loose body parts on the cart. Still it slithered and slipped back on to the cobbles like a living thing.

Now she stared at it, defeated by it, and she was suddenly so very tired.

"I've been looking for you."

Andrzej picked up the severed leg and threw it on top of the pile of bodies and body parts in the handcart. Grotesquely, it landed close to a dead old man without a leg and it almost, though very loosely, took the place of his lost limb. One of the boys with Andrzej, a spotty kid with a captured Steyr automatic stuffed in his belt, laughed. She wondered again what would become of these youngsters when this was all over.

"I've been here," she said. "Since the ... Well, since."

The last time she had seen Andrzej was yesterday, when he had walked in on her as she bathed. It seemed a lifetime ago. He turned to issue an order and she saw that the back of his leather jacket was ripped open, a loose flap showing a cloth lining underneath.

"Help with the clearing up," he told the boys with him, and they set to the task, then he said to her: "Come with me." Lidka knew an order when she heard it, and so she followed him down the ruined street to the command centre, which had also been badly damaged in the blast. Someone was knocking out jagged triangles of glass which fell to burst into sugary crystals on the cobbles below. Andrzej led her in to the building and on to the same little room she had bathed in yesterday, before closing the door behind them.

"Cat saw him," he said.

"Who?"

"The German; the one who came to Mochnackiego."

Lidka shrugged: "Just another German."

"This time he was with you."

"You believe her?"

"Yes; why would she lie?"

Lidka nodded, she could think of a reason Cat would lie. But she had not lied. She had thought Cat might have been killed in the blast. She should have guessed she would have gone straight to Andrzej. But there had been no place for Lidka to hide, anyway. She suddenly felt drained of energy. There was a low stool in the corner of the room, she crossed to it and sat down.

"Freddy's father?" he asked.

A shell fell nearby, crunching through roof tiles and wood floors, before exploding with a boom and the scatter-like sound of smashed glass and wood. The stool shook to it; she noticed that her hands were caked in drying blood. She nodded again.

"Where is he now?" Andrzej said.

"Not in the Old Town."

"Where?"

"He's gone. But he will help them," she said. "Freddy, your mother, the others."

"Help them?"

"He says the Germans plan to destroy the city, every house, every person – even children!"

Andrzej said nothing.

"Freddy," she added.

He took a deep breath, suddenly he looked tired, as tired as she felt. "It's not surprising, it's what they did in Wola," he said.

"You believe it, too?"

"What will he do?" Andrzej said, ignoring the question.

"He will take them to the Kampinos Forest, they should be safe there."

"How?"

"By truck, a German army truck. I'm to meet him at the house tomorrow, late afternoon."

"You're to go, too?"

She nodded.

"But your place is here."

"My place is with my son!"

"It's all planned out, then?" he said, softer now.

"It is," she said. "Your mother, Freddy, Sarah – they will be safe."

"But he's a German soldier?"

"Ingo is no more a soldier than those children out there are," she said, referring to the AK lads in their too-large helmets.

He looked up at the thick clouded glass of the barred little window, where tired dark grey silhouettes shifted the shadows of corpses out in the backyard, the soft thuds of bodies being tossed upon bodies the most solid thing about the scene.

"Sol Vogler will be taking his diamonds with him, then?"

"I'm not sure he has diamonds, not now," she said.

"I am," Andrzej said, still quite softly and with a little nod. "You went there, didn't you, the day before yesterday?"

"I had to see Freddy. I had to know he was okay."

"And they are okay? All of them?"

She nodded.

"You intend to go to them through the sewers, I suppose?"

She nodded again.

Andrzej said nothing for a little while, still watching the shadows behind the frosted glass, biting his lip slightly. When he did speak his manner was sharp and cold, as he said: "You brought a German in to the Old Town, teacher."

"I did not bring him, he —"

"Right now he will be telling them everything; our strength, our positions, our morale – or what's left of it."

"You don't understand, Andrzej!"

"It's Bullet, teacher." With that he went out, slamming the door behind him. She sighed. Then she heard the unmistakeable sound of a key turning in the lock.

*

371

If in doubt, get yourself a motorcycle. It might have been Ingo's motto. He found one an SS rider had left for a careless moment on the northern edge of the Saski Garden. Not far from here the SS had committed crimes beyond imagination; with that in mind stealing a bike from them seemed the epitome of petty theft. Dirlewanger and Kroh would probably hang him for desertion anyhow, if they caught him, so he figured he might as well make it worth their while.

Sat astride the DKW NZ 350 it felt just like old times – though there was no sidecar, and no Pop. He wore his helmet, so as not to look out of place, and the lightweight camouflage SS jacket, the sleeves of which fluttered in the cooling airstream. His rifle was strapped over his back and he also carried a satchel over his shoulder. It was good to feel the throb of the machine beneath him and the patter of the road through the handlebars. There was less dust in the air the further out he rode, but it hadn't rained in weeks and the smell of decomposing corpses hung around like the mist of Mrs Death's perfume. He wondered if Warsaw would ever lose that smell; doubted that he ever would. Once he had negotiated the debris and rubble that littered the streets of Wola he headed a little way south to Ochota. He rode fast, of course, and found a way in to the district that avoided most of the checkpoints. At the only one he could not avoid because he saw it too late, a Feldgendarmerie Kubelwagen parked at the edge of Plac Narutowicza, the chained dogs waved him through and he gave them a wave and a grin and rode on, up Grójecka a little further, not taking the more direct route – this way he could park up the bike and approach the house from the rear, as Lidka had suggested.

The ashy smoke from the Old Town was not drifting this way and the sun burnt bright, reflecting off the burnished cobblestones. Many of the buildings here were burnt out and there were signs of destruction everywhere. It was not as bad as Wola, but it was still bad. The bike's wheels thudded over a fan of fallen cables as he turned off Grójecka and on to Wawelska. Two soldiers stepped in to the road, one walking behind an upstretched hand. Ingo had the brakes on and the DKW came to a stop before the soldier had finished his "Halt!", the rear wheel skidding slightly.

They were Heer; infantry. They wore field grey tunics with the sleeves rolled up, because of the heat. Their rifles were slung over their shoulders and sweat sparkled on their faces beneath coalscuttle helmets that were pushed back high on their heads. Ingo did not switch off the engine.

The one who had shouted *halt* was a feldwebel with a port wine stain on his cheek that was the shape of Italy. He raised his voice to be heard over the tinny crackle of the DKW's idle.

"SS?"

"No, Gefreiter Six, 19th Panzer," Ingo said.

"But no tank?"

"I misplaced it," Ingo said, risking a smile, as he offered them his frontline ID card and his paybook.

"An SS jacket?"

"I'm attached to the Dirlewanger Brigade, they needed a dispatch rider; I have papers for the SS here, RONA I believe?" He hoped that by naming the two most feared units in Warsaw in one breath he might persuade them not to ask for the written orders he did not have – his left hand had the clutch lever depressed, his right hand was ready on the twist grip throttle, the fluttering idle of the engine alive in his piano fingers.

The feldwebel quickly studied Ingo's ID card and paybook, then glanced at the canvas satchel slung over his shoulder, which was stuffed with bread rolls. He nodded, then said: "Looks like you've been sent on a fool's errand, pal. Those Ivan murderers went too far."

"Too far?"

"Sick bastards ... Have been sent packing, out to some forest to chase partisans. Forest is the best place for animals like that." The edge of his lips curled in sour disgust as he said it.

"So, I've wasted my time, then. Typical SS, eh?" Ingo said.

The feldwebel nodded, returned Ingo's ID, then they walked on. Ingo watched them go and then rode up the street a little way, very slowly, then down a side street to meet the smaller crescent, Mianowskiego, that ran behind a small portion of Mochnackiego. He popped the bike up the steep, sloping, cobbled kerb and on to the pavement, before taking it through into a courtyard, where he parked it close to a wall. Then he made his way along Mianowskiego, entering the courtyard from the rear, and recognising the back of the house, with its now door-less garden wall, from Lidka's description. He walked across the courtyard and through the gateless gate, thudding along the flattened wooden door and scrunching up the gravel path. There was no sign of life, the curtains were closed. Lidka had given him a key for the backdoor, which he took from the pocket of his SS jacket. She had also given him a warning. And so, as he turned the key and then opened the door, he shouted the name: "Sarah!"

He walked in to the kitchen, which was dark and smelt musty.

"Sarah; I've been sent by Lidka!"

There was a light switch, but it did not work, and the click sounded loud in the dark space. He took out his Daimon flashlight and switched it on, its beam picking out pots and pans on shelves and an empty table. He stepped forward, his panzer boots crunching broken glass. He listened for signs of life, but there were none.

"Sarah, Lidka has sent me!" he shouted again.

He waited silently for twenty seconds or so, but still could hear nothing except the distant booming of the barrage from the Old Town. He opened his mouth to shout again ...

"What do you want?"

The voice came from behind him, quiet and cool and in German, and just three metres from where he stood. He turned to see her, the light from his torch reflecting off the broad blade of a knife. His rifle was slung over his shoulder and his Walther was in its holster, but he did not reach for either.

"I've come to help," he said. She stared at him with big dark eyes that shone in the light of the torch. She was attractive. But she also looked thin and frail – yet he knew from her eyes that she would not hesitate to use the knife.

"I have food," he said, and he reached in to the small canvas satchel and pulled out a bread roll, holding it in front of him; it was fresh enough to smell delicious and he saw her swallow saliva as she stared at it. He handed her the bag, and she let her knife hand drop to take it. Lidka had asked him to take some food.

"Lidka sent you?" she said, after swallowing a piece of the bread roll, her German was good.

"Yes; you're Sarah?"

She nodded.

"She gave me this." Ingo took the note, which was in Polish, from his pocket and handed it to her. She read it quickly, twice, and then she nodded. Ingo had not been able to read it, but he guessed it would explain what had been agreed.

"You're a German soldier?"

"A German yes, but never really a soldier."

"I know you now, you're the piano player," she said, before taking another crunching bite of bread, which she chewed and swallowed quickly.

"There's not much time for that these days." He did not recognise her from before and he wondered how much she would have changed during these years of hiding. She had to be about nineteen or twenty now.

"And you will take us from here? To the fighting?" The fire in her eyes ignited once more.

"To safety."

She sighed. "Yes, that would be Lidka's plan."

"Where are the others?"

"Downstairs, in the basement. Will we go now?"

"Tomorrow – Lidka will come, too."

"Then it's best they stay put."

"No, I'd like to meet them first. Please."

She thought on that for a moment, then said: "It is safer for them where they are."

Ingo unbuttoned the narrow closing strap of the leather holster at his belt and pulled out the Walther. Her pupils dilated, but otherwise she showed no sign of fear. He smiled, and handed her the pistol, butt first.

"You can trust me, Sarah," he said, as she stared at the Walther as if it was a holy relic for a moment. Then she took it, and expertly pulled back the slide, chambering a round.

"Where did you learn to do that?"

"I don't spend all my time here, and I have watched the Germans. How you have killed, and how you use these things," she said. Then she nodded sharply, twice. "I will bring them up. But you wait here; they scare easy."

She appeared again a little later, this time with five others. One was a man in his late forties at least, and there was a woman of around the same age who was clutching his arm and seemed to be his wife, both looked too Jewish to be safe on the streets, and both were clearly terrified at the sight of Ingo in his SS jacket. There was another woman – he dimly recognised her as an emaciated version of one of those who had been at the recital in this very house all those years ago. There was a boy, too, about thirteen perhaps, who coughed incessantly. Last of all there was a smaller, much younger boy, who looked a little fair compared to the others, though it was difficult to tell in the light of the torch. He smiled at Ingo and he seemed excited to be out of the basement. Ingo thought he could be no older than four or five. He winked at him, and the boy winked back, grinning a grin that was full of life. Ingo realised that this boy had to be the orphan that Lidka had told him about.

Sarah shared out the bread rolls as they came in the kitchen, not taking another herself.

"That's it?"

"Were you expecting someone else?" Sarah said.

Ingo shook his head. "Tell them they will be safe soon, just one more night in the basement," he said. He did not know what he had expected, or who. "It will be better if they keep themselves hidden for now; I saw soldiers patrolling earlier on."

"Yes, they come this way, quite often."

Sarah told the others to go back to the basement and they shuffled away without another word.

"You too, Sarah," he said.

"What about you?"

"I'll keep watch."

"Father says he has your money," she said, with a slightly accusatory tone; she would have read about all that in the note Lidka had given him, he supposed. He noticed she had said nothing about diamonds.

"I'm not doing this for money," he said.

"Then why?"

"Go to the basement, Sarah. One more night, that's all."

*

Sunshine could always get vodka and Pervitin, and Sunshine could always find girls. Pop *needed* all three, but mostly the girls. This one last time. He tried not to think about the last time, for that had been one last time, too. He knew, deep down, that he was lost, and he also knew that being drunk and high on Pervitin was no excuse. Ingo's truck? That could wait, there was plenty of time. He took another gulp of the clear spirit.

They were in a chapel that was part of a much larger church. It was always better in a church. Better even than in a hospital. The more wrong it was, the more right it felt. He did not know the name of the church; if it had one it had been blown away, along with the roof. Above him a sky of scribbled charcoal floated past skeletal beams, and out in the nave most of the pews had been blasted into chaotic geometry, with yellow bristles where the wood had fractured. In the chapel the light was filtered through dust and smoke and the jagged remnants of a large stained-glass window that threw jelly-like red, blue and green splodges on to the ash-blotched flagstones of the floor. There was a bare altar in the wide space and five rows of intact varnished ash pews with worked walnut ends and red-cushioned kneelers affixed to their backs. And there were two naked girls.

The girls were young, maybe too young; though that meant nothing here and now. It was better that they were young, better because they cried more, screamed more. They stood in front of the altar, tears carving lines in their dusty faces. They were very thin, and one tried to hide the fine hair of her bush with her hands, the other crossing small breasts with her arms, like a corpse in a coffin. That would come, too, he thought, and with that his arousal grew so that it was almost painful. Their white skin shone, even in the dim, smoky light. Pop upended the bottle and finished the vodka in one go, then let it slip through his fingers, to smash into jagged pieces on the stone floor.

The girl on the right, a particularly skinny thing, shook from fear – he could almost hear her bony body rattle, he thought. She would be his.

The first time this had happened had been in the Wolski Hospital, in Wola. He had watched Dirlewanger's men as they raped the nurses, and he had felt the arousal. Later, when Ingo had not been there, had gone ahead to save others, he had raped too; it had not taken him long, after so much waiting. And right then all those years of pain and humiliation had disappeared.

He had lost his wife because he could not satisfy her and could not give her the babies she yearned for; whenever they were together it would not work. Whenever, in this war, he had needed to kill – so many times – it had been easy for him. He had simply pictured his wife's contemptuous face, sometimes her mocking laughter, and then pulled the trigger. The Stuka tablets helped, too, as they heightened everything – although that included lust. It had been the same with whores. Some had laughed, and he had wanted to beat them, and sometimes had – like the time in Oryol when Ingo had believed he was saving the bitch; poor naïve Ingo. But he knew now that he had been right to hit them; that he needed their fear, it was the only way. For him. Even with the Pervitin he still needed the fear. Despite the fact that the drug made it so hard it hurt, the treacherous part of him would always let him down when there was a woman. Unless she was afraid of him. This he now knew. He could not blame the drugs or the drink. This was who he was. Or what he had become.

For the first time in years he had felt like a real man, when he was drunk and high, and felt like the animal he really was when he was sober. But even then, he would admit it now, in drink, it was good to know who he really was. And, in the company of the Dirlewanger men, to know he was not alone. This was why he had never once requested that he and Ingo be moved back to the 19ᵗʰ, had never bribed the wireless operators as he had told Ingo he had. He had lied to him every time, even hinted that there were no units of the 19ᵗʰ now in Warsaw; he had no idea if that was true or not. It might have been easy, really, had he tried. He would make it up to Ingo, at least a little, by taking him the truck and the papers later. He had to do that small thing, to make up for all *this* just a little. But first of all, *this*, because in the darkest part of his black heart he needed *this* more than anything.

He sometimes wondered if Ingo would kill him, too, if he knew. Like he'd killed those other Dirlewanger men. It had never been difficult for Pop to keep Sunshine off Ingo's back, for that, for he and Sunshine had become partners in this thing. They understood one another, worked as a team. It was wrong, of course, but these girls would be dead soon enough anyway. Besides, if he didn't, then Sunshine surely would … And anyhow, this would be the last time.

"You never could resist plum, Pop, right?"

Pop turned to where the voice, which echoed in the big space of the church, came from.

"Nor money," Kroh added. He had a group of heavily armed Dirlewanger men with him, two of them wearing the camouflage ski masks that had become another grisly motif of the unit. Those without masks looked as drunk as he felt, but Kroh seemed sober. As always he carried his Leica camera. In the other hand he held a peeled onion, which he crunched on as if it was an apple. He took a place on one of the pews, put his legs upon the back of the one in front, and looked up at Pop; he was trying to appear casual, but his florid face betrayed his anger. One of the girls sobbed.

Kroh placed his camera on the back of the pew then slipped his Walther from its holster and worked the slide to put a round in the breech. Then he casually shot the two girls, each of them in the head. The echoes of the gunshots rang through the church and the peppery-iron smell of the discharge filled the chapel.

"Now why would you go and do that?" Pop said, looking at the two dead girls, lying on the floor with their limbs outstretched and bent, like flat dancers.

"Noisy, the young ones – don't you find?" Kroh said. "Can't abide all that crying, when there's business to be done."

"Business?"

"Seems you've been holding out on me, Pop?" Kroh said, then crunched loudly into the onion.

"What do you want, Kroh?"

"Hauptsturmführer Kroh."

Pop nodded, sighed, glanced down at the dead girls once again. "Hauptsturmführer Kroh," he said.

With that Kroh tossed the onion away, then said: "Sunshine here knows a little more German than he lets on, right? He's also pretty good at pretending to be asleep – I suppose it's the sort of thing that passes for entertainment in those shithole Russian peasant villages. So, I know you're up to something. He knows some important German words, does Sunshine, too; words like *money*, *dollars* even, words like *papers* ... And he knows to come to me when he hears them, right?"

Pop looked at Sunshine, who smiled an apologetic smile, which would have gone well with a *c'est la guerre* shrug, and before he realised what was happening another of the Dirlewanger men took Pop's Walther from its holster. If he had not been so drunk, he might have been quicker, might have stopped him. But if he had not been so drunk, he would not be here.

"He heard nothing," Pop said, noticing that diamonds had not been mentioned, as he also slowly realised that all this was a trap; Sunshine had lured him here knowing he would not be able to resist – they could always understand each other when it came to this. Here where there were no other Germans around to see what these men might do to another German; the one crime they could not get away with, otherwise.

"You asked me what I want," Kroh said. "I want a cut."

"There's nothing to cut, the idiot's mistaken."

Kroh shook his head, very slowly, whistled a few bars of something unrecognisable in his airy way, and put his camera on the shining wood of a pew seat with a soft clunk. Then he swung his legs off the pew in front and stood up, and walked the few metres into the nave.

"You've sinned Pop, right?" he said, and he reached for a large wooden crucifix, about the size of an MP 40, which was lying face down on the flagstones of the church floor. Then he said something in Russian, obviously an order.

With that two of the Dirlewanger men grabbed Pop. One twisted his arm behind his back, and yanked it up, forcing him to bend low, as he knew it would break otherwise. He heard the heel guards of Kroh's boots clink along the flagstones, and that same airy whistle. The next thing he saw was the crucifix, and an upside-down silver Jesus swinging into his face. Jesus snapped his front teeth in a sloping line, filling his mouth and nose with the metallic taste of blood, and his head with pain.

Kroh barked out another order in Russian and the two men dragged Pop over the flagstones to a confessional that was against the wall. It was made of varnished wood with an elaborate iron pediment, and there was a low door and a curtain where the priest would sit, a half-screen to one side for the penitent to kneel behind. They opened the door and bundled Pop inside. The green curtain flapped back in place behind him.

"One thing I learnt about panzer men during my time with the 4th is that they don't like a little heat, right?" Kroh said.

Pop heard the slosh of liquid in a steel container, and then the pop of an unfastening lid. He smelt petrol.

"Recognise the smell, Pop?" Kroh said.

Then Pop heard the sound of the liquid, gushing from the clonking can, splashing over the wooden confessional. The harsh smell of the fuel flooded his nostrils, despite the blood that gushed from them. The curtain was pulled back and some of the petrol was thrown inside, covering his hair and tunic, stinging his eyes.

"Time to confess your sins, Pop, right?" Kroh said, as the curtain fell back into place. "So what's all this about dollars, then?"

Kroh waited for some seconds, but Pop didn't answer. Then he said something in Russian, and Pop heard the very familiar squeak of a little wheel turning, the almost silent breath of a tiny flame igniting.

"There's still time to repent, Pop," Kroh said, and then he started to hiss *Ave Maria* in that strange non-whistle way of his.

*

She was brought some food mid-morning by one of Andrzej's boy soldiers, surely the youngest AK 'man' Lidka had seen. It was just thin soup and a little bread and some water. She had been there all night. Had shouted for hours, to be let out, but either no one heard her, or no one took any notice. This was the first time anyone had come, as the room was a long way from other parts of the command centre. The kid was about fourteen, possibly younger, one of those lads that seemed to worship Andrzej. He wore a helmet that was too big for him, they all did, these boys, and he attempted to cover his fear in a casually cruel way that was a worse fit than the helmet.

"Where's Bullet?" Lidka said.

"Can't say."

"I need to talk to him."

The boy shook his head. He had an automatic pistol stuffed in his belt, a Luger-like Lahti. He couldn't help looking at it every now and then, as if he had just been given it and still could not quite believe it was his to hold, and maybe even shoot. But she knew there was a chance it was not loaded, bullets were even scarcer than bread and soup and water. Yet Lidka also knew there was no way she could risk taking the gun from him; she understood that a boy with a gun could be more dangerous than a man with a gun. And even if she did, what then? She would not get a message to take today, not now. And without authorisation she could not enter the sewers. There was no other way to Ochota.

The lad shook his head sharply. He had put the small bowl of soup that smelt faintly of starchy potatoes on the floor, placing the thin slice of bread on top of it. There was a tin mug of water there, too, which she really needed. But it could wait just a little while. She thought of Freddy, and hoped Ingo would stick to his part of the agreement, even if she was not there. A shell landed close by, the shock rippling the surface of the water in the mug.

It was stifling in the little room with its un-openable translucent window, which bathed the room in a sickly pale light. The boy looked at her legs, she saw, and seeing his face redden Lidka lifted her skirt slightly, over her knees. Then she unbuttoned her blouse a bit, to reveal a little more cleavage.

"It's hot," she said.

The boy tried to look away, but couldn't, her naked legs, sheened with a little sweat, were like magnets for his swivelling eyes.

"If you don't know where Bullet is, just say so," she said.

"I know where he is."

She sniffed a condescending laugh. "No you don't."

"I've been told not to speak to you."

"Who told you?"

The lad shook his head.

"Why?"

"I don't know."

"Yes, like you don't know where Bullet is."

He shook his head again, the turned to leave the room. "He's gone to Ochota, left me in charge," the lad said, and then he slammed the door behind him and turned the key in the lock.

"Ochota," Lidka whispered to herself.

*

Ingo was possibly the only German soldier in Warsaw not to possess more than one watch. Certainly, the only one with the Dirlewanger Brigade. He must have looked at this, a Heer-issue Helma, a hundred times in the last hour. Sixty times the hour before that.

"Where is she?" Sarah asked, not for the first time.

"She'll be here; soon," he said, with more confidence than he felt. It was late afternoon, nudging in to early evening, but there were still some hours of light left. Yet Lidka should have arrived by now, and Pop was overdue, too. The exchange of words he had just had with Sarah was similar to every other short conversation they had had since she had come up from the basement in the morning. He felt Sarah still did not trust him, because he wore a German uniform, and he thought she had every right to feel this way. She would feel better about the whole thing when Lidka arrived; as would he.

They sat on hard chairs by an open window in the room in which, all those years ago, Ingo had played the Pleyel piano for people he did not know, because Lidka had asked him to. Now it was bare, its walls marked with slightly brighter rectangles edged in lines of grime where pictures had once hung. Despite the heat of the day outside it was quite cool in the room. They had pulled open the curtains a little to give themselves a view out on to the street, and also to let in some warmer air, and so he could see Sarah better now in the shaft of bright light. She was beautiful, that was true. But her eyes were full of mistrust, and something else; hatred, he thought – but then he knew there were so many ways you could get wounded in this war. She wore an old green cardigan over her blue dress. It was far too big for her and had suede patches at the elbows. It had a pocket, too, the wool there now stretched by the size and weight of the Walther Ingo had given her last night.

He strained his hearing, trying to listen through the mesh of the steel squeal of his tinnitus, and the distant rumble of the battle for the Old Town; listening out for footsteps on the stairs. Sarah's brother Leon waited at the back door in the kitchen to let Lidka in. He knew it would take her many hours to get there through the sewers, but she had said it would not be a problem, said she would start out very early.

There had been a muted explosion, then another, close by, about ten minutes ago, and they had both tensed. But then an explosion was not unusual these days, even in areas the Germans had long subdued, like Ochota. Earlier he had also heard machine gun fire, then pistol shots. Dirty work, he had guessed, knowing the sounds of execution by now. He had not spoken of it, but he could tell Sarah also knew what had happened. He had his own rifle ready, across his lap, his hand around the smooth-wood grip, finger tucked inside the cold trigger guard. Sometimes Sarah would put her hand over the pocket of the cardigan she wore, as if to check the P38 was still there.

A plane passed overhead, heading towards the base at nearby Okęcie, the familiar high rasp of a Jumo 211 V12 in a Junkers 87, completing its up-and-down mission to bomb the Old Town. And then, as the Stuka started to land, its diminishing engine note was replaced, almost imperceptibly at first, by something else; rattling valves, then the pop of a steel body on cobbles, then a rising engine note and the heavy hum of large tyres.

"What is it?" Sarah said.

"*Shhhh!*" He leant out of the open window and saw the truck as it came into sight around the curve in Mochnackiego. The lowering sun was shining through the side streets, and now directly on to the flat windscreen, reflecting back in to Ingo's eyes, so it took him a moment or two to identify the vehicle. It was its sloping nose that gave it away; a six-wheeled Krupp Protze, with a black canvas cover over its open cab which extended back across the steel ribbing hoops at the rear, too, he saw as it drew ever closer. The field grey-painted Krupp came to a halt with a squeak of brakes, some way short of the house. He saw that the right front fender bore the crossed stick grenade insignia of the Dirlewanger Brigade, stencilled in white. Then, even though it was a good one hundred metres distant and the sun still splashed liquid dapples on the windscreen, he recognised Pop at the wheel.

The truck sat there for a moment or two, on the crown of the steeply cambered cobbled roadway, shivering to its rough idle, and then that rattling 3.3-litre boxer gained a steelier edge, as it was revved: Once, twice, three times. He had half-hoped Pop would arrive even later than this, knew that they could not wait long for Lidka, the truck was sure to attract attention. He now hoped his friend was in a patient mood …

"It's our ride," Ingo said. "Get the others."

*

Kampinos Forest. August 1944

Jósef had regretted his decision almost as soon as Dabrowski and Jankowski had left. A coward dies a thousand times, someone had once said. He knew now he was a coward, had always known it, deep down. And he had died a million times. Most of those deaths had been during the last two days.

He had heard no more shooting and the forest was as still as a tombstone. There was no breeze and the heat hung heavy and thick from the branches. Through the film of smeared dirt on the window the trees looked as if they were painted on to a backdrop of a forest-filtered bluey-white sky. Only the shadows of the spruces moved and an iron dark column of shade slowly crept across the tiny windowpane. He had managed to almost persuade himself, again, that the rotting smell was from the nearby swamp – it too was still, like hot ice – and was not coming from the constantly sore bullet wound in his buttock. He lay, and listened to the silent forest, because that was all he had the energy to do. He was far too scared to venture into the darkening trees, find his way out.

Jósef had hoped to surrender, but now there was no one to surrender to. Then, as he had lain on the hard ground, time's blunt chisel etched worries in him: perhaps they would never find him; perhaps, if they did, they would kill him; perhaps they would torture him; perhaps they would burn the shack and him within it – the least likely, as that would burn the forest and them in it, too, but this was by far the most frightening prospect of them all. He tried to think positively, but nothing would take hold. He was hot – even at night it was humid – he was hungry and he was tired, a heavy lead tired that made him feel nauseous, but there was nothing to eat and he could not sleep. There was little water left now, too.

Then he thought he heard something, in the forest, heavy boots in foliage. Then laughter and joking. Then gone. He listened hard, but for a while could only hear the ever-faster tattoo of his drumming heart. But no, there it was again. A whoop, of joy, some singing, too! Then a shout; he recognised it: *"Yest' chto-to!"* It was Russian … Russian!

Relief pulsed through him like an electric shock, and he felt himself start to shake, and then he began to weep. They were Russians; the Red Army must have broken through south of Warsaw; it was better than he could have hoped for. He would live, and he would not be a prisoner. He could hear them running through the undergrowth, boots clomping on hollow earth undermined by roots, the rattle of equipment, and even the slosh of water in canteens as they came ever closer. He sat up and, despite the oppressive heat, he pulled on his short, blue RAF battledress jacket with its crescent-shaped *Poland* shoulder badges.

He knew just a little Russian, but it was enough.

"Here! I am here! Polish! Polish!"

*

Ochota, Warsaw. August 1944

Sarah was the only one of them who seemed unaffected by the harsh, bright light. It was understandable, most of the others had been in that dark basement for years, seldom coming up to even take a peek out of the window or a breath of fresh air. They'd now left it too late for the latter, the Warsaw air smelt of death and burning, even far away from the fighting as they were now. But then there were fires close by now, too, burning bodies. Ingo knew the smell well. Sarah had told him that she thought some other people had been found hiding in basements, and then killed. It was not uncommon, she had said. But he knew that. It was why he was here.

It was hot, but Sarah still wore the old cardigan, which reached down to her thighs, and Ingo still wore the belted SS jacket and his helmet; he thought it best, today, to look as much like an SS soldier as possible. The older man and women, though only in their late forties or early fifties, were frail, and walked like convalescents. But Ingo did not mind if the going was slow, as he glanced at his watch once again and wondered where Lidka was. He could not leave without her; he would not leave without her. He would wait. They would all wait ...

The Voglers looked as pale as teeth and smelt of the damp of the basement and of the paraffin of the lamps they used for light down there. The other older woman, the one who was clearly not part of the Vogler family as she did not even speak to the Jews, was not so pale, and neither was the young child, the orphan that Lidka had told him they had taken in.

The engine revved again and then the truck was slammed into gear with a graunch, as Pop seemed to realise he had parked too far along the street. Sol Vogler, the jeweller, wore a hat, a pinched front felt fedora with a teardrop crown, and he carried a briefcase. It was the only luggage they had, and Sarah had told Ingo, with an edge of scorn, that it contained American dollars – and perhaps even those diamonds Lidka had spoken of, Ingo had thought. It might look better if Ingo carried the briefcase, for the others were supposed to be his prisoners. But he did not want to take it; he would let Pop bargain for the price of the Jews' freedom. Pop was good at bargaining.

The Krupp drove to meet them, and they waited; Ingo, Sol Vogler and his wife, the other middle-aged woman whose name he did not know, Sarah, the lad – who was still coughing – and the little boy, excited to see the truck, a strangely familiar smile on his face – it reminded Ingo of something; perhaps the boyish excitement he still often felt for vehicles, and still, always, felt for speed. The low sun threw the shadows of the ornate lamp-posts across the street in slanting sashes and the approaching truck, its transmission whining, heavy tyres humming and thudding across the cobbles, counted off the ticks of hard shade on gleaming black stone as it accelerated.

Sarah held the little boy's hand and he looked up at her. Ingo saw complete trust in that face. The sun shone on his blond hair. The boy smiled. Now Ingo could see him clearly he thought there was something vaguely familiar about him. Sarah bent low and whispered in the child's ear … The truck came to a halt with a squeak of brakes and the clatter of the planks on its deck … The child laughed at what Sarah had said, a high laugh, full of life.

Yes, there was something …

"Taxi?" Kroh said, from inside the door-less cab, where he had been ducking below the high rim of the dash, before jumping down on the cobbles and igniting sparks with the heel guard of one of his boots. At the very same moment a tumble of Dirlewanger men piled out of the rear of the truck, guns and equipment rattling. Ingo glanced up in to the cab, where Pop sat, pale and stooped, and hurt, one hand gripping the wheel tight, blood dripping from his mouth.

Ingo's rifle was slung over his shoulder, but he reached for it, as the tinnitus spiked like a steel bayonet stabbing within his head. One of the SS men raised his own rifle, its muzzle just three metres from Ingo's face. Ingo had his own Kar 98 almost to hand now, but he knew it was too late, as he looked along the gleaming barrel of the other gun and in to a dilating oil spill of a black pupil that was lined up with the foresight notch of the rifle. He clearly saw the squeezing curl of the SS man's trigger finger …

This close up the sound of the gunshot was deafening.

***

Brescia. May 1954

There was just a minute to go. The bowler-hatted starter kept the flag low while a timekeeper, his arm held out stiffly, concentrated on the second hand of his stopwatch. Ingo could feel the car breathe beneath him. He felt completely relaxed, and completely focussed. He looked down the road through the funnel of people that faded into the fog. He revved the engine, just a blip, and the crowd reacted enthusiastically, clapping and cheering. Many of them had been up all night, waiting for the big cars. Ingo now had 1000 miles of racing ahead of him, the rest of it he could put to one side, until they finished back in Brescia sometime this evening. He realised he was quite happy ... *Thirty seconds* ...

*

The rifle was a Karabiner 98K, fitted with a telescopic sight. It was one of many ex-Wehrmacht Mausers used by the Israeli Defence Forces. On its receiver the Nazi proof-mark stamps had been partially erased and Israeli stamps had been added, a common practice. Whoever found the rifle used to kill Ingo Six would be in no doubt about the nationality of the assassin. Yitzhak rested his elbows on the back of the chair and pressed the waffled butt of the rifle in to his right shoulder, aiming at an acute angle at the ramp to his left. Sarah sat behind him in the darkened room. They had agreed she would guard the door, but she could not miss this. He could not miss, either. For Yitzhak, this was an easy shot.

Ingo Six was bathed in the glow of the floodlights, a bright patch burning through the fog, even brighter when the flash guns of the photographers flared. His was to be a very public death, she thought. She imagined how he would look intersected in the crosshairs of the Zeiss Zielvier sights. The car's short, swept-back windscreen was Perspex or glass. Yitzhak said it would make little difference at this range and elevation. There were just 20 seconds left. Through the corner of her eye she saw Yitzhak's finger slowly tugging the first of the sniper rifle's two triggers until it set with a very soft click. Then he just about touched the hair trigger. He took a long, deep breath. Sarah concentrated on the driver of car number 532.

*

Ten seconds ... Ingo stretched his fingers out, curled them, and then stretched them again. Then he gripped the steering wheel lightly, but firmly. There was a sudden flash.

Ingo blinked out the harsh light of the camera's flash bulb. The flag dropped and he lifted the clutch, eased the Condor down the ramp, being careful not to scrape the underside of the rear end on its downward slope, and then hit the accelerator pedal. The open exhaust let out a crack that soon settled into a crisp rasp as Ingo worked the car up in to second gear, the rear wheels spinning slightly on the damp, black road as he fed in the power. He guided the car straight on to Via Venezia, fenced in by bulging black hedges of people, hooked third, then jammed the throttle to its stop, the bark of the open exhaust bouncing back off the roadside buildings, the fast cold air flooding his nostrils and clearing his head. Somewhere, three minutes down the foggy road to Verona, was Otero in the Scuderia Verde Ferrari. He would not have to overtake him to beat him on time. But he had every intention of doing just that.

*

"Why did you stop me?" Yitzhak's tone was not accusatory, merely curious. He would know Sarah had a reason. But he would not understand that reason.

So she said: "I was not sure. I didn't want to make the same mistake again."

"You mean Nice? But we know it's him; that car, that time, that driver?"

"It's the right driver, yes; but I'm not sure it's Ingo Six," she lied. "I'm not sure this man is him."

"Not sure?"

"It could be him. I need to make sure, first. I need to talk to him."

"How?"

"There are ways. If he sees me, he'll talk to me. Then I'll know for sure."

"And then you will need me?"

"No, Yitzhak, it's finished now, for you. Take the rifle, get away from here, out of Italy."

She stared out of the window as she said it. There was another car, a red car, on the yellow ramp. This time the driver did not stretch out his fingers before he gripped the steering wheel, just as though he was about to settle down to play Chopin on a Pleyel piano ...

"So, after all this, he might live?"

She just shook her head sharply. Then took her small case off the bed and left the room, while the bark of the next racing car echoed along the street below.

***

Ochota, Warsaw. August 1944

The shot still echoed in the curving street; the sulphurous, burnt smell of the discharge tugging at Ingo's nostrils. Sarah held the pistol in two hands. Hands that were not shaking. Kroh also held a P38, its muzzle pressed against the little boy's head, while he had a fistful of the boy's hair tight in the other hand, pulling up on it so the child had to stand on tiptoes. One of the women cried, as did the older lad. But the little boy did not. All the other guns were pointed at Sarah and Ingo.

"Drop the gun; you too Pup," Kroh said, and Sarah looked at the little boy and then did as she was told. Ingo did too, his Kar 98 clattering on to the cobbles at his feet. Kroh let the child go and he run to Sarah, hugging her legs tight. The Dirlewanger man Sarah had killed, saving Ingo's life, lay in the street beside the Krupp truck. The blood from his head wound trickled on to the cobbles, filling the cracks between them like tiny canals to form a brief lattice of scarlet on burnished grey-black, before it overflowed into an ever-expanding pool. The rifle he had intended to use to kill Ingo was lying in the gutter.

None of the SS men seemed concerned that the girl had killed one of their comrades. But then life was cheaper than bad luck in Dirlewanger's mob. Kroh pushed his tattered old Gebirgsjäger peaked cap to the back of his head, rearranged the strap of the camera that was hung around his neck, then said: "Fucking dumb Ivan peasants, right? Told them not to shoot until I gave the say-so."

"Pop, you okay?" Ingo said, looking up at his friend on the far side of the truck's cab. He did not reply, did not even look at Ingo. He wore no hat, and his thin copper-coloured hair seemed wet, his bald patch shining, and there was blood around his mouth and nose. Ingo could also smell petrol.

"What have you done to him?"

"Just business, Pup," Kroh said, turning to Sol Vogler. "I'll take that." He grabbed the briefcase. It had no lock and Kroh unclipped the latches. He did not take out the money and whatever else might have been inside, probably because he did not want to let the other Dirlewanger men know how much there was, and after a moment or two he snapped the case shut. Vogler took off his fedora and was now passing it through his hands, kneading the brim with his bony fingers. Ingo again looked up at Pop, still gripping the big steering wheel tightly with one hand. Then Pop glanced at him. He shook his head, slowly, looked away again.

"Not much, is there?" Kroh said to Ingo, putting the case on the floor.

"Sorry to have wasted your time."

Kroh rattled out an order in Russian and two of his men went to the far side of the open-sided canvas-covered cab and pulled Pop out, letting him slide to the ground with a meaty thump and a simultaneous moan. Then they forced him to his feet and led him around the long, sloping snout of the truck. Pop opened his mouth and Ingo saw that his teeth has been broken along a neat sloping line. Now he was out of the cab of the truck the smell of petrol was even stronger, and Ingo realised Pop's uniform was soaked in gasoline. He was swaying slightly, back and fore.

"I'm sorry, Ingo," Pop said. He sounded drunk, but that might have been because of the broken teeth. But then again, his eyes were glazed.

Ingo looked at Kroh. The tinnitus now singing solid in his head, its volume rising. "What happened?"

"Pop confessed, didn't you Pop?" Kroh said

"Sorry, Ingo," Pop slurred, again.

"Had a lot to confess, did Pop. Dirty little bugger, likes them young; likes them scared, does Pop, right?"

"What do you mean?" Ingo said.

Kroh laughed, shook his head. "I'll let him tell you himself, if there's a later."

"Look, you have the money now, that's what you came for, isn't it?" Ingo said. "Let's call it quits. You can keep it; keep it all."

"I know that," Kroh said. Then he turned to look at the cluster of people stood behind Ingo. "I have my money, and you have your Jews. But then you didn't come here for Jews, did you, Pup?"

Ingo was still looking at Pop, saw him taking in a deep breath that whistled slightly through his broken teeth.

"Tell him, Pop."

Pop said nothing.

"Tell him!"

"They killed Lidka, Ingo," Pop said.

"No ..."

"It's true, they were waiting —"

"*We* were waiting, Pop – *we*. And it was you who told us she was coming through the sewer, right?"

Pop nodded. "*We* were waiting for her, Ingo. When we heard her arrive at the drain on Filtrowa, Kroh threw a grenade in."

"Hauptsturmführer Kroh, Pop."

"Hauptsturmführer Kroh threw a grenade in."

"She might have —"

"No Ingo, it was a tight space, and we heard her scream when she saw it. Then the explosion; then he threw another grenade, too. There was no chance."

"No, it's not true," Ingo said, but he also remembered the muted explosions he had heard.

Pop moved his mouth to speak again, to say sorry once more perhaps, but seemed to change his mind. Ingo heard a snivel behind him, and he turned; it was one of the older women. He looked at the child, who was also looking at him. The little boy seemed afraid now.

Kroh came closer, so that Ingo could smell the raw onion on his breath. "Did you a favour, Pup. She would have smelt pretty bad after wading through all that shit, right?"

"Dead?" Ingo said, finally; but beyond the hardening of the steel in his head it almost sounded as if the words had come from someone else.

Kroh snapped out an order in Russian. Two of the Dirlewanger men rushed at Sarah, pulling her from the child's grasp. One of them peeled the cardigan off her and then he ripped open the top half of her blue dress, the upper part of the cream slip beneath it coming away at the same time, both hanging down like aprons in front of her. Her pert white breasts were bright in the stark light, the nipples dark and erect. She spat at the man, and he punched her hard in the mouth, a trickle of blood curved across her chin.

The noise in Ingo's head grew louder.

"You know what happens next, right?" Kroh said.

"Leave her!" Ingo heard himself say over the screaming steel, as loud in his head as an express train, its brakes slammed on in an emergency: steel, on steel, on steel.

Kroh gave another order in Russian and the SS men stepped back from Sarah. Then he said to Ingo: "You know how these lads kill?"

"They don't kill, they murder."

"Let's not forget the rape and torture first, right?" Kroh said with a smile. "Isn't that right Pop; rape, and torture?"

Ingo looked at the child, who without Sarah's hand to hold seemed lost now, upset to see her hit, shining tears brimming in his big blue eyes.

"I could have you shot, Pup. Right here and now. No mercy for deserters, right? Maybe I will, later," Kroh said. "But first, why don't we give these Jews a nice clean death? Not that any dirty Jew deserves that, eh?" He started whistling *Erika*, it sounded like a punctured tyre. Then he stopped abruptly, and said: "You know, if there's one thing I've found disappointing about this rather wonderful war, it's been your inability to join in with the fun, Gefreiter Six."

Kroh looked at Sarah, she was still defiant, making no effort to cover her naked breasts. Ingo knew what they would do to her.

"I want you to kill them, Pup."

Ingo shook his head.

"But I hadn't finished. You kill them; or the lads will kill them; kill them in their way, slowly and with great feeling."

Ingo again shook his head.

"So, you can live with that, can you, Pup?"

Ingo said nothing.

"What about Pop? Should he live?"

Ingo looked at his friend and he saw the fear on Pop's face. Kroh must have nodded, or made some other signal, for now Sunshine stepped forward, picked up the Walther Sarah had dropped and placed its muzzle against Pop's temple, pressing it tight, so that his head was forced to tilt to one side. Sunshine said something in Russian, softly and with a smile, so that it might easily have been "no hard feelings, eh?"

"So, here's the thing, then," Kroh said. "You kill them, or Pop gets it."

Ingo still said nothing, did nothing. There was the sound of a car, the distinctive rattle of a Kübelwagen in a nearby street. He hoped it was a patrol; Kroh would never kill a German with other Germans around, he knew that, it could be his chance.

"You kill them, and you might even live yourself, right?"

"Might?" Ingo said, listening out for the Kübelwagen, not hearing it now; instead hearing a distant explosion. Lidka ... Dead ... He remembered.

"Please Ingo," Pop said. "Do as he says, it's our only chance."

Kroh grinned, and said: "Kill them, Pup."

"Why are you asking this of me?" Ingo said.

Kroh laughed. "Well, I could say I want to get my own back for that stunt you two pulled with the Horch, but I reckon that you, at least, have paid enough for that, right? So, let's just say that I reckon it's about time you got your hands dirty."

"Ingo …" Pop said

Ingo nodded, and then picked his rifle up off the cobbles. An acid thought burned through the screaming steel that was slowly crushing his consciousness – turn it on Kroh and the Dirlewanger men. But there were ten of them, five with MP 40s, he would be dead by the time he had taken one of them, even before, and as he thought it he realised that every gun, except the pistol aimed at Pop's head, was trained on him. To shoot them would be to kill himself; and then Pop would die, too, while Sarah, the child, and the rest would die a hundred times before they breathed their last.

Ingo Six knew what had to be done. The edge of the tinnitus seemed to dim, as it always did, these days, when that moment of crisis he had recognised, was reached, and then passed … and all that was left was to live out the decision he had taken. The only decision there was to take.

Kroh must have recognised something in his eyes, for his barbed smile spread across his face as Ingo gripped his rifle. "No, out in front of the truck – the light's much better," Kroh said, taking the lens cap off his Leica. "Against the side of that white apartment block; the blood will show up well. And take off your helmet, you've never been one for hats, or haircuts, so why not show off those flowing locks of yours, eh?"

Ingo took off the coalscuttle helmet and dropped it onto the cobbles with a tinny clang. Then he pointed his rifle from the hip at the group of six. The older lad had started coughing again. One of the middle-aged women pissed herself, yellow urine running down her legs to splash and steam on the hot cobbles, the ammonia smell of it high in the heat. "But I am not a Jew!" she shouted, in bad German. "They are Jews; filthy Jews! Kill them, not me!" Ingo aimed his rifle directly at the woman, and then she was quiet.

"Get a move on Pup, we haven't got all day!"

Ingo led them through a low gate and a little way down the side of the building. Then he lined them up against the whitewashed wall, directing them with little nods, or by pointing with the barrel of the rifle.

"Shoot them in the head, Pup," Kroh ordered, getting into position with his camera. "I want you to look into their eyes – it's so hard to enjoy a death if you don't see the lights go out, right?"

Ingo pressed the butt of the rifle into his shoulder and aimed at the first in line, Sol Vogler. He hesitated; still hoping a Heer patrol would come along.

"Do it, Pup!"

He thumbed the safety tab at the rear of the breech and bolt, and took a deep breath, to steady his aim, concentrating on what had to be done, trying to shut out everything else. Sol Vogler still had his hat in his hands, and he now held it in front of him. His eyes were swimming with panic and tears raced down his pale cheeks.

"Shoot, Pup – or shall I say the very same thing to Sunshine?"

Vogler whispered in German: "I'm sorry, I was not going to hold out on you, I swear; my hat, they are —" He stretched out the hand that held the hat. Because he was not wearing the fedora it made it easier for Ingo to aim at Vogler's forehead, which was barely two metres in front of him. Kroh was right, it was impossible not to look into his eyes ... as he fired.

The Mauser kicked brutally, punching his shoulder, and the crack of the discharge was loud, but not loud enough to cover the sound of the round hitting Sol Vogler's forehead, like a stone thrown in to ice-crusted snow. The bullet came out of the back of his head, painting the white wall behind with a pudding mix of blood and brains. Vogler's legs turned to over-boiled leeks beneath him, and a bloody smear on the wall marked his death slide to the ground.

Ingo stepped to the side. He worked the bolt and a spent cartridge was ejected, smoking as it fell to the floor where it pinged against a paving stone. He killed Mrs Vogler next, saw the resignation and slight relief in her eyes as he pulled the trigger, heard the click of Kroh's Leica, the soft rasp of its winding mechanism. Then Ingo killed the woman who had said she was not a Jew; she closed her eyes tight and prayed aloud; and then he killed the coughing and crying lad who also closed his eyes, as if to shut out the bullet. Now there was just Sarah and the boy left. He worked the Mauser's bolt once more, ejecting another empty case.

Sarah looked him straight in the eyes. She did not look afraid, but defiant, her breasts were bare but she had made no move to cover them with the torn cloth of her dress. Ingo aimed at her forehead, looking in her burning dark eyes as he did so, and then he took up the first pressure on the trigger. There was a sob to her left, and he glanced at the boy by her side.

He was looking up at Ingo now, with those big blue eyes. Ingo quite suddenly knew the truth. Lidka's child.

Sarah started to speak ...

***

Brescia. May 1954

It was a long walk to the railway station, and the crack and snarl of the racing engines followed her all the way, echoing through the streets. Sarah walked fast. She might have taken a taxi, but she needed the walk, and the cleansing feel of the cold air, while the small suitcase she carried was not heavy, as it only contained a change of clothes and a large envelope. In her other hand she carried her handbag, which contained the things she really needed, including a Beretta automatic. She knew the times of the trains, it was all part of her preparation – she had originally planned to use a train to escape, it was an understated method that had worked before. There would be an express to Bologna soon enough, and from there she knew she could pick up another to Florence.

Brescia station looked like a Tuscan-red castle from the outside; one with big neo-classical arched windows. The crenelated towers suited the fog; the fog suited Sarah's confusion. She believed she knew why she had stopped Yitzhak. She thought it was because Ingo Six had looked so happy, as he stretched his fingers, just as if he was settling down to play a piano. Sarah had not wanted him to die happy. That would have been too easy. For him. But she was not sure that was the entire reason, and that doubt gnawed at her now.

The station was not busy. It was early and most of those awake in the town were at the start of the Mille Miglia, or trying to get some sleep, perhaps pressing pillows to their ears to muffle the sound of the racing cars. The church bells would not ring for an hour. Sarah was tired, too tired. But Italy had a remedy for that. There was a small coffee shop in an alcove just inside the station building. It had a long zinc-topped counter and was the sort of place where Italians would stop for a quick shot of espresso, standing by the bar. The coffee smell was rich and warm.

There was a man sat on a tall stool by the counter. It was the only stool. He did not wear a hat and the top of his head was hideously burnt. In the reflection of a long mirror behind the bar she caught his reflection between the gleaming pipes of the coffee machines. His face was badly burnt, too. The burns looked old and terrible; she had seen burnt people before, many in Warsaw, but most of them had been dead. This one looked like he should be dead, and as he rasped a pitiful cough she could believe he was indeed dying. She did not want to catch his eye, but it was too late …

His eyes were a curious green-grey, and bright, and they burned with frustration, or pain, then something else … She turned away from him, and made a show of looking for service.

"Lidka?" The voice was like tearing sandpaper. It was the first time she had heard her real name spoken aloud in years.

***

Kampinos Forest. August 1944

They were laughing, but he did not understand the joke, which made them laugh all the more. Jósef had been right, they were Russians. But their laughter was taunting, he realised now. One of them, a man with a single blackened tooth in his mouth, reached for his wrist and skilfully undid his watch, which he placed on an arm that was already striped with five others. They wore a strange mix of very dirty uniforms and many of them were in shirtsleeves, while their breath stank of alcohol. The soldier who had taken his watch carried a Schmeisser, which was slung over his shoulder on a piece of rope. His trousers, beneath the filth and stains, were field grey.

Each of the men wore an armband, on which there was a black cross on a red and white shield and the Cyrillic letters: *POHA*, or RONA. One soldier pushed in from behind the others. He was wearing a German field grey tunic with its buttons undone and a coalscuttle helmet, and his chin carried a scar that was in the shape of a smile. He too spoke in Russian, with a Russian accent, as he fixed his bayonet to the muzzle of his German rifle.

Józef tried to remember some Russian words, he wanted to tell them something, anything; tell them in which direction Dabrowski and Jankowski had gone, tell them which village the doctor who had treated him lived in, to tell them anything to save his life.

The bayonet entered his gut, but he did not feel pain until it was pulled out, with a vicious twist and a slurping sound. It was the purest of pains and he screamed. Then the bayonet entered him again, higher – and another bayonet, too – both sharper pains. He knew now he would die, as he was stabbed again ... again ... again. But there was no panic now, just a sudden peace, a pang of regret that he would not live to see his son. And a slight relief – his very last thought before the fog of death filled him – that he had not been burned to death.

***

Ochota, Warsaw. August 1944

The pressure of the P38's muzzle against his temple had diminished little by little as each of them had died. Now, the pistol was not touching him, but Sunshine was still aiming it at his head. Like Pop, he too, watched the executions. The other Dirlewanger men also looked on, as they trained their guns on Ingo. Even now Pop could not stop looking at the girl's naked breasts. She started to say something, but Pop did not catch it, and Ingo had shot her before she had finished speaking. The girl's expression did not change. Even as the bullet entered her head she looked defiant. Ingo ejected the cartridge and lowered the rifle, all five rounds now used up. Five people dead.

Pop's nose had started to bleed again, and he sniffed through his blood-clotted nostrils, smelling the petrol that soaked through his clothes. Some of it had seeped through to his skin, burning it slightly, but not as surely as a flaming confessional would have. He had not thought himself a coward, but every man has his limit, and he had found his earlier that day. The inside of his mouth tasted of blood and he could not stop his tongue from tracing the clean ridge where his teeth had been broken by the silver Jesus.

Now only the little boy was left alive. He was staring at the girl's half naked body, as if he was unable to comprehend what had happened.

"The kid, finish it," Kroh said. Ingo had emptied the internal magazine of his Kar 98, but Pop knew he had some stripper clips of ammunition in the top pockets of his SS jacket, and he also wore his buttoned-down holster, which would contain his P38. Ingo reached for a clip.

"No, Pup. You don't need bullets for kids, you were in Wola. You saw how it was done, right?" Kroh said.

Use your pistol Ingo, do it quickly, Pop thought, moving his lips to the unvoiced words.

The boy looked up at Ingo. And Ingo looked at him. There was no expression on Ingo's face, nothing at all. Pop knew exactly what Kroh had meant. So would Ingo …

He did not believe Ingo could do it.

The Walther, Ingo …

"I will get a good picture – smile Pup!" Kroh shouted.

Ingo did not smile. But he did do exactly as Kroh had ordered. He dropped his rifle, which clattered on to the paving stones, then swiftly bent low, lifting the boy, and then turning him round and taking him by the ankles. The child cried now, panicked and wriggled, like a puppy held by the tail. The kid was small, probably very light, and Ingo easily swung him through one complete turn as if he was a throwing hammer and then stepped towards the wall the second time he spun around. The boy's head hit the painted bricks with the clocking sound of a coconut, which Pop heard quite clearly. It broke like a coconut, too. Ingo let the child drop to the floor, with hardly a sound. He was now just a pile of ragdoll stillness. Kroh had photographed it all.

"No Ingo … No …" Pop said.

"Get back in the truck, Pop," Kroh ordered. Then he drew his P38 and pointed it at Ingo's chest.

***

Brescia. May 1954

Pop had only ever seen her picture. He had thought her pretty then, when he had often looked at it, stuck to the inner steel of a Panzer IV, or propped up beside Ingo's bunk. She looked better now, he thought, a beautiful woman, no longer a pretty girl. Age had treated her well. Except for her eyes, which seemed almost dead, the lustre dimmed – even in black and white they had seemed so full of sparkle, he remembered. But Warsaw in '44 could do that to someone, he knew. That and more. He had always thought it had been more for her too; always believed Kroh's stick grenades really had done for Lidka in the sewers below Ochota.

The small café smelt strongly of brewing coffee and cigarette smoke. It was too much smoke for his liking, and breathing, and there were far too many mirrors, for him. But he had been up all night watching the cars depart and he had needed an espresso. He had not had much of a view of the Condor through the crowd, just its rounded rump before it disappeared down the other side of the yellow start ramp; after that he had managed to find a taxi to bring him here. Her perfume just about cut through the rich coffee aroma and the smoke; it smelt of flowers and citrus, and something he could not quite place. He wondered what it would be like to sleep with a woman like this. It would kill him, even if he could possibly manage it, he knew. But then there were a million and one worse ways to go.

There was thirty-five minutes until the train to Bologna, from where he would somehow find a way to get to the passes. There he would see what he had come all this way to see. There were few in the small alcove the coffee bar filled, and those customers did not stay for long, just sinking quick coffees in the Italian way, before hurrying off, puffing out cigarette smoke like the trains they rushed to catch. Even if they had stayed longer they would have probably understood little of the conversation between Beauty and the Beast, for they both spoke in German – it was the first time he had spoken his native language aloud for almost seven years, he realised.

"What happened to you?" she said. Lidka had not recognised him, of course, they had never met, but she had known who he was when he'd introduced himself as *Pop*. Then again, he thought, no one from then would recognise him now. She asked the question matter-of-factly, not skirting around the obvious.

"C'est la guerre," he said.

"Where?"

"Warsaw."

"How?"

"Molotov," he said, and that was the truth. "It's why I couldn't meet Ingo," and that was a lie. "I knew about all that, see."

"Yes, he told me you might help."

"I let him down."

He expected her to say something like, *you couldn't help it*. But she didn't. He had not told her the truth; how he had betrayed Ingo when Kroh had threatened to burn him, and how fire had not taken no for an answer. And how part of him had wished he had been burnt to death on that day and had wished this every day since. But he could not tell her that, and he could not ask her how the hell she was still alive – he remembered well the scream, when the grenade had plopped into the sewer, and then the explosion.

She finished her tiny coffee and left a small smudge of lipstick on the thick white china. An engine let off steam then chuffed once or twice besides one of the platforms; further away steel wheels shrieked against rails. A tinny announcement mentioned *Milano*, but that was all he could make out.

"How did it turn out; for those people?" he said.

"Not well," she said, but he knew that. She ordered a second espresso, having sunk the first like an Italian. The barista looked up from his newspaper and nodded, and then the coffee maker also whooshed out steam. Pop sat at the zinc-topped bar on a tall stool; he could not stand up for too long these days. She stood and looked him in the eyes in the mirror. Most people would not look at him for more than a moment. He was used to that, though. Not this.

"Have you spoken to him?" she said.

"No, I don't think he knows I'm alive. I didn't know he was, until recently."

"Did you look for him, after the war?"

"No, I hid from the world," he said. "But before that, I fought on, after some months in hospital, towards the very end. I was burnt, but I could sit in a panzer and shoot its gun, I was still good at that, and you can bet I wasn't the only reptile in the Panzerwaffe; burning tanks are good for cooking tall pork, you see. Besides, I wanted to die, but didn't have the guts to do it myself, wanted the Tommies to do it – I've never understood why they say suicide is cowardly, you know? Mind you, they gave me another Iron Cross, 1st Class this time."

"You should be proud," she said.

He had not expected sarcasm, but he smiled his tight little burnt smile. "I was wounded again then taken prisoner by the British, another hospital at first, in Carmarthen – they hardly knew where to start with me – and then a prisoner of war camp in Llandysul, both in Wales; it has been my home since the war." He paused then, realising for the first time with a little shock that he would not go back to Lampeter, Dai Twice and the lovely Gwen, not now. "They made us work on farms, and when it was time to come home, I stayed on."

"A German in England?"

"Wales, Lidka. It's important, for some reason. Anyway, it was not a problem. I have a Polish name, Szcześniak. Always hated it, never got round to changing it, like some changed their so-called Slav names when the Nazis came along. No one could pronounce it, it was easier to call me Pop, or later – in hospital, in the camp, in Wales – it was always just Joe; Joseph is my Christian name, you see. There were quite a few Poles living in that part of Wales, when the war finished, and many assumed I was one more; and I never talked much by then anyhow. Suited me, I didn't want to be a German anymore."

"But why did you not look for Ingo Six, you were his friend?"

"I always thought he'd been killed," he said, noticing the way she used the full name.

"Why?"

"Many were." It was a weak answer, he knew. But better then saying he had betrayed Ingo. He had heard that Ingo had been sent to jail, for desertion. Kroh had wanted him executed, for that and for destroying the Panther, but Hauptman Schulte, a top lawyer before the war it had turned out, had managed to save his life. Though he found it hard to imagine Ingo thriving in prison. Last he heard he had been in a penal battalion, and few survived them, even if they were faster than a bullet. He had heard no more and had thought Ingo dead; until that day in the doctor's surgery in Lampeter.

"So, it was a surprise for you; to find out he was alive?" she said.

"Yes, a surprise. I saw his picture in a magazine. Different name and he looked different, yes, but it was the way he stood, a thing of his – the palms of his hands on the car, as if he was thanking it."

"He was the same with a piano."

"Yes, and a motorbike. Even a panzer."

They were quiet for a little while. The tiny cup of coffee was placed in front of her, and she looked down at it, the first time she had taken her gaze off his burnt face in the mirror since she had arrived.

"Have *you* talked to him?" Pop said.

"No."

"He thought you were dead, you know?"

"Why would he think that?" she said, looking at him in the mirror again.

He shrugged. It pulled at his burns, so he seldom did that, and he saw the flash of pain on his own face in the mirror. She showed no sympathy. He did not go into details. Did not want more pain. "I don't know," he said.

"*Will* you talk to him?" she said.

He did not answer. He had thought about it. But could see no point. He had betrayed Ingo, both on that day and the days before it, as he had never once tried to get them back to the 19th, because he had had *better* things to do then. Besides, he would die soon anyway. Pop had come for something else. He took a sip of coffee instead of answering. Then said: "Will you?"

"No."

"Then why are you here?" he said, as he put the tiny cup down.

Lidka picked up her small suitcase, opened it, and took out a large envelope. She reached inside and then pulled out some photographic prints which she placed on the counter. The harsh electric lighting reflected off the grey and white surface of the pictures, but they were very clear and in sharp focus. Pop recognised Ingo immediately; and the scene. It was just as it has been – one thing about Kroh, he took a damned fine photo. As Pop looked at each of the pictures it all came flooding back, as it often did, in his nightmares. One of them showed the girl, her breasts bared, and although he knew Lidka watched him in the mirror he could not help but linger on the image. He felt arousal, painful as always, then put the picture beneath the others. Then there was the last of the photographs.

Ingo had the child by the ankles. Kroh had caught the exact moment when the little boy's head had hit the wall. Ingo's face was clear in the picture; but now, as then, Pop could find no trace of emotion there.

"I cannot read you, Szcznesniak, but I sense this is not a surprise?"

Pop took a deep burning breath, then said: "You're right, I was there."

"Then why did you lie?"

"It's not something I like to recall," Pop said. "The kid, he —"

"The *kid* was my son."

He dropped the photograph onto the others. He remembered the child; he had often thought about him. "I didn't know ... Ingo didn't know."

"And that makes it okay?"

"It wasn't so simple, you have to understand, Lidka – he had no choice."

"So, he was simply following orders," she said. "I've heard that before, you know?"

"If *he* didn't do it, *they* would. Believe me, he was saving them from something far worse."

"Only him? Why just him?"

"It was because of the man who took these pictures; it's hard to explain," Pop said. "It was his way of hurting Ingo. There was history, there."

"It's always history with you people, isn't it?"

"Things were complicated —"

"Not complicated, Szcześniak," she said, jabbing at the photograph with a finger. "It is simple, it is there – in black and white."

"Nothing in Warsaw was black and white."

"No, everything in Warsaw was black and white."

"You're wrong," Pop said. "And there was another reason. He also did this to save me."

"And you deserved to live; you deserved to live more than they did? More than my son did?"

"No, I did not," Pop said. "I do not," he added. "But don't you see, they had no chance? If Ingo had not, then you can bet one of those animals would have killed them, and worse!"

"They would not have killed my son, he was blond, blue eyed – they never killed boys like him," she said.

"Dirlewanger's lot would, stuff like that meant nothing to them."

"But Dirlewanger's men didn't, did they?" she said. "Ingo Six did."

"Yes, but —"

"And he did it like *this*." She nodded at the photo.

He sighed, feeling the passage of air scraping within him. "He had to."

"Even in Wola they used pistols," she said.

"Not always."

She nodded slightly, she knew this, he could see. "And yet he had a pistol, you can see the holster," she said.

Pop shook his head. He had often wondered why Ingo had not used his Walther. It would have been the work of a moment.

"Why Szcześniak? Why like this?"

He took a sip of his coffee. It had gone cold. He noticed that the tiny cup shook in his hand. He saw that she noticed, too. "Things weren't normal then," he said.

"That's no excuse."

"There was the drug."

"Drug?"

"Pervitin," he said. "We were given it at the start of the war, and some of us developed a taste for it. I talked to a doctor about it once, I've talked to lots of doctors about many things. He told me it was methamphetamine hydrochloride, and it's highly addictive – though I didn't need him to tell me that." Pop had never been able to find the stuff in Wales, and had never been able to figure out if he was pleased about that or not.

"Ingo was addicted to it?"

"No, he'd only tried it in Warsaw, in '44"

"And you gave it to him?"

"I only mention it because that stuff could do strange things to your head; made you think in a different way. It helped some people kill, *made* them kill, I know that."

"And who did you kill, Szcześniak?"

He almost shrugged again, but instead took another sip of his cold coffee, then said: "People died, it was war."

"Soldiers die, in war. *People* are murdered."

"It's never so simple, when you're there."

"But it is when you're high, or drunk – yes?"

"I never said that."

"And is it a defence, for murder, to say you were high or drunk?"

He had asked himself the same question, so many times, had no answer that could possibly help, and so he pretended to listen to another announcement he could not understand, and then changed the subject "He thought you were dead, you know."

"Yes, you said."

"They waited, at the drain, tossed grenades in; there was a scream —"

"It was another girl, she had taken my place. I think she had wanted that for a while," Lidka said. It might have been a cold joke, but there was no indication that it was.

"Poor girl."

"You have given me many reasons why Ingo Six did this, Szcześniak. But I'm not convinced. You're making excuses for the inexcusable; because you are his friend, were his friend. Either way, you will not betray him."

"I've betrayed him already."

She shook her head. "Why did he do this, Szcześniak?"

"I've told you, there are many reasons. But you choose not to believe me."

"What about the diamonds, the money?"

"That was taken, I think, but not by Ingo."

"Then why?"

"I've told you, Lidka. But you don't *want* to believe me."

"You're not convincing."

"Is that it? Or is it that you need someone to blame; and the only man *really* responsible for all this is not so easy to find?"

"The only man to blame is here, in Italy, driving a racing car."

"It's funny how guilt makes us think, Lidka – and believe me, I was in the German army, I know a lot about guilt."

"I have no reason to feel guilty, everything I have done has been just."

"You were not there, Lidka."

"I could not be there."

"But perhaps you *should* have been there?"

She looked at the picture again, sipped a little coffee. Then shook her head, sharply. "Guilt makes us hide, Szczneśniak – and Ingo Six has been hiding."

"Ingo is not the only one who has been hiding from the past," Pop said. "Besides, it's easier to forget the war if you're as far away from it as possible – and last time I checked a globe there was a lot of blue between Germany and Argentina."

"There are more reminders of the war in that place than you could ever guess, Szczneśniak. But we're good at getting rid of bad memories."

"We?"

Lidka glanced at her wristwatch, then nodded very slightly, as if agreeing to a decision she had at that very moment made, and then she said: "After the uprising I was taken prisoner. By that time they realised they could not kill us all; even the Nazis had their limitations – but this was a purely practical decision on their part, of course. Ingo Six had been wrong about that, but right about the city, they destroyed much of it. I was sent to Pruszków and from there to one of the camps at Auschwitz. I survived, any way I could. After the war I went back to Warsaw. But there was no place there for anyone who had been in the AK, the Communists were jailing us, executing some, too. We should have known it would come to that when Stalin left us to fight alone. So, I escaped to Germany, the west. From there, I started my search."

"For Ingo?"

"Not then." She took a sip of her coffee, then continued. "I thought he had been killed on that day, had been told as much. That had made sense, and so I did not question it as I should have; perhaps I did not want to know the truth?" She nodded at the picture. "But I knew a captain in the Dirlewanger Brigade has been in charge, had ordered this. I found his name; that was not so difficult, not then. I found other Nazis, too. Then they died."

She said it casually, and with that Pop quite suddenly realised he might be in danger, and he quickly looked down at the photograph again, not wanting her to see the sudden fear in his eyes, the only part of his face that could give him away. He realised how absurd it was as he did it. Why should a dead man fear death?

"Soon I realised I was not the only one taking revenge," she continued. "But there were not many of us, not many at all. I decided to work with others, Jewish survivors of the camps mostly. Then, thanks to a man I met while I was with them, I was sent to Israel, a new group. I cannot talk about that. It was good work; but unofficial work."

"Killing?

"Of course, killing."

"But the war was over?"

She ignored that, and he realised it was not over, for some. "I was not Israeli nor Jewish, and at first it suited them. But soon it was better to be a part of it, it gave me protection; and they were the only people I could see who were interested in justice. I married a Jew, converted to Judaism. It's only a label, I was in Warsaw, I know there's no God. My surname was the same as my husband's, that's all, merely convenient. I did not really want a family, but …"

"But?"

"That's over, now. They'll be better off without me," she brushed it aside. "I took a Hebrew name, as was required, to marry, to become Israeli. I chose the name of the girl in the photographs, *Sarah*. I thought that fitting, she would have agreed with what we've been doing, it was what she had wanted from her life."

"You changed your name, your whole life?"

"You changed your life, too."

"No, it was burnt from me."

"It was the same for me," she said. "Anyway, it was worth it. They understood revenge, and they helped me to hunt down Christian Kroh."

"That scum," Pop said. "I hope you found him?"

She nodded. "We found him, in Argentina. He was eliminated."

"There won't be many grieving."

"No, but he was generous in his will. He left pictures, many; it was a hobby of his. Tourist photos."

"Yes, I remember."

"It's where these come from," she said, taking the photographs and slipping them back inside the envelope. "Our man made sure to sneak into his house and go through his things before he killed him, we've found many Nazis with pictures like these, and Kroh had hundreds of them. And the best of the pictures, or the worst I suppose, came back to Tel Aviv."

Suddenly the smoke in the bar proved too much for him and he started to cough uncontrollably. She said nothing, but the barista offered him a glass of water. When he had finished coughing and had drunk a little water, she continued, as he tried to steady his breathing.

"I had believed Ingo Six was dead," she said. "But it's not quite true that I did not look for him. There was always a nagging doubt; I'm not sure why, I suppose I needed to be sure. And so I tried the Army Information Office in Berlin, but that was no use; at that time there were one point one million Wehrmacht personnel missing, did you know that? I sometimes wonder how many they eventually found; hope it wasn't as many as we did." She almost smiled, at that, he thought.

"When things had settled down a little, and the German POWs had started to drift home, I went to Munich. I had never known his address, but I'd always known his family had a piano shop, and when I'd seen him again in the

Old Town in '44 he told me it was called Wagner's, so I looked it up in an old business directory. It was on Wagmüllerstrasse, but it was bombed out and deserted by then. I could find no one who knew Ingo Six in the area, or what was left of it. So, I then tried the Bavarian Red Cross, I was looking for his family too, by then. But nothing. Later I hired a private detective, a German, he was from Munich, too, and for him it was easier to ask other Germans questions; he had the right ID card, I did not. But he told me everyone who had known Ingo Six thought he was dead. He found his parents, living with relatives in the country, near Tegernsee. He had told them he was a former comrade. But they had not seen Ingo Six, thought him dead, too. Now I sometimes wonder if it was this detective's questions that scared him off."

She shook her head. "But, of course, it was only when the pictures turned up that I realised that he, too, might have a reason to find a new name, a new life. Anyway, eventually we found him."

"How?"

"He was betrayed. But by then our group had been shut down, partly because I had made a mistake."

"What sort of mistake?"

"Costly," she said. "But then, people die."

"And now you've found him. What will you do?" Pop said, after a pause.

"As I said, our group is no more," she said. "Which is why I can tell you these things."

"And what if I tell, too?"

"If you were with Ingo Six in Warsaw, you were with Dirlewanger. That's not the sort of company a man should brag about. Besides, I felt the need to tell someone."

"A confession?"

"No, Szcześniak, I'm a Jew now, I don't have that need, do you?"

He shook his head. Wished he had not brought up the subject of confessions.

"Sometimes, someone just needs to talk to a stranger, after so much secrecy," she said.

"I'm dying, you know?" he said.

"I can't say I'm surprised, nor sorry."

There was a pause for a few moments as a man in a raincoat forced his way between them and ordered a coffee.

"I know what you're thinking," she said, after the man had taken his coffee further along the bar. "You could warn him. But I'm not sure you're fit enough to catch the train you're here to catch, never mind a racing car."

"I won't argue with that."

"Besides, it will make no difference, he's already on his guard. It's obvious someone has tipped him off."

"But your group, you said it's no more?"

"The Group is finished."

"So, *why* are you here, then?" he said.

There was an echoing announcement over the public address system and Pop picked out the words *Roma* and *Express*. She glanced at her watch again, and quickly gulped down the rest of her coffee, although he knew there was plenty of time before that train departed as he was taking it himself, as far as Bologna. She clattered some coins on to the zinc counter then she put the envelope that contained the photographs back into the small case.

"Why did he do it, Szczneśniak?"

"Perhaps he just wanted to live," Pop said. "Is that such a crime?"

She nodded, and then picked up her case.

"Wait," he said.

"Yes?"

The coughing came again, with no warning, and he held a handkerchief to his mouth. There was no stopping it, he knew. She left, without saying goodbye. When the fit finally spluttered to an end Joseph Szczneśniak looked at the hanky, now bright with blood, then the clock on the wall. There was still eleven minutes before his train left for Bologna. He would not be able to walk to the train without resting halfway, to somehow suck some air into his tattered lungs, so he, too, would have to leave the coffee bar soon. From Bologna he planned to find his way, somehow, to a place where he could watch Ingo drive the Condor as a car like that should be driven. It was the last thing he wanted from life, and also the last thing he would take from it, he knew. He did not know what she wanted from life; or if she had finished taking from it.

*

The Adriatic coast, Italy. May 1954

The sun had burnt through the fog and the rain had stopped. They were three hours in to the race now, and on the fastest part of the course, the long drag southeast along the Adriatic coast. It had been raining through Verona and Vicenza, but it had stopped by Padua. By then they had used up enough fuel that the understeer was no longer a problem and Ingo had not had to drive around it; while the wet road surface had also meant the front tyres had not suffered so much in the early stages.

At the end of the main street in Padua Ingo had taken the tight right-hander in a big slide, the cold tyres slithering against the equally cold, greasy cobbles, the side of the car so close to a shining wet wall that Ingo could have reached out and stroked it. He had then passed the dark green Aston Martin that had started ahead of them. He had gone by on the long straight road that arrowed south out of the city; with conical hills to the right, flat green arable land gouged with slim canals to the left, and rocket-shaped church spires that pinned the villages to the verdant tapestry of the land.

They had blasted through Ferrara and on to Ravenna, where there had been a control. Ingo had slowed the Condor to walking pace as Carlo held the route card on the side of the car – the card was attached to a small board tied to Carlo's handrail by a cord to make sure it did not fly out of the Condor. An official had rubber-stamped it, the metallic *dong* a starter pistol for Ingo. On the road to Forli Ingo had passed the next car that had started just in front of them, the Maserati, on a causeway at 120mph, with just half a metre between them and a four-metre drop into the fields. Carlo had then shown him a hand signal they had not agreed on, and his pirate grin.

They were passing much slower cars all the time now; drivers who had started many minutes and even hours earlier and would usually get out of the way when they glimpsed the rapidly expanding blue patch of the Condor in their mirrors, or when Carlo jabbed at the dash-mounted horn button, which also flashed the headlights, fitted for just such occasions. But the next of the bigger cars ahead of them was Otero's Ferrari, now just a pinprick of scarlet, and Ingo had a feeling it might take more than a honk of the horn to pass that one.

The road here was straight, pinched at the distant horizon. The red dot in front of them was getting no bigger. There was no way the Condor could overhaul the Ferrari here, for while it had a decent top speed of 160mph, the Ferrari had at least 10mph in hand on the straight, and Otero was many things, but a coward was not one of them. And right now this was all about bravery. Bravery and velocity.

The Condor's accelerator pedal was jammed to the vibrating bulkhead, while his left leg was braced against the footrest. The chassis buzzed to the speed, the wheels skipped over the always far from smooth road, and Ingo read the ever-changing surface like braille through those piano fingers on the steering wheel. The hot air from the engine was mixed with the buffering slipstream, bathing him like a warm shower; oil and dust beginning to coat his face, tightening the skin slightly as the oil dried in the wind. The road seemed to expand right in front of the thick, low, moulded Perspex windscreen, as if they raced through a shimmering, blurred funnel of speed.

Then there was a slight kink ahead, and Carlo gave him the signal for 'flat', a little karate chop close to the steering wheel, just inside Ingo's peripheral vision. He took the kink without a lift, letting the car drift to the fringe of the road. The sun was climbing higher in the sky and he felt its warmth on his left cheek.

He was suddenly somewhere else: *The throttle was wide open, there was not a millimetre of space left in its travel, it was jammed to its stop, his wrist bent back a little on the twist grip, the engine note a high, steely rasp. The motorcycle and sidecar combination could go no faster. This was perfect.*

Carlo nudged him, but it was not a signal to warn him of an impending hazard. He glanced at Carlo, who was smiling wide, and Ingo realised it was because he himself had been grinning like a lunatic.

Driving flat out along a road for spells of twenty minutes and more had its own demands. You could not afford to ease off a millimetre, could not afford to leak a drop of speed. He concentrated on the road ahead, feeling his eyes bulge in his head through the effort of it. Every few minutes he was catching slower cars now; a Jaguar saloon here, a Lancia Aurelia there, and Carlo would use the dash mounted horn button to warn them. They caught a Porsche 356 by surprise, and Ingo had a moment as he feathered the edge of the road, kicking up stones and dust. He could smell the sea over the hot baking engine, and the rubber and burnt-brake odour of cars that had gone before, and every now and then he would catch a snatch of something at the edge of his vision: glimpses of the Adriatic to his left, silver-blue and shining, or sometimes granite grey, chipped with white flecks, glistening dark rocks poking through the shimmering membrane; lattices of shadow where fishing nets dried; people, too – always them – lining the route in many places. Sometimes trains would flash by in the opposite direction on the railway line that ran parallel to the road. Often there were towns up high to the right, like Loreta with its distinctive tower and dome, and more often still there were fields of gnarled olive trees, which reminded Ingo of the dead of Warsaw, burnt brittle and twisted after a Nebelwerfer attack. He let the speed wash that image from his head – cleansing speed, always pure, always simple.

Carlo touched his arm and made the signal for a hump in the road; his palm down, hand curved, then held up one finger to show the severity. Ingo remembered this one from the practice runs. Carlo had reckoned it could be taken fast, but with a dab of the brake, though Ingo had thought Carlo had been cautious. Ingo did not bother with the brake, but did come off the throttle a smidgen, to bring the nose of the car down slightly …

They hit the hump at around 155mph. The car took flight like a 75mm shell from the gun of a Panther. He kept the wheels dead straight, for to move them now could mean disaster on landing, and a second or so later the Condor touched down with four almost simultaneous scuffing kisses, as tarmac welcomed rubber home, the suspension compressing wheezily, but Ingo still holding the car perfectly straight. He thought they had flown for about fifty metres, at least.

Soon enough they were in Pescara; Ingo luxuriating in the corners, sliding the car just enough, allowing it to drift without fighting it; piano fingers caressing the dimpled wooden rim of the steering wheel, feet dancing a quickstep on the pedals. There was another control in the town, and this was also where they had planned to have their first fuel stop. The idea was to put in just enough to get them across the Apennines and on to Rome – seventeen and a half gallons – so the car would be light and agile in the mountains. He guessed that Otero would do the same, and then fill up in Rome, whereas they would just fill to three quarters again. The Condor was a lighter car than the Ferrari anyway, handled better too, while, Ingo knew, it also had a better driver. He was looking forward to the mountains. They would also take on new Buchanan tyres here, and the mechanics were busy knocking off the hub spinners with rubber mallets. While the fuel was glugging into the tank behind Ingo's seat and the Condor was raised on a jack, Carlo quickly climbed out and gave the car the once-over. Ingo took the opportunity to gobble down a peeled banana one of the mechanics handed him and drink some orange juice, while another cleaned the dead flies from the low Perspex screen.

He did not have to ask how far Otero was ahead of them, he had seen him drive away from his own stop, his Ferrari coupe shining like a polished red apple in the sunlight. He thought Otero had looked back to see where he was; he was sure of it. Guido, who was in charge here, gave the signal for him to go – these mechanics had done their work for the day, just twenty-nine seconds of it, and Varela had paid them very well for that. There would be another crew for the stop at Rome, one-hundred-and-fifty miles away, where they would take on new tyres and fuel again. Then the same in Florence, then Bologna. But before all that there were the Apennines to cross. It was here that Ingo planned to pass Otero.

The road out of Pescara was straight and fast but it soon entered a rocky valley and there were more corners, many of them flowing curves, and Ingo quickly found the groove, the car working well, tiny flakes of brake lining sticking to his skin like little flies on flypaper as he worked the brakes harder. They had only really gone quickly in the Alfa along this section, and that when sharing the road with daily traffic, and so they had failed to note the severity of the camber on one very fast corner. Ingo took the turn in a drift, but when the car slid across the crown in the road at this far greater speed it acted as a take-off ramp, and for a stretched moment the car was flying sideways at 110mph, its suspension sagging, and the rear wheels clawing at nothing but air. It landed right at the edge of the road, which was lined with a stone wall, and Ingo applied the throttle and a turn of opposite lock, deftly driving them out of the ensuing slide. One extra coat of blue paint and they would have scraped the wall. An extra inch of steel and they would be *in* the wall. They both quickly glanced at each other, laughed, then Carlo looked back at the plastic covered page of his notes, signalling a fast turn a little later.

Ingo momentarily caught sight of the start of the mountains towering in the near distance, scabs of bare white rock flashing in the green, before a grey veil of cloud gently descended to obscure the scene. Carlo was signalling continually now, like the conductor of an orchestra, as the corners came thick and fast; upraised hands; three fingers; a fist, for heavy braking, and two fingers, while Ingo used the kilometre posts that lined the entire route as points of reference.

Soon the red car in front was in sight, briefly, before disappearing around turns, and then it seemed to grow a little bigger after every corner, such was the time Ingo was taking out of it. The Ferrari was sliding more now, too, Otero over-driving, so Ingo was sure he knew he was on his tail, was worried; the boy always over-drove when he was flustered. But Ingo also knew that he would have to be careful; he knew Hector Otero was not above running a man off the road to win a race. Hector Otero was not above running a man off the road to finish last but one ...

They thundered over the Bailey Bridge that crossed the Pescara river at Popoli, the tyres humming over the jointed deck, and then climbed steadily, Ingo still eating into the Ferrari's lead. He could make no headway once they were on the long fast road that dissected the eerie plateau above, speeding beneath a sky thick with grey cloud, the air frigid now so the heat from the engine that washed over him was welcome. The Ferrari was able to inch ahead, slowly getting smaller, but before they reached the control at Aquila the character of the road changed. And the fog returned.

Otero's Ferrari hit the wall of fog and disappeared – except for the firefly flicker of its taillights. Ingo switched on the headlights at the very same time the Condor also entered the frayed extremities of the fog bank; the mist so thick both him and Carlo tensed, as if they were crashing into it. The air was suddenly cold and damp and the note of their own engine, and that of Otero's car in front, changed; seemed deeper.

The road was serpentine now, and Ingo had to rely largely on Carlo's hand signals to brake for the many corners. Trees and houses seemed to suddenly appear, to almost un-dissolve out of nothing, to jump into solidity. The road was slick, too, not having had the chance to dry in the sun. But that was not a problem. Ingo had the car on the very limit, guided by the hand signals, and also guided by the sizzling red patches in the fog that were Otero's taillights, and the violent branding burn of his brake lights; too often, and on too long. He caught him in no time. When they were a few metres back Carlo jabbed at the dash-horn, the tone of the trumpet honk now different in the thick fog, but Ingo knew Otero would take no notice, and he could see no way past the Ferrari. They raced in to Aquila in tandem, Otero locking up and sliding past the chequered black and white strip painted on the road beneath the sign that said *Controllo*. Ingo had to wait a moment while Otero's car was cleared first, then the route card Carlo presented was stamped, too. The stop meant they were a little way behind when they left Aquila, enough that the red taillights had faded to nothing in the fog, but Ingo soon caught up again. And once more they were stuck behind the wide, and getting wider, Ferrari.

Ingo tried everything he knew to pass. He made one move out of a tight left, where Otero had gone in deep, then panicked and put too much power on, the Ferrari's headlights slashing through the cotton of the fog and throwing a blanket of bright light on to a grass bank on the inside. Ingo's line was cleaner, and although the car slithered on the wet cobbles at the apex of the turn, he managed to put its nose alongside the other car at the exit, level with the door.

It was a more metaphorical door that slammed shut, forcing Ingo to stamp on the brakes, and Carlo to shout a curse that was audible over the rasp of the engines and the slither of the tyres on the wet road. Ingo caught the resultant slide and hooked a lower gear. Otero would not get far ahead, of that he was certain. But how would Ingo pass him?

Just then Carlo reached over to the portion of the dash that was close to the steering wheel. He flicked a steel switch. And turned off the lights.

Ingo's first reaction was to reach for the switch, but Carlo slapped his gloved hand away, and in the very same movement he showed him a fist then held out three fingers, to indicate heavy braking and the severity of the next turn. Ingo concentrated on the road ahead, what he could see of it, just twenty metres or so. But he could also still see the taillights and the flickering brake lights of the Ferrari, and Carlo's hand signals. It was, he now saw, enough.

Ingo also realised, with a smile, that Otero would not now know they were there, as they were hidden in the fog. He would think they had dropped back, broken down, maybe crashed …

Ingo knew exactly where he would overtake Otero. There was a longish, fast drop into a left-handed hairpin above the village of Antrodoco. He remembered the sequence of hand signals before it, and he remembered the road. He felt now as if his every sense was stretched to snapping point, but he savoured it; the noise of the downchange blips and the silky swish of the rubber on the wet road; the judder of the suspension fighting against the pitted, weatherworn asphalt; the smells of wild thyme licked by damp fog, hot brake linings, oil and fuel; the flickering red of Otero's brake lights, not so panicky now that he obviously thought Ingo was no longer behind him. He would not hear the Condor until it was too late; for he was in a closed Ferrari, and the thunder from the 4.5 V12 in front of him would be more than enough to fill his ears and those of his co-driver.

Otero was just a little cautious on the run down the hill to the hairpin, past a roadside house on the left that threw the rude noise of both cars back in their faces, and then another house on the right, and Ingo closed up steadily, aiming to be behind the Ferrari when Otero was concentrating on slowing the car on the slick surface to take the tight left-handed turn.

Ingo left his braking later, much later, and shot up the inside at the very last minute, just as Otero was turning in. The inside of the hairpin was, again, cobbled, its outer apron concrete. The cars almost touched, but such was Otero's shock at the sudden appearance of what had been an invisible Condor that this time he reflexively turned away from the contact. Ingo took the corner cleanly, except for the inevitable understeer on entry, and fed in the revs slowly at the exit, with just a small wriggle from the rear of the car as the tyres struggled for purchase.

Carlo leaned over and switched the headlights back on, the fog in front suddenly silver-white, then he signalled with a bent hand and then two upturned fingers that a tight right was approaching. Ingo risked a peek at his face; his grin alone was bright enough to light up the fog. Ingo smiled back, then slowed the car for the next turn, taking it round on the throttle. Otero was right with him now, but by the time they had negotiated the twists of Antrodoco his headlights were dimming to little yellow bruises in the wall of fog behind the Condor.

Once they were beyond Rieti the fog lifted, to reveal a field grey sky mottled with flak-burst like dark clouds. It started to rain soon after; falling on the bonnet and carving little twisting aerodynamic arabesques along it, before splashing against the low Perspex screen through which they peered, turning grime Ingo had not noticed into muddy splats. His goggles steamed up, and so he switched them for his spare pair. Some of the rain fell in the cockpit, finding gaps in his jacket, it also soaked the backs of his driving gloves. He shivered just a little from the icy water, but this was nothing, Ingo Six had endured much worse when it came to the cold. They unwound a veil of spray behind them as they raced on, and Ingo forgot about Otero, hidden far beyond that curtain, and concentrated instead on the slippery surface of the road, feeling for the grip with his front tyres, partly steering the car with the power through the rears, the Condor soaring off the Apennines in a series of controlled slides.

Soon they were on the road to Rome. He felt confident that he would be able to stay ahead of Otero before they headed north towards Viterbo, Siena, Florence and the passes beyond, especially with what would be a shorter stop for him for less fuel and fresh tyres in Rome. For the first time he allowed himself to wonder where they were in the overall standings. Otero had slowed them, but they had passed two fast cars by then, and no one had passed them; not Marzotto in the Maserati nor Mantovani in the Ferrari, Mille Miglia specialists both, who had started the race just after the Condor. Ingo felt quietly confident that they had already left their mark on the Mille Miglia.

The road into the Rome control, on the eastern outskirts of the city, was long and fast, so he knew Otero would steal back time here. It was also slick and slippery. But neither of these things was a problem. The problem was the people. There had been spectators almost everywhere along the route so far, even in the mountains. It was one of the reasons why Ingo had felt safer in the car despite Kroh's warning. In some places, like Brescia, the crowd had been five deep. But everywhere it had been more or less controlled. Except here.

At any other time Ingo would have been driving at about 150mph and maybe more on a road like this, even with the rain. But today there were just too many people. People who did not seem to mind the weather; people who did not seem to mind dying, either. The road before Ingo seemed as narrow as a path in places, hemmed in by the wheat fields of humanity who swayed and jostled and pushed; and somehow melted back just in time to make a gap for the Condor to pass through, horn blaring, Ingo weaving a little to scare them a step or so further away from the car. Carlo kept his finger pressed on to the horn button, and the faces of the spectators shone pale in the headlamps like the ghosts they surely aspired to be. It was impossible, and Ingo slowed the car down, until he was going just eighty miles per hour – but even this seemed too fast. On two occasions some machismo hand touched the side of the car. The second time this happened Ingo looked in his mirror to check if he had left some poor soul lying in the road. And there was the red Ferrari coupe with the green nose band, closing on them; closing on them very, very quickly, growing bigger in the mirror like a balloon filling with air.

Otero cared for no one, except himself, and so Ingo was only slightly surprised when he pulled out to pass the Condor. The crowd in front were ready to make way for one car, they had been doing so for hours, but they were not ready for two. There was panic, and some tripped over others as they stepped back, one girl fell and lay in the road. Ingo braked hard, a front tyre snatching and skidding on the wet surface. Otero was past him in a blink. He missed the girl in the road. Just. But the front fender of the Scuderia Verde Ferrari clipped the heel of a man who was diving out of its way, sending him spinning in to the fleeing crowd, and them falling back on to each other like toppled ranks of toy soldiers.

They had knocked off enough revs through slowing that Ingo could hear Carlo as he shouted: "Looks like we'll have to pass him all over again!"

"Well, we won't be able to use your fog trick, he'll be ready for that now," Ingo shouted back, angry at Otero, but glad that he could see in his mirrors that the lad that had been hit by the Ferrari was getting up and seemed okay.

"Not my trick, my friend. Tazio Nuvolari's. He did something similar to Varzi in the 1930 Mille Miglia; in those days it always finished in the dark. He was catching …"

Ingo did not hear the rest of the story, as he worked the Condor up through the gears, the 2.7-litre V12 roaring then briefly hiccupping to the smoothly fast shifts. Even with Otero carving a way recklessly through the crowd ahead it was almost instantly filling in behind the smoothly sculpted rear of the Ferrari, and Ingo had to make his own way through. He kept his speed down. He did not want to kill anyone. Not again. They had to take on tyres and fuel, straight after the Rome control, Otero would have to, too, and more fuel. But he was getting away from them now, building a lead by risking the lives of others, a buffer that would give him extra time at the stop. Carlo was dead right. They would somehow have to pass him on the road again.

***

Ochota, Warsaw. August 1944

The child was dead at Ingo's feet. A small red scuff on the white wall of the apartment block showed where his head had hit it.

"Always knew you had it in you, Pup," Kroh said, and Ingo turned to see he had levelled his Walther at his chest. In the background Pop was climbing into the cab of the Krupp truck while the Dirlewanger men were slinging their rifles and MP 40s, ready to move out. One of them came over and picked up Ingo's Kar 98. He checked Ingo's holster, too, saw that it was empty.

"Thing is, desertion's desertion, right? The lads know you went missing for a couple of days. They're not sophisticated, like me and you, Pup – so wouldn't do to give them the wrong message now, right?"

Ingo could see the concern paint Pop's face as he settled back in the driving seat of the Krupp. He felt a sudden flash of fear, an electric shock of it – he still did not want to die, he realised, even if it meant living with what he had done. Ingo Six still wanted to live.

Kroh started to whistle *Erika* again. He was holding the pistol in one hand, the camera in the other. Ingo wondered how many photographs he had taken. But now his focus was on Ingo, and the pistol he pointed at Ingo.

The bullet hit Kroh in the thigh with a meaty splat, he spun round once, then fell, pulling the P38's trigger at the same time, but his aim was spoiled and the pistol shot missed Ingo by a metre and thwacked into a bloodstained patch of wall.

Right then the cab of the Krupp erupted in flames. Ingo knew it was a petrol bomb immediately; had heard the tinkling of glass and the whoosh of the explosion. The flames engulfed the cab and Ingo heard Pop's screams, high and loud.

Rifle and pistol fire sparked off the railings in front of the apartment block and smacked against the cobbles out in the street, throwing chips of stone into the air. One of the Dirlewanger men was caught in the chest with a thudding bullet and he fell. The rest dived for cover and reflexively searched for the source of the firing, then returned fire with their MP 40s and rifles. Kroh had one hand over his thigh, blood seeping through his fingers, as he crawled for cover behind the low wall, Ingo forgotten for now. Ingo had instinctively hit the ground when the first shot was fired and as he turned he found he was now eye to eye with the dead child. He looked away; back towards the cab of the truck, which he could easily see over the low railing-capped wall. Black-orange flame was billowing from it, the fire and smoke so thick he could not see Pop within it: within the cab, and within the inferno. He knew there was no more he could do for him. This had all taken seconds ...

Ingo ran.

He rolled on to his feet and then hurried past the row of six dead people – dead because of him – and when he came to the last in line, Sol Vogler, his eyes prised open in the shock of his death, an acid flash of memory burnt bright in Ingo's mind. He reached down to scoop up the fedora the man had offered, crunching it tightly in his fist. Then he sprinted around the back of the building and was in cover in an instant, without a shot or shout chasing him, as Kroh and the Dirlewanger men fought their attackers who were, Ingo realised now, shooting from across the street. He ran as fast as he had ever run, his rubber soles squidging loudly on the cobbles of the courtyard as he made for the place where he had parked up the DKW.

There was a walkway through the building on one side of the courtyard, like a brick-lined tunnel just wide enough for two to walk holding hands, and he ran through it, his footfalls echoing in the tight space. He came out of the darkness and into the bright light that flooded one of the side streets.

Suddenly the arched entrance to the narrow walkway was filled with flying splinters of brick and stone, and sparks danced off the cobbles in front of him, while bullets stitched a stony ellipsis on the wall to his right.

He stopped abruptly, his momentum almost pitching him into the middle of the street, and teetered on one leg for a moment as rounds whipped past his body, feeling the pass of one in his hair, and then he ducked low and dived back in to the cover of the walkway. But he had had time, for a moment as he turned, to snatch a glimpse of who was shooting at him; a young man in a leather jacket with an AK armband. A young man who knew how to handle a sub machine gun.

Ingo ran back into the courtyard then turned left, the shape of the cobbles punching through the soles of his panzer boots, his heart hammering to keep up, sweat now pouring from him. He could hear the echoing slaps of his pursuer's shoes on the cobbles as he followed him though the arched walkway. Ingo crossed a street, then ran alongside a house and into another courtyard, then crossed it, before suddenly finding himself on a street that he did not recognise; a street that had seen a lot of fighting. He could hear the man chasing him, keeping up, but not gaining, unable to risk stopping to take the time needed to aim, unwilling to waste ammunition by firing on the run or at long range. This one knew his stuff.

There was an apartment block at the corner of the street that had been badly hit; holed like a Swiss cheese and nibbled by machine guns. As he had seen in other parts of Warsaw, there was a pile of bodies in front of the building. There were men working there, Sonderkommando. It had been the same in Wola, and elsewhere, stacking the bodies from the pile in that special way, that some cold and sick mind had devised, so that they would burn well. The corpses had been civilians, colourful summer dresses flashing like flares in the gloomy broken streetscape. He guessed they had been executed recently, but in the heat the smell of death was already choking, as his hard-working lungs sucked it in. Then he spotted the SS guard, overseeing the forced labour Sonderkommando, just one man, because each of the men he was responsible for looked nearly ready to join the heap of death they had started to rearrange into a neater stack.

"Help!" Ingo somehow shouted through burning lungs, and he wondered, as he ran, if those he had killed would add to this pile ... then the bullet drilled into his boot.

The hit of it twisted his leg to one side, as if he had been tripped, and he fell face first on to the warm cobbles, sliding along them on his belly. It was only then that he felt the searing pain, yet he forced himself back up on to his feet, turning at the same time to see his pursuer yank the empty magazine out of the side of the sub machine gun and let it drop on to the street with a tinny clatter. Ingo did not see him slot a replacement magazine into the Sten, as he concentrated on putting weight on his wounded foot, feeling the ooze of warm blood begin to fill his sock, and pain fill his being.

Now the SS man was running towards them, his Luger drawn. This distracted Ingo's pursuer, who hit the SS guard with a short burst before he had a chance to fire, bright rosettes of blood dappling his field grey tunic.

But Ingo had only caught this through the corner of his eye, as he hopped and ducked inside the apartment building, its doors long blasted open. He hobbled through the pain and into a dark stairwell, still gripping the hat tightly. Every other step was spikey hot agony now, and the sound of his pursuer's footsteps soon echoed up the stairwell behind him. Then slowed, as the man – clearly no fool or novice – readied himself for an ambush. But there would be no ambush, as Ingo had no P38. He had given that to Sarah yesterday, to help win her trust. Now she was dead. Ingo then thought of Pop, dead Pop, then Lidka, dead Lidka. But Ingo Six was still alive. This spurred him on, he hobbled faster still, using the cold iron rail of the narrow banister to help him up the stairs; second flight, third flight, his ragged breathing echoing in the dark shaft of the stairwell.

He thought that if he could get to an open flat he might find a fire escape out the back, but the doors he quickly tried on each landing were locked. Then, on the fourth and final floor, there was a doorway without a door, fringed with a corona of bullet holes, and he almost fell inside. The way ahead was choked with debris – bricks mixed with dismembered furniture and a decapitated china spaniel – but he was able to clamber over the wreckage and then through a gap that had obviously been blown through with explosives during the fighting, and on in to another apartment and a smashed-up living room. The one door that led out of the room was blocked because the ceiling had collapsed and lay in the room like a thirsty, dust coated tongue. There was also a large rectangular hole in the front wall, as if someone had carelessly enlarged the windows, knocking them into a single ragged-edged opening, through which he could still hear the sounds of the gunfight on Mochnackiego, the more distant battle in the Old Town, and a familiar rattling and clanking.

Ingo peered over the edge of the huge hole in the wall, the clatter of his pursuer as he made his way through the debris in the adjoining room ever louder. Four storeys below was the pile of corpses, from this high angle looking like a puddle of death. He climbed up on to the ledge of the gap, the bricks loose under his hands and feet, his wounded foot now slick with blood and thick with pain. The Sonderkommando had now fled, their guard dead in the street, and there was no sign of anyone alive below.

He heard the man come in behind him; allowed himself a brief look at his face – swollen with hatred – and then Ingo jumped.

It amazed him how fast he fell, and yet how long it seemed to take, before he finally hit the pile of dead bodies with a slappy thud, breaking his fall and not his neck, an already skeletal dead man's arm snapping as he fell on it, a twisted dead elbow knocking what wind was left from his heaving lungs. The pile of corpses seemed to moan as he hit them, and then he sank in amongst them, as if they dragged him down to die with them, part submerged in the tangle of limbs, until he settled; eye to eye with a dead old woman who had the shadow of a grim smile cut deep in to her throat. A cloud of fat flies filled the air around him like buzzing blue shrapnel, and the shifted bodies he was entangled with farted and hissed as the gas trapped within them was released.

He was able to turn his head and look up above, and see the man in the leather jacket leaning out of the building through the ragged gap Ingo had jumped from, looking strangely tall, as he took aim with the Sten, pressing the steel-frame butt to his shoulder. He fired a single shot that *phutted* into a corpse just centimetres from Ingo, and then adjusted his aim. Another gunshot, a sharper crack this time.

He had seemed so far up, so far away, maybe 20 metres. But now he was closer, closer, falling, the distorted-T-shaped Sten twisting away to one side like a winged seed in autumn … The man landed alongside Ingo with a rude thud, shifting the pile of bodies again, his face now just a half a metre from him. Surprise painted that face; that and the blood and slime that gushed from the hole where his left eye had been.

Ingo struggled to sit up, tried to clear himself of the grabbing dead limbs. There were shouts, in German, from soldiers, running towards him now, and a Panzer IV was rattling along the street, its tracks shrieking against the cobbles, the vibrations shaking the dead he lay with, as if they trembled from a fear that was far too late. He recognised the green and mustard tiger stripes of the tank's camouflage; the 19th. Then Ingo suddenly realised he had dropped the hat as he had jumped from the building. By some joke of the gods it had landed on the head of a woman with no lower jaw and dead eyes that looked like painted dots. Ingo took the fedora from her and placed it on his head.

***

Via Cassia, Italy. May 1954

They overtook one of the faster 2-litre Ferrari 500 Mondials just after leaving Rome, where the road passed between raised stone walkways, its driver waving them through, recognising the Condor as the quicker car, as is the way in road racing. But this was not Otero's way …

The Via Cassia had seen plenty over the centuries, and it had witnessed the speedy passage of the greatest drivers over more recent decades. But whether a man was at the reins of a chariot or the wheel of a sports racing car, Ingo doubted this noble road had ever seen anything quite as pig-headed as Otero's attempts to keep him behind. It was dangerous – sure – and it was stupid. For Otero slowed himself as much as he slowed Ingo. What made it all the harder to stomach was that when they had checked in and fuelled up in Rome they had been told they had been in fourth place overall at Pescara, behind the Lancia D24s of Piero Taruffi, Alberto Ascari and Eugenio Castellotti. That feat alone would see the Varela Condor order book begin to fill, he thought. But Ingo also knew they had lost time bottled up behind Otero over the Apennines, and they were losing more time now. He had originally merely wanted to pass Otero on the road to humiliate him, but now it was also a matter of having to pass him to have a chance of taking the fight to the leading Lancias.

The cloud had lifted again, the asphalt was dry, though badly pitted and potholed in places. The way ahead was flowing drivers' roads; lined with terracotta coloured houses and pinched tight in places by trees – around one of which a Peugeot 203 was almost folded in half like a penknife, near Settevene. There were other casualties, too: a Fiat 1100 on its roof in the centre of a steeply sloping field near Vigne Nuove; a cream and white Lancia Aurelia parked in the window of a flower shop in Pianetti, yellow blooms dripping from its roof, broken glass sparkling like diamonds around its wheels; like a crashed wedding.

Now they were hurtling through Sutri at 130mph, Otero's Ferrari and the Condor nose to tail, the exhaust fumes from the red coupe catching in Ingo's throat. It was hot in the car, and the temperature gauge was beginning to creep up too, as because of the Ferrari that was blocking their way not so much fast air was going through the radiator grille. Ingo knew he would need to drop back soon, to give the car a chance to cool. But he hated the idea. He caught snatches of antiquity through the corner of his eye: temples carved into rock, a stone theatre, Roman steps; as if the past had been shaken back to life by the seismic passage of the two racing cars.

There were many spectators here, though they were better controlled than those outside Rome had been. The Condor had not been overtaken by anything yet – except for Otero's trick on the way in to Rome – and Ingo thought they were among the first of the bigger cars to come through. It explained the welcome they were given, every man and woman and child waving and silently shouting, their voices lost in the bellow of the open exhausts.

He kept with Otero, letting the temperature rise just a little more, and chased him up through a staircase of tight curves through Capranica, both cars sliding as power was applied uphill on the slick weather-worn tarmac, the Condor's transmission tramping as the car bucked against the potholes. Yet Ingo exited the last corner cleaner than Otero and almost got the car's nose alongside the Ferrari once again. But Otero had the extra horses, and used them, out-accelerating the Condor while slamming the red door in its face. They blasted through the rest of the town, caramel coloured houses melting in the smear of his peripheral vision. The sun was high, splashing scallops of light across the bonnet of the Condor, shining bright in a dazzling pinprick of gleam on the smooth trailing edge of the Ferrari's roof. He had been looking at the rear of this car for too long, Ingo thought, but he could see no way past before Florence.

Then, as they came around a third gear curve between dusty houses, both cars sliding in four-wheel drifts, some way beyond the snarling snout of the Ferrari in front of him Ingo saw that someone was, quite calmly, walking into the middle of the road.

The person was distant, though at this speed that would not be the case for long, but Ingo could clearly see that he, or even she, was carrying something. But the Ferrari that had blocked his way and his view for the last twenty miles or so made it difficult for him to see exactly what this was …

***

Old Town, Warsaw. August 1944

The key turned in the lock. It was dark, and the person who opened the door had a small flashlight which dazzled her, so she did not know who it was at first.

"Chopin," he said. "I have been looking everywhere for you." Lidka recognised Lightning's voice. He put the small rectangular torch on its back so that a cone of light reached out for the corners of the ceiling. He smelt of the sewer, which was something more than merely shit. It was a smell she would always recognise, and a smell she was used to. She had not seen Lightning for a while and the fat had melted from him during these past few weeks.

She realised what he had said: "Didn't Andrzej send you?"

"Bullet's gone."

"Dead?"

He shrugged. "Probably."

There was an explosion outside, an incendiary landing some streets away, and an orange flash briefly suffused the thick frosted glass of the small window.

"How?"

"He told us we had a job. Top job, important mission," Lightning said, with a sigh. "Out in Ochota; to grab an SS man – just one, he said."

"Lightning, tell me; my son?"

He ignored that. "But it was more than one, many more; maybe ten. We arrived after the Germans had, they were in a truck, a Krupp, I think, parked up the street some way. It had insignia on it, crossed stick grenades?"

"Dirlewanger," Lidka said, and she felt a cold foetus of fear squirming within her belly.

"Yes, that would be about right," Lightning said. "We had been held up in the sewers. Cat said she knew the way, but we still got lost a few times. They drop grenades and —"

"I know."

"Well, Cat knew too, but that didn't save her."

"Dead?"

"Yes, she'd gone forward on her own to check for a way out; we were pretty close to where we wanted to be, she seemed to think. But the Germans were waiting at a drain, with grenades."

She nodded. Cat was not the first to die in the Warsaw sewer, and she would not be the last. "Please Lightning, tell me; my son?"

Again, he ignored the question, looked away from her and continued: "It seemed we were late, by the time we found another way out of the sewer. There were too many of them. But we took our positions anyway, in an empty apartment, opposite your place; the house where we met when this all started."

She nodded, and a distant machine gun beat a sharp tattoo.

"There was a group of civilians, six of them."

"My son?"

"The truck moved, and we saw it was going towards them."

"Tell me, Lightning."

He paused, then said: "One child, at least, of that I'm sure, but I couldn't say with certainty it was your son, Chopin, I saw him only once, and I had a lot on my mind then."

"But he was blond?"

Lightning nodded. "There was one German soldier with them, he was wearing one of those camouflage SS jackets our lads are so fond of, so maybe SS, too."

Ingo, Lidka thought. "Then what?"

"The truck pulled up in front of the house and so they were hidden from our view. Some SS men piled out of the back, there was a shot and one of the soldiers went down; dead, I think. We could not see well, but we thought it was the one who had been with the civilians, though we had not had a clear look at him; he still lay there when they moved. One of the boys reckoned he might have been AK, but Bullet told him to shut up."

Ingo, Lidka thought again. But then said: "What then?" she could hear the dread in her own voice, feel it spread through her like a heavy oil in her veins.

"They moved down the street, out of the cover of the truck now, so we could see them, but then we could not shoot at the Nazis for fear of hitting the civilians." He shook his head sharply, as if that had been an absurd notion. "They were taken around the corner of an apartment building – the white one with the lime green balcony rails?"

"I know it."

"Bullet left, without a word, and we, of course, well, we followed him, found another empty flat in the same building but further along – there are plenty of empty apartments in Ochota now, alright – and this one gave us a better view, though we were still at an angle and quite far off. But we were too late, anyway."

"Too late?"

"They had killed them all, we had heard the shots as we moved between apartments; five shots."

"Five shots, but there were six of them?"

He took a deep breath, then said: "I've seen too much of this bloody war, Chopin, but I will not forget what I heard, and what I then saw." Lightning shook his head.

"Tell me?"

"No."

"Tell me."

"No!"

"Yes!"

He nodded: "One of the SS men; he took the child by the ankles, dashed its head against the wall."

"Dead?"

"You told me to tell you," he snapped, then he massaged his forehead with thumb and forefinger and added, quietly now: "I'm really not sure it was your child, Chopin. Not sure ..."

Lidka thought he *was* sure.

"The man who did this, did you get a close look at him?"

Lightning shook his head. "No, but the bastard who seemed to be in charge, I could see him. He was wearing a cap, and he was a captain, Bullet said that; he had binoculars so he could make out much more of it than the rest of us. This captain took photographs the whole time, as if it was a day at the beach! Bullet had sent one of the lads out with a Molotov, when it hit the truck that was to be our signal. We fired, of course, but it was stupid, there are far too many Germans in Ochota. By then Bullet had gone, where I don't know. I don't know why he abandoned us, can only believe it was for a good reason. We fought them, the boys fought, anyway, and probably died. I ran, and lived."

Tears now ran down Lightning's dirty cheeks. Her eyes had adjusted to the light and she could see his lazy eye, the large patch of its white a bloodshot web.

"Am I free to go?" she said.

"Who's to stop you?" he replied. "Bullet didn't even tell us you were here; if it wasn't for that stupid kid with the Lahti I would not have known myself ... What was Bullet thinking?"

He might have been thinking of money, or diamonds, he might have been thinking of other things. She did not know the answer. Lidka shook her head. She thought she should cry now. But she could not. She felt completely numb. It was like the illusion the split second before a shell hits, when the world seems silent – a trick of the mind – when life seems to freeze. But she knew that could not last; she knew that the shell always exploded.

"I'm sorry," Lightning said. "What will you do?"

"There's still a battle to fight," she said.

"Even now?"

"Especially now."

Lidka stood up, stretched the stiffness from her limbs. Then she walked out of the small room and back in to the war.

***

Capranica, Italy. May 1954

The level crossings were marked boldly in the notes, in red ink, each and every one of them. It rarely happened but everyone knew that if it did then someone's Mille Miglia would be well and truly ruined. It would not be the driver's fault, of course, for who would be crazy enough to ignore the man with the red flag; the red flag that meant you were about to share the approaching piece of road with a speeding train?

Ingo saw the flag soon after the man who had carried it into the centre of the road waved the cars down with it. Otero slowed, Ingo catching the snarling shape of his mouth in the Ferrari's wing mirror as he cursed. Carlo had his hand up, the halt sign. Ingo braked, too, but then he saw the cloud of steam billowing into the air.

Ingo dropped down a gear, then accelerated.

The houses were built up close to the level crossing, so he could not see the approaching train itself, only the tarnished silver steam from its funnel that was being dragged over the rust-red rooftops. He jinked the Condor around Otero's Ferrari and pressed the pedal to the vibrating bulkhead, as the maths problem between life and death was set in front of him. The two red and white bars that were the barriers were dead ahead of them. Both closed. The flattened cloud of steam puffed ever closer. The Condor was closer, too. They seemed to be on an inevitable collision course, but Ingo kept his foot down. A group of people by the level crossing clapped their hands to their mouths so quickly it seemed as if they had slapped themselves in the face. The man with the red flag kept waving it, as the Condor sped by, his jaw turning into stone and weighing his mouth open in disbelief. Ingo glanced at Carlo – his eyes bulging behind his goggles with fear and confusion – and signalled for him to get down. He did so, bending low, just as Ingo shifted up another gear.

The car was metres from the level crossing when Ingo saw the dirty black locomotive, to his right, over Carlo's bent back. Its whistle shrieked, and Ingo also bent low in his seat, so that his head was just level with the top of the dash.

The lip of the Perspex screen of the Condor hit the pole hard, with a *crack* that reminded Ingo of rifle fire, and the pole bounced up and over them as they went beneath it, the hit shown in a lightning flash of cracked Perspex that ran diagonally across the screen. The car skipped a little on the light hump of the crossing, the revs singing as the wheels spun while it was on tip-toes, then it went beneath the second barrier – all in an instant – with another sharp smack as the sloping screen hit the pole, causing it to jump up high against its hinge and wobble at the perpendicular. Immediately Ingo's wing mirror turned black with racing iron, and then the striped pole fell back into its place with a bounce, and a string of dark steel trucks pulsed by after the steam engine, blocking the view of Otero and his Ferrari still on the far side of the level crossing.

Ingo switched his focus to the road ahead, which ran between two walls to a junction, where old women in black clothes crossed themselves and young men in bright shirts cheered. He crisply shifted up a gear and drove on. He was relieved that the level crossing was the same design as the one he had had a good look at near Argenta, when they had gone around the course in the Alfa, but not surprised, as most had been. He had noticed then how much slack there was in the operating wires, enough to allow a low car like the Condor to sneak under – though he hadn't planned on doing so at quite such a high speed, or with the train so very close. Ingo risked a quick look at Carlo. He was shaking his head. Slowly. And laughing.

*

Florence. May 1954

Ingo had driven the Radicofane Pass perfectly, the car seemingly fused to the nerve endings within his fingertips and his right foot, so that it was as if it was responding to his thought, rather than his inputs. He doubted he had ever driven any better. They had then blasted through Siena and the Tuscan countryside, where single files of towering cypresses guarded the ridges of the smoothly rolling hills and the road gouged a steely grey, clay-edged scar in the verdant land. Now they were on the outskirts of Florence.

The road into the city was in a pretty poor condition, and a number of times Ingo thought the Condor would bottom out and rip out its sump, or a spring would break, as it clattered and thumped over those potholes he simply could not avoid. But then Carlo could make a racing car that would get to Peru and back, and had done so, Ingo reminded himself, as he threaded the car through the suburbs, where in some places people who were tightly packed into tottering balconies looked directly down into their cockpit as they passed beneath.

They crossed the bridge over the eternal green-brown flow of the Arno and raced into the now smoothly paved streets beyond, Ingo drifting the car sideways across a square then slithering over a grid of glistening tram tracks at a junction, the bark of the open exhaust echoing back from the stone of the old buildings, before he slowed for the control, sited on a wide tree-lined avenue. The route card was stamped without Ingo quite stopping the car, and then the tyres squealed against the road surface as he drove on to the row of pit stalls just beyond.

Ingo brought the car to a skidding halt and the mechanics fell on it with a jack and their wheel hammers, knocking off the hub nuts which rang out as they spun clear and fell on the asphalt, while Ingo and Carlo climbed out and the Condor was jacked up, the gravity tank already glugging its life juice into the fuel tank, the smell of the gasoline cutting through the tang of the hot brakes and the acrid pong of the clutch. Varela was here, and he called Carlo over, ignoring Ingo.

It was now that the pain and weariness hit Ingo. Now that he had stopped driving his arms felt as if they had been pumped full of heavy rubber, his left leg as if it had been hit, over and over and over, with a hammer, from its constant work on the stiff clutch pedal, while his right foot was so hot from the conduction of heat through the throttle pedal he felt as if it might be burnt. He was very thirsty, too, the inside of his mouth like sandpaper. But above all he badly needed a piss. He had been able to ignore it at speed, for the last seven and a half hours, but now the pressure on his bladder was painful, and Carlo had often told him it was dangerous to race with a full bladder; he had emptied his own in Rome.

There was a sign for a toilet with an arrow pointing to a roped off corridor between the ranks of the pressing crowd. He did not have long, so he jogged up the pathway, his legs heavy. Not many of the race fans shouted over to him for his autograph, but some did, which seemed to reinforce how well they were doing in the race, as before today he doubted any would have even heard of Enrique Hohberg. At the Siena control they had seen the damage being bottled up behind Otero over the Apennines had done, after Pescara they had dropped to sixth by the time they arrived Rome, still behind the three Lancias and now a couple of works Ferraris, too. He wondered where they were in the race now; knew that their position could only have improved since passing Otero, but he also knew that they would have lost plenty of more time whilst they were stuck behind him before that stunt at the level crossing.

The toilet was reserved for drivers so was very close to the service area. The relief of it was almost worth the pain, he thought, as he left the place. The crowd seemed to be closer now as he hurried back to the car; people smelling of wine, garlic and sweat, calling for his attention, some beyond the rope barrier congratulating him he realised as he jogged back to the Condor. Despite the tiredness and the iron aches in his bones he had a sudden urge to be out of there, in the clean fast air again, as he worked his arms a little, loosening some of the stiffness from his muscles. Right then one voice in that crowd rose above the others. Not because the call was any louder; but because of the name it uttered.

"Ingo."

*

"It can't be?"

"It is."

He sounded different, had taken on the accent of the place where he had hidden, a natural thing perhaps, or perhaps not. Hiding is not natural. When Lidka had called out his name he had stopped dead, then he had crossed under the rope barrier and come to her, pushing past people, quite aggressively.

"I thought you were dead, I was told …" He trailed off, shook his head. In the background a car accelerated away from its stop, adding to the smell of burnt rubber, hot steel and the chemical reek of friction. The air felt gritty against her skin, like it had in Warsaw that August, almost ten years ago. His face was coated in black oil but was white where his goggles had been, a little like a panda. It starkly emphasised the shock in his eyes.

"You have done well, Ingo."

"And you?"

"I have survived."

He looked completely stunned, and he kept blinking, as if to make sure she was really there, and not a figment of his imagination. They were surrounded by people, some of them pushing past roughly in the throng. And yet it felt to Lidka as if they were in the middle of a desert, her and Ingo Six.

He kept staring at her, shaking his head slowly.

"Some did not survive, Ingo," she said.

"Many."

"The people you were to help, they were killed."

"They were killed," he said, and his eyes suddenly brightened with tears.

"You killed them, I know it," she said. "You killed them all."

She thought he might deny it, then, but he said: "Yes, I killed them."

"In cold blood."

"No, it was not like that, I had no —"

"You killed the child."

He said nothing.

"He was my son, Ingo."

Now he dipped his head. He sighed, and after a pause he said: "Yes, your son, I —"

"*Our* son, Ingo."

With that she turned and pushed her way into the dense press of people. She did not look back, but she half expected to feel his hand on her shoulder. But there was nothing. The Beretta was inside the handbag she carried. She would take it to Brescia, catching the same express, this time coming up from Rome. Vengeance could wait just a little longer, she thought. This would give him time to realise exactly what he had done. She remembered the way he had appeared on the start ramp, as if he was about to play Chopin. She had not wanted him to die happy. That would have been too easy. For him. He would finish his race, and she would be waiting.

She then made herself remember the time when she had found out for certain that it has been Freddy; when all hope, for her, had been snuffed out. It had been casual, that was the way those kids of war were back then, and it had been Badger, who had escaped the gun battle on Mochnackiego "It was your son, I am absolutely sure of it," he had said.

She thought about the look in Ingo' eyes when she had told him about his son. She had killed men, directly and indirectly. Many, many times. But she had never so utterly broken a man before. It gave her no joy, she realised. Revenge never did.

*

Rage filled him. His blood had turned to it. His head was bursting with singing steel, leaving no room for thought, and so he did that one thing that came naturally to him. Varela was glaring at him now, pointing at his watch, panic painting his fat face. He saw Carlo was staring along the line of pit stalls, pacing; looking at another car, a red Ferrari.

Ingo barged past the mechanics and jumped over the low door and in to the Condor. He pressed the starter, depressed the clutch and took first gear simultaneously as he slid into the bucket seat. He just caught Carlo's startled expression as he powered away, the rear end kicking way out of line with wheelspin as his anger took control of him, and the car.

Another racing car was just coming out of the pits and was up to speed, blasting past. Ingo had no idea how long he had been talking with Lidka. But he knew for sure that that was Otero's Ferrari, passing him once again.

As he left Florence, driving in the wake of the Ferrari, the crowds were nothing to him. He did not use the horn, nor flash the lights, he just drove the Condor as fast as he possibly could, in the hope that he could force the image of the dead child from his mind. On one corner he slid wide, hitting a pile of straw bales and crashing through to the spectators lined up beyond it. The wing mirror caught the arm of a spectator who was too slow in scattering. Ingo could actually see it fracture, in that split second of split bone. But he did not care, could not care, there was no the room for that in the steel scream of his mind.

The car slewed widely as he wrenched it off the pavement and back on to the roadway. He had not replaced his gloves and the bones of his knuckles showed white through the stretched skin as he gripped the steering wheel so very tightly. He crunched into third gear, felt the shock of the mistimed change through his wrist and arm, and he drove on.

On the long steep climb out of Florence he ran out wide on another turn, but here the road was lined with walls rather than straw bales. The Condor scraped itself along the stone, raising a cockscomb of bright sparks that he could see in his mirror, while Ingo was dimly aware of the broken blue stripe he had left along the length of the wall. But he did not want to think about the damage; he wanted to drive, he wanted to let the anger drive, he wanted to hide in that anger. To hide, again. From all he had done.

*

Raticosa Pass. May 1954

When he was in the army before the war, back when it was just playing soldiers, Joseph Szcześniak had hated the route marches. The worst bits of them was always towards their end, the last kilometre or so, when your mind was telling your body it was nearly done, and your body was agreeing. It was like that now, but this time his body knew it was almost over, and his mind was asking it for just one last thing. One kilometre further.

He hated route marches, and he hated priests, too, had for a long time. But he had been glad to stumble upon this one. Though, in truth, the stumbling had been on to the floor, in a fit of thorny coughs, while searching for a bus that didn't exist in Bologna. He had not been able to breathe for a while, thought he would die on the floor of the ticket hall. The priest and some others lifted him up, put him on a bench. The priest spoke English, listened to what he had to say, said he should go to a hospital, but finally agreed to help him when he pleaded. Pop wondered if he would have still helped him if he'd known what he had done. He was grateful, but he told himself the priest was only helping him – clearly a dying man – to help feather his nest in the afterlife. That made him feel a little better. But it was just another reason why he hated priests, they did everything for their souls, literally selfish, if you subscribed to that line of thought.

His name was Father Bernardi. He was very thin and his long cassock hung on his wiry frame like a black pipe. He was not a young priest, maybe Pop's age, 45 now, and he smoked like Warsaw in '44, which meant Pop coughed his way inside out as they made their way up to the pass in Father Bernardi's old beige Fiat Topolino, the interior of which smelt like an ashtray. It struggled to make it up the road that led to the Raticosa Pass from the east – after taking the long straight road out of Bologna that traced the ancient Via Aemilia first, and then turning off to navigate a muddle of poorly surfaced country roads to loop around and on to the Mille Miglia course. The pass sat at close to one-thousand metres and the priest had to stop once to allow the little car to cool down.

Smoke always reminded Pop of Warsaw, and as Father Bernardi puffed on his Nazionali he thought back to that day: remembering how he had fallen from the cab of the Krupp and into the street, and how Sunshine had put out the flames with the truck's fire extinguisher, ignoring the bullets; had saved his life. He often wondered why he had done that. Often wished he hadn't, too. Sometimes, he also wondered if Sunshine had survived it all. Could not see how; they were all doomed, one way or another, Dirlewanger's Russians. It was perhaps their excuse. More than Pop had ever had.

Well before they got to the top the road was packed with abandoned cars, parked at angles with wheels in the verge, as if they were dropped toys. Father Bernardi carefully threaded the little Fiat through and when they were near the summit a race official and a policeman, good Catholics both, took pity on the badly burned invalid and helped the priest to park the car up in a space alongside an ambulance and then to find a way through the crowd of spectators.

Pop had told the priest he wanted to see this before he died, and that much was true. The priest had no interest in racing cars, but still he agreed to take him to the pass. It was a Sunday, his busy day, and every now and then he glanced at his watch. Pop did not care if he stayed long, or if he stayed at all. All he cared about was seeing Ingo Six driving the beautiful car like it should be driven.

He did not deserve this one last thing, he knew, but he was glad of it. Ingo had asked him, once or twice, during the war, why he had stopped racing. He had always said he had been transferred to the army from the NSKK, and with that the opportunity to compete had gone. But that was not the truth, for while he knew *how* to drive and ride fast, he had never really been quite good enough, quite quick enough, and maybe even not quite brave enough. When his wife finally left him and the offers to race dried up, he had *asked* to be transferred, and when the training depot had proved boring, and war looked certain, he had *asked* to be sent to a frontline unit. It was never anything to do with an oberstleutnant's daughter, as he had told Ingo, he had merely thought it might help replace the respect he had lost, being a soldier in a war. But all it had brought was fear and horror. That and, eventually, the thing very few men find in life; a total understanding of who, and what, he really was.

After the war he had never felt the need to seek out racing cars, for these machines burn, too. Besides, there are always many people at race meetings, those after sensation, thrills, freak shows. He could not have borne the staring. Some of the Italians he shared this grassy bank with, which was above the junction and the small yellow restaurant at the top of the pass, stared too, before quickly looking away. But he did not care about that now.

The junction was edged with straw bales and formed a left-hand turn for the cars, nicely cambered and marking the change from uphill to downhill. Climbing the grassy bank overlooking the turn had almost finished him off, but because he was with a priest, he thought, some people had helped him. From here he had a good view of the exit of a fast left curve that led uphill towards him, edged with a double red and white steel guardrail held in place by square, very thick, stone supports. Before that there was a gently winding saddle that joined the more Alpine-like Futa Pass with the Raticossa, one of the spectators had explained, the priest translating this, and Pop could hear the cars now making their way along it, through the villages, towards where he sat on the damp grass, glad of its soothing coolness. He could also see part of the way down the road the other side, where it plunged in the direction of Bologna; though this view was obstructed.

The sky was a bright pearly grey and the air was clean and cold, and stung his tattered lungs. It also seemed thin to him, and he wheezed hard. But there was a breeze, too, and that soothed the old burns on his face a little. Everyone was here for the cars, except for Father Bernardi, who was probably here for Pop's soul. Most of the spectators had made their way up the pass in the early morning. The smell of the many cars that had already raced through – hot tyres, hot brakes, hot oil – still hung thick in the mountain air, yet was so obviously not a part of that air that he felt it should have colour, or form. He liked the smell, and he had missed it. He had not seen a racing car driven hard since before the war. Yes, he had missed it. The simplicity of that life. Be the quickest, if you can. He was glad that his friend Ingo had found it.

He had already watched a few saloon cars through the corner, wallowing on their soft suspensions like fishing boats in a swell, their tyres wailing like Nebelwerfers beneath their heavy chassis, motors rasping through thin pipes. But now a much louder car was making its way up the road, its engine note steely in the cold air, echoing through the valley from the direction of Futa. On the downshifts the engine crackled and spat, and then he watched the car as it emerged from the fast left-hander, crisply cutting the line, drifting out close to the protruding guard rail supports. It was a red coupe with a green nose band. He did not know the marque and model, it had been a long time since he had taken notice of such things, but he knew that red meant Italy – though he would have known that from the reception the spectators gave the car, too; the cheering, shouting and clapping.

The car came in to the left-hander at the crest on a close to perfect line, its nose dipping as it braked, puffs of black dust snorting from the wheels, the engine revving sharply between the gear changes; barking harshly through the open exhaust. The turn-in was aggressive – this was a driver who bullied rather than persuaded – and the car was taken out of the corner with too much throttle, the tail whipping out wildly and the rear tyres pawing up dust at the edge of the road at the exit. The spectators liked it, but it was not the driving of a maestro.

The car's number was 529. It would have started three minutes before Ingo. Pop began to think the awful thought; that he had missed him. For he could not believe Ingo would not have taken three minutes out of that driver since the start, well over seven hours ago. But if he had missed the Condor after all this, well wouldn't that be life's last sick joke? He could only hope the car had been delayed for some reason. It would be too cruel if it had retired, or crashed. But he knew he deserved nothing.

There was the sound of another engine from far below. The revs were dancing, frantic, and the noise cut through with the shriek of tyre-squeal. This could not be Ingo. Ingo would be smoother, as he always was. And by now Ingo would be even better, because he had everything Pop had taught him and experience to go with it, too. Yes, Ingo could only be better ...

The car came into sight, it was blue. He blinked. Still blue. It came through the fast left turn in a rear-end skid. Not a drift, where all four wheels slide and the car is beautifully balanced, floating through the apex, but a bad-tempered power slide, the tail now kicking even further out and tagging a stone guard rail support, lifting a bullet-hit of white stone dust. Then the car shook its head, straightened, and raced on up the hill, ballooning in size in time to the rise in the volume of its engine's angry snarl. He could see the yellow band on its nose now, too, as well as the ugly scrapes and dents that embellished the paintwork on the Condor's flanks, so that when the pale light hit it it no longer looked quite so beautiful, but rather hurt and sorry for itself. Many of the Italians were cheering wildly, thinking this was a car being driven fast, being driven well, but it was a car that was being over-driven.

But wait, there is just one man in the car, the driver, no co-driver ... Ingo had a co-driver, Carlo Rossi, Pop remembered. He let out a breath of relief, surprised that he had been holding it, for he needed every breath he could take.

The car approached the corner and the driver left his braking suicide late, thick black smoke poured off the linings like steam from a dirty loco, while white-blue smoke came from a locked tyre which flashed a patch of bright canvas where the rubber had worn through. The gearbox crunched to a mistimed downshift and the rear wheels grabbed for a moment, tyres shrieking in panic.

Then Pop belatedly read the car's number, painted in white on the bonnet: *532*.

"Oh Pup, have you forgotten it all?" He said it aloud, and in German. Until earlier that day, when he had talked with Lidka, he had not spoken German for years, and it still sounded strange to him. It took him back to dark places.

Pop saw the driver clearly now. He had seen most emotions in eyes before; evil, hate, lust and greed. But he had never seen such naked rage. It was Ingo, of that there was no doubt – even behind the beard, the googles and helmet and the black coat of oil on his face, he was sure of it. But it was not the man he was. Or had been. He wished right then that he had never made this final journey.

The Condor was thrown in to the corner, rather than turned in, and held in something approximating to a state of control by animal wits alone, the rear swinging out to overtake the front, like a second hand racing backwards around a clock face, before hitting the straw bales at the edge of the corner and knocking them back with a surprisingly loud thump, then a shiver and scraping noise as the dry grass in the bales slid across the rough road. Pop then realised the hit had also stopped the skid and bounced the car straight, saving it from the spin that had looked inevitable. The rear tyres then painted a long, wayward eleven on the road before traction was gained and the Condor headed off down the hill, trailing its V12 roar behind it. Most of the spectators clapped, thinking it was a fine trick, but they knew no better. Pop did. And so, he had always thought, did Ingo.

Pop had just two things left to do in life. To die and – since there was a priest here – to confess. He asked Father Bernardi to listen to his confession. He agreed with a sort of earnest relish and slowly helped him back down to the little Fiat. It was not as ornately carved as the last confessional Pop had sat in. Nor as flammable. They both sat in the front seats. He told the priest it had been almost 15 years since his last confession.

He then told Father Bernardi everything. How he had beaten the prostitute in Oryol, and others, when they had laughed at him; how he had executed prisoners; how he had raped and killed in Warsaw; how he had lied to Ingo about trying to get them back to the 19th; how he had betrayed his friend; a friend who had committed his own sins now, just one of them being to drive as he just had. He told him in detail, and it was very hard, physically difficult to talk for so long, and often he had to stop to suck in a breath. The priest did not smoke as Pop confessed. And did not question a thing he said. He could not. And he could give no penance, no forgiveness, when Pop had finally come to an end, now feeling slightly better, to simply speak of those things. No, Father Bernardi could say nothing, and give no penance; because Pop had confessed it all in Welsh.

*

Ingo had never driven so fast. He was sure of it. And yet there was still no sign of Otero's Ferrari. Without Carlo's hand signals he had to rely on memory and instinct. And the rage that drove him on. He knew that if he slowed that would be it, he would think, he would stop. So he let the rage win; let it persuade him to take the engine revs a few hundred over the redline; to tell him the rapidly softening brake pedal would come back to him; the tyres could take just a little more punishment. He thus discovered that he had always had more speed to give; yet he had only found it by not caring if he crashed. In a sudden burst of clarity he remembered the last piece of advice Pop had given him. *Never take rage into a racing car.* Pop had been wrong about that, too, he now thought. And yet he still could not see the red Ferrari, Otero's car, that he knew was ahead of him.

The engine was very hot, and the heat was radiating off the bulkhead, so that he was coated in slick sweat. The car now smelt of burning steel and rubber, just like the battlefield at Teploe. But he ignored that. It was hurtling along the sweeping roads off the top of the Raticosa. He had his foot flat to the floor in third gear now, the chassis vibrating so much his vision was blurred, the screaming song of it buzzing up his right leg, numbing his thigh. There was a turn approaching, blind because of the grassy embankment of the slope to his left. But he remembered this one, he thought, it opened out …

Ingo Six hardly slowed the car for the corner.

The turn tightened.

The Condor had no chance of making the curve and the brakes went completely soft beneath his foot as soon as he stamped on the pedal. The car smashed through a white-painted concrete rail at around 90mph as if it was balsa wood, the engine still roaring, the wheels still turning, and the next instant it crashed through the roof of a house built on the slope below the road, the impact slowing it and snapping Ingo's head back. Sharp broken shards of mud-red tiles fell in to the cockpit as Ingo realised he was flying through an attic space, and then out the other side of the roof – more smashing tiles and rifle cracks of shattering timber – before the car had completely flown through the now demolished apex of the house.

Then the Condor was in clear air for a moment, hanging high on nothing but its momentum, wheels still spinning and the engine screaming on the overrun, before it seemed to realise it could not fly after all. It fell steeply, nose first, the jagged, rocky ground of the valley's slope rushing up to meet it like a knuckleduster punch.

*

Brescia. May 1954

... Witnesses say the Varela Condor CR1 never looked like it would take the corner and, tragically, it does seem that Hohberg, who was now driving without his co-driver for reasons we have not yet been able to establish, completely misjudged it. At such speed the car easily smashed through the barrier and then speared through the top part of a house before landing, it seems, nose first on the slope beyond. It appears that it then tipped over lengthways until it came back into the sight of those who watched from the distant hillside, before falling on to its side and rolling down the slope like a log. The fuel tank exploded while it was rolling, and flames wrapped around the car as it continued to turn over and over before it stopped at the bottom of the valley. The Condor was completely immersed in fire by the time anyone managed to reach it, and we are told that there was no sign that Hohberg had been thrown clear of the car, even after an extensive search. The opinion of most witnesses we have spoken to is that he was probably trapped within it. It seems impossible, as this is written, that he has survived the accident. It is a sad end to an impressive Mille Miglia debut for Enrique Hohberg, also known as El Tímido, *and also for the Argentinian Varela Condor team, for the car had been ...*

The report in the *Giornale di Brescia* continued, but Lidka read no more of it, she had been through it many times already. She thought about the phrase *completely misjudged it* and wondered again if he had crashed on purpose, if it had been suicide. If so, she had killed him. And that was good, that was what she had come here to do. But revenge is never sweet, it is bitter like the espresso she now drank. Yet like the coffee it kept a soul awake; alive. She did not know how she would live without it; without the need for it.

Lidka was in the same coffee bar in the Brescia Railway Station in which she had talked to Szczneśniak the day before. Now she was waiting for the train to Milan. From there a flight to somewhere, she did not yet know where for sure, but she knew there was nothing waiting for her in Tel Aviv. That, too, was over. Had served its purpose.

It had been over a year since a woman had walked into the PFA office in Tandil. Jewish policemen are not common in the Federal Police, Lidka had since learnt, but one had been on duty. He had taken notes; and a name. The police officer knew his superiors would not be interested in a man, possibly a war criminal, seemingly hiding in Chillar, that was just another Nazi, and there were many of them. And so he sent a letter to the Israeli Embassy; he had contacted them before and was considered a reliable source. In the letter he said the woman had seemed unsure, but also angry. That had been a warning from him that this might, after all, be more emotional than anything else. He was obviously a good cop, which was rare, and good at being a cop, which was even rarer, as he took detailed notes; notes that were word perfect. The woman had told him: "Why would a man hide if he had done nothing wrong? Why did he disappear when his photograph was in a magazine? Why so many secrets? He didn't even tell me that he played piano; that his father had a piano shop, in Munich, until the very end."

"Why now?" he had asked her, as it seemed clear she had known him for a long time. "Until now I never believed he could be so cruel," she had then said. "Until now I had always believed it was to do with money, nothing more. But now I know he can be cruel. Very cruel."

The PFA officer had also noted, after checking with the local police in Chillar, that the woman was a prostitute. She had given him her name, because he had insisted: Maria Aguilar.

That letter had been filed under *H* for Hohberg and forgotten about. But when Ingo Six raced in Buenos Aires in January, under his pseudonym, one of the Mossad men in the embassy saw a news report on the race and remembered the name they had on file; he had known another Hohberg, long ago, and so it had stuck in his mind. He had then sent a memo to Tel Aviv; with those scant details, and some newspaper cuttings. The Mossad did not hurry to pass on the information to Gabriel, even though they knew he was looking for a man who played piano, but more importantly whose father owned a piano shop in Munich – that was the key, as it was on the short file she had written up for Gabriel to pass on to the Mossad. The reason they did not rush was probably because, for them, this Ingo Six was not very important, in the evil scheme of things. But the memo and the cuttings were eventually sent to him, some months down the line. Gabriel forwarded the information and the newspaper clippings to her. In one of the pictures this bearded man pressed his palms against the bonnet of a beautiful racing car. Despite the beard and the grainy picture, she recognised Ingo Six instantly. After that it had not taken Gabriel long to track him down, and then to discover that he would be in Italy for this race.

Lidka took a sip of the espresso. She rarely drank strong coffee, never in Tel Aviv, but she had not slept so well these last few days and she had found the Italian stuff helped to keep her on her toes. She liked the smell of it, too, though there was a peaty stink of cheap pipe tobacco that was beginning to fill the alcove coffee bar and spoil that. She thought Gabriel would like this place, this coffee, and then she wondered what he would make of the news; the news that Ingo Six was dead. But then she remembered that Ingo Six was her project; small fry, when compared to some who still walked free. They had told the world who he was, what he had done, but none of that had come out yet. Maybe that would have only been a story worth telling if they had shot him on the start ramp, rather than him dying in just another racing car accident. Perhaps Yitzhak had been right about that.

Outside it was raining hard, she could hear it hit the ground, that and the whirr of an electric train that smoothly cut through the panting of the steam locos. She glanced at her watch, there was not much time before the Milan train would leave, then she once more looked at the newspaper folded in front of her. The story of Enrique Hohberg's death did not take up many column inches, he was not a well-known driver, though the journalist hinted that he might have been, if he had lived. But then they always say things like that of the dead. There was a photograph accompanying the text; the Condor on the starting ramp. The other man, with the moustache, who in the picture looked so very happy to be there, just like Ingo Six did, had not been in the car when it had crashed. This, too, made Lidka believe it had been suicide. That she had killed him with the truth, as surely as Yitzhak would have with the rifle. But that, she realised now, would have made one hell of a photograph …

"Strange business," a man who stood alongside her suddenly said.

She ignored him, not sure he was speaking to her anyway.

"Yes, very strange."

This time she turned, and the man nodded at the newspaper that was spread open on the zinc counter. His breath smelt of last night's booze and his eyes whipped along her body; but she didn't care about that, that's what it was for. Or had been.

"What's strange?" she said, her defences down.

He smiled a yellow smile. He was a middle-aged man with old man's skin and hair. Maybe disease, maybe war; both much the same, Lidka knew. He smoked the pipe that had been annoying her.

"The Argentinian." He once again nodded at the paper in front of her.

"It's a dangerous race, drivers are sometimes killed."

"Oh, so you haven't heard?"

Her heart froze. "Heard what?" she said.

"The fire burnt for a while, the car had been refuelled at Florence, you know? And it was upside down. It took a long while to get the equipment needed to turn it over, down there, amongst the rocks," he said, before pausing to suck on his pipe.

"And?" she said, as he took his time.

"There was no burnt body. No body at all, in fact."

"What do you mean?"

He shrugged, looked at his watch. "Must have been thrown clear, though he's not turned up yet. No doubt some dog will sniff out a corpse soon; it will get easier as the days go by, believe me." With that he gave a grim smile, finished his coffee, put on his hat and left to catch his train.

Lidka walked in the rain. She had no hat or umbrella, and she carried the handbag in which she kept the Beretta pistol and her little blue suitcase. She had left in a hurry and yet she had no idea where she was hurrying to. She just wandered the streets with her hair streaming wet, her train to Milan forgotten. And people stared at her. She supposed she still searched, in a way, a desperate way. But it made no sense, she knew. He was gone.

She trod the slick, gleaming cobbles of Brescia for hours. Then, mid-afternoon, she suddenly felt quite cold. Lidka stopped. She was in the Piazza Paolo VI. She stared at the Duomo Nuovo for a little while, watching gusts of rain washing the white marble and the statues of the Virgin and four saints high up along the pediment, with their blank and blind eyes; unseeing and unseen. The rain was falling on her face, now that her head was tilted back, but her makeup had already run to ruin anyway. She turned back in the direction of the station. She went through Piazza Della Vittoria, walking along the colonnaded pavement for shelter. Here workmen smoked cigarettes while they waited for the rain to stop so they could take down the advertising banners that had decorated the square before and during the race. She did not know the city well, nowhere near as well as Yitzhak had, but she had a general idea of what direction to take to get back to the station. She bought an umbrella, to stop people staring as much as to keep dry – it was far too late for the latter – and the rain crackled against the tight drum of its fabric as she walked down Corso Martiri della Libertà, the grand old building of the Banca San Paolo palely reflecting headlights from its rain washed walls. A bottle green OM truck splashed in a kerbside puddle and the water slapped coldly against her already soaked stockings.

Then, she heard the music.

It was Chopin, *The Raindrop Prelude*; the same piece Ingo had played that first time, when she had heard it from the Market Square in the Old Town back in 1939. But with the noise of the rain on her umbrella she could not quite tell from what direction the sound was coming. She tossed the brolly aside, then ran on down the street, following the music, she thought, her heels clacking loudly. She pictured him, as he was back then, at the piano. But she no longer enjoyed Chopin, hadn't for a very long time. She reached into her handbag to make sure the pistol was still there, the cold feel of it steeling her.

She then thought she had gone too far, for the music now seemed to be coming from behind her and was more distant. She turned, and this time she did not run, but walked, back up Corso Martiri della Libertà until she was again outside the bank, and the music was clearer. She thought it was emanating from one of the tight side streets, but there were four leading off from here alone. She stopped and listened more carefully, trying to home in on it.

It was then that she realised how foolish she had been. It was Chopin. But it was not played well. Only adequately, perhaps not even that. Her new umbrella still sat abandoned on the pavement, rocking lightly to the breeze. She looked at her watch. There was fifteen minutes until the next train to Milan. Lidka picked up the umbrella and then walked towards the station.

*

Ingo stopped playing Chopin. The pain in his right wrist was just too much, and he was playing very badly because of it. He looked at his wrist, it was red and swollen and almost seemed to pulse with the injury. But he not been able to resist the widow's piano, perhaps because he knew that racing was now over for him, and this was all he had. He was in the parlour of the small apartment where he had rented his room; old furniture with an old smell, and many old photographs crowded on walls and surfaces, sepia fragments of a life shattered by a death. His face felt strange, cold even, and he reached up to touch the smooth skin; skin that had been covered by a beard for nearly nine years.

He had been lucky, very lucky. After the Condor had smashed through the roof it had then landed on its nose a little way down the slope beyond the house. The concrete barrier the car had burst through, and the beams within the roof of the house, had robbed the crash of some of its impetus, but the car had still hit the mountainside with a shriek of buckling steel. Carlo made a strong car, though, and while Ingo's wrist was injured when the front wheels dug into the ground and twisted the steering, it could have – should have – been a lot worse for him. He had then been thrown clear as the car pitched over, and the tumbling Condor had narrowly missed him and the spiky bush he had landed in. That bush had broken his fall, maybe saved his life.

And the crash had brought him to his senses.

He had survived, and Ingo had found right then that he still wanted to live. His only injuries were the badly sprained and perhaps broken wrist, a very sore neck, lots of bruising and many cuts and grazes from the thorns in the bush.

Ingo had realised then that it was unlikely anyone would have seen him being thrown clear of the car; all the spectators seemed to be the other side of both the house and the road, and as he watched the Condor rolling in flames to the foot of the valley, he saw that this was his opportunity. People would think him dead; *they* would think him dead. The car might burn for hours, it would give him time, and with no body to find on the mountainside everyone would assume he was still trapped within the Condor. It was sad to see Carlo's car wrecked like that, but there was nothing he could do about it. That part of his life was over.

He had made for cover quickly, remembering things he had learned in the war. He had then hidden his helmet, kidney belt and goggles under another bush. Then he had found a small stream of icy water where he washed off as much of the oil and grime from his face as he could. He had then made his way around the edge of the mountainside, out of sight of those who only looked at the burning Condor now anyway. He had found a remote house, with no one home as its occupants were probably watching the racing cars, and he had broken in. He had cut and then shaved off his beard there, using scissors and another man's razor, and taken some old grey clothes that were not as distinctive, or as ripped, as his flying jacket, yellow polo shirt and blue trousers, and also a hat like the one worn by the man on the Birra Moretti labels. He had hidden his own clothes and made his way back to Brescia, hitching lifts to Bologna and taking the train from there. He had then slept rough, in a small park.

He had waited until the old woman had gone out and then let himself in; he knew she visited her sister all day on a Monday. He still had some money here, he had always made sure there was enough cash in case he needed to run. There were no diamonds left now, though, but in return for the last of Sol Vogler's stones he had had Kroh's warning; and he had taken it very seriously. Ingo had known this would be his last race. His small bag was packed and ready.

Running again. Hiding again. He had escaped to Argentina when he found out someone was searching for him. Kroh he had first thought, assuming then that he knew there had been diamonds. If not Kroh, then maybe someone who had seen Kroh's photographs; there were many hunting war criminals like him back then – and he would never deny that that was what he was. There was nothing in Germany for him by then anyway, nothing that could do anyone any good. He had never been captured by the Allies, and so was in a sense on the run already; Ingo Six could not face life in a cage.

He had already had a taste of that. It had been soldiers of the 19th that had saved his life, Pop had been wrong about them leaving Warsaw. But he had also been wrong about other things, Ingo had soon realised – very wrong. Kroh had made a noise about Ingo deserting, from the field hospital bed where he was recovering from his wound, but Hauptmann Schulte refused to have him shot – it was then that Ingo had discovered that Pop had never requested they be transferred back to the 19th. He eventually realised why, but even now could hardly believe it. While Schulte had saved him from the firing squad – even some senior SS officers believed Dirlewanger had gone too far and so fleeing that lot was understandable – he could not save him from military jail, and from there, and it had been a relief at the time, he had been sent to a penal battalion.

At the time Schulte had asked him where his things should be sent. He thought that they would search the hat thoroughly at the prison, and so he asked that it, and some of his very few belongings, be sent to the 19th Panzer Division depot in Hanover. When the German army retreated into the Fatherland and many units were cut down to nothing, merged into battle groups, then cut down again, he had managed to get to the depot, and retrieve the hat; though it had been a big risk and he had come close to being shot on the sport for desertion – again. He had also bumped into Woof at the depot, and from him he had learned that Pop had lived, but he had also been badly burned. Woof had had no idea what had happened to him after that, but Ingo had not wanted to see him again anyway. Pop had betrayed him and lied to him, and Ingo owed him nothing; he had repaid him in full, on that day in Warsaw. He sometimes wondered if he still lived, but he doubted that. Ingo had also heard from Woof that Kroh had been asking after him, once he had recovered from his wound, but all they could say was that he was in military prison, because that's what they had believed.

Ingo had deserted from the battle group he had found himself in the week the war ended, before it surrendered to the Americans. Then he had buried himself deep in the Frankfurt underworld, in the US zone, where he could always find someone willing to buy an illicit diamond. He had sold a couple of them far too cheaply, to begin with, but then he had learnt more about the stones. Sol

Vogler had only kept the very best; none of them weighty, carat wise, but some of them – including the last one, the one that Kroh took – very good when it came to the three other Cs: cut, colour and clarity.

He had discovered he was being hunted, way back then, because after a while lying low in Frankfurt he had thought it might be safe to go looking for his past, in Munich – which was also in the US zone, so not so difficult to get to. He had then found that his father's piano shop had been destroyed in the bombing. He had asked questions, pretending to be someone else, of course, always in the night and with his disguise of hat and beard, while trying to avoid those who might recognise him from before the war. He had not been the only one to ask questions about the family of this Ingo Six, he had then learned. He still did not know if his mother was alive; but he did know that if she was then she would be better off thinking him dead. That had been a difficult decision. One he had to take if he was to live, if she was to be safe.

And so he had forgotten about Munich and his past and had gone to the Brotherhood, those that helped the 'old comrades', SS men running from their dark pasts. He had had the money and so it was not so difficult for him to get in touch with them, introductions can always be bought. There weren't so many who admitted to being Nazis right then, and there certainly weren't so many declaring they had been in the Dirlewanger Brigade. So, the Brotherhood believed he was running and hiding for the *right* reasons.

Through the Brotherhood he was put in touch with a Catholic priest. The priest, and other priests, helped him travel through Austria and on to a safe house in Genoa. He had never understood why those priests helped hide Nazis. In Genoa the Brotherhood had given him a refugee's Red Cross passport bearing his new name, and then put him on the ship to Argentina.

Now Ingo Six would have to run again. Hide again

He thought of the child he had killed, almost ten years before; his son. He believed what Lidka had told him. He also believed she did not want to see him again, he had seen that in her eyes, and in the way she had walked away from him in Florence. He wondered how long she had looked for him, to give him such news. He believed he was dead to her, and Ingo could not blame her for that. Maybe she had a family now, someone to love. He hoped that she did.

Rage had almost killed him yesterday, and he thought that might have been just. But he had lived, and he would now have to go on living, with the knowledge of what he had done. He had been faster than the bullet, but bullets are not the only things that can destroy a life.

THE END

Author's note

I had never had a huge yearning to go to Warsaw, mainly because I'd read somewhere that much of it had been rebuilt, brick by brick, after the war, and that made it seem as if its historical sites were almost fake, in a way. When I did go – I can't remember why, a cheap flight, a new country – I saw that this was the most fascinating thing about the place (it's actually a wonderful city for many reasons, I'd recommend a visit). With an idea already in my head about someone hiding from their past, Warsaw during WW2 then suddenly seemed the ideal setting for much of my story.

Also, the Warsaw Uprising story has often been neglected, I feel, perhaps because the Allies were a little bit embarrassed about the way the Poles were treated after the war, or at least they should have been. In fact, at the end of WW2 Britain seemed to forget why it went to war in the first place; though in fairness jumping straight into WW2 part 2 against Stalin was probably not in anyone's interest then, not even the Poles.

But that's complicated stuff, and it's up to others to argue about it. I'll stick with the happenings in this book, and the people; like Ingo Six.

I always wanted a pianist in this story. Mainly because there have been some notable classically trained piano players who have turned their talented hands to racing – François Cevert, Adrian Sutil, Elio de Angelis – and I'd often wondered whether there was a connection, something to do with 'feel' perhaps? Then again, maybe it's just because rich kids learn the piano *and* they race karts and cars? Yet Gilles Villeneuve was also good on the keys, and he certainly didn't have a privileged upbringing. I've long been intrigued by this, and what's a story set in Warsaw without a little Chopin anyway?

In this novel Ingo aims to start his career on motorcycles – or at least that was Pop's plan – and this was not so unusual in the 1930s in Germany; Bernd Rosemeyer came straight to Auto Union from bikes, as did Georg Meier and Hermann Müller a little later. Pop teaching Ingo the art of racing with regular bikes and cars might seem unusual, but then again a few years ago I spent a day with renowned driver coach Rob Wilson for a magazine feature I was writing. At the time he was advising seven Formula 1 drivers, and the car he coached them in was a regular Vauxhall Astra, which seems to show Pop's method might work just as well today. Because, as Pop would know, the basics, especially weight transfer, can be taught in pretty much anything. Also, of course, there's nothing like driving on snow and ice for honing car control.

Talking of Pop, the use of Pervitin by the Wehrmacht is no secret. It's better known by its chemical name of methamphetamine, and more widely these days as crystal meth. It was issued to soldiers and pilots early in the war to help keep them awake, but that stopped when the clear damage it was doing to them was noted. After that it was up to medical officers to prescribe it when they saw fit, and many, many of them often did on demand. The more research I do into warfare in the 20th Century the more I find myself coming to the conclusion that everyone was either drunk or high on drugs for much of the time. Then why wouldn't they be?

Some have argued that Pervitin played its part in fuelling atrocities during the war. Perhaps it did, sometimes – though as Sarah Malka says, it's certainly no excuse – though it's far from clear if this was so. But what *is* clear is the sheer brutality (it's not a strong enough word, there is none) of the German response to the Warsaw Uprising. There is nothing in this book that is exaggerated on that score, not even the character traits of Oskar Dirlewanger, a man so rotten you hope for the sake of humanity that he really was insane. I think he probably was.

You might also think it insane to hop aboard a bombing mission for a jaunt, too. But it certainly wasn't unknown for non-combatants to go on an operation, with the crew turning a blind eye, especially at the beginning and then towards the end of the war. In fact, an RAF man wangled a ride in a South African Liberator dropping supplies on Warsaw. It got shot down and he ended up a prisoner of war. But at least he had a tale to tell his grandkids.

I have tried very hard to stick as close to history as is possible in this work – though it's amazing when you start to dig a little deep just how often history disagrees with itself – and many of the happenings in this book, such as the Wawer massacre for instance, are real. One place I have compressed the passage of events a bit, as far as the 4th Panzer Division is concerned, is at the Battle of Kursk, just for the sake of the narrative. Incidentally, when it comes to the battles, I've relied heavily on first-person accounts for research, especially war diaries, as they always seem to me to be less distorted by the prisms of victory or defeat.

As for talking to drivers competing in historic racing, I found this a bit frustrating, as most seem to see it only in the context of today; so the brakes are poor, the suspension soft, steering sloppy, and so on, which of course might not have been the opinion at the time. Luckily, I know a little bit about race driving myself, so I could extrapolate to a certain extent, while there were two classic books I was able to lean on to get an insight into the challenges a driver faced and the methods employed in the 1950s: *The Technique of Motor Racing* by Piero Taruffi, and *The Racing Driver* by Denis Jenkinson.

A word on Warsaw street names here. Jassy, my wife, found a map of the city from 1939 on another visit we made there for research, so I've used these names when it's a Polish perspective. While many street names were Germanised/Nazified during the occupation, most Poles would have used the older versions. A good example is Gdansk Station, which the Germans called Danzig Station. Another small language point, I've written mate, as in the Argentinian drink, as maté, simply because it's quite confusing, and sometimes comical, without the accent.

That's a small thing, though, and a much bigger thing in this novel is revenge. There were Jewish hit squads operating after the war, for some years. The Nakam is the most well-known, largely because of its plan to poison reservoirs in a bid to slay millions of Germans. It later killed hundreds of SS prisoners by poisoning their bread supply. There were also other groups involved in vengeance, which is what Nakam means.

A quick word on attitudes here. These were different in the '40s and '50s, and this is *historical fiction*. It seems strange to have to write this – then we live in strange times – but the thoughts and beliefs of characters in this work are not my own, in fact they're often *very* far from that. This *should* be obvious, really.

Talking of strange times, the production process for this edition of the book was hit by the Covid-19 pandemic and as a result there have been some small issues with formatting, so apologies for that.

As far as the 1954 Mille Miglia is concerned, those readers with an interest in motor racing history might be aware that Enrique Hohberg was not the only driver to duck down and drive under a closed level crossing barrier at speed; Hans Hermann did the very same thing in his Porsche 550 Spyder. Then the Mille Miglia was like that, a proper road race, a real adventure. As part of the research for this book we drove the route, which is the only way to get a feel for it, and after doing so I was in no doubt that this really had been a race for heroes. As to whether Ingo Six was a hero or not, that's something you will have to decide for yourself.

Mike Breslin, London 2020

Acknowledgements

Special thanks should go to Leslie Gardner at Artellus literary agency, for her advice on this and many other projects over more than 20 years now. During the writing of *Faster than the Bullet* I talked to countless people in the world of motorsport, far too many to list here and usually as part of broader conversations/interviews, but I would like to single out Ian Wagstaff for helping me with one knotty little detail on 1950s sports car racing. Also, big thanks to German WW2 and classic motorcycle expert John Landstrom of Blue Moon Cycles in Georgia, USA, for his insight into riding 1940s era motorcycles with sidecars. Also, thanks to Julian Hoseason (www.polandinexile.com) for help on the very complex subject of communications between the UK and Poland during the war.

The Warsaw Uprising Museum also deserves a mention here, not just because its staff were very helpful during the visits we made, but also because there's no better way to get an understanding of this much neglected episode in World War II history. Other museums more than worthy of a shout are the superb Museo Mille Miglia in Brescia and the small but informative collection at the Automóvil Club Argentino in Buenos Aires.

Appendix: Himmler order, 1944

1. Captured insurgents ought to be killed regardless of whether they are fighting in accordance with the Hague Convention or not.
2. The part of the population not fighting, women and children, should likewise be killed.
3. The whole town must be levelled to the ground, i.e. houses, streets, offices — everything that is in the town.

Orders from Heinrich Himmler for dealing with the Warsaw Uprising.
Source: *Warsaw 1944*, Alexandra Richie

ABOUT THE AUTHOR

Mike Breslin is a freelance writer specialising in motorsport, motoring and travel. He is originally from south Wales but is now based in London. A former Formula Ford racer – who cleared thousands of pounds of racing debts with one spin of the roulette wheel by betting everything he had on number 11 – Mike has published four other books: *Pieces of Silver* (fiction, 2014) *The Unfair Advantage* (fiction, 2000), *Road Trip* (non-fiction, 2020) and *The Track Day Manual* (non-fiction, 2008). Mike loves to travel, especially in Africa, and when he's not writing he can often be found in his local pub planning his next adventure or road trip. For more on Mike Breslin go to www.bresmedia.co.uk

Also by Mike Breslin

Pieces of Silver

English racing driver Westbury Holt sees the Auto Union grand prix cars as nothing more than his chance to be the fastest. To him the Nazi involvement is just politics, nothing to do with sport and speed. But others see the access West has to superior German technology through his links with the racing team as an opportunity. He is soon drawn into a web of intrigue that is as dangerous and unpredictable as the 520bhp racing car he drives.

With the coming of World War II the boundary between right and wrong becomes blurred, and friends become enemies. But will West, now at the controls of an RAF Hurricane, find that the past is the most dangerous foe of them all?

From the race tracks and the record runs of pre-war Europe, to the bullet-laced skies of Crete and the frozen killing fields of Russia, Pieces of Silver is a 200mph journey through a world of speed, love, war and betrayal.

*

"The story develops at a cracking pace and the mix of characters, historical and technical facts combine to provide a compelling read." *Classic Car Weekly*

"It's an enjoyable page-turner ... Breslin's enthusiasm for his story is genuinely engaging and you soon find yourself wanting to know what happens next to his colourfully drawn characters." *Motor Sport*

**** "Full of twists" *Auto Express*

Made in the USA
Middletown, DE
06 January 2021